Dear Reader:

This book is essentially true and historically factual. These things happened, these people existed —however incredible and violent they seem. I used poetic license only to protect the living and the innocent.

At a young and impressionable age I personally witnessed a savage Mafia bloodbath which has never been erased from my memory. My family, like many others, suffered the hardships and fears of the great depression. Ours, however, was compounded by the daily menace of the Mafia until my father finally gave up a promising political career, rather than cooperate with the Mafia and their corrupting influences.

The current stereotype of the Mafia as a glorified hoodlum is a sham. They are more sinister and terrifying than can be imagined.

The oral history and old diaries I received as part of my Sicilian heritage compels me to set the record straight. *The Godfather* told only the second half of the history. This is the first part, how it all began . . .

GLORIA VITANZA BASILE

The Godson

by Gloria Vitanza Basile

PINNACLE BOOKS • NEW YORK CITY

THE GODSON

An original Pinnacle Books edition, published for the first time anywhere.

ISBN: 0-523-00719-1

First printing, February 1976

Cover illustration by Steve Karchin

Printed in the United States of America

PINNACLE BOOKS, INC.
275 Madison Avenue
New York, N.Y. 10016

Dedicated to My Three Sons

Louis
Robert
David

BOOK ONE

PROLOGUE

The inexorable Sicilian sun was far from its zenith on that twenty-eighth day of July, one year after the birth of a son to the Marquis Marco de Leone.

Under the impressive coat of arms affixed to the domed archway of the centuries-old chapel at the villa, a small, solemn party had gathered at the impromptu baptism of the male child.

Father Bonaventura made the sign of the cross—*"In nomini patre et figlio et spiritus santus . . ."*—as he sprinkled holy water on the dozing infant who kicked and screamed, spitting out the foul-tasting salt which had been thrust between his velvety lips. ". . . I baptize thee Dolcetto Fiorenzo Marco de Bernadotte de Cordova de Cantanese de Leone."

Overhead the sun's rays filtered through the stained-glass windows, casting fragmented explosions of color in every direction. Mixed scents from the floral offerings to the many sainted statues, combined with the musky smell of incense, permeated the chapel.

"He'll be a prince among men, this son of yours, Marco. *Che bellissimo!*" exclaimed Dottore Alberto Pietro, Godfather, as he held the screaming infant in his arms. "See, already he roars like a lion." The infant held onto his Godfather's hand tenaciously. "And see his strength? Truly, he'll be a worthy descendant of the House of de Leone. No?" The Godfather chuckled and patted the baby's backside. Alberto Pietro's complacent blue eyes smiled tolerantly as he handed the infant back to the nurse.

Marco de Leone had watched the ceremony with mixed feelings. Since the untimely death of his beloved wife Mariolina, eight months before, he had been inconsolable, neglecting everything and everyone including his son Dolcetto.

That very morning, Father Bonaventura had chastised him for this total neglect and insisted the child be baptized. The priest, a kindly, temperate scholar, pushed to distraction by Marco's unusual behavior, could take no more.

"How can you allow your son to exist from day to day locked in mortal combat with original sin? The child is one year old today. We can't allow this to continue, Excellency."

Reluctantly, Marco agreed. He'd been wrapped in a cloak of self-pity for too long, too unconcerned to care. Nothing

1

had been planned or thought out in advance. Because Dr. Pietro happened to be at the villa when the priest issued the ultimatum, Marco asked him to be Godfather. Once the ceremony ended, Marco grasped Dr. Pietro's arm and in a strained voice, he urged the new Godfather: "Promise me, Alberto, if anything happens to me, you'll be his father in God. Dolcetto is now as your own flesh and blood under God's law."

"Don't concern yourself, *compadre*. As long as I live, nothing shall happen to my Godson, that I can prevent."

The physician, a few years younger than Marco, gazed at his Godson. He pursed his lips and made squeaky sounds and chucked the baby's chin. When the child gurgled and cooed, the Godfather laughed, pleased with the response.

Watching them, Marco's anxiety abated. He felt reassured. It was fitting that Dr. Pietro be the child's Godfather. He should have attended to it sooner.

Birthday and baptismal gifts were lavished on the child by smiling *contadini*, the peasants who worked the estate, the *latifondo*. Liqueurs, sugar-coated almonds, honey-soaked *sfinghi* and *piniolatti* were served, and the people toasted the godson, Godfather and father. Without offending anyone, Marco de Leone let it be known that he would have to be excused early.

Understanding his heavy heart and the reluctant gaiety of a man beset with so much sorrow, the people paid their respects and returned to their cottages, hoping and praying that soon Signore Marco would once again be their spirited leader, their Lion.

Roberto Argento, Marco's chief agronomist and dearest friend, reassured them as they left. "Give him time and he'll be his usual self. When the mourning periods ends, I'm sure he'll return to us." Roberto permitted no one to sense the doubt fermenting in his own heart. Tomorrow, he promised himself, I'll renew all my efforts to draw Marco out of his solitude.

Standing quietly to one side of the small salon, Paolo Nicosia, skipper of the *Marchessa*, one of the cruisers owned by the Lion, waited to speak to Marco. Watching the Lion sitting as still as death staring out at the Madelaina Gardens, he coughed slightly to attract Marco's attention. Marco turned to him. "Paolo, what is it? What are you doing here? I thought you'd left."

"I couldn't go without giving the child his birthday gift." The well-built, sandy-haired seaman shuffled awkwardly. He extended the package to Marco.

"Ah," said Marco remembering. "It's the child's birthday

2

as well." A soft smile tugged at his lips. "I thought you'd be in Palermo catching the biggest fish in the sea."

The Lion's hazel eyes lit up in astonishment when he saw the exquisitely carved golden lion in the velvet case. He held it up to the light, letting the thick golden chain entwine about his fingers. "Paolo! How can I accept such a costly gift?" As soon as the words escaped him, he saw the hurt in the seaman's eyes.

"Please, Excellency." Paolo held up a restraining hand. "Please accept this for Dolcetto, in the name of the son I can never have. Ever since he was born, I've loved the child as if he were my very own. It would be a solace to me to think I might have been the boy's Godfather."

Of course! Paolo should have been asked to be Godfather. Marco felt a pang of guilt. *Why didn't I think? Paolo took Dolcetto for walks, played with him as I should have done. But it is too late now.*

"Excellency, I leave for Palermo tomorrow. I will say my goodbyes."

Marco stood up and embraced his friend. Tears stung his eyes. "I thank you for many happy memories, my friend. *Dio de benediggi,* God bless you and care for you."

Nicosia left. Marco sat down again and stared out at the gardens. He felt deep compassion for the young man. Still clutching the golden lion tightly in his hand, he arose, walked along the gleaming tiles to the end of the corridor and entered his son's bedroom.

In the partial shadows of the candlelit room, his son slept peacefully under mosquito netting in a hand-carved crib. Gina Contiguilia lay asleep in a rocking chair, rosary beads clutched in her brown, coarse hands. Walking soundlessly to the side of the crib, Marco rolled back the netting and stared down at his son.

"*Povero bambino,* you'll never know the touch of your mother's hands. You'll never smell her sweet perfume, never kiss her good night, never know a mother's love."

He dabbed at a truant tear that spilled down his cheek. As he did, the jeweled lion slipped through his fingers and dangled freely on the chain. Light from the flickering candle reflected in the glistening jewel. Watching it sway from side to side, Marco felt its hypnotic effect.

I've been feeling sorry for myself, thought Marco. *Self-indulgent and foolish, the very thing Mariolina would have detested.* He inhaled a deep breath. He felt as if a stone weight had been lifted from his shoulders. *I must return to the world of the living.*

The child stirred, breaking his mood. When Marco bent over to smooth the child's coverlet, the baby's eyes fluttered open as if he sensed his father's presence. He cooed and gurgled, his drowsy eyes blinking dreamily until he awakened fully. Then his bright emerald eyes fixed on the gold lion swaying back and forth above his head.

Marco smiled. "I haven't been much of a father to you, have I? It's not the legacy I planned for you, the next Lion of Sicily. You'll understand when you grow older, when you find that *one* love that makes all others unimportant. I've mourned too long, my son. Your own mother, *buon arma*, wouldn't have wished this. You are the legacy she left me. In my sorrow, I've been too blind to see it. When Paolo gave me this golden lion for you, I knew I'd neglected my duty.

"My son, from this day forward, I'll do everything in my power to see that you become the king of all Lions. Perhaps then, you and I shall end the black scourge that keeps our nation in bondage. The House of de Leone shall raise its colors. Destiny has decreed it! And like Destiny, you shall be invincible!"

"Dolcetto! Antonio! *Aspetta!* Wait!"

They turned in their saddles, glanced in the direction of the greenhouse. Roberto Argento came limping toward them. His incredibly blue eyes, the color of the azure sky, reflected a hundred lights in the hot, dazzling sunshine.

"Be careful today," he told them gently, trying not to alarm them. "The hills are alive with bandits."

Dolcetto nodded, gazing about him beyond the gates into the green hills. He remembered the peasant's warnings. *"Banditi* so fierce, they'd kill without provocation." He turned his attention to his temperamental horse, trying to calm him. The frisky white Arabian with an arched tail and flowing mane snaked sideways and fought the restraint of tightly checked reins. He snorted, angry that the black mare ridden by Antonio had galloped ahead without him.

"Dolcetto! Wait a moment!" Marco de Leone called to his son. Strutting toward him with a Garibaldian air of self-assurance, the titled *latifondisti* crossed the tiled fountain courtyard carrying a *lupara,* a wolf gun, double-barreled and capable of immense destruction. He was followed by two of the four Great Danes that roamed the villa. Marco reached up to steady the white stallion. *"Alleggio, alleggio,"* he purred as he stroked its head. Then Marco expertly buckled an ornate gun holster onto the hand-tooled leather saddle and slipped the *lupara* into it. He gave it a tug, made sure it slipped in and out easily, then tucked the pellets into a container on the outer side. Roberto watched every move with a critical eye to make sure the gun was hitched properly.

Dolcetto watched his father with curious interest. Then he leaned down to cover the long, slender, well-tanned hand with his own. His eyes met the steady gaze of his father and asked silent questions.

"Just for protection, my son," Marco said reassuringly. "You two stay together and use only the familiar roads."

Dolcetto smiled and grasped the reins tighter in his hands as the temperamental stallion backed up and jerked his head from side to side in protest. *"Alleggio. Alleggio."*

"I'll see you later at Lamantia's," shouted Roberto with just enough concern in his voice and eyes to disquiet Dolcetto.

"If you'd rather we didn't go, father . . ."

"Nonsense. Go along, both of you. Don't miss the grape harvest. Just be careful." Marco slapped the horse's rump and the stallion bolted forward. He laughed aloud and his whole being lit up with pride as he watched his son ride off.

"*Va biene*," shouted Dolcetto. "See you tonight at dinner, father." Unable to hold back on the reins, Dolcetto gave the stallion head to join the impatient black mare, where Antonio waited near the main gate. The two riders shouted and waved to the two men they left behind. "*Ciào*."

Roberto's troubled eyes darkened as he watched them ride through the main gate of the stone wall bordering the sprawling estate and into the open fields.

"Do you think it wise for them to ride alone in times like these?" he asked Marco.

"You worry too much, like a woman, my friend." Marco lit a thin, brown cigar. He puffed on it until it burned evenly. Then he fanned out the match and slipped the pack back into the pocket of his open-necked silk shirt. Without averting his head, he raised an arm high into the air. Immediately from behind the stables at the far end of the court came two armed horsemen.

"They'll be under constant surveillance."

Roberto didn't smile, but he was relieved. "*Aloura*, Dolcetto can take care of himself," he said. "Antonio, too." Of late, Marco was preoccupied with a brooding uneasiness. Although outwardly he appeared self-assured and fearless, he was plagued by recurrent, intuitive feelings which had prompted him to double the guard and increase the security at the villa. Just now, a premonition had urged him to arm his son.

But Marco kept his uneasy thoughts to himself. Not even Roberto Argento knew how he felt. The *contadini* had accepted the militant coaching and drilling as precautionary measures against the bandits who'd been spotted roaming the hills of the *latifondo*. It was a way of life in Sicily. The people of the Villa de Leone lived precariously poised between catastrophes, never certain from one day to the next what earth-shattering calamity Destiny had in store for them.

"Come, Roberto," said the Marquis, his spirits suddenly brighter. "From the looks of this splendid day, the harvest shall be *fantastico!*" The sun's rays caused the jeweled lion's head signet ring on his finger to sparkle brightly when he embraced his friend with *maschiezzo*, an air of manliness.

Both men moved across the courtyard dressed in the casual manner of Spanish Dons, having discarded the usual drab attire of English country squires, the current vogue among the *latifondisti*.

"Are all preparations for Dolcetto's birthday party complete?"

"Everything," said Roberto.

Before they entered the elegant villa, Marco paused

again. He gazed eastward toward the Terra d'Oro. Shading his eyes, Marco squinted into the distance and saw the two riders, Dolcetto and Antonio, etched against a blazing sky. He allowed his gaze to wander to the west toward the lush rolling hills beyond the villa complex, where men worked and sang and watched and waited, alert to any change that might mean danger. He turned south, scanning the neat row of cottages, the storage buildings, the L-shaped greenhouse within the enormous stone walls. A few women milled about near the brick ovens. Beyond them, in the fenced corrals, a herd of prize Arabians pranced playfully. Further away, in the highlands, cattle lowed and grazed, content in their boredom. Beyond the wall, promising new rich vines, not yet ready for harvest, shone the color of a sparkling green sea. In the distance, the chaotic Mt. Etna ruled imperiously with stoic indifference since her last tyrannical eruption several years before.

Marco's eyes were deeply shadowed. He no longer smiled, his expression somber and fixed. As his eyes roamed over the many armed guards along the great stone walls of the feudal estate, he sighed heavily, full of silent despair.

"Will there ever come a day when the villa can be without arms? Will this killing and greed over land ever end, Roberto?" He shook his head dejectedly. "Is it possible that one man with true dedication in his heart can really annihilate the *mafia,* wipe it out, erase it from the face of the earth? Year after year, all this uncertainty . . ."

"Marco? What is it? What's troubling you? I've never seen you like this."

His mood broken, Marco stared absently into Roberto's trouble eyes.

"*Niente.* It's nothing. Just talking off the top of my head." He affected an easy smile. "*Amonini.* Let's get started."

"Now that you mention it, the *contadini* claim they've heard talk in the Messina markets. Ever since you declined the efforts of their *gabelloto*—those damned hired caretakers give themselves too much power—the men claim their relations with the purveyors have been touchy."

"It's not the *gabelotti* who give themselves too much power, Roberto. It's the *latifondisti* who hire them and shove their own responsibilities upon them. They've tasted the power of the feudalists, *amico.*"

"And now they've become drugged by it. Is that it?"

Marco shrugged. "It's a heady elixir. Highly intoxicating."

For most of the day Dolcetto and Antonio had ridden indolently through the verdant hills of the enormous *latifondo,* the largest feudal estate in northeastern Sicily, a few kilometers from Messina. They had waved to most of the *contadini*, and the peasants, pausing in their work, waved back to the familiar figures on their Arabians. The two cousins said nothing, but both had grown keenly aware of the arms the peasants bore.

Through flats and highlands, through ancient ruins of bygone civilizations, through wood and glade, they were constantly aware of the heavily armed guards posted in groups of twos and threes, scanning the horizon with high-powered telescopic lenses. These they could accept. It was seeing the peace-loving, benign *contadini* carrying arms that was unsettling.

They were aware they had been followed since leaving the villa, but somehow, in taking short cuts here and there on the way to the Lamantia vineyard, they had inadvertently lost their silent escorts. For the first time that day, Dolcetto felt uncomfortable. Both knew the *latifondo* intimately, yet there were areas which they hadn't ventured into and so far had no desire to explore. Men had disappeared in some of the desolate interior areas. Dolcetto would have backtracked to look for their escorts, knowing they acted upon his father's orders, but it was getting late and the festivities were more appealing.

As the riders approached the northwest sector, layers of pulsating crimson crossed the sky like ribbons, sprayed alternately with yellow golds and tangerine pinks. The beginning of a breathtaking sunset hung from the heavens like a huge canopy, changing here and there only as vague shadows of twilight filtered through its spectral rays.

Dolcetto and his cousin were hot and exhausted and covered with dust by the time they rode into the draw. Preparations for the evening's festivities had already commenced. Caught up in the festive mood, they soon forgot their earlier concern.

Dolcetto's attention was captured by the wasp-faced Signora Lamantia, a frail woman in her late thirties and her last month of pregnancy. She worked with one hand and supported her bulbous stomach with the other. The other women laughingly referred to her as the Leaning Tower of Pisa. With a bouquet of *basilico*—a fragrant mixture of wine vinegar, crushed garlic, oregano, and other exotic herbs—she basted the browning side of veal cooking over an open spit. There was loud hissing and crackling as the meat juices dripped into the open fire. The flames shot up in spurts of brilliant red and orange accompanied by thick black smoke. The air was filled with tantalizing aromas.

In the manner of a highborn country squire, Dolcetto walked along the improvised, dirt courtyard. He waved to

8

the pleasant-faced Signora Amalfi whose exotic brown eyes tilted up at the corners like an oriental's. She was busy making *stratto*—a thick tomato paste. Across the way, Signora Micci, an older heavy-set woman with large pendulous breasts, was cutting zucchini and tomatoes. There was wine in great abundance, and homemade beer and tables laden with fresh fruit. Several peasant women moved about, busily engaged in one thing or another, chatting noisily.

For Dolcetto, the harvesting of the rich amethyst grape was synonymous with the making of a succulent grape delicacy called *farinada,* a dessert that he loved. To him harvest meant nothing else and he'd usually end up making a glutton of himself. The women knew that whenever *farinada* was made, the young Lion would seek them out as he had every year since he was a small child and had first delighted his senses with the tasty aspic. Now, he held up a restraining hand as Signora Lamantia moved in to give him yet another helping.

"*Mangi, mangi,*" she said, grinning shyly. "Eat."

"*Tante grazie,* Signora. Please no more. Already I'm stuffed like a suckling pig." Although Dolcetto spoke perfect Italian, French, and Spanish, he always reverted to his native Sicilian dialect among the *contadini.* He loved their warm-hearted, generous, and pleasure-filled ways, and in return the peasants felt honored and pleased that he'd favor them with his company.

Attracted by singing and the sound of mandolins, Antonio had long since deserted his cousin in favor of the young girls who were stomping grapes in a giant wooden wine press at the other end of the makeshift courtyard.

It was hot. Stifling hot. No breeze had blown in from the north to cool the air. But it wasn't the heat that made Antonio flush with pleasure and caused his temperature to rise. It was one of the beautiful young girls dressed in colorful shifts who made scintillating movements as they stomped barefooted on the purple grapes. Lilliana, the daughter of Guido Amalfi, caught his attention and held it for nearly an hour. With fresh flowers in her long, thick, black hair, she had been tossing petals promiscuously to nearby admirers from time to time. A doe-eyed beauty with flashing brown eyes, a dainty uptilted nose, and sparkling white teeth, she had captured his heart completely. She would cast her flirtatious eyes invitingly, then obstinately pretend the object of her attention didn't even exist. The handsome, dark-eyed Antonio wasn't usually shy and retiring, but this girl had him completely dazzled.

Watching them, Dolcetto laughed to himself. *There he goes again.* He could always tell when Antonio was ready to fall in love. It happened at least once a week. *Yes,* thought Dolcetto, *it has been a good day.*

In the midst of his reverie, Dolcetto glanced lazily up at the skies and gave a start. *Porca miseria!* They should have started back before this. Even if they hurried, it would be dark before they arrived at the villa. He stood up and brushed the dust from the seat of his Spanish-style riding pants; tight fitting to the knees and flared out over his boots. As he shouted to his cousin, he heard a voice calling him.

Alfredo Lamantia, a short, stocky, dark-skinned man with black agate eyes that made him appear more Turkish than Sicilian, shuffled along the dirt path toward him, pausing to place a large crate of over-ripe tomatoes at his wife's side. He patted her stomach affectionately as she flushed and shyly averted her head. He laughed and continued toward Dolcetto.

"What are you two young bucks doing here?" he asked with a crusty Sicilian accent. "Signore Roberto left over an hour ago, thinking you had already departed." He wiped his dirt-caked face, leaving muddy streaks from the streams of sweat pouring down his face and neck. His good-natured smile revealed broken lines of uneven teeth. He unslung his *lupara* from his shoulder and leaned it carefully against his left leg, frowning slightly as he glanced at the sky.

"Stashi vashieno scouro foro. It's getting dark and I don't want His Excellency to worry about you two."

Antonio spun around and walked in the opposite direction. "I'll get the horses," he called to Dolcetto. "I promised Gina that I'd help her with your birthday cake."

The women smiled with delight. "Ah," began Signora Amalfi. "How old will the young Lion be?"

Occupied by the fact that Alfredo also wore holstered guns, Dolcetto hardly heard the woman speak. He turned to her with his usual polite reserve.

"How old will the young Lion be?" repeated Signora Amalfi.

"Domani? Sixteen years old."

"Sixteen years old?" The women marveled and nodded. "It's hard to believe that only yesterday . . ." Sicilian women were all alike. Although they knew that children did grow up, they still refused to believe it.

Bowing from the waist, Dolcetto smiled graciously. "Alfredo, Signora Lamantia, my cousin and I wish to thank you and your family for the cordial hospitality you've extended to us."

Alfredo was both enchanted and amused. The young Lion was indeed his father's son—a precise copy.

10

"Prago, Seignieurino. Prago."

"Signora." Dolcetto paused to dramatically kiss his finger-tips with a flourish. "No one in the entire *mondo* cooks like you. My family and I shall pray for you and your new *bambino*."

The tiny woman flushed with embarrassment. In her shyness, she partially hid herself behind her husband. She was mildly surprised that he had mentioned her pregnancy. Sicilian children were supposed to be blind in matters of the flesh. They all waved and shouted, *"Ciào."*

Dolcetto and Antonio hurriedly mounted the Arabians and cut across the open fields.

Dolcetto's stallion was the color of snow with imperious coal black eyes that shone luminous and proud. A year ago, when he saw the colt born, he had named him *Imperatore*. As part of the elaborate bridle regalia, the horse wore bizzare-looking brass bells and assorted amulets: a two-tailed lion ridden by a crowned virgin, two-tailed sea horses, ox horns carved in brass and silver and polished to a mirrorlike gleam, all designed to ward off *u malocchio*— the evil eye.

Antonio's ebony mare, Empress, had a sleek coat which shone like black satin in the daylight. She possessed a subdued spirit of womanly coyness and flirted outrageously in the presence of the white 'stallion. Both horses had been given to them by the Royal Lion two days before. They'd been so excited at the prospect of having them for their very own, all other things seemed dull and unimportant by comparison.

By the time they reached the central sector and slowed the sweating, panting horses down to a walk, the sunset had faded into twilight and the moon had begun its rise over the hills, lighting their way like an enormous spotlight.

Dolcetto experienced a curious feeling of uneasiness when he glanced around and saw none of the guards he'd seen earlier. Perhaps it was the twilight playing tricks with shadows. The tinkling brass bells on the horse's bridle echoed in the early night air as they walked the horses.

Not wishing to alarm his younger cousin, Dolcetto teased him. "Why didn't you talk with her, Nino? We were there long enough."

"Who?"

"Who? You know who. Guido Amalfi's daughter, that's who."

"Why should I talk with her? I hardly know her."

"You'd like to know her better, wouldn't you?"

"She doesn't know I exist."

Dolcetto couldn't quell the feeling that something was

terribly wrong. *It's my imagination, I'm sure*. His eyes scanned the area time and again, trying not to reveal his concern to Antonio.

"She doesn't, eh? She flirted with you all day."

"How would you know? You were busy eating all that *forinada*. You'll be sick later and when you throw up, who'll have to help you? Me, that's who."

Dolcetto laughed nervously. "Don't change the subject. I know you're sweet on her." He peered straight ahead. They'd be out of the thicket soon and into the clearing. Thank God.

"Her *name* is Lilliana. And don't you start in on me." Dolcetto was a tease. Once he started, he wouldn't give up. *I should be used to him by now,* Antonio thought.

"You hardly know her, eh?" Dolcetto affected a light lecherous tone, emulating the older men who'd kidded them both unmercifully since they'd been home on summer vacation. "I'll bet you've already done the . . . job . . . on her like you did on Maria Theresa at school."

"Cazzo on Maria Theresa! Balls on her!" Antonio struck the mare. Both horse and rider lunged forward and disappeared through the woods.

Dolcetto laughed heartily, partly to ease the tension mounting within him and partly at his cousin who was always so touchy when he became infatuated with a girl.

He turned his immediate attention to *Imperatore* who snorted in protest at the separation from the mare. He checked the reins tightly. The strenuous ride had already caused the stallion to sweat too much. He stroked the silver white mane and spoke reassuringly. "Don't worry, we'll catch up to your sweetheart, you hot-blooded stud. Can't separate you for a moment, eh?"

Suddenly Dolcetto was shaken to the core. An inexplicable feeling came upon him, one so intense that he gave the stallion his rein. When they reached the clearing twilight had melted into night. Managghia! *Where in hell is Antonio? Usually if we separated, we'd meet here.* He turned around in his saddle and tried to pierce the shadows with his eyes. It wouldn't be difficult to get lost in the thicket especially at night. *Where is that* pezzo de shekko? *The jackass! Didn't he know I was only fooling with him?* The apprehensive young Lion proceeded cautiously towards the bluff. Instinctively, he felt alongside his right leg, next to the stirrup for the powerful *lupara*. He breathed easier.

Suddenly from out of the clearing, Antonio came toward him at breakneck speed. His voice filled with frightening urgency. "Dolcetto! Dolcetto! Hurry, come quickly!"

Without hesitation, Dolcetto spurred the Arabian and followed his cousin beyond the clearing up the rocky incline to the top of the ridge, where they both pulled hard on their reins to halt their steeds. They could see the entire estate, including the villa proper and all the buildings within the complex, lit up with the supernatural light of an all-consuming fire.

The luminous glow of the enormous golden-orange July moon was dimmed by the brilliant flares of the amber red fire as it spurted up and out across the heavens, lighting up the entire countryside. The horses reared and spooked, their nostrils distended and their eyes flared in terror. Each time the bursts of fire shot into the skies, fragmenting like uncontrolled fireworks, the horses whinnied and backed away from the rocky ridge.

"*Banditi! Brigante!*"

The boys tugged at their horses and galloped across the fields without thought or care for the crops underfoot. Some fifteen minutes later they arrived at the outer perimeter of the villa where thick curls of congested, black smoke had already covered the moonlight, limiting their visibility. Without thinking, Antonio headed toward the main entrance.

"No! Not that way. To the south, behind the stables," shouted Dolcetto.

The breathless and shaken youth understood immediately. Both had been taught which emergency measures to employ in such circumstances.

The distance to the wall surrounding the complex was nearly three-quarters of a mile. They avoided the main paths and took one known only to the villa residents. Seeing the empty stables shocked them, nevertheless they rode past without comment. They slowed down as they approached the two tower structures at the southwest gates which were usually kept locked. Cautiously they walked their horses, staying well hidden, using the murky shifting shadows for cover. The towers appeared deserted.

Dolcetto dismounted and crept to the gate. The lock was broken. He gave it a hard shove and beckoned to Antonio to lead the horses through to the other side. Antonio left the horses under a cluster of trees at the rear of the peasants' cottages. They walked stealthily behind the row of buildings, inching their way along the wall toward the greenhouse. They heard only the roar of the blazing fire running its course.

Dolcetto stopped suddenly, frozen in his tracks. He saw them first and tried to prevent Antonio from seeing the blood-soaked bodies of several guards, who lay dead with knives buried in their chests. He recognized Mario Lamantia,

13

Alfredo's son. He closed his eyes at the sight. *My God,* he thought, *how ironic. One son dead, another to be born.* He knew the others were also young sons of the *contadini.*

Both boys shook noticeably as they crossed themselves. They crouched down, out of sight in the inky, suffocating darkness and inched their way on all fours along the top of the broken wall that rose higher as it approached and hugged the outer wall of the greenhouse. It was too silent. None of the Great Danes could be heard. The chickens, the baby calves. Where were they? Only the crackling fire swirled around them, devastating everything in sight.

Here, a burst of fire shot into the air like a rocket. There, a cottage snapped in two like a wooden crate, bending and splitting into bright embers. The air, which nearly scalded their flesh, felt like the inside of a raging volcano heated to unendurable intensity.

They climbed higher and higher on the wall until they reached a position which afforded them a view of the fountain courtyard and portions of the cottages. They stared in stupefaction, powerless to stave off the insatiable flames.

Antonio shook like the last autumn leaf caught in the chill of a winter wind, trying against all odds not to disintegrate. He grabbed his cousin's arm as if to reassure himself, to see if this terrible and awesome sight was a nightmare or a reality. Only that morning things had been so peaceful.

Suddenly there was a distant cry and the thunder of hoofs. The earth seemed to tremble under them. From across the courtyard behind the storage bins at the westernmost point of the villa grounds came a galloping horde of horsemen.

"Over there. Look!" cried Antonio.

They came on swift stallions, brandishing knives and guns, swinging their razor-sharp machetes, *lupara* slung over their shoulders. The most ferocious-looking men the boys had ever seen rode into the center of the courtyard within feet of them.

Dolcetto and Antonio watched in utter fascination as the riders crowded into the area and formed a moving circle. They laughed and shouted cries of triumph, their dark eyes glittering with strange maniacal lights.

"*Banditi! E a verita.* Bandits for sure," hissed Dolcetto. Antonio nodded in astonishment. His dark eyes reflected the blazing firelights and a rising nervous excitement. He was both fascinated and wholly terrified at the sight.

Three of the riders cut out from the circle and came rushing at them. The boys crouched down, their hearts pounding. They held their breath, not daring to move. They peeked over a ledge.

14

"Madre de Dio!" whispered Antonio. His face paled and he crossed himself again. His forehead glistened with perspiration, his shocked eyes dilated and transfixed. Now he grabbed at his cousin.

"Dolcetto!" He gestured with a quick jerk of his head. "Look!" They both blinked, unable to believe the incredible sight before them.

In the center of a concentrated spotlight of blazing crimsons and torrid yellow firelight, a swarthy bull of a man sat on a powerful beast that stood higher than the rest. The bizarre and barbarous-looking creature stared straight ahead of him, his glistening black eyes fixed stonily at a point directly in front of the greenhouse, out of their line of vision. Crackling, multicolored flames fanned out around him like a penumbra of power, creating a supernatural effect. *Demonio!* He was something else, this inhuman-looking savage.

Astride the muddied, sweating black stallion, the malevolent bandit looked like an earthshaking giant looming up from the bowels of the earth. He was naked to the waist, except for a silver-studded, highly ornamented, black leather vest, worn like a badge of honor. Each wrist of his muscular arms was strapped with black leather bands. Around his forehead, he wore an Indian-style leather band studded with *malocchio* amulets. His glistening shoulder-length black hair contrasted dramatically with his shaggy, bright red beard, which gleamed like flaming copper snakes.

Here was the living legend of the mountain people. Here was the legend who had evoked paralytic fear thoughout Sicily. Here was the man who had killed more men than the dreaded malaria. Here was the man the ruthless-*carabinieri* couldn't hunt down or capture. Yes, thought Dolcetto as he gazed upon the man, Matteo Barbarossa, unholy bandit of Mazzarino, arm of the Mafia, was more ferocious, more appalling than legend claimed.

With a hair-raising, blood-curdling cry, the red-bearded terror of Mazzarino savagely spurred his horse. The animal reared in protest, turning rakishly from side to side, bucking and rebelling. The whites of its eyes bulged and flared in fright. Barbarossa struck at his horse again and again until the beast leaped forward in desperation to escape the bandit's wrath. Gripped tightly in his dark-skinned hand was a shining, two-edged saber hacked off half its normal size.

To the shouts and urgings of his men, Barbarossa took quick and sudden aim and struck fiercely at an object before him. The black balls of his eyes were immobile in their glistening whites, fierce and frightening to look upon.

The barbarous and brutal bandits laughed and cheered

15

with savage abandon. They formed another circle on horse-back and shouted and yelled as in a primitive victory rite. They were joined by more gargoyle-faced brutes, even more gruesome than their companions.

Their horses reared, rebelling at the abusive treatment they received. Their eyes were wild and dilated, foam dripped from their mouths, and their nostrils flared in protest at the intense heat and the fearsome fires. The lathered horses spooked and jumped into the air, coming down stiff-legged. Others snaked back and forth in every direction, straining against their masters. They whinnied and snorted, making terrible agonized noises.

Thick, black smoke burned the bandits' eyes. As their yells died down, they coughed and sputtered. Satisfied that no help would come to the villa, the renegades shouted triumphantly and followed the arrogant Barbarossa out of the compound without a backward glance.

Dolcetto and Antonio covered their noses and mouths with handkerchiefs and slid cautiously off the wall. They ran to the first cottage untouched by fire. Inside they found the frightened Lamponi family. Mother, father, and two sons, Salvatore and Bastiano, had been tied and gagged in the center of the room, left to be burned alive. Petrified with fear, they had struggled in vain to undo the ropes, and when they saw Dolcetto and Antonio, their tormented faces lit up with new-found hope. Tears of joy sprang into their eyes as they waited to be freed from the jaws of death.

Dolcetto unslung his *lupara*. As he and Antonio untied the Lamponi family, Dolcetto began shouting orders as natural-ly as if it were routine for him.

"Lamponi, find the others and help put out the fires. *Subito!* Use the water from the storage tanks. We have no choice. Understand?" He saw the trembling old man hesitate, but the assertive young Lion gave him no time to argue. "I must find my father. Where are Calo and Ciccio?"

Shaken by the anticipation of a fiery death, the wild-eyed peasant shook his head uncontrollably, dumb anguish in his hollow eyes. He couldn't respond. Words failed to form on his trembling lips. Salvatore came to his father's aid, while his younger brother helped his mother to her feet.

"He'll be all right in a moment. Try the storage bins, *numero siete*. Earlier they were there with Roberto and Guido Amalfi."

"Go quickly," urged Dolcetto. "Send for all the help you can find."

"*Si*," cried Signora Lamponi with bravado. "Go! *Vatini!* Help the others. I'm fine."

16

Dolcetto, with *lupara* in hand, handed Antonio a smaller shotgun. "Use it if you must, Nino."

With fires spreading endlessly in all directions, they crossed over to the path leading to the greenhouse. Their eyes burned as they blindly felt their way through the inky maze, coughing, sputtering, and choking on the thick smoke. Suddenly a hoarse, rasping scream pierced the air. Dolcetto leaped back into shadows for cover. He fought to see through the congested air. There, just a few feet away, stood Antonio, the expression of a madman on his young face. He pointed to an object he'd stumbled upon. Frozen, his lips quivered as if to speak, but no sound came forth.

Dolcetto moved in closer, his smarting eyes searching to see what his cousin pointed to. When he realized what it was, Dolcetto's eyes widened in horror at the obscenity before him. Sickened by what he saw, he averted his head from the ghastly sight. When he could, he looked again at the decapitated head of Roberto Argento.

"Sainted God! No! It can't be!"

But there it was, blood-soaked and streaked with black dirt, vacant blue eyes staring sightless; eyes that only hours before had been joyful and vibrantly alive. The facial expression had twisted into a leering look of hatred and defiance, his last look at the world before Barbarossa chopped him in two.

The young Lion fought rising waves of nausea. He swayed unsteadily and hugged his writhing body. When he caught sight of Antonio, he forgot his own palpitating heart. He quickly grabbed his cousin, slapped him hard across the face to quell the rising hysteria in the younger boy who fell faint in Dolcetto's arms.

Over his shoulder, a shifting breeze blew aside a black patch of smoke, revealing Roberto's bent and misshapen body, hung by the feet in front of the greenhouse. The sickened young Lion averted his head and shut his eyes as blinding, burning tears spilled down his cheeks.

A Lion doesn't cry. A Lion doesn't cry . . . doesn't cry . . .

Dolcetto had just locked horns with fear. In the first round, fear emerged the victor. In losing momentary control, he had wet his trousers. He felt shame, but then he started to feel the weight of his cousin's body, and he quickly forgot his own dilemma.

"Are you all right now, Nino?" he asked, forcing a calm.

Antonio nodded. He wiped away the tears from his soot-smeared face and pointedly avoided looking at Roberto's remains. In those moments, both young boys had become men.

"Come, let's find my father."

17

As they fought for self-control while moving swiftly through the smoke-filled villa, they found themselves reverting to instinct.

Beyond the storage barns to the west of the villa, they saw some of the *contadini* working feverishly to subdue the raging fires with water buckets and dirt. The women wailed, the frightened young children cried and moaned, some prayed, others flung themselves prostrate on the ground when they discovered bodies of friends and loved ones. But most worked diligently to do what they could to help.

Dolcetto heard Lamponi cry out, "Forget the others. There's no hope for them. Look how the fires have devoured them."

Dolcetto swallowed hard. His throat was parched and the intolerable heat grew worse. He glanced in the direction of the main villa. Miraculously, the fires hadn't spread in that direction. With a sudden surge of courage he called out to his shaken cousin.

"Find Guido Amalfi. Tell him to send to the northwest sector, and every other place he can, for help. See if you can find Calo and Ciccio. I'll go in the opposite direction and we'll meet back at the villa. Understand?"

Antonio nodded and left his cousin's side.

Calo and Ciccio had to be someplace. Marco's bodyguards hadn't left his side since before Dolcetto could remember. He glanced around not knowing where to go first. He raised two fingers to his lips and blew shrilly.

The white stallion appeared at the far end of the courtyard. He came across the cobblestones with loud, echoing sounds as he galloped toward his young master. As *Imperatore* tossed his white mane, his glassy black eyes, the color of reflected fire, bulged with fear. Dolcetto mounted him and stroked his mane and spoke reassuringly. "It's all right, Imperatore, I'll take care of you."

In a matter of seconds, horse and rider kicked up clouds of dust as they cut across the vineyards, through the burning fields, toward the central supply depot. Dolcetto flung himself from his horse and searched in vain for his father.

"Papa," he shouted into the emptiness. Not even an echo responded. Signs of destruction were everywhere. Promising vines had been cut, trampled on, uprooted, and ruined. The sheep at the Grazianos' were slain. Heaps of glowing embers and sparking cinders lay piled up where only that afternoon had stood immaculate cottages and buildings. There was no telling if the entire Graziano family had been cremated in the rubble.

Where the winds had shifted, a few cottages stood untouched by the decimating fires. Dolcetto opened the doors and found emptiness. *How many were dead? Missing? Who was alive? My God, Papa, where are you? Why can't I find you? You've got to be someplace. Where?*

On the doors of some cottages he found the headless, bleeding remains of various types of fowl. Graziano had been a breeder of pheasants and peacocks and had amassed an enviable collection. Now, they lay everywhere, strewn about, stiff with death. Even the haughty peacocks had been reduced to the humility of a pointless death. Years of hard work and love destroyed in moments by savage, barbarous butchers. Bastards! Whoring sons of bitches!

Dolcetto's heart hardened and he turned cold as he perceived the devastation around him. Only that morning he had rhapsodized to his cousin about the richly verdant countryside, alive and ripe with abundant harvest. Now the rolling hills quivered in a death rattle. The devil had moved in swiftly with wild abandon and painted black and barren, large patches of earth. Never! Never would he forgive such ruination of the lands!

He covered his nose at the putrid stench of death which violated his senses and etched itself vividly in his mind to be remembered forever.

He rode on past the endless chaos. Despite the inferno-like heat, cold sweat poured over his hot, flushed body. He trembled involuntarily. Waves of nausea rose in him again, and he quickly sprang from his horse and spewed vomit onto the ground. In his second encounter, fear had once again emerged victorious. When it had passed, he called to his horse and rode to the only place which had miraculously escaped the fires.

The villa, dark and deserted, seemed remote, not a part of its quickly dying outer world. It was too quiet he told himself as he slipped out of his boots and crept soundlessly across the cobblestones of the fountain court. He stumbled and nearly fell over the bodies of two guards whose necks had been broken. Dolcetto crossed himself, took a deep breath, and continued past the flower beds, slipping easily inside the carved wooden doors. He heard nothing and no one. Only silence and hollow emptiness greeted him.

In the elegant baronial drawing room, hand-painted deities, angels, and cupids stared down imperiously from their reclining positions in the cloudy mists on the domed ceiling. Marco's study, a magnificent room with an enviable collection of stuffed wild birds, rare first editions, and highly prized guns, now looked alien and uninviting.

Dolcetto's young body ached from holding the weighty *lupara*. Distressing anxiety, mad thoughts, and uncertain fears took a stranglehold on him. Once more he broke out

19

into a cold sweat. *Don't let me be sick again, God. Not now.*

Finding no one upstairs, he crept to the back stairs which led to the kitchen. Suddenly, he cocked his head and listened with the instinctive bent of a bold lion approaching its foe. Muffled sounds drew him like a magnet. Taking a firmer grip on the *lupara*, he moved slowly, a step at a time, as cautious and as intent as a cat. His eyes became the translucent eyes of a lion in the night.

He inched soundlessly to a small crack of light that shone from the slightly open kitchen door. The blood pulsed furiously through his veins as a vague, indiscernible image of someone sitting in the rocking chair in the kitchen came at him. He was about to kick open the door, when the outside door pushed open with a quick violent thrust, and Antonio rushed inside.

Dolcetto breathed easier until he saw his cousin's face fill with stark terror. Antonio had stopped abruptly in his tracks, his bewildered and horrified young eyes darted slowly about him then fixed themselves on a point out of Dolcetto's line of vision. He walked slowly into the room until he, too, saw what made Antonio recoil in terror.

Gina Contiguilia sat in a rocking chair, staring vacantly into space, in a state of catatonia. She rocked in endless motion. On the table next to her were the remains of Dolcetto's birthday cake, a *pane spugnio*, dishes of fruit and chopped nuts, overturned, upset in terrible disarray. Dolcetto walked around to face her.

In her hands she held a razor-sharp knife used for the butchering of calves, still wet with blood. Her arms, face, and hands were caked with blood. At Gina's feet, dead by her own hands, lay a once beautiful woman in a spreading pool of blood. Her face remained untouched. From her neck down to the pubic hairs, her body had been sliced open leaving a gaping wound.

In that split second, he remembered thinking how much like an animal's were human intestines. His legs trembled under him, and he felt for the wall to steady himself.

Dolcetto's mouth felt dry, his lips were horribly parched, and his throat felt like gravel. He looked at the unseeing housekeeper who never stopped her monotonous rocking.

"Gina!" There was no glimmer of recognition, no response. He shook her gently at first, then with more force.

"Gina. What's happened? Can you tell me? It's Dolcetto." Her eyes were glazed over and vacant. "Seignieur Marco. Have you seen him? Where is my father, Gina? In God's name, Gina, talk to me! Don't you know me? I'm Dolcetto."

The woman was temporarily lost in a less painful world

where the stark reality of the moment couldn't touch her. Before he could ask again, he heard Antonio's warning cry.

"Dolcetto! Look!" He pointed to the small earthen-floored storage room off the pantry, where cheese was oiled and stored, and sausage hung to dry. Dolcetto picked up the *lupara* and inched his way toward the door.

He saw the door open and a blood-soaked hand reached out from behind, struggling desperately to hold onto something. He jumped to the other side of the door and kicked it open with his foot, his gun aimed directly on target.

The body of a man, covered with blood, crept out on all fours. It took several moments for Dolcetto to realize that the bloody mass of human suffering lying prostrate before him was the mutilated, outraged body of his father. He'd never seen the Lion reduced to such degradation.

Dolcetto sank slowly to his knees. Stricken, he stared with horror at the pain-filled, abused body of his father. Blood oozed from Marco's eyes, his nose, and his mouth, like small fountains which wouldn't stop. Dolcetto felt numb, bewildered, transfixed.

Every nerve in Antonio's body went dead and caused a sinking feeling unlike anything he'd experienced before. He managed to whisper hoarsely, "Uncle Marco . . ."

"Papa," rasped Dolcetto. "Papa . . . Papa . . . Papa . . ." His voice was just above a whisper. The life was slowly draining from him and he felt numb as one who'd been anesthetized. He tried to lift his father to cradle him in his arms, but the Lion was too heavy. For an instant, he thought he saw a flicker of recognition in Marco's eyes just before the wretched man shuddered into unconsciousness. "Papa! Papa! Oh, no, please . . ." Totally helpless, the aggrieved young Lion lay his face gently on his father's blood-soaked chest.

With a sudden burst of energy, Antonio ran frantically and wild-eyed into the night calling for help. Dolcetto barely heard his screams. He hardly saw Gaetano Lamponi and his sons enter the room. He just lay still, like a baby cub next to its parent, seeking reassurance, warmth and love, and security from fear.

Although they had dealt with various unexpected experiences in their life on the *latifondo*, the Lamponi family couldn't contain their horror at seeing what they encountered in the kitchen.

Salvatore Lamponi blinked his eyes hard and stared from the bloodied knife in Gina's hand to the body of the dead girl at her feet. There could only be one like her. His eyes widened in recognition. Fifteen years had passed but there was no mistaking her.

21

"By the whores of Lucifer, Papa," he shouted. "It's Diamonte!"

The old man glanced sharply at his raving son from where he stood over Marco's battered body, then at the prostrate form at Gina's feet. His smoke-stung eyes focused on the dead girl for a moment. *Santo Dio! My son is right,* he thought.

He crossed himself, torn by the awesome spectacle, unsure of his next move. What to do first? What to do? He directed his concern to the motionless form of the beloved Lion at his feet. Filled with urgency and a sudden efficiency, he called to Antonio who stood by like a frightened waif.

"Run, my boy! Run swiftly and call my wife. When Signora Amalfi returns, make sure she's told to come here immediately. She'll know what to do until the doctor arrives." He turned to his younger son who stood shaken by all his young eyes had seen that night. "Bastiano! Fly like the wind. Get someone to take you to Messina. Find Dr. Pietro. And find Padre Bonaventura!"

The boy nodded dutifully, but his feet wouldn't move. His eyes were glued to the spectacle of death at Gina's feet. His older brother shook him roughly.

"Bastiano! Listen to Papa! Go now!" shouted Salvatore.

The younger boy snapped out of his reverie. "Yes, yes, I'm going."

"Dolcettino," called Lamponi gently. "Come dry your eyes like a brave young Lion. After tonight, no one can say you aren't a man." Lamponi wondered how to convince a sixteen-year-old he must react like a man? He had things to do to the lad's father that could hardly be understood by a boy.

"There's little for you to do here. Go help the others. Tell them to heat water in the brick ovens for the doctor when he arrives."

"No. I'll stay with my father," replied Dolcetto.

Lamponi shrugged. *I've no time for this; I must hurry.* He signaled his older son to do his bidding and moved swiftly. He gathered candles, lit them, and placed them on the floor to illuminate his work. His hands slid expertly up and down Marco's body, searching for other injuries. Finding none, he leaned over and placed his ear to Marco's chest, listening for a heartbeat. His brooding features filled with concern. He grabbed one of Marco's blood-caked wrists and rubbed it gingerly between his brown, veined hands. He glanced furtively at Dolcetto, but he could delay no longer. Pray he understood.

He doubled his right hand into a fist and pounded hard on Marco's chest several times. The loud, dull thuds startled Dolcetto, and he filled with livid anger over what appeared

22

to him an inhuman act against a pain-filled, dying man. He knew Lamponi would do nothing to hurt his father, however brutal and primitive the act appeared. *I only pray it's effective,* he told himself.

"Thank God!" shouted Gaetano Lamponi. "Your Father lives! Quickly now, find me some brandy and bring me white sheets or bandages from the dispensary . . . no, sheets are better."

Lamponi looked at the woman rocking in the chair but a few feet from them. *She must be in shock. There's nothing I can do for her.* The tenant farmer had only seen what others had done in such circumstances. He was from the remote inland village of Gangi which had no medical facilities; the villagers had had to trust in their own occult, healing potions, and voodoos.

By the time Dolcetto returned, Lamponi was ready for him.

"Tear the linen into three-inch strips," he ordered as he cleansed the bloody wounds with a brandy-soaked cloth. In some areas he poured the liquid freely over the wounds. As he packed and bandaged and made tourniquets, he tried to keep his face from betraying his feelings. He didn't want to alarm the cub who remained at his father's side, but he held little hope for the Royal Lion. *It's a miracle if he lives. A miracle!*

He wondered why someone else didn't come to help him. Where were the others? And where were El Leone's bodyguards, Calo and Ciccio? How could they have permitted such a thing to happen to His Excellency? Outrage and anger replaced Lamponi's concern. *Goddammit! There's a limit to what I can do in these circumstances. Where the hell are the others? Why don't they come? Cretins! Whoring bastards! Those bandits! Curse upon them! Curse their black stinking hearts for what they brought upon El Leone!*

He wrapped Marco's swollen, bleeding face until it resembled a mummy. His son Salvatore returned and together they carried the broken Lion upstairs to his chambers.

"God bless you both for what you've done for my father," said Dolcetto quietly.

Lamponi couldn't find the words to reply. He had to avert his head quickly so the young Lion wouldn't mistake profound hurt and dismay for cowardice when he saw tears fall from the older man's eyes.

Antonio walked into his uncle Marco's room, and he and Dolcetto sat in chairs a few feet away from where the Royal Lion lay still as death. Their sad, hollow eyes were fixed on the waxen features of the man on the large, canopied four-poster bed.

23

2

Father Bonaventura was a pear-shaped man with a fat belly, a cherubic face, and salt-and-pepper hair worn in a short brush cut. He had grown soft and flabby from indolent living habits, good food, choice wines, and a fawning housekeeper who waited on him hand and foot. His profession had placed him in a lofty position, for in Sicily members of the cloth are revered, respected, and treated like deities, second only to God.

Each morning he officiated at mass in the small lavish chapel on the *latifondo*. He handled baptisms, communions, confirmations, and weddings in the nearby villages as well as those on the estate. At harvest when some of the workers couldn't leave their work to pay their respect and homage to God, Father Bonaventura would hold mass al fresco. For the past two days, this diligent, soul-saving man had been in the hills doing God's work in the remote inland villages.

Riding home on his mule, the priest had seen the devastating black skies as far away as Tortorici, near Bronte. The tedious sluggishness of his burro only increased his anxiety. When he finally got to the Villa de Leone and saw the smoking ashes and charred ruins and smelled the stench of death, he found it too incredible to believe.

The priest had been the first to arrive after Signores Amalfi and Lamponi, and he was quickly rushed to Marco's side. Seeing the Royal Lion lying motionless on the bed in the dim shadows of flickering candlelight affected the priest more than all the destruction he had encountered at the outer perimeter of the *latifondo*.

Approaching the bed silently, he made the sign of the cross. In Latin he prayed for Marco's soul and asked God to spare this great man.

"Happy is he that always hath the hour of death before his eyes and daily prepareth himself to die . . . Labor now so to live, that at the hour of death thou mayest rather rejoice than fear . . . Who shall remember thee when thou art dead? And who shall pray for thee?"

The priest's voice broke. The litany stopped and a huge sob tore from the man. On his knees at the side of the bed, he forced himself to look upon the colorless face of his longtime friend as the hungry jaws of death drooled overhead.

Sara Amalfi and Nina Lamponi, both midwives and quasi practical nurses who had often helped Dr. Pietro in the dispensary, had worked diligently to improve on what Lamponi had done. Once most of the blood had been cleaned away, bluish-purple bruises and angry welts appeared. Both the Lion's eyes were swollen shut and surrounded by ugly cuts and abrasions.

"Has the doctor been here yet?" asked the priest softly. "What is his condition?"

"It's a miracle if he lives, Padre," whispered Sara Amalfi. "He's lost too much blood." Leaning toward her patient, she quickly blotted the blood that trickled from his lips. "See, he bleeds internally. I'm at a loss until Dr. Pietro arrives. Pray it's soon." She dabbed at the tears on her cheeks. "He's such a good man. He doesn't deserve this fate," she said quietly, not wishing the boys to overhear.

The priest nodded and rose to his feet, shaking his head sadly. Moving across the room to where Dolcetto and Antonio sat, he placed a comforting hand on each boy's shoulder, then quickly had to retrieve a handkerchief to wipe his nose and tear-stained face.

Antonio raised his round innocent face and gazed at the priest without a flicker of recognition. His dark, tousled hair fell over his haunted eyes. He was covered with soot and dirty smudges. Slowly he turned his head away and withdrew into his own private silence.

Dolcetto's somber eyes had turned a murky green and never left his father's face. Not a muscle moved. He sat, fixed as a statue, empty of all emotion. Like his cousin, he, too, was covered with grime, blood, and sweat, but he neither cared nor appeared to be aware of it.

The bereaved priest took a chair next to Dolcetto and wept with inconsolable sadness. He didn't want to perform the last rites yet, but he knew he was only delaying the inevitable. Perhaps when the doctor arrived and informed him it was necessary . . . No, it wasn't that. He didn't want to face the possibility of Marco's death despite all he was supposed to preach about death really being the beginning of life, to be approached with rejoicing. *Listen,* he told himself, *right now as you sit here, and at other times, for as long as you've lived, you've been stripped of any supernatural contact with God. Don't perpetuate the farce and think of yourself as the chosen emissary of God. Damn! Don't delude yourself further. There isn't a damn thing you can do to prevent death.*

Watching his father hover between life and death, Dolcetto felt a sense of the unreal. The last few hours had been ghastly nightmares. What shook him most were the distorted images filling his mind. Roberto's decapitated body took on surrealistic, grotesque proportions, not at all the way he wanted to remember him. But most excruciatingly clear was

25

the recurring image of the red-bearded devil, Matteo Barbarossa.

I'll never forget him. If I live to be a hundred, I'll never forget his face before he decapitated Roberto.

A powerful surge of hatred seared the young Lion's soul, and his features distorted with thoughts of vengeance.

The priest blew his nose loudly. Startled by the unexpected noise, Dolcetto gave a start. He noticed the priest for the first time. He experienced a terrible feeling of guilt for harboring such black thoughts of hatred in those brief moments. He felt as if a mirror had been held up to his soul and Father Bonaventura had discerned the malevolence lurking there.

Four hours later, there was still no change. Why hadn't his Godfather arrived? What could have happened to Calo and Ciccio, his father's bodyguards? Why didn't someone think to inform him of something? Anything! Was he not the young Lion? Does everything have to take so much time? Time! Everything takes time! How much time does my father have? How much?

Curled up in the wing chair, a gradual change came over Dolcetto. Concern over his father's fate transformed into concern for the responsibilities which faced the Royal House of Lions. Slowly the heavy cloak of depression lifted, baring the cloak of responsibility. The son of the Royal Lion had to think like the Royal Lion. Was it not for such a moment he had been trained? How, he began to ask himself, had the men coped successfully with the fires? What was the extent of the damage? How many had died? Who were the survivors? The dead? Who among them was fit to lead the rest? What had precipitated this outrageous assault of the Mafia upon the Royal Lion, on Roberto, on the House of de Leone? How had they dared?

Marco would want his son to take his proper place, give courage to the *contadini* who had suffered, to the women who mourned their dead, to the fathers of dead sons for whom they had such high hopes. But who would give courage to Dolcetto?

Dolcetto felt strongly that Destiny moved everything into place according to her scheme of things. Believing this, Dolcetto knew his life had been preordained. From the time he first remembered, he heard Marco tell him, "You, my son, shall be the king of all Lions, the Lion I could never be." Instinctively, Dolcetto's hand slipped inside his shirt, groping for the golden jeweled lion he wore around his neck.

"A man who loved you as a Godson gave the lion to you, son," Marco had told him when he was old enough to comprehend. "It is a symbol of strength, power, and absolute rule over men who will look to you for leadership and direction. Guard this trust well, Dolcetto. Don't abuse the trust or the loyalties of any man, and choose with infinite caution those men in whom you place responsibility."

Dolcetto fingered the jewel as he recalled his father's words. He slowly turned to look at his cousin, Antonio, and felt an insurmountable surge of compassion for him. In a quick gesture of love, he put his arm around him in an effort to comfort him and give him added courage.

"Don't worry, Nino, he'll pull through. You'll see." Dolcetto whispered in a voice heavy with bravado, which Antonio detected immediately. The dark-haired boy nodded quietly before he left the room on Signora Amalfi's advice to clean up.

A moment later, Dolcetto thought he saw his father move. Quick as lightning he flew to his side. "Papa?" he whispered. "It's me, Dolcetto. Can you hear me?" He picked up his father's lean, tanned hand and held it between his. It felt cold as ice.

"Be patient, my son. His life's in the hands of God." Father Bonaventura stroked the boy's curly brown hair. There was no movement from Marco, and the lad sat back on the bed, dejected.

The priest pulled a chair closer to the bed and sat down. He remembered how close Marco and his son had been. Strange how the mind picks out certain episodes and makes them appear more clearly than others. He vividly recalled the truths spoken between father and son.

Marco had never permitted Dolcetto to be treated like an immature or foolish child. Knowing that the responsibility of being a Royal Lion would one day weigh on the boy's shoulders, he never allowed him the luxury of making the same mistake twice. He'd been more demanding of Dolcetto than Antonio, more explicit in the instructions concerning Dolcetto's rearing than Antonio's.

Father Bonaventura had taught them theology in private sessions. The religious lore and superstition perpetuated by the *contadini* were not part of their schooling. Both had been taught logic and ethics at a time when their peers might be learning the alphabet. As they grew up their studies were continued in northern Italy under the tutelage of the Jesuits.

A huge sob wracked the priest's body. Again he blew his nose and dabbed angrily at his eyes. He arose and walked to the French doors that overlooked the Madelaina Gardens. It was difficult to see, for night was still upon them and the fires which had lit up the night were under control.

27

What a miracle the villa proper hadn't been ravaged by the fire, he thought. A real miracle! His mind rolled back to the boys' youth. That sonofagun, Dolcetto. What a bright young man. By the time he was seven he could shoot a gun as well as a grown man. Taught by Calo La Bolla, he became an expert at *caccia*—hunting. Antonio who detested guns never mastered them. The priest recalled the expression of ineffable delight that passed over Marco's face one day when target for target, Dolcetto matched everything Calo did.

Marco kept both lads at his side whenever he rode the hills of the *latifondo*. They listened as Marco spoke with his people. His ways became their ways in their fierce desire to emulate Marco's soft-spoken, gentle strength. From him they learned respect for their fellow men. From him they learned the importance of carefully evaluating problems, avoiding hasty decisions that could prove costly. From him they learned to be Lions.

As they grew, Antonio seemed a youth without humor, more serious than Dolcetto. He maintained a quiet reserve, was more introverted, and served as an equalizer for Dolcetto's more outgoing, demonstrative ways. The *contadini* treated Antonio as one of their own and showered him with love and affection. Dolcetto, on the other hand was looked upon with benevolent fascination, awe, and respect.

But they were inseparable. They loved each other dearly and shared their joys and sorrows as one. It was to his heir, Dolcetto, who would one day assume Marco's role, that he was the most stringent taskmaster.

Only two days before Marco had confided to the priest that the boys wouldn't be returning to Lake Como in the fall. Marco had enrolled them in a private school in Switzerland to prepare them for the subtle changes taking place in Italy.

"We'll have to rearm the villa again, make it a veritable fortress," Marco had told him. For many months the *contadini* felt as if they were sitting atop Mt. Etna waiting for her to erupt. Horns of the devil! It finally happened!

Father Bonaventura hadn't had time to learn how the bandits had penetrated the security of the villa, how they'd seemingly caught everyone off guard. *Let the militants worry about it*, thought the priest. *I can only give solace to the people. If that's what God's work is all about, that's all I can do. But how? Where do I start? I can't even bring solace to Dolcetto.* The crestfallen priest suddenly felt much older than his forty-five years.

He returned to Marco's bedside. Dolcetto was still there

in his vigil. The priest sighed inwardly. Perhaps it had been wise of Marco to have prepared the young Lion for such enormous responsibility. Only time would tell of this wisdom. He knelt and made supplication to God in the only way he knew. He prayed that God in his mercy would allow Marco to live so that the weight of so strenuous a role wouldn't burden Dolcetto so early in life.

When the priest opened his eyes and glanced at Marco's motionless form, he marveled that life should continue to flow in a body so horribly assaulted.

At that moment, a tremendous struggle ensued within the body of Marco de Leone. Faint stirrings of consciousness tingled within him. Dimly at first, then with great awareness, came the sensation of a terribly dry, burning, parched mouth. His nose felt stuffy, swollen many times its normal size. Images came and left him faster than memories. And those were just as elusive. He wanted to say something. *There's a ball of fire in my throat. Water. Please someone give me water. The fire is burning like a torch.* There were indiscernible shapes and heat. Such heat! Rasping, hissing sounds! He tried to move. His body refused to take orders. Dull throbs, like a pounding anvil, accompanied each heartbeat. *Oh God, help me open my eyes! They feel glued together, weighted down with stones.* Images continued to form and fade, bouncing away from him to converge at some distant point. Finally a sliver of light appeared. *Is that you, Dolcetto? Is it your voice I hear? What is that rasping sound? That hissing? That hot torch in my throat?*

"Papa?" Dolcetto's alert eyes had seen the faint stirrings. "Can you hear me? Papa? Papa!"

Marco's lips trembled as if to speak. His mouth opened slightly and blood spewed forth from each corner of his mouth, down his chin onto his chest. His eyes, glazed with pain, filled with an agonized look of frenzy and he lost consciousness.

Those rasping, hissing sounds gurgling from his throat had struck terror in the priest, Signora Amalfi, and Nina Lamponi. Dolcetto simply stared from one to the other, unable to comprehend. Their eyes told them one thing, but their hearts stubbornly denied it. The priest was first to confirm the truth. "May God have mercy on him! They've cut out his tongue!"

Nina Lamponi flung herself to her knees, crossed herself, and babbled an incoherent prayer. Sara Amalfi choked back the hot stinging tears and bit back her anger at the abominable act. Then, in the manner of an efficient nurse, she quickly pulled Marco up and forward, opened his mouth to let the blood drain out, packed him with linen squares, and reached for the morphine syringe with which to inject him. Thank God he hadn't choked to death on his own blood!

Father Bonaventura stood transfixed, his eyes like those of a madman. He wanted to comfort Marco, reassure Dolcetto, offer up prayers, conjure up mystical powers of communication with God. At the same time, the enraged priest felt a profound urge to kill, to avenge. He wanted to fling off his priestly garb, pick up a gun, and destroy. After all he was a man, wasn't he? But he just stood there, impotent, while his blood turned to ice.

For the third time that night Dolcetto locked horns with that demon—fear. This time fear was merciful, for everything that had begun to spin around the room dissolved into sweet blackness for the young lion.

Outside in the fountain courtyard, just beyond the portico, Guido Amalfi and his sons, Tonuzzo, Giacamo and Giovanni, stood talking animatedly with Lamponi and his sons, Salvatore and Bastiano. Benjiamino Paradiso stood off to one side consoling a red-eyed Tomasso Micci, who was bereaved at learning of the death of his son. Slightly apart from them stood Mario Massina, a moose of a man with a long sad face, a gentle giant who'd been Roberto's assistant for the past five years. Next to him, faring badly at the news of his son's death, stood Alfredo Lamantia. The men stood talking in a group, using animated hand gestures. They were understandably angry, and their hatred was directed at one solitary man, dressed in the garb of a bandit, who stood off by himself, sullen, morose, and uncommunicative.

Beneath stony eyelids, the bandit Mario Cacciatore's black eyes blazed with a malevolent cunning. His hands were tied firmly behind his back, and his cocksure pose infuriated the *contadini*. Their frustrations materialized in the form of cuss words and threats.

"Filthy beast!" hissed Micci, spitting at him, then cupping his mouth with his hand as if even the gesture contaminated him. "You'll pay for the death of my son. I'll skin you alive! Hear?"

"Villainous bastard! Son of whore's whore!"

"That's enough!" ordered Guido Amalfi who stood taller than the others. "Calling this viper names will not bring back our loved ones, restore our crops, or rebuild our homes . . ." Amalfi broke off, unable to continue. His daughter Lilliana and two of the other young girls were missing and they feared they'd met with foul play from the departing bandits.

"Then shoot him!" shouted another.

"Shooting's too good for this accursed son of a contaminated snake!"

"Then skin him like a rabbit! Even that's too good for this horn toad viper!"

When Guido Amalfi saw that these remarks did nothing but evoke sneering contempt from their captive, he couldn't resist the overpowering compulsion to smash his fist into the man's face. He connected solidly, for Cacciatore hadn't had time to duck the blow. Blood spurted from a gash at the corner of his lips. The bandit bent his head to his bare shoulder and wiped the warm blood on it. When he saw the blood, his sardonic grin vanished. He gave Amalfi a look that could curdle blood, one filled with silent menace.

"Where are your companions?" asked Micci.

"Tell us," commanded Massina, "or you'll receive the same fate you gave to Argento." Massina pushed the box at his feet out into the circle that had formed around Cacciatore and he removed the towel that covered it. The men averted their heads at the sight of Roberto's head which had swollen to twice its original size.

The sneering, overly confident bandit spat maliciously at the head. Another fist flew at him, deflecting off his temple. He winced slightly.

"Goddammit! You whoremaster! *Schifoso!* Have you nothing to say?"

"Stick it up your ass!" said the bandit.

"Shoot him!" called one of the men. "Here's my gun."

The men grew increasingly angry. Tempers boiled over and mob violence began to manifest itself in these peace-loving peasants.

"I'm giving you one more chance to tell us where we'll find the others."

"Stick it again. This time in your mouth!"

Amalfi's fist connected again, this time flattening Cacciatore's nose. He felt the crushing of bones under his powerful fist. Guido felt a sudden exhilaration. No remorse.

From a different direction came another fist pounding the bandit's back. Then he was assaulted heavily by flying fists as the men vented their wrath on him, but he gave no indication of any discomfort.

Incensed, the peasants doubled their fists, shouted curses, made threatening gestures, but nothing intimidated him. His imperious attitude only increased Amalfi's fury. He raised his powerful fist, and with all his strength he smashed it in the man's face time and again.

Finally, the culprit winced in pain. His nose swelled up and streams of blood flowed onto his chest and dribbled to the ground. It was a tense moment. A hush prevailed as

31

Cacciatore slowly lifted his hate-filled ebony eyes, leveled them at Guido Amalfi, and committed his image to memory. It was the power-saturated look of a man who is sure of himself and aware of his own strength. It was a look which promised revenge.

Dolcetto awakened to the muffled sounds of these angry voices outside. He glanced out his bedroom window at a world still bathed in the darkness of night. In the distance he heard the sound of barking dogs. He was astounded to find he'd been bathed. He smelled clean and fragrant. He flushed with embarrassment wondering who had tended him. Memory came to him and with it the pain of anguish over his father's plight. He dressed in haste.

Everything in his room reminded him of Roberto Argento: special cases skillfully handmade to hold his hunting trophies and books, a bas-relief map of the *latifondo* that had taken nearly three summers to complete, hand-tooled leather belts, gun cases, everything. Now Roberto was gone. He paused to trace a finger lightly over these treasures, feeling the texture and contour of each and remembering most of all how much love went into these labors. He swallowed hard and choked back the threatening tears. *A Lion doesn't cry. A Lion doesn't cry.*

Five minutes later Dolcetto was at his father's door. He knocked lightly, grasped the handle, and turned, but it was locked. He knocked again. Now he grew more aware of the angry voices outside. Outraged, he cursed inwardly. *Damn! Have they no respect? Don't they know Marco is inches away from death? Va biene,* he'd have to instruct them in some manners.

The door to his father's room opened. Nina Lamponi slid her plump frame through the slight opening, denying him admittance.

"The *dottore* is with your papa, Seignieurino. You are not to enter."

"Haven't I already seen the worst, Signora? How is he?"

"He's alive, Dolcettino. He's alive."

"When may I see him?"

She made a disorganized gesture that could have meant anything. "I must go. I'm needed inside."

Dolcetto felt like a stranger in his own home. He walked toward the west wing of the upper hallway. Priceless paintings and sculpture graced the arched alcoves, but he saw none of them, for he was drawn by the loud, angry voices and emotional outbursts coming from the fountain courtyard. He descended the spiral staircase that fanned out into a semicircle below him, leading to the right of the three main salons.

Dolcetto felt an unusual inner tranquility. He had no way of knowing that his Godfather, Dr. Pietro, had administered a sedative to relax him and quiet his emotions. Never before had he experienced this surge of inner strength and sense of well-being. It was marvelous how he felt. Even knowing what had happened to his father didn't twist his stomach into knots as it had earlier. He seemed to view it in the proper perspective.

Standing at the top of the landing looking down at the gathering of men, he saw the surly-faced, battered frog of a man who unflinchingly stood his ground. Dolcetto could understand the fury of the *contadini*. He noted how courageously the bandit resisted intimidation. He also noted the mad gleam in the eyes of the thick-necked, middle-aged bandit, the profusion of ugly scars across his face and upper torso, the mad glitter of teeth as he smiled mockingly at the men.

Dolcetto weighed the man's actions carefully, noting how he took blow after blow from the incited peasants with no sense of fear, no concern, almost as if he were immortal. He was either a brave man or a furtive coward effecting bravado. Which was he, wondered the young Lion. Which?

Before he approached them, Dolcetto noticed that visibility was still poor. Smoke still clung to the air. Now he refocused his attention on the scene below him. The sound of his leather boots against the cobbles drew their attention one by one.

When they first saw him, their compassionate eyes softened, filled with grave concern and profound sorrow, and they prepared to offer their sympathies and undying devotion. But something about the way he looked in the glare of the torches stopped them.

"Look at this . . . Look at this . . . *Demonio!*" whispered Lamponi to his sons.

Dolcetto locked his eyes firmly on the bandit and walked right through the men who moved aside, allowing him to pass. How silent it became. No one stirred. Nothing moved. The men stared in stupified wonder.

The Lion stopped a few feet from the bandit. His eyes, cold as green jade, stared compulsively into the contemptuous eyes of the odious, scar-faced man.

"Who is this man?"

"A captive, Seignieurino. One of those whoring obscenities. A Mazzarino."

"Where did you find him, hiding in the outhouse?" Dolcetto sniffed the air distastefully.

"No, Seignieurino. Calo La Bolla captured him as he tried to make his escape," said Guido Amalfi, watching the Lion in utter fascination.

"Turn him over to the *carabinieri*. They'll fix his tail," insisted Micci.

"No!" Dolcetto's voice was firm. "He'd only be released before morning."

The ghastly ogre of a man laughed, a raucous animal-sounding laugh.

"This boy is wiser and braver than you unmanly eunuchs!"

"I'll kill him with my bare hands!" shouted Massina. "I'll kill him!" He moved toward Cacciatore but was held back by Guido Amalfi, who still couldn't take his eyes from the young Lion.

But he wasn't the only one intrigued by Dolcetto's new pose. Cacciatore thought about him, wondering why the circle of men paid him such respect. *Seignieurino no less, Not the usual Signore? He must be the son of one of these fucking barons. Phew! I've had my fill of them.* He spat into the dust indicating his feelings toward such men.

Once again the men's voices rose in an uproar and they advanced toward him.

"*Basta!*" Dolcetto's face seemed older and harder. "Take him to the utility courtyard, next to the brick ovens," he commanded.

The bewildered men faltered, unused to taking orders from a mere slip of a boy. Yet, there was something about him. Something . . .

"I gave you an order! Move!" commanded the Lion once more. "And you, Amalfi, have they located Calo or Ciccio?"

"Dr. Pietro is tending their wounds."

Dolcetto glanced swiftly at him. "Are they all right?"

"Full of holes, Seignieurino, but they'll live," said Guido.

Dolcetto moved through the circle of men and searched out Salvatore Lamponi. They whispered in hushed tones for several moments. Salvatore's eyes smoldered excitedly as he nodded, seemingly in accord with what the Lion told him. Filled with marked excitement, he departed to carry out Dolcetto's instructions.

"Tonuzzo, go find my cousin Antonio. I want him here at my side."

The boy disappeared up the portico steps, out of sight.

3

Having moved across the heavens, the moon now sent a long beam of light into the hollow of the courtyard. Torches cast giant shadows across the mall. Dolcetto had gone there ahead of the others to be alone, to think. He stood gazing into the burning fires of the circular stone pit. He was breathing hard. The palms of his hands were moist. His flesh quivered and his mouth felt cottony as he sought to reinforce his courage for what must be done.

What little wind had risen was clearing much of the smoke. Tomorrow it would be very hot, no different than any other day during a Sicilian August. He sighed heavily and thought about the many things Marco had instructed him concerning the ways of men.

"Always remember, young Lion, that there are many breeds of men. Some men can be won and swayed by words, a few with gifts. Among the educated and knowledgeable men, you can win by reason, at times, logic. Then there are those men who fear nothing, not even their own consciences. These are a special breed of men who must be dealt with in a manner only they can understand. You must meet a man's reality in order to reach him. Raise or lower your thinking but meet them at their level, for only when you have the key to a man's thinking can you conquer him. Above all, remember, no man dares contest the resolve and forebearance of a brave Lion."

Flames shot out from the open pit, their light revealing the mixed emotions on the faces of the men congregated around the fire. Some were filled with awe and enormous respect for this young giant. Others indicated marked disapproval of his bold, authoritative manner, and some, anxious to see what would follow, tried to mask the undercurrent of excitement generated by his aggressive behavior. A few of the older men stared stonily ahead without expression, seemingly passive; their eyes had seen everything in a long lifetime. What else could happen?

There they were, all those men who'd escaped death in the bandits' raid and the ravenous fires. In their midst was the symbol of their hatred and vengeance, the bandit Cacciatore. They moved in closer to him, closing the circle.

Gaetano Lamponi scratched his bald pate, then replaced his cap. He couldn't forget that it had been the young Lion who had saved his family from certain fiery death. *Managghia,* what courage! How could he quarrel with the cub? He held him in too high regard. Guido Amalfi also held Dolcetto in high esteem, as did Mario Massina and Micci and most of the heads of the families, for they knew him best.

Dolcetto was occupied giving last minute instructions to Salvatore and Giovanni.

Ping! A shadowy figure standing on the roof over the St. Sebastian Court fired a rifle. The first shot caught Mario

Massina's right shoulder. He pitched forward and dropped to his knees, almost unnoticed except by those immediately next to him.

Zing! The second bullet whistled through Guido Amalfi's left wrist. He felt the hot sting and stared wonderingly at the blood oozing from the holes on either side. *Goddammit! It's real. I've been shot,* he told himself. As spasms of pain shot through him, he dropped to his knees, searching for the gun.

Bang! The third bullet grazed Micci's head from the rear. Instinctively, his hand traced the searing crease that traveled across his skull. He, too, gazed about the darkness in bewilderment.

Bang! Bang! Two more bullets missed their mark and promiscuously screeched over the heads of the scattering men.

Boom! A final bullet parted the bandit's hair. Blood spurted in trickles across his forehead. Unperturbed, he stood his ground, searching the darkness for the source of the gunfire. His black agate eyes spotted the shadowy form which gave rise to new hope that the Mazzarinos had returned for him.

The assailant's shooting arm shot up into the air. Passing the outside alcove in the upper portico, Sara Amalfi had seen him. She reached him seconds before Dolcetto did. Shaken by his failure to kill the bandit, the man sobbed. "I couldn't even shoot the bastard! I couldn't even hit that obscenity!"

"You always were a lousy shot, Nino," said Dolcetto comfortingly, placing his arm around his cousin. Thanking Sara Amalfi with his eyes, he took over. Hugging Antonio warmly, he spoke reassuringly and led him toward the fiery pit.

"Don't feel badly. No one could have done too much damage from that distance."

Antonio was instantly forgiven when the others learned of his intentions. Still shaken, the men circled in to listen to the young Lion who addressed the gathering before him. He jumped up on the butt end of the stone pit and leveled his vibrant eyes on them. How that golden jeweled lion around his neck glowed, they thought, like the powerful amulet of a god.

"*Amici,* this misfortune that has befallen us has taught us a lesson we'll never forget. To waste time lamenting would mark our annihilation," he began.

The men nodded. They agreed so far. This is what the Lion would have said.

"My father, who loves all of you and Sicily with uncon-

36

testable passion, lies upstairs in the hands of God, savagely mutilated."

A disquieting murmur arose among the men. There was more, they could feel it. Dolcetto reached down to place a steadying hand on Antonio's shoulder.

"My father cannot be here to resolve the fate of this savage, so it is I who will attend to it." He swallowed the lump in his throat, and with a catch in his voice he said, "You'll never hear the sound of my father's voice again."

"What did you say, young Lion?" asked Massina aghast.

Dolcetto repeated his words, watching to see what effect they would have on the renegade, who began to have second thoughts about the lad. So! This was El Leone's son? He studied the tall, slim youth with the penetrating green eyes. Goddammit! He had to admit the lad was courageous. He stared at the jeweled lion around his neck, then spat contemptuously into the dirt at his feet. The *contadini* snarled at him.

Dolcetto continued. "His Excellency, my father, no longer has a tongue. It was torn out of his head by butchers like this man who stands before us."

Reacting violently to these words, the men took menacing steps toward the viper. Cacciatore's expression changed considerably. He paled and grew apprehensive.

"No! Stop! Listen to me," called the Lion. "Hear me out."

Cacciatore backed away from the violent men. Humiliation shook him to the core. *Goddammit! To be thrust into near paralytic fear by a mere lad? Me? Cacciatore? What the hell's wrong with me,* he asked himself. Every move he made, the ropes binding him cut like hot razors. He ached from all the bruises and welts forming on his body.

Antonio couldn't stop trembling. Uncle Marco without a tongue? The nation's most formidable legislator unable to speak? What irony was this? Mario Massina's shoulder pained him, but this news shot through his heart like a saber. Guido Amalfi eagerly fingered his knife with his bandaged hand. The rest were in a state of shock. What should they do? What could they do? This was the final outrage!

"Remove his shirt," ordered Dolcetto, waving his arms at the men.

Salvatore Lamponi stepped into the circle and with his Bowie knife slashed off what remained of Cacciatore's shredded and blood-stained shirt.

"What do they call you, bandit?" asked Dolcetto.

The sullen killer glared in silence.

Instantly, a thin wire garrote was slipped over the bandit's neck, snapped tightly like a noose, jerking his head back. Calo La Bolla, a powerfully built brute of a man with his upper torso swathed in bandages, tightened his grip on the wire and shouted hoarsely, "Swine! Answer when the young master speaks." His bruised face with its raised welts and abrasions made him look fiercer than the Mazzarino.

Cacciatore couldn't have spoken even if he wanted to. He gasped and coughed and strained against the garrote. Dolcetto signaled Calo to relax his hold. The peasants, watching with profound curiosity, backed away from La Bolla, but he demonstrated unwavering loyalty to the young Lion. Why contest the Lion?

"Speak your name," demanded Calo.

Coughing, sputtering, eyes bulging, he managed to mutter, "C-acci-at-o-r-e."

Cacciatore! the dreaded name was out. Staring in shock, the peasants suddenly understood his apparent fearlessness. Here stood the most dreaded man in Sicily. His cold-blooded brutality and gruesome murders surpassed even those of Matteo Barbarossa. This was Barbarossa's butcher. He was real. He was here in flesh. He was the hawk who swooped down on unsuspecting sheep. He was the buzzard who ate a man's flesh. He was Cacciatore. And they had contested him? Would he strike back? Would he? They knew the answer and backed away from him, hoping he'd recognize none of them.

At that moment, Salvatore Lamponi, a wide grin on his face, raised a branding iron from the fiery flames to show Dolcetto its molten tip. The Lion nodded. Salvatore set the iron back into the fire and moved swiftly behind the bandit to insert a bamboo rod between the ropes at the man's wrists.

"On your knees, whoremaster!" A savage twist on the bamboo brought Cacciatore swiftly to his knees. Young Salvatore grinned diabolically. What a Lion!

The *contadini* glanced in bewilderment from Dolcetto to Cacciatore to the branding iron. They could hardly believe their eyes. They backed away confused and uneasy at what he was about to do. Is the Lion crazy? *Managghia!*

Cacciatore stared aghast at the branding iron. Sweating profusely, he panicked. Surely the boy didn't intend to brand him?

Calo La Bolla grinned wickedly. *"Va biene! Va biene!* The young master is ingenious! What a King among Lions you'll be, Dolcettino," he said. Now he waited impatiently to see how valorously the young cub fared. Grinning with maniacal delight and pride, he watched the Lion don a thickly insulated glove.

Dolcetto talked to the bandit. "Whatever it is you call yourself matters not. You'll be free to return to Barbarossa and his *mafiosi* with a message from the Royal Lion of Sicily. The entire island of men like you will know and fear the name of the Royal Lion. Heed my words well, bandit. If you don't, I swear by all that's sacred and holy to me to seek you out, if it takes all my life." Dolcetto picked up the molten iron and held it close to his face. The luminous glow from its tip lit up his face and carved it with harsh, black planes.

"You will tell Matteo Barbarossa and his *mafiosi* never to set foot on de Leone soil. Make it known to them that the Royal Lion will protect his lair with every means at his disposal. And I, Dolcetto de Leone, will not rest until I see Barbarossa brought to justice. Tell him that if my father dies, my men and I will hunt him to the ends of the earth, where I shall disembowel him and hang his balls at half-mast below the Lion's banner. You understand? There's no question?" He raised his arm high into the air. His eyes were like green ice, his young face set hard.

With a quick movement taught him expertly by Roberto Argento when branding cattle, he plunged the fiery iron into the man's back. As the iron sizzled his flesh, the furtive coward screamed out in agony.

"That's for my father," he said calmly, moving about to face the culprit.

"This is for Roberto Argento." He shoved the iron into the man's chest. The stench of singed flesh filled the air.

Cacciatore screamed with excruciating pain. He fell over onto the dirt and rolled over onto his side, his knees drawn to his chest time and again as pain spasms shot through his body. His legs jerked in painful frenzy.

"And this," cried Dolcetto loudly, his eyes ablaze like fiery emeralds, "is for all the peasants you've killed and maimed and tortured. Let's see how well you fare, Cacciatore, with the stigma of the Royal Lion of Sicily branded upon you for the rest of your days." Dolcetto drove the branding iron into the man's groin with as much detachment as he'd have in branding an animal.

The iron burned deeply into the man's flesh. He screamed agonizing screams until he blacked out.

The courtyard filled with the acrid stench of burned human flesh. The *contadini* stared with mixed emotions at the broken man on the ground. Antonio averted his head and buried it in Guido Amalfi's arm. Amalfi placed a protective arm about the sensitive boy. Calo grinned with perverse pleasure. He couldn't wait to tell Ciccio Pontiface about the brave and resourceful young Lion.

From the second floor of the villa, Dolcetto's Godfather, Dr. Alberto Pietro, had heard the screams of agony. He rushed downstairs, out the door and toward the congregated men. He pushed his way through the small gathered crowd and saw his Godson staring down at the bandit, still brandishing the smoking iron in his hands. He saw the rapidly blistering welts and the blood oozing from the shriveled flesh. Glancing from the victim to his Godson, Dr. Pietro evidenced indescribable shock and displeasure at the act.

"Dolcetto! Mother of God! What have you done?"

"Only my duty, Godfather. Only my duty. Am I not my father's son?" He dropped the iron to the ground, removed the cumbersome glove, and walked to Antonio's side. He put his arm around his cousin and together they disappeared inside the villa.

The utterly dumbstruck peasants turned away from the branded man. If Dolcetto had plunged a knife into the man or shot him with a *lupara*, they would have accepted it without qualification. But this! Branding a man like an animal! It was inhuman!

It left them totally different men. He's made a big mistake, this young Lion. He should have killed Cacciatore. Hadn't they seen the pain and terror in the *schifoso*'s eyes turn to quenchless black rage? Hadn't they seen the violent hatred turn to fires of revenge? Suddenly they were afraid for Dolcetto and for themselves.

The next afternoon, Dolcetto sought out Father Bonaventura. He asked the strained, overwrought priest to take his confession.

In perfect Latin, Dolcetto began. "Bless me father, I confess to almighty God and to you, that I have sinned . . ." The priest began his chanted response and listened. "I did willfully injure and maim a man."

"Do you feel remorse, my son?"

There was a long pause. "No."

"Will you sin against man again?"

"If I must, I shall, Father. I can't accept penance for this act."

"But my son, that is not the way of God."

"No, it's not. It's the way of man. Since God is not of this earth, I must act in the ways of man."

"That's blasphemy! If you continue to think this way, man will have made little progress in his attempt to civilize the world. You'd be no different than the barbarians of centuries past."

"Do you call what happened to my father—to our people—civilized?"

"No."

"Then we haven't advanced far from the days of our barbarous forefathers."

"In every civilization there are those who don't advance."

"Should the world then be at their mercy? Better we all remain barbarians. Let the same laws apply to one and all." It wasn't coming together. He pressed. "Padre, I can't believe if someone cut off God's arm, he'd simply extend the other arm to them," Dolcetto said on impulse.

"No. God would simply grow another." Would Dolcetto fathom his last remark?

"And that would be the way of God?" Dolcetto found it too incredible.

"Yes, I believe so."

"Ah, then that is not the way of man. Man has no such powers."

They were back where they started. The circle would always remain incomplete. No one had the answers, reasoned Dolcetto.

"Some men would reason otherwise. Perhaps one day the answers will come. Things your mind can't grasp now will suddenly become clear. You'll see. Your thoughts will change and so will your life."

"Destiny has already altered the course of my life, Padre. I know what to expect."

"That's sad. That's very sad," said the priest heavily.

"Why? Most men never know what Destiny has in store for them. I do. It makes living that much easier."

"If you say so," replied the priest.

"You might wish me felicitations, Father. Today is my birthday."

4

For weeks Marco de Leone lay on his bed, his body swollen and rigid as a corpse. Dr. Pietro had worked feverishly using all his surgical skills to save the Royal Lion.

The villa filled with motionless groups. Shutters had been drawn tight rejecting the intensity of the early September heat. The *contadini* whispered behind closed doors and shook their heads ominously. Many other *latifondisti* came to pay their respects. From Messina came the bankers, the statesmen, and friends of the Royal Lion. When news reached his enemies, even they came wearing false masks of grief to mourn him.

Dolcetto and Antonio looked upon everything with fascination. They had never witnessed the strange, primitive customs of their people, wearing their *malocchio* amulets, more prevalent than ever, gesturing with their hands, making horns after each guest left.

Dolcetto had been outraged when some of the guests drank too much, laughed, and joked, especially in those early dark hours when Marco's life hung precariously in the balance, closer to death than life. He wanted to shout at them, reprimand them for their callous behavior. Then he'd recall Marco's words.

"You must respect the ways of a man in his own world, no matter how quaint and improper they may seem to you. Meet their reality." As a son of the Lion, he couldn't reproach them for their behavior. "One doesn't upbraid a man for succumbing to traditions he's been born to respect."

Dolcetto was forced to contemplate a life without his father. The thought, at first, appalled him. How could he assume all the duties at the *latifondo?* What of the business holdings in Rome and Milan and abroad? He shook his head at the absurdity of such thoughts. Yet the enormity of such questions pressed on him like a stone. He felt alone and without consolation.

Antonio had fixed himself to Dolcetto like a powerful adhesive, marveling at his cousin's composure, unaware of Dolcetto's inner turbulence. He knew Dolcetto would never be the same as he'd been before the Mazzarino raid.

As they sat having coffee in the sun-soaked solarium a few feet from Marco's bedroom, the physician studied his Godson. Antonio had scampered off to bring Gina a small bouquet of flowers, which had become a daily ritual with him. Even though she hadn't recognized him or acknowledged him, he kept up the daily visits.

For several moments, both Godfather and Godson remained quiet. They hadn't spoken since the night Dolcetto branded the bandit Cacciatore. Dr. Pietro gazed beyond the boy, past the Madelaina Gardens of the flower courtyard at the rear of the villa which afforded a magnificent view of the northern section of the *latifondo*'s rolling hills. It all looked so peaceful that it was difficult to believe that the raid had been a reality.

"You'll be going back to school, won't you? Promise me that nothing will interrupt your schooling."

"I can't make any promises, Godfather, until I'm sure that my father will recover."

"That's understandable." He sipped his coffee. "You appear to have grown up overnight, Godson," he began as he adjusted his glasses. He leveled his sky blue eyes on the boy and placed his heavy gold watch on the marble-topped table,

42

noting the time. "I think you're old enough to try to understand a few things. You must try to think of what life will be like for Marco if he lives through this."

When he saw the glimmer of hope brighten Dolcetto's eyes, he held up his hand and waved him off. *"Aspetta, aspetta.* Wait. Don't build your hopes too high at this moment. I said *if* he lives. He will never be the same man you remember him as being.

"When a man loses an arm or a leg, he succumbs to shock. Some men adjust well, take it in their stride; some take a longer time, because they cannot adjust mentally. Others never adjust. They remain defeated souls who berate God, Destiny and themselves."

Dolcetto nodded. He'd already seen some of these very people his Godfather described. They had become invalids for all their days, broken in spirit, full of self-condemnation. Doing little or nothing productive, they had become millstones around the necks of their families.

"If your father survives, long after the scars heal and the bruises no longer appear, the problem of helping his mind to adjust to a new life will be monumental. I dare say Marco would have preferred having both limbs severed to what they did to him." Dr. Pietro paused to pour more coffee into his cup.

"Here let me, Godfather." Dolcetto quickly arose and poured the remains of the hot coffee into his cup. He offered sugar and cream.

"Thank you, my boy. We both know Marco's iron will and strong resolve will help him overcome the infirmity. But what his reaction will be when he becomes aware that his tongue has been severed . . ." The Godfather shook his head. "He'll never be the same. His life will be so different. Without Roberto to help him through this . . ." He paused again. Not knowing the outcome, the physician was sparing with words for he didn't wish to give one prognosis, then have to reverse himself. "Make no mistake. This is probably the cruelest, most threatening period of his life."

"Then it's settled. I must stay here with him. I can't leave for school knowing my father will face such difficulties."

"If you really love your father, that's precisely what you mustn't do."

"I don't understand."

"If you remain here, he'll be forever dependent upon you. It will be too easy for Marco to lean on you. He'll refuse to stand on his own strength, to be resourceful and inventive. That's exactly what he'll have to do when he can't speak.

"It will be convenient for him to fill with self-pity. His

43

brilliant mind will atrophy. He'll cut himself off from friends, from the outside world. Without the power of speech, he'll grow frustrated, angry, destructive. Perhaps violent when he can't speak to his men. Indignant if they have no patience with him. Emotions will cloud good sound judgment. He'll resign from the legislature, give up, and become a vegetable.

Dolcetto shook his head sadly. He couldn't imagine his father as described to him by his Godfather. "No. He'll do none of these things. He has a stronger will than you think. He won't give up because they mutilated him." Dolcetto couldn't bring himself to say the words *cut his tongue.* "I can't leave him, Godfather. No matter what you say. I love him too much. My respect for my father has no bounds. My duty is here with him."

"No. Your duty is to carry on with your life, to perpetuate your father's work. You must prepare yourself for life, just as Marco did when his father was tortured and killed. If you have a dream for the future, you must set your course for that destination. Every man must follow his dream." His blue eyes were vibrant, more alive than Dolcetto remembered.

"Being near my father is the only responsible thing to do. He needs me now more than ever. Perhaps later, after he adjusts to his condition, after he realizes Roberto will no longer be around, I shall return to school." He sipped his coffee. "You see, Godfather, I prepared all my life for the role I am destined to assume. I proved that I can be depended upon in a crisis."

A vision of his Godson standing that night, brandishing the hot iron over the agonized heap of the bandit's pain-wracked body flashed through his consciousness. He frowned noticeably. "You proved you can be an *animale* when among other *animales.*"

Humiliation coursed through the young Lion. His eyes blazed with indignation and he stared at his Godfather.

"An *animale!* That's what you call me? An *animale!*" Dolcetto stood up and kicked back his chair. His fists clenched and unclenched. "And what were they? Those villainous bastards who caused this destruction and heaped calamity on the House of de Leone. My father lies in the next room, mutilated beyond belief, and you call *me* an animal for what I did?" His Sicilian temper flared.

"Calm yourself, Godson, and sit down," began his Godfather. "Let me tell you what I meant."

"No. Let me tell *you*, Godfather." He spat the word venomously. "My father taught me to meet another man's reality. And I did. I did to the savage only what he could

44

understand. If I, in vengeance, killed him, what would it have meant? He'd be just another dead bandit. That would have accomplished nothing. A dead bandit in a country where lives don't seem to count would be forgotten too quickly. But a man who bears witness to an inhuman act and lives to bear the shame of his experience will remember he's not as eternal and indestructible as he might have deluded himself into thinking.

"I watched that swine among our men and saw no fear in him. None at all. I saw contempt in his eyes for their cowardice. He knew there wasn't a man among them as fearless as he. I knew then, I had to instill fear and respect in him. It was important that I communicate with him at his own level. If it meant becoming an *animale,* then I suppose that's exactly what I did."

Dolcetto fixed his gaze on a distant hill beyond the villa.

"One can justify the actions of Lucifer if need be," said Dr. Pietro in a detached voice that irked Dolcetto.

"Camoria!" cursed the lad. "Can a deaf man hear my words? You have one opinion. I have mine. I did what I felt was right at the time." He turned to the physician. "And you condemn me for this?"

They were interrupted by the excited and elated Sara Amalfi who called aloud, *"Dottore, Dottore,* come quickly."

The physician disappeared inside.

Dolcetto sat on the lion's-head balustrade, momentarily hurt and confused by the caustic criticism heaped upon him by his Godfather. He didn't feel deserving of his harsh remarks. Things would never be the same between them.

"Dolcetto, come quickly," Sara Amalfi called excitedly.

His father was sitting up in bed when Dolcetto reached his side. His emaciated face revealed the extent of his suffering. His eyes, dull and glazed, were still puffy and swollen with black circles sunk deep in their hollows. His skin had the pallor of wax. Eagerly Marco turned toward his son, tried to raise his arm to touch him, faltered shakily in midair, then dropped it weakly on the bed at his side.

Marco's lips trembled when he opened them to speak. They saw the powerful struggle as the lips moved, confusion when no words came, heard the gutteral, gurgling sounds deep in his throat, and watched his bewildered eyes. Marco raised his trembling hands to his lips while his eyes searched the physician's cool, nonchalant eyes.

Why can't I speak, he wondered silently. His eyes blinked at the disorder of his mind. *Will someone please tell me what's wrong? Why are the sounds in my throat so strange?* His hands touched the area of his throat. *Ah, that's it. Something's wrong with my throat. The area is tender.*

45

He winced at the dull, constant pain. His lips were swollen and dry as a desert. He wanted to moisten them. Why couldn't he? He turned to his son, pleading with him to tell him what was wrong. Marco saw tears well up in the boy's eyes. He grew concerned and quickly directed his eyes to Dr. Pietro. He watched him prepare a syringe for injection.

Dolcetto looks pale and frightened. How long have I been here in bed? What happened? My head feels strange and numb.

"Well, well, my *compare* has decided to join the world of the living. Welcome back, Marco." Dr. Pietro's voice became clinical and superficial while he injected the potent narcotic into Marco's arm.

"Don't try to talk for a while, Marco. It will be painful." He signaled to Sara Amalfi to moisten Marco's lips with water.

"When the narcotic takes effect, you'll feel less pain."

Dolcetto took one of his father's hands and placed it between his own. He didn't remove his concerned eyes from Marco's face. Vaguely he heard Dr. Pietro speak in a matter-of-fact tone.

"You're going to be fine. In a few weeks you'll be fit as ever."

The physician's outrageous statement left Dolcetto flabbergasted. Catching the expression on his son's face, Marco knew then that something was drastically wrong.

What are they keeping from me? He closed his weary eyes and allowed the warmth of the narcotic to flow through his tired, frail body. When he opened them, he noticed that Sara Amalfi had slipped a wide restraining band of linen across his legs. Another band strapped his waist snugly against the bed. He glanced at the silent physician who gave no indication of his intentions. When the ties were secured, Dr. Pietro sat down alongside of him and held his other hand.

Marco fought the drug. Weightlessness and a sense of well-being gripped him as the narcotic lulled him in a painless, hazy world. Dolcetto's face began to recede further and further from him. *Don't want to sleep. Been sleeping too long. Want to be awake.* His eyelids grew heavier and heavier. *Can't keep them open.*

"Marco, can you hear me?"

Of course, I can hear you, Alberto. Why can't you hear me? He wanted to shout "I'm not deaf!" Instead, he nodded wearily.

"*Va biene. Aloura,* I sedated you because your condition is exceedingly weak. You mustn't become unduly excited, *capeeshi?*"

Marco nodded dreamily. He felt giddy, lightheaded.

Dear God, thought Dolcetto. *He's going to tell Papa. How do you tell a man his tongue's been cut out?* Dolcetto took a deep breath and stared at his Godfather with new-found respect. He trembled and cleared his dry throat.

"Marco, you must accept what I tell you with as little emotion as possible," began Alberto Pietro.

A faint smile tugged at Marco's lips. *Alberto, do get on with it. So long to make your point . . . Preface always too long . . . Sara Amalfi is pale . . . Why does Dolcetto shiver? . . . I'm floating . . .*

"Marco, listen carefully." Dr. Pietro glanced at his watch, didn't put it back into his vest pocket, just let it dangle freely from the thick gold chain.

"Do you recall anything that happened the night of the bandit raid?" His voice became monotoned and flat.

Marco's eyebrow raised languidly, then dropped softly back into place. His eyelids fluttered gently.

"Excellency," he cleared his throat, "a part of your body was mutilated, beyond hope of repair." The physician watched for a reaction and whispered to his Godson.

"Prepare yourself, Dolcetto. If he reacts violently, hold his arm tightly. Don't relax your hold for a second, *capeeshi?*"

Dolcetto nodded. His face dripped with perspiration. He saw his father's eyes flutter open in an effort to fight the effects of the drug. His head moved forward. Wild-eyed and panic-stricken, he stared at his hands, moved his legs under the cover, and fell back against the pillows, limp, somehow satisfied. His eyelids fell shut like soft balls of cotton bouncing in the wind.

"Marco, *your tongue was cut out,*" announced the doctor clearly and firmly so there could be no mistaking his words.

Marco's eyes snapped open, filled with frenzy at first, then pacific.

"Do you understand me? You no longer have a tongue. You have lost your power of speech."

Dio malodetto! How many times does he have to tell him, shuddered Dolcetto. *Stop! In God's name, stop!* He felt nauseous. *Dear God, why this . . . to my father? Why?* Dolcetto sat frozen, staring at his father's pale drawn face as it filled with unspeakable torture.

They've cut out my tongue . . . No power of speech . . . No tongue . . .

He struggled against the doctor's restraining arm, against his son's viselike grip. He should have guessed when he felt the swollen emptiness in his mouth. He moved his head from side to side in a wild frenzy of mad denials. He heard those

47

gurgling, alien sounds deep in his throat. His body went completely limp as sweet oblivion engulfed him.

"You can relax your hold now. He can't hurt himself."

Sara Amalfi, shaken from the terrible strain and tension, wiped her moist forehead and breathed with relief.

"Did you have to be so brutal? So cold and unfeeling?" hissed Dolcetto coldly.

"I did what I knew had to be done."

"And you called me *animale.*"

Dr. Pietro glanced up at the boy. He would never reproach him again.

The next few months were spent in the monumental task of rebuilding the devastated villa. The final assessment revealed the destruction hadn't been as extensive as it first appeared. Of the 450 peasants who lived on the *latifondo,* seventy-five were either dead or unaccounted for. Lilliana Amalfi and her two young companions were never found. It was as if the earth had swallowed them up. Guido Amalfi was prostrate with grief along with his wife and sons. But no more so than all the other people who also suffered great personal losses.

The immense storage bins of wheat, milled flour, and corn had been razed to the ground. The underground cellars which had been built after Diamonte's departure had been spared. They held ample food to take them through till the spring. Most of the cattle had been stolen. Only a few stray heads were rounded up in the hills. The horses, all prime Arabians, had disappeared. Most of the sheep had been slaughtered. It would take a while, agreed the heads of the families, but working together they'd restore what had been destroyed.

Grim-faced, tight-lipped and determined in their efforts, the *contadini* forged on, but everything they did, every gesture, indicated they missed Roberto Argento more than they could have believed possible. Without his encouragement, his enthusiasm, and his special genius with the earth, the men found their tasks laborious and unending.

The *contadini* pledged themselves to re-create what had been, if only to honor his memory. Roberto Argento's remains were buried in the family Camposanto on the small hill overlooking Terra d'Oro in the de Leone crypt. Guido Amalfi asked Father Bonaventura to find out what special services were read for the dead of Jewish faith.

On the day when special services were offered for Roberto Argento, the priest, not having found a Rabbi, performed the rites in his Catholic litany, and when he finished, spoke a few words which he had practiced in Hebrew:

You were one special man among men. One perished by fire, another by the sword, another by the plague, another slain by thieves. Thus death is the end for all and man's life passes away like a shadow. You Roberto Argento, a Jew among Sicilians, were more Sicilian than any of us. We shall remember you and pray for your soul so that your spirit may find more happiness than your body endured upon earth.

5

"Gina, if you should tire, let us know," said Father Bonaventura, patting her hands reassuringly. "Can you tell us who killed your daughter?"

"I did," she said dispassionately.

The cool detachment of her reply stunned the small gathering in her cottage. They were silent, sober-faced, and attentive.

"Why?" asked Guido Amalfi.

"She brought all the bandits to the villa. The deaths, all the destruction, it was her doing."

"How can you be so sure?" asked the priest.

"She told me, Padre." Gina wondered at the people who filled her cottage. "Where is His Excellency? In his chambers?"

Guido Amalfi nodded, unsure of how much to tell her, since Dr. Pietro had warned them she might lapse back into shock.

"First, tell us about Diamonte. It's important that we know how the bandits penetrated the security of the villa. *Capeeshi*, Gina? When did you talk with your daughter?"

"That same night." She smiled wanly at Dolcetto and Antonio, who sat on footstools at her feet. "They are both dead, I know. There is no way they could have survived. Signore Marco sent me to ring the *campanelli*. But, you see, by that time it was too late." She shook her head sadly.

"Only Roberto is dead, Gina," said the priest. "His Excellency lives."

The old woman, her snow white hair pulled back into a tight bun, crossed herself. *"Santo Dio."*

"Tell us about Diamonte," urged Guido Amalfi, lighting a cigarette.

Gina nodded and quietly began to tell her story. Along with what Marco de Leone had been able to add to the events of that terrifying night of July 28, the story began to take shape.

49

Gina had finalized dinner preparations. The birthday cake, a light, delectable *pane spugnio*, the sponge cake Dolcetto loved, was cooling on a nearby table. At the work counter, she had completed stuffing Dolcetto's olives and had set them on the counter to marinate, when suddenly the rear door to the kitchen opened. Gina glanced up and expressed the surprise of her life to see her daughter Diamonte walk in as if she had left only yesterday—not fifteen years before.

"Well, old woman, I see you're still doing the menial jobs around here." The dark-haired beauty with the porcelain china blue eyes spoke as harshly to her mother as she had in the past. Her beauty was marred only by her acid tongue and the hardness she had acquired over the years.

"What brings you here?" asked Gina, fighting to control her rising excitement.

Diamonte helped herself to the olives. "I'm not sure I can tell you yet. Mmmm! You're still the best cook in the world, old woman. Listen," she said confidentially. "I want you to come and live with me, mamma."

"After fifteen years of silence, you ask me to live with you? Hah! What devilment are you starting now?" Gina avoided her daughter's pale blue eyes and acted busy, forcing herself to look realistically at the motives behind such a request. "Besides, I'm content here. This is my home."

"Listen, old woman, I'm giving you a chance to save yourself. I don't know why I even bother with you." Strutting before her mother in trousers, an open-necked white shirt, and a leather vest, the sound of her leather boots clicked smartly against the tiled floors. "I must be *pazza!* Crazy to bother with you. Right now as I waste time talking with you, my men have already started their destruction."

"Destruction? What destruction? I don't understand. Are you still possessed? Crazy as before?" snorted Gina, losing all patience. She busied herself washing fresh *fragolles*—strawberries—anything to keep busy.

"You'll see how crazy I am, old woman. Tonight we finish what I started years ago. You don't think I've forgotten?" snickered her daughter.

"Listen, why don't you turn around and leave us? We've had peace since you left," began Gina. "Go before anyone sees you. *Santo Dio!* Why did you have to return? It was you who tried to kill Signora Mariolina, you daughter of the devil! Don't think we didn't know, you . . . you murderess!"

"Murderess? She didn't die at my hand. But she did die, didn't she?" Diamonte's voice dripped sarcasm. "Any other mother would have arranged my marriage to Marco. But not you, *cara mamma*. Not you. You wanted me to be a servant all my life. Well, mother of mine, that life was not

50

meant for Diamonte. Not the life of a servant who is resigned to cleaning chamber pots for the rest of her days." She spun about impatiently. "Are you coming with me or not? Will you at least help me save you?"

"This is my home. This is where I stay," retorted Gina, not fully grasping her daughter's meaning. "Save me from what? *Che demonio!*"

"As usual, stupidity annihilates your common sense. I sometimes wonder if you are my mother at all," said the exasperated young beauty.

Suddenly, unable to contain herself, all the pent up fury and frustration Gina had harbored for a lifetime exploded. "Whore!" she spat. "Daughter of the dèvil! From the moment you were old enough to talk and I saw the evil of your soul, I should have ended your life. Oh, your beauty had me fooled, just as it deceived the others. That beauty of an angel which I convinced myself was God's creation. *Santo Dio!* How wrong I was! It took a while before I learned that beneath that outer cloak of beauty lurked the soul of Lucifer. Oh, how well I learned! Just as God conceived Jesus in the womb of Mary, Satan conceived you in my womb that day I was raped and left for dead. Only the devil could disguise his ugliness under so much beauty. I curse the day Signore Marco saved my life, and yours along with it!"

Twelve years of hatred, loneliness, self-condemnation, and frustration surfaced in Diamonte, and she raised her hand and struck her mother across the face. As angry red welts surfaced on Gina's face, a feeling of guilt came over her. But further action was halted when two gargantuan brutes shoved Marco de Leone through the kitchen doors and pinned him against a concrete wall while they searched him for concealed weapons.

When Marco de Leone caught sight of the white-faced anguish on his housekeeper's face and the angry streaks on her cheek, he made a move in her direction. The quick hard blow of an upthrust fist caught the side of his head. "Don't move, dog," growled one of the bandits. "Not if you know what's good for you."

The Lion blinked his eyes several times trying to clear his head, then scanning the room, he caught sight of the woman in man's pants. Only when she turned to face him with her incredibly blue eyes, did he recognize his Godchild. "Diamonte," he whispered. He'd know her anyplace.

Diamonte melted when she saw the hurt expression of disbelief on the face of this man she hadn't stopped loving. But just as quickly she retreated behind her hard facade. "Well! If it isn't the mighty Lion!"

51

"Why are you here with these men?" he asked in a guarded voice.

"You'll see soon enough."

"*Strega malodetta!*" hissed Gina. "Vile witch! Daughter of Satan!"

"Gina!" reprimanded the Lion. "*Silenzio!*" Marco recalled hearing rumors about a woman of legendary beauty who had joined with terrorist bandits, but he had discounted them as wild imaginings.

Listening to the bandits speak, Marco recognized their accents. Mazzarino bandits! The most dreaded and vicious of the island bandits; arms of the *mafia* whose marauding and pillaging took place in central and southern Sicily on the interior *latifondi*. What the hell were they doing this far east? Had they joined sympathetic forces? Why hadn't he heard? Why hadn't his spies informed him of such diabolical developments?

Only an hour ago, concerned that Dolcetto and Antonio hadn't returned to the villa, he had sent his bodyguards, Calo and Ciccio, to search for them. Roberto's return to the estate without the boys had increased his concern. To keep from worrying, they had focused their attention on other matters. Roberto had gone to the greenhouse to work on his experiments, while Marco retired to his study to write to members of Parliament about the land reforms he was fighting so desperately to get passed. The *mafia* had illegally gained control of numerous *latifondi* in the west, so Marco was pushing for government intervention. Subsidizing the financially insecure estates would reduce the danger of *mafia* control. *One day they'll wake up,* thought Marco, *if it's not too late.*

The acrimonious voices of two women upbraiding each other interrupted his thinking. When the voices grew so distinct that he couldn't concentrate, he decided to investigate. In the hall, he was suddenly accosted by the two brutes who dragged him into the kitchen.

Now it all fell together. Only someone with an intimate knowledge of the villa and the feudal fortress could penetrate its security. *Diamonte!* Diamonte had led these despicable killers, these blood-thirsty brutes to the villa. His Godchild! The child he had raised as his own. *Santo Dio!* What to do first? How to warn the others? By now they'd be at supper, relaxed and unsuspecting. Merciful God!

"In case you're wondering, the dogs were put to sleep," said Diamonte, reading his thoughts. "The horses have been taken away, the cattle scattered, and most of your peasants are dead. There's no way the Royal Lion of Sicily can alter the course of Barbarossa's Destiny." She turned to the two men. "Tie them up," she ordered sternly. "If they resist, kill them!"

How easy she issued these orders. If they resist kill them. Marco was appalled. This from the child he'd bounced on his knee? It was too much to contemplate. Why, he asked himself. Why? But this was no time for conjecture.

Marco felt the thundering vibration of horses before the others heard the distinct sounds. Diamonte rushed out the door. Flushed with excitement, she shouted, *"Va biene,* they've arrived." Gina sat in the rocking chair, solemn and silent, but when Diamonte returned, Gina spat at her daughter. About to raise her hand, to strike the older woman, Diamonte changed her mind and glanced contemptuously at her instead.

"Go call Cacciatore," she instructed one man. "He'll know how to handle these two." She took one of their knives, slipped it into her belt, and told the remaining gargoyle, "I'll find Matteo. You stay here." She walked out into the night.

Tied to the honing post between the storage room and pantry, Marco struggled against his bonds. With one eye warily cocked in the direction of the renegade who was helping himself to some food, he managed to strain and tug and yank until he felt the rope slacken.

The silence of the night was split by raucous noises, loud yells and shrieks, and the sound of galloping horses clattering against the cobbles.

The sound of gunshots and ricocheting bullets increased Marco's determination to free himself. The immediate threat was the revolting bandit who stared at him from time to time, but suddenly the bandit grew bored with his captives and decided to investigate the exciting sounds of action outside.

Marco made his move. Although his hands were still tied, he freed himself from the post, edged between an overhead knife rack and the pantry door, and used his head to dislodge one of the sharp butchering knives. One wagged sideways and swiped at his ear, splattering blood over his white silk shirt. Finally he was successful, but the knife clattered noisily to the floor. He froze at the noise, exchanging glances with Gina.

Satisfied no one had been alerted by the noise, he fell to the floor, pushed the knife against the wooden cupboard, and worked the rope at his wrists over it. The knife cut into his flesh time and again before it ultimately severed the ropes. Blood dripped freely from his ear and lacerated wrists as he cut the ankle ropes and crept across the floor toward Gina. He sliced through her ropes and shouted hoarsely, "Go, sound the bells. Ring the *campanelli* at the church. In God's name, be careful!" He shook his head at her sternly when she insisted on binding his wounds first. "There's no time. Do as I say. We must warn the others."

Gina left to do his bidding. Marco ran quickly to the anteroom where guns were housed. Grabbing a powerful shotgun, pellets, and a flaregun, he ran back into the villa and out into the utility court. He lost no time in shooting the flares into the air. Reloading the gun, he repeated the process twice. They burst and fragmented in myriad colors, lighting up the estate. Marco paused a moment and cocked his head. There they were. Chapel bells! *Grazie Dio!* Gina had made it!

Marco's momentary exhilaration was for naught. How could he have known it was too late for any signal. Caught by surprise, many of the peasants had already been slain. The guards at most checkpoints had met gruesome deaths by garrote, knives, or in some cases, both.

A sudden explosion burst in Marco's head. Struck full force from behind with the butt end of a *lupara*, he slid down into an abyss of bright lights and staggering pain that mercifully turned into a pit of blackness.

Ten minutes later he regained consciousness and found himself back in the kitchen. Vague, shadowy images came at him through dull, glazed eyes that didn't feel as if they belonged to him at all. Voices sounded far away. One more familiar than the others came at him.

Diamonte's voice reached him. "You sure you have the right one? The *biondello*? Light hair and crippled?"

"Yes," replied an awesome red-bearded, black-haired demon. "He hangs by his feet waiting for me." His crude, coarse voice filled the room.

"Now, what do you say, Matteo? In a short time, the mighty Lion will have fallen. The House of de Leone no longer can deter your plans. Sicily is yours! Have I done my part well?" she asked with a gleam of triumph in her eyes.

Barbarossa grunted. "Let's finish the job before we rejoice." Moving toward Marco, Matteo Barbarossa kicked him as if he were a dead dog. "Who's this?"

Diamonte walked toward him, a mark of disturbance on her face. Kneeling down, she grabbed a handful of his thick, graying hair and jerked Marco's head off the floor. The Lion remained as still as death. Diamonte studied his bloodied face in a prolonged silence. "Only a dead peasant," she said, laying his head back gently on the floor.

Impatient to finish the job and be off, Barbarossa headed out the door. "Listen, wench, you wait here. Be ready to beat it the hell out of here at the signal. Move!" he commanded Cacciatore. "Move!"

Satisfied that they were alone, Diamonte worked swiftly. She poured water from a pitcher into a bowl and proceeded to bathe the bloody mass at the base of Marco's skull. Her pale lips trembled and her hands shook. "Oh, *caro mio*, if only you had chosen me, how different things could have been," she whispered softly. "Why didn't you know how much I loved you? You, so brilliant a man, were you not able to perceive the depth of my love, the desire in my heart?" She cradled Marco as one would a baby. Giant tears spilled down her cheeks.

Unknown to Diamonte, all her movements were being observed by the most cunning and vicious of ruthless killers, one who had had little use for her since they'd met. Having doubled back, he sneaked into the house unnoticed and stood behind the door leading to the earthen storage room. Alerted by the gentle manner in which she had released Marco's head earlier, he now peered at her with curious fascination through a crack in the wooden door. Cacciatore, who saw everything and said little, recognized the man on the floor to be no ordinary peasant. She could fool Barbarossa with whom she slept like a whore, but never Cacciatore. Why had she lied to Matteo? Who was this man she held so highly? *Bitch!* he thought. *She's up to no good.*

Marco's eyes fluttered open. He could hear Diamonte's words, but he couldn't move. He had no way of knowing he'd suffered a mild concussion.

"Thank God you're alive," whispered Diamonte, clutching the Lion tighter to her bosom. Tears of remorse welled in her eyes. "Forgive me. I didn't know it would be like this. The destruction, the ruin of all you worked so hard to create. I'm so ashamed, Marco. So ashamed!"

A dark shadow fell between them. Diamonte's head suddenly jerked back. Pulling her by her long black hair, Cacciatore forced her to her feet. "So!" he snarled. "A dead peasant, eh?" He slapped her hard across the mouth. Time and again he backhanded her until blood spurted from between her lips. Welts appeared on her pale face, and Marco noticed she froze with paralytic fear. "You can fool Matteo, your unsuspecting lover, but not me, you whore!"

Life surged through Marco. Still weak from the loss of blood and still dazed from the paralyzing blow, he took a few moments to steady himself before he rolled over and caught Cacciatore from behind with a forceful blow struck at his knees. Caught temporarily off guard, Cacciatore released his grip on the girl's hair, stumbled backwards, then sprang quickly back to his feet.

Diamonte screamed, "He'll kill you, Marco! He's a beast! An *animale!*" She backed away as the two men circled each other like stalking animals.

Cacciatore, his knife drawn, drew his lips back over his teeth in a soundless snarl. His face, dark as midnight, was awesome. The hatred between them was as pure as the hatred of one animal for another. He lashed at Marco from left to right, taking portions of his shirt with each swipe. Marco leaped away from him at each lunge. The odds were against the unarmed Lion until Diamonte tossed a knife across the slippery tiles toward him. The odds dropped in that instant Marco reached for the knife, for he escaped a hard thrust of Cacciatore's knife which might have decided the outcome.

Moving with more assurance, knife clutched expertly in his right hand, Marco's offensive thrusts cut through clothing, sliced off buttons, and drew blood from the astonished bandit. Furious that Diamonte had intervened to aid the Lion, Cacciatore grew guarded with a fierce animal instinct. Bitch! He'd have to watch her, too! He side-stepped, spun about, and grabbed Marco's head, slamming it hard against the wooden chopping block. He pounded Marco's right hand furiously against the table's edge until his grip weakened and the knife fell from it. Somehow, Marco managed to reverse the advantage and pin his foe against the table.

He slammed the evil man's head against the table until his black eyes bulged in pain. Cacciatore wound his stocky leg around Marco and with the other he jackknifed a swift kick to the Lion's groin. His balls exploded like a rocket, and when Marco doubled over in excruciating pain, the bandit clasped both fists together, shoving them under Marco's chin with tremendous force, and knocked him against the door to the cellar.

Grasping his knife, Cacciatore went after Marco with the fervor of a psychopathic killer. Time and again he made mad thrusts and swipes at the Lion, leaving a bloody trail of gashes and cuts on the Lion's body.

During this commotion, Gina entered the kitchen unnoticed. Etched on her face was a horrified expression. Having just witnessed the beheading of Roberto Argento, she now stared as Cacciatore mercilessly beat her master. Stunned into immobility, Diamonte hadn't noticed her mother. She could see none of the madness, the frenzy, horror registered in Gina's eyes. She didn't see the maniacal expression as Gina flashed the rapier-sharp knife clutched tightly in her raised arm. All the passionate hatred and bitterness she felt welled up in that one instant as she moved soundlessly toward her daughter and with a few expert moves slashed Diamonte open from neck to stomach.

Diamonte felt nothing at first. She lifted her azure blue eyes filled with childlike innocence and fixed on her mother's impassioned stare. A stinging sensation crawled between her breasts. Glancing down, she noticed her shirt and camisole had been sliced open revealing a clean laceration between her firm breasts. There was very little blood at first, but the trickles grew until they became a pulsing gusher. Gina's upraised hands became a frenzied blur of whirlwind thrusts and jabs intermingled with flashes of glittering steel. Diamonte felt powerless against this sudden and unexpected squall. One final expert thrust sunk the steel into Diamonte's heart.

Her incredibly blue eyes lifted to meet her mother's. Softened and dulled in silent anguish as the pain tore through her body, she whispered almost inaudibly, *"Perdonna me, mamma.* Forgive me." These were her last words before she fell to the floor in a crumpled heap at her mother's feet. Gina sank into the rocking chair, totally lost to the world.

Marco saw the atrocity. Powerless to intervene, he called out foolishly, "Gina! No!" In the split second in which Marco ignored his formidable opponent, Cacciatore caught him across the face and smashed the Lion's head against the concrete wall.

A succession of shapes and forms whirled round him. Stunned, his vision blurred, Marco felt the effects of jackhammer punches. Blow after blow struck at him, rendering him unconscious, and a merciful blackness sucked him under.

Cacciatore dragged Marco inside the storage cellar to finish his sadistic job. Flushed with exhilaration of his victory, the craven and depraved beast decided to inflict his own brand of justice upon the silver-tongued orator. What could be more justified than cutting out the man's tongue so he could no longer rail against the *mafia?* Pleased with his logic, he set about his task. Then afterward, satisfied with his demoniac handiwork and his own audacity, Cacciatore flushed pleasurably. For a moment he was fascinated by the bloodied, splotched tongue; he stared dispassionately, then flung it from him without expression.

His thoughts centered on Diamonte. Traitorous bitch! Wait until Matteo learns of her betrayal. He moved stealthily back into the kitchen, arrested by the monotonous rocking of the old woman's chair. Now, for the girl, to finish her off. Wiping his blade, still warm with the blood of the Lion, he approached the old woman. Suddenly he saw the disorganized heap lying in a pool of blood at the older woman's feet. In the split seconds it took to size the situation, he fingered the warm knife with the zeal of a depraved madman. Black eyes darted from mother to daughter, his own mind and heart pounding with excitement. Hesitantly he advanced a grimy, blood-stained hand and passed it before Gina's staring sightless eyes. Not a muscle flinched in her, nothing. She didn't know he existed.

Cacciatore, a man who seldom laughed, broke into a paroxysm of laughter. He kicked at Diamonte's lifeless remains and stared at her exposed intestines and patch of curly pubic hair. Leaning down, he cut off an ear pierced with a golden spider earring given to her by Matteo. He placed it in his pocket. He'd need proof for Matteo. His diabolic laughter echoed through the villa like a giant obscenity amid hallowed halls.

Less than an hour later, Cacciatore was captured by Calo La Bolla.

Some time passed before the *contadini* could adjust to the new conditions at the Villa de Leone. The story of what had happened in the kitchen that terrifying night had filled them all with mixed emotions. Most found it difficult to believe that Diamonte could have perpetrated such vengeance against the Royal Lion who had done nothing but good for Gina and the girl. The superstitious older women recalled that when Gina first arrived at the villa, for a time she had been considered a *jettatore*, a person who unwittingly brings disaster to those people around her. But Marco had quickly quashed such rumors. When a series of minor disasters did occur, he was able to explain the reason for each mishap as having been simple negligence on the part of the men.

Faced with the monumental task of reconstructing their houses and recouping their losses, the men resigned themselves to a future without Roberto to guide them. How far could they advance now? Without the sound of Marco's infectious laughter their days would be endless.

"I should have killed him," uttered Dolcetto bitterly when he learned it was Cacciatore who had tortured and mutilated his father.

"Easy, young Lion," said Calo La Bolla gruffly. "You think what you did didn't take courage? *Managghia!* You were superb! Not even I would have thought of such treatment," he said with fierce pride in his eyes.

Dolcetto wondered why it was only Calo seemed to think his actions praiseworthy. One thing was certain: The names Matteo Barbarossa and Mario Cacciatore were etched in his mind for all eternity.

In the days to come, Marco de Leone was to learn just how accurate Dr. Pietro's prognosis had been. Tormented and filled with hatred at the powers who rendered him speechless, at first he refused to accept his fate. Alone, in the privacy of his room, he attempted to form words, to speak, grimly determined that if he practiced, he could miraculously grow a new tongue. The strange guttural sounds coming from his mouth frightened and appalled him, offending both his mind and his soul. He called on the Sainted God of the Universe, even the powers of Lucifer. In his state of mind, he'd have bargained with any available saint or demon to help restore his powers of speech. But no one accepted the challenge. Not one cent of the vast fortunes of the House of de Leone could restore what had been brutally plucked from him. He would see no one except Dolcetto and Antonio.

Three months of this self-imposed incarceration of spirit and mind ended abruptly one day when Marco agreed to see visitors. And how they rejoiced at the news! They came in droves every hour of every day.

The Lion listened as the men told of Dolcetto's bravery and resourcefulness; he was proud that his son had brought honor to the House of Lions. Rumors, they told Marco, spread rapidly among the illiterate, fear-ridden peasants, and now, when Dolcetto rode on the *latifondo,* they nodded to him with the reverence paid to a god.

Every accounting of Dolcetto's bravery was colored by each man's emotional involvement. Lamponi spoke with tremendous pride and grateful humility, for hadn't the lad saved his life and his family from the burning jaws of death? Massini, baffled over the lad's bravery, marveled, "What a Lion he'll be one day!" Guido Amalfi spoke reservedly, still ambivalent over the branding, but he wouldn't let Marco know his head still swirled with confusion. Tomasso Micci could not contain himself when he described Dolcetto to his father. "That night, he walked like a king! He appeared to have grown a foot in stature. When he looked at us with those green eyes that glowed like a lion in the night, we were all amazed and dumbstruck! *Che molto bravo,* Marco! *Molto bravo!* What courage!"

Although he was ecstatic that his son had risen to the occasion and comported himself wisely, Marco felt pangs of remorse that a lad of sixteen should have been exposed to such contemptible and barbarous acts.

"It was an inhuman atrocity, Marco," stormed Dr. Pietro. "And by a mere lad! Imagine, your son—my Godson—branding a man as you would an animal!" The only one to contest Dolcetto's behavior on that night was his Godfather who was outraged that the boy should be so revered.

Annoyed that the physician would berate his son, Marco looked scathingly upon the doctor for the first time in their acquaintance. His inscrutable eyes blazed like jewels in the candlelight. Why, he wanted to ask, was it perfectly acceptable for a barbarous horde of bandits to violently brutalize civilized man without fear of reprisal. Yet, if civilized man retaliates, his act becomes an abomination punishable not only by law but by man's judgment of him? There was something wrong in such a system, he told himself.

"You'll make sure, won't you, that Dolcetto's schooling won't be interrupted by this terrible *infamita* done to you and your *contadini?*" insisted the Godfather.

Marco grew weary. Perhaps Alberto was right. How easy it would be to insist the boys stay with him. How well they'd fill the loneliness and inactivity of his convalescence. But Marco knew that when the time came he'd insist they return to school. He couldn't deprive them of their youth. A feeble gesture indicated the Lion's reluctance to continue the conversation.

"*Va biene, compare,*" said Dr. Pietro. "I'll return tomorrow to look in on you. Consider my words, Marco. If you keep Dolcetto here during these crucial years, he'll turn out no better than that dog Barbarossa. The next time he won't stop at . . . branding a man." Pietro's blue eyes stared in an attitude of remote contemplation. "I saw him that night. Such savageness! Totally without conscience!"

Marco sighed. The trouble with Dolcetto's Godfather was that he didn't understand Dolcetto's inheritance. The House of de Leone and their descendants came from a long line of conquerors whose ingenious talents and special abilities to lead men had made them formidable warriors. Having learned his lessons well, Dolcetto had an uncanny insight into the nature of men. Marco closed his eyes and pretended to doze off.

When Marco heard the news, he wailed in anguish and hatred. His uncontrollable sadness prompted one of the most agonizing, heart-rending sounds ever to echo through the stately halls of the villa. For days, that scream tore at the hearts and souls of the peasants who had heard it and knew what it meant. They dropped to their knees and prayed God would ease Marco's anguish.

The Royal Lion had just learned of the fate of his dearest friend. *Roberto? Not Roberto! Not him! Why should he have received such a fate?* Huge wracking sobs shook his body and for weeks he remained inconsolable. *You've taken*

60

everyone I've loved! cried his inner voice to a faceless deity. *What will I do without Roberto? Life on the* latifondo *will never be the same. I know it and the* contadini *know it. Goddamn! Goddamn! Goddamn!* shrieked another voice inside Marco, filled with a terrifying vengeance. *Damn you God!*

No Sicilian had contributed what Roberto Argento, a Jew, had contributed to the nation in the field of agronomy, and to have been brutalized by beasts not worth the dirt under his fingernails was the greatest infamy of all.

The warm October sun caressed the rolling hills and shone brightly behind Dolcetto's bronzed features as he sat reading a letter his father had painstakingly written.

What a splendid young man he's become, thought Marco as he sat opposite him on the balcony off his room. Dolcetto's green eyes were the color of crumbled emeralds, and the gold lion at his neck swung freely through his open-necked shirt.

The letter read:

Son of my heart:
It pains me not to be speaking these words as I have in the past. Because my heart overflows with love and a fierce pride at having a son demonstrate courage, strength, and self-reliance beyond expectation, I can't allow you to indulge in this childish fantasy of remaining at the villa instead of returning to school.

You are of the family of Royal Lions, a de Leone. With the name comes a responsibility to our country and our people. My affliction strengthens my desire to tighten our bond of love, but I'm forced by conscience and intelligence to do what is contrary to my desires. The grave matter of your future must not be conditioned or guided by the heart.

The retaliatory feelings you experience are understandable, yet, if I encouraged you to confront our enemies at their level, in the manner they choose, you'd be no better than they, no more entitled to live a free life than those who choose to live as blood-sucking cowards, preying on the weakness of others. You'd be less equipped to survive, for a de Leone was not weaned on the sword, but on the pen and the power of the word. I've not encouraged you to become a brave Lion to be slain in the field of battle.

A knowledge of our laws and a power beyond wealth—an intimate knowledge of men and the ability to lead them—will qualify you to guide our people to a better life.

The punishment you meted out to the barbarian Cacciatore made me fiercely proud. You mustn't let the unsolicited remarks and criticism of bystanders cloud your judgment, fill you with remorse, or undermine your soul. A leader must make decisions. Right or wrong he must make them. All life is trial and error, but from it evolves the gems of learning. These are the most precious rewards.

I shall miss you more than the power of speech, my son. You and Antonio are the very beat of my heart. But you must return to school, both of you. In your absence, I shall endeavor to protect what is, while you, young Lion, must envision what could be.

I know the next Lion of Sicily understands and will not contest these few words from a loving father.

The letter was signed in Marco's bold decorous script.

Dolcetto folded the letter, placed it in his shirt pocket, raised his eyes, and met his father's inscrutable gaze.

"If these are your wishes, father, I shall not cause you further discomfort by opposing you." Suddenly he was only a child. He sprang from the balustrade, dropped to his knees before the patriarchal Lion, and hugged his father dearly.

"Papa! I hate them for what they did to you. I hate them! One day when I've grown up, truly grown up, I shall avenge these deaths. I swear, they will pay for what they did to you and our people. I swear!"

Marco stroked his son's head, fought to control the tears and couldn't. For several moments, both Lions wept. Marco caught sight of the golden jeweled lion that hung suspended from a chain on his son's neck and fell across his knee.

He picked it up and gazed at it. *What a heavy burden this golden lion placed on Dolcetto. It's not an easy task to become a Lion among men, much less a king among Lions.*

6

Vendetta was the legacy that had been handed down from generation to generation in the House of de Leone. The vendetta, between the Royal Lions and the Mafia had erupted into a cold-blooded war of brutality and slaughter. It was the curse that turned Marco de Leone into a moody, unpredictable, overprotective Lion. But he had waged a war using silver-tongued oratory, a moneybelt, and intelligence as devastatingly as his enemies had used bullets, knives, and torture. Hadn't he learned all the things *not* to do? Hadn't he been taught by masters in the art of self-preservation, his forefathers?

The Royal Order of the Lion granted to the House of de Leone by the Spanish King Ferdinand, complete with crest and coat of arms, had for the past two centuries included landed estates, generous dowries, and royal land grants. These properties as well as active political service had placed the de Leone family in high esteem. Most of the de Leone men studied law in northern universities and entered politics or became royal advisors. A few preferred the life of feudal land barons. Induced by excellent marriage contracts, the women of the family had married powerful, affluent nobles, thereby perpetuating the family wealth.

In October, 1850, the Marquis Fiorenzo de Leone arrived at the Palermo Court. He found the excitement of its social and intellectual life infinitely more preferable than the remote life afforded him on the *latifondo*. Finally, the distinguished man of letters felt at home.

Within a few months, however, the Marquis became more disconcerted each day, for he could see that the tremendous amount of graft and corruption he had stumbled upon while serving on the medical boards was spreading like a malignancy. It was clear that the *mafia* had infiltrated every phase of government.

Appointed by the Prime Minister as Director of the Bank of Sicily to investigate fraud and misuse of funds, the Marquis learned enough about the Mafia's venality to alarm him —forgery, false acquisition of land, manipulation of credit. What more would he learn of this new breed of shrewd and conniving men whose credo was never to put in an honest day's work if they could outwit and manipulate their neighbor into increasing their wealth for them? The Marquis was appalled to learn that these recipients of illegal credit protected themselves from prosecution by making sizable contributions to the *right* parties. However, Fiorenzo had no idea how extensive this protection was or how high up it reached, so he prodded and sifted through tomes of information and eventually completely unraveled the entire embezzlement scheme. He now faced the problem of what to do with the information. There was no one he could turn to in the vast and gaudy Palermitan Court. Around him glimmered a confusing array of obsequious and false smiles. Whom could he trust? His decision to go to Rome and meet with the Prime Minister resulted in a curt dismissal as bank director. The one man, a subordinate, to whom he finally confided his mission to Rome had been elevated to the prestigious position of bank director. All this before he had even left Palermo! Fiorenzo hastily retreated to his villa near Messina and reflected bitterly on his short tenure of office.

Fiorenzo felt sure his destiny lay in politics, but the demands of his own morality superseded those political ambitions which could be his for the *right* type of cooperation. In his frustration, the Marquis sat up long hours writing extensively on his findings of corruption in *mafia* interests, including the system by which they actually squeezed property owners off their lands. But before he could submit these reports to his family members in the Italian Parliament, he was kidnapped and held for ransom.

For Fiorenzo the long months of brutal nightmares and torture began. There were moments when the pain became so excruciating he would have gladly agreed never to write another word of his findings. But out of the darkness came the words of his father and his father's father: "We are nothing without the people. We must champion the poor and underprivileged and remove the monsters who hover over them like flesh-eating buzzards."

A ransom note delivered with a crude package containing the Marquis' left arm, severed at the shoulder, brought quick results from the family who paid handsomely for his return. There could be no mistake—on a blood-soaked finger was the family signet ring, a jeweled lion worth as much as the ransom itself.

It was six months before Fiorenzo, emaciated and weakened by the ordeal, was returned to his family. Only then did the Marquis permit himself the luxury of self-preservation. Plans to turn the estate into a feudal fortress were immediately set in motion. A wall, twelve feet high and four feet wide was constructed around the outer perimeter of the villa. Every fifty feet a small cubiclelike tower housed a man bearing arms. Nearly a hundred men taking shifts around the clock formed part of the first security system.

But suddenly it was upon him once more, that desperate need for self-expression which again drove him to work late into the night. There was no stopping Fiorenzo now. He became a fanatic. He set forth in writing the remainder of his works, hoping to shed some light on the corruption that ate through Sicily like a cancer. He'd made a solemn oath. This would be the legacy his eldest son Marco would inherit. This would be his retaliation against the men who had so brutalized him!

Marco and Guillermo were away at school in the north. He kept his third son, Danilo, constantly at his side, taught by private tutors until he was of university age. His wife, the Marchessa, having suffered a heart condition during the kidnapping of her husband, had developed nervous disorders and kept herself confined to her apartment, seldom venturing into the villa proper.

A year later, Fiorenzo was surprised by a visit. Well-meaning friends and politicians courted him, hoping to rekindle his political aspirations. "We're specifically interested in the Bank of Sicily investigations and the Mafia's involvement," they told him. "We aim to strike a blow to cripple their operations."

Fiorenzo flatly refused. "Isn't the empty space in the sleeve of my smoking jacket vivid enough to convince you I want no further involvement?" he asked.

"But you're of the Royal House of Lions," they said almost as if they were accusing him of cowardice.

The Marquis snorted with disgust. "Which one of you seven brave men will change places with me?" Their silence reinforced his position. "Sometimes it takes more bravery to stand still and do nothing," he told them. "My word is final!"

Before the end of the following week, suddenly and quite mysteriously, his private papers disappeared. An exhaustive search of the villa proved futile. He dispatched a courier to his sons in Rome. "Be careful of treachery. Your best friend might prove to be your enemy. Trust no one."

The news spread like an uncontrollable fire. Certain highly incriminating papers had been sent to Parliament, papers which threatened to create political upheavals and repercussions that would be felt throughout the Two Kingdoms.

Before Parliament actually received the inflamatory papers, they were intercepted by certain unknown parties and disappeared.

Marco and Guillermo de Leone returned from school that summer in time to attend the funeral of their mother. A week later the villa fell under the siege of Mafia bandits. The Marquis, brutally mutilated, suffered indignities beyond human endurance before they gouged out his eyes and left him less than a vegetable. Danilo vanished, never to be seen or heard from again.

Marco de Leone and his brother Guillermo, savagely beaten and left for dead, miraculously survived. Marco, the new Royal Lion, was filled with hate. These atrocities would be reckoned with! His black thoughts roiled with unspeakably savage forms of retaliation. But during his convalescence, time, intelligence, and a genius for survival annihilated his bloody thoughts of retaliation. Still grimly determined to avenge the brutal murders, Marco hit on another plan, a cunning plan designed to thwart his enemies in a manner they wouldn't understand. He would avenge these deaths with life. Yes! Fight death with life!

65

Silent, meditative, and gravely concerned, the tall, sun-bronzed Lion moved among his people dressed like a Spanish Don, in the manner of a king. Wearing a soft leather jacket about his shoulders to cover his thickly bandaged upper torso, he stared somberly at the wounded men who filled the small first-aid dispensary set up to temporarily aid the wounded. His clear hazel eyes suddenly sparked with bright intensity at the plans forming in his mind.

He began by recruiting every available able-bodied man over the age of twelve from the surrounding villages. He offered them room and board and steady jobs if they'd live on the estate—an unthinkable act in those days.

For hours each evening, after the farming chores were done, Marco drilled them. With twenty-two men, twenty-two workable guns, and twenty-two temperamental Arabians, the Royal Lion began his own personal form of retaliation. He drilled them, old and young, until they dropped in fatigue. He taught them to ride, saddles or none, like the fighters of Genghis Khan. With the help of Calo and Ciccio, he taught them to shoot until they could pierce a bulls-eye blindfolded. Although they were illiterate, these *contadini* weren't dumb. They weren't stupid or blind. They were industrious and could follow orders. It was a revelation to know what kind of men he would deal with. By the time he was ready to return to school in the fall to face his final year, Marco's small army had mushroomed to 150 sharp, tough, hard-riding, and fast-shooting men.

His dream would come true, by God! His eternal vision, his reason for living was the emancipation of the Sicilian peasant. It remained for Marco alone to carry forward the standard first lifted by his great-grandfather Emiliano. He shut his eyes to the possibility that he, too, might one day fall in battle. He had no time to worry about such an eventuality. There was too much to do.

In addition to becoming the new Royal Lion, Marco had also inherited the coveted title of Cavalier of the First Order to the King of Italy. Now, he was privy to the politics of the royal court and much valuable information. Staunch friends who had only contempt for the many insipid millionaire land barons in Sicily and their frightening politics became his allies. Marco laughed amiably when, upon completion of his formal education at Rome's university, well-meaning friends urged him to stay in Rome where a civilized gentleman could live and prosper in refined gentility—not among those uncouth Sicilian barbarians.

But Destiny had already staked her claim on the Royal Lion. His life would be dedicated to an even greedier mistress, Sicily, where his knowledge, his power, and his might

66

would one day be used to help his nation lift its head with proud dignity and join the ranks of other nations which had recovered from centuries of oppression and bondage. Sicily had been raped enough!

It was obvious to Marco that the primary objective of every conquering nation including the Papacy had been acquisition of land. Greed had begun over the land, therefore it must end over the land. Those ancient laws permitting any red-blooded man to claim uncultivated lands had been a travesty. When lands ran fallow, how many starving, hopeful peasants had staked their claims only to find themselves brutally beaten, severely maimed and punished, or delivered dead to their families? In this way, the corrupt feudal land barons, the Mafia and the Papacy had grown land-rich over the centuries.

The summer prior to his graduation, Marco encouraged the *contadini* to participate in a farfetched plan, later to be identified as a farming cooperative. "He must be crazy," said the peasants to one another. "Crazy!" But then, inspired by this magnetic man, hadn't they been just as crazy thinking that by bearing arms and defending themselves they could outwit the *mafia* and other baronial princes? What the hell? The pay was good and they didn't have to walk those exhausting miles each day back and forth from their village to the *latifondo*. What would it hurt to tell this *fanatico* they'd go along with him?

Whatever else they thought about their *padrone* at this time, they were to learn he was a man of his word, a man who could make miracles happen. Look at the changes in the *latifondo* already! Imagine building houses for the peasants to live on the land? Only a crazy man would do such a thing. Never, they told themselves, never would they give up their houses in the village.

To the Lion, a farming cooperative seemed the only way to stave off the greedy *mafiosi* who were rapidly infiltrating the feudal estates with their *gabelotti*, and successfully subverting the powers of the *latifondisti*. Already there were rumors of pro-Mafia legislation being passed in Parliament. "Over my dead body!" cried Marco de Leone. "Never will this legislation pass!"

Moving in and out of political circles in Rome, the Lion exchanged ideas with agronomists from all over the world. Naturally, he became more democratic in his views than his Sicilian peers who scoffed at his revolutionary ideas. A farming cooperative, indeed! What the hell is this Royal Lion thinking of? Why didn't he just give his land away outright to these foul, stinking peasants he felt the need to champion? "He's a crazy fanatic! Just like his father and his father before him! He ought to be stopped!" came the cries from the Mafia-controlled *latifondi* and from the Mafia-controlled bankers in Palermo. These cries even reached the mafia lobbyists in Rome. "We'll keep our eyes on him," they promised their wealthy constituents.

It was disappointing for Marco not to be able to infect the other *latifondisti* with the common sense of a farming co-operative, but try as he might, his enthusiasm was looked upon as something horribly distasteful by these shortsighted nincompoops. Very well, he promised. He'd show them how it's done. Just let them come to Marco de Leone's bank in Messina for loans! He'd have his answers ready for all of them!

Convinced his way was right, Marco moved forward alone. His next step was to educate the Sicilian peasant away from the superstitions and fallacies by which he'd lived for centuries. That would be only the beginning.

One morning, fifteen years later, Marco awoke to the most exciting sight of his life. He looked all around him and he smiled. The cooperative had been a fantastic success, the envy of all the *latifondisti* who remained too steeped in old traditions or too lazy to change. Nothing in all of Sicily equaled the magnificent sprawling estate of the Royal Lion. The villa itself, reminiscent of a Spanish hacienda, had been constructed around three courtyards. The fountain court-yard at the main entrance sprawled around a magnificent bronze statue of Marco's great-grandfather, Don Emiliano de Cordoba de Leone, first of the Cavaliers of the Royal Order of the Lion under Spanish rule. In full regalia he sat astride a gleaming bronze steed. Glistening hand-set mosaic tiles covered the walkways, corridors, and porticos of the two-story villa. Behind the villa, facing north, was the flower courtyard, where roses of every known species had been carefully planted and cultivated among several perennials which served to keep one strong scent from abusing the fragrance of another. Breathtakingly beautiful, they were named the Madelaina gardens in honor of the woman who conceived them, Marco's great-grandmother, an outspoken woman of impeccable taste.

To the west of the villa stood the Courtyard of St. Sebas-tian, a covered portico leading to the chapel and quarters of Father Bonaventura. To the left of this courtyard were the enormous outdoor ovens, open pit roasting areas used to cook large quantities of food. Beyond this area, the household servants lived in small *casitas*.

Inside the villa were marbled halls with terrazzo flooring, high domed ceilings, floor-to-ceiling fireplaces, exquisite Austrian and Venetian chandeliers, thick Persian carpeting, priceless paintings, and rare objets d'art.

An elegant spiral staircase fanned out from the upper hallway down to an oversized foyer. To the right of this stood three enormous formal salons. At the end of these rooms, the area had been converted into an apartment for Roberto Argento. To the left of the foyer was Marco's study, a high-ceilinged solarium, and a small dining room overlooking the Madelaina gardens. Down a long hallway to the left of the study were the pantries, butter rooms, kitchens, and larders.

Southwest of the fountain courtyard, beyond stone walls and abundant shrubbery, lay the modest individual cottages of the *contadini* who worked the lands. There was nothing like this in all of Sicily. Workers of the *latifondo* never lived on the estate. They were usually forced to travel by foot or mule some seven to fourteen miles a day. The houses, kept immaculate with tender care, were bright and cheery. No animals were permitted to roam indiscriminately through the houses, a measure which effectively cut down on the incidence of sickness and disease.

Next to the chapel was a medical dispensary, an innovation planned by Marco and manned by two of the peasants' wives to provide first aid and dispense medication for small injuries or illnesses diagnosed by Dr. Pietro, who came each week from Messina to check on the children and disabled.

Along the northern perimeter of the fortress wall was another cluster of houses. Enclosed pens behind the main *casitas* were especially constructed for breeding chickens, pheasants, peacocks, and doves. The cattle and sheep were kept in pasture lands to the west of a central sector where enormous barnlike structures housed olive oil vats, bins of nuts, fruits, and seasonal produce. Wheat and other grains were stored near a modest flour mill. Natural wells furnished most of the water which was stored in gigantic cisterns.

Mt. Etna stood beyond the southern boundary of the estate, the frothy blue-green waters of the Tyrrhenian Sea beyond its nothern shores, the Ionian Sea to the east and the whole of Sicily to the west. It was a lush paradise on earth!

To the north of the Madelaina gardens was a special place, a plot of ground called Terra d'Oro, golden land, which Marco had chosen not to cultivate. It would wait for that special something that he felt worthy of growing on such hallowed ground. It was here that the Lion could be found, lost in contemplation, when the need for soul searching became intense.

And those proud and glorious Arabian horses! Prancing in the sparkling sunshine in their own special corrals, they were one of Marco's proudest achievements. A man could feel like a king just watching them!

What a glorious feeling to know he had succeeded. What a marvelous sense of accomplishment and victory. What more could a man want? Being no great drinker or carouser of women, Marco spent the long nights at the *latifondo* in interesting discussions with Roberto, who was always a fount of information. Or they played chess. Even in Rome Marco denied himself the company of lovely ladies and made no commitments.

Long ago he had told himself he'd never marry. What kind of a life was this for a woman? How could he ask anyone to share such a life where the daily uncertainties would wring out her guts? How well he knew the meaning of loneliness. So many times he'd gaze upon the peasants and their families and wonder, how do they manage? Are their skins tougher than mine? Their hearts less hardened? Or is it because they don't live under the curse of the Lions that they can go about the simple act of living an uncomplicated life? He didn't know. He did know something was lacking. Some natural part of him cried out wanting to be whole. Fanatic? Crazy? Crusader? He was all those, but he hadn't stopped being a man. *Managghia!* Is there never to be peace for me?

7

Cesare Ruffo was tall and fashionably dressed in a gray morning suit with black velvet lapels and a conservative cravat. He fingered his handlebar mustache delicately as he scanned the file in his hands. Genteel, with a natural graciousness, he had the unmistakable look of a continental. Marco had taken to him the first time they'd met, ten years before and hired him as bank manager at the Banco de Messina, another de Leone asset.

The distinguished man with glints of steel in his dark hair glanced up with warmth in his eyes when he saw the Lion enter the bank shortly before noon.

"Good day, Your Excellency," he called to the Lion. He rose from his leather chair, excused himself to his client, and approached Marco. For a few moments they talked. From time to time Marco paused to study the elderly man seated next to Cesare's desk, then nodding, he followed his bank manager back to his large oak desk.

"How can I be of assistance to you?" asked Marco.

Ruffo made the introductions. "Permit me to introduce Don Catanese from Catania. He has applied to us for a loan to bring in his harvest of grapes and wheat on his *latifondo*."

70

Marco frowned. It wasn't his policy to sit in at loan preliminaries.

"If you will, Excellency, permit me to show you the file. Here you'll see three loan applications made at separate banks. Note the dates of previous loans . . ."

Marco scanned the notes. He quickly recognized the names of Mafia-controlled banks. "Since he already has his money, Cesare, why come to us?"

"The banks are foreclosing on Don Alfredo's notes before maturity. They are forcing him to sell his land because he can't pay off the loans until the crops come in."

Marco extended his arm. "Please, let's retire to the conference room where we can be assured of privacy." Marco wanted to be sure that this was no Mafia Don.

Alfredo Catanese had a cherubic face, a ruddy complexion that seemed unreal until Ruffo explained the older man suffered from the sugar disease and felt flushed all the time. It was a somewhat expressionless face, one beset with problems that he consciously tried not to let bother him. His white hair was combed neatly off his face, and his portly figure moved in a cumbersome manner indicating he felt some distress,

"So, Don Alfredo, tell me. Are the lands free from lease?" asked Marco.

"All but a few hundred acres are leased. The rest of the land lies fallow.

"Do you employ a *special* overseer?" asked the Lion subtly.

"Listen, Excellency," said the Don flushed with anger, "no goddamn *gabelotti* darken my properties!" He wiped his forehead with a handkerchief and fanned himself. "It's taken too long to build my lands into the richest in Catania. I wouldn't defile them with such men."

"That's his problem," interrupted Ruffo tactfully. His steadfast refusal to do business with the *mafia* or to capitulate in the manner of the other *latifondisti* is causing them to put the squeeze where a man can't take the pressure."

"You should have considered this before doing business with a bank controlled by this *honorable brotherhood*," said the Lion coolly.

"I didn't know they were involved. The men I did business with to secure the loan were not the men who have come around to enforce payment."

Marco puffed on a cigarette through a slender gold holder, his eyes intent on the contour maps and other documents. Natural wells . . . ideal location . . . He studied the titles and land grants. Moreover he listened intently to the Don.

"The property was in my wife's family for many years.

71

She was the Baroness de Grazzi. Originally the land belonged to the Royal Order of the Jesuits. In 1786, the Bourbon king expelled the order on the grounds of worldliness and corruption and confiscated the lands. Original plans to break up the Jesuit estates into smaller holdings failed and only the wealthiest of the titled class acquired the rich and fertile lands. Please, Signore, may I trouble you for a glass of water?" He glanced at Ruffo.

Instantly Ruffo reached for the water carafe. "The Don suffers from the sugar disease," he hastened to explain to the Lion.

Marco liked the old gentleman. Glancing at his watch, he suggested they retire to Lucchesi's restaurant. "It's just that I cannot break the appointments scheduled for later, so it's best we continue through the siesta.

Over lunch, the Don lamented he could no longer enjoy the foods other men ate because of his health. "I have a daughter, Excellency, who watches me like a hawk. *Managghia*, what a watchdog! 'Don't eat this, papa. Don't eat that.' I'm not master of my own life anymore." He smiled good naturedly. "I've half a mind to sell out to those *brutti schifosi!*" He sipped his water while longingly eyeing the red wine in Ruffo's glass. "If it were up to my daughter, we'd sell. She keeps nagging me to sell everything and move to America. You see I have a brother in America. A physician in Buffalo. She has some silly notion I could be cured of this nagging infirmity if we went to the new land."

"You'd consider an outright sale of your lands?" asked Marco showing interest.

"Never!" he said spitefully. "Wouldn't give them the satisfaction."

"You misunderstand," smiled Marco. "I mean sell them to me."

Don Alfredo's expression changed as he weighed Marco's words. *What would I do without land? I may not take well to America. Many Sicilians emigrated to the promised land and returned with considerable money to invest. But why have they not chosen to remain in America?* He shrugged. "I'm getting old, Excellency. This body no longer functions as it once did. I have only memories now. But oh, what memories! There was a time . . ." He sighed. "There was a time when I would have crushed these blood-sucking insects with a blow of my fist. But my blood no longer flows with the courage and impetuosity of my youth. My head tells me yes, but this old body makes me aware, too aware, that I have passed my time. *La morte*—death—awaits around the corner. No, no, don't contest these words. I've always been a straight talker. My concern only is for my

72

daughter. How could she cope with these *schifosi?* She's a woman, Excellency. At times she has the balls of a bull, but not against these vipers."

Marco was silent, disturbed by the man's outlook. He knew the Don spoke, not to evoke pity or compassion, but as a man concerned over the future of a daughter.

"Ah, *buon giorno,* Don Catanese. I see you're a long distance from your home, no?"

The trio glanced up into the shifty eyes of Don Tricario, a shrewd, small time, ex-gangster, once active in Black Hand operations in New York's Little Italy. When it was discovered he was in America illegally, he quickly shuttled back to his native land and became active in Mafia affairs.

Ruffo's refusal to stand made it clear the *mafioso* was being ignored. Marco looked at Don Catanese, as if he hadn't seen Tricario. "You were saying, Don Alfredo?"

Glowering darkly, Tricario nodded imperceptibly and walked away.

"*Schifoso!*" spat Ruffo.

"Now, now, we must be tolerant of our less fortunate brothers," said Marco placatingly.

Don Alfredo glanced from one to the other, amazed that they had the audacity to make an enemy of this Tricario. But then he wasn't used to being in the presence of a Royal Lion.

"I find it difficult to share your views on scum like Tricario. I've dealt with his kind too long," said Ruffo. "Bloodsucking leech with the venom of an asp!"

"That's some combination," smiled Marco tolerantly. "But I think it useless for three adults to waste precious time talking of such a man."

Ruffo stood his ground. "You know what I mean. News of Don Alfredo being with us will reach Catania before he does. That scum is a regular wireless who spouts pus from his lips! He must sit up nights thinking of ways to part a man from his money!"

"And what are your thoughts on the matter, Don Alfredo?" Marco had been watching the older man as he suppressed a smile at Cesare's emotional outburst.

"Only that I agree with your bank manager. I've had my fill of such men and as you said earlier, why should we waste our time talking of such scum?"

"*Va biene.* Let's get back to business," said Marco, finishing his prociutto and melon. He sipped his espresso and poured anisette into it. "Ah, that's better." Marco opened the manila folder a moment and then repeated his earlier question about the Don's considering an outright sale of the property in Catania. "Consider my proposal, Don Alfredo.

Take your time in making the decision. Name your own price. I shall be in Catania in two weeks. You can give me your answer then. Is that sufficient time?"

Marco caught sight of several Mafia Dons who stared in their direction. He frowned noticeably and looked at Don Catanese, adding quickly, "In any event, if we don't reach an agreement to buy your lands, we shall loan you the monies you need."

"But what of the *mafiosi*. They won't wait two weeks. They've given me until next Thursday."

"Do you have the notes, Cesare?" Ruffo nodded. "Pay them."

"What of collateral?"

"I need no collateral." He extended his hand across the table and shook the older man's firmly. "I have the gentleman's handshake."

"But Excellency."

"Pay them. All of them."

Don Alfredo beamed. Now, there's a man. "Excellency, it will give me great pleasure to meet with you at my villa in Catania. I can't thank you enough."

Marco nodded and rose to leave. "It displeases me to leave so soon, but I have pressing business. Good day."

He bowed to Ruffo and walked through the restaurant nodding to some and waving to others, most of whom flushed with pleasure that the Royal Lion had acknowledged them. Following him closely were his bodyguards, Calo and Ciccio, who converged behind him instantly and followed him out the door.

Two weeks to the day, Marco arrived in Catania and for the best part of the day was taken on a tour of the Catanese *latifondo*. At four o'clock they headed back to the main villa. Mariolina Catanese had been expecting them. Petite, dark-haired, seeming taller than her five-foot-four-inch frame indicated, she looked like a sloe-eyed oriental, but her independent temperament didn't match her retiring features.

"Papa," she called to her father. "Are you feeling well? You shouldn't have stayed out so long. You know what happens when you overtax yourself." She scolded her father, unmindful of Marco de Leone's amused expression as he dismounted and handed the reins to his men.

As Mariolina handed the reins of her father's horse to the stable boy, she turned back and her eyes caught the look on Marco's face. Lowering her eyes demurely, she explained, "Papa doesn't know how to relax. He thinks he's still a young stallion." She shifted her attention to the rotund

74

servant that approached. "Angelo, take off his boots before he swells up."

"*Basta!* Enough," said Don Alfredo. "Mariolina, you aren't being courteous to our guest." The Don apologized. "You must forgive my daughter's lack of manners. It seems that I've allowed her to run me as she does the villa. May I present my daughter, Mariolina de Catanese, Excellency?"

Marco bowed, kissing her outstretched hand lightly. "Signorina." He stared at her intently, from her shocking men's pants to the tip of her leather boots. Her costume unnerved him less than her audacious manners. Sicilian women were usually shy and retiring. But this was modern Catania, he reminded himself, the progressive university city where most Sicilian morals were ridiculed by the intellectuals. Mariolina blushed under his gaze.

"My dear, this is His Excellency, the Marquis de Leone." Don Alfredo scowled at his daughter's lack of respect. For two weeks he had daydreamed about marrying her off to this gem of a man, but she was hopeless.

"It's a pleasure, Signore. *Piacere.*"

"That's the trouble with educated women, Excellency. They have no respect for their elders."

Mariolina studied the Lion coolly as he dismissed his bodyguards. For two weeks she had heard nothing except his name from her father. In her classes in political economics at Catania University, the name de Leone was often mentioned in discussions of Sicily's progress. He had been instrumental in passing many land reforms favorable to the peasants. But a lot of good it did! Those *mafia* butchers made sure the laws couldn't be enforced. Mariolina noticed him staring at her outfit with disapproval, and she stifled a small giggle.

"Please, Signore, will you take coffee and anisette with us? Did you enjoy your tour of the *latifondo?*"

"It is breathtaking, Signorina. Simply breathtaking. More beautiful than I had imagined it. My only disappointment was seeing so much land lying fallow. Don't you believe in crop rotation?"

"Oh, I do, Signore. Believe me I do. But try convincing these hard-headed *contadini* of the merit of such a plan." She rolled her eyes upward.

"I sympathize with you. It's not easy to dissuade men from doing what their forefathers have done for centuries. Perhaps now that your father has agreed to sell the land we can encourage the *contadini* to learn new ways." He sipped his coffee.

"You'll stay to dinner, Excellency?" asked Don Alfredo.

"I think not. I have a young bridegroom with me, married only a week and Ciccio itches to return to his bride."

The Don nodded knowingly, thinking of his bridegroom days. "Then he mustn't be kept away too long, eh, Excellency?" They laughed.

"Your father tells me you attended the university here and set a precedent for women to be accepted for general enrollment."

Mariolina glanced at him in mild surprise. Then she laughed at some secret joke. "It wasn't easy, eh, papa? *Demonio!* They considered me mad."

Don Catanese laughed with her. "What a furor she caused. But despite the odds against her, she made it."

"For two years I incurred the wrath of every man at school, including my professors. All those men . . . I suppose I threatened their manliness." Her smile widened, then she quickly sobered.

"You must admit, Signorina, most women seldom bother to do more than what is required of them as women."

Hardly hearing him, Mariolina said with bitter reflection, "I was the only student in class not permitted to make a mistake. Do you know what that's like? Not to have the luxury of being wrong?" Marco nodded and sipped his coffee. "Once, only once, I gave the wrong answer. Everyone laughed with a smug what-can-you-expect-from-a-woman look. From then on I knew it would be suicide to go to class unprepared."

The Don excused himself. "It's a drowsiness I can't control. When it comes upon me, I must rest."

Marco rose to his feet. "Is there something I can do?"

"No, thank you. Pray don't leave until I return. I need only ten or fifteen minutes."

Marco felt a twinge of guilt at being left alone with Mariolina. In most of Sicily, leaving a young unmarried woman with a man without a chaperone implied she was a whore.

Sensing his discomfort, with a modicum of surprise, Mariolina took her coffee to the stone wall overlooking the Ionian Sea. The gigantic tangerine sun had dropped toward the horizon, streaking the sky with shades of pink and pomegranate red. It was a spectacular sunset reaching into a fiery twilight.

Marco walked to her side and followed her line of vision. The pounding surf below the high cliffs and the supernatural lights that looked more like a painting than reality blended together in an awesome panorama. The gentle tinkling of small goat bells wafted up to them as a light breeze ruffled the golden carpet of gleaming wheat below. He sighed in deep appreciation. The intrinsic beauty of the place appealed to him almost as much as the Terra d'Oro. He suddenly felt a strange rushing over his heart.

"It's truly beautiful this Sicily of ours," he said breathlessly. "At times like this, when I see such magnificence in nature, I wish the entire world could share in it." He turned to his young companion. "Doesn't it make you feel rather special to be a part of such a grand heritage?"

Mariolina spun around and faced him with dark eyes that flashed brightly and filled with youthful rage. "You, Signore, are a dreamer! How can you call this land of ours beautiful? Special, you say . . . to have been a part of this heritage? Hah!"

His words echoed back to him, strange-sounding, mixed with contempt, disgust, and anger. She paced back and forth around the patio, her dark eyes darting furtively about like those of a wildcat.

"Surely, *you* of all people aren't blind to what goes on in this land? It's incredible to me that a man of your bent could have made such an asinine remark. In this world of evil, poverty, disease, and almost total illiteracy, how can you only see beauty?"

If he hadn't been so astonished at her brass, he would have put her in her place, but she gave him no opening. She continued with a fierce passion. "The whole of Sicily despairs at the black scourge that poisons the hearts of our youth and kills them before they bloom. Ignorance, fear, and superstition chain them to the past. There's no future in Sicily, only a decadent past. Is this the heritage I should deem so special?"

Suddenly he looked at her in a different light. "But you're a woman despite the fact that you deny it with every word you utter. Your future lies in choosing a husband who makes his own future."

Mariolina was aghast. "Are you telling me a woman can have no future of her own? That she must rely on a man to do her thinking? Is she not a human being with human rights and thoughts and drives and needs which must be met as well as those of a man?"

He would have liked to have said, You're damn right that's what I'm saying! But he didn't. "In my world of lawmaking and politics—primarily a man's world—an outspoken woman is a rarity," he said diplomatically. "You must admit, Signorina, there is a decided shortage of women spouting political oratory."

Suddenly Marco smiled indulgently, his eyes twinkling in merriment. "Tell me, Signorina, are you perchance an exponent of the socialist, Gianotti? Do I detect his influence in the words you speak?"

"For whatever your reasons, yes."

Marco nodded knowingly and suppressed a smile.

"I detect disapproval in your attitude."

"It's just that most Catanian intellectuals are followers of this crafty politician who knows just how to incite an un-suspecting public. He keeps a tight menagerie of propagandists."

"I resent your speaking so disparagingly about a fine man like Gianotti."

"Signorina, it is not my intent to ridicule your ideals." He shrugged. "What amazes me is that so intelligent a woman as you appear to be could be hoodwinked by a chameleon who supports the socialists in Catania and simultaneously backs the antisocialists in Palermo."

The astonishment on her face was incredible. Marco soft-ened. "How does it happen that such a lovely young woman troubles herself with such things?" When he saw the dis-turbed look on her face, he hastened to add, "Meaning no disrespect, of course."

Feeling patronized, she became infuriated. "I have eyes. My ears also work. Behind this face is a mind that thinks. And to me anyone who thinks of Sicily in terms of beauty is not only blind, but a fool. Meaning no disrespect, of course."

His first impulse was to put her in her place. But he was becoming a bit bored with her, and out of respect to Don Alfredo, he remained polite. "Have you ever traveled to the north? To Messina?"

"No. But I've seen the corruption in Palermo. In Trapani, I saw starvation, lost hope in the eyes of the people. I've seen filth and squalor and the degradation of mankind in Corleone."

Managghia! There is no stopping her. She acts as if the plight of Sicily is my fault. Marco searched for an avenue of escape. He glanced coolly at his gold pocket watch and wondered how much longer Don Alfredo would be.

"Perhaps, one day, you'll visit my estates with your father, my dear." He walked back onto the patio and put his coffee cup down on the marble-topped table.

She recognized the curt dismissal in his voice and sensed his displeasure. Mariolina shrugged and drew her full lips tight into a pout.

Marco tried to be gentle. "It's difficult to make a per-son see through the eyes of another."

"Only if they are complete mutes or totally insensitive. I

78

see women will have a lot to overcome before they can enter the world of man."

God forbid! thought Marco.

With a sigh of relief, Marco saw Don Alfredo approaching. "Signorina, it's been a pleasure chatting with you. Perhaps one day when experience has mellowed you, you'll know why I prefer to see our country through its beauty rather than its blatant imperfections."

Mariolina's eyes smoldered with indignation as she watched him kiss her hand with polite reserve. She should have known the older generation wouldn't understand young modern day thinkers.

She saw him embrace her father warmly after they finished their business and said their farewells. Disappointed, she decided that contrary to what she'd heard about Marco de Leone and his advanced theories, he was of the old school. She promptly dismissed him from mind.

Unfortunately for Marco, he couldn't dismiss Mariolina from his mind and he couldn't understand why not. Hadn't her impertinence, abandonment of social mores, and outspoken views annoyed him? And hadn't he found her brash, impudent, and unthinking to have condemned him to the role of a fool? She had judged him too harshly, that little baggage! He boiled with resentment. But, he told himself, if she had upset him so, why couldn't he dismiss her from his mind? Why did he give her a second thought? Certainly he was more disciplined than this. But when he considered it further, he discovered something in himself that surprised him—her words had angered him whereas a man's words would have rolled off his back. That puts things in a different perspective, Marco, old boy, he told himself.

Time passed. She invaded his thoughts more than he cared to admit. Surprisingly, as he viewed her through different eyes, he discovered they had much in common. When he began to envision her as his wife and mistress of the Villa de Leone, it took all his strength to forcibly eject her image from his mind. He offered himself all the old arguments including a few new ones: the difference in their ages, their temperaments, anything to discourage those inner whisperings that grew more and more insistent.

When he began to see her face everywhere—in the gray dawn of early morning, in the black of night, in the fiery sunsets—he was like a man dying of thirst. When his thirst for her became all-consuming he barely spoke. He sank into a morose silence that no one could break. He thought of their first encounter, a near disaster, many times. Mariolina had said everything she could to discourage and frighten off the ordinary man. But Marco was no ordinary man, even when his willpower dissolved and she began to occupy his dreams, he tackled the situation like the real man he was. The time had come to commit himself to a meaningful relationship, he told himself. Sparked by inspiration, the Lion sat down at his desk and wrote a letter to Don Catanese, respectfully requesting the hand of his daughter in marriage.

8

"Marco." Roberto's voice pierced the air. Marco turned as his crew lowered a dinghy into the frothy green waters. The *Marchessa,* Marco's opulent cruiser, had just weighed anchor in the Bay of Catania.

"*Si,* Roberto. What is it?"

"Have you lost your senses? Calo and Ciccio tell me you won't let them accompany you to the Catanese Villa."

"Not today. There's no need," replied Marco softly. He turned his attention back to the busy men below.

"I won't let you do this. You can't throw caution to the winds. It's sheer idiocy. No, it's madness." Roberto's usually gentle manner had been fired with passion, and he showed his exasperation. His thin face paled with annoyance, turning the nearly invisible scar on his left cheek livid.

"Look, *amico.* I don't feel like having bodyguards with me today. There are some things a man must do alone. Can't you understand?"

"I understand that since you've fallen in love, your senses have dulled. Your memory can't be that short."

"Do you really think I could forget what happened to my family? To me?" Marco looked gravely at his blue-eyed friend with sandy blonde hair tousled by the wind. He relaxed and smiled. "Look, I promise. I'll be fine. What can happen to me? No one knows I'm here."

"I wouldn't be too sure."

"*Basta,* Roberto! No more, now."

Roberto pursed his lips stubbornly, tossed his arms in the air, and moved with a noticeable limp toward the two bodyguards who stood not far away fussing with inconsequential mooring lines, anything to keep busy.

Marco turned to watch as Roberto limped away. Oh, how he loved that man! What an incredibly warm spot he held in his heart for this dear friend. Smiling now, more tolerant of his friend's concern, he turned his attention to the two seamen in the water. *Managghia!* How long does it take to ready the boat? He called to them, "Ahoy, down below. How much longer?" One of the sailors held up ten fingers. *Delays! Always delays!* Marco scowled impatiently.

Marco's two bodyguards stood amidships listening intently

to Roberto and showing obvious disapproval of Marco's decision. Calo La Bolla was a thick-necked, heavy-set gargantuan, but his fat jowls and widely spaced buckteeth gave him the appearance of an overgrown kid. He was blessed with uncanny vision and he could spot movement at a hundred paces. His expertise with a *lupara* could blow a man's skull apart. Tough, cynical, a man of few words, the mercurial Calo had the power of a Hercules in his muscular torso.

By contrast, Ciccio Pontiface was a small gnome of a man who wore his thick black shock of hair parted in the center and slicked down to a patent leather gloss. He always wore a white starched shirt, maybe without its starched collar at times, but always with a pair of snappy red satin garters around his upper arms, a present from a whore in Marseille. Ciccio had been known to crack the heads of two men. Not only was Ciccio an enigma, he was a contradiction. With his deceptively small arms he could inflict severe wounds on any man, for as a lad, Ciccio had stowed away on a ship and spent ten years in the Far East where he learned the oriental martial arts. He and Marco met in Marseille, where Marco had gone on business. When the Lion was attacked along the waterfront by two eely characters who intended to rob his purse, Ciccio intervened, and Marco saw the wonder of wonders take place before his eyes.

This tiny man, standing under five feet, displayed the strength of Samson as he picked up one man and hurled him over his shoulders, then came down on the other with two swift chops and a kick or two thrown in for good measure. And when the other came back for more, Ciccio shot out with a knee kick that burst the man's balls. The thief gave up the purse, and holding on to his fractured privates, limped off with his stunned and bewildered partner.

Marco's infectious laughter echoed through the deserted waterfront alley. He couldn't stop laughing even when Ciccio retrieved the wallet, and with a certain panache, bowed and handed it to the Lion. The incongruity of these towering beasts bested by what might be affectionately referred to as the runt of the litter tickled his fancy. On the spot, Marco asked him how much money he made. Ciccio told him straight. "I'll triple that, give you living quarters, the contents of this purse, and a good life if you'll come to work for me—and in your spare time, teach me a few of those miracles. *Va biene?*"

Both these men were loyal to Marco. Fiercely loyal! They loved him with undying devotion. No one dared say a word against *their* Excellency and not fear the consequences. Now, as they listened to Roberto's instructions, they retreated to the stern of the ship muttering, "He's crazy. That's what Excellency is, crazy." When had love and brains ever mixed?

Roberto was frowning when he returned to Marco's side. "Marco, they don't like it. I don't like it. Can't we persuade you to change your mind?"

"*Va, va!* You worry like a woman, *caro mio*," said Marco, embracing Roberto in a brotherly fashion. Roberto refused to be infected with the Lion's happiness. Seeing his long face, Marco gave in. "All right. All right," He compromised. "Just so I won't have to see your long sad face all the way to the Villa Catanese, let's agree on a few things. In two hours, send a boat back for me. If I'm not on shore waiting for you, send the men to the villa. Does that satisfy you?"

"A lot can happen in two hours," said Roberto dryly. "But it's agreed," he added quickly before the Lion could change his mind. "Do you have the papers? The marriage contracts?"

Marco felt his breast pocket and nodded. They embraced. The Lion descended the ladder to the dinghy bobbing up and down in the water below. He looked back up and waved to Roberto, then shouted orders to his men.

Watching the boat move through the colorful array of vintage fishing boats and yachts in the harbor, Roberto leaned over the ship's railing with a sinking sensation. The two sullen bodyguards moved alongside him.

"What do you think, Calo?"

"What do I think? What does it matter what I think? I'm only a gun, a knife."

"He's in love," said Roberto simply.

"*Amore. Amore.* Who but the insane can enter that world and make sense?" asked Ciccio. "And believe me, it's from experience I talk."

"Since he made the decision to marry the Signorina, I haven't been able to reach him. Cesare Ruffo told me how angry the *mafiosi* were when they learned the Catanese villa had been sold to the House of de Leone."

"You know how bad they wanted the Catanese property? Phew!" said Calo with the appropriate hand gestures.

"But how is it you know this? It was some big secret," said Roberto.

"Some big secret? Are you crazy? My cousin Shortino told me long ago. 'Look,' he says. 'You better be careful with your *padrone*. You think they'll let this pass?' Then he told me how long Don Catanese opposed the *mafia*, how he fought against allowing a *gabelotto* on the lands. My cousin told me that once they couldn't sell their goods to the market, even though their prices were lower than those set by the *mafia*. But in those days Don Alfredo was in better health. He fought them off good. But he couldn't fight the way our people do. The *latifondisti* are not advanced like the Villa de Leone. They are *embecile*."

Roberto wrestled with his conscience. "Ruffo also said the *mafiosi* would retaliate. They consider it a contemptuous insult dealt them by the House of de Leone."

"That's what they said?" asked Calo. "El Leone will cut them in half at every turn." He grinned and flicked his cigarette into the bay.

"Calo? Who is Matteo Barbarossa?"

Both men turned to stare at Roberto as if he were an apparition. "You never heard of Barbarossa?"

"Only what Cesare Ruffo mentioned of him the other day."

"A son of Satan," said Calo as if that explained the man.

"A Mazzarino," said Ciccio with deliberation.

"And that my friends tells me nothing," said Roberto.

Calo grew restless and touchy. "He eats men like the *latifondisti*, three times a day." Clearly depressed, he tried to explain about this obscenity, this immoral *disgraziato* who had carved a career for himself from the countless deaths and killings he'd masterminded.

"He is a butcher, Roberto," said Ciccio tersely. "It's that simple. Why make so many words?" he asked his partner with a shrug of his shoulders.

"Aye, he is a butcher—and more. He's the leader of the Mazzarinos, uncontested, I hear."

"Mazzarinos? Who are they?"

"*Mah che demonio?* You don't know them? The Mazzarinos are . . . uh . . . the Mazzarinos! The most ferocious bandits in the history of Sicily. Worse! They are the arm of the *mafia*. Bought and paid for by the *capomafia* in Palermo. They do killing for the *mafiosi*. What else can I tell you." Calo shrugged.

"This Barbarossa has the cock and balls of a stallion," said Ciccio. "He's got plenty of brains, too. When they massacre and slaughter it is always with a purpose, Signore Roberto. Always with a purpose. I have studied their ways, listened carefully to the reports of their bloodbaths and soon after, I always hear of more power given to the Mafia. This Barbarossa is no ignorant savage."

"I should have forced Marco to listen!" exclaimed Roberto. "Dammit! Am I a friend or a rabbit?"

Before the two oarsmen had returned from shore, Roberto gave the bodyguards new orders. Well armed, they left for the Catanese Villa.

"No matter what he says, you are not to let His Excellency out of your sight!"

"*Va biene. Va biene,*" they said, fully spirited.

Marco paid off the driver and walked briskly toward the gate of the villa. Suddenly, two mountainous brutes with buckteeth and skin the texture of crocodiles sprang out at him, poised with hair-trigger carbines aimed at his heart. Then one of them lowered his carbine and searched Marco.

"Why am I being searched before entering this villa?" he asked icily.

Without replying they nudged him ahead with the snub-nosed barrels of their guns. Marco tensed, returned their hard stares, and fought to subdue his rage. *Damn! I should have brought Calo and Ciccio. Roberto was right. Love can make a man do foolish things.*

Inside the courtyard he sobered instantly. Everywhere were signs of mourning. Windows were shuttered and draped in black; an immense floral wreath was fastened to a huge oak door; and servants, wearing black arm bands were packing and moving crates of household goods in the far courtyard. He stared, stunned and bewildered.

"*Firmate!* Stop!" called Angelo as he shuffled toward him. He held his short fat arms in a halting gesture. He nodded to Marco as he talked in hushed tones to the imposing brutes. They relaxed their weapons and stood aside on the sun-baked clay tiles of the courtyard, offering no apologies. Their black-eyed fierceness dissolved into disinterest, and they allowed Marco to pass.

"Your Lordship." Angelo bowed obsequiously. He wrung his pudgy hands and shook his head sorrowfully. "With your permission, a thousand pardons for this shocking *comedia.*" He gestured to the grotesque centurions.

"What manner of greeting is this, Angelo?" asked Marco with stern reproval and not a little curiosity in his voice.

"There's been a shocking tragedy, Seignieure. A terrible, calamitous tragedy." He paused, stepped aside and allowed Marco to pass before him.

"Don Alfredo was murdered five days ago. Murdered. In cold blood." Angelo crossed himself and peered cautiously about to see if they were being observed.

"Bandits sent by the *mafiosi,*" he hissed. His face was white with fright. "It was them, I know. First, they warned us by slaughtering six sheep. Next they cut the choice vines of the Lacrima Christi grapes. God help us! Then they murdered little Felipo, the son of the foreman, Excellency. His little body was mutilated and sent to Don Alfredo on a cart with a letter attached." Angelo broke down and sobbed loudly.

"Calm down, Angelo. Calm down." Marco paused, calming himself with effort. "Tell me, where is the *Signorina* Catanese?"

Angelo pointed to the courtyard. "She's already ordered us to pack. She wants to flee the villa and go to America. Oh what a calamity. *Buon armo,* Don Alfredo, such a good man." He continued to shake with convulsive sobs.

"Pull yourself together, Angelo. Now, who was it? Did you see any of them? What did the letter say?"

Filled with torment, the poor man peered cautiously about the courtyard and beckoned Marco toward the *casa*. "One can't be too careful, Excellency. Understand I would talk to no one else, only you."

"I understand. Take your time. I must know everything before I pay my respects to the Signorina."

"*Si.* One week after your last visit, three of them came here. Don Trappani, Don Sperro, and Don Villalbano."

"Go on."

"Don Catanese gave them a bank draft in full payment for the mortgages. You think they were happy to get their money? Phew! They looked at the draft as if it were *carta bacauzzu*—toilet paper. They quarreled. 'Sell us the land,' they insisted. Not once, not twice, *managghia!* Over and over and over. 'Sell,' they cried. 'Impossible,' he would answer. *Aloura,* the *schifosi* left fuming with rage. Two days later they returned like Vesuvius. Everything all over again, Excellency. They pressed. Don Alfredo resisted. By then, he could take no more. You know how they are when they get something up their asses? 'Listen,' *mi padrone* told them. 'Let's end this farce. The estate has been sold and that's finished!' Oh, *demonio!* You should have seen them. Don Sperro's eyes fell from his head. And that cigar in Don Trappani's mouth looked like *mierde*. And that cretin Don Villalbano . . ." Angelo strove to control himself. ". . . if his tongue had been a machine gun, we would all have been killed that day. I told *mi padrone*, 'we haven't seen the last of those whore's bastards.'

"Six days ago we found his body. Dismembered like Shortino's son. It was not a sight fit for human eyes, Excellency. Butchers! Slaughterers! He had been missing some three days, when one of the shepherds entered the butchering shed, intending to skin a few jack rabbits. What a sight greeted him! What a sight! All that remained of Don Alfredo. Excellency, with your permission, I am going to be sick."

"They'll pay for this. They'll pay," said the afflicted Lion.

"It will not bring Don Alfredo back, Excellency. Shortino's small child can't be made whole again."

"No. None can ever be resurrected," replied the Lion. He began to experience uneasy sensations. *"Prago,* announce me to your mistress." Angelo left to do his bidding.

Marco's senses were now alert to danger. His eyes darted furtively about. Something was wrong. What? Riding up in the carriage he'd seen no workers in the fields. Only a few servants milled about. In view of what had happened there should have been more guards posted. Something was drastically wrong. He sensed it and his mind told him he was right. He ground out his cigarette with the toe of his boot when Angelo called to him.

The sight of Mariolina, seated at her father's desk in complete darkness, shocked him at first. Slivers of fragmented light flickered along a tapestried wall from a lone candle before a religious icon. He could barely make her out, until she spoke.

"You shouldn't be here, Signore. Not at a time like this."

"Signorina, no words can convey the outrage I feel at this vile act. Is it the truth Angelo speaks to me?"

"It's the truth."

"Then we must concern ourselves with your safety." He could see her now, his eyes having adjusted to the dark. She was dressed somberly in black, her pale skin drawn taut. Dark circles under her eyes had turned to black hollows. It pained him not to be able to reach out and comfort her in his arms.

"How is my safety of concern to you, Signore?" she asked tremblingly.

Hadn't Don Alfredo received his letter? Surely by now it would have been delivered and discussed. She acts as if I'm less of a friend than I was when we first met. Before he could respond, her voice came at him like a knife.

"I can no longer remain here, knowing what happened to my father. I leave for America within a week."

He felt a dull thud over his heart. He couldn't let her go, not now. Not out of his life for good! "With your permission, it is my concern. They won't stop with your father, Signorina." Mariolina raised her stricken eyes. "It is not my desire to alarm you, but as the last survivor of the Catanese estate, your life is in jeopardy. You shouldn't remain here."

Mariolina allowed his remarks to roll off her back.

"Nonsense, Signore. It was my father they wished to dispose of. He told them you purchased the lands, but when they couldn't find the deed recorded in Palermo or Catania, they refused to believe him. They'll believe me."

"I'm afraid not. We took special pains to record the

86

deed transfers in Rome, so papers couldn't be forged here. But in our agreement, your father's and mine, you are a principal stockholder until the titles clear. In the event of your death, God forbid, your signature could easily be forged. It would be simple to convince the Palermo courts you sold your interest to them."

"Then they killed him to get to me?"

"With the Catanese *latifondo* in Mafia hands, the other *latifondisti* will capitulate." Marco sat forward in his chair. "The land must not fall into their hands, Signorina, or the end of the Sicilian peasant will come to pass, and you'll see more corruption and more poverty than you ever read about in your textbooks. Surely you'll not give them what your father fought against? If you stay here or go where there's no protection, they will have succeeded. Come with me to the safety of my villa. Let me exercise the legal powers at my disposal, and they'll never own the Villa Catanese."

Mariolina protested for nearly an hour, but finally, she could no longer deny the logic of his reasoning. She packed a small valise, taking only money, important papers, and the family jewels with her. Marco insisted she take nothing else. Her departure from the villa was to look like a short business trip into Catania.

Interrupted by the sound of angry voices coming from the courtyard, they both tensed until Marco recognized familiar voices. A relieved smile formed on his lips as he led Mariolina through the corridor to the front entrance. Beyond them, in the floral courtyard, Calo and Ciccio had the drop on the two guards.

"It's all right, Signorina. They're my men. You remember Calo and Ciccio?" She nodded, and he left her side for a moment to instruct his men.

Mariolina called to the young stableboy, a sullen lad of fifteen who'd been dozing under a shade tree. At the sound of her voice, he scrambled to his feet.

"Hurry! Get the carriage for us, Ernesto."

He disappeared around the corner of the courtyard and within a few minutes the carriage was hitched to two horses and brought to the front entrance. Angelo came running toward them in baffled agitation. "Signorina, you can't be thinking of leaving the house!"

"We are going into Catania," said Marco. "The Signorina's signature is needed on some documents."

"But," he protested, "the Signorina is still in mourning. It isn't right for her to be seen in public. It will bring disgrace to us. The people will shame us." He appealed to Mariolina. "Signorina?"

Mariolina lowered her troubled eyes. Knowing it would be the last time she saw him, she didn't want to betray her feelings.

Marco raised a silencing hand. "Don't concern yourself. She's in good hands. And Angelo, double the guards here immediately. Recruit only those peasants you can trust, *capeeshi?*"

More confused than ever he dared not contest His Excellency.

As Ciccio jumped into the front seat of the buggy, Calo approached the older man. "Listen, tell my cousin Shortino, there is *molto doloro,* a great sadness in my heart, at the loss of his son. I will write to him."

Angelo nodded vaguely. "It was my curse to be the bearer of such bad news. I will tell him. Go with God."

"*Si. Ciào.*"

On board the *Marchessa,* Marco introduced Mariolina to Roberto and Capitano Paolo Nicosia. When he explained the Signorina's plight, the compassion they expressed toward her made Mariolina feel less tense, less guilty for leaving her house.

"With your permission, Signorina, accept my sympathies for the death of your father. I know His Excellency held him in high esteem. Be assured you're doing the right thing. Trust him. The Lion has wisdom in these matters."

They all stood on deck in a solemn silence waiting for the crew to get underway. The setting sun flooded the scenic harbor with blood-red lights and the sky flamed with coral and pink fire. Mariolina shivered slightly despite the balmy July day. Marco removed his coat, wrapped it tenderly about her shoulders, and felt a warm response from her as their eyes met. In the brilliant light, Mariolina was literally breathtaking. He couldn't take his eyes off her. Her raven tresses hung loosely about her shoulders, fluttering slightly in the sea breeze. Her brown, almond-shaped eyes were fringed with thick lashes. For the first time he noticed an intriguing beauty mark over her left eyelid. She flushed under his steady gaze.

"Forgive me," he whispered. "I can't help thinking what a remarkable woman you are. Not at all maudlin. No wailing and beating of breasts for you. Signorina, you have my most profound respect. You are truly made of iron."

She self-consciously turned from him, thankful the others hadn't heard his comments. She didn't feel made of iron. Inside, she felt like water, no strength at all. Her eyes caressed the harbor scene, the spectacular sunset, wondering if she would ever see this part of Sicily again. She turned for a last look at her villa, high on the cliff, and uttered an audible gasp. *"Maria Santissima!"* They turned to her, alerted by the tone of her voice. "See? There above the cliffs!"

Marco's face blanched. Roberto glanced at Calo and Ciccio and all three made the sign of the cross. The seamen and deck hands ran to the port side of the yacht and stared aghast at the giant snakes of crackling fire slithering across the pink skies, lighting up the area with more brilliance than the sunset. Continuous bursts of fire ignited the surrounding brush and in moments devastated everything in its path. Mariolina couldn't believe her eyes. One minute there was her house, her villa and all she'd grown up with. The next moment there was a shell, a skeleton, and now even that was crumbling. Black clouds of smoke billowed into the skies, darkening the surrounding area, obliterating the sight. They stood grim-faced and mute, helpless and shaken by the intolerable flaming skies and limitless ruined earth.

"Poor Angelo and the others. God, pray they escaped the fire," she muttered.

Marco slipped his arms about her and held her tightly. "Yes, we'll pray they did escape. Don't look now. It's best to remember it as it was."

"No, Marco." She spoke his name for the first time. "I want to remember. I don't ever want to forget what those swine did to us. I'll rest easily knowing there are compensations for everything in life."

His estimation of her soared even higher. As the boat traveled further away from the harbor, fire filled sky, paled and faded from sight. Mariolina withdrew into herself and remained uncommunicative for the balance of the trip to Messina.

Once secure at the Villa de Leone, Marco reflected on the death of Don Alfredo and took it as a personal and direct attack upon himself and the House of de Leone. He lost no time in sending a coded communiqué to his cousin, the Duke of Tuscany, who held a seat in the Senate.

Your Excellency:

The Catanese Villa we spoke of has been destroyed. Don Alfredo was brutally murdered at the hands of three *mafiosi*, Don Villalbano, Don Trappani and Don Sperro, who used the Mazzarinos to do the detail work. Check into the illegalities of land appropriation initiated either by these three men and/or their banks, the Catania and the Mezzo-Giorno. Have aides in Catania check into the extent of damage done to Villa Catanese. I'll dispatch my men to the villa upon clearance from you.

My love to you and your family,

MdL

Marco stamped the envelope with the Seal of the Royal Lion and dispatched Ciccio to Messina to personally post the letter. There could be no more slip-ups. Enough damage had been done.

Mariolina had been given the guest suite overlooking the Madelaina Gardens with its view of Terra d'Oro. He gave Gina instructions that she be cared for with tenderness and understanding. The older woman listened as he spoke.

"Gina, please see that the Signorina is not disturbed. She's been through a terrible ordeal with the tragic murder of her father." He mentioned no last names; he wanted no information of her whereabouts rumored or whispered about for the time being.

When he finished the middle-aged housekeeper nodded in obedience and went upstairs to meet the new guest.

Marco busied himself with notes on the meeting he was to have with Guido Amalfi, Mario Massina, and the other *contadini*. They were to meet in an hour in the greenhouse and review the new process of irrigation and soil conservation Roberto had been working on and was ready now to demonstrate to the men.

Inwardly he brooded bitterly over the calamitous affair at the Catanese Villa. God! Will it never stop? Never? He evaluated the situation and he came up with several possible solutions, but primarily he marked time, waiting for an answer to his inquiry.

The only sunshine in his life was the thought of Mariolina being under the same roof with him. It brought him closer to his personal goal.

9

The arrival of Mariolina de Catanese at the Villa de Leone created a great deal of curiosity among the *contadini*, but no questions were as frequent and as exhaustive to Gina as those from her daughter. Diamonte had grown into a voluptuous eighteen-year-old beauty with skin the color of pale ivory, ebony hair and spectacular eyes the color of sapphires, ringed with a deeper blue—a phenomenon in a world of dark exotic eyes and the object of awe and wonder by all who gazed upon her.

Within the province, shepherds and flutists were inspired to compose songs about her unusual beauty. When she grew old enough to understand the reason for this attention, Diamonte would flush with pleasure, and her narcissistic behavior increased. The ancient feudal system in which the landowner became Godfather to the first-borns and to fatherless children provided that Marco de Leone become Diamonte's Godfather.

If she had been his own flesh and blood, he couldn't have spoiled and adored her more. He doted on the child, encouraging her to read and write and taking her with him on his tours of the estate. He'd strap the remarkable beauty onto his saddle and point out places of interest as if she were his own child. It was incredible how beautiful she was.

Unquestionably, she became the source of considerable speculation and pain for Gina, whose growing concern over the child's beauty took on frightening aspects. As she continued to grow, it became even more obvious to Gina how easily Diamonte manipulated men. Her beauty got her whatever she wanted, from the choicest fruit in the basket to favored treatment by all who admired her. It was positively frightening for Gina to see the control she had over men. At least she had the satisfaction of knowing she had raised her daughter in a most stringent manner. Of late, however, when Gina tightened up on the reins, Diamonte chafed at the bit and protested with greater fury.

During the last six years, ever since Diamonte had become a woman, Gina hadn't had a moment's peace, knowing how easily a girl could get trapped and pay a lifetime penalty for an indiscretion. She prayed that St. Sebastian would watch over her daughter. Perhaps he'd dim that overactive imagination of hers and take some of those fancy notions from her head. My God, what fancies she dreamt up!

When most young girls felt the stirrings of womanhood and looked to prospective husbands, Diamonte thought only of Marco. Her fantasies included becoming his wife and mistress of the villa. In the grandeur of the villa, she created her own wonderland. And what a wonderland! The magnificent marbled halls and grand salons were her stage as she imagined herself serving at tea, entertaining at a gala, introduced as the Marchessa de Leone. She would order the servants to clean and polish the splendid silver service with its two-headed lions and the jewel-encrusted goblets of cut crystal. It was her face she saw in the portraits of the de Leone women, while she imagined her beauty being praised by courtiers, noblemen, and statesmen.

She dressed in the old gowns belonging to the former

mistresses of the Villa de Leone and stood before the Venetian glass mirrors admiring her own beauty. It was in these moments that she felt sure Marco belonged to her, and in her world he did.

It mattered not to her that Marco never considered her anything but his Godchild. In her world the thoughts and feelings of others were not relevant. As she grew older, Diamonte failed to set aside her childhood fantasies and face reality. She clung to her dream day after day, year after year, until the day Marco returned to the villa with Mariolina.

"Who is she? Tell me who she is, mama!" demanded Diamonte in brooding anger. "You must know something!"

"I know nothing, my daughter," sighed Gina, wondering what brought on this latest outburst.

"It isn't possible that Marco wouldn't tell you. He trusts you with his life."

"You snarl at me as if you'd like to kill me," Gina told her. "Better you should calm yourself."

"Curse you, mama! If you'd been the right kind of mother, you'd have arranged for my marriage to Marco."

Gina was struck dumb. "Marriage to His Excellency? You? Are you crazy, child? In the past you've said many wild things, many insolent things to me, but I've let them pass as the ravings of a growing child. But you are no longer a child. You're old enough to face the responsibilities that come with maturity. Enough of these insults and vain imaginings. I've got work to do. If you had any concern for me, you'd get busy and help me."

"Help you? Goddammit! You go to hell! You go straight to hell for all I care! And stop overprotecting me! I'm suffocating. You're smothering me with your jealousy and hatred. Don't think I don't know how much you loathe me. You never wanted me! I spoiled all your chances and you've resented me ever since!"

"You're crazy!" said Gina, aghast at the girl's outburst. As she busied herself making cookies, she wondered about this strange and mysterious child who was given to fierce and malicious temper tantrums. Diamonte had learned how to cover her fiendish nature by performing overwhelming acts of love and behaving solicitously in the presence of others.

When the two of them were alone, Diamonte treated her mother like a slave, casting indignities upon her and constantly berating her. She made only superficial attempts to help her mother when Gina's work grew burdensome.

"It's my fault. I should have sent you to a convent. They'd teach you," said Gina quietly. She'd learned to calm herself in the wake of Diamonte's anger, to subjugate her temper in the face of the other's fury.

"You always say that when you can't think of the right answers. Are you so stupid that you don't understand what I'm saying?"

"I've never been tutored by the Royal Lion, my daughter. I can't even read or write. I went only to the third grade and I went to work to help support my family. I know nothing of these high and mighty ideas that you have in your head. They confuse me and I do not understand those demons who pursue you. Perhaps, if you'd go to the chapel and ask Padre Bonaventura to help God guide you, perhaps these notions would subside and you'd come to terms with yourself."

"Listen, you find out who this woman is, you hear? All you have to do is ask."

"It's not my affair, Diamonte. What His Excellency does and who his guests are are no concern of mine. Now leave me in peace. I have work to do."

As she completed mixing the ingredients for the cookies, Gina was struck by her daughter's wickedness, and she finally realized the extent of Diamonte's ambition.

"Certainly you have *some* rights," protested her daughter angrily.

"What rights? I'm only an employee here," replied Gina calmly, rolling the *biscotti* dough.

"If you'd used your womanly gifts, you could have been more than a servant."

"*Basta!* Stop!" ordered Gina. After an hour's harangue, she'd had enough.

"Hear my words, old woman. Whoever *she* is, she'll not have Marco. I'll be mistress of this villa one day!" She stalked the kitchen like a tigress. "Me! You hear? No one else will have him. My beauty will get me that and much more."

In that instant Diamonte no longer looked the beauty of legend. Her eyes glittered madly and her ugly nature showed through.

Gina kissed the cross at her neck and lifted her eyes to the heavens. "Dear God! Please don't listen to her! She doesn't know what she says." She quickly returned to her work as if there'd been no interruption at all. Gina rolled the dough into long, snakelike ropes. With her knife she slashed the dough into three-inch strips, then, with a quick wrist movement, each length was magically transformed into a two-headed seahorse.

Loud contemptuous laughter sounded deep in Diamonte's throat.

"Go ahead, old woman, call on your God. Call on any

god to stop me and they won't hear you. Look at you! You're nothing but a dried up sack of old bones resigned to cleaning chamber pots for the rest of your life. Well, that's not for me. Not for Diamonte, you hear?"

Gina dropped what she was doing and for the first time in her life she struck the girl across the mouth. "Daughter of Satan! Daughter of the devil! I can't believe you sprang from my loins! I curse the day you were born! I curse that obscenity who planted his seed in me! I curse you all!"

"If you think a *bastinada* will stop me, old woman, think again." Diamonte traced the light sting on her cheek with her long slender fingers. With a slight toss of her head, she pushed her disheveled hair off her face. Then the insufferable girl laughed again and swaggered out the door muttering, "Strega."

Gina closed her eyes to force the burning tears back. Never in all her life had she been so angry. Not even when she'd been raped and left for dead on the slopes of Mt. Etna before Marco found her and had his people nurse her back to health. Even when she discovered she was pregnant by that marauding pirate, she hadn't felt the outrage she felt at this moment. Shame, humiliation and terror, yes, but not outrage. *Why, God, did you bring such a demon into my life? Why didn't you let me die? Why punish me?*

Gina had to sit down in the rocking chair. Suddenly she was unable to move or catch her breath. She clutched at her heart in an attempt to subdue its erratic beating. Was this really her daughter who talked to her with such degrading lack of respect? In the past Diamonte had said many bad things to her, and in a mother's way, she'd forgiven the child. She dabbed at her tear-brimmed eyes and shook her head in dismay. It was the first time in her life that Gina had ever experienced an inexplicable urge to kill anyone. That she should feel this way toward her own daughter terrified her. "Forgive me, Lord," she begged as tears streamed down her tired face.

Whatever gave Diamonte the idea that the Marquis would marry her? Had he encouraged her in some way? She thought back over the many years she'd worked for the Lion. Not him. Diamonte was the sorceress who could tempt a man. Oh, the shame of it all!

Outside, Diamonte walked past the chapel and waved to the guards at the west gate. She tried to escape the broiling hot sun by remaining in the shade of the silvery leafed olive trees that grew along the low stone wall next to the peasants' cottages. She raised the hair off her neck to cool herself and reached into the pocket of her cotton shift for a hairpin which she speared through her hair to secure it.

Already she had dismissed her mother from mind. She had more important things to consider. Since her mother wouldn't tell her what she wanted to learn, she would approach Roberto Argento.

At the fountain she splashed cool water on her face until the welts diminished. As she tucked fresh daisies into her hair, her thoughts focused on the genius agronomist. She could handle Roberto all right. But, oh, how she hated the stinking smell of all those fertilizers in the greenhouse. She shuddered.

Bright enough to know that even Roberto eyed her with desire, she always acted shy and retiring, with all the innocence of youth. She indulged him only because he was so close to Marco. Knowing he could be an ally, she had learned even as a child to manipulate Roberto. She had to brace herself before entering the greenhouse.

For several moments he didn't notice her, he concentrated so closely on his experiments.

"Ciao, Roberto."

"Ah, Diamonte. Come in, come in," he said, glancing up from his work. "See what I have here?" His vivid blue eyes lit up with a sense of accomplishment. "Now we'll see if Sicily must tolerate vast uncultivated lands. I've used the same soil five times, changing the seed, and have produced perfect results each time. *Managghia!* What a victory! What a victory!"

Roberto saw instantly that his fervor wasn't appreciated, so he set aside his flats of seeded soil to turn his full attention on her. "Well, *beda,* what's on your pretty mind?"

"Where's Marco?" she asked lightly.

"Out somewhere with Emilio Graziano and Guido Amalfi. Why?"

"He keeps to himself a lot these days."

"No different than usual. He has much on his mind." He sighed and returned to his work. *It's always the same with her. Marco . . . Marco . . . Marco . . .*

"When does he return to Rome?"

"The usual time—when the Parliament is in session."

"Does he not make an imposing Senator, our Marco? Why does he not prefer the finer life of Rome to the one he lives here at the villa?"

Roberto lifted his soft blue eyes and fixed them on her. *Always Marco!* She stood very close to him now, and the sweet floral scent emanating from her reached him. Those colognes and soaps Marco sent her from Rome were not wasted on the *latifondo,* at least not on him. How many times he'd fantasized making love to this wench. True, she was half his age, but there was more worldliness masked behind those innocent blue eyes than she let on. *Stop this,* he told himself. *Don't allow yourself these self indulgent dreams. You know you can't cope with rejection.* He thought of himself as a hopeless cripple and felt he couldn't be the man he was with her. He sprinkled limestone on the soil samples.

"Marco is his own man. He is everything he wishes to be," he said flatly.

"But why does he choose a lower life when he could live among kings?"

"What makes you think Marco considers all this . . ." He waved his hand in a wide, sweeping gesture, ". . . the lower life?"

"Well, it is. Peasants! Dirty land! Livestock! Ugh! Even his troubles with the *mafiosi*." She grimaced. "He doesn't need this. In Rome he could live a life of elegance, go to the opera, the theater, you know."

"Is that what you would choose for Marco? The elegance of Rome?"

"For Marco I would choose he be king."

"Does it not matter, Diamonte, that a man live in peace and comfort doing what he feels to be more worthwhile than being king?"

Suddenly Roberto grew angry with himself for talking to her as if she might understand such philosophical thoughts. He didn't feel like indulging her any more, and turned gloomily to his work.

"Who's this woman he brought to the villa?" she asked in a voice which masked her true feelings.

"Signorina de Catanese. The woman Marco is going to marry." He flushed at his sudden vindictiveness. *That should put her in her place,* he thought. He suddenly wanted to strike back at the silly little girl who'd caused him so many sleepless nights and couldn't see him for dust.

She dropped all attempts at pretense and paled excessively. "Marco plans to m-m-arry?" Her voice broke. "I don't believe it." She drew herself up angrily. "Marco will marry no one but me!" she stammered.

So that's it. Roberto's lips twisted into a cruel smile. Suddenly he was unable to control the burst of laughter that escaped his lips. If he had known how long she had built this dream, he might not have displayed such contempt.

"You've a lot of growing up to do before Marco would ever consider you as his wife, *cara mia*. Besides, the wedding date is set. The Marquis will marry the Signorina. It is she who'll be mistress of the Villa de Leone." Such vindictiveness was against his very nature. Never had he provoked anyone in this manner. *What the hell's wrong with me? Damn her anyway!* He turned from her with a scowl on his face, unprepared for her next words.

"You say that only because you're a miserable, impotent cripple! And you're trying to make one of Marco too!" She spat at him.

Her brutal candor pierced his heart like an icicle. Sadistically he forced himself to return her cruelty. He tilted his head indulgently. "I see. You're in love with him. Well, it won't do you any good. He loves this woman. I should know. Ever since they met he's been a different man. She has him enchanted and holds him spellbound. *E'molto encantatu.*"

"You lie! I don't believe you."

Roberto shrugged imperceptibly and walked away from her. She ran after him, tugged at his arm, and made him face her. "Tell me you lie. You're making this up."

Roberto had never been this close to her before. He felt the hot blood course through his body. His manhood sprang to life taking full control of his senses. Without thinking he embraced her savagely, forced her to look into his eyes, and kissed her. Not the kiss he'd practiced so many times in his imagination, but the kiss of an inept and bungling idiot. Why, he was to ask himself a thousand times later, why had he done it?

She pushed him away fighting to break his viselike grip on her. The look in her eyes was one of evil triumph.

"Tzoppo!" she screamed. *"Povero tzoppo!* You poor, crippled excuse of a man!" She freed herself and scratched his face like a wildcat. Her eyes gleamed wickedly.

An apology formed on his lips but disintegrated as three streaks of blood surfaced on his face and stung smartly. Cold rage and vengeful fury distorted her face, and in that instant the ugliness of her soul was revealed to him. She wiped savagely at her lips as if his had imparted venom to hers.

"Don't ever touch me again, you hear? Pig! Filthy swine! If you were ten Marcos, I wouldn't let you touch me. If you had ten times more *scudi,* you'd never measure up to him. And I'll tell you another thing. I am the one Marco will marry—or he'll marry no one!"

Their eyes met and held. For several moments they stood like statues, immobile as granite. Neither spoke. Off someplace in the distance, the soft refrain of a flute could be heard. Inside, the room was as still as death. Both Roberto and Diamonte saw the black hatred between them. Diamonte knew that having declared herself, she had made a mortal enemy of Roberto, an enemy who silently challenged her, warning her he'd show her no mercy from this moment forward.

"Cunning, moody, narcissistic bitch!" said the anxiety-ridden Roberto in a muffled voice.

After watching them both from the doorway for several moments, Guillermo de Leone strode boldly into the green-house. "Well, what have we here?" He stopped abruptly, sensing their hostility.

"What's this between you two?" asked the bon vivant. "Is this the way a traveling man is greeted on his home-coming?" His friendly brown eyes tried to infect them with his gay mood. He turned to embrace Roberto affectionately.

"How are you, cousin?" He'd called Roberto cousin from the moment they met. "And don't tell me . . . This simply cannot be Diamonte. My, how you've grown!" His appreciation of her charms brought a smile to her lips.

Guillermo's attention delighted the girl. She forgot her anger with Roberto and ran to Guillermo. He kissed her lustily on the lips and pulled back, staring wondrously at her when she kissed him back. *She has grown,* he thought.

Watching them, Roberto felt a twinge of jealousy and a profound hurt. He averted his eyes, stared out the window, and fixed his gaze on the rolling hills of the estate, beyond the villa. Then, suddenly, he turned and limped out of the greenhouse. At the entrance he cast a backward glance and saw the glazed look of triumph in her sparkling blue eyes. She tilted her head back and glanced at him with imperious and haughty disdain. She played her silly game with Guil-lermo. "What did you bring me this time?" she asked brazen-ly.

Alone in his apartment, Roberto shook noticeably, fell into a sweat, and doubled over on the bed. It was nearly sunset when he got up and washed his face with cool water from a crock on the dresser. As he wiped his face, he stared at his reflection. It was a handsome face that stared back at him, but to Roberto, it was ugliness encased in a wretched, warped body that grew more burdensome each day. He turned away and searched in a dusty black bag for his old narcotics case which had gone untouched for thirteen years. Even though the pain in his leg had disturbed him, he had promised Marco he'd never again indulge in opiates.

But this time he needed the drug for the annihilation of a bigger, more excruciating pain, one he couldn't run to Marco about. Angrily he threw the useless needle and dried up remains of the drug across the room where they both shattered into pieces. *"Porca miseria!"* he shouted furiously. "Goddamn the whole fucking world!"

From Terra d'Oro, Marco saw him in the carriage whipping the horses at a furious pace, kicking up swirls of dust behind him. *Where the hell is he going at such a late hour,* he wondered. In an effort to catch up with him, he waved Amalfi and Graziano off and wheeled Sultano off the golden land and tried to head Roberto off at the turn beyond the wheat fields. He was too late! He could barely make out the puffs of dust in the distance. He let Sultano dance a bit, then wheeled him back toward the villa. Odd, they'd been talking about Roberto moments earlier. Amalfi was telling them that Roberto was attempting to cross-graft grapes into a seedless fruit. Imagine that? Seedless grapes? Phew! That Roberto, what a gem! What a genius! He smiled warmly on the ride back.

Tired from the exhaustive hours spent with his men that day, Marco kicked off his boots and lay back resting quietly in the sanctuary of his study. The den contained everything he enjoyed. Behind the massive hand-carved desk with its ornamental lions hung the family coat of arms. Hunting trophies adorned the high shelves that had been built especially to house the silent, glassy-eyed pheasants and other wild birds. A collection of rare first editions covered the walls at either side of the open hearth fireplace. There were books on law, shipbuilding, bullfighting, as well as the works of Pirandello, Shakespeare, the Greek philosophers, and others, covering a wide variety of subjects from politics and history, to agronomy and zoological studies. Special glass cases contained crests and plaques of high honor awarded to the Lion by various government officials and King Emmanuel of the House of Savoy. The massive, sturdily constructed furniture was covered with pliant leathers from Spain. It was truly a man's refuge.

Gina's swollen eyes were the first indication that something was amiss. She served him coffee in his study and he saw an errant tear trickle off her cheek.

"What's causing the tears?" he asked gently.

She shook her head and stubbornly pursed her lips. Marco rose to his feet and said consolingly, "Tell me, Gina. Perhaps I can help."

"No one can help, Excellency." His gentleness provoked a rush of tears and she found herself confiding her fears. "Someone has cursed Diamonte with *u malocchio!* I'm sure of it!" Earlier Gina had convinced herself that this had to be the reason for her daughter's devilish thoughts.

"In what way? What makes you sure she's under the spell of an evil eye?"

"The things she says and does. Her thoughts! I don't know

her anymore. She acts as if she were possessed by a demon. Oh, Signore, if only you could hear her talk. What ideas! What crazy ideas roast in that head of hers. She has become a stranger to me. Her own mother!"

He smiled tolerantly, hoping to assure her she had nothing to worry about, that she shouldn't believe these old wives' tales. Not Gina, of all people!

"Don't you know every child becomes a stranger to their parents as they grow older and develop their own ideas? It's a curse on each generation, Gina. Since the beginning of time, parents have complained that their children are strangers to them."

"Pe d'avero? Really?" she asked. His Excellency would never speak untruths to her. Oh, if only she could make herself believe this—what peace!

"With Diamonte the problems are greater because of her beauty. Throughout history all beautiful women have had more problems than the plainer ones. Give her a little time. She'll find a husband and settle down soon, you'll see."

Gina glanced toward the door when it opened and quickly exited through the patio doors, before thanking Marco for his reassurance. She moved so swiftly, it took a moment before he saw his brother walk into the room.

"Guillermo! It's really you?" He moved across the room and embraced Guillermo warmly. *"Managghia!* You look better to me each time I see you, you scoundrel!" He stopped short. "Is everything all right? There's no trouble?"

Guillermo grinned impishly. "No, no trouble. "It's good to see you, too."

Diamonte slipped in behind Guillermo and stood quietly to one side while the brothers talked. Marco nodded at her, acknowledging her presence.

"The life of a bon vivant agrees too much with you. When will you settle down, eh?" He turned to the girl. "What do you think, Godchild? Guillermo grows more handsome each time he returns to us, no?"

Diamonte demurely lowered her eyes and refrained from answering. Surprised by this sudden coyness, Guillermo reached over and slapped her playfully across the buttocks. Marco recoiled slightly at the sudden familiarity between them. He noticed an exquisite pearl drop around the girl's neck and discreetly said nothing. But for reasons he couldn't explain, he felt a protective flush of anger. "Diamonte!" he said sharply. "Go help your mother. She has enough to do with all the guests we have."

His abrupt tone startled her briefly. Then she curtsied submissively and mocked him, *"Si, padrone. Subito."*

Her reply drew a sharp glance of annoyance from Marco,

then he softened. "I wish to speak with my brother in private, child. Please leave us." He turned to his brother, as Diamonte left the room. "You're not home a moment and you've captivated the most beautiful creature around," said Marco in amusement. "Still the same cocksman, eh, brother?"

"Marco," his brother said soberly, "if there's anything between you, I'll back away. Just tell me." Guillermo had seen all the changes in Marco.

The Lion stared at his brother. "What ever gave you that idea? Of course not. What a ridiculous thought." He shook his head. "Goddamn! She's young enough to be my daughter."

Guillermo breathed a sigh of relief, and devilment returned to his eyes. "In all of Europe, I've not seen one more beautiful than Diamonte. *Che bellissima!* She's wasting her time here. She'd be the toast of all Roma."

"Don't go putting crazy ideas into her head. Her poor mother needs her here. One day, she'll marry and raise children. That young rooster, Lamponi's oldest son, Salvatore? Yes, Salvatore. Well, he looks at her like . . ." Marco laughed suggestively. "What I want to know is how long you'll stay?"

"Two, three weeks, perhaps, until my gypsy feet itch and I decide to leave. Does that sit well with you?" He stretched out on the sofa. "Did I hear you say you had guests?"

"Not guests, brother dear. A *special* guest. The woman I intend to marry."

"I don't believe it! It's finally happened? Marco the Lion has been ensnared?" His astonishment evoked peals of laughter from Marco.

"It's finally happened." He began telling his brother about Mariolina de Catanese and spoke of nothing else for the rest of the day.

Later that evening, after Roberto returned from Messina, he lay on his bed waiting for the warm reassuring effects of the opiate to course through his veins. He heard the violent hammering of his heart, the throbbing at his temples and his neck, and felt the atmosphere swim around him while his body took on a feeling of weightlessness. His eyes shone like the depths of the sea, a deep, probing blue. The cares that earlier projected him into an abysmal state of self-condemnation began to float away, and they disintegrated into sweet, peaceful, and forgetful sleep.

He sensed his presence before he actually saw him. Then he pushed open his heavily lidded eyes. Marco sat on the edge of the bed staring at him. He held a syringe containing the remains of the opiate. His eyes contained an indescribable sadness. The Lion leaned forward slightly and set the hypodermic on a nearby table. He wanted to smash it against the wall, break it into a million pieces. Instead he pretended not to be moved by the scene.

"We've waited dinner for you. Will you be long?"

"Not tonight. Guillermo's here. Perhaps the two of you have things you'd prefer to talk over alone." He avoided Marco's eyes.

"Guillermo and I have no secrets you haven't shared. You're a brother to both of us." Marco's fists were clenched tightly. "Do you want to tell me about it? What prompted this?" He indicated the syringe. "How did it happen? Why?"

"No, I don't want to talk."

"You'll feel better."

"Not tonight, Marco. Leave me in peace."

"Very well. For tonight, peace. Tomorrow, we talk, agreed?"

Roberto nodded, but his heart wasn't in it.

Gloom had settled over Marco. First, the business with Gina. Then, Roberto. Now, Guillermo excused himself early. He had discreetly refrained from telling Marco he planned to take Diamonte out riding in the carriage. But there were other things occupying Marco's mind, too. Many things. He set about his usual after-dinner occupation, working on an oil painting of Diamonte he had begun several months earlier. Surprisingly talented, Marco could have become an artist of merit. Possessing no burning dedication, he contented himself with painting as a hobby. The concentration needed to perfect each stroke, to select the right values, and mix the oils properly took his mind off other problems and became an emotional release for Marco.

It was nearly 2 A.M. This night's painting had afforded him no relief from the problems besetting him. Mariolina disturbed him greatly. Her mourning period was taking too long. They'd been in the same house, under the same roof, for nearly four weeks and he hadn't seen her. Not once! The more he considered this, the more angry he became. *What the hell am I? Am I not a man? Dammit! Well, this has got to end,* he told himself.

Suddenly Marco tossed aside his brushes. With grim determination scrawled on his face, he strode out of the study, scaled the stairs three at a time, and stood breathless at Mariolina's door. His heart was the only noise he heard in the silence of the villa. He took a deep breath and knocked on the door. Only silence. He knocked louder. More silence. His knuckles smarted. Still no answer. All was silence. He grasped the lion's-head door handle and opened the door.

In the pale shaft of moonlight shining through the open French doors of the balcony, he saw Mariolina sitting upright on the bed. Her long black hair, caught to the side with a ribbon, hanging lazily over one shoulder. Completely nude, she hastily gathered the sheet about her full rounded breasts. Marco caught his breath, but full of resolution, he asserted his *maschiezzo*. He spoke directly. "You, Mariolina, will join me for breakfast tomorrow morning at 10 A.M. on the terrace facing the Madelaina Gardens. *Capeeshi?*"

"*Capeeshi, si.* I understand," she said softly. "I wondered how much longer you'd put up with me."

Quickly he searched her eyes, uncertain he'd heard correctly. He had. A warm flush surged through him. "Then you admit you've kept me waiting too long?" His heart raced again.

"I admit only that I've inconvenienced you too long. I must be on my way to America, where I will live with my uncle's family."

"Not that again?" He experienced a sinking sensation. "I felt sure you'd given up that thought. I mean . . . well, I thought surely by now . . . Listen, put something on. We're going to talk."

"Did you forget I brought nothing with me?"

"Of course, why didn't you say something?" He pulled the comforter off the bed. "Put this around you. I'll meet you on the balcony."

The fragrance of the roses from the garden below wafted up, intoxicating their senses on this balmy night.

Damn, thought Marco, *I should have brought matters to a head long ago. I should have told her of my intentions, about the letter, the proposal, everything. Some legislator I am when I can't even legislate my own emotions.*

"Must you go immediately?"

"It's best I go as soon as possible."

"But why? He threw caution to the winds. "Signorina, you must listen to what my heart is trying to say, even if my tongue doesn't speak the right words. What I'm trying to say is . . . uh . . . I don't want you to go away, not until you've heard my heart speak." He fixed his love-filled eyes on her. They both felt the air become electric.

"You leave me speechless, Signore. If you mean what I think you're trying to tell me, I can only say that I . . . uh . . . have other plans." She lied. For some strange reason, she felt compelled to play a game with him. Pulling the ribbon from her hair, she shook it out and fanned it away from her face.

Marco had paled considerably. "Of course. How careless

103

of me not to have considered such a possibility. There is someone else. It was presumptuous of me."

"No. There is no one." She smiled faintly and glanced about the darkness.

Marco took hope. The full moon had already risen higher in the sky, and crickets chirped in the distance. Soon the *vaccari* would be rising.

"What can I say to convince you to stay longer?"

"My plans are made. I cannot impose on your hospitality any longer, Excellency," she said with a slight tremor to her voice.

"Don't you know what my heart is trying to say? Can't you tell? I've waited to allow a respectful time to elapse since the death of your father, Mariolina. I know of no other way but to tell you straight. Circumstances do not permit the usual protocol, and time is so essential, I must dispense with the usual amenities. Therefore, I respectfully ask you for the opportunity to become better acquainted with you. Then, if we should find ourselves in accord, if you feel for me what must be written into every gesture, every word and every breath I take . . ." He paused suddenly, so overwhelmed with emotion that he no longer recognized himself. He looked deeply into her eyes.

Mariolina trembled inwardly. Her dark, shining eyes threatened an honesty which in the past had been her undoing. She was about to tell him she had already read his letter to her father, hundreds of times, knew its contents by heart. And she wanted to tell him that circumstances over which she had no control prevented her from marrying him, or anyone else for that matter. But for the first time in her life, Mariolina reacted like a real woman, a woman with frailties, design, and guile. She wanted Marco desperately. She needed his strength but had no idea of how to lure and entice him, never knowing she had only to say yes. A light breeze ruffled her hair, the comforter slipped from her shoulders and in trying to gather it up, she moved toward him as if she'd lost her footing.

Marco reached out for her and steadied her in his strong arms. Eyes melted into eyes, lips into lips. Their bodies clung closely together and passion surged between them. Breathless, they moved slightly apart and searched each other's eyes again. Marco's eager body had grown hard against hers and the need to apologize was more frustrating than the feeling of his manhood springing to life. "Please, Mariolina, forgive me. I mean nothing disrespectful," he said in his pure victorian manner. "I assure you, generally, I'm in better control than I've been these past few moments."

Angry at himself for this unworldy naivete, this stumbling love-sick calf attitude, he took time to light a cigarette. Then his voice grew stern and authoritative. "Now, listen, isn't it time we end this charade and place things in proper perspective? After all, I am speaking with an educated woman, not a dim-witted, designing, empty-headed doll. I've stated my intentions. Will you or will you not grant me the time to show you my life, my heart, my lands and what it will mean to you to become mistress of the de Leone *latifondo?*"

"Yes, Marco. I will," she said softly.

"It isn't anyone who can become mistress to so many responsibilities." Oblivious to her answer, Marco kept talking. "It isn't something I would ask of anyone. It has taken me all my life to select the right person, the woman who has the courage and spunk and stamina necessary to endure the rigors of being married to El Leone. You know what it's like to be married to a legislator? We'd be living in Rome during sessions. We'd be forced to travel to fulfill our obligations with our diplomatic relations in Spain and Austria, and we'd travel to France and Switzerland and wherever de Leone Shipping has offices. You'd be forced to entertain in our villa in Rome whenever the occasion arises. The servants there and here would be your responsibility. But, you must know well in advance that my heart is here in Sicily. Here, on the *latifondo* is where we'll spend most of our time. You'll not be able to speak as freely as Catanians are used to speaking . . ."

"Yes, Marco." She smiled at his antics.

"It's not America, you know. We're still mid-victorian here in Sicily. We'd have to concern ourselves with problems on the *latifondo*, not the latest in Paris fashions. And I thought . . . I thought . . . Well, since you're so articulate on the problems facing our nation, those of the peasants and the land reforms . . . even that boob Gianotti, whom I intend to prove to you is a two-tongued viper . . ." Marco paused, arrested by the twinkle in her eyes and smile on her face. "Did you say yes?" She nodded. "You mean you'll stay?" he asked wondrously. "You'll really stay?" He was ecstatic. He was delirious. He went sailing through space. And before he said or did anything to change her mind, he walked her back into the bedroom, kissed her forehead, and took his leave.

"At breakfast, then?"

"At breakfast."

After Marco left, Mariolina cried until she had no tears left to shed. Filled with dread, she had paced the floor of her suite until dawn. She stood on the balcony for a time gazing out past the Madelaina Gardens at the peasants already at work in the fields. She blinked at the dazzling brightness of the sun, stretched her arms out lazily, and suddenly paused in midair, straining to hear the far off sounds of a wailing flute. Now she listened intently, enchanted at first by the heartrending sound, wild and savage, yet lonely, touching her heart with aching fire. Tears fell onto her velvety cheeks. Again the overwhelming sadness and loneliness gripped her. She sighed wistfully and told herself, *you mustn't live in the past, for there is the sure death!*

The sounds of the flute grew closer. It was beautiful, sad, and defiant; her mood shifted, bending to the will of the flute. When the music stopped, she felt overwhelmed with sorrow again.

Inside the bedroom she sat before the ornate French provincial dressing table and stared unseeing at her reflection in the gilt-edged mirror, detached from the moment. She felt alien, a stranger in a land of strangers, as if she didn't belong to any part of the human race. Why couldn't she be happy? Why couldn't she be as free a spirit as those peasants working the lands, working side by side with their husbands and children? Why had she been driven to seek knowledge? The accursed pain of it and the pangs of conscience that spring from expanding intelligence are far greater than any physical pain a man endures. She knew she was only rationalizing, delaying the inevitable.

She tortured herself as feelings of dread and anxiety took possession of her once again. "Oh my God! What shall I do? What shall I do?" she cried aloud. "How can I tell Marco what happened? I've kept it to myself all these years like a deep, dark secret, from which I shall never be liberated."

She wanted desperately to be what God intended, a mere woman. She wanted to be able to respond to Marco as a woman should, but she grew frightened at her own soul-stirring desires.

"Oh, mamma. Where were you when I needed you?" she cried in anguish.

10

"So you're the woman who has captured the mighty Lion's heart?" said Guillermo de Leone after the introductions at breakfast. "I'm happy for both of you." He bowed and kissed Mariolina's hand, holding onto it as he searched her eyes. "I like you, Mariolina de Catanese. I like you

106

very much. Now listen to me, and hear me well. I've a few pointers for you. No matter how loud the Lion roars, love him, care for him, and you'll be happier than you've ever dreamed. There's no one more wonderful than Marco."

"Guillermo!" The Lion's tone reprimanded sternly.

"I know. I know. You've already told me nothing's been spoken between you." He waved his brother off and winked slyly at the girl. "That's what he thinks. But, you and I, we know, don't we?" He released her hand and pulled out the chair for her.

Mariolina laughed irresistibly. "How well you know the ways of women."

"Hah!" Marco laughed good-naturedly. "Truer words have never been spoken. If Guillermo knows anything, it's women."

Mariolina took to Guillermo instantly. He moved toward the buffet table, lifting covers from silver chafing dishes, sniffing, and rolling his eyes appreciatively. "Nowhere in all the world is there food like that prepared at the Villa de Leone," he said. "Sausage and eggs, Mariolina?" She nodded and he proceeded to fill a plate for her and returned to his place.

"Thank you," she said. In that moment her eyes met Marco's and held.

"It's good to see you at breakfast. Next to you, the Madelaina roses pale."

Mariolina flushed pleasurably. For several moments Guillermo glanced from the Lion to the girl and felt the excitement between them. "Where's Roberto?" he asked finally, devouring the sausage and eggs on his gleaming silver platter.

Marco shrugged. Mariolina felt something had suddenly filled the air like a chilling blanket of snow.

"It's not like him not to join us for breakfast. He wasn't at dinner last night either?"

"Something's troubling him," said Marco lightly. "I expect to talk with him today."

"For what it may be worth . . ." said Guillermo, looking hesitantly at Mariolina, ". . . there's poison between Diamonte and Roberto."

Marco's eyebrows arched delicately, and he lifted his eyes questioningly to meet his brother's.

"Perhaps I'm wrong. What do I know?" He sipped his coffee, wiped his lips with a napkin and announced, "I'm going into Messina. Can I do anything for you while I'm there?"

Marco shook his head. He was still absorbed in his brother's earlier remark. If Guillermo hadn't countered his first statement with a denial, he would have let it pass.

"You can do something for me, Guillermo," said Mariolina, glancing at Marco. "I need a few clothes. Gina has laundered these more times than God intended."

"Of course! How stupid of me." Marco tapped his forehead. "How good are you at selecting clothing for women?" As soon as the words were spoken both brothers laughed uproariously. Considering the many bills Marco paid to fancy women's shops in Rome, Guillermo was most expert in this field.

"Give my brother your measurements, my dear, and I promise you will be the best dressed woman in the province."

Mariolina excused herself to get a list of the things she needed.

"Managghia! I like this woman of yours. *C'e bellezza!* I must admit these Catanians are a bit more daring than our people." He referred to the trousers and boots she wore. "She must cause a hundred heart attacks a day in those clothes."

Marco laughed. "Daring? Perhaps, but just remember when you're shopping, you are buying for the future mistress of the House of de Leone, not the madam of a bordello." They both laughed. Then on a more serious note, "What did you mean about Roberto and Diamonte?"

"I found them staring at each other with death in their eyes. I never knew Roberto to fill with such venom."

"He couldn't."

"He did yesterday. If you could have seen him . . ."

"I don't have to see him. There's no venom in Roberto."

"What does he have against the girl? Why does he hate her? She cried most of the afternoon."

"Most of the afternoon?" Marco's eyes darted to his brother questioningly. "Didn't you arrive at dusk?"

Guillermo blushed uncomfortably. "You know how it is with me and women. She made me promise not to tell you, Marco. After all, we're brothers. No secrets between us, eh?" He forced a weak smile under Marco's hard look.

A protective, fatherly instinct swept over Marco. For an instant he felt like smashing his fist into Guillermo's smug face. Then, surprised by his own feelings, he averted his eyes. In that second, the worldly Guillermo knew his brother's thoughts as if he'd read his mind.

"Marco. I wasn't the first with her." He saw his brother's fist clench tightly. *"Dio buono!* I thought you knew or at least guessed it. If I'd known you'd react like this, I wouldn't have mentioned it."

Guillermo felt annoyed that a mere slip of a peasant girl

could have deceived his brother. Diamonte was easier to read than most girls. He felt uneasy under Marco's strong look of disapproval and sipped the remainder of his coffee in silence.

Behind his silence, Marco's thoughts ran rampant. Could Diamonte be as promiscuous as his brother indicated? He could understand her falling for Guillermo's charms. But his brother said he wasn't the first. Could it have been Roberto? His first impulse was to negate the thought. Then he reconsidered. Why not? Roberto was a man. Is that what happened to Roberto? What provoked him to use opiates again? His thoughts about the girl annoyed him. He'd felt a father's pride in her beauty and accomplishments, but now he felt betrayed by her actions. *There's more to this devilish creature than meets the eye,* he thought, cursing his own sentimentality.

"Here's the list, Guillermo," called Mariolina, returning to the terrace. "I hope you can make it out. Just a few essentials . . ."

"Take Calo and Ciccio with you," instructed Marco. It was an order. "And another thing, mention to no one—but no one—not even Cesare, that the Signorina Catanese is our house guest." He poured more coffee for them.

This brought a surprised glance from Mariolina until she realized his caution. Guillermo scanned the list and smiled at her.

"Sometimes, I'm grateful I don't live here as you do," said Guillermo. "I enjoy freedom in the north away from these *strange* people." He placed the note in his vest pocket.

"One does what one must," said Marco resignedly.

They both waved to Guillermo as he disappeared into the villa.

"Is he always so incorrigible?"

"You mustn't mind him. He means well."

"Mind him? Guillermo? I don't mind him at all. I find him refreshing. Unpretentious, unaffected, he is what he is and makes no pretense or excuse."

"He's all that and more." Marco placed a fingertip over his lips meditatively. "I've been waiting for Roberto to arrive. I thought you might enjoy a tour of the estate."

"I would enjoy that. But even more I'd enjoy seeing the sadness removed from your eyes," she said quietly.

"I can see I won't be able to keep anything from you." He smiled. "You'll like Roberto, Mariolina. He'll be a match for you. I remember how you enjoy debating." They exchanged knowing smiles. "He's really the backbone of the *latifondo.* You know, a veritable genius with the earth. He's done things with the soil that will revolutionize farming in Sicily. Remind me to show you the citations and awards he's received from the Department of Agronomy in Roma. Lately he's been working a new type of crop rotation, and with the help of chemical fertilizers, he's reduced crop losses from attacking parasites. And, his theories on antagonistic symbiosis are amazing. You must have him tell you about it. Perhaps one day uncultivated lands will be a thing of the past."

"Remarkable. He must be all you say."

"And more. He'll come for you in about an hour. Will you be ready, *cara mia?*"

She felt as if her heart would burst when he called her that. "Yes."

Reluctantly he tore himself away. "Until tonight at dinner?"

"Until tonight." She watched him leave until he was out of sight.

She stood at the landing at the top of the staircase dressed in a black silk gown selected by Guillermo. Her dark hair, piled high atop her head, was caught with diamond hairpins, belonging to her mother the Baroness. Circlets of diamonds set in gold pierced her ears, but nothing ornamented the gown. Descending the spiral steps with the poise of royalty, Mariolina walked into the arms of her stunned suitor, who for several moments remained speechless, totally taken by her.

"You are astonishingly beautiful," whispered Marco. "I've never seen you dressed like a woman . . ."

When he recovered, he took her arm and walked through the foyer. "I've sent everyone away. Tonight the villa belongs to us, you and me." He walked her through the elegant candlelit room and steered her toward the flower-filled terrace. Strains of soft Sicilian music reached them, but it wasn't until they reached the edge of the terrace that Mariolina saw the musicians, nestled into a corner of the Madelaina Gardens. Several *contadini* played their guitars, mandolins, flutes and pipes. They both recognized "Melodia d'Amore," an ethnic love song from her *paesi,* and she smiled at his thoughtfulness. Later a rich tenor voice was raised in song:

> *Vido mare come' bello*
> *Spiri tanto sentimente*
> *Un perfumo come' bello*

Mariolina was compelled to look at Marco, unable to remove her love-filled eyes from him as he nodded to the musicians and acknowledged their graciousness in playing this evening. Dressed in a black velvet dinner jacket over a

110

white silk shirt with solid gold lion's-head studs and matching cuff links, he looked every inch the Royal Lion. The touch of gray at his temples and his sun-bronzed skin enhanced his handsome features. His hazel eyes, more green than brown, reflected only an overwhelming love for the woman who had occupied his desires these past few months.

Her dark eyes lit up pleasurably when she saw that the main salon had been prepared for this special event. She stared in open-mouthed amazement at the massive gothic pillars and stunning crystal chandeliers. "I had no idea all this grandeur existed anywhere except the old palazzos in Palermo," she said in stupefied appreciation. "Marco, truly it is *fantastico!*"

"It's subordinate only to your beauty, *carissima.*"

She was too overcome to speak. It felt delicious to be a woman. *What have I been missing,* she asked herself. She knew the answer. Nothing! She'd missed nothing. God! What in the entire world could equal this moment with this man among men? For a moment she lowered her eyes, and when she raised them to meet his, it became a moment in which their hearts stood still, a rare moment for lovers when words are superfluous and the heart has a way of communicating the magnetism of love. It was a moment Mariolina would recall many, many times when their love would support her through the agony of hell.

Deeply moved, Mariolina was the first to break through the mood. Taking his lean strong hand in hers, she walked to the edge of the terrace, watching the musicians as they came to life under the enormous orange harvest moon.

Marco walked to the sideboard laden with wines and champagnes. He poured two sherries. He gave her one and held his glass in a toast.

"To us, *carissima,*" he whispered.

"To us," she echoed back.

They sipped the amber liquid. "This is traditional, *cara mia.* Sherry, that is. Now if you like, after the first drink—champagne? What is your pleasure?" He moved his arm in a wide sweeping gesture.

"This is fine. Thank you." She was unable to take her eyes from him.

"You must know I feel for you an overwhelming love," began Marco, somewhat awkwardly at first. "I had planned when the time came to speak of love, to do so more uniquely than any other man may have done. I find, instead, my senses dazzled, my tongue refuses to form words and my babbling, inarticulate mouth can only say, I love you. It repeats itself, I love you. *Io te amo moltissimo, cara mia.*" He paused and tilted her uplifted chin so their eyes met.

111

Then with a huskiness to his voice that made her senses quiver, he continued.

"Mariolina, I beg you, spend the rest of your life with me as my wife, mistress to all I own, and mother to whatever children God decides to grant us." He placed a lean sun-bronzed finger over her soft, sensuous lips. "Before you reply, you must know I'm thirteen years your senior. Does that disturb you?" Before she could move to reply, he removed her wine glass from her hands and held both of them between his. *"Sonno encantado.* I am truly enchanted with you."

She didn't have to answer. The look in her velvety brown eyes told him what he wanted to know. He drew her close and kissed her, gently at first, then with increased fervor until she kissed him back. Suddenly, he drew back and stared incredulously into her eyes, startled by her unabashed response. As their eyes melted into each other's again, he kissed her passionately until they were both breathless, infected by the unmistakable blending of chemistry and soul. Then, somewhat embarrassed by his naked passion, he pushed her gently from him, afraid his feeling might be construed as too bold. He was anxious to abide by all protocol, as if he sensed an obscure haunting in her out of a dim past.

"Carissima," he whispered over and again. Unable to keep his distance, Marco drew her closer to him. They kissed again, soulfully, as their bodies began to move rhythmically to the rapturous music.

> *Amore mi, Il tempo per L'amore*
> *E il tempo per l'amore*

Music, mood and the moon blended into an intoxicant of love. They danced for several moments, closer than they should have. They clung to each other longer than they should have. They were in love, perhaps more than they should have been. At any moment the fires igniting between them would burst into an uncontrollable blaze. The singing stopped. Only the soft refrains continued, heightening their romantic mood. Soon they, too, stopped, and dinner was announced.

Dinner was a masterpiece, but they hardly touched their food or noticed the magnificent opulence.

Immediately after dinner Marco took her to the small sitting room off the Madelaina Gardens where, in the romantic mood of candlelight and music and wine, he presented her with a five-carat diamond solitaire and the string of priceless matching pearls he had intended to give her in Catania.

Seated before the flower-banked fireplace where scented candles enhanced the fragrant atmosphere, Marco reached tremblingly for her slender hand and slipped the Tiffany-mounted stone upon her finger. Mariolina raised her shadow-filled eyes to his and held for several moments. Swallowing hard, she courageously removed the ring and placed it in the black velvet box. Marco glanced at her, looking startled and confused.

"I don't understand, *carissima*. What is it? Don't you like it? Doesn't it meet with your approval? Did you want a larger stone? It can be arranged. I had little time. It is the ring my father gave my mother when they were betrothed . . ."

She smiled. *"Caro mio,* it's nothing like that. It's exquisite. Anything you might have given me would have sufficed. But before I can accept this ring or your proposal of marriage, it is necessary that I tell you a few things." She averted her head, unable to look at the hurt expression in his eyes. She rose to her feet and moved toward the fireplace, the folds of her gown rustling about her. "Guillermo has excellent taste, don't you think?" She picked up a slender Venetian vase.

He nodded. His eyes were fixed expectantly upon her. What was so monumental that it weighed on her conscience. There could only be one thing. Had she been a murderess, a thief, a demon of another nature? What?

Mariolina replaced the vase carefully. It was difficult to get started and she had to select the correct words, so he would understand. *Pray God I'm doing the right thing.*

"Please try to understand that what I am about to tell you has been locked up inside me since my childhood. Since I've come to know you, respect you, and love you, I hold you in such high regard that I can't deceive you."

"Sainted God! What can be so terrible?"

"Try to understand. If when you met me, you thought me to be lacking in the feminine graces—no, please don't contest me, it was true—it was simply because I chose to emulate my father rather than my mother. What a beauty she was. Red hair the color of an orange-gold harvest moon, complexion like rich cream, eyes that reflected the sea at sunset—none of which I inherited—plus the emotional depth of a flea. The Baroness thought only of the Baroness. She lived totally absorbed with herself, in a world of countless vanities and selfish demands. She had no interest in me. Starved for her love, jealous of her beauty, I grew up hating and resenting her because she gave me no attention and acted as if I didn't exist.

"I even resented my father for lacking the courage to in-

113

struct his wife on being a good mother. At that tender age, I had no understanding of the passion between man and woman. It became obvious I couldn't penetrate their adult world and share in their delights, so when I was shuttled off to a convent, I was resigned to the world of misfits along with other girls in my predicament.

"The Convent. Everyone thinks of a convent as a place of purity and goodness, no? What a laugh! What a travesty! It was a cold place, strange and deceptive in appearance, and inside it was worse. But I suppose even now, my recollection of the place is colored by my experiences.

"I shared one room with eleven others. We were curious young girls, concerned and preoccupied and even worried about the rapid changes taking place in our growing bodies. But there was no one to explain the mysteries and beauties of the body, except the Sisters, those *good* sisters of merciful kindness," she spat venomously, "who made us feel considerable shame and humiliation if we raised our hands to ask why Maria's chest was suddenly swelling up more than ours or why Teresa left blood spots on the floor one day. Why did we feel peculiar inside us when the boys from the village stared at us? Why were we not permitted to talk with boys? What was so bad about them that brought punishment to those who didn't avert their eyes when they passed?

"Where could we go to learn? Who'd answer our questions frankly as they should be answered? We were taught to feel shame for every emotion and natural biological response except urinating and defecation. Since there was no one, we turned to books, the kind that are hidden in lockers and under mattresses, the kind young boys somehow find to help them understand the difference between the sexes and what to do if they're aroused physically.

"One day I was reading such a book, trying desperately to understand what was happening to me, for I, too, found myself becoming a woman."

A warm flush of embarrassment surged through Marco at the intimacy of the subject. These Catanians were certainly blunt. Frank and straight. No subtleties about this woman. *Managghia!* His desire to understand this most frustrating and traumatic period in her life caused him to listen intently and hang on to her every word.

"As I was reading the book, all at once, a shadow passed over me and disturbed by what I thought to be a dying candle, I glanced up terrified into the eyes of the Mother Superior's assistant, Sister Mary Good Counsel. She was a witch! A sorceress! The devil's disciple! A whip-cracking, tough, desk-pounding, ruler-slapping . . ." Mariolina

114

caught herself. "Forgive me, even today, my memory of her is such that although I've tried to forgive and forget, I find it isn't finished in my mind. I thought it was. Well, I'll not tarry . . ." Mariolina paused to sip her coffee and continued. "The usual took place. Marched to her office, she lowered my bloomers and proceeded to give me a *bastinada*. It was only later that I learned this was a most unusual *bastinada*, but at that point it was simply a humiliating, painful and degrading act. In the middle of my pain and anguish and tears, I turned to this fiendish woman, intending to plead with her, to ask her forgiveness for being so wicked in reading such a book. It was the look in her eyes which arrested me. Nothing I'd ever seen before. It wasn't anger or fury or disgust or the frustration of having to impose discipline upon an errant school girl. None of these. It was the look of agony. Her eyes were filled with curious and strange lights. She was moaning and groaning and writhing like a snake. Oh, I know now what had taken place. But at twelve, what does a child know of such things? That agony and ecstasy could be one and the same? Pleasure and pain synonymous?"

Marco's face paled. A grim tightness had set in around his lips. Absorbed in her story—almost sensing what was to come—his curiosity became insatiable. He glanced at the diamond in its box. Apprehensive, he wondered, what could be so terrible? What was this monstrous shadow that suddenly loomed between them?

"I learned many things that day and for days to come. How can I explain this with any degree of delicacy? There is no way except to tell you straight as it happened, Marco. If it should offend you or if you find it in poor taste, I can only apologize in advance. I want you to know and understand. If you don't, well, that's another matter."

"Please continue, Mariolina, but only if you feel you must. I'm concerned with what you appear to be reliving at this moment. It seems to cause you considerable pain. Rather than subject you to such torment, I prefer you dismiss it from your mind."

"No. I can't. I must tell you. You must know all about me. Every person is entitled to examine the goods he buys and pays for."

"Mariolina! I've chosen you to share a life with me. I'm in love with you. I don't understand such an attitude." Marco rose to his feet and paced angrily before her. *"Managghia!* You Catanians are really something else!" He could never recall being so confused and angry at a woman.

"You don't know me at all!" she said flatly.

"I know enough to want you."

"Will you understand if I become moody and remain in my apartment for weeks without seeing you as I did when I first arrived? What happens if I reject you?"

"I wouldn't tolerate it," he said with arrogant *maschiezzo*.

"But what if you can't control it? What if suddenly I go mad? Crazy? Out of my head?"

Marco paled and stared at her. "Are you trying to tell me . . . are you trying to say . . ."

"There's insanity in my family?" She smiled. "No."

"I believe you. But don't scare me like that again." He sighed, relieved.

"Then, listen. Hear me out. You must know all about me. You have to know what to do with me at certain times."

The Lion turned to her and submissively sat down again. The distance between that diamond solitaire and Mariolina's finger suddenly seemed so vast.

"Where was I? Oh yes. Sister Mary Good Counsel! Even the name evokes such devout goodness. *Aloura*, not understanding her moans and groans—stupid that I was—I mistook that expression for one of considerable pain. Little did I know it was pleasurable pain. In my girlish naivete, I squirmed off her lap and threw my arms around the woman, asking her forgiveness for having pained her so greatly. I hugged her and I kissed her and promised I'd never do anything to bring her such pain again. The astonishment in her eyes remained a mystery to me. Later, she became gentle with me and began to shower me with favors. I was teased by my classmates who wondered what magic I had spun to convert this wicked monster into so gentle a woman.

"She even bought salve for my bruised bottom which she insisted upon applying herself. I had no suspicions. None at all. But one day, I began to feel strange stirrings in my stomach, and all over, from her manipulation of my body. Well, the inevitable happened. I was molested by this woman, time and again. But you see, I never knew it was bad. How could anything the good Sister do be labeled bad?

"One day, while being *medicated*—that's the word she used—we were caught by Father Andrew. She panicked. We both saw the shocked expression on the priest's face, then, the sudden transition as he locked the door behind him. They talked together in hushed tones. I could see they were not as alienated as they seemed at first, which I learned later was only a pretense, a sham, an effort to keep up a front of holiness.

"Now, it was something different with a man in the room, and a priest at that. I suddenly became aware of my nakedness. This Father Andrew couldn't take his eyes off my body. He began by speaking softly to me, trying to make me understand. He'd not betray me or the good sister, he said. But would I mind if he partook of the pleasures? Could I refuse a priest? Who dared contest or deny a priest? Aren't they emissaries of God? Aren't they His chosen disciples? Besides, and I say this in all humility, up to then it had been a pleasurable feeling. I felt no sense of shame, because it had been demonstrated by a nun. How's that for logic by a twelve year old?

"Father Andrew was undressed before I even nodded my head. I had never seen a naked man before ever in my life. Not even a baby. I had only known my body. My fascination was the fascination of a twelve year old. My astonished eyes fixed upon his enormous sex organ evoked laughter from his lips and a glassy-eyed expression when he reached for my hand and placed it on his manhood. To my astonishment, it grew in size right before my eyes! He inserted it into the nun's body and I became amazed, amazed by his excitement and the manner in which his body moved so erratically on the body of the nun. I was even more amazed at the moaning and groaning that went on between them. But when he finished with her and he withdrew and I saw his organ had miraculously disappeared. I recall asking, 'How did you do that? What magic did you perform? Where did you leave that big thing you had before?' He broke out into laughter. Even the nun smiled and averted her head so I wouldn't see her. 'Do you want to see the magic again?' asked Father Andrew. 'Oh, yes, I do! I do,' I said excitedly.

"He promised he'd rework the miracle. But first he wanted the good sister to make me feel good. 'But keep an eye on my magic box,' he told me. I did. As she began to massage me and manipulate me again, I saw him get larger and larger again before my very eyes. It was a miracle, I thought. But then something happened. He moved in closer to the nun and placed his sex organ in her mouth and began to caress my breasts. That changed and suddenly he was on top of me. I heard the sister protest, but the priest paid her no mind.

"By then, the kindly Father Andrew was no longer kindly, but a beast who brutally tore into me. He seemed to lose all control of himself. He tried to put that enormous organ inside my young body and made such powerful thrusts, I remember screaming in pain. This wasn't pleasure! This was torture! Agony! Apparently his brutality succeeded in rupturing the uterine wall and blood gushed out. You think the animal backed off? Hah!" she said bitterly. "Stimulated to greater heights of ecstasy, neither hearing or caring what

117

happened to me, even after I'd fainted, I later learned he had continued with me.

"I heard the Sister scream, '*Basta! Basta! You'll kill her!*' My eyes fluttered open and vaguely I saw the priest reach out to her, even as he was still inside me. He bit at her breasts with such ferocity that he was oblivious to what he was doing to me. '*Basta!*' screamed the nun. This time she swore at him and swung at him so brutally, he seemed to understand. One more savage thrust at me and I felt him shudder until the bed trembled. As long as I live I shall remember the animal cries that arose in his throat before he lay still on top of me. By then I had fainted again.

"I awakened in another room in a clean bed with clean sheets. A stranger was looking at me. It was a doctor who'd been summoned. He had examined me, packed me with linen bandages, and when questioned I could only tell him I felt numb from my neck down. The expression on the kindly doctor's face was one of violence. Soon I heard him tell Father Andrew and the Sister what he thought of them. 'Bumbling butcher of a priest!' he called him. 'How you get away with these acts of violence is beyond my comprehension. You and your oversized cock have just done another near-lethal job. Villains! Both of you! Poor child. What could she be? Twelve? Thirteen? Goddam you! Both of you! Now, quick, give me the information I need, so I can leave this foul place! What's the child's name?' he asked.

" 'She's an orphan,' said the Sister.

" 'Just like the last one, eh?'

" 'Just like the last.'

" 'I trust you'll be discreet, *dottore*,' said Father Andrew.

" 'By God, this is the last time. The final atrocity you perform—or else.'

" 'Yes, yes, good, *dottore*. I promise. The very last time. I swear to you. In the name of Jesus Christ, I swear!' the priest replied.

" 'Child-fucking son of a whore! You'll continue to violate young girls until your tool withers and dies away. Already you've filled half the fucking country with your bastards. And those ignorant bitches believe they are carrying a probable messiah in their hot bellies!'

" 'Send the girl home to her parents. You know what to do,' said Father Andrew after the physician left. By the time I was sent home, I had been thoroughly brainwashed by the crafty Sister Mary Good Counsel.

" 'You've been lucky to have been loved,' she told me. 'You wouldn't want to see any of us suffer, would you my child? When you grow older, you'll understand more.' She instilled the fear of God's wrath in me. She implanted the

118

idea that I'd be considered a very bad sinner if I told the true story. 'Your soul will burn in hell if you speak against members of the clergy!'

"I obeyed her instructions like a dutiful child, knowing my mother would believe the church before she'd believe me. I could never confide such an experience to my father. So I lived with the secret buried deep inside me where it traumatized and shocked me into retreating from the outside world. I never knew until much later that a letter signed by Father Andrew had been sent to my parents. It said little except that I was an exceptional student who needed private tutoring, away from convent atmosphere. That I'd been ailing of late and in view of my weakened condition, I should be treated with care and concern and should be protected from overtiring myself. Oh yes, he enclosed his usual best wishes and the united blessings of the Convent, the Church and the orphanage for the generous endowments made by the Catanese family . . .

"Wait, there's more—only a little more. I never regained my strength. If I walked for more than an hour, I felt tired. At home, I studied with private tutors, became an avid reader, and poured my frustrations into books. At seventeen, I still preferred solitude and books to the companionship of other girls my own age. I refused a gala my mother wanted to hold in honor of my debut to society. At eighteen, I astonished my father by requesting entrance to the university. You know the results of that involvement.

"I never set foot inside a church again. I haven't gone to confession. If a priest or nun has crossed my path, I deliberately avoided speaking to them and have remained deaf to my family's pleadings to do otherwise.

"After my mother's death, my father encouraged me to become a free thinker, hoping that in so doing I might bloom into natural womanhood, meet an eligible young man, and give up all thoughts of soap box oratory. His last hope was that I'd settle down to be the woman God intended I be.

"I discovered many things about myself, Marco. By being so fiercely competitive, I had unwittingly given vent to the fear, hatred, and contempt I felt for all men, even my father. I loved him dearly but never really forgave him for sending me off to live in a convent where all those terrible things happened to me.

"My life, filled with nightmares and vivid recollection of Father Andrew reinforced my abnormal fear of men. In this fear I was determined to outclass them mentally. I made it a point to learn all about anatomy. The impressionable child of twelve hasn't existed for a long time.

119

"Knowing the importance our society places on virginity in marriage, I long ago gave up all thought of marrying. Even in my most reckless moments, I couldn't imagine telling a prospective bridegroom about the manner in which I'd been deflowered. I told myself there were other things in life besides marriage. Devotion to a cause or to a people for instance. I found that if I concentrated long and hard enough, I could subordinate all my sexual drives. That is, until you entered my life.

"Your gentle ways and manliness fascinated me from the first, even though I attacked your ideals like a hot-headed campus radical. And when you took matters into your hands after the holocaust descended on my villa, I found myself inescapably in love with you. My self-imposed period of mourning was spent carefully regarding my predicament and how I could ever bring myself to reveal my soul to you. When you came into my bed chamber last night, I ached for you as much as I felt you ached for and desired me. If I'd been any other woman, I wouldn't have let you go.

"So I had decided that, rather than tell you the sordid details, I'd leave for America. It would have been much easier for me than staying and telling you all this. Yet as I contemplated my dilemma, I convinced myself that I owed you the truth. If you couldn't handle it, I would leave. The problem was how and when would I find the guts to tell you.

"Deception is not one of my traits. I gambled. If you sent me packing, then Destiny hadn't intended our marriage to be consummated. It is legend how much Sicilian men revere chastity and a virginal wife. I didn't assume you'd be different. But on the other hand, if you accepted me with all my imperfections, then it could only be you who would make me come alive as a woman. It's a chance I had to take, Marco."

She had been watching him closely as she talked and had seen him undergo several changes. He no longer seemed in control. Marked agitation, heavy breathing, and chain smoking had consumed his time. Now it was apparent he was livid with rage and had difficulty containing his anger. His eyes had turned into the ferocious eyes of an animal and Mariolina grew frightened.

At first she took his rage to be directed at her. In many moments of sinking sensations, the fear of losing him distorted her reasoning. At that moment she knew losing him would be the most difficult thing she'd have to face. She paled noticeably and trembled as she sat down next to him waiting for his verdict.

"Villiachi!" he cursed aloud. *"Brutti villiachi!"* His hands

gripped the armrests on the red velour chair. He sprang from the chair and began to pace the floor.

Dismayed, Mariolina said, "I've overestimated the Lion's tolerance. After all, you are a man, not a god without imperfections. Why would you take this any other way? I'm a spoiled piece of baggage in any man's eyes. You above all have the right to expect your wife to be untarnished." Very well, she had gambled and lost.

"What are you saying?" He turned to her, faced her, and stared at her through new eyes. Mariolina felt the flush of embarrassment sweep through her. Her eyes wavered from the intensity of his gaze, and she averted her head as tears spilled over her saddened cheeks.

"Oh, *cara mia!*" he said, suddenly overwhelmed with compassion. "You don't think for a moment I have a quarrel with you? That this could affect the love I feel for you?" He rushed to her side, placed his arms tenderly about her, reached up to stroke her face tenderly and gently cradled her. He thrust her from him and forced her to look into his eyes. He brushed away the tears with his handkerchief. "It's not with you I feel this blinding anger," he said as he stroked her face with the back of his fingers. "Our love does not perish in the first gust of wind that comes along. Sainted God! What you must have endured! What courage it took not to tell your *genitori*—your parents. Why didn't you tell your father? Don Alfredo would have whipped those two *dishonorati* to within an inch of their lives. Priest or no priest! Nun or not!" Marco felt the pain and anguish as if it were his.

"It's done and in the past, Marco." She felt the warm surge of love sweep through her once more where only moments before had been an icy void.

That night she discovered that Marco de Leone had indeed loved her in a way she could never hope to understand and with a depth beyond which she dared to hope. Mariolina had feared the worst, hoped for the best, and when the best happened, her utter amazement, incredible love and adoration for this godlike man swelled her heart and imagination beyond its limits.

11

Several conferences between Father Bonaventura and a Papal emissary from Rome brought immediate results. Within three weeks, the family rode to Messina where the banns of marriage were announced four times in one day.

With preparation for the marriage underway, Mariolina asked Gina to take her on a tour of the villa. By now

121

Guillermo had been held fascinated under her spell, and she and Roberto had become soul mates.

From the first she responded to Roberto. She found him to be a brilliant and warm human being. His love for Marco and his dedication were unimpeachable. They got into long discussions on every imaginable subject and she found that Marco had been fair in his assessment—Roberto was truly a genius.

On the other hand, Roberto found her to be astounding—for a woman. Her equestrian prowess, indefatigable spirit and knowledge of the management of the *latifondo* dazzled him. His profound knowledge, at its best when besieged with countless questions, had never received such stimulation and her ego-inflating responses brought him back to life again. His encounter with Diamonte had faded dimly into his mind and he pointedly ignored her now. He was happy that Marco became so occupied with Mariolina. He'd not brought up the opium incident again.

For Roberto, the next two weeks were sheer delight. He took Mariolina on a daily tour of the *latifondo* and she couldn't believe what she saw. She simply didn't believe such a place could exist in feudal Sicily. Her awe and utter amazement at what Marco and Roberto had accomplished intensified her curiosity.

Contadini living on the very lands they farmed? What an ingenious innovation! How much more productive. It was new! Exciting! Revolutionary! Nothing like this was taught in Catania University.

Many things intrigued her. The rapport between the peasants and landlord baffled her.

The faces of these *contadini* were not the half-starved, backward, animalistic faces of men and woman she'd seen in central and western Sicily. If such a cooperative worked here, why not in the west? Why not all over? The marked contrast between other *latifondos* and that of the Lion startled her into a cold sobriety. What magic did Marco employ to transform these lands into such remarkable productivity? How had he generated such profound love and warmth and respect from the same people whom other *latifondisti* treated like animals? No one in Catania would believe her if she told them.

One day she broke into mirthful laughter. Roberto glanced curiously at her and she told him of her first encounter with Marco. "What a fool Marco must have thought me. He had every right to speak of his country through the eyes of love. Evidence of his love is everywhere."

"He couldn't have thought you too foolish, he's marrying you, isn't he?" They both smiled.

Everything Mariolina saw both delighted and disturbed her deeply. Even the fact that Dr. Pietro came on a regular basis to the *latifondo* was most revolutionary. When did any landowner ever give a fig over the health of his workers? Any thinking man would have to be crazy not to see the merit in such an enterprise. If Marco would permit it, she'd give anything to stand before the Senate and laud efforts like these. Her enthusiasm was so pronounced, she had to force herself to simmer down and remember that she'd made the choice to be a woman. A woman and a wife without political aspirations is what she had chosen for herself. But she could still think, couldn't she? She listened carefully as Roberto explained each phase of the operation.

"Marco imported the latest in farming equipment from England. He financed my trips to Rome and London to study political economy in agricultural science," he told Mariolina. "I, in turn, instructed the men. You know, Mariolina, the peasants can work miracles with their hands!"

"Tell me how the cooperative works," she insisted. "Do the peasants lease the lands? What?"

Having found a willing listener he told her of the de Leone ideals. "Each family is given an equal share of land, from five to ten acres depending on the crops they select to grow."

"Can they choose anything they wish to grow?"

"Only from a selected list. Some time prior to planting, the men meet and decide what each will grow. Each year they rotate and select a different product."

"Ah! Then they can learn from each other what idiosyncrasies each product presents in various stages of growth?"

"You catch on fast," grinned Roberto. "Each person passes onto the next grower all he's learned including all pitfalls."

"And there's no jealousy or competition among the men?"

"We have no time for jealousies. And competition? In the final analysis we see who grew the best crop and learned the most from his predecessor. The final product is the proof."

"Do they earn enough to satisfy them?"

"If they didn't, the cooperative would have been a failure. One-half the yield is retained by the *contadini* to do with what they wish—keep it, sell it, or give it away. The other half goes to a central depot to be taken to market and sold to the vendors in the cities."

"Aren't there price controls?"

"Of course. *Mafiosi* infiltrate wherever they see weakness. But the wholesale markets in Messina are perhaps the only free markets left in the land due to the de Leone cooperative. Independents are all at the mercy of the *mafia*.

123

Until they learn what it's taken us a long time to learn and achieve, and have the guts to do it as we did, they will always be at the mercy of scum like those."

"What happens to the income from the sales?"

"It pays the taxes, pays for necessary repairs to equipment, until the more mechanically inclined learn to do it themselves. It buys tools and new equipment. Incidentally, all purchases and expenditures are authorized by a body of six men elected yearly by the *contadini* themselves.

"Marco has the unique quality of being able to recognize another man's potential along with the ability to draw it forth. He believes, as his father did, 'The plow is the arc of peace that will unite the civilized with the uncivilized. A man who has plowed the earth is not bent on heaping it with corpses.' Knowledge of the earth is vital to the peasants. They couldn't exist without it."

"I can't believe the dissension between the other landowners, Roberto," she told him when he mentioned their petty jealousies and their inability to unite on a common ground for the betterment of the people and their country. "One day their petty bias and stupidity will do them in. The sorrows of Sicily, the majority of them at least, can be laid at the door of feudalism. Tell me, have the other *latifondisti* given you much trouble?" she asked as they headed back to the villa.

"No. Not in the sense you suggest."

"Can't they see the difference? I find it hard to believe they won't concede that you and Marco have accomplished something close to the miracle that Sicily's needed."

Roberto laughed. "Remember, *cara mia,* Christ was never considered a prophet in his own village." Roberto pulled down the visor of his brimmed hat, shielding his intense blue eyes from the glare of the afternoon sun. He kept the horses at a slow canter, never in a hurry to leave her.

Mariolina smiled faintly. "You're a strange man, Roberto. I've never met anyone quite like you."

"The world is full of men like me. It's Marco who's unique."

"It's easy to see the strong bond of love between you."

"If it weren't for Marco, I'd probably still be a book clerk in Rome. Perhaps worse."

"Is that where you met?" He nodded.

During the past weeks, a deep affection had sprung up between Mariolina and Roberto. He was a private person who said little or nothing about himself. How many times she wanted to ask about his leg, to discover if that was what made him so reserved, but what right did she have to pry? Perhaps Marco would speak of it someday. Yet, he baffled

124

her. Always cheerful, witty, and remarkably handsome, she wondered many things about him. Especially one.

"Why haven't you married?" she asked him.

At first he resented her question. When he thought about it, he responded. It had been a simple question with no malice intended.

"Perhaps, like Marco, I'm too difficult to please." It was meant as a compliment. She knew it and flushed with pleasure. "Marco waited a long time to find you, Mariolina. Somehow, I feel you both are right for each other."

"Even I have come to believe there is something special about our love," she told him, then changed the subject. "Tell me about Diamonte, will you?" Mariolina regretted the question instantly when she saw the change in him. His lips tightened and his jaw set hard. He stiffened suddenly and a wall sprang between them. *Guillermo's right,* she thought. *There is something between them.*

"What do you want to know?"

She eased up. "Why don't we see her around? Once in a while I see her looking up into my balcony from the gardens, but when I wave to her, she moves away into the shadows as if she hadn't seen me at all. What an incredible beauty this child has. Don't you agree?"

"That depends on how you define beauty?"

"Oh, come now," laughed Mariolina. "She's a raving beauty. Would that God had endowed me with such a face, and those incredibly blue eyes!"

Roberto pulled up on the reins with such force the horses whinnied in protest. "Don't ever say such a thing," he told her. "You have more beauty in your little finger than she has in the whole of her!"

Startled by his sudden outburst, she remained quiet for the remainder of the ride to the villa. She wanted to ask many questions, but couldn't. The wall between them was back in place.

12

"Why haven't I seen you before this?" asked Mariolina.

Diamonte shrugged indifferently.

"Are you kept busy helping your mother?"

"Si."

"What do you do in your spare time? Do you read? Have you gone to school?"

"Signora Amalfi taught us to read and write. But my Godfather taught me before."

"Your Godfather?"

"Marco is my Godfather."

125

Mariolina smiled. "Then I'll be your Godmother after the wedding, won't I?" She stared at Diamonte and caught her breath at the girl's beauty. The milk white satin of her bridal gown next to Diamonte's tanned skin gave it an opalescent glow like golden moonstones. Her black hair the color of a moonless and starless night set off the whiteness of the silk. And those eyes, thought Mariolina. Never had she seen the color of azure so blue.

She had persuaded the girl to try on the gown so she could alter it properly. At first Diamonte's eyes turned cold with superstitious fright. "No!" she shouted excitedly. "If I try on your wedding gown, I'll never have one of my own."

"Nonsense. You don't believe such foolishness, do you? How else can you tell if a gown fits you, if you don't try it on?"

Diamonte's suspicious, brooding eyes studied Mariolina as she pinned the gown, then slowly she turned to gaze about the room. The orange blossom headpiece with tiny seed pearls and yards and yards of silk illusion veiling lay draped over the bed. As she caressed the shimmering satin and Alençon lace of Mariolina's gown, she tried to subdue the fiery indignation that seared her soul. *If it weren't for her I'd be wearing this gown. I would be walking down the aisle to marry Marco.*

She gazed enviously at the array of new clothing, furs, velvets, hats with ostrich plumes, and jewelry, all waiting to be packed into steamer trunks and valises. Choking back the torturous feeling of hatred she felt for this woman, she wondered what Marco saw in her. *I am the most beautiful. He should have chosen me.*

As she gazed at her reflection in the mirror while Mariolina put pins in the gown, Diamonte thought, *She may think she'll marry Marco but she won't. Not if I can help it!*

"Wouldn't you like to go to school where you could learn more than reading and writing, Diamonte?"

Diamonte eyed her rival suspiciously. *Why was she trying to be so nice? She'd like it if I went away. I wonder what she'd say if she knew that Marco bought me many books and wanted to send me north to a finishing school, that I refused because I wanted to stay here with him.*

"No, I wouldn't."

Suddenly Mariolina felt drained of energy and lightheaded. The fitting completed, she asked Diamonte, "Please, *cara mia.* Be a good girl and ask Gina for some hot black coffee and a few *biscotti.* She told me they were baking today."

"*Si, Signorina,*" said Diamonte removing the gown carefully. She slipped into her shift, smoothed it into place, and quietly left the room.

Why am I so tired of late, sighed Mariolina as she lay back on the chaise longue. The shopping trips to Messina kept her busy everyday for the past few weeks. *So tired . . . So very tired.* She thought about Diamonte. *How gorgeous she is. Why does Roberto feel so strongly against her? I will talk with Marco about sending her to school. It would be a pity to keep such beauty from the world. Now I understand why Marco has attempted to immortalize her on canvas. Her beauty is as rare as her name—Diamond.* Slowly her eyelids grew heavy and closed.

"What took you so long?" she asked Diamonte when the girl returned an hour later with her coffee and cookies. Mariolina glanced at the porcelain clock as the chimes struck the hour. She frowned. "It's too late now. Dinner will be served shortly," she told her. "Take it away."

"No," she assured Mariolina. "Dinner will be late tonight. Mama was very upset that I didn't return soon enough to help her, now everything is delayed. Drink the coffee while it's hot. It's just the way you like it. The *biscotti* are fresh from Signora Amalfi's oven."

"*Grazie molto.* Please apologize to your mother for me."

"There's no need. I explained. Dinner will be at least two hours. Take a little nap."

"That long?" Mariolina frowned. She'd be late for the chess game she planned with Roberto in Marco and Guillermo's absence. "Very well," she sighed, "I am suddenly so tired."

She sipped her coffee and watched Diamonte spread out the folds of the gown, caressing the rich fabric gently and allowing it to slide gently in her fingers.

"When you marry you shall have the gown, if you like."

"Oh, no! It's too beautiful. I'd be frightened to wear such an expensive gown."

Her affected humility touched Mariolina. "Nonsense. It's yours if you want it." Mariolina made a wry face. "*Managghia!* This coffee is bitter." She broke a gaily frosted green *biscotti* in two and dunked it into the cup, hoping it would sweeten the coffee.

Diamonte watched through cool appraising eyes as Mariolina leaned back against the chaise longue. She saw her reach over to wind the key of the exquisite hand-painted music box Marco brought to her from Messina. The miniature Roman temple's door opened as small porcelain figures came out on a track, pirouetted, and turned and went back inside the temple before the refrains of the aria from *Aïda* ended. It was Mariolina's favorite possession and she played it constantly.

Diamonte poured the rest of the silver carafe of hot coffee. "Finish this, Signorina, and I will take it back to the kitchen."

Mariolina did her bidding and watched as Diamonte slipped out of the room closing the door behind her.

Roberto paced the study for better than a half hour waiting for Mariolina. Earlier when faced with the prospect of dining alone, he felt glum and expressed his sentiments to Gina. "Why must I eat alone? Where is everyone?"

"The brothers are in Messina and won't return until morning. The Signorina Mariolina was tired. She worked all day on her bridal gown. Diamonte took a tray to her about four o'clock."

"Did you see her?"

"No. Diamonte was with her. I hope the Signorina doesn't fill her head with too much nonsense and fancy ideas. As it is she is impossible to live with."

Roberto glanced sharply at Gina, his eyes searching hers for some sign. He sipped the delicious soup made with *badotteri,* small succulent meatballs, grated cheese, and bread crumbs. After two spoonfuls, however, he pushed the dish from him. His appetite had vanished.

"Che c'e? Non e buono? What's wrong? Isn't it good?"

"As usual it's delicious. I'm not hungry. I'll take my coffee in the study."

In Marco's den, Roberto began to set up the ornate Florentine chess figures; his eyes caught sight of Diamonte's unfinished portrait.

My God, the bitch is truly beautiful! Marco's caught the essence of her loveliness, but the mouth's all wrong, thought Roberto critically. *Marco depicts her as an innocent.* Roberto saw her as a seductive whore with a cruel mouth. Marco painted the eyes of a Madonna; Roberto saw her with the eyes of a demon. *No wonder he's been unable to complete the painting. He's unaware of her duality.*

Angry at himself for harboring such thoughts, he forced himself to return to the chess table. When Gina brought him his coffee, he asked casually, "When did you see Mariolina last?"

"Mezzogiorno. Around noon."

"Did you fix the tray of food for her?"

"No. I was at the Amalfi cottage to help Sara ice the *biscotti.* It was baking day for all the women."

"Aloura, who fixed her food tray?"

They both were struck by the same horrifying thought. Gina clasped a hand over her mouth to stifle her words, as if it would harness her thoughts. *"Dio buono!* Dear God, no!"

128

They both ran from the room, crossed the foyer, and ran up the stairs. Hampered by his bad leg, Roberto was out of breath and shaken as he got to Mariolina's door moments after Gina had knocked on the door and, receiving no reply, entered.

Mariolina lay on the chaise longue, her face drained of color, as motionless as death. Roberto reached her side, raised her arm, and let it fall limp over the armrest.

"Quick, black coffee and brandy. *Fa subito!*"

He rubbed her wrists and felt for a pulse. It was there, remote, faint, and irregular, but there. "Mariolina. Mariolina," he called. He pulled her to her feet. "Come on. You must walk. Walk, I tell you, walk!" She fell into a heap. Then again and again, he repeated the process. "Dammit! Get up! You've got to walk! Walk, I tell you! Walk!" It was useless. He lay her back on the chaise, and for the first time he noticed the remains of the coffee and *biscotti*. He raised the cup to his nose and sniffed its contents. Puzzled, he dipped his finger into the remains and tasted the liquid.

Gina returned with the brandy and hot coffee. Roberto grabbed the bottle and poured it directly into her mouth, spilling it over her chin down onto her breasts.

"Signore Roberto!" shouted Gina. She pointed to the *biscotti*. He didn't understand until she told him, "We didn't frost the *biscotti* with green food coloring—only white. We've been out of coloring for some time."

Roberto heard her but didn't grasp the significance immediately. When he realized what she meant, he reached for the fancy-shaped sea horse and nibbled at the frosting and smelled it. He spit out the frosting at the faint scent of bitter almonds.

"*Jesu Christo!*" he exclaimed. "Gina, force the brandy down her throat. Forget the coffee. Do what I say until I return." Moments later, cursing his crippled leg, Roberto struggled into the greenhouse and scanned the cabinet where he kept his chemicals. Everything looked intact until he spied small granules of green powder in the flickering illumination of the candle. Only yesterday he had mixed a new compound with the white cyanide crystals, turning it to a pale green. It was a deadly poison; his only hope was that it had been used sparsely. He searched like a half-crazed madman. Finding the book he needed, he turned the pages to the antidotes for cyanide poisoning.

Back inside Mariolina's room, he instructed Gina, "Get some eggs and vinegar. She's been poisoned. We must make her vomit."

"I'll get Sara Amalfi. She'll know what to do."

"No, there's no time."

Roberto rubbed Mariolina's hands, trying to wake her.

I will say of the Lord He is my refuge and my fortress . . . God don't let it be too late. Not now. Marco just found her. You can't fill his life with any more sadness.

Gina returned with the whipped egg whites and vinegar and forced it down Mariolina's throat. They both prayed and worked feverishly.

Several hours later, when it was all over, Roberto sat next to Mariolina's bed, spent and perspiring. Gina sat opposite him, her eyes staring at Mariolina without expression.

"We must tell His Excellency, Gina. You know that?"

"It's my responsibility," she said, her face resembling a death mask. "I'll attend to it."

Gina searched the entire villa for Diamonte. She asked everyone. No one had seen her. Unable to locate Father Bonaventura at the chapel, she took a moment to light a candle and pray for her mistress. As she knelt at the altar, Gina's wrinkled skin took on a sudden softness in the candlelight. Her body, heavy and shapeless after the years of neglect, had never bothered her as much as it had her vain daughter. It never entered her mind to improve on God's handiwork. What God had neglected in the endowment of physical beauty, he compensated for by creating a soul of beauty. Kind and thoughtful, Gina had never uttered an unkind remark against another, except at her daughter, who constantly provoked her.

As she thought of Diamonte, her eyes filled with a glittering, unfamiliar wildness. Why? Why, dear God, had the girl tried to kill Mariolina? Filled with shame and heartache she wept aloud in heart-rending sobs. With all her heart she hoped Roberto had misjudged Diamonte, that he was wrong. Her heavy heart told her different. *Santo Dio,* how could she face His Excellency?

Gina blew her nose, brushed wisps of gray hair from her face, and walked slowly out of the chapel, a defeated old woman. She retraced her steps toward her small *casita.* For a brief and wild moment, she felt she'd find her daughter there. All she found was emptiness. A quick look through her things caused the truth to choke her and leave her with a strangled feeling of futility. Several items were missing. Too heartbroken to take an accurate count, Gina sat in the rocking chair and in the darkness rocked endlessly in monotonous rhythm, weighed down with enormous feelings of guilt, profound sorrow, and disgrace.

"You will *not* tell Marco about this," insisted Mariolina to both Gina and Roberto. "I don't want him to have any more problems than he already has. Just put the incident out of your minds."

"You're wrong, my dear," insisted Roberto. "He's bound to find out about it someday. And he won't appreciate your silence."

"It will hurt him deeply to think such things of his God-child," she implored. "Besides, I don't want our wedding day to be marred or shadowed in any way."

"Diamonte is nowhere to be found," said her mother tearfully.

"Then tell Marco she's visiting Signora Lamantia who's expecting her firstborn."

As luck would have it, it was Dr. Pietro who inadvertently brought the matter to Marco's attention after all their hasty plans to keep the matter secret. He arrived in the morning for his usual monthly rounds and at Roberto's request, he looked in on Mariolina. Before Roberto could caution him not to say anything about the nature of her illness to Marco, the door opened and Marco came rushing into her bedroom filled with concern.

"*Carissima*, what's wrong?" he asked solicitously. He sat on the edge of the bed, stroking her pale face and pushing away the long strands of silken hair from her face.

"It's best you allow her to rest," said Dr. Pietro touching his shoulder lightly. "She's been through a terrible ordeal. If it weren't for Roberto's quick thinking, she'd be dead. How did you know it was cyanide?" he asked the pale blond man who had forgotten to caution the doctor. He glanced at Gina in alarm. It was too late now.

"Cyanide?" Marco stared in bafflement. "Cyanide," he repeated. "What are you telling me? Cyanide!"

"Let's go downstairs to the study," suggested Roberto quietly.

"Tell me now." Marco was in no mood to be put off.

"I'll send Signora Amalfi to relieve you, Gina," said Dr. Pietro. "You look tired. Go get some rest."

The weary, frightened woman nodded.

"I don't believe it. That child wouldn't bring harm to me and my house," stormed Marco when they were forced to explain.

"Does it matter now?" asked Roberto. "What's important is that Mariolina is alive."

"Why would she do such a thing?"

Dr. Pietro smiled at his friend's naivete. It seemed nearly everyone knew of her crush on him except Marco himself.

"I treated the child as if she were my own daughter. Why would she do this to someone I love?"

"She wasn't a child any longer, Marco, or hadn't you noticed?" Roberto's voice dropped softly.

131

"So that's what's disturbed Gina?" said Marco. "Were you aware of her feelings, Roberto?"

"Never to the extent she'd kill for your love."

"I want her found. No matter how long it takes, I want her found and brought to me," said Marco, filled with a curious mixture of disbelief and anger. "What of Gina? She must feel dreadful."

"She's stricken with grief. If it hadn't been for her curiosity about the green food coloring . . ." began Roberto. "Well, thank God, we caught it in time."

"Yes, thank God," agreed Marco. "Thank God!"

Dr. Pietro snapped open the lid to his gold watch. "*Aloura.* I must be on my way. I've much to attend to."

"Why not spend the night with us, Alberto," suggested Marco. "I hear the hills are infested with bandits once again."

"Again?" Roberto looked up questioningly.

"There are rumors. A herd of cattle was stolen from the southwest sector, and I heard in Messina from Cesare Ruffo that the uncultivated lands of the Duke of Nelson were claimed by peasants. Once again rivers of blood flowed. The duke's lands are bound by ours near Bronte." Marco looked tired. His fervor waned and he fell into brooding.

"No matter how many times peasants and landlords meet on the battlefield, no matter if human blood flows like wine, life goes on," spouted Dr. Pietro. "I have a midwife sitting with a prospective mother who has joined forces with the devil and refuses to relinquish her unborn child. It remains swollen and truant in her fat belly for longer than it should. Already she's a month past due." He waved his hands about the air in a gesture of futility. "Who can understand the riddles of life?"

Marco laughed suddenly. "You know what the old Sicilian adage says, Alberto, 'The pear won't fall off the tree until the fruit is ripe.'"

"All I need today is Sicilian logic," snapped the physician wryly, as he busily wrote out a prescription.

"Mariolina will be well enough for the wedding?" asked Roberto with reserve. He could never warm up the detached physician.

Dr. Pietro nodded. "Make sure this is filled. She is to take it like a tonic."

"*Va biene. Aloura,* we'll see you on Saturday, *dottore.*" He waved them both off and limped off toward the greenhouse.

Marco walked Dr. Pietro to the front entrance, where the physician's horse and buggy waited in the courtyard. "*Tante grazie,* Alberto," said the Lion, glancing at the prescription. "Why this?"

"It's just a tonic, Marco. Just a tonic. Mariolina will be all right. Just make sure she gets all the rest she can. Capitano Nicosia tells me you intend taking the boat to the mainland on your honeymoon. Will you be gone long?"

"Two or three months. Why?"

"It's just that . . . well, perhaps it's nothing." He shook his head. "Forget it."

"You know I won't now. What is it?"

"It may be nothing, but when you get to Rome, see if you can get Mariolina to see this colleague of mine." He fumbled through his billfold for a card. Then he searched the pockets of his suit, and after shuffling through a mess of scattered memos, he found what he was looking for.

"A peculiar appearance to her skin and the discolored portions of her eyes disturb me, but it will take tests for which we have no equipment to determine if my diagnosis is correct. Dottore Simoni is a specialist in female disorders, a good man, truly a genius. He hopes to open a clinic in Switzerland shortly. It doesn't hurt to have such a man check her out, eh, Marco?" He patted the worried Lion on the shoulders and bid him farewell. "Saturday, my friend. Oh, by the way, before I forget, will you order these three books for me in Rome?" He tore a memo from his small black book and handed it to Marco. "It will take forever if I send the order in through the mail."

Marco scanned the contents of the list and smiled tolerantly. "You still pursue that dream, Alfredo?"

"You didn't give up your dream, Marco. And look what happened. It became a reality." He waved his arms in a full sweep indicating the *latifondo.*

"I don't mean to make light of it, Alfredo. Really. But you must admit, not every man is dedicated to finding a lost treasure belonging to some distant prince."

"I thank you for that, Marco. And trust you'll be discreet and not mention it to anyone. It would sound foolish to any man who has lost the art of dreaming."

Dr. Alberto quickly got in his carriage. He attached a yellow and black flag to the upper portion of the buggy, waved and cracked his whip. The horses took off smoothly, rounded the courtyard, and disappeared through the main gates of the estate. Dr. Pietro flew his yellow and black talisman immunizing him against bandits. His horses didn't wear the usual evil-eye amulets, since Dr. Pietro had no respect for superstitions entertained by the Sicilian peasants for *u malocchio.* He was also no believer in Destiny, choosing to believe a man captains his own soul in life. Secretly

133

he read Nietzsche and felt strong leanings toward the works of Arthur Schopenhauer.

In his study, Marco wondered why he felt so heavy of heart, considering there were only five more days until his wedding. It was time for rejoicing, for pleasure and excitement. He had busied himself getting last minute preparations out of the way. Roberto would take over the running of the *latifondo* in his absence. He had no qualms. Guillermo remained in Messina to help Captain Paolo Nicosia to ready the yacht and planned to return to officiate as best man at his wedding.

For a time Marco glanced at the unfinished portrait of Diamonte. He was unable to believe it was she who attempted to poison his beloved future wife.

She's my Godchild. I favored her more than the others. I loved her as my own child. What was it Roberto said, "She isn't a child any longer."

Indeed she wasn't if Guillermo spoke the truth when he insisted he hadn't been the "first" with her. She had grown up and he hadn't really noticed.

13

Never had there been a wedding like that of the Royal Lion and Mariolina de Catanese. It was all she could have hoped for in view of the circumstances and recent death of her father. She stood gazing down at the frolicking peasants who always enjoyed such festivities with great passion and expression. Dressed in a stunning black velvet traveling costume and an Empress Eugénie hat, she waited for Marco. Having entered the room silently, he stood behind her and kissed the nape of her neck. As she spun around and melted into his arms, he kissed her forehead and held her tightly.

"Ready, *carissima?*"

"Ready, my love."

Pelted with rice and flower petals, they descended the spiral stairs and made their way to the fountain courtyard and stepped into the awaiting carriage, waving happily at the throngs of people who had attended the wedding ceremony. When she found out that Calo and Ciccio would be accompanying them on their honeymoon, Mariolina was dismayed. Would Marco have to fear for his life so far away from Sicily?

Their wedding night was spent aboard the cruiser *Marchessa*. Marco kissed his wife and made passionate love to her, and she returned his passion in a way she never dreamed she could. He'd been tender, and loving and so inflamed by love that he infected his bride with the same delirious quality, making her feel like a woman for the first time in her life. But between them was a wedge of darkness —the malevolent priest who had held her in the intimacy of sex. It tore at Marco's heart like a searing flame burning all his flesh.

Ironies to end all ironies, Marco had told himself many times after hearing Mariolina's painful story. She had made him promise not to take any action against the priest, "because he'd come to his own undoing one day." Marco never told his wife it had been Marco's grants to the orphanage that had permitted Father Andrew to become a priest. In time he pushed the episode from his mind and became susceptible to her wit and charm, innate sweetness and intelligence.

Watching the *Marchessa* cruise out of the harbor, Roberto Argento slapped Guido Amalfi on the back. To help him forget the emptiness and loneliness he would face over the next three months, the agronomist made a suggestion.

"Since we are both dressed in our fine formal attire, it would be a shame to waste such elegance by not seeing a bit of Messina. What do you say we visit Angelo's *Birreria* before we return to the villa, eh?"

Dressed in a vintage tuxedo, awkward and ill at ease, Guido had never been in Roberto's company socially before, and the prospect awed him enough to accept. *Contadino* and landlord? Goddamn that was some combination.

At the pub, Guido gawked like a wide-eyed tourist. He was impressed by the courtesy and aplomb with which Roberto was treated by headwaiters who knew him from his frequent luncheon visits with Marco and other business associates. Guido was suddenly bursting with pride as he walked through the crowded bistro. When Roberto saw the expression of shock on the peasant's face as he caught sight of the nudes displayed on the walls, Roberto grinned with amusement. He patted Guido reassuringly on the back as he sat down in the chair next to him.

"*Managghia*, Signore Roberto! Is this the way the nobility live? With decadence, shame, and immorality staring them in the face?"

"What's so immoral about a nude woman? You, a married man with three children and one in the oven, talk about immorality in the nude body of a woman?"

"*Che demonio?* What are you saying? But, of course! Never! Never have I seen my wife completely nude! You think I have intentions of burning in purgatory for allowing temptations of the flesh to sear my soul and forever lose faith with God?"

135

Roberto was astounded. He stared at Guido. "I don't believe it! These words from a physical and sensual man like you?" Wisely enough he let the subject drop. He'd learned enough from Marco to know not to try to dissuade a man from what he believed. The task, a hopeless one at best, could only bring mistrust and suspicion. *It's remarkable to have worked as close to Guido as I have all these years and never really know the man,* he told himself.

He almost welcomed the unsolicited intrusion of a man of medium build in his forties with scrawny dark features and a look of arrogant indolence who swaggered cockily toward them. A waiter managed to place swiftly two Stregas on the table and blurt, "Compliments of Don Tricario."

Guido's face turned red. The *mafia gabelotto* from the Duke of Nelson's estates! Son of a whore! This was the treacherous cockroach, who a while back had boasted he controlled the Lion's estates, and the word had spread like a malignancy. As a consequence of these rumors the de Leone cooperative experienced costly delays at the wholesalers' markets, and while the false rumors spread, their products had been boycotted. It had taken Marco's quick presence of mind to sift through the grossly inaccurate rumors and shrink them down to fact. When he had discovered the source of the lies, he whipped the man with his bare hands and marched him through the streets until he retracted his statements.

"If ever you do such a thing against the de Leone cooperative again, I'll reckon with you differently, you cretin," he had told the man, much to the dismay of his own bodyguards, Calo and Ciccio.

"You should have killed him, Excellency," they had counseled him. "One day he'll return and cause real harm. Like a cancer, you must excise him completely or you'll live to regret it."

"I've come to ask that bygones be bygones," said the beady-eyed man with a thin, hooked nose like a bird's beak.

Roberto placed a restraining hand on Guido's arm when he saw the outrage in his companion's dark eyes.

"Let's hear the man out, *amico.*"

Guido pulled in his horns and whispered, *"Faciemo le fica."* He thrust two fingers in a downward motion under the table in the gesture of *cornu.*

"Well, if it isn't the illustrious Don Tricario," said Roberto with outward amiability. He was certain the Don wouldn't detect the irony in his voice.

"Aloura, what do you say we bury the past?"

"Only if the past is dead," admonished Roberto. "If as

they say, all's fair in love and war, why not in business as well, eh?"

"That's what I admire," exclaimed the Don. "A fair man." He'd learned much from his years in New York's Little Italy.

"I hear His Excellency has taken a bride. Anyone we know?" asked the *mafioso*.

"How quickly news travels," said Roberto lightly. He raised his glass. *"Cienti anni."*

"Cienti anni," replied the Don, tasting the wine. He smacked his lips together and placed the glass on the table.

Amalfi made no move until Roberto kicked him under the table. *"Cienti anni,"* he muttered. *"A cazzi te,"* he added so only Roberto could hear.

Roberto nearly choked on his drink and quickly pulled out his handkerchief to catch the dribble on his chin. Unaware of the interplay between the other men, Don Tricario made his move.

"I've a proposition to make to you, Argento. How much money would it take to tempt you to leave the Villa de Leone?"

Guido sputtered in astonishment and glanced at Roberto. He saw him shrug his shoulders imperceptibly, raise an eyebrow, and purse his lips as if he were truly considering the matter. He shook his head as if the thought hadn't entered his mind, but he might not be closed to such a suggestion.

"You don't intend to work for another man all your life? Wouldn't you like some land of your own? A wife and a family, perhaps?" asked Don Tricario persuasively.

Guido Amalfi had learned his first lesson in mental gymnastics that day. Without uttering a word, Roberto conveyed his interest in what the *mafioso* proposed.

"May I speak freely?" The Don jerked his head toward Guido.

"Speak freely, by all means." Roberto snapped open his gold watch that played the Polonaise.

"Would 500 acres of land and enough money for a lifetime suit you?" The Don glanced at the tinkling watch in annoyance. Roberto pretended to be impressed. "You'll consider it?" Roberto pursed his lips and tilted his head, giving the impression that he might think about it. "Can I at least tell my people you're considering a deal?" Roberto shook his head apprehensively. "Ahhhh," the Don sat back in smug assurance. "Everyone has their price. You want more, is that it?"

Astounded by this dialogue, Guido Amalfi's peasant mind couldn't grasp its significance, but his peasant's instinct warned him. He didn't like this game and couldn't contain

137

his alarm. The contradictions in Roberto's behavior made no sense to him. No sense at all.

Don Tricario's premature thoughts of victory dazzled his imagination. *If I can snag this Jew bastard from de Leone's fold, I'll have won where all others have failed and become* numero uno *with the* capo *in Palermo.* If he could just convince this Jew, tempt him with enough money to ditch the Lion, he'd uproot the very core of the cooperative. He hadn't learned the ropes for nothing in New York. He'd show them they didn't know everything.

"You need more time? Is that it?"

Roberto nodded. He snapped the gold watch case shut, cutting off the music.

"Va biene. It's a pleasure to know such a *gallanuomo* as you," said the Don, lighting up a cigar. He puffed contentedly for several moments.

"Even if I'm a dirty *Jew bastard?"* asked Roberto mockingly.

The question struck home. Don Tricario had spread ugly remarks that Roberto's being a Jew was an abomination to the soil, to Sicily itself.

Don Tricario's face turned purple. His beady reptilian eyes darted around for some avenue of escape. He felt like a fly, baited and trapped by a spider. He no longer smiled. His transitions were evil and fascinating.

"So? What if you are a *Jew?"* The cunning, evil man was not without resourcefulness. "I got nothing against *Jews."*

"Really. I was told you're a *Jew-hater."*

"You see how I'm maligned? You see? I'm continuously misquoted and misunderstood. A man in my position becomes a target for vicious rumors. In truth, Signore Argento, I swear, the truth is . . . My limited knowledge of the Jew is that of a merchant, a moneylender, nothing as demeaning as a tiller of the soil."

This insignificant fly has a way with words. Listen to him twist words to suit his purpose. Roberto watched him with fascination.

"Now, I ask you? Does that make me a *hater of Jews?"*

"How does one answer such a question, Don Tricario? You have the profound ability to maneuver another through a sieve without his knowing it." He was sure the Don wouldn't understand him and he was right. "Misunderstandings do occur from time to time."

"Oh, they do. Yes, they do. I can see you've got plenty upstairs. It pays to use your head. I like that. I respect brains." He smiled cunningly, happy to have survived the situation unscathed. He turned to give Amalfi a long hard look, which at first had the overtones of polite indifference. "What do you do?"

Before he could open his mouth, Roberto interrupted.

"Amalfi is my right hand man." His eyes lit up mischievously. "Now if you really want a good man, one who knows the business, Amalfi is your man. I don't make a move without his approval."

Guido stared in stupefaction at this incredible exaggeration. The Don frowned, and perhaps for the first time he sensed the jocular deception.

"Perhaps you haven't understood me, Signore Argento." He cleared his throat and proceeded testily. "We want a good man . . . *not* to do his job. You."

"Ah," said Roberto as if he just got the message. "The man wants me *not* to do my job, Guido. All this time I felt certain he wanted me for my many accomplishments. I thought he needed a man like me to help his country and his people."

Don Tricario's smile evaporated. He grimaced. He wasn't sure what was happening. Roberto raised his arm, signaled a waiter, and ordered more drinks. He was beginning to enjoy the game.

Across the room, seated at another table with his companions, Cesare Ruffo had been watching. He recognized Roberto immediately, knew Guido Amalfi from the villa and felt disturbed that they should be on such apparently friendly terms with the likes of Don Tricario. When he could no longer contain his curiosity, Ruffo excused himself from his guests and walked toward Roberto's table.

"*Buona sera*, Roberto," said Ruffo. He nodded as Guido hastily scrambled to his feet out of respect.

"*Piacere*, Cesare," said Roberto warmly. "May I present Don Tricario?"

Ruffo nodded curtly and quickly ignored the *mafioso*.

The Don stood up and laid his cigar in an ash tray. "Perhaps we can complete our business at another time, Argento," he said visibly annoyed by Ruffo's presence. He left abruptly and returned to his own table.

"You must be crazy to be seen with that black-hearted *mafioso!* Don't you know he's more deadly than an asp? He's the most avaricious, cruel, and despotic *mafioso* in the province," exclaimed Cesare Ruffo. "I simply can't understand your consorting with such a man."

Guido took his seat again and for the first time in moments he began to breathe easily. Roberto laughed.

"We were just having a little fun."

"If it's fun you desire, Roberto, I can lead you to a place that will supply you with more than you can handle. One

139

does not have *fun* with a viper." Ruffo wiped the perspiration from his brow. "You gave me heart failure."

"He propositioned me. Tried to get me to leave Marco. For a time I pretended to go along with it. It was all in fun."

"Nothing is *fun* with Tricario. Don't be fooled by his innocent or condescending ways. The man is full of treachery and deceit. He is an ambitious man. *Molto ambizioso!*"

"*Aloura*, Cesare, *basta!* There was nothing more. Right Guido?"

"No, Roberto said nothing. It's the truth. He said nothing." Guido thought for a moment, then added, "It's what you didn't say that worries me." Roberto raised an inquisitive eyebrow. Cesare looked interested. "We Sicilians speak volumes by remaining silent, just as you did with Tricario," explained Guido. "What you *didn't* say, I am sure Tricario assumes you did say, even though your tongue was silent."

"But it was all a joke."

"You better discuss this in full with Marco," said Ruffo. "In the event of repercussions, he'd be prepared."

"*Managghia!* You'd think I committed murder."

"You misunderstand, *amico*. We're concerned over your safety. If word gets out you've consorted with a *mafioso* in these parts—and you can bet such a rumor will start—it will become unsafe, even dangerous for you in certain quarters. We in Messina do not condone *mafiosi* as they do in Palermo. You face a double danger from both sides."

Roberto shrugged off the preposterous suggestion.

"There's another matter, Roberto. Signorina Diamonte Contigulia came to the bank to withdraw her dowry money recently. Since the papers were in order, I didn't bother to notify Marco, didn't want to disturb him just before the wedding." He caught the look on Roberto's face and hastily added, "I trust I acted prudently." He glanced from one to the other and knew something was amiss.

"How much did she withdraw?" asked Roberto. When Ruffo told him five thousand he whistled at the amount.

"Is something wrong?" asked Cesare.

"Just make sure Marco hears of it when he returns. Did she say where she was going?" He knew the answer would be no. Where could Diamonte have gone? She knew no one, had never been off the *latifondo* except to visit Messina for a festival once.

Roberto excused himself, and he and Guido returned to the Villa de Leone, leaving a worried bank director to re-examine the release papers. Roberto didn't have to tell him he'd done the wrong thing in turning the money over to Diamonte. It was written all over his face.

140

Nearly two months passed before Roberto sensed that something was wrong at the villa. He noticed a marked degree of aloofness among many of the peasants and actual hostility from others. Before an obscure misunderstanding could turn into disaster, he called a meeting of the family heads and the dissenting peasants in their usual meeting room behind Roberto's office in the greenhouse. Guido Amalfi, Mario Massina, Alfredo Lamantia, Tomasso Micci, Gaetano Lamponi, and Benjiamino Paradiso sat at the head of the T-shaped table in the unpretentious room. The rest of the peasants sat at the foot of the table facing them.

"Listen," said Mario Massina in his usual straightforward manner. "I don't like why we're here, but you got something on your minds, so speak up."

Only silence greeted him. Sullen and withdrawn, the men stared at their hands, their cigars, their feet, anything rather than face him squarely.

"Well, speak up. Speak up." Massina, a man short on temper and impatient with men who wouldn't speak their minds, burned with indignation that Roberto should be subjected to such obvious lack of respect from men not worth his little toe. He slammed the table top loudly. "Goddammit! Speak! You try my patience. With so much work to do, you sit here playing deaf and dumb? Speak or I'll adjourn the meeting. Then if anyone has any bellyaching, he'll have to abide by my word."

"We know your way, Massina," said one of the peasants. "A good stiff fight that you always win. You're bigger than we are and can lick the shit out of us. But not this time." He nodded toward two retiring men who shuffled awkwardly toward the head table with documents in their hands. Tulio Raffa, a short, cocky man, and Nino Grasso, tall and slender with thoughtful and troubled features, approached Massina.

"We wish to terminate our leases," said Raffa boldly.

Roberto frowned as he stared out at the sea of hostile faces and leveled his eyes on the spokesman. Massina and the other titular heads stared at Raffa.

"You're on a probationary lease and you wish to terminate?" Massina roared at the utter absurdity of the idea. Then he asked soberly, "Why? What the hell's wrong with you?"

Raffa shrugged. "We all wish to terminate." The men nodded their heads in agreement.

The heads of the families remained impassive. Roberto grew perturbed, wondering what had brought this on. *Damn, if only Marco were here, this nonsense would have ended before it took root.* This situation demanded the Lion's presence. Sicilians never fully trusted foreigners and that's

141

precisely what he was to them, a foreigner. And a Jew at that, which worsened his position.

Mario Massina ran his fingers through his curly salt-and-pepper hair. He stood up and paced the area behind the head table, then leveled his gray eyes at Raffa. He was angry. "What's wrong? Does it hurt to see your children well fed, clothed, and healthy for the first time in your life? Can't you stand the clean, comfortable cottage that doesn't leak in the winter or grow unbearable in the summer? Does it offend your nostrils to live in a clean house instead of one that reeks of piss and shit, eh? Many of you are on probation. You're the last to join the cooperative but the first to lodge a complaint. Tell me, have you suddenly experienced too many luxuries?" He turned back to Raffa. "Have you forgotten who came to you in that filthy hovel when your children were starving and two had died of malaria and all of you were disease-ridden, with no clothing or food? Is this the thanks I get? You want to quit without giving me a reason. None of you even deserve to be heard if you want to know the truth. I regret that I even bothered to help you. Goddammit! I should have known better!"

Raffa's dark, moorish features jerked, and he shifted from one foot to the other in obvious embarrassment. "Our quarrel's not with you, Massina, so you can keep that acid tongue of yours in your mouth. It's with that *Judas* over there. Argento."

Roberto's blue eyes widened in astonishment. *Judas? What is this?* In all his years his loyalty had never been questioned. Why now, with Marco away?

"Judas?" Massina's powerful voice shook the rafters. "Judas?" He took a threatening step toward Raffa but was held back by Roberto. "Now, Goddammit, you've gone too far."

"Just a moment, Mario. The man's charged me with being a Judas. I believe I should be permitted to talk with him." Roberto leveled his cool eyes on Raffa.

"You called me Judas. I'm not sure why I've earned such a disgraceful name. But, for the sake of argument, let's assume you're right."

A low murmur escaped them, and a look of smugness crossed their lips. Didn't he just admit it? Hah!

"I didn't say you were right. Let's just pretend you're right. You are all God-fearing men. I know, because I see you going to church, confessing to Father Bonaventura, taking Communion each morning, and praying for the forgiveness of your sins. But you are unwilling to practice the teachings of Jesus Christ. You refuse to honor him, although you pretend you do so the world believes you are virtuous

142

men. Since I seem to have done something terrible, don't I at least deserve the right to answer your accusations?"

"Listen, leave Jesus Christ out of this. And God, too." They didn't understand Roberto's logic and muttered amongst themselves for a moment. Antonio Grasso finally stood up and spat the word, *"Mafioso! Mafioso, fittuso!"*

"What's that?" asked Roberto in astonishment. "You call me *mafioso?* His forehead creased in puzzlement. "But why?" He suddenly recalled Cesare Ruffo's words: *If word gets out you've consorted with a* mafioso *and you can bet such a rumor will start . . .*

It's what you didn't say that worries me, Guido Amalfi had told him.

As Roberto waved his hand in the air for silence, Lamantia suddenly recalled some stupid rumor he'd heard about Roberto in the markets of Messina. Because he'd believed none of it, he'd put the remarks out of his mind.

That day, Don Pollo had asked Lamantia what they intended doing now that Roberto had decided to leave the Villa de Leone.

"What devil's work are you spinning today?" asked Lamantia, paying him little heed.

"Then you don't really know?" asked the Don. .

"What the hell are you talking about, man?" asked Lamantia suddenly annoyed.

"Argento works for Don Tricario," he hissed confidentially.

"You're crazy!" Lamantia waved him off. "Crazy! That wouldn't happen in a million years. And if you'd clean out your hairy ears, I'll tell you something else. Signore Argento wouldn't waste his time shitting on a man like Tricario. *Mafiosi* aren't his style!" Lamantia had gone about his business leaving the red-faced produce broker chewing his cigar to shreds.

Lamantia had had no reason to mention the incident to Roberto or any of the family heads because he knew the remark was utterly absurd. A man didn't pursue the gossip of women. Now he regretted not having squelched the rumor before it festered. His thoughts were interrupted by the sound of Roberto's voice.

"Guido, will you tell these men just what happened that day at the *birreria* after we saw the *Marchessa* off?" he asked the amiable man.

In the flamboyant manner of a storyteller, Guido described his reaction to the nude paintings on the wall, and in so doing, provoked laughter and relaxed their anger. He followed this with a verbatim account of how Roberto had made a jackass of Tricario. "What else could that *schifoso*

143

do but try to save face by spreading false rumors about Roberto, eh?"

"Dammit to hell!" continued Amalfi. "I was one damn proud man that day. Roberto acted like a true Sicilian. And you call him a Judas?" Guido snorted his contempt. "This Jew has more balls than all of us put together."

After they heard the full story, the dissenting peasants squirmed at their blundering and were forced to laugh at their stupidity.

The six heads of the family did not laugh. They were relieved, but only for the present.

"Listen, Roberto," said Massina after the meeting. "This is one stinking situation. I don't like the looks of things. They sure managed to get our men stirred up. I wonder what the hell they're up to, these *mafiosi, schifosi,* eh?" He watched the complainers take their leave.

Roberto begged off. "Not now, *amico,* my head is full to bursting already. Let's talk later, eh? I wish to hell Marco was here. When did I say he'd be back?"

Massina shrugged. "A week, maybe? Two? I forget what you told me."

Roberto nodded and shrugged as if the matter held little importance. Inside it tore him in two. He glanced out through the greenhouse windows at the darkening sky and grabbing a jacket from a wooden peg on the wall, he went outside and began to walk along the inner perimeter of the estate. It could have been a stinging defeat. Thank God it wasn't.

It was brisker than usual. The winds chilled him now that winter approached. Soon the rains would come.

"The Lord is my God . . . No Harm Shall Befall Me . . ."

Why, now, suddenly, did he think of these words? It had been such a long time. A very long time.

The prospect of rains each year were constant reminders of that day a lifetime ago. A time he'd never forget.

BOOK TWO

14

"Kill the Jews!"

A rock came crashing through the candlemaker's window startling Jacob Silverman. But he seemed more anxious over the frantic screaming and wild shouting outside the small ghetto shop than the destruction inside. In the streets he saw Jews scampering in every direction, desperate in their search for cover.

The dimly lit lanterns hanging from rafters overhead swayed and the old tenement structure shuddered at the approaching sound of thunderous horse's hoofs on the cobblestones. Jacob Silverman's face turned the color of lead, his piercing blue eyes clouded in thought, and he suddenly grew enormously excited.

"The Cossacks!" He mouthed the words almost dreading to speak above a hoarse whisper. He thought about Sara, his wife, and of their two sons Simon and David, who would be returning soon from Rabbi Goldman's seminary.

"Kill the Jews!"

Would it never end? Jacob glanced outside into the dismal downpour of rain. Despite the torrential, wind-ravaged rain, they rode through the streets shouting their obscenities, screaming their hatreds, smashing windows, dragging every Jew they knew by sight into the street where they beat them savagely and without mercy, then left them in the gutter to die.

It all happened so fast. Before Jacob could move, the door to his candle shop was kicked open. Two fierce, black-haired Cossacks wearing crimson coats with golden braid and buttons grabbed the frail old man and hurled him out onto the street. His small gaunt body went flying from the tremendous thrust and his skull crashed against the hard cobblestones. Blood oozed from a cut at his temple and his startled open mouth. He gazed up at his attackers. Their thick beards, wet from the pouring rain, resembled curling black snakes, like a medusa.

They beat Jacob Silverman with their whips until no breath was left in his pain-wracked body. They mocked him with their coarse brutal manners and kicked at his head with rough mud-soaked boots. Then they strode away, their brutal eyes searching furtively for other Jews to persecute.

As Simon Silverman and his younger brother David neared the ghetto, they heard the commotion.

They instinctively fell back into the bleak alleyway which led to the open court across the street from their father's shop, and remained hidden until they felt it was safe. Simon ventured forth, followed by David, who clung to him as they skirted the edge of the ghetto. To reach the shop they'd have to cross the street now littered with dead and dying bodies.

"You stay, David, until I return for you." Simon knew immediately what had happened. Crouching down on all fours, he crept slowly over the dead bodies, filled with sickening terror. Suddenly, his eyes stared out at the body of his father. He was stricken with disbelief. Disregarding all precaution, he stood up and began to slowly walk to his father's side. He stared at his father's blood-soaked body, hypnotized by the immense power of death.

Why? Why this perpetual hatred for the Jews? When would it end? What had they done that was so terrible, so earthshakingly wrong that the universe refused to let them live?

Simon stood stone still, his eyes fixed on the incredibly grotesque figure of his father. He didn't see the Cossack advancing on horseback. Watching the scene, the warning cry froze on David's lips when he saw the rider coming at his brother with a raised saber in his outstretched arm. David heard nothing, saw nothing except the quenchless hatred in the Cossack's eyes, the mad glitter of white teeth, the uplifted arm holding the shimmering wet blade.

David stood transfixed with horror. One moment his brother Simon stood staring down at his father, the next, a headless body stood motionless, his severed neck spouting rivulets of crimson. Then the body toppled over like a felled tree and sprawled over his father's body.

The Cossack disappeared at the end of the street and the sound of his horse's hoofs faded in the distance. David moved in a trance toward the bodies of his father and brother. The rain beat down on the dead and on David. By the time he reached the decapitated body of his brother, he was in a state of shock, drained of all feeling. Clutched in his father's lifeless hand was a Star of David. He leaned down to pick it up when suddenly he heard a shrill scream pierce the air. He ran like a frightened hare into his father's shop and slammed the door behind him.

The place was a shambles. David crouched behind an overturned table shaking with terror. The place reeked of paraffin; a large vat had overturned and most of the wax had hardened on the floor. The boy peered cautiously about the darkened room. He heard a second scream, closer this

146

time, coming from the family living quarters at the rear of the shop. He crept forward, keeping in the shadows, and there behind a large packing crate he saw his mother.

Her naked body twisted and contorted as she valiantly fought off a leering Cossack. The brute raised a powerful fist and struck viciously at her. Her hands clawed at him. Scratching and pounding, she left a mass of bloody tracks across his craggy face.

"Jew bitch!" he cried hoarsely and clutched at his face.

David wasn't sure what the Russian intended, but seeing his mother without clothing shocked him into a cold sobriety. When the Cossack entered his mother and Sara Silverman screamed in agony, David picked up a large silver candlestick mold and swung it with all his force. It caught the man at the base of his skull. For an instant, the spindle-legged, bare-assed Cossack bolted upright with a startled look on his livid face, then he groaned and fell over in a dead weight over the woman's prostrate form.

David tried with all his might to dislodge the bulky form from his mother's body, calling, *"Mammila! Mammila!"*

Sara Silverman's agonized eyes flickered open in recognition. *"Dovilla,"* she whispered hoarsely. "Go. Run and save yourself. Find Rabbi Goldman, he'll help you." Blood trickled from her lips and her head sagged to one side.

"Mammila!" he cried. *"Mammila!"* He grew frenzied. Before young David Silverman could make a move, he felt a crushing blow at the side of his head. The room spun around and images rushed at him. Hate-filled Cossacks leered at him shouting, "Kill the Jew bastard! Kill him!" Then all was darkness.

When David regained consciousness, he felt the rains whipping at his nearly numb body. His blond curls clung to his head. From his position, hanging from his wrists from a hangman's scaffold, he gazed down and recognized the entrance to the ghetto. His body swayed like a reed as the rains and winds kept up their fury. How long have I been here? he wondered. The streets were deserted and it was nearly dark. His arms ached and felt torn from their sockets. Each movement, deliberate or accidental, tore into him like searing flame. He began to pray.

The Lord is My God . . . No Harm Shall Befall Me . . .

Once again he heard the savage cries of approaching horsemen, riding swiftly down the street coming toward him. Be still, he told himself. If they think I'm dead, they won't bother with me.

The triumphant Cossacks reined their horses and glanced contemptuously at the lad's body swaying in the rising winds. The half-naked young Jew's circumcision had been left exposed. "We'll just let him hang. Let them all see the lad and learn we'll not stop until we kill them all."

One bloodthirsty, vodka-soaked Cossack felt a sudden omnipotent surge of power and struck at David Silverman's body. The razor-sharp saber missed the boy's head by hairs, slashing through the rope. He fell to the cobblestones below like a dead weight.

David bit back an impulse to scream as agonizing flames of pain shot through his body. He stuffed his wrist into his mouth and bit down hard until blood spurted out. Only when he heard the horses move away did he take a deep breath. In the fall, he'd crushed his foot and ankle; the pain was so excruciating that he fell unconscious.

When he awakened, it was pitch dark and he saw only the shadowy forms of the dead still strewn about the deserted streets. His ankle and foot had swollen to twice their normal size and the pain throbbed unbearably. When he could, he crawled along the wet streets toward the window of a cellar, several yards away. He removed a shoe, broke the pane of glass, reached in and slid the bolt. Pushing in the window, he eased himself through the opening into the darkness. His scream was stifled when he fell onto a pile of stacked leather hides. The pains shot through his body and once more he lapsed into unconsciousness.

Hungry, cold, and filled with pain, he awakened and gazed about in an effort to orient himself. Shafts of light came in through the cellar window and he saw packing crates, fur pelts, and leather hides, bundled with baling straps. Everywhere fat, black rats crawled about in the darkness, leering at him. One moved close to his wrist, smelling fresh blood, and he shoved it from him in utter revulsion.

If he lay motionless, he could barely stand the pain. If he moved his leg slightly, the pain grew acute. He kept hoping for a miracle, that someone would find him and save him from this dungeon of death.

If I stay here, I'll starve to death.

The Lord is My God . . . No Harm Shall Befall Me . . .

David reached for the nearby furs and wrapped his wet, cold body in them. Hearing no noises from the street above, he reasoned that the Jews were staying well hidden until every murdering devil left. He had no way of knowing that three days had passed and that the Cossacks had left long ago to terrorize another Jewish ghetto in a nearby city.

"*The Lord is My God . . .*" said David as he swatted at the glassy-eyed rats who stared at him with an unnerving patience. Knowing they were hungrier than he was, he couldn't fall asleep again. Pains at the base of his spine spread out in tentacles of fire.

David vaguely recalled once seeing his father fix a splint for a stray dog that had been run over by a cart. His eyes searched the area for the makings of a splint. He found wooden stakes from a broken crate and with leather thongs from the baling, he proceeded to do as he'd seen his father do with the dog. He wrapped his ankle with the leather strips, until it felt firm. Then he placed the wood on either side of the bone and bound it with the narrow leather strings.

When he tried to stand up and found he still couldn't walk, he lay back dejected and filled with dismay. He thirsted for water and his stomach ached for food. For the next three days and nights, David chewed on the leather strips and for a time his thirst abated. As he chewed, he imagined that he ate the finest beef and boiled cabbage and soon his hunger pangs weren't as bad as they'd been the first few days.

By dawn of the seventh day, he began to hallucinate. He knew instinctively he'd have to do something or in the battle between himself and the rats, the rats would win. It was time for him to leave the cellar. Pain or no pain, it was time to move.

It took two hours for him to slide across the cellar and struggle up the rickety steps. Once at the top of the stairs he pushed against the door with all his might and was astonished to find himself inside Olinsky's haberdashery. It was a high-sounding name given to a simple shop that sold used clothing and other furnishings.

Crawling about the shop, he found suitable clothing and wrapped himself in an oversized overcoat. Pulling himself up against a wooden counter, he tried to stand on his one good leg, but the spasms in his lower back caused him to double over and wince painfully. *Oh Lord, please remove the pain. Please!* When he glanced up, his eyes rested on an umbrella stand containing an assortment of walking sticks. *That's what I need,* he told himself. He managed to slip one under his left arm and another under his right, then hunched over, putting his weight on them, he was able to move.

Mrs. Olinsky used to keep a cache of sweets somewhere. Where? Where could they be? He searched and located them, greedily shoving the hard sugar candy into his mouth, making a mental note to thank the Olinskys for their generosity at some future date. He found an open cash drawer with a few shekels. Grasping them in his fingers, he placed them in his coat pocket.

Moving out from behind the counter, the youth stumbled over the bodies of both, Mr. and Mrs. Olinsky, staring sightless at the ceiling, hands clasped together in death. Feeling

149

worse for having been an interloper, David removed the coins from his pocket, lay them on the counter with the candy, and hobbled out the door as quickly as he could.

Outside a steady drizzle poured from overcast skies. It was late, dark and dismal, and a forlorn feeling came over him. Across the deserted street, past the entrance to the Jewish ghetto, he saw a covered wagon. *Perhaps if I can hide in the wagon for tonight, I'll feel better in the morning. At least there'll be no rats to feast on me.* He huddled in a corner and pulled the thick blankets around him. He ached all over and the weakness returned.

The Lord is My God . . .

When David awoke, the sun was shining and he felt movement under him as the wagon bounced and bumped along. He peered out through the flap at the rear and was startled to see the greenest hills he'd ever seen. A sweet scent of clover and new-mown hay struck his nostrils and he inhaled deeply. The wagon had traveled many miles south of Warsaw. Weak from hunger and pain, he'd fallen in and out of consciousness several times. Three weeks later he awakened to find himself in a comfortable bed of down between clean sheets, so fresh and sweet he kept inhaling them and touching himself to make sure he was alive.

"*Leibling,* you're awake at last," said a robust, rosy-cheeked woman with enormous breasts and cheery blue eyes.

"Leopold!" she called to someone out the window. "Leopold, come quickly. The boy is awake."

"You had us so frightened, *leibling.* You haven't moved since the doctor came."

David smiled weakly. He didn't understand a word she said for she spoke Austrian. But he understood the love on her face and the softness of her voice. He asked her where he was.

She shook her head and shrugged at the language barrier, but left the room and returned with a steaming cup of broth.

"Food?" she asked. As she began to spoon-feed the greedy youth, she laughed and said, "Gently now, not too fast. You must sip it slowly."

David Silverman spent six of the best years of his life with the Austrian-Jewish couple who passed for gentiles in a country which hated Jews. Leopold and Anna Schiller owned the small farm they lived on and tried to exist in a frightening world which they couldn't always understand. From this wonderful couple, David learned much about animals, the soil, and the crops they grew. Fascinated with all forms of life, David watched the fruits of his labors as he helped Leopold till the soil and grow a variety of crops. He had his own room, a mansion to him, filled with books which Leopold brought him each time he went to the village.

They never asked him how he happened to be in the wagon, or how his leg was injured. When Leopold saw the ankle, he had removed the crude bindings and realizing the foot had been broken beyond his own ability to repair it, he simply made a sturdier cast for it and kept the boy off his feet until the injuries healed. Having knit improperly, it was obvious he'd always remain a cripple. At first it didn't bother David. Although it was cumbersome for him to move about —the ankle lacked elasticity and it sort of flopped as he walked—he ignored it for there was no one around to stare with curiosity. He learned to live with the pain.

The Schillers never mentioned the Star of David indelibly stamped on his left forearm. He saw no menorahs, no Chanukah candles for the holidays. Leopold wore no yarmulke. There was no Seder Torah for him to study and he found no mezuza to kiss at the door. Yet David knew Leopold was a Jew. He'd seen the man's circumcision once when they both went for a swim in the river bordering the farm. He never mentioned it.

The fact was David enjoyed living without the pressures of being a Jew. No one called him a *dirty Jew*. He heard no more terrifying cries. He didn't have to carry stones in his pocket as he did in Warsaw for fear he'd be accosted and would have to defend himself. More important he didn't have to live in a ghetto. During these years away from the Jewish traditions, David couldn't find any real reason to practice his faith again. What had his faith done except to bring him sad anguish and memories?

One day after his sixteenth birthday, Leopold's brother-in-law, Eli Poltacheck, stopped to visit the Schillers while en route to Italy where he intended to live as a writer.

Although he grieved to learn of the death of his sister, Leopold was delighted that Eli could at least realize a portion of his life's ambition. The family spent a wonderful week together recalling events in their childhood. Soon the day came for Eli to depart. He mentioned how pleased he'd be to have a lad like David accompany him to Italy, for he'd been struck by the lad's bright agile mind.

Anna Schiller exchanged conspiratorial glances with her husband and nudged him, "Leopold, speak up."

"Do you mean what you said about David? Would you take him with you?"

Knowing their love for the boy, Eli asked, "Is there some problem?"

151

Tears welled in Anna's eyes. "Several of the people in the village know the boy is a Jew. I never cautioned him to keep his arm covered. One day while he helped Leopold load supplies, he rolled his sleeves up in the heat and I am certain that Frau Mueller, that gossipy witch with Satan's tongue, who always has bad things to say about the Jews, saw the Star of David on his arm.

"One never knows about women like Frau Mueller," continued Anna Schiller in her thick Austrian accent. "Oiy, such hatred in her heart for the Jews. 'They'll take our homes from us. Our businesses,' she tells the people. 'They rob us blind. Their interest rates are usury.' I tell you, Eli, I envy your leaving like this. It is frightening for all of us who hide our religion."

"And you're worried now, Anná?" asked Eli.

"Yes. I want no trouble for the boy. He's suffered enough."

"Won't you miss him?"

"I would rather miss him and know he's alive than to mourn him because he's dead."

"Then it's settled. He comes with me."

They quickly packed his clothing and belongings, together with a large basket of homemade bread and relishes and sausages to eat on their long journey. And a bewildered David Silverman found himself saying farewell to the wonderful, loving family with whom he'd felt such peaceful security. He couldn't hide the hurt and dismay he felt when he thought they no longer wanted him, for they hadn't explained the reason they were willing to part from him.

"My boy," said Eli as they drove off toward Italy, "if we're going to spend some time together, it's best we begin with only truth between us." Eli told him why he'd been shuttled off to live with him.

"They loved me after all."

"More than if you were their own flesh and blood."

Lake Como with its surrounding snowcapped peaks and crisp dry air became their home. Eli leased a villa, hired an Italian couple to cook and clean for them, and in no time they both began speaking Italian like natives. The Italians had difficulty pronouncing Silverman and it came out Seel-vairmahn—a real tongue twister. When David told them the name Silver was Argento in Italian, they fared better, and he became Signore Argento. The name David was harsh to pronounce and somehow, no one recalls how, he found himself with the name Roberto, probably from his middle name Rabin. He gave up correcting anyone and soon the name stuck. He was Roberto Argento.

Five years passed in which Roberto became Eli's chief researcher. His phenomenal memory was a constant source of amazement to Eli. Once having read the material, Roberto seldom had to refer to it again.

Overnight Roberto's world was shattered by the unexpected illness and sudden death of his friend and benefactor, Eli Poltacheck. Since Eli hadn't bothered to make a will, the estate was tied up for many years until the probate courts could ascertain if there was a legal heir. Being a foreigner didn't simplify the situation.

Tearfully but efficiently, Roberto handled all funeral arrangements, remained at the villa until the lease expired, then left for Rome with his few worldly goods packed into one bag.

By sheer luck, on a bright sunny day in April, shortly after Easter, he strolled by the university and saw a sign in a bookstore window reading, *Clerk wanted*. The handsome, blue-eyed blond with a noticeable limp was hired on sight by the elderly Campanellas. They took to Roberto immediately and offered him room and board in the back studio, which he accepted at once. "We want to retire," they told him. "We expect a full accounting every three months. You can send the money to this address in Naples," they instructed him. "What's left over, above a certain amount, you keep as wages or a bonus. Run the shop as if it were your own. Our accountant will contact you to explain the details."

By this time Roberto spoke Italian without a trace of accent. Rome was exhilarating! He loved the people, found them warm, compassionate, and open. Having traveled some and having met many of Eli's literary friends, Roberto saw that people existed well enough without being driven by their religion. In Italy, Catholicism predominated, yet the Italian didn't permit it to be his motivating force. Roberto had come to agree with the more liberal that it was more fulfilling to keep God in your heart than on your coat sleeve. He drifted away from any one religious concept and became more universal in his theory of God.

Rome! Having read so much about it, he felt sure he knew it inside out. At last he was in the romantic Eternal City, and it was natural for Roberto to seek the companionship of the opposite sex. But because Italians were quite strict with their virginal daughters, he had little opportunity to meet available young girls his age. Except for the company of the whores at Madama Roulettini's which one paid for, an eligible young man had to be invited to social functions by friends or acquaintances of the family.

Once Roberto saw and became smitten by a beautiful

young woman, but when they were introduced, she stared horrified at his crippled foot and turned away from him, pouring her charms on some dolt standing nearby. When the same thing happened a second time, Roberto swore he wouldn't let it happen again. His lameness began to eat away at him like a rotting fungus, affecting him emotionally and mentally.

His feelings of inadequacy grew; he felt he was a socially unacceptable outcast. *Face it! Don't knock your head against the wall. You're a freak of nature!* He felt that all eyes were focused on his deformed ankle. *Well, fuck them! Fuck them all! Who needs them! Who has time for their petty intrigues and supercilious attitudes!* He became a recluse, sublimating his sexual drives by pouring his energies into reading.

Physicians had told him there'd be times when the pain in his foot would recur. When it grew unbearable one night at Madama Roulettini's, Roberto had his first encounter with a reliable friend—opium.

In her bordello on the Via Pompeii, Madama Roulettini catered to every taste and every size bank account. On this particular night, Roberto was especially vulnerable. He'd been rejected for the second time, and in his depression he'd done a foolish thing. At home, he'd taken a fireplace poker and struck at the cause of his hatred, his deformed ankle. Time and again he struck in a mad, blind fury. When his passion abated, the pain in his foot grew unbearable. With no pharmacies open, he hailed a carriage and sought out the Madame.

"I guarantee, Roberto, it will take away all the aches and pains as even the best of women can't do," said the dark-haired, elegantly dressed woman, who looked more like a mother than a madam, as she handed him a pipe.

He lay back, inhaling the fumes, and prayed for some magic balm to cure his ailments. Nothing happened.

"Give it time, my sweet. Give it time," said the Madame as she left him to his world of dreams.

First came the feeling of floating and weightlessness. His world expanded and took on new dimensions. He felt exultant, as if he'd escaped the shackles of earthly entrapments. Whether they were dreams, fantasies, or actual expansions of his consciousness, Roberto found momentary solace in his opium adventures. For a time they satisfied him and enabled him to live normally. His only objection to the opium pipe was that he had to return to the world of reality too often.

Almost a year after his arrival in Rome, Roberto met Marco de Leone. They appraised each other from a distance

154

at first, then their communication was instantaneous, as mysterious as it was unmistakable. Marco de Leone entered the bookstore and immediately stood apart from the rest of the students who frequented the shop.

Rome was at the height of its rainy season on the day Marco first came into the shop, flung off his rain cape, and wiped the raindrops from his face. When he saw the crowded tables, his bright eyes dimmed in annoyance. He waved to a few people, nodded at others, and found a place at a corner table for his books. As he glanced about for a place to hang his dripping cape, Roberto walked toward him.

"I am Roberto Argento. May I take that for you?" he offered pleasantly.

A pleased expression crossed Marco's face as he studied the fair-haired man with inordinately blue eyes. His expression caught Marco's eye and he liked him right away.

"Hello, de Leone! Come join us," called one of the students from across the room. "We want your opinion on the Sicilian situation. We're going hot and heavy today."

Marco wagged a finger and laughed. "Not today, *amici*. I regret this day must be spent entirely on the elusive Etruscans. *Il professore* refused to declare a moratorium. Tomorrow he puts our brains to the test. Since I must speak on their behalf tomorrow, today I must study them."

"Etruscans?" asked Roberto.

"*Si*. You know about the Etruscans?" Marco's eyes lit up hopefully.

"It's possible. We have many books on the subject. What do you need? The culture? The people? The politics? Arts and crafts? What?"

Marco wagged a finger again. "No. No books. What do *you* know about Etruria, the Etruscans and their times?"

Roberto glanced at him through tilted eyes. "That's a tall order, too broad a subject to explain in just moments. An extemporaneous speech on Etruria would take all day unless you ask specific questions . . ."

"Fair enough," smiled Marco, demonstrating a willingness to sit back and listen.

That's how their relationship began. For nearly five hours, interrupted only by an occasional sale or a question from a customer, Roberto expounded on the Etruscans. He spoke of the Greek influence, both culturally and politically, and of how Etruscan kings ruled Rome in the sixth and seventh centuries B.C. He explained how the Etruscans colonized southern Italy and how they incorporated Helenistic influence of Greek culture into their own. "We owe a modified

155

version of the Linear B script to the Etruscans. Rome later modified it and the world uses it today," said Roberto.

Marco was both fascinated and amused by the bright young man. He learned more from listening to Roberto than if he had cracked the books all night. More than once Marco showed his astonishment.

"Have you ever thought about teaching?" he asked.

Roberto laughed. "I couldn't put up with the gross stupidity of an uninspired student. If he looked at me and drew a blank after I lectured to him, I'd lose all patience."

"Well, *amico*," said Marco. "You certainly seem to know your Etruscans. Tell me, what other subjects are your specialty?"

Roberto shrugged self-consciously. "Would you like some coffee?"

"Yes. As a matter of fact, I'd like that very much." He paused. "I don't know your last name."

"Argento. Roberto Argento."

"Marco de Leone, at your service." He bowed curtly, like royalty.

"Piacere."

"No, Roberto. The pleasure is all mine." He grew thoughtful for a moment. "Roberto Argento . . ." He mused over the name. "Are you Italian?"

"No. Polish. When I arrived in Italy . . ." He told him the story of how he acquired his new name.

"I'd call that expeditious of my people, wouldn't you?"

Roberto laughed. He liked Marco without reservation.

Over coffee, he told Marco about the research he'd done for Eli and how much he had enjoyed the work. Marco noticed the limp as Roberto walked about the shop closing it after the last customer left. He said nothing about it. But he politely listened as Roberto told him a few things about himself.

"You shouldn't make light of such talents," said Marco. "To retain information as you do, you could sit in command of your world."

"Plenty of people retain what they learn."

"Be modest if you will. You've a talent that should be put to good use. What do you plan to do with yourself?"

"I don't understand."

"Your life. Surely you don't plan to work in a bookstore all your life. You must have other plans?"

"Not presently."

"Well, *amico*, you will. You will." Marco finished his coffee and stood up. "I have to leave now. Remember? The Etruscans."

"Ah, yes, the Etruscans," grinned Roberto. "Tonight you study."

They both laughed as they walked to the door.

"Thank you again for the coffee and the information. I'll let you know how I fare on the examination."

He gave Marco his rain cape. *"Ciào, amico."*

"Ciào."

He noticed two burly men step out from the building and fall into step alongside Marco when he left. For a moment he was tempted to call out and warn him, but Marco seemed to know the fierce-looking men. He shrugged and changed his mind. He liked Marco and for the first time since he arrived in Rome, he felt stimulated by a conversation.

Two weeks passed before Marco came to the shop again, and when he did he brought a small package and thrust it at Roberto.

"Open it, Roberto. It's for you."

He opened a small white card embossed with the Seal of the Royal Lion first. Written across it in Marco's bold script were the words: "In consideration of your splendid services and your infinite knowledge of the Etruscans." It was signed Marco. He stared at the exquisite, gold pocket watch with a lion's head encrusted on the cover, which, when opened, played Chopin's *Polonaise*.

Roberto was speechless. "But I . . ."

"Thanks to you, *Il professore* was startled by the paper I turned in." He glanced about the shop. "You're busy I see. I wanted to pick your brains on agronomy."

Roberto grew serious. "What phases? Soil depletion? Crop rotation? Irrigation? Seeding? What?"

Marco turned to him stunned. "I don't believe it." He tossed his books on the table. *"Managghia!* You're incredible! Absolutely incredible!"

Whenever Marco had free time, he and Roberto went sightseeing in the art galleries, the museums, wherever they could go to saturate themselves with Rome's amazing history. They viewed the spectacular works of the Great Masters in awed silence. It became difficult for Roberto not to notice the constancy of the two bodyguards who always followed wherever they went. Marco didn't bring up the subject so Roberto refrained from mentioning them.

One month later, a fiery political debate took place among the students gathered in the bookshop. The discussion centered around Risorgimento and Garibaldi, the hero who unified Italy and Sicily. Marco had entered unnoticed, paused to listen, then shaking his head in mild amusement over their idealistic rage, he moved toward Roberto.

"They're too involved for my blood today. Do you have any coffee brewing?"

Before Roberto could reply, the room became suddenly silent. It was as if a dark cloud had passed over the room. Felipe Santiago, a young Spaniard and once a promising student, had entered the shop, obviously drunk. In recent months a drastic change had taken place in Felipe. He drank heavily and had alienated friends and acquaintances by appealing too often for loans against his monthly allowance. It became obvious to both Roberto and Marco that the other students ignored him, averting their heads as if he didn't exist.

"Edoardo?" Felipe's bleary, red-veined eyes turned in the direction of a slim youth whom he'd befriended in the past. He leaned over and whispered in his ear.

Edoardo shook his head, removed Felipe's hand from his shoulder, stacked his books, and stalked out of the shop.

"What's wrong?" asked Felipe slurring his words. "Now that Felipe is broke, you won't talk with me? When Felipe had money in his purse, he was friend to all. Now, *va futta*, eh?" He weaved back and forth on his heels and turned his pockets inside out. He turned to another friend. "Eh, Martino! Can you spare a few *scudi?*"

Martino followed Edoardo out the door. In a flash of rage, Felipe grabbed the student nearest him and swung a powerful, but reckless blow, unaware that he'd singled out the university's most athletic young man. The athlete responded with a blow that sent Felipe sailing across the room.

Unhappy with the odds as others came toward Felipe, Marco jumped into the melee, shouting, "Leave him alone!" Another student struck out blindly and caught Marco on the side of the head.

Instantly, Marco's two bodyguards moved in, pinning down one student and holding two others. The other students scrambled toward the entrance. Many others had congregated in front of the large window and stood gawking inside at the action, all flushed with excitement. Everything happened so fast.

Roberto felt certain the two bodyguards would have killed the youths if Marco hadn't intervened.

"*Basta!*" he shouted, oblivious of his quickly swelling eye and puffy lip. "All right, my friends, the shop is closed for the day," said Marco. He helped one of the scrappers to his feet. "No hard feelings, eh? *Va biene?*" He escorted the last of them out of the shop, shut the door, and bolted it. He signaled his men to take Felipe into the back room.

"I hope you don't mind, Roberto, if we use your apartment." He tossed a stack of lira on the counter. "This should compensate you for the loss of business."

"That's not necessary. Please follow me." He led the way to his living quarters.

They plied Felipe with hot black coffee and when that didn't help, Marco steered him over to the balcony overlooking the rear court and dumped a pitcher of water over his head. "I think the plants need watering, eh, Roberto?" he grinned.

Startled, Felipe blinked his eyes and shook himself. Marco handed him a towel, and the two stood on the balcony talking in hushed tones. Roberto couldn't hear them, but he saw Marco thrust a fat stack of bills into Felipe's pocket. He patted the Spaniard's back smartly and walked him to the front entrance.

When Marco returned, he apologized for Felipe's behavior. "Santiago's going through a bad time, a terrible tragedy. He'll be all right once he stops feeling self-pity."

The bodyguards attended to Marco as if he were royalty. Roberto wondered about Marco. Who was he? Why were these men constantly at his side? After they helped him into his jacket and overcoat, Marco felt his bruised eye only because the other two fussed over it.

"I'm fine," he assured them.

"Was it wise to give Felipe so much money, Marco?" asked Roberto. "He'll only go out and get drunker."

"*Amico*," said Marco tolerantly, "there comes a time in a man's life, if tragedy strikes, he's entitled to get drunk and feel self-pity until he hits rock bottom. When he sinks that low, a good man will find himself. Then he'll be his own man forever. No one will ever own such a man. Felipe will be fine, you'll see." He paused. "Oh, by the way *amico*, since you'll be seeing much more of them, may I present Calo La Bolla and Ciccio Pontiface." He turned to his men. "This is my dear friend, Roberto Argento, of whom I've spoken so often."

The men nodded politely and stood as silent as sentries; the only movement was in their active, all-seeing, all-knowing, non-committal eyes.

The last semester of school, Marco seemed detached and unduly quiet. He took Roberto to Rudolpho's on the Via Condote where many business men and politicians dined.

"What do you know about the *mafia*, Roberto? Perhaps I should call them, the Honored Brotherhood."

"Political corruption? Peasant oppression? Land Appropriation? What? What do you want to know?"

Marco's astonishment bloomed into good-natured laughter.

"Tell me, how the hell do you know so much? I don't believe it. You are an enigma."

"I've told you. I've little else to do but read."

Marco nodded absently. "I'm waiting . . ."

Roberto glanced questioningly at him. "About the *mafia?* Are you serious?"

"I'm serious."

"Are you personally interested or is this an assignment?"

"Why? Would it color your answers?"

"No."

"Well then?"

"I'm against any form of oppression," began Roberto. "As a young boy I lived with it. From the beginning of time, my people have been oppressed. My parents were killed by such men. I'm a Jew, Marco. Didn't you know?"

"I never gave it much thought," he replied. "A man's religion isn't the making of a man. What he feels or thinks in his heart, his reaction to his fellow man—these are important. All else is incidental. You don't happen to have a brilliant mind and a good heart because you're a Jew."

"I'm not sure I agree with you on that point. The Jews have been a hated people, a persecuted race for so many years. Perhaps because of this hatred and tyranny, Jews have evolved into a people who had to develop their minds. Because we've never been accepted, we try for achievements the ordinary man has no reason to pursue."

"But why? Why haven't they been accepted?"

Roberto no longer smiled. "I really don't know. Being born a Jew means living in an entirely different world than yours. One you couldn't hope to understand."

"Try me. I'm a good listener. The Jewish problem has intrigued me for years. When you take into account the countless Christians who were persecuted by the Romans and so many others who refused to allow them to worship as they chose, you wonder how they managed to survive without the necessity of clinging together in ghettos. You wonder why the Jews haven't managed this same acceptance you talk about—the way other persecuted people have done through the ages."

"The world won't allow it, it seems."

"That's no answer. I had hoped for deeper insight. Does it bother you, being a Jew?"

"Why do you ask?"

"I detect a slight hostility in you, my friend. Perhaps only a surface hostility, nevertheless it's there. I've seen it often enough."

"It's not because I'm a Jew," said Roberto evenly. He knew what Marco was driving at.

160

"Then why? Because you're a *cripple?*"

For an instant Roberto paled, then he flushed with color. "I wasn't aware I wore my feeling on my face," he said with a trace of bitterness. "I'll have to do something about that."

"What's wrong with your leg?" asked Marco, filled with concern. "You never speak about it, never mentioned it in all the time I've known you. Don't you think it's best to get your hostilities out in the open where they can do you no harm?"

"Will you be returning to your home after graduation? Or will you settle here in Rome?" asked Roberto, pointedly changing the subject.

"Were you born with a faulty leg?" persisted Marco.

"No."

"Then, there's hope?"

"No. I think not."

"You've looked into the matter with specialists?"

"I tried one or two, years ago. It's too late now."

"See this man," said Marco, scribbling on a lion crested card. "Tell him I sent you. There will be no fee."

"I can't impose upon you for such a service. No. Really."

"You're not imposing. I've known you some three years now. Soon I'll be returning to my native Sicily and I ask you to return with me. You can be of great use to me, Roberto, and I can be of use to you." Marco smiled. "Besides you'll have no one to pick your brains if you stay here in Rome."

Roberto was astonished. He shoved his veal *piccante* aside and gazed at his friend. "What would I do there?"

"On the *latifondo?* I've already decided. You'll be my chief agronomist."

"Your what?" Roberto was stupified. "I know very little about . . ."

"You know plenty."

"On the *latifondo,*" said Roberto flatly. He shook his head. "No."

"On the *latifondo*—yes," repeated Marco assuredly.

"All right, so I grew a few plants once and crossbred them and they thrived. That doesn't make me an expert."

"That's true."

"What then?"

"You'll learn as I'll learn. Look, *amico,* you're talking to a man who knows you. I've talked with you long enough to know that in your head is stored more information than any ten scholars collectively. You may not be formally schooled in agronomy, but I'd wager a small fortune on your ability to experiment, with the proper tools at your disposal. With your brain, you're bound to come up with amazing ideas. Perhaps, though, you might think such a profession is a boring one? Well, I dare say it isn't. When you told me some of the happiest years of your life were spent with that nice couple you lived with and that you enjoyed working with the soil, well, I just thought you'd be the most qualified man. It takes love to nurture the soil. So? What do you say? I'll more than compensate you for your efforts. I've a special feeling about you. When I put my faith in a man, I'm never wrong." Marco paused. "Am I going too fast for you?"

"Too fast?" Roberto laughed. "Your mind's like a bullet— swift and sure."

"Forgive me. *Managghia!* You don't even know who I am. What I am. It was presumptuous of me to assume that on the basis of a friendship, I could change the course of your life."

"I wasn't thinking that."

"Allow me to finish." Marco lit a small black cigar and puffed on it thoughtfully as a waiter freshened their coffee.

"I doubt I've spoken to you about my personal life, away from Rome, that is. As a rule, I don't talk about myself. You've never asked me about Calo and Ciccio, though I'm sure you've wondered." He drew himself up regally and his demeanor changed. "I'm Marco de Leone, son of Fiorenzo de Leone, the Royal Lion of Sicily."

"And I am David Rabin Yosell Silverman, son of Jacob and Anna Silverman of the *not* so royal order of candlemakers of Poland, alias, Roberto Argento of Rome."

Marco burst out laughing, relaxed somewhat, and filled with a good-natured humor. "Was I so pompous?"

"Worse."

"You never heard of me?"

"Sorry, Marco. If you come from a family of lions, one would never know. Your disguise is perfect. If you hadn't told me, I'd swear you are human."

They both laughed heartily.

"Look, I'll give you a few weeks to decide. I can see I won't be able to talk seriously with you until we get to the villa. Please understand, any time after you arrive at the villa and decide it's not to your liking, you'll be free to leave. But I warn you, I'll work you until you drop. I'll never stop picking your brains. I'll demand more of you than you think you can give. I have a dream, *amico,* and I'll need you to make it come alive."

"How much time will I have?" asked Roberto. He opened the lid of his gold watch and listened to the *Polonaise.*

"We leave in three weeks."

"When do you want my answer?"

"As soon as possible."

162

"I'll have to contact my employers to make sure they have a replacement."

"Then you'll come?"

"*Sì*. I'll come." Roberto closed the lid and slipped the watch into his vest pocket. "With such a challenge, how could I refuse?"

"*Bravo*, Roberto! *Bravo!*"

The next day Marco came to the bookstore. Calo and Ciccio took their usual positions at the front of the shop.

"Don't say one word, Roberto. We have to talk. You must be serious with me. Yesterday I got off the track."

"I understand, *El Leone*."

"How do you know that?" Marco's eyes turned smokey and he seemed suddenly defensive.

"You told me yesterday. Remember?"

Marco relaxed. "Yes, I recall. Now yesterday we talked of the *mafia*. It's important you know what you're getting into before you make your decision to return with me."

Marco told him about his family and their hatred of the *mafia*. He explained what it would be like living on the *latifondo*, the dangers posed by the bandits and the *mafiosi*. He told him of his plans for Sicily and his people, and how life had exacted such a terrible toll on three generations of de Leones in their fight against the oppressors, how his father and mother suffered at the hands of the Honored Brotherhood. He held nothing back.

"So, you see, Roberto, I couldn't ask you to join me in the life of uncertainty that's become my inheritance. I can't let you give up your life here, letting you think that life in Sicily would be as gay as life in Rome. You've suffered too much in your young life to be inflicted with any more tragedies."

Roberto now realized the affinity between them—two men from different backgrounds, both of whom suffered tremendous losses, endured physical hardships, and mental sufferings. But where Roberto had no desire to fight back at the oppressors of his people, Marco was strongly motivated to fight back, and would employ every means at his disposal to prevent the *mafiosi* from controlling his people and his country.

"My tactics are not to fight the *mafiosi* in open warfare. My campaign will be defensive. Within the well-guarded feudal fortress, I intend to form a cooperative farming venture. Handpicked people, banded together with the sole purpose of elevating themselves from oppression, will become a free people who'll fight feudal injustices with every breath in their bodies instead of perpetuating a tradition of passive resistance. When our intentions are discovered, and

163

as soon as we show progress, it's quite likely we'll come under attack—physical attack!"

Roberto listened with rapt attention and marveled that one man was powerful enough to even contemplate such a project.

"No one could be more barbarous than the Cossacks."

Marco's troubled eyes darted quickly to Roberto's cool and calm blue eyes. *Tu si pazzu, amico.* If you accompany me to Sicily, you're crazy."

"No more than you for going."

"You crazy bastard! Do you realize what you're asking for? You'll never know from day to day when they'll send their terrorists to maim and kill. The *mafiosi* are despicable, satanical, marauding killers, who can kill with little or no provocation, totally without conscience."

"If they're good enough for you, it's not fair to deny me the same pleasures."

"Will you be serious for a moment?"

"I've never been more serious. Look, you were right. I do have an active mind, perhaps too active to be confined in a bookshop all my life. Since Destiny brought us together, I've had a different feeling about life, even about myself. Yesterday you told me what you thought about me. You held a mirror up and I saw myself for the first time through another's eyes. I saw a worthy human being who might have something to contribute, somewhere, somehow, to this life of ours. A few moments ago, you mentioned your plans for your country and your people. You gave me the idea that I can contribute something, that I could be a part of those plans. Somehow, Destiny has moved me about in this world for some purpose. Who can tell? It doesn't matter that your people are not my people. What's important is to help make our world a better place. Who knows? Perhaps in another hundred years, what little effort I may have expended might indirectly prevent some of my people from being persecuted. Good seeds germinate in strange places, and the results can be miraculous. If you want me, I'll go to your country with you."

"Yes, but you must know the dark side of the offer."

"Surely you don't expect a bandit raid the day we arrive?"

"Pray it *never* happens."

"We leave three weeks from yesterday? I'll be ready."

"Be sure you have everything together and my men will make sure they get aboard the *Marchessa.*"

"The *Marchessa?*"

"My cruiser."

"You never mentioned you had a cruiser."

"You never asked, *amico*." Marco grinned amiably.

Whatever reservations the young Jew may have had about their agreement melted in the fraternal handshake, hug, and welcome which the Royal Lion of Sicily gave him. Future generations and an entire nation would feel the consequences of this alliance. It would create fury and havoc in Senate halls, stir up greed, jealousy, and vendetta in the hearts and minds of Mafia-feudalists. It would raise private armies, destroy lives and properties, and leave a trail of blood from one end of the island to the other. And finally, it would culminate in the elevation of an obscure *mafia* aspirant into one of the greatest feudal overlords the nation ever produced.

Fifteen years passed swiftly and without incident despite Marco's emphatic warnings. Marco had become a Senator, and when the Senate was in session, commuted back and forth to Rome and took a residence there. Land reforms passed through his diligent efforts forged a semblance of peace between *latifondisti* and peasants in the east. In the west, slothful land barons continued to view the Lion's efforts with disdain, and prophesied doom for his progressive cooperative despite rumors of his success. They continued to borrow money promiscuously and indulge in extravagances, refusing to give up their selfish practices. Living the life of absentee landlords, they mortgaged their lands to the hilt to pay for their caprices. In so doing, they formed an alliance with the *mafiosi* who grew more sophisticated, more knowledgeable, and shrewder with money and properties. They set up complicated marriage contracts, which included sugar-sweet cash dowries, to entice the nobility to overlook the illiteracy of their backward daughters and accept them in marriage. The earthy young women made fantastic bed partners, and with a little tutoring, became fairly presentable in a declining society. Because the nobility sought only to perpetuate their stagnant, antiquated prejudices, they enabled the new breed of *mafiosi* to gain a foothold and form a rising middle class of *gallantuomi* who slowly eased the nobles off their lands. In gaining control of the precious lands, they got what they were after—power.

Roberto Argento, totally engrossed in problems of the soil, faced the centuries-old problem of uncultivated lands. He worked untiringly and made giant strides in the field of agronomy. While social changes were brought about in the west, the House of de Leone continued to prosper. No lands ran fallow. Abundant crops were produced. Young men of the cooperative who showed promise were sent north to school on scholarships provided by the Lion and his agronomist. The original twenty-six families had swollen to fifty-three. Signora Amalfi set up a small schoolroom in which the young children were taught to read and write.

The de Leone *latifondo* flourished, and it became known throughout the province and most of the island that Roberto Argento, a Jew, born with green fingers and a genius with the soil, had turned the de Leone lands into the most fertile in all Sicily.

Yes, thought Roberto, life had been good to him, considering his early beginnings. So far he had outwitted Destiny and avoided the fate usually meted out to a Jew in his time.

One evening, just before Easter week Marco and Roberto were sitting out on the portico. Spring had bloomed and love was in the air. Young lovers strolled side by side with chaperones trying to keep pace with them. Marco considered the fact that Roberto hadn't taken a wife.

"You should be married, living a normal life and raising a family," he told his agronomist.

"Are you trying to convince me or yourself?"

"It's different with me. I have a destiny to fulfill. How could I subject any woman to the uncertain world in which I live?"

"Marriage isn't for me, Marco. I couldn't bear to have the woman I might love shrink from me when she sees the leg I'm forced to carry around."

"The *right* woman would never shrink from you, no matter what happened."

Marco recalled what the medical specialist had told him about Roberto's leg. "It can never be mended to heal properly. In a few years, medical advances might change things, but right now surgery would be a waste of time. It would just cause more pain and suffering. Let your friend remain on narcotics if it eases the pain. Of course it would be best for him to avoid them entirely. They only serve as a mental crutch anyway." Marco had never discussed the physician's words with Roberto, but, whenever he saw the loneliness within the clear blue eyes of his friend, he'd recall these words.

"You shouldn't have to live as I do, Roberto. I'm used to the solitude which a leader of men must endure."

On this night, Roberto opened up and poured his heart out to Marco about his miserable and unhappy experiences with women.

"Why allow another's fear to destroy your life," said Marco. "You must be lenient toward these people who've

166

hurt you. People discovering unfamiliar things that they don't understand react in fear. And that fear forces them to overcompensate by bullying or ridiculing others. Fear has many faces. It can make a man withdraw from life and become a defeated soul without hope.

"A physical handicap isn't the worst thing that can befall a man, Roberto. You have a great mind. A brilliant mind. One that sets you apart from all other men. Put your gifts to use. Don't concentrate on the depleted minds of lesser men."

Little did Marco know that these same words would be spoken to him at a future date, when his despair became greater than Roberto's.

15

Marco de Leone paced the deserted Messina waterfront peering about the darkness with increasing annoyance. Why hadn't someone met the *Marchessa?* His instructions to Roberto had been explicit as to the time of their arrival. Now, with Ciccio and Mariolina, he waited for Calo to find a carriage to transport them to the villa.

Disturbed by the fact that his wife had grown weaker and paler as the days passed, Marco had cut the honeymoon short. His grave concern over her mysterious malady only increased his anxiety and shortened his temper. He glanced up in relief at the sound of wheels and horses' hooves clacking against the cobblestoned streets.

Wrapped in a fur robe, Mariolina sat back in the carriage, looking exceedingly frail. She lay her head on Marco's shoulder as soon as he entered the coach. The carriage moved off into the night with Calo and Ciccio riding shotgun. They said nothing, but they didn't like the looks of things. What kind of a Christmas was this going to be, eh? Roberto, Massina, or Amalfi should have met them. Someone at least.

An hour later, the lathered horses arrived at the villa. The estate was in total darkness. Marco glanced at his watch. It was 10 P.M. It's not *that* late, he thought. Calo and Ciccio had already jumped off the coach. Guns gripped firmly in their hands, they advanced cautiously toward the entrance.

The wind swept through the trees, swaying leaves and bending branches. It shook the carriage and Mariolina awakened.

"Are we home yet?" she asked sleepily.

"Yes, *cara mia*. I didn't wish to awaken you, you were resting so comfortably." He breathed easier when he saw

Calo and Ciccio returning to the carriage. Marco silently searched their eyes. Calo nodded, indicating all was well.

"It's good to be home," said the new Marchessa de Leone.

"Yes, dearest, it's good," said Marco, helping her from the coach.

Lights went on. The huge portals opened and standing there en masse with warm welcomes on their lips were Roberto, Guido Amalfi, Mario Massina, Micci, Lamponi, and all the heads of the families with their wives, shouting, *"Benvenuto! Benvenuto al casa!* Welcome to the newlyweds! Welcome home!" Musicians struck a chord, and the foyer filled with gay music and a sea of happy faces.

Roberto and Marco embraced warmly. Noticing that the Lion heaved a sigh of relief, Roberto searched his face critically and said, "How good to see you, *amico!"*

"We've both missed you dreadfully," said Mariolina, embracing him warmly.

"Not as much as I missed you both," replied Roberto, concerned by the excessive paleness of her face. *Perhaps they are both tired,* he told himself.

Mariolina slipped out of her traveling coat and hat and smoothed her hair into place. "Dearest, I can't leave them now." She handed her things to Gina and began to circulate among the guests.

"Is everything all right?" asked Roberto, noting the concern in Marco's eyes. "She's been so tired lately. I don't know what's wrong. It's like watching a rose fade before your eyes." He had a sudden thought. "Did a letter come for me from Milano? From a Dottore Simoni?"

"Yes. As a matter of fact, it did. Shall I get it for you?"

"No. I'll read it after she goes to bed. Let's not keep her up too long."

"I understand," said Roberto.

Suddenly, their conversation was interrupted by a shrill scream. The music stopped. The dancing halted abruptly and all heads turned in the direction of Mariolina de Leone. The young bride had crossed the foyer to close the front doors which she thought had been forced open by a gust of wind. Rooted to the spot, she stared out the door in horror. Marco and Roberto rushed to her side as she fell faint. Holding her tightly in his arms, Marco glanced over her shoulder and saw the decapitated head of his bank manager, Cesare Ruffo, impaled on the door with a saber. His swollen eyes protruded in their sockets, staring sightless into the night.

Later, the men gathered solemnly in Marco's study.

"Why Cesare Ruffo of all people?" asked Marco.

"You remember, Roberto?" asked Guido Amalfi ruefully.

"It was Signore Ruffo who interrupted Don Tricario that night at the *birreria*. Perhaps he blamed Signore Ruffo when you failed to get in touch with him."

Marco glanced inquiringly at Roberto. Very quickly Roberto filled Marco in on his encounter with the Don and what happened subsequently, including his confrontation with the *contadini*.

Marco shook his head. "Don't concern yourself in that respect. There's more to it than that. The *mafiosi* who killed my wife's father and burned her estate have been apprehended and jailed for their fraudulent land appropriation. Their arrest was initiated by my own men in Rome."

"Ah," said Roberto excitedly. "Then some action was taken after all?"

The men sipped their coffee in silence.

"They just selected Cesare Ruffo to get back at me in some way. That has to be it."

A knock at the door interrupted them. It was Sara Amalfi. "Could I please speak with my husband," she asked. Guido excused himself and stepped out into the corridor. Before she could speak, Calo and Ciccio burst through the front door. Calo carried the body of the nine-year-old son of Emilio Graziano in his arms.

Guido and his wife stared as the two men strode past them. Sara gasped and held her hand over her mouth to stifle a scream. Guido fell into step behind the bodyguards.

"Listen to me, Guido," began his wife, pulling at his arm. "Listen . . ."

"No, I must see what happened." He tried to pull away from her grasping arms.

"That's why I came. Listen!"

He turned to her questioningly.

"The baby heifers have been slain. Most of the livestock has been killed off . . ." She grew hysterical.

Guido reached out to console her. "Go," he said. "Get the other women together, get all the *lupara* and all the weapons you can find and go to the storage shelters. I'll join you as soon as I've told the others. And Sara . . . be careful."

"You also, be careful."

Guido returned to Marco's study. Graziano sobbed unashamedly as Marco solemnly read the note pinned onto the child's *camissa*.

"Take the child to his mother and call Father Bonaventura," he instructed Calo. He turned to Graziano. "You should be with your wife at such a time." He put his arms around the man. "Please tell your wife my heart couldn't be more pain-filled if the child were my own son. Tell her

169

I will not rest until the boy's murderer is apprehended."

Graziano couldn't stop sobbing as he followed Calo out of the room. Roberto took the note from Marco's outstretched hand. He read: *Death to the enemies of the brotherhood! Those who defy us shall be considered our mortal enemies. Reconsider! Leave the pride of the Lion before it's too late. His days are numbered and so will yours be—if you stay!*

The men looked to Marco for some word, some sign. It was a sorrow-filled, crestfallen Lion who stared back at them. He had no words of solace to offer at this moment.

Guido Amalfi spoke up. "My wife tells me, Excellency, the heifers and most of the cattle have been slain."

Marco glanced sharply at him, but remained silent.

"And?" asked Roberto, sensing the Lion's mood.

"I told my wife to gather all the women and weapons and move into the storage shelter."

"Very good," said Roberto. He turned to the others. "Go. Let's assess the situation before making a decision on what action to take." The men nodded and left.

"It's that diabolical Tricario. I know it. I should have listened to Cesare," cursed Roberto.

"Don't punish yourself, Roberto. Tricario is only someone else's tool, like the other Dons who follow orders." Marco grew meditative. "There's something underfoot. I heard the rumors in Rome. They tried to tell me we have more enemies than even I dreamed. The *latifondisti* have watched the cooperative more closely than we thought. In Palermo, over five weeks ago, at a meeting with the *capo-mafia*, Don Calomare, the *Principessa* Maria Scarletto, and her fellow *latifondisti* declared our system too democratic. She's concerned it will cause dissent, even anarchy, among the peasants." Marco snorted with indignation. "It seems she and her cohorts are determined to destroy the cooperative." Marco paced the floor, puffing furiously on his cigar. "They are upset by our success. Hah! What they don't know is that they're playing with dynamite. This Don Calomare is no uneducated bum. He controls the money that's been loaned to the *latifondisti*. It is Don Calomare who buys up all their notes before the ink dries on their signatures—just as they did with Don Catanese."

"Surely they must know?"

"Who knows what the other *latifondisti* know or don't know? They'd sell their souls for the money to pay for their extravagances. As long as the *mafia* will run their estates, they're content."

"How can they be so incredibly ignorant? For educated men to be so naive is unbelievable. Don't they know the *Principessa* is Don Calomare's mistress?"

170

"Ah . . . you know that too?" He seemed surprised. "They won't face reality. They are totally out of touch."

"Then they deserve their fate," said Roberto with disgust.

"It's not that simple, *amico*," said the Lion. "If the *latifondisti* fall so falls Sicily. No matter how bad conditions appear to be, they're better than what might result if the *mafia* takes over. The peasant would be lost forever. It's easy to fight oppression if the oppressor is not your brother or if he comes from another world. But how do we pit brother against brother, Sicilian against Sicilian without a civil war. History has proven our people have no stomach for killing."

"You don't include the *mafiosi* in that category?"

"*Mafiosi* are a special breed unto themselves. They exist for their own kind, spawned into hybrid Sicilians by those *latifondisti* who preceded us. It is the average Sicilian peasant I fear for, the underprivileged, the man I've dedicated my life to help. Without guidance or leadership, or someone to care for his welfare, he'll be eaten alive."

Roberto could almost feel the power he generated as he spoke.

"By God, if it's war they want, they shall have it!"

Suddenly he remembered Mariolina. He shuffled through the stack of mail, paused at the one he had anticipated, opened and read it. The color drained from his face. His arm fell over the chair in a dead weight, the hand holding the letter grew limp, and the paper fluttered slowly to the floor.

"Marco! *Che c'e?* What is it?"

Marco didn't answer. Roberto walked to his side, picked up the letter, and leaned toward the candelabra to read it in a better light.

The letter referred to blood tests done on Mariolina in Milan. His eyes skimmed over the technical portions of the letter and came to rest on prognosis.

It is with profound regret that I advise you that, unless her blood condition can be remedied, your wife's life expectancy will be greatly reduced to perhaps a year at the most, providing no complications set in.

Roberto's heart sank. He stared at the letter, stunned. He could find no words. He sank into a chair, leaned over, and buried his face in his hands, fighting hard to control his feelings. What a black day! First Cesare, now Mariolina!

Marco glanced at him and said softly, "He did say 'unless her condition can be remedied'? We'll get the finest doctors available." He floundered, not wanting to believe what he read.

"You don't mind, Roberto. I'd like to go upstairs to see her before the others return."

Marco opened the door to her bedroom, moved silently across the carpeted floor, and sat quietly at his wife's side, his eyes intent on her still form. Fragrant scents from the Madelaina Gardens wafted into the chamber. Moonlight burst through the latticed windows, throwing a variety of patterns on the floor. Mariolina lay motionless on the pillow, her face as pale as the shimmering white sheets, her thick hair shining in the light of the flickering candle.

Gently, oh so gently, Marco stroked her moist forehead. Her eyes fluttered open as if in a drugged sleep. It took a moment or two before she held him in focus. He leaned back against the headboard, and Mariolina moved quickly into his arms. He wrapped his strong arms around her and held her tightly. He could feel her heart quicken. All at once, Marco choked back a sob. The doctor's words were etched into his brain like acid, and they came at him like whirling images . . . *A year at the most . . . Deep and profound regret.*

They'd been honest with each other, but Marco couldn't bring himself to tell her what the letter contained. There would never be a clear future for them now.

Mariolina leaned away from him and studied him with intent eyes.

"Marco, what is it? I know how terrible you must feel about Cesare Ruffo. We all do. It was a terrible shock, but you must not take it to heart. It won't help you with the others. For them, you must be strong."

Marco gazed at her with love in his heart, somewhat startled by the courage of her words. It was good she thought his anguish was for Ruffo and not for her. He smiled tenderly at her. She wound her arms about his neck and lay her head against his wildly beating heart. Together they lay still in the great silence, not talking, just listening to each other's heart.

"Beloved," he said finally. "It's nearly dawn. I must leave you for a while. I'll be back before the holidays, I promise. Roberto will be here with you, so you must promise not to be frightened if anything develops in my absence. I want you to rest now."

"You aren't telling me what's wrong, Marco. I'll not let you go until I know and hear it from you."

He couldn't spare her. They'd been too honest with each other. He told her about Graziano's dead son, about the slaughtered cattle, the threats to the other *latifondisti*, and the warning in Rome. He avoided her eyes for fear she might sense his own agony over the doctor's letter.

Pulling back the covers, she made an effort to rise. "I must go to Graziano's cottage to offer my consolation, Marco," she began.

"No!" His loud command startled her. "This night belongs to the family," he added softly. "There'll be time in the morning after you've rested," he assured her, pulling the coverlet back into place.

"Of course, dearest. As usual you are right."

"Va biene, carissima. Dorme. Sleep now, my love." He leaned over and kissed her forehead. Her white face frightened him.

"You won't leave until we say goodbye?" Her eyes fluttered drowsily.

He nodded and tried to swallow the hard lump in his throat. He closed the door behind him and leaned heavily against it. *Santo Dio!* Why? Why?

"Does she know?"

"No. And I don't intend to tell her. Promise me, Roberto, you'll say nothing to her. Nothing!"

Roberto shook his head in bewilderment. "I can't believe it. Pray my feelings don't betray me."

"She is to know nothing," insisted Marco feverishly, holding his friend's arm in a viselike grip. "Where are the others?"

"In the office, waiting for you."

From the study came the sound of angry voices raised in heated debate. Marco and Roberto entered. The Lion sat behind his desk with Roberto at his right and asked for their reports.

"The vines in Lamanita's sector have been cut, destroyed completely," reported Guido Amalfi with a sickish look on his face.

"The storage tanks look like a sieve, full of holes. We're lucky if there's enough water for morning coffee. Those sons-abitches shot up everything in sight," reported Massina in an ugly mood. "Fucking vermin!"

"Demonio!" spat Lamponi thoroughly disgusted. "Whores of the devil! Three bins of filberts squashed like cockroaches. Totally destroyed. If they had stolen it I'd feel better. But to see such waste. *Figghi de butani!* And the prickly pears? All squashed to a pulp. I fear, Excellency, we'll have no crop for the holiday markets this year."

The doors to the study burst open, kicked in by Calo La Bolla. No one had to tell Marco. Bad news was scrawled over the sweat-stained face of his bodyguard like graffiti. "Four sentries have been found with their throats slit!"

The forty-six-year-old Micci jumped to his feet and stared numbly at Calo. Sainted God, his only son stood guard that evening!

Calo's huge hairy hands reached out to steady the trembling man. Their eyes met in mute understanding. "I'm sorry, old friend," said Calo, displaying rare compassion. Micci was numb with disbelief.

Marco moved from behind his desk and placed an arm about the man. "Ricardo was my Godson, Tomasso. I loved him like a son. Go to your wife," he said, trying to be a comfort. The older man shook his head.

"No. I will stay." Tears welled in his eyes. "I will stay."

Marco lost little time in outlining his intentions. *"Aloura,* it's happened. What we've dreaded has finally come to pass. Within the families there are more than 200 able-bodied men and women who'll fight as we fought once before. Good fortune and prosperity has made us soft. It must cease! In a few hours, Capitano Paolo Nicosia and I leave for Milano. I have several friends there whom I shall persuade to return with me. By God, I promise you we shall avenge this *infamita* done to us. We shall become warriors once again. Are we in accord?"

Then Marco said something which disturbed Roberto. "Since your losses supersede mine," said the Lion, talking to heads of the families, "it is your decision by which I shall abide. If you prefer that we do nothing and turn the other cheek, I shall respect your wishes."

Marco maintained that men who volunteered made better soldiers than those who were conscripted, and in moments Roberto was to learn the merits of Marco's action. It was Guido Amalfi, in his crude, peasant manner, who spoke on behalf of the others.

"Listen, Excellency, you know me. With words I am not good. So have patience." He stood with his cap in his hand, twirling it around and around. "We've been with you . . . *managghia* . . . Who counts the years? From you we learned human dignity and respect of ourselves. No longer are we the animals the other *latifondisti* call the peasants. We do not eat among the swine and sleep with goats and chickens. From you we learned a way of life that is worth dying for, so that our children can grow up . . ."

Tomasso Micci sobbed loudly, *"Ricardo, sanguo dei mio sanguo!"*

". . . and live an even better life. You say the choice is ours, Excellency," continued Guido. *"Aloura,* my family is as yours. We stand by your side in this. *Capeeshi?* That's

174

all I gotta say for now." He sat down stiffly and glanced compassionately at Micci. The others tried consoling him.

"I also remember the old days, Excellency," said Lamponi, removing his cap. "Those coyotes must be taught there are others who can howl. My family stands as yours!"

"Mine, too," came the replies one after another. Micci nodded, indicating his cooperation, as he blew his nose.

Their decision to stand with Marco was unanimous, and because each man felt as if he'd made the choice without coercion, their solidarity was so powerful, it infected all the peasants on the estate. Discretion, caution, and utmost secrecy were stressed by Marco. "You'll not breathe a word of our intentions to another soul until I return," cautioned the Lion. The meeting adjourned and the men scattered to their houses.

Sultano was saddled and waiting for Marco. Sensing his mood, Calo and Ciccio had brought the stallion around and now they followed the Lion at a respectful distance as he broke into a wild gallop. They knew exactly where he was headed.

Alone in a silent sea of wind-swept, rolling hills, Marco sat in his saddle staring off into the distance, somber and silent. Terra d'Oro, his refuge in a storm, the place where he came to sort out angry emotions and violent thoughts, was soundless except for a gentle wind and the shuffling noises of the white Arabian as he grazed on the tall grass.

What was it his father had told him about the land? How precious it was, that the hope of mankind was in the land. "Care for it and nurture it, for from it comes the very life of man," he had instructed his son.

Communing with nature in this vast vista usually helped Marco to adjust his perspective. It was here that the Lion came to realize how insignificant one man by himself could be. Once, his father had told him, an empire stood on this very spot, pulsing with life: temples, marketplaces, universities, and villas with magnificent gardens. Men had rejoiced, wept, loved and hated and procreated here. Conquerors stood at battle with legions of soldiers. Wars were won and lost. Colorful victory banners that had waved in the breeze had long since crumbled and blown away. Cowards and heroes who had died side by said lay buried far below the earth's surface. Phoenicians, Egyptians, Moors, Carthaginians, Greeks, Romans, Spaniards, French, Austrian, British—what was left of them? Nothing! All were covered by the shifting sands of time.

Why, then, he asked himself, *does it matter what I decide* to do? Do I, one man, mean anything to this world. Can one man's decisions make a difference in a lifetime? What is it that drives me? Revenge? Hatred? Vanity? Lust for power? Immortality? He'd asked himself these questions many times in the past. Each time he filled with despair. How easy it would be to give up, now. Marco's heart pounded with uncertainty and he asked himself, *What is there for me in being the Royal Lion? Am I never to enjoy peace and contentment? Am I not entitled to love and be loved, to have children and share in their pleasures and delights as do other men? What more must the House of de Leone endure?* Santo Dio! *Mariolina! Mariolina!*

For a time he bent his head and let the reins slip from his fingers as if he'd fallen asleep. Sultano, sensing his master's torment, remained perfectly still. Calo and Ciccio watched their sad Lion in the saddle. They knew why he had come to Terra d'Oro, but they couldn't know the utter desolation, grief, and heartache that he felt.

All the Lion had ever known was an overt compulsion and insatiable need to protect his people. *Am I part of an unrelinquishing destiny who allows me no volition of my own*, he asked himself.

Suddenly Marco came alive. He stood up in his stirrups and gazed about. It was as if the earth opened and from its depths he heard a voice, not his own, but one more powerful, filled with a resonance that shook the earth. He sensed another presence, but when he looked there was no one.

Calo and Ciccio both felt a peculiar movement in the earth. Their horses grew skittish. They looked but they saw no one except the Lion, who seemed intent, as if he were listening to something supernatural.

The inevitable fate of all mankind is death and utter desolation buried under a barren earth, blown about by the winds of time. Each soul is like a seed, to be scattered upon the earth, where it will spring up again in another time, in another place, in another lifetime. Nothing is for naught.

Marco sat straight in his saddle. His answer had come. He knew now that what he did was vitally important. His spirit would live on in the heart of any man who chose to be free, who stood up for his human rights with pride, dignity, and strength. Fired and uplifted by these unseen forces, Marco de Leone knew there'd be no turning back. In a few days he'd be in Milano with his old friend, the *Falconiero.*

16

Felipe Santiago hurried across the courtyard of his villa outside of Milano. The forty-two-year-old Spaniard lived in
semiretirement away from the hubbub of city life and rarely
saw people or encouraged encounters with them. Since yesterday, when a message of grave importance had come
from his dearest friend, Marco de Leone, Felipe's excitement had been uncontainable. He ordered an elaborate
feast prepared in the Lion's honor. Watching three figures
approach on horseback, he felt a warm surge of happiness.

Santiago, a tall, craggy-faced man with a powerful phy-
sique and the dark piercing eyes of a falcon, wore the garb
of his countrymen, the attire of a Spanish Don: tight-fitting
pants flared over charro boots, a soft white silk shirt, a
leather jacket, and a kerchief tied at his neck. All that was
missing were his big rawled spurs, which he removed unless
he was riding. If it weren't for the cartridge belt and double six-shooters that he wore, Felipe could pass for any
wealthy *haciendado* or landowner.

While he watched his guests approaching over the horizon,
Felipe smiled and recalled how he first met the Lion.

Born near Andalusia, Spain, Felipe came from a long
line of Basques, many of whom were shepherds. When, at
eighteen, he fell in love with the daughter of Don Diego de
Fuentes, the wealthy nobleman bribed him with substantial
sums of money and a fully paid education in Rome to give
up all thoughts of the young girl so she'd be free to marry
in her own class.

Nothing could have tempted the ambitious young man
more than so fabulous an offer. What was one girl when he
could pick from a continent full of them, he asked himself.

In Rome, during his second semester at the university,
Felipe learned that the girl, Maria Rubia, despairing over his
callous, opportunistic ways, had killed herself. For a time
he pretended to be unmoved by her suicide, but soon, he
began to party more than usual, drink to excess, and live a
high life as if pursued by demons. The guilt he felt over her
untimely death ate away at him like acid and soon turned
him into a domineering boor who offended all his associates
and classmates. In time, doors once open to him slammed
shut. No longer sympathetic to his moods, his friends cut him
off abruptly.

His handsome looks dissipated into the perpetual hag-
gardness of a drunk and he grew slovenly in appearance.

Shortly after the fracas at Roberto's bookstore in Rome, Felipe had disappeared. What was worse, no one cared or asked about him. It appeared as if the earth had opened up and swallowed Felipe Santiago, for no one heard from him.

In Marseille on business one day, Marco de Leone and the manager of de Leone Shipping lines, Henri Duval, had been walking along the waterfront in the direction of his offices. Marco stopped in his tracks when he caught sight of an unshaven man whose mass of curly dark hair had grown to almost shoulder length. "I think I see someone I know," Marco said vaguely. "I'll see you back at the office."

"It's dangerous in these quarters, Monsieur de Leone," Duval protested. "It's unsafe without protection."

"Here, too?" said Marco with a tinge of bitterness. "I assure you, Henri, I can handle myself."

Before the Frenchman could protest further, Marco had crossed the narrow cobbled street and entered a shabby waterfront bar. It took a moment for his eyes to adjust to the dimly lit interior, and then he spotted the familiar face slumped over a table, unable to hold his head up. He walked to the man and laid a hand on his shoulder. "Felipe?" No recognition glimmered in his dull, red-veined eyes. Totally uncoordinated, he attempted to light a cigarette with his shaking hand. Marco held his hand and steadied the flame. "Felipe?" He tried again. "It's me. Marco de Leone. Don't you know me?" Marco had to avert his head as the rank odors of vomit, urine, and stale alcohol wafted up to his nostrils.

"Monsieur, s'il vous plait, buy a beggarly man a drink."

"Felipe . . . Felipe. It's Marco. Remember Professore D'esti?"

The wretched drunk blinked his swollen eyelids trying desperately to connect this man to a face and voice out of the past.

"Black coffee, waiter!" called Marco snappily. He began to work on his old friend.

An afternoon of black coffee and hot steam baths followed by a massage and icy showers began to restore the memory of the dazed, protesting Felipe. Vague images of Marco came at him, but with his sobriety came more remorse. "Maria Rubia is dead," he murmured over and over again. A barber clipped his hair and shaved him. A manicurist transformed his grubby unkempt hands. At a haberdashery, Marco had him completely outfitted. Slowly the haze began to lift from Felipe Santiago's mind. The image that bounced off the mirror at him was a Felipe from the past, but inside, he still held himself cheaply.

178

"It's over now," said Marco sternly. "You've felt sorry for yourself long enough. It's time you stopped wallowing in self-pity."

"Nothing you can tell me will remove the guilt, Marco. Maria Rubia died because I abandoned her love. The blood of her suicide is on my hands."

"Ah, *mon ami, mon ami* . . . have you not learned that no one can prevent what Destiny decrees? You may have been able to prolong her inevitable end, but you couldn't have prevented it. Believe that, Felipe, and your pain will dissolve. Do you not wonder why your own life has been so directed? Can you not see there is a lesson to be learned in everything? Out of all the anguish, torment, and pain you've endured, there has to be some reward."

Felipe glanced at Marco as if he'd lost his senses. *Caramba!* A lunatic yet! He'd play along with this do-gooder for to-night, wheedle a few francs from him, and by tomorrow, he'd pawn these fine clothes and bury himself in his miseries again.

But if Felipe thought he was dealing with a harmless do-gooder, he was in for a surprise. Marco didn't let Felipe out of his sight all night, and the next day he brought him to meet Henri Duval.

"Here's the man we've needed," he told his French associate. Henri was delighted with Felipe, who spoke four languages fluently.

Nervous and unsure of himself, Felipe protested to his benefactor. "You're a fool to put your trust and faith in me. What will prevent me from going out and drinking all over again? I'll fail miserably. It's too great a responsibility."

"Let me worry about the risks, Felipe." Marco's warm, reassuring voice gave him hope.

Marco explained Felipe's plight to Henri and cautioned him not to push the Spaniard too hard. "He's made of tough stock and he'll come around. Let him develop his wings and he'll soar like no one else. Go easy with him and you'll have a man of considerable worth."

Henri, taking Felipe under his wing, introduced him to a friend who was an expatriot. Over dinner one night the friend spoke about his many escapades as the leader of a special group of professional freedom fighters. They'd fought in Spain, France, Austria, and recently in Corsica. Impressed with the man's dedicated life, Felipe came alive for the first time in years. Difficult as it was, he asked Henri for time off to join the band of guerrilla fighters. Knowing he'd never really tame the restless Spaniard, Henri reluctantly agreed.

Felipe had finally found his niche. At last the sun shined for him. The world was his oyster.

"Buenos días, amigo! Buenos días!" cried Felipe, tears brimming in his eyes for the man who had made his world possible. They embraced warmly. "Goddammit! It's good to see you, Marco! You're a sight for these tired eyes." He led him across the courtyard with a certain flair.

"Felipe, old friend, you bring joy to my heart," said Marco, accepting the goblet of wine his host handed him.

Seeing the vast shadows in his friend's eyes, Felipe said wisely, "Let us forego the usual amenities, *amigo.* Tell me what brings you to the lair of the *Falconiero?"*

When he heard the Lion's story, Felipe said quietly, *"Todas los muchachos están listos."*

"Bueno, compadre. Muy bueno."

Two hours later, Felipe and fourteen of his men boarded the *Marchessa* en route to Sicily. By morning of the next day, the yacht had docked in Messina's harbor and in less than two hours they arrived at the Villa de Leone. The *Falconieri* were flabbergasted at the magnificence of the feudal estate.

"Dios mios, Marco! Had I known you were so affluent, I'd have charged you an extra lira for my services!" exclaimed Felipe, laughing amiably.

The *Falconieri* lost no time in getting to the business at hand. Heads of the families were rounded up and Felipe Santiago talked to them personally.

After explaining their intentions, Felipe and his men organized the peasants, men and women, into fifteen squads of twenty each. At first there was resistance from the Sicilian men who objected to their women doing *man's* work. Felipe put their *maschiezzo* at ease.

"In such times there is no distinction between men and women. We are all human beings fighting for a cause. Who among you prefers his wife and daughter be raped or violated because she never learned how to use a knife or gun to ward off her attacker?" He received no arguments from that day forward.

They drilled by day. They drilled by night. The peasants drilled until they could drill no further. Men and women alike, tested for various aptitudes, were placed where their services could be best put to use. Soon the metamorphosis took place. Those who never held a gun before became expert marksmen. Their senses became sharper, their powers of observation keener, their trigger fingers more sensitive. The *contadini* became a different people. Unskilled hands

180

grew receptive to the feel of different blades. The men were taught to disarm an enemy soundlessly, using the element of surprise. They learned both offensive and defensive fighting with weapons and their bare hands. Soon the peasants swore they could see from the back of their heads. What a sense of achievement they felt! What expertise they developed! *Managghia!* They lifted their heads with a sense of fierce pride.

The *Falconieri*, despite their profession, believed in the dignity of death and in fighting the enemy on their own terms. They found they had no stomach for the *lupara* and its needless violence, yet, somehow, they rationalized its use. The women were taught to melt lead into triangular pellets for the weapon.

How fast the months passed. The Christmas holidays came and went, dampened by the recent deaths and the slow deterioration of Mariolina's health. Marco had only to gaze upon her pale face to know that her life was slowly being snuffed out. Standing by helplessly, watching her spirit disintegrate, corroded his guts and ate away at him like a cancer.

Mariolina took her medication religiously. Furious with Dr. Pietro for refusing to discuss her ailment, she vowed that she'd go to Messina and seek the diagnosis of another physician. She knew nothing of Dr. Simoni's prognosis.

Her devotion to her husband won the admiration of all those closest to them. Often Roberto would walk into the study and find them together. Amused by her wit and dazzled by her charm and laughter, he was often forced to turn away lest the trembling of his heart would give him away.

To Mariolina, Felipe Santiago was a champion. It was the closest she had ever come to hero worship. This Spaniard was El Cid, da Gama, and Cortes rolled into one. Felipe agreed to dine with the Marquis and his wife out of politeness, but he insisted he was no better than his men and, for the preservation of unity and the strength of the group, he could not accept any special privileges. He dined with his men and the other *contadini* after that.

Mariolina not only understood, but she prevailed upon her husband to permit all the men to dine together at a long banquet table in one of the salons. This proved to be an excellent idea, and Marco, overjoyed at the prospect of being closer to Felipe, praised his wife's perception. Too soon this proved unacceptable.

Each night the salon filled with more than two hundred people, and since the duties involved were shared, it was not inconvenient. But Mariolina soon realized that the men felt inhibited with women present. Sensing their discomfort, Mariolina encouraged the women to permit their men the pleasure of dining alone. Reluctantly, they agreed. A guest of Felipe's caliber was a rarity at the villa and she would have liked nothing better than listening to tales of his vast experiences. Instead she contented herself with hearing the stories secondhand from either Marco or Roberto.

Felipe Santiago was at a loss to understand why the other *latifondisti* sought to destroy Marco. He listened as the Lion told him of the generations of hatred between the House of de Leone and the *mafia,* who controlled most of the feudal estates. "Is there nothing you can do through legislation to control such a situation in your country?" he asked the legislator.

"If there were another avenue to pursue, Felipe, I wouldn't have resorted to training a private army. Don't misunderstand my words. The *fascisti* in the north are making progress, and in time Il Duce may do wonders for the nation. But they are so concerned with their own problems, they don't give a damn about the football at their toe.

"You think Rome cares who kicks the football around?" Marco continued. "Raping, pillaging bandits cause endless destruction. Does Rome do anything? No! So what if the *mafia* is the second government in Sicily? It's not Rome's concern! She's too far away to get involved. You know something, Felipe?" asked the Lion confidentially one night. "There are men who sit with me in the Senate who believe and state unequivocally that there is no such thing as a *mafia* in Sicily. Having deluded themselves constantly over the possibility of corruption in Sicily—something the Mafia lobbyists work in earnest to convey—my supercilious associates laugh. Laugh, mind you! They argue, 'If it's true that something called a *mafia* does exist, Rome can only look into the situation *after* her own affairs are in order.'"

"Goddamn! That's the straight of it?" asked Felipe.

"That's the straight of it! These obtuse mentalities bring stinging defeat to my highest hopes. Worse! They add to the sorrow and heartache of my people. My inability to convince these hypocritical asses of the true state of Sicily's plight has led me to these measures. Now you see why I need your help?"

"Fight fire with fire, eh? A continuation of feudal priorities which will make you uncontested overlord." Felipe spoke his thoughts freely.

"I have no other choice. It's that or annihilation! The

182

government won't help, so by God, I have to help myself and my people!" Suddenly on the defensive, Marco stopped cold. "I've asked myself where I've gone wrong? How I have failed to convince my senatorial peers of Sicily's urgent need? Truly, Felipe, I could not find that I'd done anything wrong except to expound my beliefs to the point of sounding fanatical."

"Perhaps what those stuffed toads need is a southern vacation and a few weeks under the fiery sting of a bandit raid," said the Falcon wryly.

Marco smiled and the smile broke into light laughter. "You know I never thought of that!" He nodded to himself. "My dear Felipe, what a gem of an idea!"

They both laughed.

January 1 was a cold, wet day. Roberto buttoned his sheepskin jacket as he rode alongside Marco. The rains would threaten on and off for another month or two before spring would burst forth. The trails were muddy and rutted and made a hell of a mess as horsemen galloped through them.

"By now the *Falconieri* know the *latifondo* like the backs of their hands," said Marco, scanning the horizon with his binoculars.

"They're remarkable men," replied Roberto. He was fascinated by those insane belts they wore which concealed a half-dozen or more implements: knives, garrotes, fingerless gauntlets, brass knuckles, an assortment of wires, and of course, bullets for their service pistols.

"They're getting restless."

"I can see they might with no action."

"At breakfast this morning, I asked Felipe to remain until the end of February," said Marco quietly. "I have a feeling that something will happen before Lent."

The Lion's instinct proved right. On February 10, one month later, everyone at the villa was edgy for no apparent reason. The *Falconieri*, who could smell the approach of an enemy, were especially agitated. Before nine that morning Felipe gathered his men and the leaders of all the squads and went over every phase of their plans until they could recite their instructions backwards.

The excitement mounted and the tension tightened. Six o'clock came and went. Marco looked questioningly at Felipe. "This tension is eating at everyone."

"They're out there, Marco. I can smell them. My men know just where they are. We must wait. Be patient."

That night, under the full of the moon, the bandit Scolezzi and a gang of thirty diabolical killers came riding in as if from hell. They entered through the main gates, purposely left open and unguarded, and broke up into separate groups, each heading for a vital section of the estate.

Six bandits rode to Amalfi's cottage. Waiting for them were Guido's wife Sara and several other women who cut the men in two with their well-aimed *luparas*. Recovering from their initial shock, the women stepped quickly, recovered the bandits' horses, and led them to an enclosed corral; the other women reloaded their *luparas* with garlic-dipped pellets.

Six more bandits nosed their horses toward the west gate, dismounted, and crept stealthily in the direction of the compound where the olive oil tanks and lots of expensive equipment were stored. The bandits crept inside. Instantly the *contadini* moved in behind them, closed off all the exits, and bolted the doors from the outside. Only after the bandits had lit their torches and tossed them into the vital machinery and storage tanks, did they realize that all exits were barred to them. Weeks before, the valuable olive oil had been removed and transferred in secret to Messina.

Eight bandits arrived at Lamantia's vineyard with machetes and *luparas* slung over their shoulders. As they approached the draw, one by one they struck at their horses spurring them into a gallop, and one at a time, horse and rider fell into the well-camouflaged crevice dug deep enough to hold a dozen men and their horses.

From out of the shadows came men and women who dumped vats of crude oil into the trench. Then lit torches were hurled into the oil-soaked ditch. Short bursts of flames exploded, turning the trenches into raging pits of hell. The cries and shouts of terror were horrifying.

Instantly, the stench of burned flesh permeated the air. The putrefying odors nauseated the peasants as they stood rooted to the spot, unable to move. Their staring dark eyes reflecting the fiery devastation were somber. There were no wild cries of victory.

Under the express orders of the Falcon, both Marco and Roberto sat out the battle. Marco had deferred to Felipe's logic when he explained that it was imperative that the peasants themselves handle the major portion of the fight. "It will imbue them with a sense of pride. Besides, they must learn not to depend on you, Marco. If you should be absent from the villa when another such problem arises, they'll need to be resourceful."

The confusion and pandemonium had been total. The

bandits were so surprised, they became disorganized. Of the thirty who initiated the raid, nine escaped to tell the tale of that unforgettable night. Farfetched stories spread across the island faster than a malaria epidemic. By the time the stories reached the villa of *capomafia* Don Calomare, in Palermo, they'd been distorted and and blown all out of proportion.

"An army of a thousand warriors using professional military tactics came at us. Phew! Such an army! El Leone knew in advance all details of our plans! Why didn't you tell us they would have cannon and machine guns? You sent us into a massacre!" said a few sullen survivors. "There were generals and soldiers and enough ammunition to blow Sicily off the map!"

Don Calomare called for a regrouping of his Mafia Dons. This stinging defeat was embarrassing. To save face, they cried aloud in outrage, "We have spies in our midst. We must take action." And they did. A complete purge of the Scolezzi camp followed. Most of the *mafiosi* used this disgraceful defeat to rid themselves of personal enemies, even those innocent of the affair.

Victorious, cheering, and tearful, the *Falconieri* left the villa, filled with fond memories and sincere hopes they would never be needed again. They hadn't been gone three days when a series of puzzling events began to happen. A letter arrived postmarked Trapani, Sicily. Inside the envelope was one name: *Oriello Vincenzi*. It was signed *Amici de Amici*, friends of friends.

"What do you make of this?" asked Marco, showing the letter to Roberto.

Roberto shrugged. It made no sense at all.

Ten days later another envelope arrived postmarked Gangi, Sicily. The name enclosed was *Amelio Petrocino*. It was again signed, *Amici de Amici*. Marco placed this letter with the first. A third arrived, then a fourth and a fifth until nine names had arrived, each from a different location. After the ninth name arrived, a letter came from Castelvetrano, Sicily. Marco read the letter with profound curiosity.

El Leone:
  You've received the names of the nine surviving black-hearted villains who raided your villa in February. Each of these men can be found hiding in the villages postmarked on the envelopes. This is our way of informing you the Brotherhood had no part in the atrocious attack on the Royal Lion.
                                        Amici de Amici

"Do they take me for a complete fool, Roberto?" exploded Marco. "What devious ploys the Mafia uses to absolve themselves. They are so treacherous they turn on their own kind. A simpleton could detect their plan."

Marco did nothing to bring the nine culprits to justice. He didn't have to. The Mafia saw to it that they were apprehended, and before the poor fools could make statements to the *Securrete Polizia* or the *Squadistras,* squads of secret police on special assignment, they were murdered.

One man named Loccorno, from the village of Randazzo, heard of the treachery that befell his companions, escaped, and made his way to the Villa de Leone, seeking audience with the Lion.

Prostrating himself before the Lion he begged for mercy, blaming those who sought to destroy the House of de Leone. "Now they turn on us, cloaked in the innocence of our blood!"

"Just a moment, Loccorno," interrupted Marco. He remained cold and unmoved. "If this is a confession, understand that it in no way pardons your guilt. You'll not receive amnesty from me."

"Yes, I understand, said Loccorno, regaining his composure. "I expect only to be treated justly for my crimes. To be marked for death by the very men who maneuvered me to do their bidding by threatening my family is not my idea of justice. Don't you see? Dressed in the garb of angels, they sprout wings and the halos of sainthood, pretending to be sanctimonious and virtuous friends of the Royal Lion." Loccorno's anger gagged his throat.

Calo and Ciccio stared at their master in stony silence. Roberto, disturbed by what he read in their eyes, shrugged compassionately in favor of the man Loccorno. Marco frowned darkly. He disliked traitors on every count. Yet, he could understand a man turning against the factions that betrayed him.

Dammit! What a dilemma! What to do with Loccorno? Turning him over to the authorities meant the Mafia would deal with him in their own way and torture his family as well. The information Loccorno brought to Marco was nothing he didn't already know. Damn! Why had he come at all? Marco knew that his decision would be unsatisfactory to all concerned, primarily to his own men, who were apt to hold him in contempt. But when had this ever stopped him in the past? the Lion asked himself. He looked at the trembling little man who stood opposite his desk, then thanked him with icy politeness and told him he was free to leave.

Loccorno paled visibly. Calo and Ciccio made their displeasure clear. Roberto was surprised. He glanced swiftly at the bodyguards, who avoided his eyes, then nervously lit a cigarette. *What in the world is Marco thinking,* he wondered. *What madness!*

"You mean I can go? You aren't going to order me shot?"

"Sir," said the Lion drawing himself to his full height. "I am not a murderer. Nor am I a law enforcement agency. I thank you in God's name for having the decency to come forward to do what any good citizen would do when he possesses information that might help his fellow man. Outside of that I have no claim on you."

"I don't understand. I'm hunted by the law in my village. And you will press no charges?" The bewildered man filled with a curious mixture of anger and fear.

"Then let the law find you and deal with you. See that the man has food to eat," Marco told Calo. "When he's rested, give him a horse and let him go in peace."

Calo and Ciccio, unable to understand such generosity, left with their charge. Calo vividly recalled carrying Graziano's dead child in his arms. And El Leone set this man free? *Butana u diaoro!*

Roberto excused himself and returned to the greenhouse. Marco remained shut up in his study where he was interrupted several hours later by Calo and Ciccio with the news that Loccorno had been found near the east gate, hanging from a tree. A note in his pocket read: *God forgive me for what I've done.*

Calo confided to Ciccio that night that Marco possessed the wisdom of Solomon.

17

"Signora, I thought I made myself clear a month ago. Now you return and I find you're with child." Dr. Salvatore was furious. "I refuse to discuss this further with you. I insist upon seeing your husband."

"You ask the impossible, doctor." Marco hadn't known she'd solicited the advice of another physician. Each day she'd grown weaker and Dr. Pietro refused to say anything except pat her hand and tell her she was improving. "My husband's in Rome. You'll have to tell me the nature of my ailment."

"You have a particularly rare form of anemia, a peculiarity of the blood cells, in which an abnormal amount of leucocytes are prevalent. It's a disease of blood-forming tissue in which the white cells far outnumber the red cells."

"What exactly does that mean?"

"Among other things, it's extremely dangerous for you to be pregnant."

"That's all?"

"No, Signora, that's not all." He stood up and ran his fingers through his wavy brown hair. His eyes flashed angrily as he lost patience with her. "Apparently you didn't listen to a word I had to say before. Did you discuss this with your husband at all?"

"No." Mariolina thought for a moment. "How dangerous is it? Will the baby be all right?"

Dr. Salvatore tried once again. "I really don't wish to alarm you. Perhaps it would be best to send for your husband, so that I can speak with him in a more objective manner."

"I don't wish my husband to be disturbed unless it is of the utmost importance. It isn't necessary that he be alarmed."

"It's necessary, Signora," the doctor said very gently. He lowered his dark eyes, breaking the connection he held with her.

Mariolina began to flutter her handkerchief back and forth in the air around her. She suddenly felt warm and flushed.

I see, Mariolina thought, *it's that bad.* "How long before further complications set in?"

He shrugged imperceptibly. "If you stay in bed—and I mean in bed—take prescribed medication, rest, eat properly, who knows?"

Her inscrutable dark eyes stared into his questioningly.

"Signora, I'm not the creator." He apologized to her. "I just don't know." At times like this he hated being a doctor. If his tests were correct, she couldn't last a year.

"One more question, please. Will I have time to go to America, say for three months."

"You must be mad, Signora!" His hot Sicilian temper had been stoked. "During a pregnancy, traveling any distance is always a risk. In your case it would be suicide. If you contemplate traveling such a distance, you'll compound the dangers ten-fold. In your condition, I say, no. Your mustn't take chances like that."

Mariolina's own temper sparked and ignited as she sat listening to him talk to her as if she had taken leave of her senses. She was so infuriated at his talking down to her that she grabbed her wrap and stormed out of his office.

She returned a half-hour later, soaked with perspiration, considerably paler. When she staggered into his office, he jumped up and helped her to her chair.

"Doctor, I'm truly sorry for being so childish. I think it best you be entirely truthful with me and I shall reciprocate. You see, I'm not who I said I was when I first came to you. I'm the Marchessa de Leone, wife of His Excellency Marquis de Leone."

His face burned in anger. "Why was it necessary to deceive me? I'm a doctor. A patient-doctor relationship is sacred to me."

"Do you know my husband?"

"He's well known here. I'd have to be an ostrich not to have heard of him."

"Then you know of his dedication to his people and to Sicily?"

He nodded.

"Could you . . . would you understand if I told you that I do not wish my son to be born here in Sicily?"

He glanced at her sharply. Had he heard correctly? "The Lion of Sicily's heir to be born in another country? Another world! *Managghia!* I'll have no part of this!"

"I don't want my son to be born with the profound dedication to Sicily and its people my husband has. Does it seem strange? Unreasonable? Traitorous?"

Dr. Salvatore understood a mother's fears. But this was too much. He couldn't answer her.

"This may sound primitive to you doctor and perhaps it would have to me a few years back. I must talk with someone about these dreams or visions I've had, or I shall lose my mind." Mariolina's head ached and she felt dizzy again.

"Are you feeling all right?"

"Yes, yes, no different than I have for the past few months. I'm used to this dizzy, light-headed feeling."

"Visions are not my specialty, Signora. My hands are kept busy with physical ailments. Those of the mind are beyond my ability to diagnose. Marchessa, I regret, there are many patients in my office that need my attention. Perhaps another day, when you bring your husband . . ."

She opened her small brocaded bag, removed several large bank notes and tossed them on the desk before him. "Will this compensate for the time I'm taking?" Her voice was edged with sarcasm. Then she lowered it again. "You know I can't find time to come here often. I must travel over rough roads to get here and as you said, it's not safe to travel. Please just a few more moments of your time."

He looked from the bank notes to her face. There was well over a month's rent on the desk. Before he could respond, she began her story.

"You see I keep having the same dream over and over and over. I see the villa and all the lands blazing with fire. The crops destroyed, the lands all razed to the ground. In the center of the devastation stands a burning cross, like a crucifix. On the fiery cross are the remains of a decapitated body. The head at the foot of the cross, overflowing with blood, belongs to someone I know." She didn't mention that it was Roberto's head she saw. "My husband stands alongside watching the fires sweep across the *latifondo* as blood pours from his eyes, nose, and mouth like faucets. It's always the same."

Dr. Salvatore placed a slender hand over his lips meditatively. "I told you earlier, I'm no *psichiatro*. I'm not qualified to interpret what you say. What goes on in your mind belongs to you and you alone." He stood up, walked to the window, and looked out at the busy square. Several people milled about, and many carriages stopped at the smart shops across the street. Why couldn't she be a simpleminded patient? Why did she have to be so deep and complicated?

"You know, Signora, the figments of an overactive imagination can at times be so real that people often believe in their visions more than they do the realities of life. Sicilians are masters at this phenomenon. I deal only in scientific realities, even though these change daily."

"That's all you can say to me to help me understand this ah . . . phenomenon, as you call it?" Mariolina felt trapped, as if she were going to suffocate. She needed help, some answers to these strange premonitions.

"I can't endorse what I have no faith in, what I don't believe," he offered as an apology when he saw her dilemma.

"No, I suppose not." She'd felt terribly let down. Now she knew more than ever that the answers must come from her. She'd go to America as she'd planned. No matter what happened, her son must not be born in Sicily, to remain chained to it as Marco had, for the rest of his life. Her son was entitled to a better fate.

He knew what she felt and thought. It was written on her face as clearly as if she'd spoken the words.

"Do what you will, Signora. I can see that no matter what I advise, nothing will change your mind. But I assure you that I'll have no part in this folly if you persist."

Their eyes met, hers filled with stubborn determination, his with futility and defeat.

"You realize you're gambling with your life and your child's?" He shook his head sadly as his eyes scanned the reports of her various tests.

"Nonsense," she scoffed. "I'll be fine. My uncle is a fine doctor. I'll be in excellent hands." He shook his head. "Really. He's excellent. He's a specialist, you know. *Un ostetrico.*"

He smirked and continued to shuffle through the papers. If it weren't for that large concentration of white cells, he'd feel a little better. The trip to America might be therapeutic for her and could possibly do her a world of good. Damn! She was abnormally possessed about her son's future.

Long after Mariolina had left his office, Dr. Salvatore thought about her. He'd given her a prescription with a long list of do's and don'ts, which he felt sure she'd ignore. He was less than optimistic about ever seeing her again, even though she promised she'd see him when she returned from America. He felt terribly depressed. What would happen when the Royal Lion discovered what his wife was up to? That his only son might not be born in his beloved Sicily?

Roberto was in Marco's study involved with the large contour maps of the northwestern sector when Mariolina returned from Messina with the news.

"Carissima! I'm so happy for both of you." He embraced her and led her to the comfortable leather divan. *She looks so radiant,* he thought. *Perhaps the doctor in Milan had made a mistake.*

"When will Marco return?" she asked as Roberto helped her with her wrap and pulled out an ottoman for her to prop her feet upon.

"Not until the Senate retires at the end of the session. They're working hard to block the pro-Mafia legislation. Perhaps two more months."

"That long?"

"Why? Is there something wrong?"

"Roberto, I must go to America," she blurted. Her face flushed again. Little beads of perspiration formed on her brow.

"Why?"

"I have an uncle there who's an excellent physician. I'm hoping he'll help me."

It sounded reasonable to Roberto. She certainly wouldn't get the treatment she needed here. "Does Marco know?"

"No. I don't wish to disturb him."

"Disturb him?" He was stupefied by her remark. "He'd be terribly disturbed if you didn't tell him. Mariolina, don't you really know how much Marco loves you? How much he adores you?" Roberto sounded profoundly hurt.

"Yes! Yes, of course, I know." She almost snapped at

191

him. "You don't understand. I'd be gone and back before he finishes in Rome."

"You can't mean that you'd leave without telling Marco?" Roberto's hurt turned to astonishment, then slowly doubt filled him. "I don't know. Your husband would be furious with you. And I can't say that I'd blame him." He felt like a conspirator.

"Does he have to know?"

He studied her, disbelieving what he heard and what he felt she meant.

"Oh, no! Don't ask me to deceive Marco. No!"

"Please, Roberto."

"No! I can't! I won't aid you in this deception, even if I thought you were right in this . . . this insane plan of yours."

Mariolina sat back in her chair, somber and petulant. *I should have known it would be futile. I shouldn't have confided in anyone. Leave a note and go. That's the way to do it.*

"Marco doesn't know you're carrying his child?"

"Not yet."

"Don't you think he's entitled to know first?"

"There'll be plenty of time when I return."

"You've made up your mind then?" She nodded. "With or without my aid?"

"Yes."

"You're making a grave mistake, *cara mia.*" He threw his hands up into the air in a helpless gesture and let them drop at his sides. "But, why? Why are you embarking on such a long journey without Marco?"

"Because," she retorted in an unguarded moment, "I don't want my son born here in Sicily!"

Stunned by the remark, Roberto stared incredulously. "Mariolina! Do you realize what you've said?"

She quickly averted her head. She got up and walked to the balcony, overlooking the terrace of the Madelaina Gardens. She bit her lips savagely. *Managghia!* She hadn't meant to let it slip.

"You don't intend to return by the time Marco finishes in Rome. What do you have planned in that mad head of yours?" Roberto felt impelled to question her further. "How long are you with child?"

"Just before Christmas."

"Did Dr. Pietro give you permission to travel, now, in your condition?"

"*Cazzu* on Dr. Pietro! He won't tell me why I feel so

badly. Why I'm so weak. Why I lose strength from day to day."

Gina came in with coffee for them and Mariolina's bottle of medicine. "Signora, time to take your *tonica.*"

"*Si, si, capitano!*" retorted Mariolina in a regimental manner.

Gina glanced sharply at Roberto and shrugged her shoulders in a helpless gesture.

"There's no need to take your anger out on her," said Roberto gently. "She's only trying to help."

She took her medicine dutifully, made her apologies to Gina, then sulked unhappily. "I can't help it, Roberto. I feel so helpless. I can't breath. I feel I'm going to choke on Marco's obligations to Sicily, to his people, his insufferable dedication."

"Is that why you *don't* want your child born here?"

"Isn't it evident?"

"I don't understand. This is your land, your home. Yours and Marco's. Why wouldn't you feel a fierce pride in giving birth to your son here?"

"Roberto. Oh, my sweet, gentle Roberto. You, too, are filled with dreams. Do you think I could wish our life on our son? Our fathers and our fathers before them have lived under tyranny, despotism, never knowing from one day to the next whether they'd live to see the light of the next sun. Do you think I wish that on my son?"

"You're forgetting who you are! You, the wife of the Lion of Sicily. A man who *is* Sicily!"

"No! I haven't forgotten! If only Marco *was* Sicily. I'd be proud to have his son born here. Do you want to know who is Sicily? I'll tell you. The *mafiosi*, they are Sicily. They have seeded it with their poison, infiltrated it with black-hearted corruption and evil. They've inculcated into the hearts and minds of each and every peasant, the very essence of their malevolent greed and thirst for power, any way they could. That's who is Sicily!"

An indescribable sadness constricted his heart, gagged him; he couldn't breathe. She was being emotional now, thoroughly emotional and unrealistic. She needed Marco. She'd never talked like this in his presence. What had come over her?

"Guillermo has the right idea. He stays away from Sicily as much as possible. He handles other business for the family away from here, far off in Rome, Milan, and Florence. Why can't Marco do this? Why must his life be dedicated to such a hopeless cause?" Roberto saw her fight for control as tears welled inside her.

"Why not talk this over with Marco?" Roberto sank back in a chair alongside her and began to light a small thin cigar which he rarely smoked. "With your permission?"

She nodded absently. "I have no time. You know that, don't you?" she said quite simply and honestly.

Roberto averted his sad blue eyes. "I would travel to the ends of the earth for you, *cara mia,* but please don't ask me to deceive Marco." He rolled his cigar over and over in his fingers, staring at it.

"Very well then, I'll find another way."

"Mariolina . . ." he pleaded. "Please reconsider."

"It's not your concern." Then, in a way that women are so expert at, she closed him from her thoughts.

In the year he'd known her, there had never been a cross word between them. Now a rift as wide as the ocean stood separating them. Roberto stood up, bowed and left her to her misery.

Roberto paced aimlessly up and down the dirt floors in the greenhouse, looking at soil samples, changing boxes from one location to another without purpose. He watered some, fed others, added and deleted certain chemicals, noting quantity, time and specific dosages. In his laboratory he began to arrange a structure of copper tubing which he'd been working on to invent a more expedient and economical irrigation method.

But he couldn't concentrate. He knew he must do what he had to do. He sat down and wrote a letter to Marco, telling him to return as soon as possible. "Take no cause for alarm, but make haste!" He signed his name, addressed the envelope to the "Honorable Marquis Marco de Leone" and scribbled across the envelope: *Deliver to Senate on arrival! Urgent!*

A month passed before Marco received the letter and by the time he was able to return to the Villa de Leone, June had slipped by. Mariolina had left almost immediately following her conversation with Roberto, so Marco knew it would be futile to try and catch up with her.

It took three weeks for the crossing by the *Conte de Savoia* and when she first saw the Statue of Liberty, she was too ill to give it much notice. Met by her aunt and uncle, she was taken by train to Buffalo and immediately admitted to the hospital.

On July 28, under the sign of Leo, Mariolina gave birth to a premature baby boy. Emergency transfusions helped prolong her life until she returned to Sicily with her son and

194

a nurse, Amalfiah Cario, who traded her professional skills for passage back to her homeland.

Before she left, her uncle told her the blatant truth. He saw he couldn't convince her to remain until both she and the child were strong enough to make the trip back. "Since you're hellbent to make the trip, you must know the truth, Mariolina. Not even the latest in medical science can aid you. There's no cure for this rare blood condition you have."

"I know, uncle, I know. They told me in Messina. What do I have? A few more months?"

How could he hurl the final blow at her and tell her she'd be lucky if she made it home. Instead he said, "Only God knows the time and place."

She arrived home at the villa early in September and presented her son to Marco. He wept with tears of joy that she was safe in his arms. He played the part of an adoring father, but inside he felt tormented by her foolishness.

"Am I forgiven?" she asked weakly when Roberto kissed her.

"You imbecile," he whispered. "Don't you know Marco would have gone with you if he knew how strongly you felt?"

"Is that the truth?"

"Of course. You only succeeded in keeping yourselves apart all that time, especially when you told him you felt better than you really did. He was ready to take the next boat to your side; then, concerned you might somehow miss each other, he remained here waiting. What tortures you put him through. But what of you? What does your illustrious uncle say? That you'll outlive all of us, no doubt." He tried to be gay, but he already knew the ending to the sad story.

She smiled wanly and turned from him. She watched Marco strut across the enormous drawing room showing off their beautiful son with his startling emerald eyes and brown curly hair.

"*Cara mia,* I dread to think what will become of Marco when . . ." Roberto stopped, his face the color of cherries.

"You know?" She reached for his hand. "Does Marco know?" Her eyes were unduly bright. She turned again and stared at her husband.

"He's known for a long time," whispered Roberto.

She felt a catch over her heart. "He's known? For a long time?" She placed a hand over her lips to choke back a sob. "I've been a fool then. To have wasted four months of precious time we could have spent together."

"Don't cry, Mariolina. If nothing else, Marco understands dedication to a cause. Remember? He's the Royal Lion."

"Dear God! What have I done?" She averted her head. She felt feverish.

"Only what you had to do. Destiny would have had it no other way," he sighed despairingly.

Later that night after nurse Amalfiah had put Dolcetto into his cradle in the solarium next to their room, Marco spoke with the young woman. He asked her to stay on with them until other arrangements could be made. At least until after . . . He couldn't bring himself to speak the words. Amalfiah understood and nodded.

"Yes, of course, *Signore.* I'll remain as long as you need me."

Mariolina sat in the chaise longue in the master bedroom, next to Marco. They'd been there for nearly a half hour, just sitting, quiet and still, listening to the many unspoken words of their hearts. Marco held her like a fragile doll, guarding her like a most precious jewel. His face was a study in complexities. He'd wanted to scold her for stealing such precious time from them, but he couldn't. Having lived with the knowledge that she'd soon die, he remembered he'd have to continue to act as if she was eternal.

And now there was a son, a son she'd risked her life to bring into this world. Since that day on the Terra d'Oro when he came to terms with himself, he'd been determined to live each day as it came. It had been his obligation and duty to go to Rome, the passing of the land reforms were vital. Why couldn't she have waited for him to return? If Dr. Pietro hadn't discouraged him, he would have taken Mariolina to Rome with him. Between his duties, he could have seen that she was occupied doing the things she enjoyed. Now it was too late.

How wonderful it would be if one knew in advance what Destiny had in store. No matter what man did to thwart her, Destiny always emerged victorious. Of one thing Marco was certain. Destiny had never intended to fill his life with happiness. He could count on his fingers the real moments of happiness he'd experienced in his lifetime. Meeting and knowing Roberto was one, marrying Mariolina another. Mariolina stirred in his arms.

"Are you comfortable, *carissima?* Tell me, is there something I can do for you?"

"I'm fine," she said, her voice above a whisper. "Dearest, before it's too late, let me tell you how much I love you. With all my heart and soul. I never wanted to hurt you."

"And you haven't, *cara mia*. You've given me the happiest year of my life."

"A year? Has it been a year?"

"It's been a lifetime, for both of us. We couldn't have asked for more."

"Marco." She hesitated a moment. "Will you marry again?"

"That's not a question I'd have thought you'd ask."

"Don't make fun of me. I'm not trying to be witty."

"I was sure you'd ask me to fund a scholarship for the shackled women who need liberation."

She smiled faintly. "If you told me you loved me, I wouldn't have believed it more than those endearing words you just spoke."

Marco looked at her and his heart broke. He couldn't let her see how he really felt. He tightened his arms around her. She lay back for a few moments and became so still that, for a brief wild instant, he grew alarmed.

"Mariolina!" He removed his arm from her shoulder and held her, facing her.

Her eyes fluttered open. When she saw his grave concern, she smiled vaguely. "Not yet, beloved. I promise I'll let you know. I won't leave you until we've said our farewells."

"Oh, my dearest, my beloved." He moaned softly and lay his head against her heaving breasts. She reached up and stroked his head tenderly. They'd had such little time together. *Oh God, what have I done that you should take your vengeance out on me? My only crime has been loving Marco with the spirit of my being. Why do you bring such sorrow upon him? Hasn't he suffered enough?*

Two days later Mariolina asked to be brought downstairs where she could sit on the terrace facing the Madelaina Gardens. She'd been playing a slow game of chess with Roberto. Her soft brown eyes sunken in their hollows glowed with unnatural lights and she spoke in hushed whispers.

"*Caro mió,* will you call Marco? Ask Amalfiah to bring my son to me."

He ran from the terrace to do her bidding, for there was something frightening in her pale, drawn face.

Several moments later, she looked at the sleeping form of her infant son laying in her arms. "Dolcetto," she whispered. "Take care of your father. He'll need all the love and care you can give him." She kissed his strong little fist and nodded to the nurse. "Take him now.

"Roberto, dear, dear Roberto. Will you watch over both of them? Teach Dolcetto to be a strong brave Lion like his father."

197

Roberto stared at her with giant tears streaming down his face. Marco burst onto the patio filled with anxiety. When he saw them talking, he drew a deep breath of relief.

"Carissima! How well you look! Is that a touch of color in your cheeks? Look Roberto, right here," he pointed. "Perhaps that new tonic Dr. Pietro gave her will work after all." Gently, so gently, he stroked her face. He glanced at Roberto. Roberto averted his head.

"I told you, beloved, I wouldn't leave you until we said our farewells," she said softly. Her lips were pale and she leaned against his hand.

Marco swallowed hard. *"Carissima . . ."* he whispered. "No, not yet!" Uncontrollable tears streamed down his face and he cried unashamedly.

"Amore mio, don't cry. I've never heard of a lion with tears in his eyes. A lion doesn't cry."

"I'm merely a man who loves his wife with all his heart, *bellissima."* He wiped his eyes and held both her frail thin hands in his.

"I had confession this morning."

"Yes, *cara mia,* I know."

"You'll tell Dolcetto I wish for him to be just like you. He must be!"

Suddenly her body grew rigid. She sat up half-erect and her dark eyes turned to his as if filled with magnificent lights.

"Amore, tu si mio cuore . . . My love, you are my very heart," she whispered to him.

Mariolina de Leone was dead the next instant.

18

Guillermo de Leone stared at the letter in his hand and looked up at Ciccio Pontiface, who had traveled to Rome, the bearer of bad tidings. His grief-stricken expression made clear what was in the letter.

Mariolina dead! It's not to be believed! The last time I saw her . . . Guillermo stopped. He rose to his feet in his office at de Leone Pharmaceuticals, summoned his secretary for last minute instructions, and left immediately with Ciccio for the villa.

Ever since he and Marco had escaped death years ago, Guillermo had passed in and out of Marco's world with a cavalier ease, never taking life seriously, playing the role of a rogue and libertine, and enjoying every minute of his life. He cared little for the traditions of his people, and of late he had begun to assume an attitude of indestructibility, a certain chronic Sicilian arrogance. His only responsibility was management of de Leone Pharmaceuticals and Chemicals, which was run by an imposing Board of Directors. Guillermo worked only as long as it didn't interfere with his pleasures.

He thought about all this en route to the villa, wondering if it was now time for him to alter his life and take some of the responsibility for which he'd been destined? He contemplated. The only love in Marco's life had been prematurely destroyed. In his grief, Marco was disconsolate. Roberto moved about in a daze. Nothing at the villa was the same. All this only reinforced Guillermo's determination to enjoy life to the fullest.

One afternoon he wandered into the solarium where the infant Dolcetto lay sunning in his bassinet. He picked up the child on impulse and held him close, making funny little noises to make the baby smile.

"Please Signore, don't awaken the child. I've only just put him to sleep," said Amalfiah, stepping into the room. "It's difficult finding a wet nurse for him. Makes his hours so confusing." When she looked into his eyes, she became confused. "Oh, I'm sorry, I thought you were Signore de Leone."

"I am . . . His Excellency's brother. Guillermo de Leone, at your service. Who are you?"

"Amalfiah, the child's nurse."

"Ah, the American." His appraising eyes assessed her femininity.

"Originally from Siragusa. I've been ten years in America."

"I can see. I can see." He noticed she wore cosmetics.

It began by his asking questions about America. Charming and more sophisticated than her Sicilian contemporaries, Amalfiah appealed to Guillermo's prurient longings, and during his stay they were constant companions in her free time. When time came for him to leave Sicily, he did so with noticeable reluctance.

Four weeks later, Amalfiah announced to Marco that she intended to leave for Siragusa. Having instructed Sara Amalfi and Signora Lamantia on how to care for the infant Dolcetto, she took her leave.

Six months later, Amalfiah Cario returned to the villa. Although he was pleasantly surprised to see her, the Marquis was dismayed to find her pregnant, especially when she named Guillermo as the father of her unborn child.

"I had no place else to go, Excellency," she told Marco. "My family is disgraced by my condition and they have for-

199

saken me. I'm possessed with fear. Because I spoke so high-ly of you and your brother, they suspect your brother of fathering my child. I beg you, Excellency, not to mention my condition to your brother. I want nothing from him. All I want is to have the child and return to America."

Outraged by Guillermo's reckless conduct, Marco in-sisted his brother would do the honorable thing. "In good conscience, I must inform him of this matter."

She protested vehemently, "He'll end up hating me, and I couldn't bear that!" Tears poured from her eyes. "Help me have the child and I'll leave him with you. I know you'll love him and care for him just as you do Dolcetto. When I return to America, life will continue as before."

Marco lost no time in writing to his brother in Rome, advising him to return to the villa on a matter of grave im-portance. Away skiing in Switzerland, Guillermo didn't re-ceive the letter for three months. By the time he returned to Sicily, his son Antonio was nearly two months old. Amalfiah had long since returned to America against Mar-co's stormy objections.

Marco upbraided his brother for being so careless and in-sisted he do the right thing by the girl. "You're thirty-eight and it's time you settled down. She's a nice young girl and her behavior clearly shows how much she loves you. What more could you ask for?"

"She doesn't inflame my heart, Marco. Surely you can un-derstand that?" He felt a pang of dismay at his brother's outrage.

"Yes," said Marco, suddenly remembering Mariolina. "I can understand . . ." He filled with silence and could say nothing more.

Guillermo doted on his beautiful son who was his image. He spent every waking moment with the child, but soon it became obvious he was anxious to return to Rome. "I'll take my son with me, of course. He's my responsibility."

The Lion studied his brother thoughtfully. "What kind of a life is yours for a child, my dear brother? It wouldn't be ideal, you must admit. Leave him with me. Two boys grow-ing up together will be better for both."

Guillermo suddenly seemed relieved of a heavy burden. Sighing deeply, he said, "As usual, you speak with Solomonic wisdom. You wouldn't mind?"

"Isn't he part of my flesh and blood as you are? Why should I mind?"

"You'd be a better father, Marco. There's no question."

"Perhaps one day, when you settle down, you may want him with you."

"Yes," replied his brother. "One day, when I find my Mariolina, I shall heed your advice." Anxious to take one last ride into the hills before leaving for Rome, Guillermo slapped his riding crop impatiently against his boots. "Do you mind if I take Sultano this morning? My mare is with foal."

Marco nodded and waved him off, suddenly preoccupied with thoughts of the work that had accumulated on his desk.

Three hours later, Marco glanced up as the clock on the mantel chimed the hour. He set aside his plumed pen, stretched his arms, and yawned. Turning in his swivel chair, he looked up into the agonized eyes of his brother. Guillermo stood frozen in the doorway, clutching at the bloody holes in his chest, an incredible look of disbelief on his face. "Marco," he gasped. In his outstretched hand he held a wrinkled, blood-smeared envelope.

By the time Marco reached his side, Guillermo had fallen to the floor. Without thinking, Marco stuffed the letter into the pocket of his jacket and knelt down to examine his brother. "Roberto!" he called. "Roberto!" He ran to the front entrance. "Calo! Ciccio! Anyone!" he shouted frantically. "Come quickly!" He rushed back to his brother.

Calo and Ciccio galloped wildly into the courtyard and flinging themselves from their horses, they ran into the Lion's study, the first to arrive.

"Quick! Call Signora Amalfi," he ordered. "You, Calo, help me put him on the sofa," he snapped angrily. "Where the hell were you two? Why didn't you follow him? You know my orders!"

"Excellency, we did. At first we thought it was you on Sultano. But he gave us the slip. That's when we grew suspicious that it wasn't you at all. You know Guillermo. He objects to 'escorts.' We were only ten minutes behind him," said Calo apologetically. He stared at the pale, silent face of the Lion's brother and respectfully tugged off his cap.

Roberto came shuffling into the room. "What is it? What's wrong?" He saw Guillermo lying in a mass of blood with Marco kneeling beside him, stroking his face affectionately and trying to wipe away the blood. Roberto grasped the table for support. "Oh, God of all gods, why?"

Calo moved in and lifted the mangled scarf with which Guillermo had apparently stuffed the hole left by the *lupara* blast. He grimaced. *"Santo Dio!"*

"Yes," said Marco. "It's bad."

"I've never seen such a wound," admitted Calo. "He must

201

have been shot at close range. I'd say no more than two, maybe three feet."

Marco glanced sharply at his bodyguard, noting the implication of his words.

Signora Amalfi lost no time in issuing orders. "Take him to his bed. Bring brandy and hot water and get my case from the dispensary."

In Guillermo's room she worked skillfully and swiftly. Morphine first. Next she cleansed the wounds and packed them with dressings to stop the bleeding.

"The wounds are serious. Excellency. Send for Dr. Pietro at once. *Madre de Dio!* What did they use—cannon? The chest injury is minor, thank God. But his stomach?" She remained silent in her vigil. *What more can happen to the Lions?* she asked herself.

Ciccio was dispatched to return with Dr. Pietro. Calo left to alert the guards to watch for anything unusual. Roberto and Marco moved across the room and sat on the sofa before the marble fireplace.

"What happened?" asked Roberto, his face strained, his lips taut.

Marco raised his arms in a helpless gesture and let them drop heavily to his sides. He felt the crumpling of paper in his pocket, and recalling the envelope, he pulled it out. "Who knows?" he said. He stared at the envelope, then opened it and unfolded the letter. His eyes darted back and forth over the lines and with a heavy sigh, he lay back against the sofa, a defeated man.

Roberto removed the letter from Marco's trembling hands and read:

> *Death to the man who violated our sister. If you don't die from today's attempt, we will search to the ends of the earth for justice. No one dishonors us or our family honor. Not even the Lions of Sicily.*
>
> Guiseppe Tricario

"What was Amalfiah's last name?" asked Marco with a sinking feeling. Before Roberto could reply, Marco rose to his feet. He addressed the nurse. "Is it all right to leave for a few moments? We'll be in my study."

"I can only make him feel less pain for now," she said simply.

In the study, Marco searched frantically through several drawers until he found the document he was looking for. He examined it critically and suddenly sat back heavily in his chair, the very life drained from him. "She called herself Amalfiah Cario. But here it is on Antonio's birth certificate, *Amalfiah Tricario*. These Americans shorten their names. Why didn't I think to inquire more thoroughly?"

"They'll kill him. They won't stop until he's dead," murmured Roberto.

"I won't let them," snapped Marco. "You'd better know that if you don't already know."

"I'm not suggesting anything else, Marco," replied Roberto despairingly.

"We'll hide him. Send him away someplace where he'll be safe . . ."

"Aren't you a bit premature?"

Realizing what Roberto meant, Marco dropped his head into his hands and sat as still as death for several moments. Finally, he got up, placed an arm about Roberto's shoulders, and together the two old friends climbed the spiral staircase to resume their vigil at Guillermo's side.

Dr. Pietro did the best he could with Sara Amalfi's help. Later, when he asked Marco what had happened, Marco couldn't reply.

"It's just lucky that scamp has kept himself in top physical condition," said the physician. "Otherwise, he would not have had the strength to survive."

"Will he live, Alberto?" pressed Roberto. "Just give us that much hope."

"With God on our side, proper attention, and a miracle," shrugged the eccentric physician. He gulped down some black coffee and left with the promise he'd return the next day.

Marco came to life, astonishing not only Roberto, but also himself. He cornered Calo La Bolla and spoke in hushed whispers for several moments. When he dismissed the bodyguard, his hazel eyes sparked with fire. Next, he sat down at his desk and began to write as Roberto watched him in utter fascination. When he'd finished, the Lion handed the paper to Roberto.

"Please see that the newspaper in Messina, *Il Popolo*, receives this and prints it verbatim, *capeeshi?*"

Roberto took the paper from him and glanced at it. Stunned, he shook his head in bafflement. "I don't understand. This is an obituary. Notice of Guillermo's death." His eyes dropped to the paper and he read, ". . . *died of injuries sustained in a fall while riding on the estate. The casket will be closed. The funeral takes place . . .*" Roberto stopped and faced his friend. "Marco . . ."

"Don't you see? I can't risk any more atrocities by those vile animals. Since the *Falconieri* left we've had peace. Our people cannot handle any more violence. Roberto, we've all

203

had our fill. I can't ask my people to subject themselves to any more violence." Marco paced the room. "Let the *mafiosi* gloat when they read the paper. Let them think they killed Guillermo de Leone. As long as they believe it, they'll take no retaliatory action."

Now Roberto understood. Marco wanted his brother alive, even if it meant he'd never see him again.

A casket was delivered the next day. In it were placed a slain sheep and a goat. Marco locked the casket himself and watched as an engraved nameplate was affixed to the elaborate coffin. A small funeral service was held in the estate chapel with Father Bonaventura officiating. Members of the press attended, Roberto spoke the eulogy, and the casket was interred in the family crypt.

Following the ceremony, several people gathered in the main salon to mourn with Marco. Marco felt terrible about deceiving the *contadini,* but he justified his action as being far more sensible for all concerned. Suddenly they could feel tension sweep through the room. Don Tricario and an entourage of *mafiosi* walked in, their fedoras in hand. As they approached the Royal Lion, the Don nodded curtly to Roberto and extended his hand in sympathy. With a look of profound sorrow on his face, Roberto made no effort to accept the Don's handshake.

Don Tricario wisely moved on to Marco, but he made no effort to extend his hand. Bowing slightly, he said, "Excellency, it grieves me that your heart should be so saddened by such an unfortunate accident. Your brother was a good man. Not like *El Leone,* but a good man in his own way."

Marco wanted to pounce on the revolting little man and beat him to within an inch of his cowardly life. Instead he shook his head sorrowfully, pretending to be overcome with grief, and waved them on.

Satisfied that Guillermo was dead, the *mafiosi* left the villa unaware that guns had been trained on them with orders to shoot to kill if they should flick an improper eyebrow.

Two weeks later Calo La Bolla reappeared at the villa after a long absence. He joined Marco in his study where they both remained in seclusion for many hours.

That night, shortly past midnight, three shadowy figures left the villa in a covered carriage driven by Calo. They arrived at the deserted waterfront in Messina, and Calo reined the horses as they neared a secluded area where a boat and oarsman waited. Marco embraced his brother Guillermo and clung to him in deep affection for several moments before he let him go. Then he embraced Paolo Nicosia, his old skipper from the *Marchessa,* and handed him an envelope.

"Paolo, Paolo, I will forever be indebted to you for this special favor."

Nicosia shoved the envelope back at the Lion. "Excellency, do not offend me by offering me money. You have done for me more than what I could ever repay. With my last dying breath I shall do whatever you desire of me. But, please, no money."

Overwhelmed with emotion, Marco could only say, "Take care of him, old friend. See that he gets to his destination without incident."

Nicosia nodded and he jerked his head toward Calo. "We go now."

The two brothers embraced again for the last time. They had said their farewells back at the villa, away from prying eyes and listening ears. Marco brushed away his tears, quickly boarded the carriage, and headed for the villa. Guillermo stepped from the rowboat onto Nicosia's fishing scow, the *Baccala,* for other ports and another life.

Marco waited three days before he confided in Roberto and even then didn't tell him everything.

"It's not that I don't trust you, Roberto. God knows we've been closer than brothers. I want no one to suspect Guillermo's alive. The less you know, the better for you. Not even Paolo Nicosia will know where Guillermo is going. He'll be dropped off at a port far from his final destination. Who knows, perhaps in a few years we can all be united again."

Roberto understood and he respected Marco for bearing the burden alone.

19

"How far does the Signorina travel?" asked Don Umberto Partenico, who was dressed in the manner of an affluent banker: gray suit, black velvet collar and lapels, and a gold watch looped through his vest.

Diamonte didn't reply. Her icy blue eyes glanced indifferently at him, then she concentrated her gaze out the window of the coach at the passing panorama of the Ionian Sea.

"The trip will be long enough, Signorina. It's best we know each other. Permit me to introduce myself. I am

Don Umberto from Godrano. This gentleman next to me is Signore Bellini who travels to Mussomelli."

Diamonte continued to ignore them. *How dare they be so presumptuous as to speak with me. What do they take me for? A tart? A whore?*

Don Umberto was puzzled. A noblewoman, no doubt. Her aloofness confirmed his theory. But to travel alone was unpardonable! Foolish!

Signore Bellini's thoughts were of a different nature. He leaned forward in an intimate fashion, placing one hand on the girl's knee. "Don't be frightened, *bellissima*. It's a long journey. Don Umberto is right. It's better if we are friendly."

Her cool blue eyes stared hard at the hand on her knee. She slowly lifted her eyes to meet his. He was so taken with her beauty, Signore Bellini didn't see her reach into her handbag. Then, quicker than the eye could see, she plunged a small, sharp stiletto into the back of his hand.

"Botto de sanguo!" screamed the man, angrily withdrawing his bloodied hand. Unable to contain his shame and rage, he sulked into a corner of the carriage and wrapped his injured hand in a handkerchief. Don Umberto laughed aloud.

Straining and creaking noisily, the carriage was pulled up the rugged mountains by sweating, lathered horses. It swayed rakishly, careening around corners and juggling its passengers unceremoniously. Diamonte experienced many bad moments. Her thoughts took her back over the two days that had passed since she'd left the de Leone villa.

Cunning enough to know there'd be no mercy after her murder attempt on Mariolina de Catanese, she took a few personal belongings and a horse and rode to Messina. She'd slept outside overnight, sold the horse, and claimed her dowry money when the bank opened. At the *modista*'s, she'd made a few necessary purchases, including a few pairs of men's trousers and shirts which she stuffed into her needlepoint carpet bag. Leaving the *modista*'s in a black travel suit and a Princess Eugénie feathered hat, she looked like an astonishingly beautiful young noblewoman.

The object of every eye as she passed along the street, she marched boldly into the travel office and purchased a ticket for Catania. The security of her money belt, attached firmly inside her uncomfortable whalebone corset, gave her both the courage and the poise to carry herself with unmistakable elegance. En route to Catania, she decided to take the southern coastal route to Palermo, and from there a boat to Rome.

A young woman without chaperone was astonishing even in modern day Catania, where she found herself with a two-hour layover. Enthralled by the splendor of the city, she became a wide-eyed tourist. The appraising glances of passersby were nothing new, but when men made obscene gestures and propositioned her and restaurants refused her admittance without an escort or a chaperone, she realized she knew very little of this alien outside world which threatened her. She grew frustrated and alarmed.

In desperation she stopped at a delicatessen and purchased some salami, cheese, olives, and a small *panetta*. Then she headed for the cool lawn in the park across the street from the Piazza Roma. With a peasant's abandon, she sat down and began to munch hungrily on the snack. Her eyes filled with the splendors of man-made wonders her young eyes had never seen. *Managghia!* It is possible? A team of horses drawn by ancient gods gleamed like gold in the sunlight, high atop the tallest building in the piazza. How, she wondered had they been carried so high across the sky? Had they been real once? Frozen into immobility at the hand of a cruel sorceress? In the pictures she'd seen of Garibaldi, he appeared as a gnome. The bronzed statue of him in the square portrayed him as a giant. *What a curious world this is,* she told herself.

The incongruity of her noble attire and her peasant behavior had drawn some curious bystanders. A few boys stood staring curiously at her. Nurses wheeling baby carriages paused to stare at her outrageous behavior. Flushed with self-consciousness, Diamonte left the remainder of her food, gathered her poise, and with an arrogant toss of her head, walked out of the park.

The city proved cold and hostile for Diamonte. There were no friendly and familiar faces to smile at her and treat her as someone special as they did at the villa.

At the appointed hour, Diamonte had boarded the coach and found herself seated across from these two insipid boors. Warned to hide their valuables and be prepared for unusual circumstances, all three passengers took the words in their stride. They didn't seem in the least perturbed when the driver announced, "We'll soon be in bandit country."

Diamonte glanced at the fancy gold watch she had purchased in Messina. If the driver didn't tarry, they'd arrive in Gela by 7 P.M. Convinced that no man would ever harm or rob her, she patted the folds of her skirt into place and ignored the other two passengers.

The road grew more rugged and the terrain more hazardous. The coach's squeaky wheels slipped in and out of muddy ruts, tossing them unceremoniously about.

Bellini shouted to the driver, "Damn you! Can't you be more careful!"

Don Umberto cursed aloud, "Goddammit, you clown! Better slow up!"

Diamonte's hat slipped off her head and rolled to the carriage floor. Her handbag slipped off her lap and she bounced off the seat several times, finally landing on the floorboards. *"Butana de shekki!"* she screamed in the acrimonious voice of a fishwife. "Whore of a jackass! Driver of sheep dung!"

No one could have been more shocked by her behavior than the two men who sat staring open-mouthed at her. This tart wasn't nobility at all. She was nothing but a common peasant who looked like a countess. Probably someone's whore. Disgusted with themselves for having been so expertly deceived, they didn't even bother to assist her to her seat.

A few kilometers away from Ragusa, it happened. The coach came to a screeching halt. Through the carriage windows they saw on horseback, six of the foulest, most ferocious, unkempt men they'd ever seen.

"Bandits!" they exclaimed in muffled voices.

The sight of these fierce and frightening blackguards both intimidated and excited Diamonte. She clutched her wildly beating heart. Signore Bellini's eyes popped in fright and he trembled from head to toe. Don Umberto sat back calmly, unaffected by the interruption. He paused only to light a cigar. Diamonte missed none of this. Thoughts that her life might be in jeopardy didn't enter her mind. Her concern was only for the money belt hidden in her corset.

The bandits moved swiftly into action when the coach halted.

"Everyone out!" shouted one of the men. "Throw down the cargo!" he called to the driver. "And don't be clever or you won't live to tell about it."

"You . . . Yes, you!" called another brute to Signore Bellini. "Strip! You heard what I said, strip!"

"But . . ." The protest died on Signore Bellini's lips and he quickly obeyed. In stripping Bellini down to his underwear, they had stripped him of his dignity and left an embarrassed coward trying to cover himself from the amused girl's eyes.

"And you . . ." Two bandits approached Don Umberto. ". . . are next. Move!"

"Don't touch me if you value your life," said the Don

quietly holding his two would-be assailants at bay with the power-saturated stare of a *mafioso*. The bandits backed off and permitted the Don to reboard the coach. Bellini stared at this in awe, forgetting his own plight. He shuddered as he realized who Don Umberto must be.

Next the bandits made a move toward the girl. Even as she shook in her boots, Diamonte imperiously leveled her vibrant eyes on her accosters, and speaking with authority, she said, "Well! It's about time! You finally got here, eh? What took so long?"

The bandits froze. Disarmed by her aggressive manner, they exchanged puzzled glances. Don Umberto's head poked inquisitively out the coach window and he stared in fascination. The driver looked at her as if he'd seen an apparition. Before any of them could recover from their astonishment, Diamonte continued haughtily, "Come, come! Don't just stand there! How long will it take to reach your camp? Am I to meet with your leader as planned?"

One bandit, not easily intimidated, ordered gruffly, "Identify yourself!"

"Listen," shouted Don Umberto. "This is one *strega* who can defend herself. Better do as she says." His words carried weight.

"I need no one to speak on my behalf," she retorted daringly.

The Don shrugged. *"Ciào strega!* Give my regards to Matteo Barbarossa."

An idea struck Diamonte. Opening her handbag, she retrieved a snowy handkerchief embossed with the seal of the Royal Lion. She handed it to a short, paunchy bandit with a sharklike face. "Tell your leader I come as emissary from *El Leone.*"

The men studied the seal of the Royal Lion. *Demonio!* She must be some helluva woman! None had ever dared to speak to the Mazzarinos as she had. She was absolutely fearless. Who could she be? Did their new leader, the red-bearded devil, forget to tell them? He was a strange man this Barbarossa, never confiding in anyone, always brooding. They'd better take no chances.

One bandit took her bags, another gave her his horse, and they waited until the coach was out of sight before they moved into the hills with this strange bit of baggage who stood up to them as if she possessed the balls of Hercules.

In the moving coach, Don Umberto considered this woman who had kept six Mazzarino bandits at bay. *Phew! What a diabolical wench!* Signore Bellini shook all the way to Mussomelli unsure of who was most frightening, the six

Mazzarinos, the *mafioso* seated across from him, or the vile witch who had injured his hand.

The seven riders rode swiftly, traversing steep ravines, winding over twisting roads, climbing higher onto the craggy tors. They passed ancient ruins of bygone civilizations, and for hours Diamonte wondered about her sanity for getting involved in such a crazy scheme. Exhausted by the endless riding, they finally passed several checkpoints and came upon an enormous grayish white boulder—etched by time and the elements into the shape of a gigantic hawk—which marked the entrance to the well-camouflaged camp.

If Diamonte had had any idea that she'd soon encounter the sadistic and cruel Mazzarinos, recognized as the most ferocious killers who had ever inhabited the island, her bold daring might have waned considerably.

It was sunset when they rode into camp. *Managghia!* Diamonte guessed there must have been two hundred people in the sprawling camp. Dark-skinned, unsmiling, evil-looking shrews, each unkempt and slovenly, paused to stare at her, cloaking their curiosity behind brooding eyes. They nudged one another and pointed to her as she passed. Dressed in dark cotton shirts and skirts and heavy mountain boots, they stood with their feet apart and their hands on their hips like men.

The savage stench in the air nauseated her. *How primitive. So foul and repulsive. Why didn't I just give them my money? They'll get it anyway! What did I get myself into this time?* she asked herself.

A tug on the reins of her horse startled her. Ordered to dismount, she was led toward a circle of men engaged in conversation. At the center of the activity stood a towering, red-bearded giant, six feet tall with hair the color of coal. Naked to the waist, he had skin the color of glistening bronze. His ebony eyes terrified her at first, but as she approached and noticed how they appraised her body, Diamonte, a woman who understood men, took courage.

She inhaled deeply to brace herself and screwed up her nose at the distasteful odors. Men at either side of her along the path turned in her direction. One man calmly unbuttoned his fly and relieved himself on the ground before her. Averting her head, she strode defiantly toward the bandit leader.

Matteo Barbarossa, a matchstick rolling between his lips, leaned back lazily against a wagon, watching her lithe movements. His eyes took in every inch of her from head to toe, then came to rest on her incredibly beautiful face. Desire

210

swept over Matteo like a tidal wave of passion, drowning out all except this vision walking toward him. Watching them both, Mario Cacciatore, a frog of a man, felt the electricity between them, and he scowled darkly, confused by the discovery that his chief was a mere mortal, subject to human frailties and passions after all.

At that moment, Destiny whispered to Matteo Barbarossa. *Be on your guard. Trust no one, Matteo. Think! What would the Lion of Sicily want with you, his sworn enemy? Why would the great Lion send a woman as his emissary?*

Diamonte quickly appraised Matteo. Here was a man she could rule by the power of her body, arms, lips, and loins. She would bend him to her will and he'd answer her commands. She smiled inwardly.

Matteo watched her without giving evidence of his feelings. He set his jaws firmly and pulled back his shoulders. His fiery eyes dilated angrily and turned cold. He asserted his manliness.

"What's your name?" he boomed loudly.

"Diamonte. What's yours?"

He ignored her question. "State your business."

"You're the leader here?"

"I ask the questions here, wench!" he growled. Every eye in the camp was upon them. The Mazzarinos strained and stretched their necks. This they had to see!

"Ah, so you're Matteo? Then it's you with whom I must speak."

"Speak!"

"Here? In front of all these people? What I have to say must be said in private."

Matteo raised a powerful arm and slapped her across the mouth. Unable to avert her head in time, she caught the full force of the blow and was thrown momentarily off balance. Coarse guffaws and mocking laughter arose from the onlookers. Phew! They were relieved. For a moment they were certain their leader had been bewitched. What a daughter of Satan!

"You lie! You weren't sent by *El Leone*. Don't be clever with Matteo Barbarossa. What is it you want? You'd best answer truthfully or I shall turn you over to the women. They won't be as gentle as I!"

"I'll say nothing until I know you are the leader here," she said stubbornly.

"*Che demonio!* I am Matteo Barbarossa, leader of the Mazzarinos!"

"Very well, Matteo Barbarossa, leader of the Mazzarinos," she mocked. "Since it's you I've come to see, where can we go to talk?" She wiped a trickle of blood from her lips, stared at it on her hands, and rubbed her fingertips together in an effort to erase it.

"Impudent bitch! Is there no fear in you? No respect? Talk!" he commanded.

"No! Alone or nothing. I have my orders," she lied.

Matteo struck the dirt with the heel of his boot like an enraged bull. Behind her and all around them, he saw the subdued mirth on the faces of his men enjoying his discomfort, the eager eyes of the diabolical women watching, waiting to see him fall under the guile of a woman. Without warning he slapped Diamonte again and again. A four-fingered welt sprang up on her pale face. She choked back the tears when she noticed the women flush with pleasure at her discomfort. She raised her hands to her face and traced the welts lightly with her fingertips, but she wasn't without resourcefulness.

"You call yourself a leader of men? Hah!" She raised her hand to strike back at him. Matteo caught her wrist in mid-air and held it firmly.

"You try my patience, bitch! Speak or I shall have you beaten!"

"And I say, alone!" Her jacket had come undone. The huge pearl Guillermo had given her moved across her heaving breasts like a pale, creamy moon of fire. Frightened, humilated, and angry—mostly angry—Diamonte held her ground. The sweet, fresh fragrance of her perfume unnerved him. Her fearlessness unnerved him. Goddammit! Always complications! Finally, he thrust her from him and signaled his men to move away from them. Then the Mazzarino leader led her to a secluded area where they could converse in private.

Cacciatore burned with indignation. He occupied himself by busily honing his blades, but his mind roiled with thoughts of Matteo and this impertinent baggage. Goddammit! He'd just ruined one of his best blades. Angry both at Matteo for being bent by a mere slip of a woman and at himself for his lack of concentration, he flung the damaged knife from him. Who the hell was she, anyway? Goddammit! She even knew his name! Hadn't she called him, Matteo? There's more to this mazurka than meets the eye! Stony-faced, he watched them until they both disappeared behind the boulder leading to a bluff that overlooked the entire camp. *Whore of the Devil! I'll find out,* he promised himself.

"Diamonte, eh?" Matteo sat on a huge volcanic rock, lit up a thin cigar, and puffed with deliberation.

"Barbarossa, eh?" She mocked him.

"Listen, be grateful you possess great beauty, else you'd already be buzzard bait."

"Ah, the villain is a man after all."

"What's this nonsense about *El Leone?*" he said, ignoring her last remark.

"Nonsense? What makes you think it's nonsense?"

He glanced at his cigar, contemplating it a moment, then, leaning forward, one hand firmly gripping his knee, he pursed his lips and waited with exaggerated patience for an answer. He watched her remove bone hairpins from her hair, shake it out, and allow it to fall loosely over her shoulders. She shrugged. "Very well, you know it's nonsense."

"Listen, don't hold me cheaply," he said, annoyed by her sudden candor. "You're speaking with the next feudal over-lord of Sicily. I know everything. One thing's certain. The Lion of Sicily would not seek out Matteo Barbarossa!" He inhaled her fragrance and studied her through calculating eyes.

"You are astute, leader of the Mazzarinos. And percep-tive, too." She flattered him and it pleased him more than he let her know.

"*Aloura,* why are you here?"

Her wits slowly disintegrating, Diamonte found herself in-escapably drawn to this raw brute who filled her with a peculiar excitement. Why? She'd never known her own fa-ther, reputedly a Greek bandit. This affinity she felt, this lack of fear, this uncanny feeling that she'd been among such people before—what was it? She just didn't know and could not sift through her mind to think, not in the presence of this man whose lean hard body could crush her in seconds.

She slipped out of her jacket and sat on the rock next to him. Something Marco had told her came back to her. She was sixteen, growing into womanhood, when he said, "A woman must learn to become important to her man and learn to flatter him at the proper time. Help build his weak-ness into strength. One day, he'll lean on this strength and never forget it's source." *Odd,* thought Diamonte, *why should I remember Marco's words at a time like this.*

"Why are you a bandit?" she asked on impulse. "Surely you don't belong here with such scum and filth. At the Villa de Leone I've seen lesser men than you hold public office, bask in positions of trust, and grow wealthy beyond their dreams."

"The Villa de Leone?"

"I was born there," she volunteered. "My mother is the Lion's most trusted servant. The Marquis is my Godfather."

Matteo laughed uproariously at the ludicrous tale. "What

213

a web you spin, little spider. Too many complications! Too many . . ."

"You don't believe me?"

"Basta! Enough is enough. What are you doing here? I tire quickly, little spider." He was still laughing.

"Then I won't risk the danger that you'll laugh yourself into convulsions, fall over and get entangled into my web," she said sarcastically. "Then for sure your men would kill me and take my money . . ." Diamonte gasped. She was horrified at her lack of prudence and wanted to bite off her tongue.

"Money? You have money?" His eyes lit up brightly.

Diamonte thought fast. "Just a few *scudi*. I'm not lying to you, Matteo. I've spoken the truth to a point. I've come here seeking sanctuary." Her voice dropped. "You see, my father was a bandit . . ." Her voice trailed off dreamily.

Barbarossa's patience wore thin. "How many stories will you tell before the truth spills from those lying lips?" He was exasperated.

"I poisoned the wife of the Marquis," she blurted out defiantly.

"You did what?" His eyes darted to her face. "Is this straight? The truth? *Che demonio!*" He saw truth in her eyes even before she nodded, and he grew guarded.

"Why? Were you mistreated? Did she beat you? What?"

"I didn't like her."

"You didn't *like* her! And you killed her for that?"

"It's not funny. I'm a hunted woman."

"And you've come here for sanctuary." She nodded. "Forget it. This is no place for you."

"Where then, in some small village jail, imprisoned by the *carabinieri*, who'll hang me or use me as they will? If this is no place for me, then it's no place for you!"

"I have plans, woman. Destiny brings me here—but only for a short time, understand?"

"You believe in Destiny?" She slipped out of her jacket in the warmth of the night.

"If I didn't I wouldn't be here."

"If you believe in Destiny, you must believe that my destiny and yours have been ordained. It was Destiny who brought me here to you."

Annoyed, Matteo dropped his cigar, ground it out with the heel of his boot, and thought about her words. He didn't like anyone being smarter than he was, and this wench talked like she had book learning. "How the hell do you figure our destinies are bound up together? I don't see that our destinies are tied together in any way."

214

"I'm here, aren't I?" He shrugged and leaned against the boulder. "That's all the proof you need. If Destiny hadn't decreed we'd meet, we wouldn't have met. I wouldn't have committed the crime I did, and I wouldn't have run away from a wonderful life like a frightened, hunted animal." Diamonte paused reflectively at her own words. A glance at him told her her words had taken effect. "If Destiny hadn't intended us to meet, your men would have taken my jewels and freed me as they did the others—no? Have they ever brought anyone to camp as they did me?"

"You deceived them."

"No, Matteo. It was Destiny who deceived them. Destiny guided me to you. How would I have found courage to face you and your people, if Destiny hadn't bolstered me?"

Matteo scowled. He didn't like people being cleverer than he was either. Maybe if he looked closer, he'd see a pattern, a pattern woven by Destiny. He relaxed a bit. Goddammit! Why the hurry? She wasn't going anyplace. This was Barbarossa's land. Here, his word was law. What did he care if she was clever. If he read the message in her eyes, she could be as clever as hell!

He stood up and walked to the ridge. Below them, the sun had set, giving fire to the earth. Her words echoed in his mind. He'd almost forgotten that there was another life beyond the world of the Mazzarinos. He'd listened to her every word, wondering as he did why he'd let this *woman* talk with him.

Matteo turned to look at her, this woman who'd thrust herself into his life. Etched against the darkening sky, his features were filled with black shadows. Whatever had drawn them together, Diamonte fought the feeling that her future belonged with this red-bearded bandit. She knew his eyes were upon her and she tried to meet his stare, but the luminous, yellow-orange sunset blinded her. She was forced to avert her head.

"The women here are *animales*," he said, trying to convince himself and her that the camp was no place for her. "They will steal everything you own, pick you apart like a plucked chicken. They can be cruel and vindictive."

"I can handle myself."

"If you survive their treacheries, jealous rages, hatred, and superstitions, you'll have to reckon with the men. They'll be around to lust after you, rape you, fight over you and with you. You won't have a moment's peace."

"And you, Matteo? Where will you be when all this takes place?"

"Where an observer should remain, detached and to the side."

"Wouldn't *you* be here to protect me?"

He cocked an amused eyebrow, walked toward her, and sat down next to her on the boulder. "I make it a point not to mix business with pleasure. If you join the Mazzarinos, you become everyone's property. Make sure you understand fully what I say. Here, we follow the law of the desert: one for all and all for one."

"What a strange law. Do you live by the same law?" Her voice dropped an octave. "Wouldn't you want me to be—only—your woman?" she whispered hoarsely.

"That's impossible. I cannot defy the law."

"Is there no other way?"

Their eyes met and held in a pregnant silence, as if they were testing each other.

"No." He felt a dull thud over his heart. He knew, from that moment on, that it would be the blackest day of his life if he ever saw her with another man.

Matteo lit another small cigar and puffed on it as he gazed out into the distance. His features jerked and his jaws flexed as he wrestled with himself. No matter how he tried to convince himself that he wouldn't care who she slept with, he knew he was lying to himself. It did matter. This very fact seemed to eat away at him.

Busy with her own thoughts, Diamonte grew animated at the prospect of making love to that ugly sea of faces she'd seen earlier; faces with no character, all of them animals, like a herd of filthy, disgusting goats. She shuddered visibly and filled with revulsion.

"Porca miseria! There must be another way. How long may I stay here with you before I'm considered public property?"

"My men and I alone determine that."

"Matteo?" Diamonte pondered a moment. "Don't some of the women ever belong to *one* man?" She'd seen a few children when she entered camp earlier.

"Only those who decide to get married."

"Well," she sighed heavily as if the weight of the world had suddenly been removed from her shoulders. "Then it's settled."

"What's this? What are you telling me?"

"It's settled. We shall marry."

Barbarossa exploded. "No woman tells me who I shall marry."

He grabbed her long black hair and entwined it roughly around his fingers. He felt the closeness of her body, her

216

warmth. He tightened his grip and pulled her head back at an awkward angle. She didn't protest. She smiled, taunting him.

"When I marry, I shall do the asking. I make the decisions." He spoke with authority. His fierce dark eyes were magnetized by the pools of her misty blue eyes. His manhood sprang to life. Diamonte felt him and knew.

"You're resisting Destiny, Matteo."

"Managghia!" he exploded. "Where do you learn such boldness?" He loosened his grip on her and she tossed her head and laughed softly.

"From those very men who aren't afraid to fight for what they believe in. I've had the best instructors in the world."

Cacciatore piled heaps of stringy, overcooked rabbit on two plates and poured wine into two tankards. Shuffling in his ducklike walk, trying to balance the plates and cups, he followed the dirt path leading to the bluff where Barbarossa and the girl were talking.

"Here, take this." He shoved the food toward them.

Diamonte glanced from the revolting mess they called food to the suspicious and hard-eyed Cacciatore. "No, *grazie,*" she said politely.

Matteo took the food and wine and promptly dismissed his hatchet man. He shoved a hunk of meat into his mouth and chomped hungrily, like an animal. *"Mangia, mangia,"* he told her, wiping the juices dribbling from the corners of his lips. "Listen, you'd better eat. Food is like gold here. A rarity. You'll get no food until tomorrow night."

"No breakfast?" she asked woefully. She was famished. But never, *never* would she touch that foul-looking slop. She watched in revulsion as he gobbled his food, making loud smacking noises. He guzzled his wine even more revoltingly.

When he finished eating, Matteo led Diamonte to a secluded area high among the rocks, isolated from camp. He tossed a blanket over his shoulders. She smiled to herself. So far it had worked. Her wits hadn't eluded her altogether. If she could keep him in this receptive mood for a day or so until she stole a horse, she could escape this absurd jungle of filthy animals.

She could hear soft music floating up from the camp. A few men sang plaintive songs of their childhood and their villages. For a moment, Diamonte felt homesick. But the sounds of loud moaning and men and women grunting like animals frightened her.

"Don't be alarmed. They sound like mountain lions when they couple to make love," said Matteo.

She'd never been that sexually aroused, and the primitive sounds excited her even more.

"Songs have been written about me. Do you at least believe that?" she asked coyly.

"I can see why." At this point he would have agreed with the devil.

For Diamonte, compliments were an effective aphrodisiac, lubricating both her mind and her body. Sometimes in the past, the nearness of a man was enough to bring on an explosive orgasm. Now Matteo's animal smell excited her immensely. She moved voluptuously on the hard blanket-covered ground, giving no indication of her discomfort. In the secluded knoll, protected on both sides by an outer cave wall, the night air was warmer.

She unbuttoned her blouse and laid her hand on his upper thigh, supporting herself as she shifted about. Gently she brushed the area of his groin and felt a stonelike hardness. She flushed with pleasure. They were both sexually aroused. A low moan escaped Matteo's lips; he tried desperately to restrain himself but couldn't. Savagely he tore at her blouse and cupped both her breasts. Diamonte sighed ecstatically. Her breasts were the most sensual part of her body. She had never felt such passion. With all her strength she pushed him away.

"Not like this," she insisted. "Not like two animals."

"Why not? This is what you want."

Diamonte had no way of knowing Matteo had been celibate for two years. Unable to take the filthy women at camp, he decided to abstain. What passions were stored inside this powerful man waiting to be released. His resolve turned to water. Nothing short of an earthquake could have prevented him from taking her. His savage lust aroused her, and she frantically tore at her own clothing until she lay naked in his arms. They impatiently explored each other, and soon she felt him inside her, hard and hot and throbbing. She heard the soft growling and moaning in her ears as his passion increased and his thrusts became more rhythmic. He rode Diamonte until she screamed, her whole body trembling with the shock of an awesome orgasm. Matteo held her with a passion that frightened him, his whole being flooded with a satisfied warmth.

Afterwards, they smoked and drank wine. Matteo, relaxed from the sexual release, reflected bitterly that he had found no virgin in her loins. He frowned and felt an icy chill. Although she was the most satisfying woman he'd ever been with, she was nevertheless a whore.

He heard a muffled sound and turned toward her. Diamonte was crying.

"What's wrong, eh? Why are you crying, little spider?"

"I wanted it to be different, Matteo. I'm so ashamed you found no virgin in my loins." Her act was superb.

"If I'd known that one day I'd meet with a man like you . . . Oh, Matteo, it was so terrible. We were so poor and he threatened to throw us out. My mother worked like a slave for him. Poor thing. If she only knew what I've done to keep a roof over our heads, she would have plunged a knife into her breasts. My mother is an angel. I would do anything for her."

"Who? What are you raving about, woman?"

"Who do you think?"

"El Leone?"

Diamonte lowered her head. She didn't have to answer. At that moment, her silence had incriminated Marco.

"It was terrible. Why do you think I've grown so bold, so fearless? Only because I've been subjected to indignities that would never have been if we weren't so poor. I tell you, one day I'll make them all stand up and take notice of me, rue the day *they* ever violated me."

"They?" *Managghia,* what sort of a devil did he have on his hands.

"He has a brother, too. And a very dear friend."

Matteo glowered darkly. "So this is the man whom the peasants of Sicily worship like a god?" He stroked her head and held her close.

"Shhh," he said soothingly in a gentle manner which surprised him. *"Aloura,* don't think about him or the past. One day he'll be reckoned with, you'll see."

Perhaps she wouldn't be too anxious to leave this Mazzarino bandit, after all. Suddenly, she remembered. She felt around the ground, around the blanket. Her slender hands groped about the strewn clothing. She panicked.

"Have you seen the white packet, Matteo? I must have dropped it." The money! She couldn't find it.

"Is this what you're looking for?" he asked, holding the envelope teasingly in front of her.

She grabbed for it a bit too anxiously. He pulled it back away from her, his curiosity stimulated.

"Give that to me!" she ordered in an angry shrewish voice. All seductiveness left her. She was like a snarling mountain lion, all teeth and claws.

The change in her was so pronounced that Matteo frowned and pushed her away savagely and looked into the packet.

He took out the money and whistled low and appreciatively. He hadn't seen that much money in his lifetime.

"Where did you get this?"

"None of your business. It's mine." When she saw his baffled look turn to suspicion, Diamonte knew she'd done the wrong thing, and said even worse. She quickly changed her attitude.

"It's my dowry money," she said quietly and truthfully.

"You just said you were poor, that your mother slaved to support you."

"That's true."

"Then how did you come by all this money."

She wanted to tell him that she didn't have to account to anyone. But she remembered all too well where she was, whom she was with, and what could very well happen to her, so she continued with the truth to see how far that would take her.

"My Godfather set up a trust for me when I was born."

"The man who . . ."

"Yes, the man who deflowered me." She lied to cover up her previous lie. "Now give me back my money," she pleaded.

"Not now. It wouldn't be safe with you. Besides, I want to check out your story, little spider."

"You don't believe me? And stop calling me that silly name."

He laughed at her, feeling more secure. Now that he had her money, he knew she'd not wander too far without it. Not this wench. She was too shrewd and calculating, perhaps even for a master like himself.

"The money stays with me, Diamonte. I am the leader here. My word is law!"

Her first reaction was fiery anger, then, thinking better of the situation, she calmed down. Very well, there'd come a time, when he'd least expect it and she'd have her money again. Nothing could have been sweeter than her voice when she said, "As you say, your word is law."

Diamonte had lived on the threshold of two separate worlds. Neither peasant nor noble, she was ill at ease in both worlds. She never knew to which she really belonged. Deep inside, she had always felt constant rejection, beginning with the father she never knew, and this seemed to set the stage for the fantasy world in which she existed, safely and comfortably. Her fantasy involving Marco probably resulted in the biggest of all rejections, a blow to her ego so monumental she couldn't cope, so she struck back at the object

220

of his love. As a highly complex young woman subject to fits of bad temper, she had learned to wear many masks, one for each fantasy.

In many ways these two, Diamonte and Matteo Barbarossa, were alike. Victims of their environments, lonely and introverted, thinking they didn't belong, they had to create their own world so they could manipulate people to satisfy their whims and demands. They were inescapably drawn to one another.

Barbarossa smiled to himself. What a wife she'd make when he became *capomafioso* of Sicily. She's as ambitious as I, perhaps more so. Then, again, perhaps he could teach her to exercise prudence and wisdom, this little spider of his.

So far Destiny had kept her bargain with him. Now that she had suddenly thrust this beautiful creature at him—for no special reason that he could see at the moment—why should he turn his back on her.

20

Diamonte awoke at dawn to the odor of strong black coffee, urine, and horse dung. She felt dirty and her body ached from the hard stony surface beneath her. Her hand groped lazily for Matteo. His place was empty.

"Here, drink some coffee."

A young girl with dark eyes and thick black braids stood over her extending a cup of the muddiest coffee she'd ever seen. Her face was sullen; her pose tough.

"Thank you." She sipped the liquid and made a face to match its bitter taste. "What's your name?"

"Teresina. What's yours?"

"Diamonte." The girl nodded morosely. "Is there a place I can take a bath?" The girl stared blankly, shrugging uncomprehendingly. "You know—a bath? *Un bagnio.* I want to wash myself."

"Ah," said the girl pointing to a large vat similar to a water trough for animals below them in the clearing.

Diamonte gagged with revulsion. "I'll not be an *animale* like the others. There must be another place—a creek or river, something. Where's Matteo?"

Leaning against the huge boulder, the young girl watched Diamonte straighten her hair. She pointed to an area Diamonte couldn't see. Walking to the edge of the bluff, she saw Matteo talking with several of the men. She ran eagerly down toward him. They saw her approach but paid no attention.

"Buon giorno," she said amiably.

The men looked away from her. Matteo turned his back and resumed his talk.

"I said 'good morning.' Can't you speak?"

Matteo glared hotly at her and walked to the bluff where they'd spent the night. Stunned, sorely confused by his alien manner, and filled with embarrassment, she followed him, taking giant steps to catch up with him.

Out of sight and hearing distance to the others, Matteo turned on her. *"Number one.* You don't talk to the men unless you're spoken to. *Number two.* You never walk into a group where men congregate. You send a messenger, if needed. Who the hell taught you these manners, eh? A woman doesn't act as bold as you."

"All right!" she sputtered angrily. "Now I know. I can't follow rules if I don't know what they are. At the villa I talk to all the men. We're like a big family."

Matteo's mouth hung agape. "I don't believe you. You lie like you lied last night."

"Yes, it's true. I tell you it's true. We stop, we talk, we pass the time of day. You don't want me to talk to the men here? Then you tell me."

"Good. Now you know." He began to walk away.

"No you don't. You stay. I want to speak with you."

"Number three! You *do not* command Matteo Barbarossa." He shouted loud enough for the entire camp to hear. "Here, I am the leader!"

Diamonte turned around and looked below them. The eyes of all his people were on him. They heard him easily. She turned her cool eyes to him. "You weren't like this last night." She tried to find the balance.

"Last night was last night. Today is today!"

His behavior was new and repulsive and confusing to her. At the Villa de Leone she could do no wrong. This was a painful and intolerable situation, but until she could retrieve her money and flee this unpredictable man and horrible place, she'd have to accept the subordinate role. Her eyes narrowed with cunning.

"If it's not too much trouble, Oh Mighty One," she mocked, "tell me what other rules you've set up for *paying* guests. Then I shall know my place in this magnificent den of thieves, cutthroats, and murderers."

She tossed her head defiantly, expecting another slap for her impudence. Her eyes fell to the ground, suddenly darting in all directions.

"Matteo," she shouted. "My bags. They're gone!"

"Who was here with you?" he asked, glancing about the rocks.

"There was only Teresina . . ." She paused, regretting her accusation when she saw his face tense.

Matteo walked to the edge of the bluff and whistled shrilly. In a matter of seconds Cacciatore appeared. They hastily exchanged words.

"Your things will be returned shortly."

"Is there anyplace I can bathe? A stream? River? Anyplace?"

He acted as if she had asked for the moon. "I told you this is no place for you. I shall have you escorted to Gela."

"And my money?" She knew the answer.

"It stays here. We need supplies and clothing."

"Then I stay. It's all I have in the world."

"Suit yourself, but don't expect special favors and treatment from us."

Cacciatore pulled the girl Teresina along by her long braids with one hand. Diamonte's travel bag was clutched firmly with the other. He tossed the bag at her feet and addressed Matteo. "What is her punishment?"

"She stole. And she disobeyed my orders. Punish her for both, stealing and disobeying."

"I forgive her this time," said Diamonte when she saw the look of frozen terror on the girl's face. She glanced at Matteo. His cold, brittle expression caused her to back off. Last night he'd been a fantastic lover; today he was a satanic monster as unpredictable as Lucifer. She watched Cacciatore place the girl's hand on a rock, and in a swift, sure movement, he raised his knife and whacked off her finger.

Teresina screamed, then fainted. The severed finger rolled over the bluff onto the rocks below. Blood gushed from between her thumb and forefinger. The two men walked off in brutal detachment.

Diamonte felt faint, sick to her stomach. In quick movements, she reached under her skirts and tore away at her ruffled petticoat. She looked about for something, opened her travel bag, and poured some cologne over the wound, grateful for having watched Sara Amalfi in the dispensary. She made a tourniquet, then wrapped the girl's hand as best she could. She cradled the girl's head and rocked her back and forth as one might a baby.

Swine! Rotten barbarous swine! She fought off the tears, until she realized she could have been killed as easily as not. She glanced up into the eyes of four hostile-looking women. They stared at her and at Teresina's bandaged hand with faces of stone, ugly and frightening.

"Help me with the girl. Can we take her to her bed?" The women didn't move a muscle. "Won't someone help me with

Teresina?" she pleaded. "She'll need attention when she awakens."

"Why do you aid her? She stole from you, disobeyed our leader, and received her just dues."

"Punishment I can understand. But mutilation for so small an offense?"

"She'll never steal again. Or it will be her hand next time," snarled one of the hags.

A red-haired woman came forward. "I'll help you. She sleeps a few feet from me. I'll watch over her."

Nodding gratefully, Diamonte managed to get Teresina to her feet with the redhead's help. Walking carefully down the path, they half-carried her the full length of the camp, past the horses, beyond the campfires along the shaded area, and placed her on a bedroll.

"My name is Petrocina. What's yours?" She covered the girl with a shawl.

"Diamonte."

"Will you be one of us?" asked the redhead with bright, light brown eyes.

"In God's name, no!" she retorted. Then, seeing color rise to Petrocina's face, she added quickly, "Excuse me, but I'd rather be dead than stay with your people."

Petrocina explained. "But don't you see? We're already dead here. What we came from was no worse."

"Where did you come from? *Inferno?* Hell?"

"You may call it that. I came from Corleone, an incestuous cesspool of corruption. At least here we have no fears of oppression, insecurity, or starvation. Here we eat one big meal a day. We know what to expect and what is expected from us. We live by the rules imposed on us, rules that don't change. We have no *gabelotto* to take away our bread and our houses. No taxes to pay with money we don't have."

"But I know nothing of such a life," said Diamonte reflectively. "I come from rich and fertile lands. No *gabelotti*, no *mafiosi* dictate to us. Peasants live on the *latifondo*, well-fed children smile and go to school. There is a dispensary with nurses to care for the sick and wounded." Her eyes stared off in the distance. "We eat three meals a day or whenever we are hungry. The women are clean. We wash before we eat and never, never do we permit fowl or animals to enter our *casitas*. They have places of their own."

"Where do you come from, girl? Paradise?" asked Petrocina, disbelief in her eyes.

"I come from the Villa de Leone, the *latifondo* of the family of Royal Lions, where *contadini* are all partners in the farming, making money and living well."

"But why by the balls of Lucifer did you leave such a heaven? Why?"

Diamonte stared off, suddenly feeling wretched. "We all do foolish things at times."

"If I came from such a place, wild dogs couldn't have dragged me from it! Not even elephants!"

They both turned as horsemen rumbled by in a flurry of excitement. The bandits were off, led by the red-bearded Matteo, his leather and silver amulets shining brightly in the early morning sun. For an instant Diamonte's heart beat wildly, and she experienced a thrill as images of their sexual intimacy flashed before her. Then, remembering his sadistic treatment of the girl Teresina and the money he took from her, she filled with loathing and profound confusion.

"Petrocina, tell me. Is it possible to love and hate at the same time?"

"One cannot love without hating and one cannot hate without loving. The two are inseparable."

Later Petrocina showed Diamonte where she could bathe. "Beware only of the men. If they catch you here, don't be surprised if you're suddenly raped or seduced, depending on your feelings in the matter."

"That won't happen. I'm Matteo's woman."

"Well! If that doesn't beat everything!" Petrocina marveled. "The entire camp believes Matteo is a eunuch. I'm the only one who didn't believe that rot." She took her clothes off and watched Diamonte shed hers and wade into the creek.

"I'll attest to the fact he's no eunuch, *cara mia!*"

Petrocina watched as Diamonte rinsed out her undergarments.

"Don't you have soap?"

"What is soap?"

Diamonte gave up. Back at her campsite, she gave Petrocina some of her floral-scented cologne. "Somewhere we've got to get soap. Meanwhile we'll use olive oil to clean off," she told her new friend.

During the bandits' absence, Petrocina told the others about this place Diamonte came from. No one believed her. Diamonte told stories of the harvest, the festivals, the communal love and respect and friendliness of her people. Only vaguely had any of them heard of *El Leone*. At times, when all she could relate about Marco was praiseworthy, she filled with remorse over her deed and longed to be back in the security of the villa. "He's my Godfather," she said proudly.

"Then why are you here?"

Diamonte grew silent and quickly changed the subject. She did her best to encourage the women to adopt cleaner habits, but they fought her at every turn with their own brand of logic.

"Why should we clean ourselves. It only makes the stench of our men more noticeable."

"But if you set an example, won't they be more fastidious with themselves?"

"Hah! You don't know the Mazzarinos. If we were to even suggest that they bathe, they'd cut out our tongues just so they wouldn't have to listen to our nagging. We're nothing to them, only tools to use as they see fit. We wash for them, cook for them, let them use us as they need us. The rest of the time we say nothing. Some of us even have their bastards, never knowing which man sired it. This is our lot in life," said Petrocina.

"If there's a God, he knows it's better for us here than back where most of us came from," said Teresina, recuperating from her punishment.

"What's this? What's this?" sniggered the women when they saw Diamonte dressed in men's trousers, shirt, and boots. They ridiculed her with their acid tongues and called her an obscenity.

"It's better than those filthy skirts you wear. They brush against goat and dog shit and human excrement, and their stench takes your breath away. And while we're on the subject, have any of you ever heard of feminine hygiene?" She explained what she meant, and when she finished, they laughed and told her she was crazy.

"If the men were clean, we could understand being clean. But when they return from these excursions, who knows what they've slept with, eh? Cows, pigs, sheep! They could have fucked anything if they found no women to rape."

Diamonte blushed at the thought of the degenerate sexual practices which these women took in their stride, but she took courage and decided to give them something to think about. "Well, I can understand how they might prefer cows, pigs, and sheep, when they have nothing better here . . ."

Diamonte must have been protected by a guardian angel at that moment. The women seethed, understanding the full implication of her remark. Their eyes burned as they fingered their knives. Petrocina came to Diamonte's rescue. She laughed uproariously and said, "You know, she may be right! What do you think of that? It took an outsider to tell us what we already knew in our hearts was true." She winked at Diamonte and said, "You think you could show us?"

226

By the end of the week she'd made some progress. Petrocina and a handful of the woman had started wearing trousers, claiming they felt freer in them. Many of the women took daily baths, indulged in more feminine habits, and even spoke softer. She taught them how to cook food fit for human consumption. When she discussed penning up the chickens to keep their excrement away from their living quarters, Diamonte saw she was moving too fast, so she put that project off.

The bandits hadn't been back ten minutes before Diamonte heard loud roars of protest. Teresina rushed to her side up on the bluff. "Diamonte! Diamonte! Come quickly! Matteo is asking for you, down at the campfire. They're waiting!"

"If he wants me, he knows where to find me," she said stubbornly.

"Oh, Diamonte, he'll beat me if you don't come."

"He wouldn't dare!" Then glancing at the bandaged hand on the girl, she rose to her feet. "I'll come. I don't want another *infamita* on my conscience."

"Well, speak up! What have you to say for yourself?" he bellowed.

"Oh, it's you," she said flatly. "Do I have your permission to welcome you back?"

"Signorina, you try my patience." He coughed apologetically and glanced at his men. "If it weren't for the fact that you presented me with news vital to our future plans, I'd have you whipped."

In the instant it took for her to understand his game, Diamonte saw the look in Cacciatore's eye. She shuddered and said nothing.

So, thought Cacciatore, *Matteo hasn't been honest with me. He's fallen for the whore. What is he covering up? What has he been holding back from the council?*

"Are you responsible for this?" Matteo pointed to a few women in pants. Now, for the first time he noticed her appearance. "Take off those pants and dress like a decent woman," he commanded.

The impact of his words were to have far-reaching effects. The women rebelled and sided with Diamonte. Sullen and uneasy, their manliness hovering in the balance, the men stood next to these partially liberated women, looking first at Matteo, then at Diamonte.

"I'll dress the way it pleases me."

"You'll do what I say if I have to do it for you!"

"Really, Barbarossa! You go too far!"

Matteo picked her up bodily, tossed her over his shoulder

227

and as she struggled and kicked and screamed, he marched up the path to the bluff. The Mazzarinos screamed triumphantly, and following Matteo's lead, they pursued the women who had scattered in all directions.

Matteo's resolve melted when he smelled her sweet, fragrant cleanliness. He wanted her desperately. He wouldn't tell her how much he missed her, how each night away from her was sheer torture, how he had longed to touch her, taste her, and ravage her. His manner softened. Gently he raised her face to his to kiss her, but she slipped from his embrace.

"Don't you touch me. I'm not a woman you can humiliate then turn to to satisfy your lust."

"You mustn't mind the way I talk to you before the others." He smiled patiently. "It's the way we are together that counts, little spider."

"Not in my eyes. I care how you treat me in the presence of others even if they are animals. I care how you treat me when we're alone also. If you're a coward and can't wear your feeling about me openly, then I don't want you. I can't love a coward!"

"You *dare* call me a coward?" He stepped menacingly toward her.

"Does it puff you up to let your men think you treat me like a dog? Is that what you call bravery? Where I come from *real men* are gentle to their women. That makes them giants in the eyes of their women and also among other men."

"Hah!" he snorted contemptuously. "You come from a world of sniveling dogs. Cowardly men without the guts to fight for their rights, men who hire *gabelotti* to do their dirty work for them."

"Not where I come from. You're wrong. Dead wrong. My world is full of brave men who stand on the side of the law and what's right." How confused she felt in this disorganized world. Santo Dio! *If only I could undo the wrong I did.*

"Listen, wench, those are men I crush with a blow of my fist."

"And they crush you with a movement of the pen."

He glanced swiftly at her. "A movement of the pen, eh?" Matteo pondered this. "A movement of the pen?" He liked that. That is power, he told himself. To her he said something entirely different. "Listen, you better get this straight. As long as you are my guest here you will not fill the women with fancy tales about a fantasy world of your creation, hear?"

"It's not a fantasy world."

"I'm telling you not to do it, hear?" He flared suddenly.

"Is that an order, oh, high and mighty one?"

"Yes, that's an order! And this nonsense about pants. You will not wear them in my presence. Do I make myself understood?"

"Why?"

"I don't know why. They offend me. That's enough."

"But why?"

"*Ancora?* Why? Why? Why! *Porca miseria!* Does there always have to be a why? I don't know why! That's why!" Matteo paced back and forth. "Why do you do this, eh? Each time we talk you mock me and torment me. If you were anyone else, little spider, I'd have you beaten."

"And chop off both my hands, no doubt!"

"*Ancora?*" He made a disorganized gesture and shook his head hopelessly.

"You don't understand. Before I came to lead these people, they lived by certain laws. If I change these laws there will be many complications. Nothing was dependable where they came from. Here, they feel secure. I have no intention of changing their world. For me this is only something temporary; it's not my world. I only rule this world for a time. I am their leader."

"A real leader can make and establish his own laws."

"Goddammit! Leave me in peace, woman!"

"Whatever you say, your lordship." Diamonte moved to leave.

"Where the hell do you think you're going?"

"You just told me to leave."

"Bitch!" he cried hoarsely. "This is what you want and you know it!" He kissed her savagely on the lips until she began to respond. Then he grew easier, more gentle. Having missed each other more than either would admit, they lusted after each other.

Later, Matteo lay back, his arm about her, content and thoughtful.

"Why can't you be like this all the time, Matteo. When you're gentle with me, I melt faster than snow on molten lava. When you become savage, I want to kill you. I freeze like ice on the mountaintops in winter."

"A man can't be the same all the time. There are reasons for the things he says and does."

"A real man can control his emotions. Not be a slave to them."

"What are you that you should know so much about men?"

"I'm a woman. Who knows more about men than women? Yet you are different than most men, Matteo." She touched his face and stroked his fiery beard. He felt a shiver run

229

through him. Hot blood shot through his body and his manhood sprang to life. Her tenderness set him on fire. He'd never been gazed upon with such desire by a woman of such great beauty. Certainly the whores in Godrano had never infected him with such passion. To Matteo, sex had always been a simple matter of physical release.

"Well, tell me what makes me different?"

"Ambition, perhaps. Something that burns in you that doesn't live in other men. It's a rare quality. Most men, content to live each moment, give no thought to tomorrow. Only men of tremendous stature have their sights set on tomorrow."

He thought about her words, but when he looked, he saw reflected in her eyes the image of another man, not himself. Matteo said nothing. After a while he got up and dressed. "I'll see you at the campfire," he said. "It will be time to eat soon. We brought back a lot of supplies."

"Did you think to bring some soap?" she asked suddenly.

"Yes," he said quietly, "I brought soap."

Winters came and left. Men who left on raids, returned with the injured, who were nursed to health. Some died and never returned. New men arrived to join the Mazzarinos: young men with burning ambition; old men with none. A few new women joined the men. Diamonte remained.

With her at his side, Matteo grew more sure of himself. His fierceness took on new dimensions, and he began to think it was time for him to assert himself with the Palermo Don Calomare. He had done all he could as a Mazzarino. He itched to prove himself at something more worthy, to show Diamonte he wasn't merely a bandit.

Filled with pride at being the secret envy of every man in camp, Matteo had been delighted with Diamonte's ability to adjust. She remained aloof and cool to the other bandits and did her work. The women looked to Diamonte as their leader as the men did to Matteo. And he loved it.

One night after a bandit raid, Matteo and Diamonte went swimming down by the creek. Later she dressed in skirt and blouse to please him, and they walked back to camp, where she fixed him a plate of succulent veal.

On this night, Matteo watched her with fascination. She sat but a few feet from him, looking more desirable than ever. Even the thick black cotton fabric couldn't hide the sculptured contour of her rounded thigh, shapely calf, and slender ankles. He set down his plate, placed his hand on his heart, and looked deeply into her eyes. He'd never really told her how much he loved her.

"Why do you continue to stay here with us?" he asked. "You don't belong here among savages."

"Because you won't return my money. Why else?" she laughed seductively.

"I returned it to you long ago. That excuse is no longer valid."

"One becomes the pawn of Destiny in the game of life. I stay because it's my destiny to be with you. Sometimes we do what we don't wish to do, and at other times, we don't do what we desire to do."

"I do nothing I don't wish to do. And don't be clever again."

"You do what Destiny *wills* you to do, not what you desire to do, Matteo. And I'm not being clever. I'm stating fact."

"I do what *I* wish to do. It's fortunate that Destiny wills what I wish," he boasted.

She smiled. "Then you're a fortunate man. In the lives of many are placed obstacles over which they have no control. The wishes and desires of others must be considered."

"You're crazy as usual, little spider. Crazy like a woman," he told her. "If I permitted myself to think such thoughts, I'd have been dead long ago. Men who think such thoughts will always be conquered by men who think as I do. I believe in myself, Diamonte," he told her. "If you were wise, you'd do the same. One day I'll own this island." He rose to his feet, towering over her like a primitive god. "Five years ago, I told you my time will come. I'm not sure when. Destiny knows and I wait only for her prodding."

"You haven't touched your food. Aren't you hungry?"

"It isn't food I want."

Diamonte flushed with pleasure. "You go on ahead. I'll join you in a moment."

She watched him move easily over the rocks and disappear behind the boulders to the upper grotto. Being astute, she never let Matteo know she'd found the key to his thinking. Instead, she kept him fully excited, aching for her body, like the need for a drug. Over the years she had worked subtle changes in him.

Smiling secretly, Diamonte walked after him. She found him gazing up at the glowing stars scattered in the black heavens, so close it would take little effort to reach up and grab a few.

She lay down beside him and whispered, "I believe in you, Matteo! Oh, how I believe in you!"

Watching them from a small cove high above them was the ever silent and morose Mario Cacciatore. He'd been walking aimlessly along the rocky terrain, trying to fathom Bar-

231

barossa's infatuation with the girl. For five years he'd watched their amorous embraces. He'd seen Matteo change into a more cautious man, one he didn't understand. He missed Matteo's companionship, their plans and discussions of the future. Since this slut came into his life, nothing had been the same. His instinct told him she spelled trouble.

Mario made his way back to his campsite, brooding about the future. Everything had been so secure before. He wondered what lay ahead now. The others were playing instruments and a few of the couples danced a tarantella. Still others clapped their hands and sang.

Nothing is the same. Imagine! The women bathe daily now. Imagine! He wrapped himself in his thoughts and sat back against a tree staring into the fire's embers.

21

Mario Cacciatore was fourteen when he made his bones. Seeds of discontent, anger, and hostility germinated early in his antisocial and warped mind. Short, stocky, and dark-skinned with thickly lidded eyes that labeled him a frog of a man at an early age, he was the sixth son of an itinerant laborer and an ignorant, nagging woman who held no compassion for either her husband or her sons. She felt she was doomed from the moment she was born in the interior village of Villalba, where her family struggled under the constant threat of hunger.

A malaria epidemic claimed this morose woman and three of her sons one year, and the next year typhoid took Mario's father and two more brothers. One last brother sought solace in the priesthood, and with the pittance he received from the sale of their hovel, young Cacciatore decided to seek his fortune. With his money tucked safely away in a chamois pouch, he made his way to the edge of the village, taking only the clothes on his back.

When he was accosted by a gang of boys led by a bully named Nino, Mario eluded his assailants and found refuge among the ruins of an ancient Greek temple. At dusk, he scurried over the sun-scorched steps and crept along the hand-hewn stone walls, and finally lay exhausted among the shadows of a dimly lit cave. His wildly beating heart calmed and he reached into his jacket for a few morsels of cheese and bread to munch on.

Suddenly, his head was jerked up and back, and he looked into the leering faces of Nino and the others who chased him earlier. They beat him up, took his purse, and left him bleeding, bruised, and battered.

It took all his strength to crawl to the mouth of the grotto where he overheard Nino tell his companions he'd take the money home and divide it the next day. Mario knew what he had to do. Straggling behind, well hidden in the shadows, he followed the confident thief to his house. Later, peeking through the open window at the family at supper, Mario froze. *Che demonio!* The thief's father was the very man who had bought Cacciatore's house. He didn't have to figure it. Two and two made one hell of a stink! As bitter bile of resentment eroded his guts he waited patiently. One, two, three candles were extinguished. There went the oil lamp. *Va biene. Va biene.*

A half-hour later he made his move. Inside the silent house, he saw an array of sharp knives, picked one up, and slipped it into his belt. Moving soundlessly over the earthen floor, he crept cautiously up the steps to the second floor.

A shaft of moonlight illuminated the bedroom. Clothing was scattered in wild disarray on the bed, chairs, and floor. The money! Where was the money? Where had the thieving bastard hidden it? Besides Nino, four other children lay asleep on the rumpled bed. Nino moaned and rolled over. Mario lay flat against a dark wall, holding his breath, his eyes holding a dead bead on the thief. There it was! The money pouch, suspended from a cord around his neck. Mario moved. Carefully, very carefully, he sliced through the cord. He shoved the pouch into his pocket just as Nino's eyes fluttered open. Their eyes met and held. The next sound Nino made was a muffled groan as Mario plunged the knife into his jugular with a swift, sure thrust. Nino's head fell limply to one side, a cry of alarm frozen in his throat.

Mario felt no remorse. He opened the pouch, counted his money, and left the house, stopping only to steal some food from the pantry. Two days later, he got lost and stumbled into a bandit's camp in the mountains of Cammaratta, thirsty, hungry, and grotesquely swollen from the beating he had received. No one paid any attention to him. For a time he stood like a disoriented waif near a wrinkled old woman with a hawk's nose and white hair pulled back into a tight bun who stood stirring a stewpot. The toothless old girl glanced up and saw his haunted, starving eyes fixed intently on the stewing rabbit.

"Who are you?"

"Mario Cacciatore."

"If you're hungry, go up stream and clean up. You're filthy as a pig!"

Those were the kindest words he'd ever heard and to him she was an angel. He returned in moments, having done only a fair job of washing, but at least she could see his features. Black and blue welts, dark bruises, and scabby cuts played over his face like a crazy-quilt pattern. His swollen eyes looked like buttonholes. He dove ravenously into his plate of food.

"Not so fast!" cautioned the old woman. "You'll get sick. Where do you come from? What happened? You look like a squashed cockroach."

He told her everything except that he'd killed Nino. He only vaguely remembered it anyway. For two weeks Mario was in heaven. She gave him the only maternal care he'd ever had. He willingly helped her with the chores, and anticipating her needs, he'd get chores done without her having to ask. Signora Carcacci flushed with pleasure, praising him and rewarding him with so much food, he found himself saying for the first time in fourteen years, "Please no more. My stomach will burst."

The arrival of Pasquale Aiello and the other bandits nearly put an end to his happiness. Having fared badly in their raid, they returned weary and disgruntled. Foiled by a detachment of *carabinieri* sent out by the land barons, the bandits' black mood was not to be reckoned with.

Because Aiello might look upon Mario as just another mouth to feed and dispose of him in any way, including death, Mario was prudently kept from the man's sight. The old woman cautioned, "Stay out of their way, you hear? If they see your face often enough, a little at a time, they'll begin to think you belong here with the other children."

A week later, while the old woman plucked chicken feathers, someone asked the dreaded question. "Who is he?"

"Just one of the children," she replied.

Aiello, a fair-haired, light-skinned, brooding man grabbed Mario by the scruff of the neck with a powerful arm and held him suspended in midair. "Who are you?" he roared.

"Mario Cacciatore."

"Where do you come from?"

"I told you," shouted the old woman, fearing the worst. "He's one of the children. *Managghia!* Don't you recognize him?"

Aiello shoved her aside roughly and told her to be silent. Incensed at the rough treatment given his benefactor, Mario made a lunge for Aiello's knife which was suspended from a sheath at his waist. The knife grasped firmly in hand, Mario swiped at Aiello, slicing into his leather jacket, nearly cutting into the man himself. Stupefied, the bandit examined his damaged jacket, then turned his attention to Mario, who had scrambled to his feet and stood crouched over like an animal, knife in hand. Startled by the pure animal response in the boy, his eyes filled with a peculiar light. He circled slowly. The old woman screamed, "No, Mario, he'll kill you! Put down the knife!"

Aiello laughed. At first he was tempted to walk away, but something he saw in Mario's eyes changed his mind. He waved the others back and, falling into a crouch position, he and Mario circled each other.

The bandits wondered if Aiello would actually fight with a boy. They moved in with interest. Mario made a lunge but missed as Aiello jumped out of his path. Amusement crossed Aiello's face. Testing the lad's courage, he turned and stood a few feet away. Mario moved quickly and, before Aiello could follow, he jabbed the knife into the bandit's thigh. Disbelief on his face, Aiello glanced down at the open wound and his hand felt the hot blood seep through his fingers. His smile dissolved.

"Balls, eh? Let's see if you have a cock! Bastard! I'll teach you to stick Aiello!"

Swiftly, expertly, he kicked the knife from Mario's hand. It fell to the dust out of reach. Mario soon felt himself warding off blow after blow from the enraged bandit. The old woman moved in to plead with Aiello. "Let him be. He's only a child." She felt sure Aiello would beat him to death.

Mario was no match for Aiello. He had only intended to test the lad, but Mario held his ground, bravely bearing the crushing blows that sent him spinning into the crowd, only to be pushed back by the leering men to receive more of Aiello's angry pounding. The bandit leader grew angrier when Mario refused to beg mercy. Finally Mario had had enough. He could take no more. He spit into the dust through bloody, dirt-caked lips, forcing back tears of pain and humiliation. His head felt ten times its normal size and pains of fire shot through his battered body.

"Clean him up and bring him to me!" ordered Aiello.

"Where did you learn to fight?" asked Aiello, watching the swollen-faced, puffy-eyed, arrogant young kid who stood defiantly before him. When Mario refused to answer, Aiello asked again. "What's the matter? Can't you talk?" He watched the lad's wary eyes.

"You know why I beat you up? To teach you a lesson. Plunge a knife into a man, Goddammit, and you better make sure you finish him off. If he lives to retaliate, he'll do the job on you later! *Capeeshi?* Now sit. Take supper with me. We'll talk."

This incident began a quasi father-son relationship which

235

lasted eight years. One day Aiello returned to camp with a gangrenous wound. Before he died, he summoned young Cacciatore to his side. In eight years Mario had made no friends. He was considered a cold-blooded ogre who killed for killing's sake. Concerned for his safety, Aiello advised Mario, "Leave the camp before I die. Somewhere there's a place for you, Mario, where you'll fit in better than you do with these men who are frightened of you. Beyond the mountains of Cammaratta, past Mussomeli, you'll find a place called Mazzarino." He handed him a map and a letter and wished him well. "You're a strange man. Be long gone before I die, else you may be killed by the men who fear you most. While I live they dare not touch you."

Mario Cacciatore, a grotesquely scarred and odious man to all who encountered him, a man with crippled emotions, left the camp of Aiello. He came to learn that Aiello's bandits were cheap imitators of the Mazzarino bandits, who stood alone as the fiercest and most cunning lot of militant fugitives who ever sought sanctuary in the guise of bandits.

Cacciatore lacked one essential quality that kept him on the fringe of life—he was no leader of men; he couldn't inspire others to do his bidding. Early in life he discovered that by himself he was nothing and would amount to nothing. By attaching himself as a satellite to some shooting star of spectacular power, he would go places. He knew how to make himself invaluable, for his skill lay in following another man's instructions to perfection. Basically immature, his nature was that of a furtive coward, a bully, a cheat, and a liar. Although Cacciatore lacked the capacity to make plans and carry them out, an essential quality in a leader, he could complement a man who possessed such traits. He had been with the Mazzarino bandits for three years before Destiny brought such a man into his life.

22

Matteo Barbarossa, a few years younger than the Royal Lion, was born in the remote village of Godrano in western Sicily. Like the adjoining village of Corleone and most interior villages, Godrano was remote and withdrawn from the rest of the world. Pillaging bandits roamed freely in the nearby Ficuzza Woods. The faces changed from year to year, but the situation was always the same: year after year after year: abject poverty.

Life in Godrano was orchestrated by an iron-fisted *mafia gabelotto* who doled out work to the day laborers of the feudal estates under his terms at his own prices. Peasants

236

learned early in life to subjugate their desires to the needs of the *latifondo*. Godrano held little hope for a bright, young boy except that he enter the priesthood or follow in his father's footsteps. But the strict life of discipline and submission demanded of a religious acolyte held no fascination for Matteo whose overactive, highly imaginative mind never stopped working.

Matteo was eight years old when his father lost their land gambling. Forced to take the only job open to an illiterate, his father became the cleaner of cesspools and human excrement. Whores of Satan! What a disgrace! Humiliated and ridiculed by the other peasants, the bewildered young lad whose pride was fiercer than most ran away from home unable to face the dishonorable position in which his father had put him. The son of a shithouse cleaner! The very phrase would one day cost the life of any who dared utter it in his presence.

For four years, Matteo attached himself to a band of rebels, led by a brute named Lorenzo. Treated like an ordinary lackey, he cleaned their meager weapons, mended and polished their saddles, and at times even helped cook their food. But, as he moved about in their circle, he listened with cat ears and came to learn much about nature and men. He learned how to track an enemy, lose one, how to heighten his senses and know intuitively when danger approached.

One night when he was twelve, Matteo saw a vision of his mother so vivid that he borrowed a horse and rode to Godrano, arriving just in time for his mother's funeral. Broken in spirit, his father made Matteo promise to remain with him until he got back on his feet. The miserable old man cried most of the night, grateful at having been reunited with his only son.

Matteo was lost! He'd lived with real men, not these whining shells that boasted of the *maschiezzo* of another era. Could he renew acquaintance with his former friends? Never! Boys his own age were mere children. He was a man. Everything annoyed him: his father's increased drinking, the limited hovel they lived in, his father's constant references to the good old days, his father's rusty companions, everything! *Che demonio!* Did he ever miss Lorenzo's men, their vulgar behavior, boastful manners, and outlandish clothing! He thought about this as he ambled about the village with a long, sad face, looking for an avenue of escape.

One day when his thoughts were darkest and he was ready to take off to the hills despite his promise to his father, Destiny prodded Matteo and he found himself standing near the fountain in the piazza, listening to an argument between a dark, explosive man and three others. He recognized the dark, angry man as Don Umberto, a highly specialized *mafioso* from a particularly ferocious branch of the *mafia* called *Cancia*. Don Umberto acted as intermediary between local peasants who wanted their wheat milled into flour and the mills located several miles away.

The men argued, "The constant raids by that devil Lorenzo are making the transportation of both the raw product and the finished flour too costly. On top of this, the increased rates you impose upon us, Don Umberto, are unreasonable. We'd rather burn our wheat than entrust it to you," stated their spokesman daringly. "Perhaps we'll get Lorenzo himself to act as intermediary," declared the spokesman, "then the price will remain stable."

The trio walked off in a huff, leaving in their wake a red-faced and angry Don Umberto shaking his unique walking stick. Carved in the shape of a clenched fist with the middle finger upright in an obscene gesture, it had a razor-sharp stiletto recessed in the middle finger that could be released by a secret spring. He turned and strutted imperiously across the piazza to his small office, talking aloud to himself.

"*Managghia!* Too many shipments hijacked. Too many raids on the warehouses. If this keeps up I'll have to notify the *capomafia*, Don Calomare, in Palermo. But to enlist his aid would be humiliating. I'd lose too much respect. *Butana u diaoro!*"

Don Umberto tapped the cane along the cobbles as he strutted, head held high, giving no outward show of his inner turmoil. *Lorenzo! Son of a whore! I'll take care of you, my enterprising enemy!* But how? he asked himself. All attempts to deal with that bastard had been contemptuously flung back in his face. *Lorenzo wants too much. Too goddamn much! Here in Godrano, I'd take care of his hide, but, in those accursed woods and mountains, who could find the weasel?*

Matteo followed the fierce-eyed Don at a respectful distance, trying to work up the courage to talk with him. He watched the *mafioso* and saw the expressions on the faces of the merchants on the street who withdrew when he passed.

Several times the Don glanced over his shoulder, took note of Matteo, shrugged, and continued on his way. He paid little heed at first, then as the lad continued to straggle after him, he stopped and stared hard at him. Each time Matteo would edge up against a building. *Managghia! Che demonio!* What the devil is this? Finally Don Umberto reached inside a vest pocket and tossed the lad a coin, thinking that would finish it. He continued on his way.

No one could have been more astonished than Don Umberto to see the same coin land a few feet ahead of him on the sidewalk. The Don's eyes followed the rolling coin until it swiveled to a stop. He glanced quickly over his shoulder in time to see Matteo slip out of sight. Annoyed, the Don retrieved the coin, slipped it back into his pocket, and proceeded to his office. *Goddamn kids! What the hell gets into them?* Today he was in no mood for petty annoyances.

Don Umberto smoothed back his steel-gray hair, replaced his fedora, and entered the shabby building through a door upon which a sign had been decorously painted: *Don Umberto Partenico, Consigliori, Compania de Cancia.*

Matteo positioned himself outside the office and waited patiently. The Don stared at him from time to time until he could no longer stand the thought of this lad intimidating him. He opened the door with such a thrust the building shook. Don Umberto appeared in shirt sleeves and marched boldly into the sunlit square, grabbed Matteo by the scruff of the neck, and led him into his office.

"*Mah,* what the fuck do you want?" he yelled not two inches away from Matteo's determined face. Up close the Don's glowering eyes, thick bushy brows, and handlebar mustache looked more menacing.

"Eh? What do you want? Who sent you to spy on me?"

"No one, Excellency."

The Don reluctantly released his grip when he heard himself spoken to with such respect.

"Then what is it? What do you want of me? Eh?" He tossed the coin on his desk. "You threw this back at me. Why?"

"I'm no street beggar. I work for my money."

Don Umberto tried to hide the faint trace of a smile.

"You'll forgive a mere child, Excellency. When I heard you talking with the peasants in the square, I decided you could use my services."

"*Your* services?"

Ignoring the marked contempt, Matteo asked the Don, "How much would it be worth to you to get shipments to the mill and back without trouble with Lorenzo?"

"What the hell business is it of yours, eh?"

"I, Matteo Barbarossa, can guarantee such protection providing you pay." The Don's contemptuous laughter echoed through the dilapidated building. *Hah! How old could this young citrollo be? Ten? Twelve?* He happened to catch sight of the lad's defiant face in that moment and his laughter ended abruptly. Sobered, he grabbed the lad's shoulder and

239

leaned his sweaty face closer to Matteo, attempting to frighten him off.

"Do you know what I do with young lads like you? I eat them!"

The voice replied without humor. "Then you must have terrible attacks of indigestion."

Unprepared for Matteo's audacity, the Don laughed again. "Why are you complicating my life, eh? Go on, be off with you and I'll forget the incident. I've no time to waste on pranksters!"

Matteo snorted. "And they say you have much intelligence!" He was outrageous and bold. "You haven't even heard me out and you think I make jokes on you?"

"Whore of the devil! You try my patience!" cursed the Don as he walked away from the lad. But then, Don Umberto suddenly spun around and stared hard and long at the youth. His mind roiled with thoughts as he took time to light a fresh cigar, puffing on it until the smoke dimmed his face from Matteo's sight. Finally, waving the smoke from his face, the Don cursed again, "Goddamn the devil! I'm willing to wager you could pull it off!" He puffed again on the fat stogie. "What's your name, kid? Who did you say you were?"

"Matteo Barbarossa."

"Barbarossa . . . Barbarossa?" His face lit up in recognition. "Not the son of Bastiano u' . . ." He was about to say, not the son of the shithouse cleaner, but he never finished the words. The boy threw a wild punch, which the Don caught in midair. He quieted the enraged boy and made him sit in a chair. Then he pulled up another chair and sat opposite him.

"Calm down. I meant no offense," said the Don much to his own astonishment. He continued as if he addressed an older man. "Now, we talk like businessmen, eh?" He admired the lad's protective attitude toward his father.

Matteo watched every move the Don made, every gesture, as if his eager eyes couldn't be sated.

"Talk."

"How much is it worth to you?" said Matteo as if there'd been no lapse in their conversation.

"Can you arrange for me to talk with Lorenzo?"

"With no tricks?"

"No tricks," smiled the Don. "You're one smart kid. It's just possible you could succeed where the others have failed. I'm going to chance it. What makes you so sure you can pull it off?"

"I've lived with them for four years. We're friends. He

240

trusts me. Lorenzo will always listen to a fair deal if you're firm and honest with him."

"What have I to lose? If we don't come to terms, I'm no worse off than before. We must get together or you can tell Lorenzo, I will import men who will crush him."

"No. No threats. I've seen how Lorenzo reacts to threats. If it's war you want, that's different. But if you want to preserve the shipments and keep your business running smoothly—no threats. Just a sound business deal."

Don Umberto's mouth fell open in astonishment. "How old are you?"

"Twelve."

"Tomorrow we meet in the village square. You bring me Lorenzo's answer by noon." They shook hands.

Matteo smiled to himself. *This Don Umberto is no big, important man. This is a loud-mouthed, blustery jackal whose hand feels like a slimy dead fish.*

Riding swiftly through the Ficuzza Woods to Lorenzo's hideout, Matteo had misgivings and wondered how he was going to pull it off. From the moment he entered the secret draw, where lookouts usually signaled to him, he felt a thousand eyes on him, but saw no one. He raised his fingers to his lips and whistled shrilly. No signal was returned. He cautiously walked his horse past the craggy volcanic boulder which marked entrance to the camp. His eyes were everywhere. His disquiet increased when he saw two grim-faced riders galloping toward him at a fast clip. Silent and unresponsive, they took his reins and led him into camp.

Matteo's unsuspecting mind had anticipated a different greeting. When he spotted the cold, stone-faced Lorenzo standing silent and menacing, Matteo smiled despite the icy atmosphere, ran to Lorenzo and hugged him.

"Lorenzo! Lorenzo! I've missed you so much!"

The bandit leader held the boy at arm's length, glowering darkly. "Hah! A likely story! First you steal our horse, then, when you're caught, you come to me pretending fidelity and lie to my face. You missed me! Hah!"

Matteo shook off Lorenzo's arms and gazed at the bandit with a puzzled expression. *"Steal your horse?* No! No, it wasn't like that. I had to leave. My mother died. I had a vision and I had to go. I got there in time for the funeral."

As he listened to Matteo's story, Lorenzo sat by the fire and drank wine from a goatskin. He wondered if the boy was telling the truth. He'd been a good worker. His story sounded sincere.

"Would I have returned if I had stolen a horse? No! I

knew I'd be risking my life if I returned and you didn't believe me," he lied. "Considering I came on a mission of importance, at least hear me out."

That night, Matteo presented a clever and profitable scheme, convincing Lorenzo it would not only work, but it would also eliminate the hardship and unpredictability of the raids. A plan was agreed upon. By the age of fourteen, Matteo Barbarossa had earned a reputation of worth. As go-between for Don Umberto and Lorenzo, he learned the power of fear.

Shortly after the unification of Sicily and Italy, there was no longer a need for a patriotic underground to combat foreign tyrants. The original concept of the Mafia, primarily a vigilante type of law enforcement group, had come from the need to combat their oppressors. Now the Mafia felt thwarted. Their unique skills in murder, robbery, kidnapping, and extortion had been so well refined, they felt it a shame not to use them.

When the *mafiosi* awakened to the fact that their enemies were the titled *latifondisti*, they began to watch these indolent landowners with the eyes of a hawk and the quenchless thirst of blood-sucking vultures. Having worked the lands themselves, they knew the *latifondisti* well. Glib of tongue, the more enterprising *mafiosi*, preyed on the weaknesses of these fat-bellied land barons, offering full management of their estates without their having to stay in Sicily at all. These land barons willingly entered into *absentee* management agreements, delighted they didn't have to deal on a one-to-one basis with the loathsome, animalistic peasants.

The Mafia's power became absolute. Foolhardy people who opposed them were dealt with violently and expeditiously.

Matteo Barbarossa saw how *fear* controlled his people. He kept his eyes open and his mouth shut. Shortly after his fifteenth birthday, Matteo witnessed his first cold-blooded murder. Don Samuzzo, a crafty *mafioso*, had just shot a stubborn shopkeeper and his brother for refusing to pay protection money. Blasts of the *lupara* had been so close, the noise momentarily deafened him. In moments the quickly reloaded shotgun was turned menacingly on Matteo, who stood next to an olive tree, quietly observing.

Matteo looked from the two bodies sprawled on the ground not far from him into the eyes of the awesome man who fingered his *lupara*. Whatever it was he saw in Matteo's eyes, the Don slowly lowered his shotgun.

The middle-aged lizard of a man broke out into raucous laughter. Swinging the *lupara* over his shoulder, he moved in toward Matteo, placed an arm about him, and together they walked back to the village of Godrano.

From that day forward, Matteo's destiny in life had been set for him. The Godrano Dons took Matteo under their wing and taught him the ways of the *mafia*. At sixteen he made his bones. In two years he murdered *mafia* victims, terrorized them, tortured and beat them, kicked, slugged, and threatened them for the small pittances they were forced to pay for protection. He became a killer without conscience.

Shrewd and calculating and keenly observant of his superiors, he filed away for future reference all he learned. He could size up a man with amazing accuracy. Privy to what the Dons discussed, he missed nothing and remembered every detail. Soon he grew restless and decided he should be progressing more rapidly.

"If you really want to become a Don of importance," goaded the crafty Don Samuzzo one day, "you must earn a reputation worthy of the name Matteo Barbarossa. One known and feared throughout Sicily."

"How? Tell me. How?"

Treachery oozing from every pore, the Don smiled and from a drawer in his antiquated roll-top desk, he pulled out a bright yellow scarf with the letter M embroidered on it in black.

"Ride to the hills outside Mazzarino wearing this scarf about your neck and present it to whomever you first encounter." He pointed to a crudely drawn map of the area. "Here, at a fork in the road, beyond which there's a sheer drop of several hundred feet, you must exercise caution. The paths are treacherous and the hills of our ancestors are filled with killers the likes of which you've never encountered."

By then Matteo had committed the map to memory. "Please continue," he urged the Don. "I'm listening to every word."

"If you're stopped before you reach the designated spot, don't hesitate to show the scarf. Mind you, the scarf is your calling card. It will get you in, but once you're in the rest is up to you."

The Don blew his nose and hawked phlegm into the cuspidor. He lowered his eyes and feigned sadness. "I can't help but feel that the Mazzarinos will kill you, Matteo. Perhaps you'd better not go. Forget it. Stay here with your own people. In ten, fifteen years, you may be able to rise to the

243

position of a great and respected Don." By then he knew Matteo was hooked. Ambition shone in his eyes like tinsel.

"No. Tomorrow I go. I thank you for all you've done, *Zu* Samuzzo," he said with respectful reverence.

Knowing the *capomafia* in Palermo encouraged young, up-and-coming Mafia potentials, these crafty devils, Don Samuzzo and Don Umberto, had to prevent Matteo from coming to Don Calomare's attention, just to secure their own position. By shipping him off to the Mazzarinos who'd been sure death for every other ambitious *mafia* aspirant, they were confident Matteo would meet the same fate.

Could Matteo have guessed these men would plot against him out of jealousy for his youth and astuteness? Not even when Don Samuzzo embraced him with tears in his eyes, did he realize they were tears of deceit.

Lorenzo and his bandits had been mere child's play compared to the ferocious Mazzarinos. A band of hostile criminals, they lived deep in the moutains some distance from the bleak village of Mazzarino with their equally savage women camp followers. Hotter than the desert sirocco in summer and wetter than the ocean in winter, the area was a brooding nest of nature's treacheries.

The Mazzarinos saw little of civilization in their primitive setting. Undependable communications, except those sent by special courier, were an aggravation Matteo found hard to adjust to. He hadn't expected anything so primal and remote.

As his black hair grew longer and his beard grew in the color of fire, Matteo presented a fierce and awesome sight. Anyone who saw him never forgot him. He began to dress more dramatically: black trousers, no shirt, a black leather vest adorned with *malocchio* amulets. Subconsciously, he was building an image which would instill fear in those around him. Moving about the camp, he could sense that all eyes were upon him, staring as if he were a mighty, barbarous god.

The two Godrano Dons tragically underestimated Matteo Barbarossa when they thought they'd sent him to his death. They resented this 'punk son of a shithouse cleaner' more than could be imagined, but it didn't take long before Matteo recognized their treachery.

Matteo played the fox. For years he listened, kept his own counsel, and did as he was told with a patience which even astounded him. Extremely guileful, without scruple or conscience, this chosen Godson of Destiny set about winning the confidence of others and bided his time.

23

When Cacciatore joined the Mazzarinos, their leader was Andrade Vespucio, a rough, black-bearded brute of a man with oddly spaced yellow teeth and the round face of a perennial juvenile. He had become a favorite of the Palermo Dons when he organized his eighth-grade schoolmates and set up a flourishing business which netted him nearly twenty dollars a week, a tidy sum in those days. He came to the attention of Don Calomare, the *capomafia*, and before he turned sixteen, he had made his bones. But soon his presence threatened the Dons who'd worked hard to attain the prominence they enjoyed. Fearful he'd usurp their power, they convinced him to join the Mazzarinos in order to make a name for himself—just as they later convinced Matteo. Secretly they hoped these aggressive young men would be annihilated.

Bitter at having spent ten years of his life living like an animal, angry for not taking what he wanted when he was younger, and filled with hatred when he discovered the real reason he was sent to the Mazzarinos, Andrade bitterly accepted his fate, led the men with iron rule, and vented his frustration on his people. Then Destiny brought Matteo Barbarossa into the fold.

It didn't take Matteo as long as it did his predecessors to realize that the Mazzarino territory had become the killing and burial ground for every young upstart who dreamed of becoming a *capomafia*.

"*Disgraziati! Dishonorati!*" raged Barbarossa when it all came together for him and he came to fully realize the treachery of the Dons. "Oh, but they'll pay for this! They'll pay for these lost years!"

Matteo detested the menial tasks demanded of him as newcomer. He worked alongside Mario Cacciatore who contented himself with caring for the horses, mending saddles, chopping wood, and other low-grade work, but Matteo kept his distance from the cold, unemotional man.

"He has the biggest cock, with balls like a bull!" bragged the only bitch who permitted Cacciatore to touch her. Philomena, a pig of a woman, cooked for him and washed his clothing. For these services, Cacciatore would condescend to sleep with her when she nagged at him. When finished with the old sow, he'd spend an hour in the creek washing her stench from his body.

Barbarossa watched these antics and was filled with disgust at Cacciatore's lack of ambition. He had been there three years without advancing a hair. He found himself avoiding the Villalban as the others did, yet there was something about the man which made him continue to observe Cacciatore.

Nothing moved fast enough for Matteo. Destiny, he felt sure, had forsaken him. Smart enough to know he couldn't advance in line unless the man ahead of him either died or was promoted, his frustrations grew more demonstrative, he became desperate and disenchanted. He had no one in whom he could confide. Andrade didn't consider him a social equal. Cut off and ignored, Matteo brooded as his solitude began to gnaw at him. Out of desperation he found himself mysteriously and irrevocably drawn to Mario Cacciatore. He found him polite and cordial, yet remote. Against his better judgment he engaged the man in conversation and began to pour out the discontent that ate away at him.

"I made my bones before these men were cut from their umbilical cords. And what am I doing? Shoveling horseshit! Francesco isn't half the man I am. I can outride, outshoot, outkill, and outthink any of the men. *Porca miseria!* Why do I let myself be used in so lowly a manner?

"One of these days, Cacciatore, I will be *capomafia* of all Sicily. You hear what I'm saying? I, Matteo Barbarossa, will make the earth tremble. I swear by the mighty gods of our ancestors, the name Matteo Barbarossa will be one to reckon with. Those sons of whores will tremble in their own shit when they see me coming. Do you believe what I tell you?"

Cacciatore glanced up from the stirrup he'd been mending and nodded.

"Yes, I believe you." The words were spoken as if they were meant to appease a madman.

Barbarossa sighed and despaired even more. No one believed him.

The next day, Francesco was found with his throat slit. Andrade called a meeting of the men. Francesco's death was attributed to a jealous woman, since he was known as a fickle cocksman. Matteo was moved up in rank.

The change in Matteo was miraculous. Destiny hadn't forsaken him after all. Delighted and filled with new-found enthusiasm, he took over Francesco's horse, saddle, and other personal effects as was the custom. Now Matteo Barbarossa would show them! His skills tested, his talents were ready to be tried. How glorious it was to feel alive again!

In the coming week he enjoyed the liberties of his new position, but a thought nagged at him: Why hadn't Cacciatore been elevated to the next step in rank? One night he asked Cacciatore about it.

"I'm content to stay with the horses, until I find the leader under whom I wish to serve," he said in a strange and detached voice.

The next day another Mazzarino was found dead. Word was he slipped on the wet rocks near the well, struck his head at the base of his skull, and died instantly. An hour later, Andrade sent for Barbarossa.

"I watched you at maneuvers last week, Barbarossa. You know, you're damned good! Since Luigi's accident this morning, we'll need a new man to supervise his squadron. What do you say? Can you handle it?"

"I'm always at your disposal," replied Matteo quietly. Inwardly his heart was singing. *You didn't forget me after all*, destinu mio!

Andrade liked Matteo's reply. Not an animal like the others. He was tired of the other beasts who stank like pigs and had no manners or intelligence. "Then it's agreed. You take over Luigi's place."

"Who will take my place?" asked Matteo on impulse.

Andrade glanced up from lighting his cigar. "I haven't decided. Why?"

"What about Cacciatore?" he found himself asking, curiously inspired.

"Cacciatore? Ugh! Let that evil one stay with the horses. He's content."

"I hear he's excellent with weapons. I've seen his targets. Every shot a bull's eye. Every knife dead center. It's a shame to waste such talent."

"Every shot a bull's eye?" mused Andrade. "Knives . . . dead center?" He tilted his head in surprise. "Really? We'll see, Matteo. We'll see."

At dawn the next morning, Cacciatore sat astride his horse, holding Barbarossa's saddled stallion by the reins, waiting for him. "You spoke to Andrade. Today I ride with you."

"Va biene," said Matteo, swinging to the saddle. He shoved his rifle into a saddle holster and wheeled his horse into place behind the others. Cacciatore followed, and fell into place alongside of him, a place he would occupy for a long time to come.

Three months passed. Five more men had been found mysteriously dead. Barbarossa moved progressively up in the ranks and was now a member of Andrade's Inner Circle, a council of twelve men considered the hierarchy of the Mazzarinos who plotted, planned, and carried out explicit orders from *capomafia*, Don Calomare of Palermo.

As Matteo Barbarossa stepped into the tent of Andrade for his first meeting of the council, his smile quickly evaporated in an atmosphere of gross hostility and collective distrust. The men lost no time in charging Barbarossa with the willful and malicious deaths of the five men who'd met with foul play.

Stunned at the unexpected turn of events, Matteo grimaced angrily. "So! This is what you really think of me, eh?" He fixed his cold, black eyes on them in a deadly calm which unnerved them. As he lit a thin cigar and puffed on it, his pose was dramatic, audacious, and disdaining. He took the cigar from between his lips, stared at it, and while the smoke spiraled upward, he maintained his silence.

Andrade spoke first. "Understand this is only a meeting to get at the truth. No one is accusing you."

Matteo remained silent, still staring at the smoke curling from the cigar. His mind was roiling with the past events, sifting through the maze.

"Do you know anything about the deaths?" pressed Andrade.

Matteo shook his head. He sat on the bench facing the men.

"You had the most to gain," shouted one of the twelve men.

"You've been elevated to a council seat in less than three months."

"Strange that in all these years nothing like this has ever happened," said another.

"It's an omen," said another sullenly.

"A portent of doom," came still another.

"He did it! It has to be him. Who else has risen so fast! You can't disguise the truth any longer. We're on to you, Barbarossa!"

Matteo glanced from one man to the next until he had fixed them firmly in his mind. His outward calm evaporated and he grew incensed. He stood up and kicked back the bench, lifting his voice menacingly. "Let me understand this. You are accusing me of five deaths?"

One at a time the twelve men lowered their eyes and glanced uneasily at each other. Some coughed and cleared their throats.

"One moment, Matteo," began Andrade.

"One moment, balls! What the hell do I know of these men? I didn't even know them by name. Why don't you question the men who knew them best?"

"You *did* have the most to gain," said Andrade thoughtfully.

248

"Aha," said Matteo knowingly. "So it's Palermo all over again, eh? The *mafiosi* grow uneasy, because a *picciotto* progresses too rapidly, eh?"

Matteo's words struck home. The expressions on their faces told him they'd all been affected by the unyielding, scheming Mafia Dons.

"Let's face it. We've been had by those malignant old goats!" began Matteo. "Afraid we'll take their place and replace their old ways with new ideas, they put us where they could be sure we would annihilate each other. Just to secure their place in the brotherhood. Now, you do the same thing!"

The shame-faced council knew he spoke the truth, yet in the political storms of shifting factions and fickle loyalties that existed within the group, none dared voice his true thoughts.

"I'd be most cautious in speaking of the brotherhood, Matteo, until we learn who caused the five deaths. None of us are safe," said Andrade.

"I don't understand."

"In ten years nothing like this has ever happened. It's as if someone has earmarked us all for death." That statement exonerated Matteo.

"And you accuse me of . . ." Matteo was flabbergasted. "Ball busters! You're all acting like suckling babes! Even children have more sense," he scoffed.

"Children or not, I order each and every one of you to single out one of the men to become your bodyguard. Choose whomever you like. He will accompany you wherever you go. Understand?"

The tension eased. For the first time in weeks, they felt a sense of relief. Andrade moved on to vital business. He spoke impressively. "In a few weeks, we shall be involved in a very important raid. One with political overtones. A new group has sprung up, threatening the power of the Dons. We shall be going to Mussomeli to teach them a lesson. They will hold a plebiscite. The party sponsored by *El Leone* and the *latifondisti* in the east are trying to bring pressure against the Dons to prevent their . . . shall we say miraculous confiscation of some of the western estates."

Andrade's voice went on and when the meeting ended, Barbarossa came away with several conclusions. First, Andrade was a coward who couldn't make decisions without the approval of twelve ludicrous idiots. Second, Andrade hated his role, hated the wilderness, hated the bandits, had no heart left for the vigorous undertaking of his position, and had begun to show signs of weakness. Third, Andrade was a fool. Bodyguards, indeed! Any man there should have already grown eyes behind his head. If he didn't know his craft, he deserved to be killed!

Yet Matteo carried out his instructions. He chose Mario Cacciatore as his bodyguard. But if Cacciatore took any pleasure in the honor, he didn't show it. He bowed slightly, left immediately, and returned with his meager belongings to sleep closer to Matteo's campsite.

In Cacciatore, Matteo found a willing satellite who did his bidding well and expeditiously. He remained in the background, like a shadow, never imposing his presence upon Matteo unless summoned to do so.

The Council of Twelve sat in meeting after meeting outlining preparations for the coming plebiscite. The camp filled with an undercurrent of excitement. The women told their men what they wanted in the way of ornamental trinkets and sweets if the project fared successfully. The bandits sharpened knives, cleaned their weapons, repaired saddles, and curried horses.

Several days before the scheduled raid, Matteo Barbarossa and Cacciatore went riding in the nearby mountains, and accidentally stumbled on a secret meeting between one of the bandits and a stranger whose features were obscured by a thick veil of dust. It was obvious he'd ridden a great distance.

Staying hidden, they dismounted, tied their horses to a tree, and crept cautiously toward the clearing to observe and hear the meeting.

The young bandit, identified as Stefano, spoke with large open gestures. "I consider it a great honor to serve you, Excellency." He looped a money pouch around his neck and tucked it well into his shirt. Stefano pulled a rolled parchment from inside his boot, spread it over a large flat boulder, and began to explain the crude drawing to the nobleman. They spoke of the coming plebiscite, its importance, the necessity of deterring the *mafia* and foiling the Mazzarinos' intervention on behalf of the *mafia*. Their words were muffled, but the point was clear.

"It's of vital importance to Sicily's future," said the nobleman eloquently, "that our detachment of soldiers and *carabinieri* prevent the Mazzarinos from giving aid to the *mafiosi*."

"That's up to you, Excellency. I've done my part. These are the plans," said Stefano, gazing about uneasily. "If it's learned that I'm a spy for you, Excellency . . ." He rolled his eyes significantly.

"I understand, Stefano." He turned to the map. "Before our men cut the bandits in two—at this point . . ." He indicated a position on the map which Barbarossa couldn't see, ". . . you leave the men at this point and join us here, a few kilometers from the flat hill, before the entrance to the village. You'll never have to return. They'll think you were killed in the ambush."

Seeing that Cacciatore was about to accost the two conspirators, Matteo restrained him, silently warning him not to intervene. Barbarossa's eager black eyes had already plotted their next move. They waited until the stranger had ridden off and allowed Stefano time to return to camp.

"You should have let me kill them both," grunted Cacciatore. "You know what it means to let both escape?"

"Yes, but I have other plans. Trust me," grinned Matteo wickedly.

That night after supper, Matteo called Andrade aside. "It's time we talked." They went into Andrade's tent. In the flickering glow of the oil lamp, Andrade looked expectantly at Matteo, while he rolled a cigarette.

"What would you say, Andrade, if I asked you to change your plans for the day of the plebiscite?"

"I'd say you were mad," replied Andrade, annoyed that the cigarette didn't roll properly. "Crazy! Fucking crazy!"

"If I told you there's a spy in our midst?"

Andrade's eyes left the cigarette and met Matteo's questioningly. "I'd still say you're crazy. Every man here has been checked and rechecked, including you. There are no spies here," he snorted. "I'd stake my life on it!"

"Then you're a dead man," said Matteo. He rose to leave.

Infuriated, Andrade threw down the clumsy cigarette. "Make yourself clear!"

"And risk being called crazy for the *third time?* No thanks." He was nearly out of the tent.

"Porca miseria, Matteo! Tell me what you know." Andrade threw his antiquated service revolver on the table and began to field-strip it. Matteo's self-assurance irked the bandit leader, and he had to keep his hands occupied as they talked.

"Don't go ahead with the plans. Someone knows of them."

With the parts of the gun spread out before him, Andrade thought, *One day I'm going to fight this sonofabitch for the leadership of the Mazzarinos.* He had known it the night of the first council meeting. He'd been waiting for the first sign of dissension in the man. Was this to be the time, he wondered. He picked up the magazine and filled it with bullets from his cartridge belt.

"Except for the twelve men of the council, including you

and I, no one knows the plans," said Andrade, affecting a calm.

Watching him insert the bullets, Matteo said, "If you made a wager on that, you'd lose."

"How do you know? What makes you so sure of yourself?" Andrade's hand fumbled with the magazine, unable to insert the final bullet.

"You already put in eight shots," said Matteo. "You think it will stretch?"

Andrade tossed the extra bullet on the table angrily. "I don't need lessons on how to handle my gun. Just tell me how you know, Goddammit!"

"Today Cacciatore and I were out riding in the hills and we came upon one of our men talking with a stranger. A man he called *Excellency*. They were discussing our plans in detail."

"Just who were these men?"

"I can't answer that, Andrade. The sun was in our eyes. The stranger was dressed in black and covered with the dust of the sirocco."

"Yet you *heard* them discussing our plans?"

"I didn't say we were deaf. Only that we couldn't see." Matteo averted his eyes to hide his displeasure. *The stupid bastard doesn't believe me. The sun rises too early for this cock!*

Andrade rose to his feet, walked to the flap of the tent, and whistled loudly. Two of his men appeared. They spoke in low whispers, then departed.

"We'll see about this."

"You don't believe me?"

"Why didn't you apprehend them?" he asked as two council members entered the tent.

"Are you crazy? Without orders from you? How would I know you hadn't planned the encounter between them?" His words were two-edged swords.

"You dare call me a traitor?" He was about to pounce on Matteo when his two men returned with Mario Cacciatore. He stopped short before the bewildered council members and thundered loudly, "Now we'll find out what this is all about!"

It took Cacciatore only a second to size up the situation. Matteo stared stonily ahead.

"Tell us what you saw and heard today."

"Listen, chief, you better ask Matteo. He's better with words than I am. We were together. I saw what he saw. Didn't Matteo tell you?"

"But in your own words, tell me what was said." Andrade

stepped between the two men, blocking Cacciatore's view of Matteo with a smug look on his face.

Cacciatore shook his head. "You want word for word? Why are you complicating things, chief?" He stared at the tips of his boots. "There was this traitor, see. Plotting against us. They plan trickery the day of the plebiscite, but, chief, ask Matteo. He is better with words, believe me."

"Just who were these men you saw and heard, eh?" pressed Andrade.

"Who could tell, chief? The sun, white like fire, blinded us. Perhaps Matteo saw them? Did he say?" He leaned his head around Andrade just as the bandit leader walked away, filled with disgust. Matteo smiled to himself.

Back at the crude table he used for a desk, Andrade sat down heavily, avoiding Matteo's non-committal glance. Then, suddenly remembering, he shouted, "You called me a traitor! That I won't forget!"

"I called *you* traitor?" asked Matteo in all innocence. "You called yourself traitor—not I!"

The time had come. "I've had as much of you as I can stand!" snarled Andrade, kicking back his chair. Aching for a fight he flew at Barbarossa. Instantly the others scrambled out of the way.

Andrade grabbed Matteo's shoulders, struck his head against a thick wooden post, and chopped him across the nose. But before he could slam him again, Matteo broke his grip, lunged at him, and sent him back sprawling against the table. He rolled back and lost his balance. Steadying himself, Andrade reached for his knife. The others gasped. Unarmed, Matteo sidestepped each thrust and jumped out of range, turning and twisting at each swipe Andrade made with his blade. The fight continued outside the tent where Matteo kicked the knife from Andrade's hand. Now they relied only on their fists. Curious and tense, the men gathered around them. Excited women stood on rocks to watch the commotion.

Knocked down by a powerful fist, Andrade's hand grasped the knife again and rose to a crouch, hatred in his eyes. Cacciatore slipped a knife to Barbarossa.

Now they were even. With a knife to aid him, Matteo became a worthy opponent. Andrade found himself on the defensive. The men didn't dare encourage either man in this fight for leadership. They sensed the hatred, the driving ambition in each man, and fearing their cries of encouragement might go to the wrong man and later be remembered, they bit their lips in silence.

Matteo managed to disarm Andrade. Grinning sardonically, with an evil twist to his lips, Matteo saw the thick crowd of men watching them. In a sudden show of bravado, he tossed aside his knife. A murmur of approval from the onlookers applauded his bravery, and at the same time, reflected the contempt they felt for Andrade.

Then somehow Andrade retrieved the knife. Catching Matteo off guard, he leaped into the air and sunk the knife into his shoulder. Matteo's surprise turned to astonishment. Andrade's face contorted with horror and pain as he reached behind him, clutching desperately at his back. Andrade groaned and clawed at his back and finally fell forward into a dead heap. A knife had been buried to the hilt in his back just behind his heart.

Matteo's eyes searched the sea of faces and came to rest on Cacciatore's dark excited eyes. In that instant, Matteo Barbarossa knew Cacciatore had killed the other five men. *Demonio!*

I'm content staying with the horses until I find a leader under whom I wish to serve. Hadn't that devil spoken these very words?

Barbarossa had no time to think, he had to call an emergency meeting of the council. He asked that Cacciatore remain at his side. His face was caked with blood and his head ached from the pounding he took, but Matteo was too flushed with excitement to care.

"It's only fair that I explain to you what preceded this fight. I told Andrade that the plans for our trip to Mussomeli on the day of the plebiscite must be changed, because Cacciatore and I stumbled across a plot to annihilate us, all of us, before we arrive at Mussomeli. Andrade refused to believe me.

"Suddenly, the man turned on me. He accused me of calling him a traitor. Never have I uttered such words. Believe me, my friends, I honored Andrade. He was my friend as well as our leader. His fate grieves me. But when he came at me unjustly and forced me into an encounter, I had to protect myself. The others will attest to that fact, no?" He looked at the two men who'd been summoned to fetch Cacciatore. They nodded regretfully.

"They saw I had no knife when he came at me. Then when he lost his, I threw mine away." Matteo opened his arms in a wide open gesture, silently appealing to the council, pleading for their understanding and loyalty in what was to come.

The men nodded quietly. That much was true. With their own eyes they'd seen Matteo give Andrade more than a fair chance. They had no quarrel with him on that score. The eldest of the council asked, "This spy you spoke of, where is he?"

Matteo glanced at Cacciatore, giving him a silent signal to bring the culprit Stefano to him.

"He'll be here soon. You can question him. On his person shall be a pouch of money, unless he's hidden it elsewhere by this time. He didn't count the money in our presence, so I can't tell you the sum it contained. Soon you'll understand why I asked Andrade to change the plans."

The council nodded. They remained silent until Cacciatore returned with Stefano. Their astonishment was complete. No one would have suspected this comely young man of treachery.

Stefano entered the tent of Andrade not knowing what to expect. He was a pleasant-faced youth of medium build with an ingratiating grin and twinkling brown eyes. Around the camp he was hailed as the minstrel who sang ballads while playing his instrument.

Matteo grimaced as a painful spasm shot through his arm.

"What is it?" said Stefano compassionately. He reached out in a gesture of help.

Matteo drew back, his face filled with exaggerated hostility. "Goddammit! Don't you touch me, you traitor!" he said wrathfully.

Stefano paled and stared uneasily at the others. "I don't understand . . ."

"Tell me it wasn't you we saw in the woods today with His Excellency. Tell me," implored Barbarossa with dramatic panache. "Tell me that with my own ears and my own eyes, it wasn't you I heard and saw. Tell me, Stefano, that I'm wrong to call you a traitor." Matteo held the others spellbound with his showmanship.

Caught off guard and mesmerized by Matteo's performance, Stefano might have admitted anything. He feigned innocence with such a self-conscious stammer, he couldn't convince the council. On a signal from Matteo, Cacciatore came in from behind Stefano, held him in an armlock, and pointed a sharp dagger at his throat.

"Now, Stefano," said Matteo, holding up a set of plans. "You'll show us exactly where the ambush will take place and what time, and where you intended to meet His Excellency's men." His mood and manner changed instantly into that of a cold, hard chieftain.

"Never! I'll tell you nothing!" He spit at Matteo's face. The tent filled with silence.

Cacciatore tightened his grip; the knife drew blood on Stefano's throat. Matteo wiped his face on his shirt sleeve and

255

remained unperturbed. He turned his back to Stefano and faced the council. "Maria Theresa, Maria Adorate, Maria Helena are your three sisters—no?" He asked with just the right touch of menace. He turned to glance at Stefano, who glared at him, astonished he should have such information at his disposal, yet trying not to betray his feelings.

"If you want no harm to come to them," said Matteo gently, "I suggest you cooperate with me." With a swift movement, he reached up and snapped the money pouch from Stefano's neck. "I'll see that they receive this." Matteo bounced the gold coins up and down in the palm of his hand. "They'll be safe from harm and will have the protection of the Mazzarino at all times."

"If I refuse?"

"You'll die anyway. Your sisters will be accepted as women of the Mazzarinos."

Stefano was revolted. He couldn't risk such fate for his sisters.

"I have your word no harm shall befall my sisters? The money goes to them?"

"The word of Matteo Barbarossa is more honorable than the word of God!"

The twelve members of the council exchanged uneasy glances. This new leader was nothing like Andrade. This man had the gall to place himself above God. They felt powerless to intervene, for this man demonstrated the balls of a bull elephant.

Stefano bent over the map and pointed to an area outside Mussomeli. "Here is where the ambush will take place—in the pre-dawn hours."

"How many?"

"You will be outnumbered five to one."

Matteo and Cacciatore exchanged concerned glances. The council members leaned forward, gravely worried. A few took sips from their wine-filled goatskins and wiped their parched lips. So Barbarossa had been right after all.

"Where were you to have been met?"

Stefano indicated a point on the map. "A few miles to the south of the point of ambush."

"If you aren't telling the truth . . ." warned Matteo with deadly calm. "Just imagine your sisters being raped by all the men!"

"I swear on my mother's grave. I swear!" cried Stefano nervously. He may have held Andrade cheaply, but he believed Barbarossa.

Matteo turned away from him. He spoke without flinching. "Shoot the traitor!" Two men left with Stefano, followed by Cacciatore.

Matteo turned to the map spread out on the table before him. He studied it carefully while the men studied him.

Out of courtesy to the council members, he asked for suggestions, but he'd already decided what to do without benefit of their ideas.

They all heard the gunshots when Stefano was executed. The council members, who for the most were as tough as Matteo, sat quietly in their seats and turned to take another long look at their new leader. This was a devil! A sonofabitch of a man! What a tiger, eh?

Long before dawn on the day of the plebiscite, two hundred Mazzarinos rode swiftly through the night to the other side of Mussomeli, where armed squads of *carabinieri* and government soldiers were camped. When the soldiers and *carabinieri* awakened, they gazed into the *lupara* and rifles held by the confident Mazzarinos. One or two shots from each bandit, and the hillside was covered with sprawling bodies. Not one of their enemies was left alive. It was a wild, insane feeling. Everything was going just right.

An hour later, Matteo Barbarossa and a hundred of his men waited in ambush for the detachment that was to meet Stefano. The detachment was wiped out to the very last man.

By 10 A.M. Matteo Barbarossa and four hundred bandits walked their horses through the Mafia stronghold and deliberately set up positions at the election stations. The fear on the faces of the voters as they stared at the incredible sight reflected their final decisions.

The *mafiosi* won the election by a landslide—without one overt threat made to a single voter. This was witnessed by the government soldiers who stood guard, wetting their pants in fright as they valiantly manned their positions. They later testified, "We saw no violence. No threats were imposed. Why, it was one of the most orderly elections we've ever seen!"

Before the sun reached its zenith on that hot, hot day in Mussomeli, the town band began to play its triumphant march music. Several of the *mafia* Dons came into the Piazza Garibaldi to applaud the courageous bandits. From where he sat, high astride his gleaming black stallion like a conquering god, Matteo Barbarossa saw the Dons searching the crowd for Andrade. Shading their eyes, smoking their fat cigars, and grinning broadly at their victory, they felt secure once more.

Many Dons from Palermo and other nearby villages had traveled to Mussomeli for this very important election, which meant life or death to the *mafia*'s plans. Among those who came to celebrate the victory were Don Umberto and Don Samuzzo of Godrano. Matteo Barbarossa was the first to recognize them. They hadn't changed over the years as much as Matteo had. For a time they didn't recognize him.

The *mafiosi* looked in all directions in their effort to find Andrade. News of his recent demise hadn't reached them. They openly ignored Matteo, nodding curtly to him as one might to a servant in passing. Matteo's silent and amused eyes fixed on them as they skirted in and out among the congestion of mounted horsemen. Sitting back in his saddle with an air of nonchalance, he smoked his long thin cigar.

The *mafia* Dons asked questions of his men. One man pointed to Matteo. Accompanied by eight other men, Don Samuzzo and Don Umberto approached him reservedly, their heads held high.

"Matteo?"

"*Si*, Godfather? What can I do for my Godfathers, eh?"

"You were splendid. We were sure you'd meet with catastrophe. Word came of a plot to annihilate all the Mazzarinos and we feared for your life. Where is Andrade?"

Matteo raised a leg over the horn of his saddle in a lazy pose. "Andrade? Andrade who?"

Knowing what he meant, their dark eyes burned in humiliation. "Who else? The leader of the Mazzarinos."

"Oh, that Andrade. He's dead."

"That's too bad," said Don Umberto. "He was a good man. Showed much promise."

"Andrade was a fool."

"Then who is the new leader of the Mazzarinos?"

"Guess who, Godfather? Guess who?"

An excited rider came thundering toward them, striking at his horse with fury. Dismounting, he talked with the Mafia Dons using exaggerated gestures. One by one, they turned and gazed at Matteo Barbarossa with open-mouthed expressions, disbelief written on their faces.

"Is it true what this man tells us? You wiped out an entire contingent of *carabinieri*? Some 800 men?" asked Don Samuzzo.

"Didn't you want to win this election, Godfathers?" Matteo wheeled his horse around and led his colorful array of brigands out of Mussomeli.

As quickly as transportation allowed, the Mafia Dons rode to Palermo to confer with Don Calomare, the *capomafia*. Neither Don Umberto nor Don Samuzzo dared speak their thoughts: That Barbarossa had earned the reputation they had tried to deny him; that this man possessed some special magic, some amulet of protection; that Destiny had somehow become his mistress; that in some mystical way he had bent her to his will. —Or that Matteo Barbarossa would one day be a name to reckon with.

The Mazzarinos rode into camp, circling the campfires, shouting, and yelling cries of victory. Such feasting and drinking! Their celebration lasted three days and nights. *Che demonio!* Not one man had received as much as a scratch! Were they impressed with this new leader? He was some sonofabitch of a man, this Matteo Barbarossa! Some man!

Recalling all this, Mario Cacciatore wondered what had happened to Barbarossa's dream. Since the arrival of this whoring daughter of the devil, Diamonte, it appeared to this butcher of men that all their dreams would evaporate like melted snow. Hadn't he already seen the taming of the Mazzarino?

Although they never mentioned it, Barbarossa knew it had been through Cacciatore's efforts that he was elevated to a position where he could challenge Andrade. Over the years Matteo came to understand this cunning and brutal man whose cold-blooded killings left him shocked and appalled. He was an animal! Like Aiello, Barbarossa recognized his deadly and ferocious instincts, his unscrupulous and devious behavior, and his total lack of conscience, the very characteristics which made him important to Barbarossa. When the Mazzarino chieftain found it unfeasible to personally involve himself in a murder, he used Cacciatore as his hatchet man, personal executioner, or butcher.

There'd been times when Cacciatore's thirst for blood had so offended Barbarossa that he had been overheard saying, "One day I might have to shoot that obscenity, if I can ever find a reason. I might even kill him without a reason! If that crazy bastard interferes in my dreams once too often . . ."

Reported to Cacciatore, this conservation brought a rare smile to his thick lips. His chief could have given him no greater compliment. "My, my, imagine that?" he had replied.

Those were great days. Goddamn, sonofabitching great days! Days when the Mazzarinos' fame had reached its height. *Now he's become a lovesick bull,* Cacciatore told himself gloomily.

How was Cacciatore to know how much he'd underestimated Matteo Barbarossa? Moreover, how much he'd underestimated Destiny's plan for this special man. Didn't he

259

know that no earthly force could push or prod Destiny when she chose not to be? For a time, Matteo had to remain where he was, where he could learn of many, many things from a little spider of a woman.

24

"Fifteen years, Matteo? Fifteen years? Is it possible so much time has passed?" She glanced at the gold and diamond earrings he had given her. "How beautiful . . ." She slipped them into her pierced lobes and turned from side to side for his approval. "You like?" They were shaped like a tiny web with a jeweled spider at one end and a teeny fly caught in the trap at the other. "To think," she laughed, "I used to hate when you called me your little spider."

They sat by the fire, drinking wine, holding hands, and reflecting on yesterday's dreams. Matteo thought how fiercely proud he'd been to have possessed such a woman. Her ultimate femininity, her ability to use words—sometimes as a love potion, sometimes as a stiletto—her womanly guile and sexuality, all contributed to satisfy his needs.

In all this time Diamonte had listened prudently to Barbarossa's dreams of becoming the greatest of all feudal overlords. How adamant she'd been in the beginning to lure him until she could find some avenue of escape. Fascinated by the countless contradictions in him, Diamonte not only became powerless to leave him, she began to see in him answers to her own deep-rooted needs. Here was the man through whom she could one day take revenge on Marco de Leone, who had spurned her love, and on Roberto Argento, a man who knew her better than she knew herself.

It was no great secret to Matteo that the *mafia* had consistently tried to control all the landowners, hoping for a monopoly of land interests, which would ultimately control the politics and government in the nation. The one main obstacle preventing total capitulation of the *latifondisti* was the Royal Lion of Sicily, who fought them at every turn. Representing twenty-five percent of the landed estates, the Lion's share was enough to keep the *mafia* at bay. The Royal Lion would never capitulate. Never!

Very well, seventy-five percent of the pie was better than none, the *capomafia* had wisely decreed. Don Calomare's insatiable greed, tempered by intellect, wanted no encounters with the Lion; there were too many risks. Forced to content themselves with less than they dreamed, the *mafia* like a ship in irons, unable to move forward or in any direction, waited for the wind.

Who was this wind for whom they waited? Who was the shadow of power hovering over the golden throne of Palermo's *capomafia*? Whose strength did they feel? Was it Don Calomare? Don Umberto? Perhaps Don Samuzzo? Or were these merely the cheap imitators of that real titan who stretched and yawned in the cave of the four winds, waiting, watching, testing his strength? Only Destiny knew . . .

Matteo Barbarossa had told Diamonte many times over the years, "The man who solves this problem for the *mafia* will control Sicily."

And so it was. Certain that the time had come for Matteo to make his move, Diamonte decided to stimulate him. "What if I could show you a foolproof way to annihilate both the Royal Lion and his genius agronomist, Roberto Argento?" she asked. Her voice stimulated something in him far more exciting than his throbbing manhood. He turned to her with strange lights in his eyes.

"It wouldn't work. Don Calomare shies from locking horns with *El Leone*."

"If I prove to you it can be done?"

"Ah, *cara mia*, the moon, the sun, and the stars and all of Sicily would be ours." He replied with a tone of futility.

"You listen, *caro mio*. You be the judge. If you listen to Don Calomare or those impotent rabbits who lack the guts to move forward, you'll be chained to these mountains until only the ghosts of your dreams are left to haunt the wilderness." She sighed. "Of late, even I grow weary of these inconveniences."

Matteo listened. With every inch of his body, mind, and soul, he listened to every word, time and again, over and over. Day after day, month after month, year after year. Cacciatore was right. Barbarossa had changed, but not in the way his butcher thought. He'd not been domesticated by a whore. It was a period of hibernation, inspiration, and contemplation, a sorting and sifting of facts, a unification of one great force, the most stupendous force that would ever dominate Sicily.

Diamonte knew Matteo was ready before he did. He'd grown moody and indifferent. Her soft arms, passionate kisses, and the heat of her loins hardly moved him. Another mistress, Destiny, had spun her web of seduction over him.

Diamonte smiled as they sat by the fire one night in early spring of that last year, finalizing their plans. Something occurred to Matteo as he sat listening to her, something which he found disturbing. Diamonte had always insisted she loathed the Lion, but instinctively he knew different. On this night he could no longer bear his feelings. As she talked, his fingers entwined around her long, black hair and at one point he drew her to him savagely.

"You love him!" he accused.

"I hate him!" she replied too quickly. She stared into his burning eyes, giving him no indication of her discomfort.

Matteo tightened his grip on her hair. "You lie, bitch! You lie!"

"My wish is that Marco de Leone and his agronomist be reduced to nothing."

"In fifteen years you've not forgotten that Lion! Don't think I don't know how you've raved about your life at the villa. How *fantastico* it was. Now, you look into my eyes and say you hate him? Bah! You can't be trusted!"

"What I said about the *latifondo* is true, Matteo. Why do you suppose the *mafia* wants to break him? They know his democratic ideas will influence the peasants into wanting a better life. What's wrong with that? Only that you and your people don't want the advancement of Sicily. The *mafia* controls through fear, and fear controls the peasants, no? I am showing you a way to fulfill your dream, Matteo. What a victory for you if you succeed in taking the Villa de Leone! What victory if you crush the only enemy of the *mafia!*" She placed her slender, work-worn hands over his and released his taut grip on her hand. "You would then be the *mafia* itself."

Matteo Barbarossa's black eyes dilated with fire as he envisioned his dream. He was so close he could almost taste it.

"It's time to make your move, Matteo, before another young *picciotto* comes along to dethrone you as you did Andrade."

"What are you saying, bitch? No one will dethrone Matteo Barbarossa! You hear? When the time comes, I will appoint a successor. The Mazzarinos belong solely to Matteo Barbarossa!"

"And when will that time be, Matteo?"

"When I say so!"

In a violent fit of passion, he pulled her to him. There, under the stars, under the spotlight of an enormous moon as they had done in the beginning, she yielded to his manliness, again, and again, and again. His power, transmitted to her, increased her passion, and she did something to him she'd never considered before. He'd longed for this but never found the courage to ask her. That night, after she buried her head in his loins, there was nothing he wouldn't do for her. Just before the moment of orgasm, Diamonte paused to glance at him. Matteo sat up, and grabbing her head, he held her tight against him. His savage profile against the huge orange moon startled her. She couldn't read his mind, but at that moment, she knew he envisioned himself overlord of Sicily, *capo di tutti capi*, head of all the *mafia* Dons.

He exploded like a thousand cannon.

Destiny had prodded him at last. He felt that Diamonte's words were an omen for him to tarry no longer. The day came. Asserting his *maschiezzo*, he asked, "Where exactly is this magnificent estate of which you boast?"

"I thought you'd never ask, *caro mio*," she said. She took a stick and drew a map in the dust and described the *latifondo* in detail.

Matteo found her words incredible. How could such a place exist in Sicily?

"Just who is this Roberto Argento who incites you to vent your spleen? Why do you hate him so?"

"A Jew who knows the lands better than any Sicilian."

"A Jew who knows the land?" Matteo laughed scornfully.

"I tell you only what the peasants themselves say, that he must have had a love affair with the earth to so understand its innermost secrets. History has proven it true, Matteo." As always, her voice softened in reflection.

Barbarossa's eyes narrowed in thought as he listened to her. "A woman who speaks words her heart doesn't feel is not a person to be trusted, my little spider," he said slowly with a pang of dismay. "No, don't deny it. If I understand nothing else, I know your ambition. I know your allegiance will ultimately lie with me, because I'm the only one you can turn to. I am not educated with books as is your Royal Lion. But, little spider, I listen with my eyes, and I see with my instinct, and my heart trembles in doubt."

"Matteo, you're wrong. I love you. After all these years you question my love?"

"We'll see, little spider. We'll see." *Damn the devil! I'd better see!*

The time was at hand. "I'll be gone for several weeks," Matteo told her. "Cacciatore and I will be moving about, traveling northeast. If you need me, send a courier to Randazzo."

"But where will you be?"

"Scouting the Villa de Leone to see if your information checks out. Many things can change in fifteen years. Even I have changed, little spider. You see how I can speak without losing my composure? How much more complicated I have become? Always thinking. Always planning. Like a whirlwind."

"Take me with you, Matteo."

"No. Beauty like yours is too noticeable. Rumors will spread like fire."

"But you'll take me on the raid! I'd risk anything to see my poor old mother again."

Matteo smiled. In fifteen years, she hadn't mentioned her mother more than once or twice. "Look, Diamonte, look at that magnifico sky. It doesn't seem possible that storm clouds are gathering, eh, my sparkling gem?"

Diamonte glanced up at the magnificent sunset. She turned to him. It was the first time he'd ever called her Diamonte. She moved in close to him. "You're crazy, Matteo. Whoever heard of storm clouds at this time of the year? And what happened to your little spider?"

His black eyes were busy looking at another scene, some miles distant, a place he'd begun to dream about of late, until he felt sure he knew every inch of the lands and every man who lived in this land of make-believe.

25

"You must be exhausted. Please avail yourself of the facilities of my villa. Please! Bathe yourself, wash, anything! We must remove that savage stench from your person!"

Matteo Barbarossa's face turned redder than his famous beard. "I didn't think to bring a change of clothing. I felt what I had to say more important . . ." he began in apology, filled with awkward self-consciousness.

"And it is, young man. It is!" Don Calomare's nose screwed up in distaste. He pulled a satin cord summoning a servant. "It's just these allergies of mine," he said apologetically. "Whenever I smell the raw wilderness, I cough and sneeze and become as a man plagued by consumption."

Matteo bowed stiffly and followed the servant to another section of the Monreale Villa. There he bathed, slipped into some ill-fitting clothing, and prepared himself for his audience with the *capomafia*.

Although Don Calomare had a fringe of gray hair around his bald pate, he still walked as straight and poised as he had when he was an officer in the army of the Two Sicilies. In Barbarossa's absence he turned in his swivel chair and glanced up at the portrait of himself in uniform. That was before he'd climbed the slippery slopes of the new society of *gallantuomi*, the *mafia* feudalists who came into their own under his directives. A strange sensation shot through him

264

and he wasn't sure what caused it. He'd awakened that morning with a peculiar feeling in his guts. Certain that this day would be more unusual than any day in his life, he was unable to subdue the excitement that churned inside him.

At one time in his life Don Calomare had been guided by sham and pretense. Now, he abhorred it. Straight-talking men were his kind of men, but where to find such men? Forced to play these games men played until he could no longer stomach them, he became brutally candid, just as he had been in Matteo's case. Did he give a fuck if he offended Matteo? Hell no!

"Accept my apologies," began Matteo on re-entering the study.

"So you're the famous Matteo Barbarossa I've been hearing about?" said the *capo*, waving off his apology. "My, my, I've heard so much about this whirlwind Mazzarino! Let me take a moment to commend you on that spectacular job you did in Mussomeli. Your *amici* in Godrano have never forgotten your courage and victory that day."

I'll bet they haven't, thought Matteo as he seated himself in the straight, high-backed chair the Don indicated. He watched as his host poured a robust red wine from Venice, and he accepted a cigar from an elegant humidor.

"Valpolicella!" announced the Don, holding up his glass. They drank in silence.

"Ahhh," said the Don, smacking his lips together. "I've been impressed with the special jobs you've performed on our behalf. Your reputation has spread faster than our communication system." They both laughed at the old joke.

"Now, suppose you get on with these *important* plans you spoke of."

Matteo nodded. "First there are some conditions. This plan is not to be discussed with anyone else. It is only for you and I to know. If I could choose, only I would possess the information." When he saw the icy distrust and hostility creep into the Don's eyes, he quickly added, "I meant no disrespect. These days one can't be too careful."

Matteo's tone of authority and the presumption of his sudden elevation in class offended Calomare. He said nothing. He only nodded.

"Forgive a bumbling wild man, Excellency. For so long I've held my own counsel, this role is unfamiliar." He had no desire to offend this man as he had the Godrano Dons who sentenced him to the Mazzarinos. "If I overstep my position, you tell me. I understand. I learn quickly."

"Go on."

265

"In the past my plans have succeeded because I disclosed them to no one. I lead the Mazzarinos because my men rely on me. I am a temperate man, but I will kill for a mere infraction of our laws. I become emotional in battle only where it counts. I fight to win. Too much of me goes into my plans for me to lose only because someone has babbled when wine loosens his tongue. But why do I tell you? Surely you know men's frailties better than I."

"Go on."

"It has come to my attention that certain baronial resistance has caused you many delays in the total acquisition of the feudal estates. Particularly those in the northeast, near Messina."

The Don glanced sharply at him, listening to him with a half-smile and a mind full of crafty ridicule. "Go on."

"Most of the land barons, mortgaged to infinity, could be easily squeezed into bankruptcy. The right person, a *manipulator*, a dealer in such matters, could step in and for a pittance, buy up these notes, then, gently, oh so gently, ease these pompous asses right off their lands into the streets where they deserve to be."

The Don's gleaming yellow skull glistened with perspiration. His features jerked with insatiable greed.

"The men who own the land in Sicily, own Sicily," continued Matteo.

"My sentiments exactly!" exclaimed Don Calomare, caught up in his guest's mood. He quickly took hold of himself and contemplated the awesome bandit. "Just who do you have in mind as the *right* person?"

Matteo tilted his head and shrugged noncommittally. "You're the *capo*."

"Hrumph!" he cleared his throat. "What is this master plot? How will you carry it out?"

"With very careful planning and utmost secrecy. Very careful planning."

Don Calomare jumped to his feet, walked to the enormous bay window, and stared silently into the sunlit courtyard. Two guards stood talking next to the beautiful wrought-iron gates upon which rested an ornate coat of arms, belonging to the villa's former owner whom Don Calomare had squeezed off the place. His heart beat furiously, leaving him breathless. He was almost certain of what Barbarossa had in mind. He knew it! Just like the air before a holiday becomes electric, the air in the room pulsed and vibrated with a certain powerful force. It was almost a feat to ask his next question.

"What other conditions do you pose?"

266

"First, that I can leave the Mazarrinos and live here with you."

Don Calomare turned to him. "With me?"

"As your Godson."

"My Godson, Matteo?" He was struck by the man's audacity.

Right then, Matteo knew exactly where he stood with the *capo*. The stigma of class lay not only with the titled nobility but with the lower classes as well. Seething at the obvious effrontery, he gave the Don a simple bland look.

Don Calomare lowered his eyes. "What you ask is a matter for the family . . ."

"You misunderstand. I do not mean it literally. Only that you treat me as Godson. Teach me what you know. I want only to follow in your place."

Don Calomare, in his wisdom, said nothing for the moment, and keeping his face like a sheet of glass, he returned to his desk. "What you ask is not possible. I don't control the choice of a successor except in extraordinary circumstances. I'd like to tutor you, really, but the other Dons are not as clear thinking as you or I and will not take kindly to such a proposal. Matteo, there are nearly thirty *anxious* men waiting to take my place."

He stopped talking. Matteo saw right through his sham. A *capomafia* owes no obligation to anyone. The icy contempt in this barbarian's eyes caused him some anxiety. He *had* to know these special plans now. For him to outline such outrageous conditions, the plan had to be stellar. *I can agree to anything,* he told himself. *What I do with this insolent upstart, who dares suggest he be my Godson, is another matter. Godson, indeed!* He smiled suddenly with revolting sweetness.

"Why have you been kept away from me, Matteo? A man of your caliber should have been brought to my attention years ago. Bah! These small-town Dons! They have the brains of pygmies!" He walked to Matteo's side. He could hear the brittle hammering of his own pulse as he laid a hand on Matteo's arm. "What a keen intelligence you have, my boy. It's rare to find such cleverness in a young man these days."

"If they hadn't been pawned off to the Mazarrinos by your astute families, my Don, you might have had a stable full of bright and clever young men at your side."

Bastard, upstart, son of a shithouse cleaner! "You may be right, Matteo. With so many things on my mind, it's difficult to police each little village. But you didn't answer my question. Where have you learned such wisdom?"

Matteo laughed. *Goddammit! He has a way with words. My little spider is right. 'You must learn to use words right, Matteo,' she has told me time and again.*

"I observe, I listen, and I talk as little as is necessary. I avoid complications," he said knowing what the *capo* wanted to hear.

"Va biene. Va biene. Now listen. Suppose I told you I agree to your conditions?"

"Agreed? Everything agreed?"

"Agreed! Am I not the *capo?* Let them oppose me and I'll show them who wields the power." He raised his glass to his lips, sipped his wine, and studied Matteo critically over the rim of his glass. "Now, *Godson,* continue."

"My first plan is to destroy the Royal Lion of Sicily."

The Don almost choked on the wine. He sputtered and the wine spurted like a fountain from his lips. Matteo leaned forward and handed him a white serviette from the desk. The Don raised his eyes to meet Matteo's calm, sober gaze.

"That's a worthwhile ambition," he said wryly. "Forget it."

"It can be done."

"Better men than you have tried and failed miserably."

"They didn't know how. Besides, there is only one Barbarossa!"

"Eight years ago we deployed a band of cut-throat bandits, led by men more vicious than you Mazzarinos, to do the job. They were pitiful! To date every last man has been killed or imprisoned."

"Or betrayed? Besides, they were not like the Mazzarinos. There are only one of their kind."

The Don ignored both the innuendo and the declaration. "The Marquis is too powerful. You'd best avoid any encounters with the House of de Leone."

"Once the Lion falls, the others will capitulate. They won't hold out."

"I say no! The Lion's lands are impenetrable! We have enough in our overall plan without his domain. We can't risk bringing the Government down on our necks! As it stands we are lucky to control those who occupy the barracks in Sicily. Tamper with the Lion and we court disaster. No! I tell you, no!"

Don Calomare paced before a map of Sicily on one wall. He paused to study it with intent eyes. "Except for the northeast corner of the island . . ." He slapped the map soundly. ". . . it would be all ours! Government and all! But I say no! We can't risk it! De Leone is too formidable. His closest friends and relatives control the Senate. He resigned his position in politics for a while to devote full time

268

to his people. The man's a fanatic. Fanatics are dangerous. Mark my words."

"And I say, it can be done." Angry that he had to serve an apprenticeship by licking boots, Matteo tried to maintain his calm. They gazed at each other with impassioned silence.

"What makes you certain?"

"I know, that's all. I'm a specialist in my craft. Did you forget? The *Straggi de Mussomeli!* I thought you remembered the Massacre at Mussomeli?"

Apparently eight hundred deaths weren't enough to convince Don Calomare. "I've a complete set of plans of the Villa de Leone and knowledge of all its security," he added reluctantly.

"You have such information?"

"I, myself, have come here after a week's personal surveillance of the *latifondo*."

"You were on the property of the Lion?" Calomare's manner altered considerably. He returned to the desk and refilled Matteo's glass, while he studied him critically. "Personally, I think you a fool to lock horns with *El Leone.* You must know what you are doing, or you'd not venture into such a deed. I've heard enough about you to know you possess an uncanny wisdom. I wish to know nothing of such a plan, if you follow me. If you should emerge victorious, you shall return to Palermo on the terms you specify. I will see to it that you receive full immunity for any crimes committed against the state." He smiled. "You know you're wanted in almost every province on the island?"

"But you can take care of such trivialities with a snap of your fingers, eh? You know the right people."

"You know this, eh?"

"Everyone knows and fears the power of the *capomafia*."

"Be careful, Matteo. If you think our brotherhood is powerful, it is nothing compared to the network of information supplied to Marco de Leone.

"You aren't *sympatico* to *El Leone,* Excellency?" Matteo frowned.

"If there were more men like Marco de Leone, the brotherhood might never have had a reason for existence."

Matteo froze. He not only disliked this line of reasoning, he didn't understand it. *He speaks like a man with the soul of a woman. Too damn dangerous for my thinking.* "You don't feel sorry for your enemies! Enemies are to be annihilated! Crushed!" This evidence of weakness on the Don's part was stored in Matteo's memory, to be remembered.

"You're disturbed because I praise such an enemy? You don't have to pay allegiance to a man to recognize and admire superior qualities. De Leone is a great and mighty Sicilian, a forthright man whose personal desires remain subordinate to the needs of his people. Just because he's an opponent, doesn't mean I can't admire him."

Matteo spat contemptuously. "Would he praise or admire you?"

"What makes you think he hasn't? In the right perspective of course. I'm sure he knows all about me, perhaps more than I can even remember. A man should always know his enemies to determine the kind of man he opposes. The Lion fights for what he believes in. I fight for what I believe in. Who is right? Who is wrong?"

The last thing in the world Matteo would do or say was that he didn't understand this deep philosophy. *Who is right? Who is wrong? What kind of thinking is this for a* capomafia? *He's a nothing this Calomare! A nothing! The sooner I dethrone him, the better. How do you praise a man in one breath and sanction his death with the next,* he asked himself. Matteo's memory was short.

Don Calomare sighed wistfully. The man had nothing to offer save being a hired killer. *He's merely a savage who can fight with the strength and cunning of a voracious tiger, but an illiterate who lives by pure instinct is someone to fear.*

"When will all these plans take effect, my friend?"

"It's best only I know of such plans. Since I need only my own men, my own resources, it's best these plans are kept confidential. No disrespect meant, you understand?"

"Tell me, Barbarossa, is it true you were born with a gun blazing in each hand and a knife between your teeth as is rumored among those who know you well?"

"Che demonio, Excellency," laughed Matteo. "Such a fabrication! Can you imagine how uncomfortable that would have been for my mother?"

Don Calomare showed signs of a faint smile. He had no other words to mask the outrage he held for this brazen son of a shithouse cleaner! He wished him well, and in the usual custom of respect, he permitted Barbarossa to kiss his hand before he left.

Watching from the bay window, Don Calomare saw that Matteo was joined by a frightening, but impressively brutal man whose very presence had defiled his courtyard. He shuddered and returned to his seat at the desk in the artlessly decorated room made up of the accumulated memoirs of his life.

It had taken shrewd planning and artful boldness to pull away from those gout-infected nobles, and a firm, fierce resolve to eliminate his enemies. Calomare stepped up as *capomafia*, at a time when the *mafia* needed direction. Don Alcalmo Calomare, the first of his kind, had taught them the importance of owning land, of bowing and scraping to the baronial feudalists until they could win their confidence. Gradually, the brotherhood came to control nearly all the land in the west. He'd taught them the importance of patience, of biding one's time, and the necessity of controlling the politics and government of the nation.

Now, if this Barbarossa could pull off what he plans, what a coup! *Managghia!* What a coup that would be! But Don Calomare refused to speculate further. In the past, sweet fruits of a premature victory had turned to acid. He'd wait this time, save wear on his intestines, before he shouted joys of victory. He made a note to ride to Godrano to learn more about this uncouth barbarian without tipping his hand to the Godrano Dons. He wasn't ready for them to know of the plans initiated by the Mazzarino that day.

Matteo Barbarossa returned to the Mazzarino camp consumed by the burning hatred he felt for Don Alcalmo Calomare and indignant at having been forced to bathe before their talk. Would the stigma set upon him by his stupid dolt of a father never be wiped clean? If he had to become *capomafia* of the world, he'd get even for the humiliation done him!

26

Impotence was a new and frightening sensation for the pain-filled Cacciatore. When he regained consciousness following the branding inflicted on him by Dolcetto de Leone, he slipped away in the dark of night unaware that Dr. Pietro had injected him with a pain-killing dose of morphine. Having ridden his horse all day under the broiling sun, he began to feel the excruciating pains as the narcotic wore off. Cacciatore had nothing going for him except his grim determination to live and strike back at that young Lion who'd shamed and humiliated him, leaving him half a man.

No one could have been more stupefied than Matteo Barbarossa to see Mario Cacciatore ride into the Mazzarino camp some four days after the de Leone raid. More dead than alive, he was tied and strapped to his saddle. The horse, filthy, sweating, foaming at the mouth, was about to collapse. The men untied their comrade, marveling at his daring. Filled with incredible shock when they saw the extent of his wounds, they helped him to his bedroll where he lay moaning. How, they wondered, had he survived? The brand of the Royal Lion hadn't appeared yet—there was only blistering, infection and dirt-caked blood.

The women cleansed him with olive oil, spoonfed him soup, and forced him to drink much water, while they kept their eyes glued to the entrance of the camp, waiting for the appearance of the one person they missed the most, Diamonte. And with a solemn face, Barbarossa took to riding the hills, searching, as if he, too, waited for someone.

Two weeks passed before Cacciatore was well enough to answer questions. Well before that the women had found the shriveled flesh resembling a human ear, pierced with the golden spider earring. They feared taking it to their leader, but they did.

Holding the earring in the palm of his hand, Matteo's first question to Cacciatore was, "Where is she?"

"Dead!" spat the frog. "And good riddance!"

In his black despair Matteo would have finished the job on him. Seeing the violence in his eyes, Cacciatore cried out in anguish, "The man who lay on the kitchen floor—the one she said was just a peasant—was the Royal Lion himself! I didn't kill her! Not me! I only cut off an ear so you'd believe me!"

Barbarossa recalled how gently Diamonte had laid his head on the floor. He'd been right. She had loved the Lion all these years. All these years she had coupled with him, but she had loved Marco de Leone.

Cacciatore told him what had happened after the bandits left and gloated over the fact that he'd cut out Marco's tongue. "He'll never speak against the *mafia* again!"

What the hell is wrong now, thought Cacciatore, noticing no elation from his chief over his cunning piece of work. Sulking, he turned to the others for praise.

Barbarossa left his side and stumbled blindly along the path to the bluff where he and Diamonte had spent so many love-filled hours. Sitting on a boulder facing the vast lands of Sicily, he was overcome with inconsolable sadness. Night fell with a quiet emptiness. Matteo knew by the way they looked for her that the women would miss and mourn her, but like he did, they bore their grief inwardly, silent and brooding.

He ate nothing for days. He saw Diamonte reflected in the soft eyes of the women. Everyone had been inspired by Diamonte. Even the children were different. Everywhere were visible signs of her influence. Matteo knew then that he could no longer stay with the Mazzarinos.

He opened Diamonte's traveling case and slipped her golden pocket watch into his vest. He took her pearl and the ruby-and-diamond ring he bought her once for a birth-day gift and placed them in his pocket. Filled with anguish, he clutched her garments to his chest and moaned softly. Then, in a quick movement, he gathered all traces of the woman into his arms and flung everything into the roaring campfire, leaving nothing of Diamonte, except her jewelry which he kept, plus the one spider earring.

The next morning he put Brancusso in charge.

"The next time you receive orders from the *mafiosi*, do nothing unless they bear my sign. Understand me, Brancusso, you will take orders from no one but me."

Brancusso knelt before Matteo and kissed his hand. This supreme mark of respect filled Matteo with pride.

He took Cacciatore to Gela with him, were they both bought new clothes befitting a Don and his bodyguard. Matteo even shaved his coppery beard. He also bought a pair of dark-tinted sunglasses. He had admired them for some time but thought it too vain to wear them until he had gained some stature. Once he put them on, however, he felt compelled to wear them.

Now, as Destiny readied the next phase of her plans for this obedient Godson, these dark-tinted glasses were as vital to Matteo as were her plans. Men would come to hate and fear them, unable to see through them into the windows of Matteo's soul. For without those glasses, Matteo Barbarossa's eyes were Sicily, and his enemies could easily see his quench-less thirst for her power.

27

The Island of Sicily trembled in dumb stupefaction at the news of the barbarous assault on the Villa de Leone and the irrevocable damage done to the Royal Lion by Matteo Barbarossa and the infamous Mazzarinos. In Palermo, a gathering of *mafia* Dons was underway at the Monreale Villa of Don Alcalmo Calomare. From all directions they came, with bodyguards, hardware and muscle, to take another look at this forceful, giant whirlwind, Matteo Barbarossa, who climaxed all his endeavors with shattering victories.

Not all the Dons wore smiles of satisfaction when they discussed the red-bearded devil among themselves, but there were two who made their connection with him known.

"Barbarossa comes from Godrano. He's my Godson," said Don Umberto puffed with pride. "I took him under my wing, taught him all he knows. How to shoot a *lupara*. Handle a knife. Everything he is he owes to me!"

Don Samuzzo, stroking his gray mustache, added, "I also had a hand in his future. Who do you think made him the giant he is, eh? I taught him all the ropes." He silently challenged Don Umberto to contest this.

The Dons from Trapani and Marsala saw in Barbarossa a formidable enemy, a ferocious barbarian who lived by his own rules, caring nothing for organization or the necessary loyalties to the brotherhood.

The Dons from Corleone and Piana dei Greci were displeased. They protested the manner in which Barbarossa had climbed to the top of the Mazzarinos. Some of their own Godsons had stood next in line to Andrade. The families would not honor such a man, they protested vehemently.

The *capomafia* had wisely put his affairs in order. Listening to his associates for the better part of an hour, he finally made it known he was bringing the meeting to order. Sighing deeply, he wanted these men to understand clearly their position. Tied to the past, it seemed they'd never disassociate themselves. Nevertheless, he had to make his points.

"Amici, we are growing old. This red-bearded dog you speak of is no longer a *picciotto.* He's a grown man. I didn't call this meeting to hear you lament like women. What do we have here? Men of power or sniveling cowards? Let's give credit where it's due. Barbarossa has more *fegato*—guts— than any ten of us put together.

"Remember Mussomeli and remember it well! Think about Camporeale, Villalba, Castelvetrano, and all the other places we sent Barbarossa. Victory after victory was laid in our laps. We are where we are today, because *animales* like Barbarossa made it possible."

Don Calomare gazed at these brooding vultures. They knew he was right. Their blind absurdities, their arrogance, and the Godlike conviction of their own superiority prevented them from giving this devil his due. He continued, "We can't prevent Destiny from following her course. But I assure you, none of you should fear him. It's my position he wants. Barbarossa wants to be *capomafia!"*

A disgruntled murmur arose from the Dons. He raised his hands to silence them.

"You told him to go out and earn a reputation, no? Now he's done it! He's entitled to the respect. He merits our applause. He deserves the title. It's unfortunate that none of you understand. Nothing we can do will prevent Barbarossa from becoming *capomafia.* Fight it and I'll wager against your survival. Join him and you'll be as rich as Croesus one day. While you're deciding, I advise you to remember that he controls the Mazzarinos!" he said wisely.

274

The men grew silent and reflective as they puffed on their fat cigars and sipped their wines.

"And what of you?" asked Don Umberto.

"Thank you for asking." The *capo* replied with a tinge of sarcasm. "As certain as I am that the sun will rise each morning, I am certain that in a fortnight or less, I shall not be among you. My demise is certain and irrevocable. My affairs are in order. You will do the same. You will give the new *capo* all the cooperation he deserves and more."

"But I am next in line!" protested Don Umberto with quenchless greed. "It is I who have seniority."

"Umberto . . . Umberto," reprimanded the *capo*. "I'm still alive."

"But you said . . ."

"So I did." He showed the Godrano Don the patience you'd show a child. "You see, Umberto, Barbarossa would kill me to take my position. You wouldn't!"

Within forty-eight hours, Don Calomare was dead. A magnificent funeral, held in Palermo, brought all the Dons and dignitaries to mourn him. The most prostrate, the most disconsolate, was Matteo Barbarossa, whose floral tribute was the largest in the true tradition of *mafia* ascendancy, to advise the brotherhood who possessed the true power.

Don Matteo Barbarossa became the uncontested *capo-mafia* of Palermo, of all Sicily.

He never really realized how much he'd learned from his little spider in those fifteen years until he held the power of the *mafia* in his fist. *Capomafia* Barbarossa took to his new life as if he'd been born to it. He found himself bit by bit, becoming a confidant of the titled *latifondisti*. His ingratiating manner, coupled with the fiercest of reputations, made him an awesome figure upon whom they thrust the problems they encountered with the peasants. Hardly a day passed that the Don wasn't called upon to solve some common sense question. As long as there was a profit in it for him, Don Barbarossa never refused them.

From these associations with the nobility, the barbarian Matteo Barbarossa developed polish. He learned to speak softly. Diamonte had been right. Being polite and considerate of a woman wasn't a sign of weakness in a man. When he was invited to dine with these men, he was awkward at first, but he learned that eating wasn't an animalistic rite accompanied by loud, guttural noises and greasy hands. What really amazed him was the discovery that more could be accomplished over a glass of wine than by killing, that politeness, consideration, and patience were more profitable weapons than a gun.

All this was called being civilized. And it came late in life. He wasn't always successful in the role, but he tried.

Don Barbarossa was nearly forty when he took a bride, the daughter of a wealthy landowner from Trapani. Plain, quiet, and unassuming with dark skin and large eyes, she had the look of a Corsican peasant and crude ways. What she lacked in beauty, her handsome dowry made up for tenfold: four large estates in prime locations quartered out of an enormous feudal estate by her shrewd, enterprising father, Antonio Basconato, whom Matteo made into a *mafia* mayor in his village.

Barbarossa brought his wife into his new home, the former villa of Don Calomare in Monreale, and found making love to her loathsome. Febronia at thirty-six, in a marriage of convenience, allowed him no feeling of exultation when he deflowered her. He found no excitement in it, and the episode left Matteo unnerved and filled more with distaste than desire. Thereafter, his husbandly duties were limited to once a month.

No woman could ever be to Matteo what Diamonte had been—part of his heart, his soul, and his life for fifteen glorious years of sheer ecstasy and love. He berated himself many times for never really telling her how much he loved her.

While the enterprising Don Barbarossa made the Palermitans march to his drum beat, Destiny moved Marco de Leone ahead in giant steps. Having already compensated him for the loss of his tongue many years ago, she endowed him with a literary genius. Wielding his pen like a golden scepter, he became a reigning monarch among historical writers. He began by writing powerful letters to his colleagues in Parliament, and the Senators forwarded these letters to King Victor Emmanuel, who turned them over to his number one man, a young Fascist named Benito Mussolini.

In Rome, the very word *mafia* was viewed as something remote, a figment of someone's imagination. When Mussolini read de Leone's allegations of *mafia* corruption and power, he smiled benignly. When the Lion of Sicily referred to the Mafia as the second government in Sicily, Il Duce scoffed and wondered if Marco weren't senile.

Then, with the astuteness and sagacity for which he was credited, Il Duce investigated the accuser before checking the actions of the accused. There were no skeletons in the Lion's closets. In both public office and private life, the fierce dedication of the man and his family toward their country and people was exceptional and was held in high esteem. Il Duce himself was impressed.

But it wasn't until His Royal Highness King Victor Emmanuel, on a tour of Sicily, was hustled off to the Greek village of Piana dei Greci and forced to become a Godfather to the Mafia Don's newly born child that Il Duce took action. The future dictator of Italy, incensed at the shabby treatment of his Sovereign, cancelled the many affairs of state that were scheduled for the next month and left Rome to reckon with this growing malignancy at Italy's foot.

From the moment he set foot on Sicilian soil, Il Duce sensed the sinister atmosphere and danger. In every village—and he went inland to the remote interior villages where it seemed civilization had stopped centuries before—he was threatened, insulted, and openly ridiculed by the Mafia Dons who subtly implied that in Sicily, Il Duce was powerless.

Although he shook with rage, he maintained his silence and bided his time. Only the famous flexing of his jaws reflected the fiery indignation he felt at such insolence. He was brazenly told to dismiss his military escort, that as long as he was escorted by the brotherhood Dons, no harm would befall him. Wherever Il Duce and his entourage traveled, arrogant young militants armed with *luparas* policed his activities. Imagine that! Such punks policing Il Duce!

Il Duce wasn't stupid in those early days, so considering the odds, he left the interior and returned to Palermo. There, he visited the Bank of Sicily to make an examination of the bank's records. Although polite and cordial, the bank examiners and officials denied his request. "We'll need a court order, Signore," they told him, "one available only through the channels provided by Don Matteo Barbarossa, who just happens to be away on a short holiday." These same officials left little doubt in Il Duce's mind that even if he tried to force a full-scale investigation, the matter would in no way be resolved unless the *capomafia* himself were there to sanction the act.

A cursory check into water and road improvement appropriations disclosed that the money was gone and the work undone. Additional checks into other public offices—Finance, Taxation, Public Assistance, and many more—showed more irregularities, but a blanket of protection prevented him from probing too deeply. In one village, where Il Duce was scheduled to speak briefly to the populace, it took but a few moments to realize he'd been the victim of a

277

farce. Ordered to remain away from the piazza, the residents of the village locked themselves behind their doors, while in the piazza a cross-section of village idiots, cripples, and degenerates had been gathered by the Dons as a sign of their contempt for the future dictator.

Il Duce saw them, heard them, and felt their power, but he found it difficult to believe the mafia really existed. He and his entourage traveled the unpaved road to the lands of the Royal Lion. At the request of the king, Marco de Leone prepared other papers outlining in full detail all the *mafia's* operations: manipulation of credit through *mafia*-controlled banks, the forging of signatures on all falsely acquired corporate holdings, and the gross misappropriation of lands. Marco presented Il Duce with reams of documented evidence—the violent deaths of peasants in their attempts to claim uncultivated lands, the unfair system of taxation imposed upon the peasants, the monopolistic practices of *mafia*-controlled businesses, the takeover of the trade unions by the mafia. Contained in Marco's reports were names and places and atrocities. How he, a citizen, had to employ a private army—the *Falconieri*—to protect his estates from a *mafia* takeover.

Silent and brooding, Il Duce decided to cut his trip short. He lauded Marco de Leone for all his stout-hearted bravery and his one-man fight against this force of evil. He addressed himself to the impressive Lion. "Excellency, be assured that proper action shall be taken to exterminate this depraved menace from Sicily's shores. Sicily has been neglected for too long, left to her own fate for the last time. Trust in us, we shall restore the dignity she deserves." Mussolini smiled amiably and asked Marco, "Are you *fascisti* now?"

Marco wrote on a card. *I'm too old for politics. I'm simply a patriot who loves his country.*

"Too bad, Excellency," replied Il Duce. "We could use a man of your caliber in our progressive Roma."

They shook hands and the impressive dignitaries left the villa. Marco waved at them in parting and considered this iron-jawed giant. He was dynamic, this Il Duce, a forceful individual who believed in his ideals with total conviction. But Marco had certain reservations about the *politicos* who were quickly changing the course of history. Dolcetto and Antonio wrote from Switzerland constantly referring to the predictions by international tycoons of another world war, one bigger and deadlier than the first war which had ended not long ago.

But if Marco thought that Il Duce would forget the problems of Sicily and devote himself to more selfish gains, he had underestimated this ambitious and politically astute dynamo.

In Rome, Il Duce worked swiftly and methodically. Hand-selected for the job was Prefect of Police Cesare Mori, who had a curious loathing for the *mafia* and a great desire to please Il Duce, with whom he enjoyed a rather bizarre relationship. Mori literally plowed through Sicily, lining people up indiscriminately, *mafiosi* or not, mowing them down with machine guns, and tossing their bodies into mass graves. Genocide was his immediate solution.

God how they fled! *Mafiosi* or not they scattered in every direction! Some swore allegiance to Fascism, many were imprisoned and were never heard of again. Don Barbarossa wisely imprisoned himself in a *mafia*-controlled prison in Palermo for a few years, then one day he calmly walked out of prison with his entire file of criminal charges tucked under his arm, to disappear into obscurity for nearly twenty years.

Was this Sicily? Could this really be the land we've lived in all our lives? asked the Sicilians. In the twenty-year interim, Sicilians lived a life totally unreal to them, a life free of oppression, brutality, and fear. Internal peace reigned. New land reforms favoring the peasants were enacted. God love Mussolini! *Viva Il Duce!* There were no *gabelotti* to shoot them when they claimed uncultivated lands. Absentee landlords, forced to don their country squire corduroys or forfeit their lands to government appropriation, busily knuckled down to face their responsibilities. *Che demonio!* it tickled the peasants to see Prince Oriano riding through his estates dealing one to one with them again. And wasn't that comical Baron Tedesco a sight to behold? Forced for the first time to actually work side by side with the peasant, that sonofagun wasn't faring too badly. See? We aren't as bad as you thought! There was laughter and gaiety once again.

And then that Iron man, Il Duce, made it even better. He built schools! Imagine that? Schools for the peasants! He introduced new textbooks designed to unite the Sicilians and Italians. Only through the young would the vast difference in their thinking be bridged, he told his Sicilian constituents. But that wasn't all! There was more! *Managghia!* Where had this iron-jawed prince been hiding all these years? He granted subsidies to the peasants! That's right! Subsidies! What are subsidies, asked most the peasants, baffled by so complicated a word. You mean the government will pay us to grow wheat? *Che demonio!* What devilment is this? What trick does he plan to surprise us with? Pay us to grow wheat? *Managghia!*

The peasants planted every acre, every square inch of land, with this golden crop—and at the Government's expense! What a bonanza! Only one man protested this dangerous departure, but with all the sugar-coated promises and dazzling subsidies, no one would listen to *El Leone. Managghia!* There was too much money to be made! Their time had come. The peasants had their chance to make a *bustanza* and nothing would deter them. Besides, what did he have to say, eh? The same old thing. "Stop planting the wheat. The land will be rendered barren!"

What happened? they asked themselves, staring at the dust bowl of Sicily. A depression happens in New York and a dust bowl forms in Sicily? What irony is this? And what is this new order? Il Duce intends to confiscate all the cattle and sheep to feed the armies! What armies? The Italian army is where? Fighting in Albania? More wheat is needed? Very well, but where shall we plant it? The land is fallow. Now the war is in Ethiopia! What's the matter with that Il Duce?

And will someone tell us what's happened to the lira? Up one day, down the next! Had the whole world gone crazy? Sicily is getting too complicated. The cries were loud, protests unheard or ignored. Subsidies, those dazzling subsidies, were still being dangled before them, but for what? They could plant all they wanted, but the land grew greedier and thirstier and became a great pain to them. Now with the cattle gone, and the sheep appropriated, there was no fertilizer for the land. How were they to feed their families, eh, God? God? Are you listening to us? Have you forgotten us entirely?

What's this? Mussolini and Hitler? That crazy *chu chu* has really done it this time! Is he some crazy man? He dares oppose the United States of America? Now for sure we're doomed. From the north came the German and the Italian soldiers, taking over their country like everyone always did.

Hey, Il Duce? How come you feed the Germans and Italians and we Sicilians haven't a crumb to feed our children? And besides who can afford to pay these prices? Il Duce! Mussolini! *Managghia!* Can't you hear us? You think if we call Hitler he'd hear us? Hey Hitler! Tedesco! Can you hear us?"

There were no more cries and shouts and supplications. Sicily had grown silent. And when her sons were conscripted, Sicily wept and felt injustice was all she'd get, as in all those other centuries of inequities and bad memories. The cycle had started again. What's the use?

Don Matteo Barbarossa was sixty years old. In April, 1943, the white-haired, paunchy old man shuffled along the paths bordering his modest villa in Godrano with two English hounds yipping at his feet. He saw the mailman approach on his bicycle. *This day will be no different than any other*, he told himself. *Why do I greet this man and make him feel so bad.* Everyday it had been, "*Buon giorno*, Pasquale. Anything new today?" And Pasquale would reply, "*Buon giorno*, Matteo, *niente*." Why should mail come to him? Who knew he was alive? Who cared? Even Cacciatore had buried himself in the village of Castelvetrano so no one would recognize him. In Barbarossa's company, chances of discovery were far more likely. Since his wife's death six years ago, the Don had only the workers on the estate to talk with and pass the time of day.

Matteo Barbarossa sighed. Among his most valuable assets had been his rigid self-discipline and his ability to adjust to solitude. He had avoided any set pattern of behavior, formed no new friendships, and avoided the old ones. Above all, he waited patiently for the right moment to act.

"*Buon giorno*, Don Matteo." The voice of the mailman interrupted his thoughts.

This is all wrong, thought the Don. *It is I who usually says*, Buon giorno, *Pasquale*. He shrugged indifferently. *What's the difference?* "*Buon giorno* Pasquale. Anything new today?"

Pasquale grinned a toothless smile. He brandished a special delivery letter. "From America," he said proudly, holding it as one would a priceless possession. "You know how remarkable it is for such a letter to come in time of war?" asked Pasquale. "*Mamma Mia!*"

The Don shook as he marked his X on the receipt book. It would take too long to print his name. He held the letter, examining it from all angles. Nodding excitedly to his friend, he looked past him at a contingent of German and Italian soldiers and supply trucks rolling by with the usual supplies removed from local storehouses.

"Devilish bastards!" muttered Pasquale. "Not only do they rob us of our food, but those whoring sons of pigs steal our women as well!" He rode off on his bicycle. The Don walked into his house, locked the screen door after him, and left the dogs curled up and yawning at the door.

Inside the kitchen, Matteo made a fresh pot of coffee, sat at the table, put on his bifocals, and wondered who could have written him from Dannemora prison in New York, U.S.A.

When he removed the letter from its envelope, he glanced at the signature of Salvatore Luciano. *Managghia!* My cousin, Don Salvatore? In America he was called *fortunato*. Some *fortunato* to be writing from prison? Lucky Luciano. What could he want? How long had it been since he saw him? Too long to remember. He began to read:

> Caro Cuzino *Matteo:*
> *I know you will wonder why I write to you, especial-ly after all these years. But, listen, Matteo. I do not put you in jeopardy by this letter, so don't get up-set. Read on and you'll know what I mean. Recently I helped some* pezzinovante *with some big problems in the war,* capeeshi? *Only today, before I sit to write you, they came again. This time they ask for bigger stuff.* Managghia! *Really big stuff. (You know, I got friends among the longshoremen who helped in the effort.)*
>
> *Some lousy prosecutor got to me. That's why I write from Dannemora. That's another story. After you read the letter and understand the request, you burn this letter,* capeeshi? *After you decide what you'll do, write to me according to the instructions. It's big, Matteo.* Molto importante! *Only to you would I entrust these* pezzinovante."

Flushed with excitement the Don read the four-page let-ter, not once, but many times over, committing it to memory. Then, lighting a cigar, he set fire to the letter with the match, placed it in an ash tray and watched it burn. Now he was ready to reply. It was not an easy task, for only recently had he learned the excruciating agony and ecstasy of writing:

> Caro Cuzino *Salvatore: You are to inform your Amer-ican Generals that Don Barbarossa is courteously willing to comply with their requests without com-plications or too much cleverness. Respectfully your cuzino, Matteo.*

He sealed it, walked to the post office himself, sent the letter special delivery to the address Luciano specified, and returned home.

By now, the aging Don trembled with inner excitement. He sat alone at his kitchen table recalling other days. Throughout his beloved Sicily, now occupied by alien forces who sought to destroy her, there were others, hundreds and hundreds of his kind, who like their chief had secluded themselves over the past twenty years. They had survived, guided only by the iron-willed discipline of the man who was and still is their leader. Alone, each man had become meaningless. Together they could become a mighty, irresistible force which could erode Fascism and drive the Nazis back into their own lands. Only Matteo Barbarossa knew how to bring these indestructible forces together. Only Barbarossa could pick up the scattered pieces and reconstruct the empire of his dreams. But, this time, there would be no Mussolini to stop him. He would trust no man. Forgive no crime. His enemies would be erased from this earth. He would lie, cheat, steal, cajole—what was it the civilized people call it? Manipulate? Yes, he would outmanipulate everyone and leave no stone unturned to become the Father of Sicily, the Sicily of his almost fading dreams.

He picked up a pen and laboriously constructed another message, which he copied ten times: *The time is at hand. Be prepared. Years of the locust shall be restored.*

Matteo walked to the rear of the villa and entered an aviary, where, among the rare birds, he kept ten very special pigeons from ten areas in Sicily. In each of ten capsules, he placed a message, strapped the capsules firmly to the legs of the doves, and released them one by one, watching them flap their wings until they were out of sight.

In Piana dei Greci, Corleone, San Guiseppi Jato, Partenico, Montelpre, Alcalmo, Castellammare, Mount Erice, Marsala, and Castelvetrano, graceful doves began to circle overhead. In each area, the birds were spotted and men hastened to dislodge the capsules. The message gave rise to hope which sparked their impotent eyes. Color rushed to their pale cheeks and they came alive.

In two days you could hear the earth rumble with excitement as a twenty-year hibernation was about to come to an end. Two weeks later, they came one at a time, in mule cart, on foot, in old vintage autos, on horseback, in any conveyance possible. Twenty-three *mafiosi*, old village Dons, came out of hiding, renewed their vows, and flushed with the excitement of a bridal night when they were told of the coming of the Americans. The hour of liberation was at hand.

On July 10, 1943, the Allies landed in Gela, Sicily. Aided by the indefatigable efforts of Don Matteo Barbarossa, General Patton's Seventh Army marched into Palermo without incident. On the west coast in Mount Erice, Don Barbarossa's *mafia* underground painted the tops of Italian and German redoubts, and storage and munition strongholds with bright fluorescent paint, making exceptional targets for Allied planes.

Don Matteo was back in the saddle! He knew what he was doing every step of the way. Risks were minimal. Rewards inestimable! On the east coast where British and Canadian troops landed without aid from the *mafia,* entire villages had been destroyed, combat was fierce, and thousands were needlessly killed. It took three weeks before they reached Messina, half the distance traversed by General Patton in a day.

Italian and Nazi contingents fought valiantly but were finally pushed to the Italian mainland, while the Allies occupied Sicily and planned the strategic invasion of Italy.

With the establishment of Allied Military Government of Occupied Territories (AMGOT) in Palermo, Don Barbarossa was decorated as a hero, reinstated into power for his cooperation in the war effort, and made an important adviser to the Allied High Command.

Unwittingly, the Americans had brought about the rebirth of the *mafia.*

The Don's power became indisputable. He was given a penthouse apartment at Allied Command Headquarters, and because the *mafiosi* were definitely anti-Fascist he reinstated all his cronies as mayors of every village. In only a few weeks, he became an absolute ruler of Sicily, restoring to the *mafia* all that had been taken from it.

Matteo Barbarossa, the son of a shit house cleaner, who learned to control men through fear, a man of few words, a man of immense dignity and honor, became the ruling monarch of Sicily.

Don Matteo Barbarossa, who had remained illiterate nearly all his life, was suddenly sought out by educated men. Intellectuals marveled at his feats, listened to his every word, and impressed with the finality of his opinions, placed him on a pedestal. The Don became the head of a self-created aristocracy of the intellect. His belief in himself with the unwavering faith of a religious fanatic had been transmitted to a league of followers. Don Matteo enjoyed every moment of his new-found power. Offered the world for the second time, Don Matteo Barbarossa was ready for it.

BOOK THREE

28

One of the busiest restaurants on the Via Veneto in Rome, Rudolpho's Bistro teamed with luncheon guests shortly after New Year's, 1953. Booked at his usual table, Dolcetto de Leone, now in his forties, had grown into an exceedingly handsome gentleman. With him were his lawyer Giorgio Bocca and Lieutenant Santino Domingo of the *Guardia de Finanza*, the Italian Treasury Department.

"Why should I jest with you, Dolcetto?" asked Giorgio between mouthfuls of delicious veal *picante*. "I've been telling you all morning this property in Porto Tomasso is magnificent. Dates back to the days of Napoleon. Originally the property of some king or prince. I'm not sure. I've never done a complete title search. Whatever, it's incredible! It's a shame to see those uncouth devils get it after the owner has done so much to keep it out of their hands."

"You know better than anyone, *amico*, I need no ties in or around Palermo," said Dolcetto, shaking his head. "Why should I tempt fate?" He tilted his head, raised an eyebrow, weighing the suggestion, then shook his head again. "No, it's out of the question."

"Tell me, Giorgio," said Lt. Domingo. "Are you talking about the Vanzini Villa?" He'd been listening intently for over a half hour. "Vanzini Chemicals? Father, mother, and son found murdered in 1943 shortly after the Allies landed? Survived by a daughter whom it was rumored killed and castrated the two confessed betrayers?" His lips puckered in thought.

Dolcetto's interest was sparked.

"That's right! Exactly right! *Fantastico,* Santino! How do you do it?" Giorgio sipped his coffee and wiped his lips with the linen napkin. "The girl, Francesca Vanzini, lives the life of a recluse. Imagine what it's done to her? She was a young woman teeming with life, brilliant, well-educated, yet somewhat naive about the things women should be naive about. Now she's a woman too wise in her ways, lives in a virtual fortress, in only one apartment of the enormous palace surrounded by bodyguards. You know what I mean, Dolcetto?"

Dolcetto knew exactly what the lawyer meant. Neither he nor his cousin Antonio had ever known a life without bodyguards, without threats of violence and destruction. Despite the twenty years the *mafia* were underground during Mussolini's reign, Marco always insisted someone watch over them. He'd lived too long under their threat to know a free moment.

"I've tried to encourage Signorina Vanzini to sell the estate, but the only offers come repeatedly from Don Matteo Barbarossa. Soon his offers may cease being *offers."*

"Barbarossa? When did he crawl out of the ground? I presumed his tentacles were rendered ineffectual long ago."

"Hah!" exclaimed Lt. Domingo. "Wouldn't we give an arm and a leg for such an eventuality."

"I've been out of touch it seems," said the Lion blandly.

"I'd like to be out of touch like you, *amico,"* grinned Giorgio Bocca. He waved a hand to hail a waiter. "Three espressos, Alberto." He glanced at his companions for approval. They nodded.

"Not only does my client here maintain all the family interests, Santino . . . ." He nudged the officer playfully . . . "the Royal Lion's shipping lines, the chemical and pharmaceutical plants, the land interests, but what do you suppose has happened? He's about to become an oil entrepreneur!"

"Doesn't anything ever escape you, Giorgio?" grinned Dolcetto. "I haven't discussed the offer with you and you already know."

"I try to know everything about my special clients," Giorgio smiled and turned to Lt. Domingo. "It's not enough he's a multimillionaire, now Destiny's added rich, black oil on the *latifondo."*

Dolcetto scowled. Reference to his wealth annoyed him. He never flaunted his riches. Like his father, Dolcetto's business acumen and shrewdness in money matters was highly respected in Rome. Many other financiers looked to him for lucrative investment leads. Embarrassed, he quickly changed the subject.

"What's this about castrating two men? Literally or figuratively?"

"Literally, *amico.* Literally."

Dolcetto's green eyes intensified. "Why does Barbarossa want the Vanzini Villa? It's off the beaten path from Palermo, isn't it?"

"You tell me? Why did he want the chemical plant that Vanzini owned. It's been shut down for the past five years."

"From our point of view, it has a private harbor which makes the smuggling of narcotics less public. They can avoid detection by our agencies," offered Domingo.

"Now they're involved in narcotic traffic?" Dolcetto

seemed genuinely surprised. "Extensively?" Domingo nodded. "What you said, Giorgio, doesn't make sense. They knocked old man Vanzini over to control the chemical plants, then they abandoned the plant all together. Now you say they're involved in narcotics. It doesn't make sense, I tell you."

Domingo pursed his lips and stared at Dolcetto as if he looked right through him. He weighed Dolcetto's words very carefully.

"All I know, is that they swallowed up all the businesses and interests controlled by Vanzini. Look, for two or three years they made all sorts of offers to buy Vanzini out. They wanted everything, including the villa. That seemed paramount. The deals my client told me about included the landed estate at Porto Tomasso. He refused all offers, and I might say, they were handsome offers, more than the market value. I know because my office sent letters to Barbarossa's representative—a lawyer named Garibaldi. Primo Garibaldi. A few months before his death, Vanzini made a trip to see me. He confided his suspicions to me. I tried to pacify him, but what could I say to alleviate the man's fears, eh? I knew little about how the *mafioso* worked, except what I learned from the private papers of the Marquis de Leone, your father, Dolcetto."

Dolcetto nodded briefly, lit his cigarette with a golden lion's-head lighter, and clicked it shut.

"Vanzini insisted he was going to be killed," continued Bocca. "Before it happened he transferred title of his estate to his daughter Francesca. We recorded everything here in Rome. My anger is with myself, that I didn't have the foresight to have the corporate stock from the business transferred to her name. It would have been a simple matter, but we didn't think about it. Vanzini was murdered three weeks later."

The waiter returned with the steaming espresso.

"Immediately following his death, while ironing out the legalities, we were amazed to learn his business holdings had melted to nothing. Many documents presented to us indicated he'd transferred title of ownership to his so-called partners. The signatures on the documents, when examined by experts, turned out to be high-class forgeries. But when it came time to testify, the experts had vanished."

Giorgio paused to sip his espresso and light a cigar.

"Soon after his death, the offers poured in on the villa. Offers which far exceeded its market value. I wondered, and still do, why the *mafiosi* are so interested in the estate. Truly, it is something special, but nothing the *mafia* would want—to my way of thinking. The previous owners were

French princes, Spanish noblemen, Sardinian princes. I was told it was once the summer palace of Charles I of Anjou. That's why I wanted the House of de Leone to buy it, Dolcetto. Perhaps it could be turned into a magnificent resort, like the one Ali Khan built in Sardinia."

The Lion shrugged. "If it were in another part of the hemisphere, I might consider it, but so close to Palermo, no!"

"That's a shame. I was trying to find a buyer so I could get Francesca Vanzini out of the place. Most of the apartments are shut down. You should see the view. *Magnifico!* If I had the *dinaro,* I'd buy it myself."

The men sipped their coffee in silence.

Giorgio Bocca, a handsome man of Dolcetto's age, had the bright innocent face of a child with a smiling mouth and soft gray eyes. Well-built, with a touch of gray at his temples, he wore thick horn-rimmed glasses to impress his older, more dignified clients. A *summa cum laude* graduate, he joined the law firm of Bello, Bondi, and Barlini on Dolcetto's recommendation. Hired as a junior law clerk, he made rapid advances in the firm with the aid of a facile mind, instant recall, and a willingness to work long, hard hours. His expertise in preparing briefs was so exemplary, the other *avvocati* requested him personally. By the time he was made a full partner, he had clients begging for his services. His poised, self-assured courtroom manner was as effective as the bite of a piranha. His loyalty to a client was legend. No one ever said Giorgio Bocca could be bought. Once certain of his client, he gave one hundred percent of himself.

After fifteen years, he became a senior partner and the firm added the name of Bocca making it Bello, Bondi, Barlini, and Bocca. Primarily a corporation and international contract law firm, they were compelled on occasion to handle criminal cases. For the most part, the important ones went directly to Giorgio. Through his work in the criminal courts, he'd come into contact with many law enforcement officers and their agencies. One such special friendship had been struck with Lt. Santino Domingo.

Lt. Domingo looked like anything but an Italian Treasury agent. He resembled a mousy, studious bookkeeper, scrupulously clean but nevertheless disheveled. His dark brown eyes, enormous through thick-lensed horn rims, gave him an awesome appearance. He was medium height with a powerful build beneath his deceptive clothing. He and Bocca played a vigorous game of handball twice a week. Through this friendship, Lt. Domingo voiced an interest in meeting

Dolcetto de Leone, a casual interest, none that he pushed too hard. They'd been introduced a year ago. The three hit it off quite well and often had lunch together.

Dedicated to his work, Lt. Domingo was a quiet, soft-spoken man. Having done a few favors for the lawyer in the past, his friendship was guaranteed. In his work, Domingo, who possessed an almost photographic memory, learned volumes about the people with whom he came in contact, and he'd made it a point to learn as much as he could about the Royal Lion of Sicily and his family. Giorgio Bocca had no way of knowing that Santino Domingo's interest in Dolcetto lay beyond a simple curiosity about the Royal Lions and their way of life.

Sitting at the small table in the crowded bistro, Dolcetto stood out above the crowd. His sun-bronzed skin glowed and his eyes, which had become a deeper shade of green, still changed color when his emotions changed. He wore his curly brown hair longer than most, and he exuded warmth and friendliness. He had only a faint trace of Marco's chin cleft. He wore casual clothing, preferring suedes and leathers to the conventional, stuffy and uncomfortable black silk suits of the Roman businessmen. Like Marco, he was his own man, an extremely private non-conformist, who remained aloof and detached from his peers.

When Mussolini drove the *mafia* underground, the vendetta between the *mafia* and the House of de Leone seemingly evaporated. Grateful for the apparent exodus of *mafiosi*, the Marquis felt his prayers had been answered.

When the Allies unwittingly resurrected Don Matteo Barbarossa and with him an invading army of antlike followers, both Marco and Dolcetto de Leone realized that Destiny hadn't let them off as easily as she might have appeared to do.

The three luncheon companions were interrupted from a momentary reverie by a slight commotion across the room. Entering the prominent bistro were five distinguished-looking men who bore the unmistakable stamp of *mafiosi* and political bigwigs. They were escorted to a table opposite Dolcetto's.

The entire hierarchy of the management sprang to life and swarmed around the newcomers like bees to honey.

Giorgio Bocca leaned over and said to Dolcetto, "It's Martino Belasci, the new Premier-elect, and his flunkies."

"They're still *mafiosi!*" Dolcetto said flatly. He sipped his crème de menthe and soda.

Giorgio shrugged and glanced toward the men. One of

the cabinet members nodded to Bocca, then one of the Dons huddled with a waiter. In moments a magnum of champagne was delivered to Dolcetto's table.

"Compliments of His Excellency Minister Belasci," said Alberto, their waiter, twirling the huge bottle in a bucket of ice.

"For whom?" asked Dolcetto icily. His eyes turned the color of jade.

Alberto shuffled awkwardly at the tone of the Lion's voice. "I'm not sure, Excellency. I think they said *Avvocato* Bocca."

"Ahh," said the Lion, turning to Giorgio with an air of disdain. "Well?" he asked the lawyer in a voice that made Bocca feel like a traitor.

"We've never met."

"Send it back, Alberto," ordered Dolcetto.

"But . . . I . . . er . . . It's not wise to offend the future Premier."

"Send it back!"

Alberto's face turned the color of his red waiter's jacket, and he reluctantly obeyed the instructions. Lt. Domingo observed all this quietly.

"Martino Belasci was involved with the famous Salvatore Guiliano, no?" asked Dolcetto, changing the subject. "You think he had anything to do with Salvatore's death?" He referred to the famous and colorful bandit who held postwar Sicily in the palm of his hand for a brief six years before his mysterious and brutal death.

"Salvatore was Belasci's man until he became too powerful and threatening. You read the papers," said Lt. Domingo, secretly delighted with the Lion's guts.

"Ah!" said Giorgio Bocca finally. Intense relief flooded his face. "Now it begins!" He hadn't heard a word they said.

"What?" asked Dolcetto.

"The man with the minister is one of Barbarossa's men. For a week they've been trying to reach me concerning the Vanzini property. I'm told *Consigliori* Garibaldi is here in Rome especially for that purpose. That's why they sent the champagne."

Dolcetto glanced casually at the group. They were busily talking with animated gestures, seemingly involved in a heavy discussion.

Giorgio was the first to see her. He sputtered, nearly choking on his espresso. Taken by surprise, he stood up, wiped his mouth, and managed to express his astonishment.

"Francesca! What a surprise!" He moved to help her to a

chair, then glanced about self-consciously. Women were not permitted in Rudolpho's and he wondered how she got in.

Dolcetto and Lt. Domingo expressed their surprise and rose to their feet instantly.

"Signorina Vanzini may I present my friends, Signore de Leone and Lt. Domingo."

Francesca nodded to them without speaking, and without really looking at anyone except Giorgio. Every eye in the bistro was upon them.

"Please, please, sit down. How on earth did you get past the captain?"

"Several thousand lira and a lie. I told him I was your secretary, that it was urgent, and I'd stay only a moment. I wouldn't have intruded had I known you were with clients. Your office didn't tell me . . ."

Her voice is wonderfully thick and throaty thought Dolcetto as he appraised the woman who was dressed in a simple suit.

"Nonsense. It's all right. I'm shocked at seeing you in Rome without warning. Is everything all right? Tell me what it is that couldn't wait."

They talked in hushed whispers for a few moments, unaware that they were the center of attention. Dolcetto, in particular, couldn't take his eyes from her.

Her face was white and cold as marble. Her eyes, shadowed with violet, had an exotic cast. Her head remained averted while she spoke with Giorgio, but after a moment she began to feel the hot intensity of Dolcetto's eyes. She slowly lifted her face and turned to gaze upon him, and for a time their eyes fixed on each other in an intense silence. Her eyes dilated and turned black like fiery coals. His filled with great interest. Giorgio Bocca and Lt. Domingo glanced at each other knowingly.

"Come, Santino," said Bocca. "I can see we're not needed here." To Francesca and Dolcetto, he said, "I'll be at the office if you need me."

Both Francesca and Dolcetto sensed instinctively that this encounter was something special. She began to melt under his steady, probing gaze. Her breath quickened and color rose to her pale cheeks. She saw everyone was watching them and she became self-conscious.

"This is madness."

"Yes, isn't it?"

"Something for the Signorina?" asked Alberto politely, clearing away the other dishes.

"Cappuccino, bittersweet, if you will," said Francesca to

the waiter. Dolcetto raised a subtle eyebrow. "Forgive me, I'm so used to doing everything for myself."

"Everything?"

"Yes. And why not? The war caused many of us to do things we never thought we could . . ." She suddenly felt fearful and angry, on the defensive for no apparent reason. She changed the subject. "I don't understand why Giorgio left so abruptly."

"He left because he possesses wisdom. Perhaps he's wiser than you and I." He offered her a plate of confection *dolce*. She refused. "As a matter of fact, Signorina, before you arrived we were discussing your estate. For some strange reason, Giorgio thinks I should buy it. He feels you should be living here in Rome *a la dolce vita*."

"Giorgio doesn't understand the ways of a Sicilian."

Dolcetto found himself stammering and his heart quickened. Never had he experienced difficulty with women.

"He told me about your father's unfortunate demise . . ."

"They were all killed, Signore . . . uh . . ." She groped a moment.

"De Leone. Dolcetto de Leone. Please call me Dolcetto."

The coffee came and she was grateful for the interruption. She lowered her eyes to stare at the burnt cinnamon stick and began to twirl it. She stopped and glanced swiftly at him. "Dolcetto de Leone? The son of the Royal Lion?" She couldn't hide her amazement. Then a rush of mental images came at her. "So you are Dolcetto de Leone, the adonis of the Italian continental café society. I've seen your pictures in the Rome papers Giorgio Bocca sent to me in his efforts to lure me away from Porto Tomasso." She smiled knowingly.

"I know what you're thinking," smiled Dolcetto, "but you're wrong."

"A foreign princess slashed her wrists over you," grinned Francesca.

"Hardly."

"It was in all the papers. The actress who sold her memoirs to the newspapers and photographs to the paparazzi caused a minor scandal for a time."

"I promise, it wasn't me. Although there've been times when I wouldn't have minded such a life."

"But who? The name was de Leone. I read it myself."

"My cousin Antonio. He's the black sheep. The playboy of the family."

Francesca smiled and didn't believe him for a moment.

Dolcetto reached into his wallet, drew out several large bills, and tossed them on the table.

"You, Francesca Vanzini are coming with me."

The five smoldering *mafiosi* and the Minister of the Interior, insulted when the champagne was returned, stared at them and asked questions. Having recognized the son of the Royal Lion, they asked, "Who is the young woman?"

"*Avvocato* Bocca's secretary," replied the captain. But then, what did he know.

Francesca found herself in Dolcetto's powerful Ferrari sportscar, winding through narrow Amalfi Drive, through old Rome, high above the seven hills of Rome. He stopped at the crest of one of the hills. The air was filled with delicate orange blossom scents, and for several moments they sat in the stillness of the Eternal City, gazing at the antique ruins and sunlit landscapes in the distance.

They both felt the magic between them and could say nothing about their feelings that wouldn't make them seem foolish and premature. It was as if they'd known each other a lifetime.

He lit two cigarettes and handed her one. "Would you like to live in Rome, Francesca?"

"I'd like to live anyplace where I can experience happiness. Where I don't have to be as expert a shot as the stranger who might appear in the dark of night. Where every knock at the door isn't greeted with armed resistance, and where each night before you say your prayers, you don't have to worry about them being your last. And where I never have to lay my hands on a knife again."

"That bad?"

"Only one who knows the existence I speak of can understand."

"I understand. I, too, lived that way for most of my life."

"Everyone knows the Royal Lion has been the archenemy of that *sociata dishonorata,* dishonorable society. A *mafia malodetta!*"

"It displeases me to hear that you've been subjected to such a life. With a man it's different. But a woman?"

They talked for hours, until Dolcetto glanced at his watch, turned to her and said, "You know, of course, I'm going to marry you."

She replied quietly, "Yes, I know."

Dolcetto had the golden lion he wore around his neck duplicated for her. Embedded in its eyes were two fiery emeralds, in its mouth, a blood-red ruby, and a diamond circlet surrounded its mane. He gave her a duplicate lion's-head lighter in gold and slipped a ten-carat diamond ring on her finger. Two weeks later he kissed her deeply, holding her tightly as they waited for the plane to take her back to Palermo. There, she'd be met by her bodyguards, the Vittorio brothers, and escorted safely back to Porto Tomasso.

"You're sure you know what to do, *cara mia*? You don't make a move until you hear from Barbarossa. Understand?"

When he saw the radiance in her eyes as she gazed at him, he laughed with pleasure and they kissed again.

"I've never been so happy, Dolcetto."

"I know, *cara mia*. I feel the same. But you do understand everything we've discussed?" He filled with concern.

She nodded. "Do I have to leave you? I don't want to go back there."

"It will be only for a short while. You know what to do. We've been over it countless times, *carissima*," he said conspiratively.

"I've felt so alive with you," she told him. "For the first time in my life I feel the world is no longer my enemy, as if my life hadn't been a mistake, that I do count and I mean something."

"Oh, beloved, you do. You do. You mean everything to me. Promise you'll be careful. You'll call me everyday until we see each other again."

"I promise."

Dolcetto waited until her plane departed before he drove back to his office. He felt terribly let down, as if part of him was missing. He would have to write to his father tonight and tell him the news. He smiled as he recalled Giorgio's flabbergasted expression when he told him.

They all had work to do. Everything had to be in order, for the transfer of money, titles, and deeds from Francesca Vanzini to the House of de Leone. All had been veiled behind dummy corporations, recorded and re-recorded until it would take a master cryptologist to uncover what had transpired in the complicated transfers of property.

Dolcetto wasn't ready to announce to the world that he'd purchased the Vanzini Villa yet. Too many questions remained unanswered in his mind. Before subjecting himself to a nest of adders, he had much to consider.

Why? he asked himself a thousand times, did the *mafiosi* really want the Villa Vanzini? Why had they gone to such extremes to acquire the estate? Kill three people, take over, then close a highly productive chemical plant that could have been a legal avenue by which to refine opium to heroin. Surely they couldn't be all fired up about the place as a residence. So many palaces, closer to Palermo, could be bought for a song. Why pay triple the value of the place? He promised to have lunch with Lt. Domingo in a few days and learn more about the possible reasons the *mafia* should want the Villa Vanzini.

A week later Francesca called out to her housekeeper. "Maria Antonia!" She stepped out into the courtyard and shaded her eyes from the glaring sun. *"Maria Antonia!"*

Two tawny Great Danes, Cane and Cannelloni, jumped up from their snooze and lumbered toward her, stretching and yawning. She petted them and stroked them lovingly, and growing frisky, they began to bark. They wanted her to frolic with them.

"Go on, you two, play in the garden."

Shuffling across the baked clay tiles of the court, a gray-haired, middle-aged woman, wiping her plump brown hands on a white apron called out, *"Che c'è?* What is it?" Her brown eyes studied her mistress as she tried to push off the sniffing Dane dogs. "Go on, get away from me," she muttered with a gentle scowl. "I've no time for you today."

"Quickly, summon Gino and Pepino."

The older woman nodded dutifully and departed, both dogs at her heels barking gleefully.

The sound of Francesca's leather boots echoed smartly across the cobbles that led to the small storeroom off the alcove of the villa. She rolled up her sleeves, unlocked the door, and removed several automatic rifles. By the time she stacked them alongside the wall, the Vittorio brothers arrived, followed by Maria Antonia and two younger women who acted as her helpers.

"We're expecting visitors," announced Francesca flatly. "Don Barbarossa is sending three of his *men of respect* to talk with me. They just called from Palèrmo." She tossed some of the guns to Gino, the others to Pepino. "You both know what to do."

The Vittorio brothers nodded. Each took off in opposite directions.

The housekeeper and her helpers crossed themselves.

"Go back into the kitchen. Continue with your work as you would any other day. And you're not to enter the courtyard when they arrive, *capeeshi?"*

"If you commanded us to, we wouldn't!"

"Mafiosi! Fittusi! You dared ask them to come here?" Maria Antonia was aghast.

"You wouldn't understand if I explained. Now go and do as you're told."

As the women departed, she saw Gino walk toward her. "I need the keys to the gate terminals."

"Of course, I forgot."

"Who's coming? Did they say?"

"Cacciatore and two other Dons." She shrugged and removed the keys from the key ring attached to her leather belt. "I didn't catch the other names."

She handed him the key and disappeared inside the villa to prepare herself for their arrival.

A half-hour later the Vittorio brothers sauntered slowly with the agility of mountain lions toward the entrance gates. The refrains of Francesca's favorite music could be heard. Ever since her return from Rome, she'd been playing the same record over and again, the American song "Shangri-La."

"Let's prepare for the worst, eh Gino?" said his brother.

"It wouldn't hurt for the *mafiosi* to see the strength of the Vanzini Villa."

"Think there'll be trouble?"

"Who knows?" shrugged Pepino. "When dealing with Don Matteo, no one ever knows for sure."

They both exuded the excitement of professionals making ready for battle, never underestimating their enemy, always on guard for the unexpected to happen. Their instincts wouldn't relax, so they doubled their caution.

"The others have guns and ammunition?"

"*Si.* I gave them the M-1 rifles and the Berretas."

"What about the alarm?"

"Ah," said Gino absently. "I'll attend to it right away."

Pepino watched his brother examine the intricate alarm and signal devices that had been installed within the great stone wall which bordered the villa. God forbid they should go off suddenly and warn the *mafiosi* of their plans.

Both young men, former acolytes from an orphanage, had spent many long hours in the sun. Their skin, dark and leathery, set off their expressive eyes. Pepino, the darkest, had the pacific benevolence of a priest. He walked in short, measured steps and being decidedly pigeon-toed, his feet took on a flapping appearance. He wore his hair in a crew cut in the manner of the American GIs he emulated.

The handsomer of the two and a deeper thinker, Gino had light brown eyes which twinkled in merriment most of the time. His curly brown hair grew in corkscrews and he wore it in a mass of curls. Both men had powerful torsos and stood just under six feet.

"Everything's intact. I forgot I checked it early this morning." Pepino wiped his sweaty face with his shirt sleeve and grinned, showing even white teeth. "Better to be safe, eh?"

He slipped the M-1 over his shoulder and removed an automatic pistol from his belt and checked the gun clip. Satisfied, he shoved it back in his belt.

The cordial smiles on the brothers' faces belied the duality of their nature, for both could turn into heartless killers when provoked.

"You look concerned, brother," said Pepino lightly.

"It's Francesca. Does she seem changed since she returned from Rome?"

"To me? I see no difference. A bit more rested, perhaps. The trip did her good." Pepino sliced open an orange he plucked from a near by tree and chomped on the juicy fruit.

"She's a different person to me," frowned Gino. "She's hardly spoken a word to me since she returned." Gino swatted at a few pesky flies drawn by the smell of the fragrant orange.

"If anyone should know, you should, eh, brother?" Pepino winked knowingly and stuffed another orange wedge into his mouth. He laughed at his brother's discomfort and wiped his hands on his trouser legs.

"Don't be concerned. I'll keep your secret." Pepino lit a cigarette, careful to extinguish the match. He winked at Gino.

"*Porca miseria!* Leave me alone. Do I pry into your affairs?" retorted Gino defensively. He angrily swatted another pesky fly.

Pepino glanced at his brother. He'd been edgy all the while their mistress was away. Upon her return his nervousness had increased. He suspected Gino had been *doing the job* on their boss, but he never knew for certain. Now that he thought about it, Francesca had maintained an unusual aloofness since her return from Rome. In the past she'd been more outgoing, played cards with her men on occasion, even drank with them. Since her return they hardly saw her. She instructed them to prepare for a possible encounter with *mafiosi,* and insisted the men keep up with target practice. Security around the villa tightened and new alarms were installed. She'd requested the brothers to recheck the men for their loyalties. But that was all. She told them nothing further. It was evident something was brewing.

Francesca had taken to walking about the villa very early in the morning or late at night after everyone had retired. Yes, thought Pepino, her behavior had been different. The Great Danes came out of the rear courtyard and spotting Gino, whom they loved dearly, jumped all over him. Sensing his introverted mood, they stopped nudging him and finally lay in the shade panting excessively.

"Come on, you clowns, I'll give you some water," laughed Pepino. "You'd better get dressed," he told his brother. "They'll be here soon." The dogs chased playfully after him as he left the courtyard.

Long ago Gino concluded Francesca was a strange and special woman, so much like a man at times, his masculinity felt threatened. She could shoot a gun better than most, handle a knife more expertly, and trim sheep better than most of the hired hands. None of the peasants could cheat her with the grain count, although they tried. He recalled what she'd done to the Scalerno brothers when she discovered they'd betrayed her father. Face to face with the traitors, she had them hung upside down. Calmly, with dead aim, she fired at their heads, then symbolically took a razor-sharp knife and cut off their testicles and penises. She threw down the bloodied mass of flesh with a gesture of contempt, wiped her hands on her shirt, and walked away as if nothing had happened.

For many long hours afterward, she had walked in silence by herself. Their paths happened to cross high on the thick stone wall overlooking the sea. The moon had risen high in the starless sky, casting a pale silvery beam on the waters below them.

"Buona notte, Signorina."

Startled, Francesca glanced up from her self-imposed solitude and stared at him as if he were a mystical apparition.

"You showed a great deal of courage earlier. I wish to tell you, my brother and I feel honored to be working for such a brave woman."

Affronted by his boldness at first, she softened when she saw the genuine admiration reflected in his eyes. She sighed with a peculiar detachment.

"That wasn't courage, Gino. That was pure violent hatred and vengeance you saw."

"Whatever it was, it was remarkable and brave."

She had fallen into step alongside him. "Don't you tire of this life," she asked him. "It has to be more difficult for a young man."

"No."

"You gave up the priesthood. Why?"

"Because I couldn't believe that any one man or a group of men can be chosen emissaries of God. Most men who become priests are inordinately afraid of life and too lazy to face the challenge of living. By becoming recluses they don't have to face society or the fear of rejection. They don't have to conform to the world in general, just one small slice. They don't have to put their feelings and emo-

298

tions on the line. So they retire from life, secure in their sheltered world where suddenly they find adoration and respect from the very persons they fear. Suddenly they're martyrs! To me they're hypocrites."

"You *are* in a mood!" exclaimed Francesca taking the cigarette he offered.

"Forgive me. I forget the priesthood is sacred to most people."

They walked along the high northern wall overlooking the Tyrrhenian Sea. On the other side of the wall was a sheer drop of five hundred feet. They both paused to stare at the breathtaking sight of the pounding surf below as waves on the shore broke like the whispering wind on a velvet carpet. They could see the flickering lights of passing fishing boats going out to sea, early before the dawn broke.

"Why do you live alone like this, Signorina. Away from the rest of the world?"

Francesca felt like putting him in his place for the second time that night. She replied sharply, "That's my business." She turned and proceeded back toward the villa proper. Gino followed at her heels, silent and meditative.

Before she opened the huge oak doors to her apartment, Gino called to her. "Forgive me if I appeared forward and brash, or overstepped my position. I care about your welfare and it grieves me to see you so sad. Try if you can to put what happened out of your mind. The Scalerno brothers deserved what they got. Your father had been like a father to them. Everyone knew it." He turned to walk away.

"Gino?"

"*Si.*"

"Would you care to join me for a cup of coffee? I won't sleep for a while."

"It would be my pleasure, Signorina, with your permission."

For both it was totally unexpected. The need had been more powerful than the social taboos. Gino found her profoundly exciting. He made love to her but not as he would have liked to because he felt awkward and inept under the circumstances. Francesca experienced so many orgasms, it shook him at first. When she begged for more, he tenderly put her off and promised he'd be better, later. Bad enough he'd taken her virginity, but to find her such an uninhibited lust-filled woman both frightened and excited him. *What a woman! Too much for one man,* he told himself.

"There'll be other times, I promise. That is, if you want,"

he said gently. He began to tire of that music that played over and over and over.

"Oh, yes, I want! I want!" she had replied, brimming with passion.

That memorable night had taken place four months ago. Since then, Gino hadn't seen her so much as glance in his direction to acknowledge the intimacy of that special night. Could she file away her emotions that efficiently he asked himself time and again. Since her return from Rome, she continued to play that damnable song "Shangri-La" over and over. Each time he heard it, it stirred up powerful memories and increased his desire for her.

Listening to the refrains now, as the music wafted toward him, he imagined her as she had been that night. *Managghia! Stop this foolishness,* he told himself. *Get to work!* Sighing discontentedly he went to his quarters to change his clothing.

Dressed in a simple black frock that showed her full-figured curves, Francesca decided it was only fitting she should receive Don Barbarossa's emissaries in the same room they'd murdered her family. What could be more diabolical? She smiled to herself. But just as quickly, she panicked. *Dear God, give me courage to face these butchers. Let me be brave enough to carry out our plans.*

Facing an encounter with the malevolent Mario Cacciatore unnerved her at the outset. It was well known that Don Barbarossa used Cacciatore for all the heinous acts committed against enemies of the *mafia*. And in so doing he'd left a bloodbath of killings that stretched across the island of Sicily, covering his tracks so expertly that neither the *carabinieri* nor the security police found clues to lead to him.

She failed to mention this fact to Dolcetto when they talked that afternoon. And Dolcetto had never mentioned to her the story of a young lad who used a branding iron on the man who had good reason to hate the very mention of a lion.

In a matter of moments she'd be facing this butcher of men. The thought sent shudders through her. It was one thing to plan and formulate and boast of one's intent, but another thing to effectively carry out the plan. How brave one can be in the planning stage, she told herself.

Pacing the room impatiently, Francesca stared intently at the family portraits on one wall as if in so doing she could recharge her courage. The ornate porcelain clock encircled with smiling cupids struck the hour. She glanced swiftly at it and drew herself up regally.

Contrary to the usual Sicilian indolence, the *mafiosi* were known for their punctuality and rigid discipline. They were certain to arrive on time. For them everything was timed to perfection. The irony of her logic at such a time stoked her anger.

Outside the Great Danes barked at the sound of an approaching auto. Within the picturesque courtyard, dressed nattily in summer seersucker suits, the Vittorio brothers walked calmly to the front gate and paused. The frightened housekeeper and her helpers raced into the kitchen, slammed the door shut and bolted it, peering out anxiously from behind shutters. Six guards were positioned at strategic points along both walls at either side of the main gate, and all those in the surrounding vineyards became alert as they sighted the auto enter the outer courtyard. Gino's eyes fixed on the guards, waiting for their signal. A few feet from him, Pepino reined the barking and excited Danes on choke chains. The guards raised their rifles in a signal. Gino lifted the steel bars which secured the front gates and permitted the *mafiosi* to enter the inner courtyard.

Their barking more ferocious than their nature, the Danes snapped and snarled viciously, baring teeth. Two of the Dons glanced anxiously at them and followed Cacciatore. Older now, with dyed black hair plastered to one side of his head, but still the same pocked-marked frog of a man, Cacciatore strutted through the walkway as if no one existed but him. Nodding and extending a hand toward the entrance, the Vittorio brothers fell into step behind them.

Under hooded eyes, Cacciatore acknowledged the presence of a formidable enemy. Missing nothing including the bulges under the jackets of both bodyguards, he grunted to himself with his usual self-assurance.

They found Francesca Vanzini standing regally before a flower-banked fireplace next to the family portraits. The sight of these odious men stirred up smoldering fires of hatred and revenge in her memory. *Santo Dio,* how she loathed them!

"Signorina Vanzini?" Cacciatore acknowledged her and pointed to his companions. "These are my associates, Don Cuccio Farfalla and Don Albanese. We all knew and respected your papa."

Francesca nodded to them and fedoras in hand, they took the seats she indicated. Silence filled the room. Cacciatore's reptilian eyes darted here, there, and everywhere, anything to avoid looking at the madonna in black who gazed upon him with inscrutable eyes.

There were several awkward moments in which an uneasy

silence prevailed. It was not proper that business be broached until after the host or hostess had offered *un bicchierino* of *liquore* or some refreshment. Finally, realizing this woman was not about to offer them anything, Cacciatore took the bold liberty. What the hell! He wasn't about to sit here all afternoon, he told himself.

"Don Barbarossa asks, Signorina, with respect of course, that you reconsider selling your villa and all the lands belonging to the estate to him." He cleared his dry throat. "It's been well over a month and he hasn't received your answer. Perhaps it slipped your mind?" Words came to Cacciatore with difficulty. He lacked finesse.

"You will give Matteo Barbarossa my regrets. The villa is not for sale." Her voice was surprisingly calm, considering.

"Listen to me, Signorina, price is of no matter, see? He told me himself, the Don did, 'Give the Signorina whatever she wants. Anything she asks for, give her.'" Cacciatore paused, then continued confidently. "Name your price, Signorina." He winked slyly. "And you'll get it." He glanced at his companions. *"Aloura,* what could be more equitable, eh? It's some offer."

"Equitable?" Francesca raised an eyebrow and affected a speculative smile. "Perhaps?" She observed the three butchers, dressed in almost identical garb, with their fedoras cocked at obtrusive angles on their short squat knees. She thought they looked more like benign apes than arrogant murderers. Although Francesca seethed inwardly, nothing could have been gentler than the smile she gave them. Her long fingers entwined the golden lion at her throat.

"Why does Matteo Barbarossa wish to be so generous with me? He's never been known to display so generous a nature." Her voice dripped honey.

"Listen, Signorina," began the *mafia* spokesman, "the Don has special plans for this villa. Let's say, very special plans. I can't tell to you what they are. I can't tell the world just what is the Don's business. Who knows? An orphanage? A cloister? With the Don who can tell the direction of his generosity, eh?"

Francesca stared at him with a look of simple interest.

"Listen, since the war's end, thousands of homeless orphans . . ." Smart enough to see the weakness in that argument, Cacciatore stopped when he saw indignation threatening to rise in the woman. He waved his arms in the air in a gesture of confusion. "You see I'm sworn to secrecy. How can I reveal Don Matteo's humanitarian projects without his permission?" Clasping his hands together in near supplication, he wailed benignly. "Ah, if the good things the

302

saintly Don Matteo does for his people were known, he'd be sanctified by the Pope."

The other Dons glanced sharply at Cacciatore. Wasn't he overdoing it? *Managghia!* Yet they marveled at his dramatic flair.

Francesca recoiled. "I suggest your Barbarossa is a bit premature. The villa is not for sale."

Cacciatore glowered. Tact and diplomacy weren't among his virtues. To him words were a waste of time. He glanced noncommittally at his men. Two things prompted his next move—her rudeness and her blatant lack of social graces. Cacciatore reverted to his usual ways.

"So! The murder of your family taught you nothing, eh, Signorina? I assure you, the game you play has ended. It's a pity you're not cleverer than your papa. They told me 'this Signorina Vanzini is *molto scarta*.' I think not." He jerked his head in the direction of the family portraits, then tossed his shredded cigar into the cuspidor at his feet.

Across the room, the Vittorio brothers no longer smiled. They looked to their mistress for some sign. Cacciatore's companions shifted uncomfortably in their seats. Francesca, who'd been staring at Don Farfalla trying to place him, barely heard the *sicario*'s words.

She averted her head and stared coldly at the loathesome man. "Please repeat what you just said, I was preoccupied."

He did and she heard every word, each a dagger aimed at her heart. Her eyes bore unwaveringly into his in silent confrontation.

This woman has guts, all right, but no sense, he told himself. *Stupid bitch! She should accept the offer I made.*

He had expected to instill fear in her. What the hell kind of woman is this? Her strength didn't come from the two bodyguards who attended her. Oh, he'd already heard what she'd done to the Scalerno Brothers. News of her retaliation reached Palermo. No, there had to be another source for this kind of courage. No one stood up to Cacciatore! No one except that young Lion years before. *Aloura,* was he just too rough on her? He changed tack. *Once more! Only once more, I'll give her a chance.* He became smug.

"Don Barbarossa always gets what he wants, Signorina."

"Pe d'avero? Really?" She forced a tight smile. "Not this time." At that moment, Francesca noticed a butterfly fluttering around the flowers next to the open French windows, and it came to her who Don Farfalla was. A former trusted employee of her father. One of his betrayers.

Sainted blessed Virgin! Rotten villainous murderers! All of them!

303

She marshalled all her strength and turned to Cacciatore. "As I said, your employer will not get what he wants this time. The Villa Vanzini and all lands were sold over a fortnight ago. The deeds and all transfers were handled in Rome." She smiled knowing full well what this meant to the *mafiosi*. Deeds recorded in Rome made the prospect of forgeries showing up in Palermo remote.

The *mafiosi* exchanged nervous glances. It was a bomb they hadn't expected. At that moment, Cacciatore caught sight of the jeweled lion at her neck. In a sudden reflex he clutched at his chest where the scar of a lion lay beneath his shirt.

Following his line of vision, Francesca instinctively clutched at the jeweled lion and held it protectively from his sight. She saw the hatred in the eyes of the *mafiosi*, the quenchless rage they tried to conceal, and she became afraid. Her fear went unnoticed by her bodyguards who at the moment were thinking their mistress had been a match for Cacciatore.

"And now, if you'll excuse me. We have nothing further to discuss." She turned to her men. "Show these men to the door."

Acting on impulse, she turned to Don Farfalla and said with revolting sweetness, "Would *you* care to remain behind with me? I'm sure we have many things to discuss."

Her cordiality shook Don Farfalla and the damage was irrevocable. Cacciatore looked upon Don Farfalla with suspicion as he prodded his companions on ahead of him. At the door he turned to her. "With your permission, to whom was the villa sold?"

"You'll know sooner or later," she shrugged indifferently. "The House of de Leone from Messina. The Royal Lions."

Francesca thought the engorged veins on his neck would burst. He glanced again at the jeweled lion, a symbol he found revolting. "That's a remarkable piece of jewelry. It's a lion, no?" She didn't answer. "Did you know this king among beasts will cower at the sight of *un picolo tavelino*? A tiny tablemouse?"

Caught off guard by the inane remark and taken by the threatening innuendo, Francesca burst into laughter. "Did you know, Cacciatore, you are a believer in fables?" She turned her back on him and dismissed him, showing no respect at all.

She picked up a phone. *"Centralino? . . . Voyo fare una telefonata interurbana a Roma. Mi metta in communica-*

zione con Roma in Italia. Si, numero 711 . . . Biene grazie, Signora."

After a moment, she melted. "Dolcetto?" She smiled happily. *"Carissimo,* how I've missed you! . . . It's done. They left a few moments ago." The sound of his voice filled her with warm reassurance. "I love you, love you."

"Cara mia, I've missed you more than you'll know. I love you. Oh, how I love you, my dearest." He sighed. Then he asked, "Have you followed the plan?"

"Si. I'll contact them in the morning to make the announcement."

"Good," he told her. "I'm sending you the rest of the plans by messenger. Follow them to the letter."

"I miss you," she whispered. "With my heart and soul . . . and my body."

Dolcetto chuckled happily. "You *will* be careful."

"My men are with me night and day."

"Really? Now, listen, don't carry that *too* far, eh?"

"You know what I mean," she laughed in the deep voice he loved so much.

"In any event, double the guard until I get there, for my sake as well as yours. I won't chance anything happening to you."

They said their goodbyes and Francesca replaced the phone, wrapped up in the feeling of love she had for him.

"And now, Don Barbarossa, we shall see just how omnipotent and immortal you really are," she said aloud.

She glanced at the portrait of her parents. Tears sprang to her eyes like liquid fire. "If it's the last thing we do, we shall make Barbarossa pay for what he did to you. Dolcetto and I will never rest until we've avenged your deaths!"

Two weeks later, Palermo society was stunned by the betrothal announcement of Signorina Francesca Vanzini to His Excellency the Marquis Dolcetto de Leone, son of the Royal Lion of Sicily. The wedding had been set for one month hence. More startling was the announcement that the wedding would take place at the Vanzini Villa, in the heart of *mafia* territory.

Don Matteo Barbarossa took this news with cold detachment.

"If you had let me finish the Vanzini woman off like I did her family she wouldn't have involved the Royal Lions. Why you insist on having the Vanzini Villa is a mystery to me. Why is it so important? The private harbor below?"

The Don's cold impersonal stare evoked a hasty apology from his personal butcher. *"Mi 'scuza,* Matteo, *mah,* how can I forget what that uncivilized creature did to me, eh? Never! Never will I forget!"

Don Matteo checked the impulsive desire he had to laugh. The bloodiest butcher in Sicily was calling *El Leone*'s son *uncivilized*. He said nothing.

It was subsequently rumored that the *capomafia* had entered into a silence that lasted two weeks. When he emerged from the silence, his mind was made up. He sent for his chief village Dons, and one other person who'd been vital to his plans and instrumental in his rapid rise to riches in the past few years.

29

"Signore de Leone! I've called you all over town. What shall I do? They won't take no for an answer. Your cousin refused to see them. He insisted it was your responsibility and left for the day. Meanwhile I'm losing my mind!" Dolcetto's exasperated secretary, Dino Caruso, was a total wreck.

"Calm down, calm down, Dino. One thing at a time," said Dolcetto easily. He walked through the spacious suite of offices, through a heavily carpeted alcove housing six secretaries, nodding to them in passing.

Inside his private office, a combination of old and new world elegance brought to Rome after the war's end, Dolcetto removed his rust suede jacket, gave it to Dino, and moved across the well-furnished room to the bar where he poured himself a short glass of *compare* on the rocks.

"*Aloura,*" he said smacking his lips together at the bitterness of the drink, "tell me what's causing you to act like a freshly plucked chicken."

"Here, see for yourself," declared Dino handing him a white business card. "They were here a half-hour after you left."

Dolcetto studied the card, sipped his drink, and sat down in the leather chair behind his desk. He pretended to be impressed as he read: *Primo Garibaldi, Avvocato, Representing M. Barbarossa Enterprises, Import-Export Division, Palermo, Sicily.*

He tossed the card on the desk and sat back contemplating the situation. The sheaf of papers in Dino's hands shook noticeably.

"Easy, *amico*. There's nothing to be upset about. Take it easy." His secretary's effeminate behavior was occasionally annoying. "What did Garibaldi want?"

"With men like him, you don't ask. You just hope they

evaporate!" Dino wiped his brow. *"Aloura,* he said he'd call you this afternoon."

Dolcetto nodded. "Very well. Meanwhile we've much work to attend to. First, cancel my appointments for the balance of the day. Locate my cousin Antonio. Later tonight we both leave for Messina. Bring me the files on our Palermo office. And, yes, try to locate all you can on Vanzini Chemicals in Palermo—what they specialized in, who ran it after Vanzini's death, everything. And get Lt. Domingo on my private line."

"Lt. Domingo from the *Guardia de Finanza?"*

"Do we know any other Lt. Domingo?"

"No, sir. Right away, sir. Forgive me. You know what happens when I hear about the *mafiosi."*

"Yes, I know, Dino."

Dino Caruso had every reason to hate and fear the *mafiosi.* His family entered into a dispute with a *mafia gabelotto* in the village of Lercara Friddi near Palermo. Dino was hiding when they locked his family inside their meager house and set fire to it. Dino never forgot their heartrending screams and the stench of burning flesh that permeated the air. He vomited and retched and because he didn't want to make any noise, he almost drowned in his own vomit. Hidden by a relative, he was finally shuttled off to live with another relative at the Villa de Leone. There Marco met him and took him under his wing. The lad told the Marquis he wanted nothing to do with farming. He was sent to business school and upon completion was employed by Dolcetto in his Rome office. Fear of the *mafiosi* never quite left the frail, highly nervous man, who was otherwise extremely bright and competent.

Most of Dolcetto's afternoon was spent pouring over the files and reports he had requested earlier. At approximately 5 PM Dolcetto's inner office phone rang.

"Signore de Leone, *Avvocato* Garibaldi to see you." Dino's voice sounded more composed.

Dolcetto noted the time and frowned. Whatever he wants, I hope it doesn't take too much time. "Show him in."

Primo Garibaldi's youth took Dolcetto by surprise. He expected someone older in the capacity of *consigliori* to Don Barbarossa. Garibaldi dressed and acted more flamboyantly than most of the conservative lawyers in Rome. His pleasant expression was a refreshing departure from the usual puffed up looks of importance the men he represented usually wore. He extended his hand in a warm greeting.

"Ah, Signore de Leone. I can't tell you what a pleasure it is to meet you."

"Garibaldi." Dolcetto nodded curtly and gestured to a chair. He recognized Garibaldi as one of the men with the minister at Rudolpho's when he returned their champagne.

"What excellent taste," remarked Garibaldi gazing about the room, silently appraising its artifacts. His experienced eyes lingered appreciatively on the exquisite jeweled chest on Dolcetto's desk. "Ah!" he exclaimed gleefully. "A Phoenician relic? Or is it Carthaginian?"

"Neither," snapped Dolcetto. He wished the man would get on with it. "I have several pressing appointments, *consigliori*. Unfortunately, my time is limited. What can I do for you?" Dolcetto found his tone apologetic and this increased his annoyance. He lit a cigarette with the golden lion's-head lighter and kept toying with it, clicking it on and off.

"Yes, yes, of course," replied Garibaldi. He opened a gold cigarette case and sat down in the chair opposite the Lion. "With your permission?"

Dolcetto nodded.

While the lawyer lit his own cigarette, he studied Dolcetto as inscrutably as Dolcetto peered at him.

"I represent several business interests in Sicily who've decided to invest a great deal of money in the importing and exporting of olive oil, among other commodities. Since the war, the demand for Italian and Sicilian goods has superseded the supply, as you know. And we desire to entrust our cargoes solely to the distinguished lines of the House of de Leone. Be assured your firm shall be compensated far beyond any profits you may have enjoyed up to now. Your lines would become the largest and most influential of the Mediterranean, second to none—even the Greek Lines. I took the liberty of bringing with me a complete itinerary designating the ports your ships would enter to pick up and deliver cargo.

"You understand, of course, that the routing and rerouting of ships would, of necessity, conform to our schedule. Any other business you might solicit and enjoy would have to be second to our needs."

He placed the itinerary on the desk before Dolcetto. The composed Lion scanned it in silence. Garibaldi mistook the silence for encouragement and continued to outline the financial disbursements of his firm to de Leone Enterprises. Having listened courteously for as long as he could, Dolcetto fixed his inscrutable green eyes on the lawyer opposite him. His voice became pliant and full of shaded subtleties.

"It's a most unique olive oil that originates in Lebanon and Turkey and is then shipped to Corsica, wouldn't you

308

say?" Dolcetto smiled an easy, deceptive smile that masked his true feelings. For all intents and purposes, he allowed Garibaldi to think he was anxious to effect a deal.

"Well, Signore," began the *consigliori* sounding like a forgiving uncle making excuses for a rebellious nephew, "you see my client has other interests. I'm sure you know that. If ships are scheduled for a planned destination, what difference does it make if an additional stop is made? As long as you're compensated for all considerations, who would object, eh?"

"Obviously you don't know the shipping business. Our ships dock for special customs inspections in four of the ports you designate. I fear the constancy of these trips will arouse suspicion, possibly damage the excellent relations we enjoy with the various foreign legations. For three generations de Leone Shipping has never done anything to make us feel apprehensive about our licenses. You see, we plan to be around for a while."

"It's well known you enjoy formidable connections throughout Italy." Garibaldi finished his cigarette and put it out. "Look, we intend to divert better than ten million a year to de Leone Shipping and better than fifty million to de Leone Pharmaceuticals." Dolcetto pretended to be impressed. "In addition, my clients guarantee you complete immunity from any possible trouble."

Dolcetto smiled and replied easily. "We have that now." His expression convinced Garibaldi that he simply wasn't impressed with the figures he tossed about.

"That much revenue from one source? I doubt it?" Garibaldi was cocksure.

"Are you truly familiar with the House of de Leone, sir? Have you really taken time to investigate our business and political involvements before making this offer? Money is of no consequence to the de Leone family. Surely, counselor, I can't accept what appears to be your complete naiveté. Your schooling precludes that."

"Come, now, no one has that much money that they'd refuse more in American or Swiss currency!"

Dolcetto closed the file with finality. "You may tell your clients that the House of de Leone is not at their disposal. We have more business than we can handle presently."

Garibaldi bit on his gold cigarette holder with a subdued fierceness. His intent eyes smoldered behind the tortoise shell glasses. "If you don't mind a bit of legal advice," he faltered. "My clients have come to you out of respect. In the past, they've allowed you to scorn them, ridicule them, even cast aspersions on their good names. Now they feel an impasse has been reached. You must either join them, or they shan't be responsible for the consequences. You are aware of their power, their importance in Sicily?" Garibaldi walked about the impressive office, studied the profusion of law books, examined a model of the first of the de Leone ships, the *Barca d'Oro*, with interest. He eyed a painting with the curiosity and appreciation of a connoisseur, scrutinizing the signature—an original Chagall. "You do know they *are* the government in Sicily?" he said with emphasis.

"Do I detect the slightest hint of a threat?" asked the Lion.

"Times have changed a great deal since the war, my friend. The days of the *latifondo* are gone. Land barons no longer wield the power they did. Surely, you don't wish to become a part of the decaying old world?" Garibaldi's eyes came to rest again on the attractive chest on Dolcetto's desk. He stroked the curved lid, caressed the inlaid stones. Suddenly his eyes narrowed and he peered closer.

"Are these genuine stones?" he asked. *"Managghia!* They are!" he shouted, somewhat stupefied. "And you keep it here, not even under lock and key?"

Dolcetto ignored his enthusiasm. "You didn't answer my question."

Garibaldi averted his reluctant eyes, shook his head in disbelief, then stared at Dolcetto. "Call it what you will. I've come to ask your cooperation for what is inevitable. I've offered, on behalf of my client, a more than generous price for your services and you refuse. I've assured you of complete immunity from legal entrapments and still you refuse. What is your price? Perhaps we've underestimated you. Tell me so I can inform my client. He's a fair and equitable man, not the ogre he's been painted."

The Lion glanced up with deadly eyes. "I grossly resent the whitewashing you give a known murderer. More than five hundred deaths have been officially attributed to him, with perhaps the innocent blood of countless others on his hands. How dare you, counselor? How dare you insult my intelligence?"

Garibaldi flushed with anger. He wiped the sweat from his forehead and dabbed at his face with a white linen handkerchief.

"Let me put it to you this way, de Leone." Once again he tried to exercise his persuasive powers. "My client is a respectable business man. Since the war and the reinstatement of his power by the Allies, he's earned a position of great trust. He has many influential and high-ranking friends in America and Great Britain, not to mention the less powerful nations. For his undying loyalty and the cooperation he extended during World War II, he's received many coveted honors. His business interests are legitimate, open and aboveboard. For many years, the open hostility of the House of de Leone has been a blight on his horizon." He paused. "Do you know how easily that blight can be eradicated?"

Unknown to Garibaldi, the entire conversation was being taped on a recorder concealed in Dolcetto's desk. He'd allowed the lawyer to talk freely, let him be patronizing. Inwardly Dolcetto was seething. It took tremendous control not to throw Garibaldi out on his ass. He'd been waiting for something, some word, a sentence perhaps, information that would allow the law to cut into the nerve center of the *mafia*'s operations. What infuriated the Lion was the way Garibaldi had spoken of Don Barbarossa, as if he were immortal.

Garibaldi continued to speak in the compassionate voice he reserved for the courtroom. "A man does many things in his youth he later regrets, even though he believed his way was best for his people and himself." He stopped when he saw the look of utter boredom on Dolcetto's face.

Garibaldi found Dolcetto's passivity disconcerting. He'd heard the Lion would be a spitfire, hard to handle, difficult to approach. He'd been forewarned that all talks would lead to a dead end. The enmity between the House of de Leone and the *mafia* had been too long standing. Don Barbarossa had told Garibaldi talk would be futile, but Primo had asked to prove his point. Most of the feudal estates had collapsed since the war's end, the older generation was dying. The younger men, the educated ones, looked with disdain upon the old laws of vendetta and revenge. As the world grew smaller, there were fortunes to be made.

During the conversation Primo Garibaldi could not keep his eyes off the splendid chest on Dolcetto's desk. "*Aloura, de Leone.*" He glanced at his watch. "I've taken enough of your time. Why not postpone your answer until you've had the opportunity to review and reassess our proposition, eh?" Before Dolcetto could respond, Garibaldi dropped his defenses and he became quite cordial. "If you will, tell me why you keep this magnificent jeweled case on your desk? It's undoubtedly the most exquisite piece I've ever seen."

"Ah, counselor, you are a connoisseur." Dolcetto's eyes took on a fiery intensity. "It would take a worldly man such as you to appreciate the expert craftsmanship and many hours of labored love that went into the making of that chest. And its contents are even more precious than the container itself." His voice took on an aura of mystery.

"Really? I can't imagine anything short of a king's ransom to be more precious than the case."

"Ah, more precious than that. Would you care to examine the contents?"

"I'd consider it a great privilege," he replied in a solemn, austere voice. "Some men take to their telescopes, but personally I'm fascinated by anything historical."

Dolcetto reached over and with slow, deliberate movements, unlocked and raised the lid, inch by inch, and removed what appeared to be a miniature doll's arm.

"This, Garibaldi, is the arm of my grandfather. *Mafiosi* tore it from his body. They returned him to my grandmother maimed for life." He removed what looked like a shrunken head. "This is the head of my father's dearest friend, Roberto Argento, severed from his body by your sanctimonious Barbarossa, before my very eyes. Argento's only crime was to have been a genius, a man who did more for Sicily than any five thousand Barbarossas."

Garibaldi was rooted to the spot, mesmerized more by Dolcetto's attitude than the demonstration.

"These are the accumulated members of bodies of our friends and relatives whom your gentle, benevolent, redbearded monster of a client felt were in his way and had to be liquidated." He continued to thrust small unidentifiable objects at the *consigliori*. "And, this . . ." He thrust a small spongelike object, the shade of faded crimson, at him . . . "is my father's tongue, ripped from his mouth by a man I branded for life—Mario Cacciatore, your client's emissary and hatchet man." Dolcetto stood facing the bewildered lawyer. His eyes were deadly calm as he spoke. "Go ahead, Garibaldi. Talk to me. Tell me about the kindly old man cloaked in a mask of respectability, the gentle soul who's succumbed to the godly side of life, the saintly, righteous man who calls upon me to join forces with him in what is to be an inevitability. Tell me more about his goodness, because for some reason, I can't hear you. It doesn't penetrate!"

The office workers, preparing to take their dinner hour before returning to work for the evening, were astonished to see a man burst out of their president's office as if pursued by demons. His face was twisted with a look of horror. Papers spilled from his half-open briefcase; he dragged his coat behind him. From the inner office they heard the loud infectious laughter of the Lion.

At Madama Roulettina's on the outskirts of Rome on the Via Pompeii, the new madam, a fireball entrepreneur who knew how to cater to every male whim, had, since the war, turned the bordello into a most fashionable lounge. Here a man could discover if he were truly a man. If he wasn't, there were many deviations for his pleasure.

Antonio de Leone, a frequent visitor of late, had been drinking heavily. When the call came for Antonio, the madam was loathe to interrupt her favorite and most lucrative client.

"You'd better get your *ass* moving, if you expect to keep him as a client," Giorgio Bocca advised her. He waited patiently at the other end of the phone. He'd just spoken with Dolcetto, who'd asked him to track down his errant cousin.

"We're flying to Messina in an hour and a half. Tell Antonio I'll meet him at the airport." Dolcetto added, "Giorgio, if you need me, I'll be at the villa for approximately three weeks. Then off to the Villa Vanzini. I'll see you at the wedding at least, eh?"

"Try and keep me away."

"Va biene."

No sooner had Dolcetto hung up than Giorgio's phone rang again. It was Lt. Domingo.

"I'm trying to reach Dolcetto. Do you know where he is?" He sounded disturbed.

"Just talked with him. Try his private number. He's leaving for Messina shortly. If you don't reach him now, you won't until after the wedding."

"It's very important. Perhaps you had better stay in touch. He may need you." Santino Domingo sounded ominous.

"Why? *Che c'è?* What is it?"

"I prefer you ask him."

"Come, Santino, what's wrong?"

"Sorry, counselor. It's business. I must talk with Signore de Leone first."

The treasury agent's sudden formality threw him. *"Ciào,"* said Bocca, then hung up. Now, as he waited for the hot-blooded Antonio to come to the phone, he wondered what the hell was eating Domingo.

"Pronto. Pronto," said a lazy, bored voice on the other end.

"Antonio?"

"Si. Giorgio?"

"Get your ass on over to the airport. You and your cousin are leaving for Messina in an hour. You're to fly back with him, understand?"

"That soon?"

"That soon!" announced the lawyer with a sudden burst of

313

impatience. "What's the matter, aren't you getting enough? Now get cracking, hear?"

"*Sì*. I hear," replied Antonio, sensing the lawyer's annoyance.

"Antonio?"

"*Sì.*"

"Haven't the girls there made you forget yet?"

"They're trying, *amico*. They're trying."

"*Ciào!*" Giorgio hung up.

"By all means, *ciào*," said Antonio without expression.

Dolcetto was walking out the door, briefcase and travel bag in hand, when his private line rang. Frowning with impatience, he set his bags down, muttering a string of curses at the delays. He picked up the phone.

"Dolcetto, I must speak with you now," came Domingo's anxious voice.

"Not possible." He glanced at his heavy gold watch. "I'm flying to Messina in an hour."

"Fine, I'll meet you at the airport. We can talk before you take off." Domingo's voice had a slight edge to it. He didn't sound like his usual, friendly self.

"Is it really urgent, Santino?"

"Yes, I'm afraid it is."

"All right," sighed the Lion. "Tell Umberto at the gate that I authorized you to pass. You know where I keep the plane."

"Right. *Ciào.*"

Dolcetto eased the Ferrari out into the early afternoon Rome traffic. In no time at all, he could see the large commercial planes coming in to land. Once past the main terminal, Dolcetto headed for the smaller airstrip, converted to accommodate private planes. He waved to the guard and turned toward his own private hangar where his twin-engine Cessna was being prepared for flight.

Dolcetto talked with his mechanics for a while, then walked over to the gate to watch the enormous transports and commercial planes take off while he waited for Lt. Domingo. His thoughts gravitated toward his cousin. Antonio, certainly no businessman, had become the darling of international café society. He'd grown into an exceedingly handsome, dark-eyed, curly black-haired young man, with an engaging personality and ingratiating grin that tugged at the hearts of the many women who adored him. Easy-going, light-mannered, and superficial with most women, he never

314

© Lorillard 1975

Come for the filter...

A PRODUCT OF
Lorillard

KENT
WITH
THE FAMOUS MICRONITE FILTER

DELUXE LENGTH

© Lorillard 1975

...you'll stay for the taste.

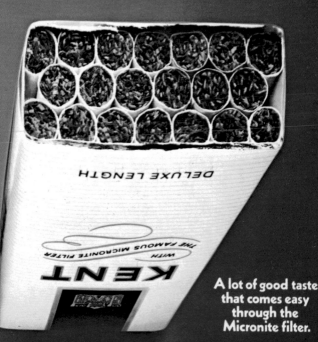

DELUXE LENGTH

KENT

WITH THE FAMOUS MICRONITE FILTER

A lot of good taste that comes easy through the Micronite filter.

18 mg. "tar," 1.2 mg. nicotine av. per cigarette, FTC Report Oct. '74.

lacked companionship, for sex oozed from every inch of his well-formed body.

Dolcetto smiled and burst into laughter as he always did when he thought of Antonio. He loved Antonio like a brother, had always been protective of him. One thing about Antonio, thought Dolcetto mischievously, he could always be counted on to entertain the frequent visiting dignitaries with aplomb. He knew every bistro, every café, every pleasure palace at any price. It took a load off Dolcetto's mind, because he didn't have the strength nor the capacity to continue living *la dolce vita* any longer.

The approach of a familiar figure in a wrinkled trenchcoat and pork pie hat interrupted his reverie. The wind from a nearby prop plane blew with sudden fury and Domingo had to hold onto his hat with one hand. In the other he clutched a briefcase. He hurried toward Dolcetto.

"Che c'e?" shouted Dolcetto over the roar of the planes. "What is it? What's wrong?"

"Where can we go to talk?" shouted Domingo.

Dolcetto motioned for him to follow. He walked to the Cessna and opened the cabin door. "Here, inside. We'll be alone.

"Well, what's the problem that couldn't wait?" He filled with friendly warmth for the agent whom he liked and respected.

"You won't like it!" Domingo avoided eye contact with the Lion. "If you only knew what I had to do to persuade the *commissario* to allow me to discuss this with you before any action is taken."

Dolcetto handed him a drink from the small but ample bar on the plane.

"No, *grazie*, I shouldn't. But it would soothe this dry throat. Well, just a sip." He tasted it, smacked his lips, felt the fiery smoothness with the accompanying glow. "The weather looks good for flying?" He looked out beyond the hangar at the blue expanse of sky.

No use prodding Domingo. Dolcetto learned long ago that this quaint but knowledgeable *Guardia* agent had to tell the story in his own way.

"Aloura, Dolcetto, do you remember when I came to see you six months ago with the American narcotics agents, Hank Rossi and Danny Moreno?"

Remember? Dolcetto would never forget that meeting. The three of them surprised the hell out of the Lion when they dropped into his office that day. After the amenities were out of the way, Agent Rossi had taken the lead.

315

"I wish to assure you, Signore de Leone, it is with much trepidation that we approach you in this manner. If it hadn't been for Lt. Domingo's effective persuasion these past six months, we wouldn't be here at all. He vouches for your unimpeachable honor, has assured us that if something were amiss in any phase of your operations, you'd want to be the first to hear of it."

"I thank the lieutenant for his faith." He nodded pleasantly to Santino. "What is it?"

Rossi dropped three glassine packets on Dolcetto's desk, all bearing the insignia and trademark of de Leone Pharmaceuticals, the golden seal of the Lion.

"On a recent narcotics haul in Chicago, Illinois, we found over five hundred kilos, worth close to five million dollars on the market, packaged by your plants in Italy. All entered the U.S.A. illegally."

Dolcetto examined the packets carefully, his face a mask of concentration. "You base your claim on more than an insignia and a trademark, gentlemen? This could be a forgery."

"It could, but it's not. Our evidence is supported by many other factors," replied the tall, well-built agent with thick eyebrows and luminous brown eyes. Hank Rossi began to read from a report.

"De Leone Pharmaceuticals and de Leone Shipping have been under constant surveillance for nearly a year. A direct tie with Mafia narcotics traffic has been established. Shipments from Lebanon and Turkey to Corsica, where crude opium converted to morphine base was traced to de Leone Pharmaceuticals there. Refined to pure heroin in both the Rome and Milan plants."

Dolcetto interrupted. "What do you have in addition to these packets?" He was abrupt and visibly annoyed.

"Much more at the office. Perhaps these will suffice for the moment," said Rossi calmly as he reached for one of the satchels Danny Moreno carried. Rossi removed a container of a well-known brand of men's talc, made by one of Dolcetto's plants. Hank unscrewed the cap, poured out all the legitimate talcum powder which occupied seven-eighths of the container. He wrestled with an inner shaft which, when removed, revealed a thin vial of plastic containing a white powder. "Heroin," said Rossi. "This vial of heroin, inserted into the center of this talc container, is packed thirty-six to a box, a gross to a carton. Each vial contains approximately eight ounces. Is your arithmetic as good as ours?"

Dolcetto's face remained like stone. He picked up the vial, wondering at the daring and ingenuity of the scheme.

Rossi placed a rectangular tin of olive oil bearing the label of de Leone Olive Oil Exporting, Inc. The bushy mane of a green and golden lion was emblazoned on its face.

"Looks as innocent as most tins of olive oil processed by your firm, no?" Rossi turned the tin upside down. "Take another look Signore de Leone." With the tip of his pocket-knife, he uncurled the seal at its base. A cone-shaped false bottom dropped out.

Dolcetto couldn't conceal his amazement. Slowly he filled with a white rage, wondering at the tie-in between the two diverse businesses.

Lt. Domingo's usually cheery face reflected the gravity of the situation. "Dolcetto, I know you're familiar with the laws required by the Italian *Commissario* of Hygiene and Public Health, limiting the manufacture and distribution of heroin to medicinal needs."

"Of course. Why?"

"Apparently the Italian *Commissario*'s office has been remiss in the licensing of each issue of the refined drug at de Leone Pharmaceuticals." Domingo averted his eyes.

"That's impossible," retorted the Lion. He looked from one agent to the other and what he saw in their eyes, caused his face to harden. His green eyes turned the color of a raging sea. Implication of criminal involvement and collusion with government officials was something that didn't set lightly with him. "I suggest you're prepared to prove these allegations."

Agent Rossi removed several papers from his briefcase and handed them to Dolcetto, who pored over them carefully. Over his head, Rossi caught Domingo's eyes. He wanted reassurance from the Italian agent that Dolcetto wasn't involved. They had taken a chance in approaching de Leone. The American agents weren't sure approaching the Royal Lion was the right thing to do. They'd been reluctant to meet him for many reasons. The prime one being the unlimited political connections the de Leone family enjoyed with the Italian Government. Proven wrong, the revelation could set off fireworks that could easily jeopardize Italo-American diplomatic relations and sever any hope for a continued alliance with the nation. They had to tread carefully, in these days of the cold war.

Many months prior to this session, Domingo had managed to wrangle a meeting with the young Lion through Giorgio Bocca. In the interim, he'd compiled a dossier on Dolcetto that left no doubt in his mind as to the relationship between the *mafia* and the House of de Leone. He then began talking to his American counterparts, trying to convince them of his findings. "If any illicit goings-on occurred at de

317

Leone Pharmaceuticals, they were without the knowledge and sanction of their owners." Finally, with great reluctance, a meeting was arranged.

For what seemed a long time, Dolcetto carefully studied the papers. Finally, he laid them down and pushed a few buttons on his desk. A section of the west wall in his office slid open to reveal an alcove containing many filing cabinets. He walked to them, riffled through several drawers, found what he needed, and returned to compare the papers on his desk to the ones in his hands. It was easy to see his reaction. His green eyes smoldered with indignation. He threw the papers on his desk with marked disgust.

"These aren't even good forgeries!" he blurted angrily. He handed the authentic signatures to Rossi, then continued. "These goddamned documents pass through the hands of at least six people at each plant before the orders can be processed. I must admit to having employed at least six blind men!" he spat sarcastically. "Or else they were passed deliberately." He pondered a moment. "Tell me, have you traced the heroin to a specific plant?"

"We were in hopes you'd tell us."

"Not unless I see the requisitions or bills of lading."

"What about the licenses? Don't they specify the city for which they were issued?"

"Not these. These were issued in Rome, a factor no doubt overlooked by the guilty parties," said Moreno.

"Or else made to deliberately appear as though the shipments came from the Rome plant."

"Such negligence is inexcusable," said Dolcetto.

"If it *is* negligence," suggested Rossi.

"I'm sure five million dollars worth can't be labeled negligence," suggested Dolcetto. "What can I do? You can be sure, gentlemen, that I'll institute a full-scale investigation in all the chemical plants—the pharmaceuticals in particular."

The agents exchanged uneasy glances. "No," said Rossi. "That's what we *don't* want you to do."

"I don't understand . . ."

"We're in hopes you'll allow us to place several of our own undercover agents into each of the plants, so we can, first, determine the source, and second, who the responsible parties are."

At that meeting, Dolcetto gave permission to the agents to place their men as needed. They couldn't be employed under Dolcetto's auspices. A change in the hiring pattern would look suspicious and any illegal activities would come to an abrupt halt.

Dolcetto discussed this incident with no one, not even Marco, who would have put his own elaborate spy system into operation.

Sitting in the twin-engined Cessna, Dolcetto turned expectantly toward Lt. Domingo, waiting for him to get on with his story. Domingo just stared at him. His reluctance to talk became apparent. He sipped his drink very slowly trying to bolster the courage he knew it would take to tell Dolcetto the earth-shattering news. Finally, he cleared his throat. He knew he couldn't stall any longer.

"It's Antonio!" Having spoken, Domingo wished the floor would open up and swallow him, rather than have to look at his friend.

"What's Antonio?" Dolcetto grew curious. The full implication hadn't set in.

"Antonio. Behind the narcotics," said Domingo with an apologetic tone in his voice. "It's in the report . . ." Domingo tapped his briefcase lightly.

Dolcetto's face blanched under his tan. Then, as the words sunk in, his face flamed scarlet. His green eyes burned with animal ferocity. He turned and leveled them on Domingo. Impulsively, Dolcetto grabbed Domingo's lapels and drew him in menacingly. When their eyes met, the Lion realized his friend spoke the truth. He relaxed his grip and released Domingo.

"Santino, I'm sorry." He waved his hand back and forth apologetically. He averted his head, unable to look at his friend. "You're mistaken. There has to be another explanation. He couldn't get involved in anything like that. Believe me, I know."

It suddenly became a job of convincing himself of Antonio's innocence rather than examining the evidence at hand. It was his own flesh and blood Domingo had implicated.

"What do you have? What evidence?" asked Dolcetto quietly.

"Here, see for yourself." He handed the file to him. Dolcetto waved it off. "No. Tell me in your own words. I have no eyes to read for the moment."

"A six-month surveillance of your pharmaceutical plants and their narcotics shipments resulted in the capture of a *mafia* henchman who'd been using a devious, well-protected trade route. Starting from your plant in Rome, he led us to Milan, then back to Rome again. From there to Luciano in Rome, then to a villa in Palermo." Domingo loosened his collar and tie.

319

"Whose villa?"

"Don Cuccio Farfalla's. The report says he was once a big gun with Vanzini Chemicals. He and a few *mafiosi* were reported to have bought it from Vanzini before the old man died, but according to Bocca, they forged Vanzini's signatures, remember? Nevertheless, our agents confiscated twelve kilos of heroin, unloaded from a superpowered cruiser called the *Arcturus II*."

"The what?"

"*Arcturus II.* Why?"

"*Arcturus, Arcturus,*" said Dolcetto over and again, trying to stimulate his memory. "Damn, the name sounds familiar. Never mind, continue."

"We procured full cooperation from one *mafioso* who was being nosed out of a deal. He gave us more information than we bargained for. When we put all the pieces together, they spelled out one name: *Antonio de Leone.*"

Dolcetto's eyes closed briefly, his jaw muscles flexed, his features hardened in deep thought.

"Antonio de Leone has been diverting massive quantities of heroin to the underworld market in the U.S.A. through legitimate merchants in Chicago, New Orleans, and New York, who in turn sell it to the Mafia. They distribute it accordingly."

Dolcetto shook his head. "Sorry, *amico*, you're wrong. Antonio's *not* your man. I'd stake my life on it. Antonio's a big-hearted buffoon, a cocksman of the first order, a ladies' man through and through. He's a man possessed by the voluptuousness of a woman's thighs. But a trader in narcotics, no! No matter what proof you present me with, I tell you it isn't true. Someone else is behind this. To begin with, Antonio hasn't enough knowledge of the pharmaceutical business to have masterminded such an elaborate enterprise."

Domingo shrugged. "Look, I'm sticking my neck out in even discussing this with you. When my associates felt you were behind the heroin traffic, I could speak on your behalf because I knew you. The suggestion of any involvement with the *mafia* on your part made me laugh, just as you're incensed at this moment at the mention of Antonio's part in this ugly business. I don't know Antonio as well as I know you. I couldn't vouch for him. Remember, Dolcetto, this investigation has been underway for a long time. Some of the shrewdest men on two continents have been working on it. Do you consider the American agents without intelligence? Certainly we at the *Guardia* are not imbeciles. Are the *Questura* stupid? I tell you, Dolcetto, already there are warrants out for Antonio's apprehension." Domingo removed his hat and wiped the perspiration from his forehead. It was hot and stuffy in the plane.

"I stuck my head in a noose coming here. My job is on the line, because I persuaded the *commissario* to allow me to tell you first. If you weren't the Son of the Royal Lion, I doubt it would have been possible."

The two stared at each other.

"All right, Santino. All right. I'm not angry with you. I appreciate your courtesy and your friendship. I'm not selling your agents short. I just say you're wrong about Antonio. He can't be implicated. That's all. At least," Dolcetto paused thoughtfully, "not knowingly . . ."

Domingo was about to ask him what made him so sure when Antonio entered the plane, looking like an overgrown kid with his black hair tousled by the wind, his shirt opened at the neck and his arms ladened with packages. He had the relaxed look of one who'd been pleasurably serviced.

"What's all this about Antonio?" he asked his cousin laughingly. "Ah! we have a visitor!" He set the packages down on one of the seats and began to remove his jacket. He cooed ecstatically. "Ah, *caro mio*, what you interrupted! If you could have seen her, you'd have delayed this trip for a month." He kissed the tips of his fingers with a flourish.

Dolcetto and Domingo stared at him with stony faces. Antonio glanced at them briefly. The looks on their faces stopped him cold.

"Mah, che c'è? What's wrong?" He spoke in Sicilian. "You two look as if the world has collapsed." His smile slowly disintegrated. "Dolcetto? What's wrong? Has anything happened to *Zu* Marco?" He seemed almost afraid to ask the question.

The Lion's probing green eyes nearly bored a hole through his cousin. Antonio's face turned red with self-consciousness.

"You aren't angry with me because I'm late again? *Vah!* I'm sorry! You know the girls at Madame Roulettina's— they wouldn't let me go," he said apologetically. *Va, vah!* If it's going to make you two so angry with me, I don't know what to do." Antonio was bewildered and totally inept in the situation. "Will you tell me what's wrong," he shouted.

Dolcetto shoved Domingo up and out of the plane. He grabbed Antonio with one arm, his jacket with the other and shoved him outside with Domingo.

"Come on, Domingo. We're going back to Rome!" He turned to his cousin. "And you, you hot-cocked stud, have a lot of explaining to do!"

321

30

In a sequestered office at the *Guardia de Finanza* where the American agents shared a desk with Lt. Domingo, Dolcetto and Antonio de Leone sat waiting for *Avvocato* Bocca to arrive. Rossi and Moreno wondered why the hell the Lion needed his lawyer's presence since no formal charges had been filed against Antonio.

When Giorgio Bocca arrived and Dolcetto told him of the allegations leveled at Antonio, the lawyer laughed amiably and shook his head at Lt. Domingo. He placed a friendly arm around Santino's shoulder.

"No, my friend. You've made a mistake. It couldn't be Antonio." Bocca smiled, then glanced at the report in his hands.

"Why can't it be Antonio?" demanded Lt. Domingo, shuffling about on his sore feet. *They hurt more than usual,* he thought. *Tomorrow for sure, I'll see the doctor.*

Avvocato Bocca motioned him to be patient until he read the report.

Domingo nodded and glanced at Antonio de Leone. Easy and relaxed, he seemed oblivious to the goings-on. He glanced back at Bocca. The lawyer's face was without expression. Dolcetto sat back in a chair observing the Americans.

Bocca signaled Domingo. He placed his arm around him again and the two walked to the far end of the room out of earshot of the others. He offered Domingo a cigarette and took one himself. Bocca shook his head.

"I promise, Santino. The man you want isn't Antonio. Trust me. We'll find the guilty parties. I see by the report, Dolcetto has cooperated with your agents a hundred percent. If you pursue Antonio in this, you'll find yourselves in a helluva mess. Not counting precious time lost."

"Why are you so positive it *isn't* Antonio?" asked Lt. Domingo. "Other men lead *secret* lives. Everything isn't always as it appears on the surface!"

"In Antonio's case, it is. He's exactly what he appears on the surface. No more, no less. By the report you're looking for a brilliant administrator who knows his way around the underworld on two continents; a shrewd manipulator . . ."

"Goddammit! Why not Antonio?" Domingo's irritation swelled.

"Calm yourself and I'll tell you. A few years ago Antonio sustained a serious head injury in a fall playing polo. For a time his behavior became erratic, contrary to his usual behavior. Specialists recommended critical surgery in Switzerland by an expert in prefrontal lobotomies. You know what that is, I'm sure."

"I'm listening," replied the lieutenant with deep interest.

"You've never heard of a prefrontal lobotomy?"

"Not exactly," replied the lieutenant.

"In layman's language, a portion of the memory is blacked out. Certain nerves were severed. For a while he was as a child relearning all the things infants learn in the growing process. At times, Antonio hasn't the ability to recall what he had for breakfast, much less what happened six months ago. Perhaps one day his memory bank will stretch to longer periods of time. The man you're looking for would have to display a phenomenal memory for names, places, and events. Well, I don't have to tell you what a mind it would take to corral this kind of operation."

Lt. Domingo glanced over at Antonio. He looked no different than anyone else in the room. "If not Antonio, who then?" Domingo winced at the pain in his foot. As a reluctant conscript in the Italian army, he'd been hospitalized when a jeep ran over his foot, crushing the bones. He was back in action soon after, but the foot never healed properly and it caused him considerable discomfort.

"Let's find out, eh, *amico?*" said Giorgio.

Lt. Domingo threw down the file with a burst of impatience. Rossi and Moreno beckoned to him and the three agents huddled for several moments while Domingo filled them in on the lawyer's conversation. Their usual stony faces fell in disappointment, their mood alternating between skepticism and profound curiosity.

Giorgio moved across the room and stood talking pleasantly with Antonio. Noting the doubt on the agents' faces, Giorgio walked across the room to them and explained.

"It's understandable you'd find this difficult to believe. Whenever you wish, I can supply you with affidavits concerning Antonio's mental health. You are free to examine these documents at any time."

"That's good enough for me, Counselor," said Rossi. "We have no reason to doubt you. It's just a letdown. After all these months of ball-breaking hard work to find the fucking case blown to hell in a matter of minutes . . ."

"Better now than in a year or after several false arrests, eh?" Giorgio glanced at them. "Would you mind if I lead off with my client? I think I can get a little further, if I direct the questioning. You see, I know him well . . ."

Giorgio Bocca removed his jacket, wiped the lenses of his horn rims, and asked, "Got any coffee around?"

Lt. Domingo brought over the pot and poured him a cup of the hot, black liquid. "Anyone else?"

There were no takers. Giorgio walked to Antonio's side and set his cup on the table and winked at him. "I see Madame Roulettina finally got to you, eh, *amico?*" Antonio grinned amiably. "Tell me, who signs requisitions for supplies in your office in Milan?" he asked gently.

"I do."

"Who signs them in your absence?"

"I do."

"No, Antonio. You couldn't. I mean in your absence, when you take a trip, you know. Who handles special dispatches or any emergency that arises?"

"When I leave for any length of time, I sign a dozen blank requisitions. Nothing can be procured or expended unless it bears my signature. It's more expedient this way. You see, we trust our employees implicitly," said Antonio.

Dolcetto's concerned eyes lit up in alarm. He leaned forward and glanced at his cousin.

"Why, Antonio?" His annoyance increased, but he controlled himself. "Who advised you to leave your signature on blank requisitions? You don't do that with commercial accounts whose orders must be processed through legal channels? The payroll? Purchase orders or sales contracts? Everything?" He tried to contain his dismay and concern.

"*Aspetta,* Dolcetto," interrupted Giorgio. "He can only answer one question at a time."

"It depends on how long I plan to stay away . . ." began Antonio.

"Where did you get authorization to leave your signature on blank vouchers?" demanded Dolcetto. "The board of directors never authorized such action." Flabbergasted that this hadn't come to his attention before this, he continued. "Everything you've admitted to is in opposition to the stringent rules set forth by the directors, the corporate charter and amendments!"

"From the Chairman of the Board, of course," grinned Antonio benignly. "Who else but you, Dolcetto?"

"Me?" Dolcetto turned to his lawyer with an expression of utter amazement. "I never signed such authorization!" The Lion dug into his memory and his eyes clouded in thought. "No. Never." He glanced at his cousin, filled with grave concern. Could his condition be getting worse? The doctor insisted he should be checked carefully twice a year.

"*Si,* Dolcetto," insisted his cousin. "It was when Amelio Molinari came to work in the Milan office. Remember when

I asked for his transfer? From the shipping lines to the pharmaceutical plant?"

Dolcetto grew reflective. Antonio had requested Molinari's transfer to facilitate the courting of the man's daughter. After checking the man's records and qualifications, Dolcetto saw no reason not to grant his cousin's request. Molinari had worked for the de Leone family well over fifteen years. Well-educated, prominent in local politics, Molinari was considered an asset. It also meant Antonio might settle down, marry, and raise a family—just the kind of stability Antonio seemed to need. Dolcetto had endorsed the transfer wholeheartedly and promoted the man with an increase in pay.

Dolcetto reached for the telephone and called Dino Caruso. "Dino, can you bring me the file on Molinari? All transactions bearing Antonio's signature for the past two years?"

"Why don't you ask me to bring the entire wall of files?" asked Dino.

"That many?"

"Siguro. For sure."

Dolcetto turned to the agents. "Can we discuss the rest of this business at my office? It appears there are far too many documents to transfer."

The others agreed.

"Aloura. Dino, meet us in my office in fifteen minutes. And try, if you can, to locate one document in particular . . ." He explained which document was needed.

"In blank!" screamed Caruso. Dolcetto held the receiver at arm's length. "You never authorized such an order!" came the filtered voice.

"Basta! Basta! See what you can find."

When they arrived at Dolcetto's office, the Lion gazed with astonishment at the array of papers strewn about the office. He placed a cigarette to his lips.

"You find anything?"

Dino's red-faced embarrassment was answer enough.

"I don't know how this happened, Dolcetto. I must have overlooked it that day as routine. If I'd read it properly, I wouldn't have permitted you to sign it."

He pointed to the date. "On this day we were busy with the strikes—the union dispute at the sulphur mines—and you had union leaders in and out of the office all day." Dino wrung his hands compulsively and his eyes twitched. "We were in the final stages with so much to do . . . If you terminated my employment immediately, you'd be justified."

Dolcetto looked at the others. "Well, there you have it! An

325

honest mistake. It was negligence, but I can understand how it slipped by," he explained. "A six-week period of tension had just ended." He turned to Dino. "You're entitled to one mistake in five years, *amico*? But—goddamn! What a mistake! You think if we look deeper we'll find any *more* of these mistakes?" he asked his secretary significantly.

Dino slunk away feeling miserable. His reputation as a stickler for detail had been shattered.

Meanwhile Giorgio perused the document. His eyes lit up as the germ of an idea struck him. "Antonio, who prepared this document for signature?"

Dolcetto glanced sharply at his lawyer and nodded. He knew exactly what Giorgio was driving at.

Antonio glanced at the document and after he regarded it a moment, he said, "Signore Molinari."

All the men exchanged glances. They all knew the road the lawyer had embarked upon.

"Molinari, eh? Was it his suggestion you sign the requisitions in blank?"

"At first, yes. When I found I could take an extra day off without plunging the office into a state of chaos, waiting signatures on routine forms, I discussed the idea with Molinari. Since I was sure he would be my father-in-law, I saw no harm. I knew he could be trusted."

"Why didn't you discuss this with me, cousin?" asked the Lion gently.

"Don't you have enough to do? You're so busy you haven't time to play any more. Surely I can be trusted to think things out for myself."

"Yes, of course," said Dolcetto, gently.

Giorgio Bocca had finished. "Who handles the licensing for the refinement of narcotics, specifically the heroin which requires special licensing for each issue?" asked Dolcetto.

"Molinari."

"You've never bothered to check him out? To see his work's done efficiently? To make sure there's no error?" asked Dolcetto quietly.

"Why? He's been responsible for bringing us unlimited new accounts. Have you checked the figures in the past year? Molinari's done a splendid job. Even though I'm not going to be in his family, I think he's entitled to a raise and a promotion. At least a bonus."

"We'll talk about that another time. Why don't you and Dino get us some coffee, Antonio?" he said gently.

Antonio scampered to his feet and went out the door with Dino Caruso.

"Did you gentlemen complete a dossier on this Amelio Molinari?" asked Bocca.

Lt. Domingo shrugged. "A brief one. How about you?" He glanced at Rossi and Moreno.

"Only what your personnel records reflect. We don't usually place a man under a microscope unless he's suspect." *Damn*, thought Rossi bitterly. *More damned delays*.

"Then I suggest you start immediately," said Giorgio curtly. "You've wasted much time."

Moreno and Rossi exchanged ironic glances. "Tell us about it," said Rossi. *All I need is a smart-assed lawyer telling me off*.

"Is there any way to handle this without publicity?" asked Dolcetto.

"Please don't do anything for a time," requested Danny Moreno.

"Nothing?" Dolcetto was outraged. "Molinari shall be dismissed immediately."

Lt. Domingo shook his head.

Dolcetto looked to his lawyer. Moreno hastened to add, "Look, man, it's not just one guy we're after." Danny Moreno, a second-generation Italian American like Hank Rossi, added, "We need time to check things out. Molinari's not in this alone. Other employees of yours must be involved. So we goofed on the connection with Antonio—but you can see someone's gone to a helluva lot of trouble to make it look like Antonio was the fall guy. Please, hear me out. The set-up takes on unusual proportions now. You said Molinari enjoys influential political connections. He's a Christian Democrat, isn't he? A staunch party member?"

"His records indicate such," said the Lion.

"This uh—former Minister of the Interior—the man who used the newspaper as a sounding board between himself and the bandit Salvatore in Sicily—he's a Christian Democrat! There was a big stink in the Communist press about the connections between government and bandits, right?"

"Martino Belasci?" Giorgio Bocca expressed grave reservations. "You're talking about the next Premier of Italy, gentlemen. You'd better tread carefully, if you're heading up that path. *Managghia!* Where's the connection?"

"Belasci has been tight with Lucky Luciano, Vito Genovese, and Gentile. They've been seen in Naples together. Listen, this isn't conjecture. It's a matter of record. All documented in our files. Well, this Belasci is also on record as being the protégé of Don Matteo Barbarossa."

"You're shooting high up the political ladder, my friends," said Dolcetto thoughtfully.

327

"Why do you think we've moved so slowly? When we thought your family was implicated we proceeded with extreme caution. We've been warned about creating international incidents!"

"Better check your facts more carefully than you did in this instance," said Bocca, soberly. *"Managghia!* What a complicated nest of snakes!"

"If you're aiming at Martino Belasci, *caro mio,* I caution you to tread carefully. Those are well-meant words of advice—not threats, understand," said Bocca wide-eyed and noticeably disturbed. "You realize, don't you, that the Premier was recently feted by your own Vice President at an elaborate affair in your own country?" He was trying to make a point.

"Yes, we know," said Rossi, catching the implication. "We know."

"You know, eh?" snorted Bocca. "Listen, I don't want to hear anymore! This isn't *our* affair. I want no involvement in this either personally or for my clients. Not in this international web of intrigue. Just get on with what you want to say about this situation but limit your words to our *possible* involvement!"

Dolcetto glanced questioningly at Giorgio. He'd never seen him so worked up.

"Very well," said Rossi, expecting such a reaction. "Understand in advance that the suspension of heroin refinement might be enforced after we nab the responsible parties," he addressed himself to Dolcetto.

"Rossi, for all I care we could cease refining the drug altogether. Our livelihood doesn't depend on the narcotics produced in our plants."

Antonio and Dino returned with the coffee they all greedily consumed.

Dino smiled brightly. "You wanted financial reports on the Rome office for de Leone Pharmaceuticals? I also brought the comparative analysis figures before Molinari's transfer and after. Also the figures reported from Milan and Naples to cover the same period."

Giorgio Bocca smiled at Dino's resourcefulness. "Good man! *Va biene!*"

Dolcetto nodded absently. His head buried in corporate profit and loss statements, he soon demonstrated considerable reaction to the figures. Despite the fact he was a master at concealing his feelings, Dolcetto's features jerked and twitched. Stunned by the contents, he handed the folders to Bocca as they exchanged meaningful glances.

Giorgio flipped through the pages casually at first. Then,

with pen in hand, he jotted figures on a sheet of paper. When he finished, he quickly checked the impulse to express his astonishment. Watching them the Federal agents sipped their coffee in silence. From time to time they exchanged non-committal glances.

"Dino, you're sure these figures are accurate? There can be no error?" Dolcetto spoke, without emotion.

"Your accounting firm prepared them—after audit."

Dolcetto flushed. About to speak, he was cut off by his lawyer. "Gentlemen, before we can make these figures known to your agency, I feel they should be authenticated by the de Leone accounting firm."

The agents glanced expectantly at the Lion. Dolcetto shrugged. "That's why I pay him such an exorbitant fee," he said without apology.

The agents stood up as if on cue. "We have your permission to continue the investigation, Signore de Leone?" asked Hank Rossi.

"Do what you will. I'll be in Messina for two weeks. Then in Porto Tomasso for the wedding."

"May I extend to you my warmest felicitations," said Lt. Domingo.

"Thank you, Santino. Gentlemen."

The agents left his office.

"Why all the mystery about the accounting firm?" asked Dolcetto of his lawyer.

"Do you have any idea what the fines alone will amount to on the heroin issued on the forged licenses? I think we should come to terms with the *Guardia* before you release these figures. You've cooperated more than most citizens would have."

"That's the way I want it."

"But not at your expense, Dolcetto. If fines are to be imposed, the *Guardia* should absorb them. You shouldn't be burdened with the tariff on the unlicensed issues."

Dolcetto shrugged.

"*Amico*, do you realize we're talking about issues in excess of twenty million dollars?" Giorgio found the sum staggering. He whistled low.

"Yes, I saw the reports," said the Lion flatly.

"I told you Molinari increased the business," said Antonio from across the room. "He's some businessman, eh, cousin?"

"Yes," replied the ironic Lion. *"Some businessman!"*

"If he increased the Rome office by twenty million, have you any idea what his take might have been in the two-year period? What a perfect setup. *Managghia!*" marveled the lawyer. "Shipping heroin into the States legally through a bona fide pharmaceutical plant. I had no idea how much money was involved in narcotics."

"Don't get any ideas, eh, *amico?* I have enough to worry about without being concerned about those dollar signs glittering in your eyes."

"You don't admit it staggers the imagination?"

"Yours, perhaps. Not mine. Presently there is someone who *does* stagger my imagination, and if I don't move my tail and get the hell out of here, she may not be waiting for me when I get there." Dolcetto reached for his jacket.

"By the way, *consigliori*, Primo Garibaldi was in to see me."

"Why?"

"He offered de Leone Pharmaceuticals an additional twenty million a year in business—plus fifty million to de Leone Shipping."

"And I said twenty million staggered the imagination?" grinned Bocca. "What did you tell him?"

"Come, Antonio," called the Lion. "If we hurry we can have breakfast with Marco." To Giorgio, he replied, "Nothing! I told him we didn't want their business."

"Goddamn! I wonder what it feels like to refuse twenty million dollars. Some oriental potentate? A Sultan? A pasha? An Emperor? What?"

"We'll see you at the wedding, *amico*," said Dolcetto, laughing amiably, in parting.

"Wild horses couldn't keep me away."

"Check with Domingo tomorrow. I gave him the tapes of the conversation with Garibaldi. Tell Santino I said you should listen."

Giorgio reached for a pad from Dolcetto's desk. He scribbled a few words. "Here, sign it. I want no misunderstandings with Santino. O.K. it in writing. What do you intend doing in your spare time, *amico?* Becoming a government agent?"

Dolcetto laughed. "I'd move too fast for them. I'd have dealt with Molinari in a far more expeditious manner. I'm a Sicilian! I have no patience for governmental and departmental red tape." The Lion took his cousin's arm. *"Va, amonini,* Antonio. Let's go."

Outside in the crisp, cool, predawn hours, they inhaled the fresh air and gazed about at the stillness of the sleepy Eternal City. Dolcetto and Giorgio shook hands, embraced, and went their separate ways.

Primo Garibaldi arrived in Palermo about the time Dolcetto and Antonio de Leone arrived at the Villa de Leone. He found the Don as usual at his table at Nunzzio's Birreria right off the sunlit piazza, close to the Albergo-Sole. Nearing seventy, his towering frame carried nearly two hundred pounds; his white hair was parted to one side; his coal-black, unyielding eyes remained alert and fearsome behind dark glasses. It was several hours before the impatient Garibaldi could maneuver the Don back to the isolation of his villa.

"*Aloura, consiglioro*, what do you tell me?"

"You were right! I should have listened to you. Dolcetto de Leone is not only unreachable, he is not to be believed. He is a man without fear."

"You explained the benefits?" Garibaldi nodded. "I presume you also explained the disadvantages?"

"He was unapproachable!" Garibaldi thought about the jeweled case. "There's no intimidating him. He's simply fearless!"

"He's his father's son," muttered the Don simply. "Too bad he's an opponent. He would have made an excellent *capo*." The Don popped a thyroid pill into his mouth. "Unfortunately, we may have to take extreme measures to teach him a lesson."

"Extreme measures?" asked Cacciatore from where he sat across the room in the Don's study. Cacciatore didn't express himself aloud, but many of the Dons were beginning to wonder about the reluctance of Don Barbarossa to retaliate. "With your permission, Don Matteo," said Cacciatore, taking sudden courage. "Why your steadfast refusal to fix the Lion for good? We've had many an opportunity."

"*Managghia u' diaoro!*" countered the Don. "How many times do I have to tell you now isn't the time. It's not possible to erase the House of de Leone without bringing the government down on our necks. The *Guardia* and the Communists would like nothing better than to find sufficient cause to wipe us out again. We've worked hard putting our men in government. Shortly we'll have everything exactly the way I've been planning since 1943. Our man just became Premier. Soon we will be able to do anything! Look how we suppressed the Red menace, eh?

"Listen, if we don't proceed with caution, all our operations will evaporate into thin air." Barbarossa chewed his cigar savagely and closed his eyelids, suddenly tired of Cacciatore and the other slow-thinking Dons. They'd never learn. Never!

"Don't think I don't recall the old days when I could have erased the Lions like that!" He snapped his fingers smartly. "I almost did, once." He hawked up some phlegm and spit it into the spittoon. "We've too much at stake to risk an investigation. Let sleeping dogs lie, *misericordia!*

He continued ruefully, "I know what you think. Don Barbarossa is not the Don of old. He's gone soft. Maybe the youngbloods could do a better job! You complain of our American counterparts—that their ways of organization haven't the cohesive unity our brotherhood boasts. But look at the progress they've made. You've enjoyed the rewards, no? You must forget the past and look to the future," insisted the Don.

Forget the past? thought Cacciatore. *How does one make a Sicilian forget the past?* Every morning before he dressed, Cacciatore saw the scars of the Lion's brand. Whenever he relieved himself, day or night, he saw and felt his limp sex organ, grotesquely scarred by the Lion's brand. Forget the past? How could he when he lived with these unrelenting reminders.

Don Farfalla, who had joined the meeting, hadn't bothered to relight the cigar that died moments ago in his hand. He kept rolling it around between his fingers, preoccupied with thoughts of Francesca Vanzini whom he felt sure knew of his participation in the murders of her family. He recalled the fate of the Scalerno brothers and grew uneasy. Even Cacciatore hadn't treated him without suspicion since that day at the villa. Finally he threw out the lifeless cigar.

Primo Garibaldi had a touch of class that made him seem out of place among the crude and uncouth *mafia* dons, who, for all their money and new-found riches, couldn't attain a look of refinement or elegant manliness. Primo grew reflective. Thoughts of those goddamned arms and legs came at him with increasing frequency. Damn de Leone anyway! He'd not forget that scene for a long time. He wondered what he was doing here with these men. If only he hadn't promised his father.

His father had been *consiglioro* to Don Barbarossa ever since the Don presented him with an ornate scroll and conferred the title upon him. Primo's father learned law from the Don who made his own laws. The elder Garibaldi wanted more than a store-bought diploma for his son. He sent him to the University of Catania. His Godfather, Don Barbarossa, had told him that upon graduation he'd be welcomed into the brotherhood. He kept his promise.

Don Barbarossa glanced at the men easily and disguised his inner thoughts. He knew they were dissatisfied. He'd soon have to make a move regarding the House of de Leone. No one knew—not even Cacciatore or his *consigliori*—that

332

spit it into the spittoon. "We've too much at stake to risk investigation. Let sleeping dogs lie, *misericordia!*

He continued ruefully, "I know what you think. Don ~~barossa~~ is not the Don of old. He's gone soft. Maybe the ~~~~ngbloods could do a better job! You complain of our ~~~~erican counterparts—that their ways of organization ~~~~en't the cohesive unity our brotherhood boasts. But look ~~~~the progress they've made. You've enjoyed the rewards, ~~ You must forget the past and look to the future," in~~~~ed the Don.

~~~~orget the past? thought Cacciatore. *How does one make ~~~~icilian forget the past?* Every morning before he dressed, ~~~~cciatore saw the scars of the Lion's brand. Whenever he ~~~~eved himself, day or night, he saw and felt his limp sex ~~~~an, grotesquely scarred by the Lion's brand. Forget the ~~~~t? How could he when he lived with these unrelenting ~~~~inders.

~~~~on Farfalla, who had joined the meeting, hadn't bothered ~~~~relight the cigar that died moments ago in his hand. He ~~~~t rolling it around between his fingers, preoccupied with ~~~~ughts of Francesca Vanzini whom he felt sure knew of ~~~~ participation in the murders of her family. He recalled ~~~~ fate of the Scalerno brothers and grew uneasy. Even ~~~~cciatore hadn't treated him without suspicion since that ~~~~ at the villa. Finally he threw out the lifeless cigar.

~~~~rimo Garibaldi had a touch of class that made him seem ~~~~ of place among the crude and uncouth *mafia* dons, who, ~~~~ all their money and new-found riches, couldn't attain a ~~~~k of refinement or elegant manliness. Primo grew reflec~~~~. Thoughts of those goddamned arms and legs came at ~~~~ with increasing frequency. Damn de Leone anyway! ~~~~d not forget that scene for a long time. He wondered what ~~~~ was doing here with these men. If only he hadn't promised ~~~~ father.

~~~~is father had been *consiglioro* to Don Barbarossa ever ~~~~e the Don presented him with an ornate scroll and con~~~~red the title upon him. Primo's father learned law from the ~~~~n who made his own laws. The elder Garibaldi wanted ~~~~re than a store-bought diploma for his son. He sent him ~~~~ the University of Catania. His Godfather, Don Barbaros~~~~ had told him that upon graduation he'd be welcomed ~~~~ the brotherhood. He kept his promise.

~~~~on Barbarossa glanced at the men easily and disguised ~~~~ inner thoughts. He knew they were dissatisfied. He'd ~~~~ have to make a move regarding the House of de Leone. ~~~~ one knew—not even Cacciatore or his *consigliori*—that

with pen in hand, he jotted figures on a sheet of paper. When he finished, he quickly checked the impulse to express his astonishment. Watching them the Federal agents sipped their coffee in silence. From time to time they exchanged non-committal glances.

"Dino, you're sure these figures are accurate? There can be no error?" Dolcetto spoke, without emotion.

"Your accounting firm prepared them—after audit."

Dolcetto flushed. About to speak, he was cut off by his lawyer. "Gentlemen, before we can make these figures known to your agency, I feel they should be authenticated by the de Leone accounting firm."

The agents glanced expectantly at the Lion. Dolcetto shrugged. "That's why I pay him such an exorbitant fee," he said without apology.

The agents stood up as if on cue. "We have your permission to continue the investigation, Signore de Leone?" asked Hank Rossi.

"Do what you will. I'll be in Messina for two weeks. Then in Porto Tomasso for the wedding."

"May I extend to you my warmest felicitations," said Lt. Domingo.

"Thank you, Santino. Gentlemen."

The agents left his office.

"Why all the mystery about the accounting firm?" asked Dolcetto of his lawyer.

"Do you have any idea what the fines alone will amount to on the heroin issued on the forged licenses? I think we should come to terms with the *Guardia* before you release these figures. You've cooperated more than most citizens would have."

"That's the way I want it."

"But not at your expense, Dolcetto. If fines are to be imposed, the *Guardia* should absorb them. You shouldn't be burdened with the tariff on the unlicensed issues."

Dolcetto shrugged.

"*Amico*, do you realize we're talking about issues in excess of twenty million dollars?" Giorgio found the sum staggering. He whistled low.

"Yes, I saw the reports," said the Lion flatly.

"I told you Molinari increased the business," said Antonio from across the room. "He's some businessman, eh, cousin?"

"Yes," replied the ironic Lion. *"Some businessman!"*

"If he increased the Rome office by twenty million, have you any idea what his take might have been in the two-year period? What a perfect setup. *Managghia!*" marveled the lawyer. "Shipping heroin into the States legally through a bona fide pharmaceutical plant. I had no idea how much money was involved in narcotics."

"Don't get any ideas, eh, *amico?* I have enough to worry about without being concerned about those dollar signs glittering in your eyes."

"You don't admit it staggers the imagination?"

"Yours, perhaps. Not mine. Presently there is someone who *does* stagger my imagination, and if I don't move my tail and get the hell out of here, she may not be waiting for me when I get there." Dolcetto reached for his jacket.

"By the way, *consiglieri*, Primo Garibaldi was in to see me."

"Why?"

"He offered de Leone Pharmaceuticals an additional twenty million a year in business—plus fifty million to de Leone Shipping."

"And I said twenty million staggered the imagination?" grinned Bocca. "What did you tell him?"

"Come, Antonio," called the Lion. "If we hurry we can have breakfast with Marco." To Giorgio, he replied, "Nothing! I told him we didn't want their business."

"Goddamn! I wonder what it feels like to refuse twenty million dollars. Some oriental potentate? A Sultan? A pasha? An Emperor? What?"

"We'll see you at the wedding, *amico*," said Dolcetto, laughing amiably, in parting.

"Wild horses couldn't keep me away."

"Check with Domingo tomorrow. I gave him the tapes of the conversation with Garibaldi. Tell Santino I said you should listen."

Giorgio reached for a pad from Dolcetto's desk. He scribbled a few words. "Here, sign it. I want no misunderstandings with Santino. O.K. it in writing. What do you intend doing in your spare time, *amico?* Becoming a government agent?"

Dolcetto laughed. "I'd move too fast for them. I'd have dealt with Molinari in a far more expeditious manner. I'm a Sicilian! I have no patience for governmental and departmental red tape." The Lion took his cousin's arm. "*Va, amonini*, Antonio. Let's go."

Outside in the crisp, cool, predawn hours, they inhaled the fresh air and gazed about at the stillness of the sleepy Eternal City. Dolcetto and Giorgio shook hands, embraced, and went their separate ways.

Primo Garibaldi arrived in Palermo about the time Dolcetto and Antonio de Leone arrived at the Villa de Leone. He

found the Don as usual at his table at Nunzzi right off the sunlit piazza, close to the Albergo-S seventy, his towering frame carried nearly tw pounds; his white hair was parted to one side black, unyielding eyes remained alert and fears dark glasses. It was several hours before the impa baldi could maneuver the Don back to the isolat villa.

"*Aloura, consiglioro*, what do you tell me?"

"You were right! I should have listened to you de Leone is not only unreachable, he is not to be He is a man without fear."

"You explained the benefits?" Garibaldi nodded sume you also explained the disadvantages?"

"He was unapproachable!" Garibaldi thought a jeweled case. "There's no intimidating him. He's sin less!"

"He's his father's son," muttered the Don simp bad he's an opponent. He would have made an *capo*." The Don popped a thyroid pill into his mou fortunately, we may have to take extreme measures him a lesson."

"Extreme measures?" asked Cacciatore from wher across the room in the Don's study. Cacciatore di press himself aloud, but many of the Dons were be to wonder about the reluctance of Don Barbarossa taliate. "With your permission, Don Matteo," said tore, taking sudden courage. "Why your steadfast re fix the Lion for good? We've had many an opportu

"*Managghia u' diaoro!*" countered the Don. "Hov times do I have to tell you now isn't the time. It's r sible to erase the House of de Leone without bring government down on our necks. The *Guardia* and th munists would like nothing better than to find s cause to wipe us out again. We've worked hard putt men in government. Shortly we'll have everything the way I've been planning since 1943. Our man came Premier. Soon we will be able to do anythin how we suppressed the Red menace, eh?

"Listen, if we don't proceed with caution, all ou tions will evaporate into thin air." Barbarossa che cigar savagely and closed his eyelids, suddenly tired ciatore and the other slow-thinking Dons. They'd nev Never!

"Don't think I don't recall the old days when have erased the Lions like that!" He snapped hi smartly. "I almost did, once." He hawked up som there was, in fact, another power behind the throne from whom the Don took orders.

For nearly ten years, every phase of the *mafia*'s operations, the phenomenal profits and wealth, had come as a result of the shrewd, enterprising ways of this silent overlord.

Don Matteo's eyes came to rest on a small instrument panel on his desk concealed by a concave hood visible only to him. The tiny red button flashed twice, then it stopped. Don Matteo stood up and excused himself. He walked through a long hallway to another room in the villa, unlocked the door, and entered.

"You heard them, Alberto?"

"*Si.*"

"There's no other way, you can see that."

"He was properly approached this time?"

"We've reached the end of the line with the Lions. They must be put into a position where their influence is no longer felt."

"It's come to that? You're sure?"

Nodding, the Don tried to clear his congested throat.

"When will you see to your throat? I've warned you many times . . ."

The Don waved the issue aside impatiently. "What of the Lion? We can't turn the other cheek, no more. These new enterprises are too precious to abandon. You know what's in this for all of us. Only three people stand in our way!" Don Barbarossa unwrapped the silver foil from his cigar and studied the man he affectionately called the *capomastro.*

"I asked you to come to Palermo not only to tell you how disgruntled the other Dons have become over the House of Lions, but also to tell you, face to face . . ." He paused, rolling his cigar between his lips, hesitant to light it because Alberto would fuss at him. "It's about that choice plum you've wanted for so long, the Vanzini Villa. *Aloura*, Alberto, it is no longer available." He kept his eyes fixed on his companion.

Alberto glanced up, his eyes dimmed, and his jaws flexed tightly. "I don't understand. You told me it was a matter of time and the property would be mine. Six long years have passed since their deaths and you still tell me it's not available? Are you the *capomafia* or not? Perhaps you didn't understand, Matteo. I want the villa at any cost!"

"And it would have been yours if the House of de Leone hadn't put in their two cents! They bought it from under our noses! Titles, deeds, all the records were handled in Rome!"

"The House of de Leone?" His astonishment was uncon-

333

tainable. "But how? I didn't know they knew each other . . ." He dug into his memory, tried to recall when, if ever, the name Vanzini had been mentioned at the Villa de Leone.

"Who handled the deal? Marco or Dolcetto?"

"Why? Does it make a difference?"

"Perhaps not. Either way, I wish to know."

"What do I say to the other Dons? They're waiting for an answer," said Don Matteo, pouring two glasses of Strega from a decanter on the desk.

"You need an answer now?"

Don Matteo shrugged imperceptibly.

"I suppose we've delayed the inevitable long enough," Alberto sipped the Strega. "Understand, Matteo, the time must be right. It must be done properly. All must be destroyed at one time."

"There's something else," said the Don. "When Cacciatore put the question to the Vanzini woman, she wore a jeweled lion suspended from her neck."

"Ahhhh! Dolcetto! I might have known. He'll always be a thorn in the Mafia's hide!" He suppressed a smile.

"There's more. There's to be a wedding between Dolcetto de Leone and Francesca Vanzini," said the Don quietly. "The betrothal has already been announced. The wedding takes place in a fortnight."

If he had plunged a dagger into Alberto's heart, the man couldn't have been more deathlike. He felt the staggering impact of this blow more than Don Matteo could possibly imagine. His head filled with myriad images. He needed time to think. Both the Don and he knew what complications would evolve from the Vanzini-de Leone union. If the nuptials were permitted to take place, it would only be a question of time before the Lion would demand an examination of the Vanzini deaths and a reexamination of their former holdings.

Alberto had worked too long, too hard to have everything blow up in their faces now. With all the pending complications, everything would be lost, unless—unless—by the belly of Lucifer! How could he order the deaths of Marco, Dolcetto, and Antonio de Leone? How?

The irony of it all struck him. No one in all of Sicily dared defy the Mafia! No one except the Royal Lions! Now he filled with reflected anger.

No one could stand in his way! Not now, not after all he'd endured!

The time was at hand. He had to make his choice. If he didn't exterminate the Lions, the Lions would devour him

334

and the others, and prepare a banquet of vengeance on them for the authorities.

Very well, the decision must be made. Alberto finished the Strega. He placed the cordial glass upside down on the desk before him. He lifted his blue eyes and met those of the *capomafia.*

Don Barbarossa arose, sighed heavily, and tossed aside the soggy cigar.

"It is done, Alberto." His eyes lingered on the overturned glass.

"Make sure, Matteo. Make sure."

The *capomafia* left the room just as he'd entered it, knowing well in advance what must be done.

31

It was 1945, the year the war ended in Europe. Everywhere was chaos, unrest, and reorganization, with hundreds of political parties vying for supremacy. Don Matteo Barbarossa, active in the Grand Council in Palermo trying to determine Sicily's political fate, was hip-deep in political intrigues with feudal landbarons trying to suppress Communism and promote Christian Democracy. Separation from Italy and autonomy fired the minds of the millionaires who promoted the Monarchy of Sicily.

Having lunch as usual at Nunzzio's Birreria, he sensed the presence of a comely gentleman standing next to his table upon which was placed a square of yellow silk; a sign in *mafia* protocol that the man wished to identify himself and speak with the *capomafia.*

Don Matteo excused himself to his companions and led the way through the crowded bistro to a back room Nunzzio maintained especially for the Don to conduct business upon occasion. Unnoticed by most of the luncheon guests, a flank of bodyguards with bulging shoulder holsters under their ill-fitting jackets converged from various positions in the room and descended upon the two men before they entered the smaller room.

The white-haired gentleman with piercing blue eyes, who walked erect with the stance of a military general, wearing a sadly-fitting black serge suit, stepped aside and permitted himself to be searched.

"My men trust no one," said the Don, pushing his dark glasses into place.

"It's understandable," he replied, following the Don into the room. "Permit me to introduce myself. I am Alberto Pietro, doctor of laws, practicing doctor of medicine in

Messina." He spoke purposely with a Sicilian accent. Glancing about the dismal room, he tried to keep his disappointment to himself.

"Piacere, dottore," said the *capomafia*, pointing to a chair. "What can I do for you? Is there a special favor you wish from Don Barbarossa? Ask! If it's in my power, I shall not hesitate, since you came to me in respect," he said with a pompous air.

A waiter knocked and entered the room. "Bring wine," ordered the Don.

Dr. Pietro's azure blue eyes remained cordial, but contained an impersonal expression. "No, Don Barbarossa. I need no favor from you." He dusted off the chair he'd been offered with apparent disdain. He lifted his trousers at the knees before he sat, then, stiffly arched, he raised his eyes to observe his host.

Imperious and vain, the Don grew alternately indignant and annoyed, but gave no outward indication of his thoughts.

This was no fawning galantuomo *who wanted to rub elbows with the illustrious Don Barbarossa.*

"What I can do for *you* is more important," said Dr. Pietro pleasantly.

The Don laughed uproariously at such a foolish remark.

"Would you consider a billion dollars foolish?" Alberto swatted at the pesky flies buzzing around him.

The Don's smile evaporated.

"Listen, doctor, I got no time for foolishness! I'm due at a Grand Council meeting. You handed me a yellow scarf. Out of respect I extend the courtesy to talk with you. Now either state your business or leave me in peace. Goddammit! I have people waiting for me." His colorful jargon had been inspired by the Americans and British with whom he worked these many years.

"Ah, you've just spoiled the illusion," said the physician with disappointment. "I was told you were a man of great vision, Matteo. A giant of strength. A man who once made the earth tremble under his feet! Not a mere child content with toys and playthings."

Addressing the Don by his first name was bad enough, but to add his personal unsolicited criticism was highly disrespectful and foolhardy.

Don Matteo's black eyes burned fiercely behind the glasses and his face contorted with rage. "Listen, you, tell me what you want and don't be clever with me."

A waiter appeared with two dishes of *granita*, lemon ice, and wine. The Don took a deep breath, which brought on a coughing spell and a cracking to his voice. He reached for the wine only to find a strong, restraining hand on his arm.

"No, not the wine," insisted Dr. Pietro. "Here, take the water."

More furious than ever, the Don was surprised to find himself complying. He gulped the water down in prodigious amounts.

"How long has that cracking appeared in your voice? Does it occur frequently?" asked the doctor clinically. He swatted at another fly.

"Goddammit!" said the Don in a thin voice. "First, you insult me, then you become a solicitous old whore!"

"How long has your voice cracked?" he persisted.

"How the hell do I know? Who the hell keeps track?" The Don waved his arms about impatiently. "Six months, a year." His voice thinned and became barely audible. "Why?" he asked suspiciously.

"Have you seen a doctor?" Alberto removed his glasses and cleaned them.

"Why the hell you asking me these questions, eh?" Before Alberto could reply, the Don exploded impatiently. *"Va! Do me a favor, will you?"* He made an obscene gesture. He rose to his feet and pushed his chair back. "Goddammit! This meeting's over!"

"If you don't take care of your throat you won't live a year." Dr. Pietro calmly reset his glasses on his nose, replaced the napkin, and raised his cool eyes to meet the astonished eyes of the *capomafia*. "Two years at the most."

"Listen, don't be clever with me, I said. I dislike clever people. What the hell do you want, eh?"

"I'd suggest an immediate biopsy. No, not in Palermo—perhaps in Naples. Yes, Naples. A colleague of mine specializes in this sort of thing." He removed a pen from his breast pocket and scribbled a name on a slip of paper. "You tell the doctor I sent you. I promise he'll examine you without delay." Dr. Pietro sipped water from the glass as if it were covered with germs. "Now, Matteo, shall we talk about the billion dollars?"

Barbarossa felt as if he'd just been castrated. He sank back in his chair, disarmed, irritated, and confused. Because he equated doctors on a par with morticians, he generally kept his distance, and he didn't fathom the mystery and reverence enshrouding physicians. Compelled to listen, he grew economical with words.

"Talk," he said.

The doctor nodded and cleared his throat. "Since the war's end, American economic aid to its World War II allies has reached giant proportions. Billions of dollars are being spent on strategic supplies in a massive attempt to rebuild war-torn countries. Now, as I see it, if we can divert these supply shipments, relabel and reroute them into special boxcars to the free port of Trieste, then the boxcars can be coupled onto other trains which will take them into Communist Yugoslavia and from there on to Russia."

"Ah," said the Don, *"Si communisto?"* He hated the Reds and found them a growing cancer in Italy and Sicily. For years, in alliance with Salvatore Guiliano, the famous Sicilian bandit, he had driven them out of Sicily.

"No, no! I'm no Communist! Like you, I'm too much of a capitalist for the Reds. I want us to both make more money than we ever dreamed possible. And since we need each other in such a venture, what could be better than forming a partnership? With money like that one need never live like a peasant." Dr. Pietro, who usually measured his words carefully, had let that last remark slip accidently. Good, he thought, the Don hadn't heard the remark. He began to swat the flies again in an effort to divert Matteo's thoughts. He caught a fly in his hand, tossed it viciously on the floor, and stepped on it. "This place is filthy! They should do something about the flies."

Alberto was wrong. The Don had heard the remark and understood the insult. But the vision of wealth was stronger than the insult.

"I have certain trustworthy contacts in the north," continued Dr. Pietro, "Italian companies that will place orders with American firms. For example, let us say they'll need several tons of copper wire, generators, engines, whatever. You, Don Matteo, I'm sure, control men in key positions in the Ministry of Foreign Commerce, who'll sign import documents for compensation. The companies in question must sign certificates attesting that they'll be the sole users of the goods. Then they'll deposit, in a bank in Zurich, cash payments for the materials which are advanced by the Economic Recovery Administration. From there on, the procedure is simple. The goods are shipped to a European port where our agents change identification and destination of the packing crates on forged bills of sale. Our agents then divert the shipment to Soviet agents for three or four times the amount paid originally, all in advance and in gold or other commodities. Later, when the Italian companies show proof they never received the goods, the money on deposit is returned to them, and we repeat the process."

Don Matteo, a fantastic listener, didn't miss a word. In fact he was several steps ahead of the physician. Nearly every office in the Cabinet of Ministers under the Premier was under the control of the Mafia. And soon his protégé, Martino Belasci, would become Premier. The doctor's proposal took on enormous significance, and visions of huge profits began to accumulate in his mind.

He took a second look at this man Alberto Pietro. Instinctively he detected a curious violence in the man's easy manner. Something obscure in the dim recesses of his mind tried to surface. He tried to place the man but couldn't. He remained silent.

"The world grows smaller each day," continued Alberto. "There are millions to be made and with your cooperation it can be done." Pietro's eyes lit up with glimpses of a secret world, known only to him, one Don Matteo would never hope to learn about.

"Before you give me your answer, I must ask that this and all subsequent conversations be held in the strictest of confidence. You'll be the only man I'll speak with and my plans shall be outlined only to you. No one must know or suspect that we even remotely know each other. It's the only way we can become powerful and influential. You deserve to be rightfully placed in government as a lawmaker—say a Senator in the Italian Parliament. It's possible now that you've been reinstated in your proper place and gained world-wide acceptance."

Instinctively the Don was drawn to Alberto by his cool and detached, yet self-assured and brazen manner.

"Why do you wish such anonymity?" he asked the physician.

"I have friends among the titled *latifondisti,* powerful political officials in the government in Rome. From time to time I hear privileged information that can help us, information that would be unavailable if it were known I had *mafia* connections. If you'd known in advance what was coming before you were driven underground twenty years ago, you might have been able to avert those lean years."

"Who can argue with Destiny? We did what we did, just as the Fascists did what they had to do. *Che sera sera.*"

"Wouldn't it be important to learn if spies or traitors are in your midst?"

"We have ways to handle traitors. They are the least of my concern."

"Yes, but always after the fact. The old way. An eye for an eye. You're missing the point." Alberto took a spoonful of the melting lemon ice.

The Don tilted an eyebrow and shrugged indifferently.

"Ah," said Alberto finding the key. "Two years ago with your cousin Lucky Luciano, you embarked on a new business that hasn't proved as profitable as you were led to believe. You travel to Corsica twice a month aboard the *Arcturus II* and pick up the contraband. And for this you receive ten thousand dollars from your cousin. Apparently you aren't aware of the market value of that white powder they refine and call heroin. You think ten thousand dollars is adequate?" smiled Alberto. "Did you know that your cousin's take was well over two million dollars? Not in lira, but in American currency deposited in Swiss bank accounts."

The Don's face turned to granite.

"The agreement was to split the proceeds three ways. One third of two million is a bit more than ten thousand, no?"

"How do you know all this?"

"Does a bird teach the fish to swim?"

"There you go being clever again. I told you, don't be clever!" The Don made a mental note to look into his cousin Lucky's affairs.

"This is the kind of cooperation I can offer you. If you wish to pursue the traffic in drugs in addition to our plan, at least let's make it profitable." Alberto spooned another mouthful of lemon ice. "I hear the youngbloods are giving you trouble." He knew it was a sore spot with the Don.

"I can handle them. They want to take over without paying their dues. When I was young, one had to earn the right to become a man of respect, a man of honor." An edge of bitterness crept into his voice.

"Matteo, let the *picciotti* take over the land interests. The *latifondisti* will soon be no more. The land giants are dying off and there's no one to replace them. The *latifondo* is no longer the power in Sicily. All this is unimportant. Money is the power! Soon will come construction, new housing, apartments, and office buildings. In the east already the foreign oil companies have leased the lands where oil shoots as high as Mt. Etna. Move with the time or you'll be left out. The world is moving fast and things that were effective twenty years ago are obsolete today. Take a lesson from your American associates; Genovese, Luciano, and Gambino have all made fortunes. Organize the youngbloods, make them Dons and lead them yourself. Don't split the factions or the brotherhood will die of old age. Rejuvenate! Move with the times. The youngbloods aren't stupid. Impetuous, yes, but not without intelligence. Listen to me, *amico*, the time is coming when to make millions of dollars all a man has to do is sit at a conference table and with a pen move decimal points to the right. The days of mass killing and vendetta are over. The public won't stand for it. The power of the pen has become mightier than the sword."

340

Goddamn! The power of the pen! That was power! Vaguely the Don recalled those words out of his past. His little spider hadn't been wrong.

Three hours of talk had covered nearly every *mafia* activity. The waiter appeared twice and twice Don Matteo ordered wine. Both times, Dr. Pietro boldly changed the order to water, cautioning him about his throat. The third time, the Don exploded. He demanded wine be sent immediately and when it arrived, he defiantly poured himself an extra large glass and placed it to his lips. Dr. Pietro glanced stonily at him and stated flatly, "Our talk has ended! There's no sense pursuing plans with a dead man!"

Don Matteo dropped the wine as if it had turned into a handful of hissing vipers. *"Botta de Sanguo!* Will you leave me alone!" he shouted angrily. He attempted to wipe the wine from his trousers and from the white tablecloth. "Leave me be!"

"There, there," said Alberto in the voice of a concerned father. "There. That's better. Take this dish of lemon ice." He pushed the watery substance toward him. "It'll refresh your throat. Don't let me see you drink any more wine until you have the good sense to see a doctor. Else the deal's off."

"Porco diaoro! Pig of a devil! What ever gave you the idea the deal was on?" glowered the infuriated Don Matteo. No one had ever talked to him as this upstart of a doctor had done this day.

"I know," smiled the physician. "I just know."

Their eyes locked and held again. Suddenly they both laughed easily. The Don slapped his thigh and laughed the loudest. At last the air cleared. Then, that crazy man with his peculiar brand of guts congested the air all over again.

"One matter, Don Matteo, must be discussed and considered properly. I must insist that the vendetta between the Mafia and the House of de Leone cease."

He heard it. But he didn't believe it! Don Matteo removed his dark glasses. The malevolent look of power that had made this Sicilian mongoose *capomafia* of all was frightening to behold. For several moments Alberto suffered quick second thoughts about his demand. But he held his ground.

The Don's beady eyes were barely visible. His face had swollen and turned purple. And he thought, *either this man is the world's biggest fool or he's a tremendously brave man.*

"With a flick of my finger I could have you killed. You dare issue ultimatums to me, Barbarossa? End the vendetta between the Mafia and the House of de Leone, indeed!" He struck a match and began to light his favorite smoke, a long

341

thin cigar imported from Cuba that he'd been hoarding due to a diminishing supply.

"No smoking, either, Matteo," said Alberto sternly. "I don't wish to alarm you but you should refrain from irritants until you see a specialist."

Barbarossa stood up and kicked back his chair with savage intensity. "No one tells Don Barbarossa what to do! No one!" His eyes were saturated with anger. His voice constricted and he coughed and sputtered and grew angrier as he tried unsuccessfully to clear his throat and regain his voice.

Alberto held his hands up in an open gesture. "What would you like engraved on your tombstone?"

No one had ever talked to the Don like this and lived to tell about it. His face twisted and jerked as he tried to find his voice. He gulped at the water greedily.

With affected boredom, Alberto fixed his patient blue eyes on the *mafia* figurehead and watched as he paced the room like an enraged bull. He saw the heated torment rising in the Don as he tried to subdue his anger. Alberto smiled to himself. *I've bagged the old moose and the old moose knows it.*

In the few moments he paced the floor, a lifetime of discipline had been tested.

"About the House of de Leone, it's out of the question," he said when his voice returned.

"Then we have no deal."

"You realize I've had men killed for less than your actions today? Goddammit! You take too much liberty!"

Alberto shrugged indifferently. He unfolded a chocolate mint and popped it into his mouth.

"You realize what you ask of me?"

"Yes."

"For what then must I humiliate myself?"

"For untold wealth. Haven't you done more . . . for less?"

"Tu si pazzu! You're crazy! For more than two centuries there's been vendetta between us."

"Ah, *si*," sighed Alberto filled with boredom. "There's always vendetta . . ."

"I have my honor to maintain."

"Is it worth ten billion dollars?" He swatted another fly. *"Dio malodetta!"*

"It's worth my life!" thundered the Don. *"My life!"*

The immovable object finally met the irresistible force and silence filled the room as they stared hard and fast at one another.

"Aloura, let me offer you a counterproposal," began Alberto, understanding the extent of the Don's dilemma. "Let

342

us take an option on our relationship. While we engage in the various business enterprises we've discussed, no harm must come to the family of Royal Lions. If the brotherhood is provoked by a Royal Lion anyplace in the world, no action must be taken against him. In exchange for this consideration, you will have riches and powers beyond your wildest dreams; a power more potent than a king. At the end of a year, when we assess our situation and find it's been most profitable, we shall decide then the ultimate fate of the Royal Lions."

"One year?" The Don temporized. "Making a deal for one year isn't as binding as a lifetime," he said. *What can I lose by such an agreement?* he thought. *Complications—always complications. One had to master them or be caught in their stranglehold.*

"Whore of the devil! How in God's name," he asked, "can I suddenly reverse a situation that has held fast for two centuries?"

"You work it out however you can, Matteo. I trust you implicitly. It is well known that Don Barbarossa's word is his bond."

The Don glanced sharply at him. *Now he mocks me! We'll see, now.*

"You've done most of the talking. Now, its my turn. Talk. You tell me, what do you want?" insisted the Don.

"I thought I made myself clear. To share in the profits."

"In what? All our holdings?"

"Only those I bring to you. Those I direct you to myself."

"Nothing else, eh?"

"Nothing I can think of."

"A high office in the government, perhaps?"

"Are you crazy? Me? Forgive my impertinence, but never!"

"What, then? There must be something. A possession, a section of Sardinia, perhaps, when I settle the fate of my country?"

"There will be plenty for me in the business I direct to you, Matteo."

"A private practice assured so no one can infringe upon your profession? Perhaps a private hospital, built by government funds. That will be no trouble, I assure you, *dottore.* You professionals always like to see your names etched in stone for posterity. That's it! The Alberto Pietro Hospital and Clinic! I knew I'd hit on it! Is that for you?"

"No. What can I say to make you understand?"

"I understand. I understand. There must be something

343

you want, Alberto. I'll not rest until I find out what it is that I can do for you in return."

"If you put it that way . . ."

"Yes?"

"Perhaps, one day, when I'm ready to retire, I shall let you purchase a villa for me. *Va biene?* Someplace where I can sit out the rest of my days and relax and probably write my memoirs of a man as great and grand as Matteo Barbarossa."

Barbarossa reset his dark glasses into place and smiled internally. *The man has a way with words all right,* he told himself. Methodically, as though he were studying some supernatural creature, Matteo Barbarossa fixed his tinted glasses on the man seated opposite him, on his ill-fitting black suit, meticulously tied necktie, scrupulously clean fingernails, gold watch fob entwined through the buttonholes in his vest. Even his manner of shaking hands before they parted offended Don Matteo. He got the distinct impression by Alberto's reaction that he'd caught something contagious from the Don by shaking his hand, for he had quickly wiped his hand with a handkerchief.

Immediately after his departure, Don Matteo recruited the efforts of young Primo Garibaldi to personally check out this man and prepare a dossier on him from birth to present day.

When Don Matteo first learned of the long standing, close relationship between Dr. Pietro and the Royal Lions, and that he was in fact Godfather to Dolcetto de Leone, his first reaction was of blind anger at what he thought was blatant deception. He reconsidered the situation, and giving time for the partnership to advance, he came to learn the mastermind and financial wizard emulated by Alberto was none other than the Royal Lion himself, Marco de Leone. And he came to understand why no harm must befall the Lions. What irony! With the Royal Lions alive, Alberto, who remained in close confidence with the de Leone family, would be free to remit vital information and effect business transactions that began producing astounding results for them almost immediately. The *capo* could have asked for nothing more.

The Don had kept this report in his confidential files at home in his villa in Monreale. Not even his *consigliori* knew of Alberto's existence and his relationship to the *mafia*.

Not one to be outfoxed, the Don used Paolo Nicosia to take him to Naples to check out the throat ailment. The mysterious throat malady, caused by some metabolic disturbance, was corrected by taking a quarter grain of thyroid.

344

He never informed Alberto that he had checked into the matter.

What Alberto Pietro promised that day had come to pass. The Don's name, as it became internationally known, made him the undisputed overlord of Sicily. The rewards? More than the balding, rotund, energetic physician had intimated. Money in Swiss bank accounts, world-wide investments, oil interests, and multimillion-dollar construction companies were only a few stamps on a roll of thousands.

In February, the Don's man, Martino Belasci, had been proclaimed Premier, having survived a complicated scandal involving the Sicilian bandits. Now, the world was theirs.

The financial wizardry of Marco de Leone's shadow, Dr. Pietro, had proved astounding!

Over the years of their acquaintance and mutual profit-making ventures, there were times when the *capomafia* felt he was sitting on a time bomb ready to explode. Not that he was worried. He employed experts who knew how to dismantle a detonator, but first the bomb had to be located.

32

For a time, Destiny felt neglected by Matteo. His loyalties to her had thinned. He now took orders from another. We'll see how he gets along, she thought in the manner of a jealous mistress. She raised her long, slender hands to her crafty lips and laughed with world-shaking mirth. She sat back on her uncontested throne and gazed with contemplative eyes at the world of her charges, moving them about as she saw fit. It had been Destiny who had nudged Francesca Vanzini to go to Rome at a time when she was sure to meet Dolcetto de Leone.

For some time, Destiny had been viewing Alberto Pietro with suspicion. She labeled him a cheap imitator of men. Alberto was no believer in Destiny. He paid her no homage and believed that a man steered his own course in life.

· Destiny had grown indignant when she saw Pietro interfering with her two most prized subjects, Marco de Leone and Don Matteo Barbarossa. She felt Albert Pietro lacked the courage and integrity of Marco's brave and honorable intentions. And he certainly lacked the courage and integrity of Barbarossa's savage convictions. His insufferable conceit inflamed her anger and she looked upon him as her arch-enemy.

After having observed him for many years using one man against the other and interfering with her plans in order to reach his ambitious goals, Destiny decided to step into the picture to move things into their proper places. She would teach this nonbeliever a lesson.

For the next few months, this volatile empress kept herself occupied with intrigues and counter-intrigues. More specifically, she looked into her universal files to take a better look at this man, Dr. Alberto Pietro.

Before Alberto Pietro was fourteen years old, he knew what he must do to leave home and prepare a life of his own. Stringy-haired and stocky with short arms and legs, a sallow complexion, and alert blue eyes, he stood apart from his dark, black-eyed brothers and most of the other natives in his home in Cagliari on the island of Sardinia.

Alberto's father, Emilio Pietro, an itinerant farmer on a feudal estate until he met and married his wife, the daughter of a quality wine grower and merchant, became a wine merchant following their wedding. The dowry money had provided the means and his own shrewd management with money and business made him successful.

Young Alberto felt trapped as soon as he learned that for a young boy, there was only one destiny, to follow in his father's footsteps. Forced into becoming an apprentice, along with his two older brothers, in a wine and bottle shop, where people from all walks of life congregated to taste a variety of wines, local and imported, it was here among the antiquated barrels and dusty bottles that Alberto first heard rumors of a strange story of mystery and intrigue that was to one day change the course of his life.

Over a century before Alberto was born, the reigning king of Sardinia had difficulty with a truant young son who was enamored of the seamier side of life. The king's only daughter, an obedient and loyal girl, had given him much pleasure and joy. She allowed herself to be married to a French prince in the hopes of forming an alliance with one of the Napoleons. However, the son, a fun-loving libertine, incurred monumental gambling debts in his desire to live in a manner more splendid than even his father's regal fortune permitted. Threatened with disinheritance and the embarrassment that follows a penniless sovereign, the young rebel pretended to mend his ways. Once before, when his allowance had been cut off, he had discovered the inequities of poverty and made up his mind to avoid such a condition in the future.

No one knew when it began, but the prince began frequenting his father's palace more than usual, taking a profound interest in the magnificent estate. Since the *Risorgimento* unified the Kingdom of the Two Sicilies, few guests visited the grand old palace as in bygone days. So, many of the treasures contained within the palace walls were being stored away for posterity. There were collections of original oils by the masters, statuary, art objects encrusted with gems of immense worth, rich tapestries and lush carpets worth a vast fortune. On the walls of many salons, in alcoves, recessed in huge vaults and along the stately halls were splendors which exceeded in worth many times the money in the king's treasury.

In the prince's mind began to form a plan to siphon off many of these priceless treasures. Who'd miss them? They only collected dust. Why shouldn't he avail himself of the luxury these things could provide? Was he not the prince? Why, with just a handful of these articles he could live the life of his own choosing. A few miles outside of the splendid Palermo Court where all royalty congregated, he acquired a magnificent summer palace built originally by the Romans and later refurbished by the French Bourbon king, Charles of Anjou. The prince couldn't have been happier with this lush palace. It was ideal! Slowly, at first, he began to decorate it with the fabulous art treasures he pilfered from the king's palace. Then, growing bolder, he managed to practically fill the hold of a cargo ship in broad daylight with enough treasures to last a lifetime. This *fait accompli* was managed without detection.

Upon the death of the king a few years later, an inventory was taken; the discovery that the treasure had been dramatically depleted by an estimated many millions sent shockwaves throughout the palace. By the time court advisers could piece together what might have happened to the fortune, and long before they were able to trace the stolen goods to the prince, the scoundrel had been killed in a duel. The jewels and art treasures were never recovered and never showed up in anyone's private collection or in a museum. Never!

How many times young Alberto listened to this incredible tale, over and over again, each time with a new twist, a new slant, more insight, less conjecture and a myriad of speculations as to where the treasure had been hidden or buried. The story began to hold particular fascination for Alberto; it filled him with profound interest and began to influence his entire life, like a distant dream to be one day fulfilled.

In Cagliari, Alberto developed a strong appreciation of art. The antiquities of the Phoenicians, the Carthaginians, Romans, the Argonnese and other ancient civilizations had left their stamp on the buildings and museums of Sardinia. Why should Alberto bury himself in a dreary wineshop when the lure of romantic museums, libraries, and ancient temples intoxicated his senses and set his imagination on fire? Emilio Pietro, however, had different ideas for this troublesome son whose head floated among the clouds. One day he looked for his son and was told he could be found as usual in his frequent haunt, the library. So enraged did Emilio Pietro become that he decided it was time for a showdown. He marched out into the daylight in his shirt-sleeves and strode across the piazza, oblivious to all he passed, up the steps and into the library, where he picked up his son by the scruff of the neck, marched him out of the library, away from an astonished collection of shocked faces, down the steps, back into the wineshop where he proceeded to give Alberto a beating the boy would never forget.

Later that night, nursing several welts and bruises, young Alberto, an expert horseman since the age of five, rode painfully for two hours along dirt roads to his grandfather's vineyards, only to learn his old ally had just died of a coronary. Although stunned and grief-stricken by the news, Alberto was happy to learn he'd been left an unconditional legacy which he demanded immediately after the funeral. That his detachment and unfeeling nature should appear callous to others didn't disturb him in the least. Immediately after the funeral, he kissed his mother goodbye, said nothing to his father or brothers, and made a trip to see the lawyer who handled the estate.

Within a few weeks he had enrolled in a Jesuit school outside of Rome. Not considered by the Holy Fathers to be a very bright lad, they nonetheless praised Alberto for his diligence. They began to consider him as a possible religious acolyte and were utterly astonished when he announced his intention to study medicine.

Priests and physicians were given special treatment and were considered closer to God than any other professionals. In either capacity he'd be free to roam about and research his pet project. Educated men, he learned, were held in high esteem by titled men, who frequently sought their company, respected their ideas, and treated them as equals, showering them with favors and gifts. Hadn't his own father taught him it was far more prestigious to be owed money by the nobility than to be paid in cash by the poor?

While with the Jesuits, he learned of a hybrid order of monks who lived shut off from the material world in a small mountain retreat in central Sardinia. Vowing to live in the strictest poverty and dedicate their lives to prayer, these

348

dedicated men became diligent historians and kept the records of the country, its rulers, and its politics.

Before Alberto left to study medicine, he obtained permission to visit this remote retreat and explore its archives, which he learned contained direct references to the lost treasure. Several members of the original Order of Stylites—monks who once lived atop of pillars to separate themselves from the world and mortify the flesh—had lived on the estate of the Sardinian king. As a matter of history, they had documented the missing art treasures, describing them in every detail and remotely suggesting that the prince had in some way been responsible for the treasure's mysterious disappearance.

In addition to the information contained in the monastery's archives, Alberto learned enough to make him study medicine at the University of Catania, spending his summers in and about Palermo. Apart from his professional studies, every spare minute of Alberto's time was spent in libraries and museums learning art appreciation.

After earning his doctorate in medicine, Alberto chose to practice in Messina because of its key location and modern facilities which included a hall of records containing trust deeds and land grants dating back many hundreds of years.

A competent physician, Alberto displayed an amazing talent for diagnosis, but his bedside manner was abhorrent. Because he could strike up no real rapport with his patients, he attached himself to the All Saints Hospital where he could keep his private practice to a minimum.

One fateful day early in his career he was asked to travel some fifteen kilometers, as fast as his horse and buggy could take him, to the Villa de Leone where an unexpected bandit raid had taken its toll. Many desperately injured people needed medical attention.

Alberto was confounded, excited, and speechless. An opportunity to meet with the Royal Lion of Sicily would certainly be a step toward the goal he sought. *Pray the Lion is alive and that I might save him!* His research had already mentioned the name of de Leone, and the remote possibility that the Marquis might shed more light on the Sardinian prince was one of the reasons he settled in Messina.

After the events following the bandit raid, Marco never forgot that it was Dr. Pietro who nursed his brother Guillermo and himself back to health. The efficiency with which Dr. Pietro and his small team of workers patched up the injured and maimed and kept long, endless vigil as the two brothers hovered between life and death, was looked upon by some of the nurses as perhaps the most humane act Dr. Pietro had performed since he joined the hospital staff.

Alberto remained at the villa for nearly three weeks, sending to Messina for additional supplies and assistance. In so doing, he'd set up what amounted to a temporary dispensary and first-aid facility. He taught the wives and daughters of the *contadini* the fundamentals of cleanliness and minor first-aid techniques, unaware that in so doing, he would spark the idea for a permanent dispensary in Marco de Leone's mind.

One night at dinner, Marco discussed his future plans with Alberto Pietro. Marco's infectious manner and persuasive personality interested the physician. He saw in the Lion many things he could never hope for in himself: supreme self-control, fearlessness, undaunted leadership, and a genuine love for his people. Alberto was astute enough to realize the Lion couldn't be swayed by flattery. Obsequiousness was a trait Marco tolerated only among the uneducated peasants who were motivated by pride in their *padrone* rather than greed or a desire for financial gain.

They'd stroll about the villa gazing at the many art treasures that had been in the de Leone family for centuries. Marco was genuinely delighted to hear Alberto expound on the techniques and the lives of the many artists represented at the villa. When Alberto mentioned he played chess, nothing could have pleased Marco more for it was a game he enjoyed dearly. Their thirty-year-long friendship began that night.

Pure astonishment lit up Marco de Leone's eyes the night Alberto superficially mentioned the Sardinian prince, and the story of the lost treasure. And when he concurred with Alberto, suggesting that he too believed in the story, Alberto's excitement was uncontainable. Having never met anyone who had taken such a profound interest in the subject, Marco was moved to speak.

"You know, Alberto, somewhere in that history is buried a family skeleton. You see, my friend," said Marco with a twinkle in his eye, "the prince's sister was engaged to marry the cousin of my great-grandmother, the Marquess Maria Louisa Bernadotte. The engagement was nullified by order of Louis Napoleon in favor of his nephew in order to form an alliance between France and Sardinia. Well, the Bernadottes were furious. From that point on they weren't hesitant to say or do anything that would discredit the Sardinians for the insufferable outrage. When rumors of the larcenous prince spread through the royal court, they were only too eager to see him caught and apprehended. Many, it seems, later tried to locate the treasure and failed miserably. It

350

would seem a monumental chore, Alberto," reflected Marco. "If one were of a mind, I suppose it might be possible to locate the prince's palace by tracing the land grants and deeds throughout the Palermo province from the time before Napoleon. Providing you learn the assumed name in which the deed was registered."

This stream of consciousness stoked, it began to pour forth. Marco shook his head. "Unfortunately, when the House of Records was destroyed by the fire in Messina, most court records were lost forever. What a mess that was! Property owners urged to rerecord their deeds were suddenly confronted with forgeries by people attempting to claim their lands. Government officials went crazy trying to untangle that mess. It took years before most people knew whose property belonged to whom. In many cases the wrong people were given title to property they didn't rightfully own. The practice became the basis for a *mafia* racket that drove most Sicilian landowners *pazzi!*"

Marco suddenly broke into gales of laughter.

"What is it?" asked Alberto.

"I was just thinking, the only other way to effect such a title search is . . ." He laughed again. "Nothing . . . it's too ridiculous."

"Please tell me, nevertheless. I'd like to hear," insisted Alberto, who clung to every word Marco spoke, absorbing them like a sponge.

"It occurred to me," smiled Marco, "if a man could give up two years of his life, the answer to your Sardinian fortune might be found in Rome's Hall of Records. Immediately following the dissolution of power of the Kingdom of Two Sicilies . . ." Marco paused a moment. "Or was it the Kingdom of Rome?" He paused thoughtfully again. "Or it could very well have been during the Piedmontese Government. Oh, well, whatever." He waved his hand in the air in a disorganized gesture. "There was a period when titles to all estates throughout the kingdom had to be recorded in Rome. Most of the archives under Papal jurisdiction were turned over to the Rome Government and recorded properly to avoid later confusion as to who gave who which land grants under which government." Marco paused again to sip his black espresso, then added in all seriousness, "If the prince lived under an assumed name, sheer intelligence would lead you to believe he would select the name of a man who wasn't among the living, perhaps a dead relative, someone he knew well. I suppose if one were interested enough to discover these vital clues, he might study the prince's family tree to learn if any names in the lineage appeared on any of the land grants or deeds or title transfers."

Marco had no way of knowing it then, but his chance remarks saved Alberto innumerable years of research. Marco also had no way of knowing the extent of the physician's dedication until many years later when he learned that Alberto Pietro had spent four grueling summer vacations in the heat of Rome, seated in the stuffy, sweltering back rooms, searching and studying, filing and cross-filing until he found his answer. As soon as Alberto found the answer, he took the first train to Palermo to promote his initial meeting with Don Barbarossa.

33

Pure insanity was the only way to describe Dr. Pietro's driving as he demonically manuevered the four-wheel war-surplus jeep over the lava encrusted slopes leading to the Villa de Leone. The abused machine kicked up whirls of dust so thick he could barely see the approaching horsemen coming toward him.

"Buon giorno, Godfather," shouted Dolcetto as they passed each other on the road. He waved to his Godson and to Antonio who rode up close behind his cousin. They wheeled their horses around and followed the zig-zagging jeep as it jogged along the bumpy road. Two apprehensive sentries had already swung open the main gates, nodding to the physician in passing. Dismounting, Antonio and Dolcetto waited as Alberto parked the jeep. After a cordial embrace the trio entered the villa.

They found the sixty-seven-year-old patriarch seated at his desk deeply involved with his writing. In the corner of the room, occupying a somewhat obscure but nevertheless visible place, hung the completed painting of Diamonte. It had turned out to be an exquisite work of art. Somehow in all those years following the Mazzarino raid on the villa, Marco had found the key to the girl's personality and was able to complete the portrait. The magnificent portrait of Mariolina, painted from memory, hung over his desk.

Marco glanced up and smiled. He rose and crossed the room to embrace Alberto. He turned to his son and prodded him gently, pointing to the physician.

"What is it, Marco? What are you trying to say?"

"What Uncle Marco is trying to say, Dolcetto will do in a moment," laughed Antonio. "First, the wine. I'll propose a toast." Antonio walked to the liquor cabinet, placed four glasses on a silver tray, and brought the crystal decanter with him.

"Well, Godson, what do you tell me? What's the mystery?"

"No mystery," began Dolcetto as Antonio passed the drinks around. "I'm going to be married."

"Married, Dolcetto? Well, well! So the young Lion's captured himself a lioness, eh? Congratulations, Godson, congratulations!" Alberto embraced his Godson and patted him affectionately on the back.

"To the bride and groom!" cried Antonio happily.

Alberto turned to Marco. "Congratulations, *compare*. At last your dreams come to pass, eh?"

Marco smiled and nodded happily. He embraced his son with tears of joy in his eyes. Then his eyes clouded. He pulled Antonio toward him, pointed to the third finger of his left hand, and feigned a slight impatience.

"Who, me?" laughed Antonio good-naturedly. "Not yet, Uncle. I'm having too much fun as a bachelor." He winked playfully at Marco and they all laughed, then settled down in the comfortable Moroccan leather sofas.

"*Aloura*, tell me. Who's the lucky woman? Anyone I know?" asked Alberto.

"I'm not sure. Signorina Francesca Vanzini of Porto Tomasso." Dolcetto reflected a moment. Her name brought a glow to his cheek.

"Ah," his Godfather nodded.

"You know the family, Godfather?"

"I've not had the pleasure. If I'm invited to the wedding, I shall meet her."

"You'll meet her. She's quite a woman."

"She would have to be to capture your heart," said Alberto.

Then because his Godfather asked, he told him how they met and how he'd bought the villa right from under the nose of Don Barbarossa. If Dolcetto hadn't been thinking about Francesca, he might have noticed his Godfather's sudden pallor when he asked, "What will you do with such a villa? Live there?"

"Me live in the heart of *mafia* country? You must be dreaming. No, *grazie tanto*, I prefer to breathe clean air. I bought it to keep it out of the hands of the *mafia*."

Marco hung on their every word. Smoking a thin cigar, sipping his wine, with his family around him, he was content. His eyes chanced to rest on Alberto and he gave a start. *Something's wrong*, he thought. *Alberto can't fool me. He plays a game of cat and mouse with Dolcetto.* He wondered why, but his thoughts were interrupted when Antonio took the floor. How he loved that nephew of his, who was the exact mold of his father Guillermo, whom Marco missed with infinite passion. He listened as Antonio began to praise Dolcetto for the manner in which he handled some business in Rome. Special agents? What was Antonio saying?

Before Dolcetto could stop Antonio, he'd blurted out the whole story. Marco listened with all his senses working at once. He noticed Dolcetto's discomfort and annoyance and his constant effort to get Antonio to change the subject. He noticed again the unusual lights in Alberto's eyes. Finally, unable to allow Antonio to continue, Dolcetto interrupted him.

"As long as you decided to publicize it, cousin, let me tell it." He hoped Antonio would see his displeasure, but he knew it was useless to scold him.

"It was nothing important, Papa," said Dolcetto noting the studied look on his father's face. "Just some silly misunderstanding about vouchers and requisitions Antonio signed."

"Nothing, Dolcetto? Then why were the *Guardia* and the American agents involved?" asked his Godfather in a matter-of-fact tone.

"Just a routine check, that's all."

Marco knew something was amiss. He admired his son's attempt to minimize the situation. Some things you don't talk about. Not wishing to be obvious, he tried to signal Antonio not to pursue the conversation, but the dark-eyed adonis didn't see his uncle's eye signal.

"Dolcetto's too modest," interrupted Antonio. "They found out Amelio Molinari is working for the *mafia*. The agents suspect he's diverted several million dollars."

"Antonio!" Dolcetto showed signs of impatient anger.

"I was only going to say they suspected me . . ." He turned and for the first time saw the warning in Marco's eyes. Overwhelmed by the disapproval he saw, he withdrew wondering what he'd done wrong.

"Let's not talk business on a holiday," said Dolcetto. He patted his cousin's thigh and stood up. "Besides, we have more important things to discuss."

Marco stood up, nudged Alberto, and pointed to the game of Monopoly.

"You want to play a few games, Marco?"

The Royal Lion nodded. Together they moved toward the game table.

"When will the wedding take place?" asked Alberto, trying to cover his distress.

"In exactly one month," said Dolcetto searching through his briefcase.

"Here?"

Marco glanced at his son.

"No," said Dolcetto evenly, searching his father's eyes. "The Vanzini Villa."

Marco shook his flowing leonine mane in stubborn refusal. His eyes reflected a mixture of alarm, apprehension, then blank refusal.

Don't they understand? Surely their memories aren't that short!

In the split seconds of Marco's refusal, his entire life of combating *mafiosi* flashed before him.

"Won't you reconsider, Papa? I know how you feel. I understand all you've been through," pleaded his son with love and gentleness in his heart.

"You must be sensible, Marco," intervened Alberto. "Times have changed. You can't live the rest of your life expecting the worst. What kind of life is that? Surely Dolcetto mentioned the Vanzini Villa is a veritable fortress."

Dolcetto spun around and stared in stunned silence at his Godfather. He didn't recall mentioning anything about the villa to him. He watched Alberto pour cognac from a crystal decanter. His blue eyes seemed warmer than he ever remembered them. Dolcetto was grateful for the affectionate consideration Alberto held for Marco, a friendship that had weathered many storms. He suddenly recalled the day Alberto told Marco he no longer had a tongue. It was a vivid impression. *Why should I think about that now?* He watched his father and his Godfather touch glasses, drink the fiery liquid, and smack their lips in appreciation. Marco set his glass down on the table, arose, and strode across the room. He flung open the French doors and stood somberly looking out at the *Terra d'Oro*.

Nothing will change my mind. Either the wedding takes place here at this villa or the wedding takes place without me. I must insist on this without hurting Dolcetto.

Antonio walked to his uncle's side and stood silently looking out past the Madelaina Gardens. "Do you recall the wine we brought you from Fregossi's vineyards last year? The wine you praised so highly. Remember? You said it gave you new life, made you think of dancing girls in your youth." He embraced his uncle. Marco's smooth, unlined face broke into a wave of smiles. Antonio always made him happy. He nodded.

"You made me believe if you could meet with Fregossi you'd convince him to part with the vines you want to plant there on the *Terra d'Oro*."

Dolcetto cast a speculative eye in Antonio's direction. He

355

picked up an alabaster egg from Marco's desk and rolled it between his hands, tossing it lightly as he listened to the conversation across the room. Alberto was playing a game of solitaire.

Marco salivated at the mention of Fregossi's wine, closing his eyes for a moment and thinking about his friend Felipe Santiago, the old *falconiero*, who bragged that his wine was the finest in the world. Having finally settled near Andalusia, Spain, Felipe devoted full time to growing grapes; winemaking had become his greatest passion. A sly look crept into Marco's eyes as he envisioned his own golden acreage prolific with the vines of Fregossi.

"Where's the wine? Is there any more left, Uncle Marco?" Marco nodded.

"Let Alberto be the judge. Has he tasted it yet?"

Marco shrugged indifferently. Wouldn't Felipe be stunned with amazement when he tasted wine from the golden grapes. That's what they'd be if grown on the *Terra d'Oro*.

Antonio moved across the room to the wine cabinet. He winked at Dolcetto with remarkable assurance. Locating the special decanter, he poured some into a wine glass and handed it to Dr. Pietro.

"Would you permit me, Marco?" asked Dolcetto's Godfather.

Marco leaned languidly against the desk and lit a thin cigar, his inscrutable eyes fixed on his friend.

Alberto rolled the liquid around in the glass, while the warmth of his hands tempered the wine. He inhaled its bouquet, placed the goblet to his lips, sipped the rosé wine in the manner of a connoisseur. He rolled the wine around his mouth, then swallowed it, smacking his lips loudly. Marco eyed him carefully and leaned in closer, studying every detail of Alberto's face. From the corner of his eyes, Alberto observed Marco and he deliberately remained silent, teasing his friend. With marked hesitation, he repeated the process. By this time, Marco was as anxious as a child. Alberto nodded, half-dubious, half-approving, as he balanced his hand in a rocking motion.

Finally Alberto murmured, *"Ah chè bella sapore.* Are you sure this wine is from Fregossi's vines? But it's not possible!" He paused for a dramatic effect. "You say there's a chance Fregossi would give you some vines?" A look of disbelief flooded his face. "No, not Fregossi. That peasant wouldn't part with the dirt under his fingernails."

"It's the truth. Fregossi told me only a short while ago that if *Zu* Marco would come to him personally in Palermo, he'd be honored to give the vines to the Royal Lion to grow at the Casa de Leone," insisted Antonio. Dr. Pietro showed his disbelief at such an incredible offer by pursing his lips and pulling down at the corners of his mouth. Marco's eyes danced with delight and nodded happily along with his nephew.

Watching the farce, Dolcetto grew sickened that Marco should be approached in the manner of a child, teased and coaxed into doing something he was adamantly against. When he'd taken as much as he could, he slammed down the alabaster egg and shouted loudly, *"Basta!* Antonio. God-father. Marco will not be coerced into doing something he doesn't want to do. Enough of this fiasco. Papa will make up his own mind. I thank you both anyway." He turned to Marco. "I'm going riding for an hour or so."

Marco walked to his son's side. For several moments his love-filled eyes were locked with the emerald green eyes of his sympathetic son. He embraced him, put a restraining hand on Dolcetto's arm, and indicated he wanted him to follow. At his desk, Marco sat down and wrote notes on large sheets of paper.

From across the room, Antonio and the physician exchanged awkward glances. They felt like schoolboys caught cheating on an examination. They wondered what Marco was up to.

When he finished he handed the first note to his son. Dolcetto read:

> *The aging old Lion still has his wits about him. I knew what they were up to. The lonely Lion has little amusement these days. I thank you for your honesty.*

Dolcetto smiled and felt a warm tenderness in his heart. He tore up the note and threw it into the basket under the desk. Marco handed him the second note that asked, *What is the security at the Vanzini Villa?* For a brief moment, Dolcetto looked intently at his father, then on impulse he crossed the room to a chest containing his briefcase. He removed a set of plans and returned to his father's side. Marco put on his horn-rimmed glasses as Dolcetto spread the plans out before him. His expert eyes scanned the layout and the scale drawings that included a contour map with elevations. Curious, Antonio and Dr. Pietro gravitated toward the desk and looked down over Marco's shoulder.

"These are the surrounding groves of olive trees," said Dolcetto as he pointed to an area west of the villa. "To the north, behind the floral courtyard, is a sheer drop of nearly four hundred feet to the sea. All is solid rock and deep ravines for two kilometers at either side of its outer perimeter."

Dolcetto went on to explain the intricate set of alarms, installed by the late Signore Vanzini, recently renovated. "Caesar's legions used these underground passageways when they fought on Sicilian soil," he told his interested listeners. "The slaves used them as escape routes leading to and from the surrounding villages. Isn't it remarkable how they engineered such complicated systems in those days?" he marveled.

Dolcetto hadn't planned to reveal these plans to anyone but Marco. Francesca told him how important it was that no one knew of these tunnels and alarm systems. He wanted to abide by her wishes. No doubt existed in his mind that Antonio or his Godfather could be anything but allies, but he couldn't deny the inborn instinct of using extreme caution. He stopped abruptly when he saw the unusual interest demonstrated by his Godfather.

Marco handed his son another sheet of paper that relieved him immensely. He read:

I'll give you my answer later. Now leave me. I'm going riding for an hour by myself. I'll see you all at dinner.

"*Va biene*, Papa." He turned to his Godfather. "I'll see you later. Antonio and I have a few things to attend to. Will you stay for dinner?"

"No, I'll stay for a few minutes with Marco. I must get back to Messina shortly."

The two older men were alone.

"You want to play *monopolia* before I leave?"

Marco shook his head. He was preoccupied.

"Chess then?"

He shook his head again. Marco pointed to the wine decanter.

"*Grazie*, no, *compare*. I've had enough. *Aloura*, I'll be leaving. I'll see you in three days as usual?"

Marco rolled up the set of plans and nodded. He handed them to the physician with an attached note. Alberto took them and read the note: "*Take these to il tipographo in Messina and have a set made for me. Understand?*" Alberto glanced sharply at Marco, watched him raise the tip of his index finger to his lips.

"Don't worry, I shall be discreet. No one will know except you and I."

Marco strode out the door, across the cobblestones to the stables, where he waited for the young lad to saddle up Rajah, the young spirited stallion sired by Sultano and

Antonio's black mare. The horse was a strikingly beautiful white Arabian with four black socks and a black and white arched tail. He had flaring pink nostrils and two coal-black eyes. Marco offered a few bits of hardened sugar in the palm of his hand and the stallion devoured them instantly. He smiled as he recalled the intense desire with which Ali Kahn and his entourage had eyed the horse a few weeks before, when they came to the villa to buy some of Marco's Arabian studs. Nothing would have enticed him to sell this animal. He was bright and frisky and displayed almost human intelligence.

He mounted Rajah and quickly they rode out into the open fields. For nearly ten minutes, he gave the stallion his head and they traveled at a full gallop until they were both breathless. In the distance were the two familiar figures who rode with him wherever he went. Calo la Bolla and Ciccio Pontiface were a little older, perhaps not as alert, but they were ever faithful.

Marco inhaled the fresh, sweet air of the glowing countryside. He sat back in his saddle and thought about his son. He loved Dolcetto with such passion it overwhelmed him at times. He couldn't have asked for a more wonderful son. Now he was at the point where he might have to disappoint him and he didn't want to stand in the way of the only real request Dolcetto had ever made.

The wedding at Porto Tomasso had to be thought out carefully. The long years of insufferable animosities and vendettas between the *mafia* and the House of de Leone had taught him one thing—not to provoke encounters. On occasion it had been necessary to reprimand his son for flaunting his fearlessness and hatred for the *mafiosi*. Dolcetto took too many chances. Either the *mafiosi* had grown softer since their twenty-year hiatus or else a guardian angel stood watch over Dolcetto. It was a miracle he hadn't been assaulted before this.

To go to Palermo in the heart of the *mafia* territory and gather the de Leone family under one roof was to invite trouble. But no matter how much he resisted or how foreboding his thoughts about attending the wedding might be Marco knew that ultimately he'd go despite his better judgment. He sighed deeply and sat motionless for several moments, staring at nothing in particular.

Marco could almost hear the sounds of artillery fire, smell the gunpowder as if it were yesterday when World War II brought life and death to the *latifondo*. He had stood in this very spot viewing the battle on the plains below like a

359

commanding general, when the British and Canadian Allies drove back the aggressive Germans and reluctant Italians. He recalled the terrible fatigue and pain of the men who lay swollen in the sun, their guts spilled out over their decaying bodies. Bombs had burst violently throughout the once fertile lands like miniature volcanos, leaving ruptures and craters in their wake. The war marked the decline of the *latifondo*.

The land would never be the same again. Soon this civilization would join their ancestors buried deep below the *Terra d'Oro*. Marco couldn't find it in his heart to forgive the shortsightedness of the Allies for reinstating the *mafia* after the war. With the resurgence of their power, the island reverted back to its former terrors, as if the twenty-year peace had been only a dream.

Mariolina had been right when she predicted there was no real hope for Sicily. The glorious days of the *latifondo* were no more!

Along with the other *latifondisti*, Marco had been forced to plant an excess of wheat. Although he protested, explaining to the Department of Agronomy the hazards involved in the continuous growth of wheat, it did no good. In a war, during a national state of emergency, one had to follow orders. All of Roberto's efforts in soil conservation and crop rotation had been lost. The land would soon render itself barren. By government requisition, cattle and sheep had been slaughtered to feed the armies of Hitler and Mussolini. Lacking in natural fertilizers and no longer enriched by chemicals, the land became unyielding. Goats replaced cattle and did even more damage. His stable of prized Arabians had been confiscated by the government and shipped north to the cavalry.

Devastating bombs scarred the earth, wiped out entire villages, and destroyed cities. The peasants, helpless and distraught, left the land for the city to try and eke out an existence. The young men of Sicily, reluctant to fight for Italy and ideals they didn't believe in, had been conscripted and very few returned. Those who did, fled to the cities to try their hands at construction or factory work.

For the first time in his life, Marco felt his hands were tied. The war left uglier scars on the land than it did on the people. The slow, tedious rebuilding of the *latifondo* never totally took hold. Now international oil companies, having bid on the lands, began to erect their pumps. Marco's world had taken on new proportions. It was no longer a land for stout-hearted lions. It was moving too fast.

360

Marco pulled up on the reins, interrupting Rajah's contented grazing. *Enough of this reverie,* he thought. *I'll return to the villa and make plans for the future. Yesterday is dead. Memories of the past should be buried with it.*

As he cantered back to the villa, something nagged at him but it wasn't until he dismounted and turned his horse over to the stable boy that his thoughts jelled. Earlier when he examined the blueprints of the Vanzini Villa, his eagle eyes had searched for some point of vulnerability. In his superficial examination he'd found none. *It's easy to overlook unfamiliar detail. If there's a weak spot, I'll find it.*

For the Vanzini family to have been murdered, something had to malfunction. With such an intricate system of signal and detection devices, how could such a violent act have been possible?

By the time he entered the villa, Marco had made a mental list of requisites. He would take four of his own trusted bodyguards and his personal servants. Calo and Ciccio had long since been put out to pasture. They'd grown old with the Royal Lion and lost their prowess with *luparas* and other weapons. Calo wore thick glasses as a result of the removal of cataracts. Ciccio, a victim of diabetes, had only recently been afforded the use of insulin. But their loyalty to Marco was undiminished, so when it was agreed they would accompany Marco to Porto Tomasso, they were delighted. They wouldn't have felt right letting the Royal Lion go anyplace without them, especially out of Lion country.

Across the island in his office in Monreale, Don Barbarossa opened a package and studied its contents. He smiled, marveling at the genius of the man.

A slip of paper contained a date and location in code. Decoded it read: *October 15—Vanzini Villa.* A complete set of plans and a reproduction of the alarms and underground tunnels, identical to those Dolcetto had given his father, were included.

Don Barbarossa studied the plans carefully for several hours before calling in the only expert qualified to do the job effectively; the only man with enough hatred in his soul to insure no slip-ups; the only man with enough vengeance in his heart to guarantee the death of the Royal Lions— Mario Cacciatore. He'd grown older, but he could still do the job better than any ten *sicarios,* hired killers, combined.

Before the Don had time to summon him, Cacciatore arrived at the villa with news of his own.

"The di Lucca brothers have just observed Paolo Nicosia with two American narcotics agents," he said breathlessly.

"So? What does it mean? Nicosia won't talk. And even if he does, who'll believe a crazy man?"

"They saw him accept money."

"Why would they give him money? They don't work like that? Were the di Luccas drinking?" Cacciatore shook his head. "How did the di Luccas know they were American agents?"

"I didn't ask."

"Then ask. I'm not concerned that Nicosia might talk, only that two American agents—if they are agents—know we use the *Arcturus* in our work." The Don frowned. "So! We've been observed!"

"Shall I bring Nicosia to you?"

"No. First check out the story. Find out who the men are, *if* they are narcotics agents and *if* they asked leading questions. Meanwhile we change our routine. Nicosia can be of no further use to us."

"You mean . . ."

"Yes. If the story checks, dispose of Nicosia."

The order came as a shock to Cacciatore because he thought a strong camaraderie existed between the old seaman and the *capomafia*. He never thought he'd hear such an order. Noting the expression on his face, the Don asked, "What's wrong?"

"Nothing. Nothing at all. What could be wrong?"

"*Va biene. Aloura.* Come here and look at this. I finally have for you the biggest job in your career, Cacciatore. I want you to handle this one personally."

The two men bent over the maps and began preliminary preparations for their night of triumph.

"You must find some weak link at the Vanzini Villa, Mario. There's not much time. Only three weeks till October 15."

Cacciatore's eyes lit up like a rat's eyes in the night.

34

Shorty after V-E Day Don Matteo answered the telephone in his study in the Monreale villa. "Talk," he said in his usual terse manner.

"You know who I am?"

"I know who you are. What do you want?"

"It's me. Lucky, your cousin. Show some warmth, eh, *cuzino?*"

"*Si*, Don Salvatore . . ."

Luciano thought that the Don was as enthusiastic as a fucking dead whale. "Something wrong, Don Matteo?"

"Nothing that concerns you," said the Don, not ready to tip his hand. He was disturbed. Damned disturbed and it all concerned Lucky Luciano, whom he'd recently learned was cheating him out of substantial sums of money. This wasn't the time to discuss the problem. "Now, what do you want, eh?"

"A boat."

"A boat? Why come to me? You think I'm a boat builder, too?"

"Only you have the power to get *this* one."

"Only me?"

"Only you." Luciano dove right in. "There's a cruiser at anchor in Palermo harbor. The *Arcturus II*. Remember Genovese's cousin, Don Ciccio from New Jersey? He brought the ship here. Unfortunately, Don Ciccio had a—let us say— an accident. He died intestate. You know what that means here in the old country, eh? Only you can get the boat for me, *capeeshi*, Matteo? Listen, don't spare the costs. The boat is the fastest in the Mediterranean."

"Consider it done," said the Don. "And, Don Salvatore, we talk, soon, eh?"

Luciano got the picture. "*Si*, we talk. But, make sure you get the fucking boat. I never thought I'd see the day Luciano would go whoring for a damn boat!"

A quick call to *consigliori* Garibaldi in which the message and information was relayed started the ball rolling. "Get the *Arcturus II* at any cost!"

Garibaldi discussed the situation with his associates in the Department of Navigation and Maritime Traffic. Within the hour came this: "The *Arcturus II* is tied up in monumental red tape and unforeseen legalities. The probate courts and local stipendiary magistrates decided to dispose of the vessel at public auction. If only you had spoken up two weeks ago," came the reply.

"If only, nothing! My client wants that boat! My suggestion to you is to make sure he gets this *Arcturus II*."

Huddled meetings in secrecy, the passage of money into well-greased palms, and Primo Garibaldi's skillful manipulations converged into the following instructions to Don Barbarossa.

"We must accept the private auction. Let them post the required notices and the day of the auction we'll be the only ones there to bid on the boat. It's a simple formality and we'll get the ship for a mere pittance."

But—

The Mafia hadn't counted on the impassioned zeal that one very special man had developed for the *Arcturus II*. Several months before the courts ruled on the disposition of the boat, Paolo Nicosia piloted his decaying relic, the *Baccala*, through Palermo's harbor when he caught sight of the sleek American yacht. After bringing the fishing scow into port and disposing of his load of sardines, he lost little time in rowing out to where the *Arcturus* lay at anchor.

For this discerning seaman, it was love at first sight. He rowed around it studying its hull and sleek lines. Many times he called out to see if anyone was aboard. Soon he was enamored of the vessel. He began to make daily pilgrimages in awe and admiration. In all this time, he'd seen no one around. One day he secured his dinghy to the raised ladder and shimmied his way up the line and boarded the cruiser. Dismayed to find her in a sad state of neglect, he began by tidying her up a little here and there. He asked questions of the Master of Port Works. No one knew about this mystery ship. No licenses were posted and inquiries led to a dead end. The *Arcturus II* began to occupy his desires and dazzle his senses. In an outright adoption, the *Arcturus* became the woman Paolo Nicosia could never have, and he began to service this new mistress daily. For three months the love affair between Nicosia and the *Arcturus II* flourished. When he was finished, she was immaculate, her accessories shined mirror bright, leathers softened and polished, salt water damage repaired. On the day Paolo started up the motors and each roared with power, he felt an exultation which he likened to an orgasm. He brought out the wine and drank a toast.

She sliced through the waters in a way that left Nicosia breathless. God! Was he happy! Three months of total ecstasy with his new possession! Never mind that he didn't own it and hadn't the right to assume such intimacy with the boat. What could a piece of paper mean? No one loved the *Arcturus* as Paolo did. Otherwise, why would they have neglected her like a poor orphan?

One day, Nicosia arrived to find the *Arcturus II* gone. His heart stopped beating. He panicked. Where was it? Where had it gone? It couldn't have vanished into thin air! He rowed back to his *Baccala*, searching everywhere in the harbor. Depression, disillusionment, and anguish twisted his guts. On land he walked up and down the waterfront along the various docks and quays reserved for those boats that needed servicing. Suddenly, his heart quickened—he saw her. As fast as his legs could move, Nicosia ran to her side, out of breath and panting hard. When he saw the notice of public auction posted on her hull and saw she'd been sealed and padlocked, he cried aloud and shook his fist at unseen forces and at God, his old enemy who'd always showered him with disfavor.

"Not again! Not to Paolo Nicosia!" he stormed and ranted. "No! No!" he yelled. "This time you won't win!" His usually docile nature was fired with pure animal rage. Eyes black with perverse fierceness, he stalked off angrily. He'd had enough with this God, he told himself, as a plan formulated in his mind.

Back aboard the *Baccala,* below deck, Nicosia pried up a loose board from the ship's hold and removed a wooden chest containing his worldly possessions. *Managghia la miseria!"* he lamented when he took stock. For all his fifty years on earth all he had to show was a miserable one thousand dollars; just enough to buy him a first-class funeral and headstone when he died.

Dejected as gloom pervaded his being and filled him with unendurable agony, he paced the floor until suddenly an idea struck him. Of course, why hadn't he thought sooner? Guido Scarpino, the baker, would lend him the money to buy the *Arcturus II.* Never mind that the interest charges would amount to more than the principal. Besides, he'd sell the *Baccala* and since that was paid for, he could come up with enough, he felt certain.

"It's not that I won't lend you the money, old friend," said the rotund, belly-scratching baker with a red bulbous nose. His calculating fish eyes laughed gently at Nicosia's request. "I'm sure you are an honorable man who'd repay the obligation. But, *paesano,* be reasonable. Practical, at least, eh? If you caught all of them, there aren't enough fish in the sea to pay for this seaworthy craft. Think of the costs! In gasoline alone, she'll drain you, eat you alive! Listen, *paesano* take some well-meant advice. You aren't a young bull anymore. Before making such an investment, you must think carefully. With inflation and things still in turmoil, how do you dare invest in the folly of such a frivolous dream . . ." Scarpino's shrewish voice faded into nothingness as Nicosia walked out the bakery door more despondent and heartbroken than before.

The money-lending baker was right. *What a foolish dream! What a jackass I've been to ever think I could own the* Arcturus! *A piece of paper does matter in this material world where feelings mean nothing; where what's in a man's heart counts nothing; where only the contents of his purse is a measure to be considered. You won again, you blundering voice of the universe! You've beaten Paolo Nicosia once more!*

Despite the bright and clear dazzling Sicilian sun that lit

365

up the verdant hills and flowers of the Conca d'Oro and the blue-green sea in Palermo's harbor, black gloom pervaded Nicosia's world as he watched the group of *mafiosi* approach the *Arcturus II* in a self-assured group, like strutting peacocks. He couldn't recall when he'd felt so downcast and forlorn. A shifty-eyed, greasy looking weasel of a man, Strunti, the apparent auctioneer, walked like a bird in flight, moving his small, wiry body with synchronized movements as he neared the rickety old dock where the *Arcturus II* had been moored for sale. On the starboard side of the boat, he set up a collapsible stand, much like that of a musician's. When the auctioneer lost his footing, he fell backward against the cruiser and left angry scratches across the hull. Nicosia flew into a rage.

"What the hell's wrong with you, you stupid sonofabitch!" he yelled, shaking his fist at Strunti. "Look what you did to my boat!"

Drawing himself up a degree or two, Strunti looked upon Nicosia with cool disdain. "Who is this uncouth old goat?" he asked his deputy as he gathered up the stand and reset it into place.

The deputy, a paunchy Sicilian with a crew hair cut and a pock-marked face without expression, shrugged indifferently. Dressed in his immaculate royal blue uniform with bright shiny buttons and an official looking badge, he glanced at Nicosia as if he didn't exist and answered perfunctorily, "Who knows, eh? Listen. You'd best get on with it. I don't like the looks of this. Too many people are attracted to this sale. Take a look, Strunti."

Strunti's face filled with surprise when he noted curious groups of onlookers congregated behind the *mafiosi*. "You're right, we'd best hurry." He wiped the cold perspiration from his forehead as his shifty eyes scanned the cold, imperious faces of Don Barbarossa's men. "Pray everything goes as smooth as silk." He nodded at the deputy's signal for him to commence.

Nicosia saw the signal and was so absorbed in his misery that when he heard the falsetto voiced auctioneer ask, "What am I offered for this splendid boat, the *Arcturus II?*" the unexpected happened.

"One thousand dollars!" cried out Nicosia in a passionate, unthinking voice.

Strunti and the deputy stared in astonishment. First, one head, then the next, and the next, turned until every eye was on Paolo Nicosia. The cold, hard stares from the fish eyed men of respect pierced his heart like icicles. He froze like a statue. Even he had the grace to blush at his own daring.

The *mafiosi* fumed! Their anger stoked to high intensity. Who dared open the bid at such an outrageous figure? The bribes alone already amounted to ten thousand dollars! They were to have made only a token bid. How dared this prickless clown do this, they asked themselves! Who had brought this joke into the picture?

The *mafia* spokesman, a man of slight build, delicate features, a supercilious waxed mustache, and the look of a squint-eyed Arab with a long beaked nose indicated to Strunti, by the flick of an eyebrow, to up the bid by one lira. If that idiot didn't get the picture by then, he'd give the nod to dispose of him quickly. Before the highly agitated Strunti could effectively close the bid, another voice was heard loud and clear.

"Two thousand dollars!" called the tall, sun-bronzed, curly-haired young man with eyes of green fire. The scion of the unimpeachable de Leone family stood a few feet away observing the goings-on, studying the interplay between the confident *mafiosi* and the poor wretch, Paolo Nicosia. Standing next to Dolcetto de Leone, unaware of the identity of the young Lion, the fat, belly-scratching baker, Scarpino, who'd attended the auction out of curiosity, had unwittingly voiced Nicosia's plight to the exceedingly handsome young man.

"What chance does my poor fool of a friend have against these cunning *mafiosi*, eh? Ah, *povero chu chu!* Poor obsessed fool! I told him he was foolish! But, he never told me who was bidding against him. Had I known, I'd have taken stronger measures to convince him of his folly! How could this clown ever think he could own such a costly boat?" he had confided.

"*Andiamo,* Dolcetto," called Giorgio Bocca, the spiffy lawyer from Rome. As always impeccably dressed, he tugged impatiently at the Lion's sleeve. "*Andiamo!* What the hell do you want with a fifty-two-foot cruiser when you have an ocean filled with them?" He didn't like what he saw on the faces of the others.

"Who the hell is this man? Who dares oppose the *mafia? Managghia!* It takes balls to oppose these *schifosi,*" came the whisperings all around them.

Dolcetto, quite aware he'd caused momentary bedlam, ignored his lawyer's words and addressed himself to the auctioneer. "I'm waiting for you, Signore Strunti." His confidence was unmistakable.

"Signore," hissed the baker with dollar signs for a heart, "if you'll pardon an old man's intrusion, but, take my advice, do not make this matter yours. You must be a stranger not to recognize Don Barbarossa's men." He lowered his voice. "It's not wise to set yourself against them. Consider your life, signore." At that moment, Scarpino noticed the jeweled lion on a chain suspended from Dolcetto's neck. He studied his regal bearing and caught sight of the Lion's signet ring. His face flushed with the excitement of his detection. *Managghia!* Is it possible? *El Leone?* He moved back into the crowd and in moments the astute baker had spread the word, *"El Leone!"* A hush prevailed.

Flabbergasted, Strunti the auctioneer became a nervous wreck. His waxed mustache twitched nervously. He glanced with disgust at the deputy for whose benefit this entire fiasco had been staged, and saw with some perverse delight that the deputy, too, began to sweat. Swiping at a pesky fly that pestered him, and dabbing at the dampness on his face and neck, he nudged the auctioneer to commence.

"If there are no further bids . . ." stuttered Strunti apprehensively.

"Five thousand," countered the outraged *mafioso* bidder.

"Seventy-five hundred," said the cool, complacent lion.

The crowd glanced from one to the other. *Mafiosi* exchanged noncommittal glances, but, from the way their features jerked and their jaw muscles clenched and their teeth gritted against teeth, it was obvious they realized the cruiser was lost to them. A quick huddle brought negotiations to an abrupt halt. Lethal glances were cast at both auctioneer and deputy, promising future retributions; these two, agitated and prostrate in their misery, grew totally disorganized under the hostile scrutiny. What else could they have done? They couldn't have openly refused a bid by an independent bidder in a probate auction, especially when that bidder turned out to be one of the Royal Lions of Sicily!

The prospect of facing Don Barbarossa's wrath weighed heavily not only on the wretched officials, but the *mafiosi* themselves. Aloura, *hadn't the* capomafia *himself ordered them to back off in any confrontation with the family of Lions?*

"Vafangule!" muttered the five *mafiosi* under their breaths, walking in a body away from the dock. There was no sign on their marble faces of the outrage they felt toward Dolcetto de Leone.

"Please, signore, step forward with your letters of credit," managed Strunti when he recuperated from the disturbing turn of events.

"Avvocato Bocca of Roma will handle the arrangements with the new owner of this handsome vessel," replied

Dolcetto; walking toward the totally bewildered Paolo Nicosia, he asked gently, "How are you called, *pescatore?*"

Nicosia glanced suspiciously at this handsome, foreign-looking man, dressed in his white pants and coat-sweater which revealed a sunbronzed chest upon which glittered a jeweled lion. He was almost mesmerized by the sight of the amulet, but something tugged at his memory. Hazy and dim, something far away tried to pierce through the veil of darkness close to his eyes but nothing tangible surfaced to enlighten him further. He regarded Dolcetto wonderingly as one might a child when spoken to by a stranger.

"Are you talking at me?"

"*Si,* to you. What are you called? Your name—what is it?"

"Why?" asked the fisherman suspiciously. Behind the Lion he saw huddled in a group several of his old acquaintances with Scarpino at their center watching the goings-on in awestruck silence.

"Come," said Dolcetto gently. "We have to make arrangements for the boat you just bought."

"The boat—I—bought? . . . But, I bought no boat!" Confused, feverish eyes sparkled with a rising excitement. "*My* boat? Did I hear you call it—*my*—boat?"

"*Aloura,*" insisted the Lion. "Your name. We must have your name for the papers, the ownership papers!"

"Paolo Nicosia," he said in a dream state.

"*Aloura,* Nicosia, come along. You're the new owner of this seaworthy craft—uh—" He glanced up at the hull and read the name. "*Arcturus II!* Even the name holds magic! The brightest star in the heavens!"

Stupefaction flooded the seaman's face. The glittering lion bounced on the young man's chest as they walked toward Strunti's stand. *If only these cobwebs in my mind would clear,* he thought, as he tried with increasing difficulty to sift through the tangled fragments. *Why do I feel such a curious stirring in my stomach?* he asked himself. Nicosia's eyes lingered on the jeweled amulet, then raised them higher and fixed them on those eyes of green fire. He felt something again but when he tried to pierce that thick veil in his mind he came up with nothing. Only what the stranger had told him mattered. The *Arcturus II* belonged to Paolo Nicosia! Think of that! To Paolo Nicosia! *Praise God and damn the devil! Is it possible I was mistaken about God?*

"We made fools of those vipers, eh, *paesano?*" laughed Dolcetto and nudged the fisherman playfully.

"Yes, yes, we did," agreed Nicosia in gleeful wickedness, falling into Dolcetto's mood.

369

Only Giorgio Bocca didn't smile, didn't think the encounter laughable, and stern disapproval reflected in his eyes, instantly dissolving Dolcetto's grin. The lawyer beckoned to Nicosia.

"We need your signature on these papers, fisherman." He turned to the Lion. "Yours, too, Excellency."

Dolcetto glanced sharply at Bocca. Whenever the lawyer was irked with him he always addressed him as Excellency.

"Excellency?" muttered Nicosia incoherently. "Excellency?" Trembling noticeably with excitement, Nicosia grew visibly humble and bowed gratefully to his benefactor. He made a swift move toward Dolcetto's hand, kissing it with a profound mark of respect and reverence. *"Te baccio le mane,* Excellency. I kiss your hand."

"Now, now, there's no need for that," insisted the Lion. He flushed with embarrassment when his eyes caught the taunting eyes of his lawyer. He cleared his throat. "Just take good care of the *Arcturus II,"* he smiled. "One day, I might want to go for a nice long ride in this *vapore magnifico, va biene?* Now, go with God, *pescatore."* Dolcetto didn't know how prophetic those words would become.

Dolcetto broke away from Nicosia, signed where Bocca instructed him to sign, and told the lawyer, "I'll be in the car when you're through here."

Scarpino the baker moved in immediately to peer at the signature. "Ahhh! You see—what did I tell you? Dolcetto de Leone, son of *El Leone!* Look for yourselves," he told the illiterate hangers-on. "Didn't I tell you it was the Royal Lion?" He turned to Nicosia. "You have me to thank, *paesano.* If I hadn't told him of how passionately you wanted this boat . . ."

El Leone's son had bought this *Arcturus* for him! Imagine that! *Go with God,* the young Excellency had told him. *God bless you!* To him, Paolo Nicosia! There was such a swelling inside his heart he felt it would burst!

Avvocato Bocca thrust several papers into his hands, snapped shut his briefcase, nodded curtly to everyone, and walked briskly to where Dolcetto waited in his Ferrari Berlinetta sports car several yards away.

Driving to the airport, through the city of Palermo, Dolcetto burst out into unrestrained laughter. It was an easy, infectious laughter, one reflecting his pleasure at the outcome of the day. Once again he'd bested the *mafiosi.* Nothing pleased the Lion more. A glance at Giorgio told him the lawyer didn't share his enthusiasm and momentary joy.

"What's the matter? Why the long face, *amico?"*

"One day, *amico,* you'll go too far," said Giorgio ruefully.

"Did you see the looks on their faces? They are out for blood. Your blood, Dolcetto."

"*Va biene.* Let them. It did my heart good to shake them. It's small compensation for the gross injustices they've perpetrated."

"You're a fool, my friend. A fool!" Giorgio brooded inwardly. It did no good to warn Dolcetto. None at all.

"Did you see the sheer look of joy on the fisherman's face? Who the hell was he, anyway? It took nerve to contest those *schifosi.* Imagine that old scoundrel. What guts, eh? Something about him—you notice he acted odd?"

Giorgio Bocca wasn't about to be pushed off the subject. He had something to say and now was as good a time as any to tell Dolcetto what he really felt. He asserted himself above the roar of the powerful engine.

"You more than most men should know, Dolcetto, that you can rob a man, betray him, best him in any encounter and you might obtain his forgiveness, even his friendship. But, if you humiliate him, laugh at him, injure his pride, strip him of self-respect, he'll never forgive you and he'll remain forever a remorseless enemy," began Giorgio.

"*Basta! Basta,* Giorgio! Don't preach ethics or morals to me. Preach them to the *mafiosi!*" He was amused by Giorgio's dramatics.

"Listen, why the hell should I preach to them? You think I give a shit for those despicable, cheap imitators of real men? I care only what happens to you."

Touched by his friend's obvious concern, Dolcetto grinned impetuously. "Don't worry. Nothing will happen to me. Haven't you learned by now, I'm invincible?" He laughed again and gunned the supercharged 12-cylinder motor and the car shot ahead like a missile. The Lion donned his dark glasses to cut the sun's bright glare. For the remainder of the drive through Palermo to the airport they were silent. Giorgio Bocca grasped the handrail firmly when the speedometer registered over one hundred miles per hour, tried to hide his nervousness by concentrating on other things—like a possible funeral and whether or not his will was in order.

Airborne in Dolcetto's twin-engine Cessna shipped from the States, Giorgio continued. "There are other ways to defy the *mafiosi* instead of flagrantly crossing them in public as you do. Your father's way has been effective and certainly less perilous. Subtle ways of blocking pro-*mafia* legislation in the Parliament where it really counts, in politics and big business, where it hurts their bank accounts.

"Think, Dolcetto, one motivating force which superseded even that of acquiring riches, is their burning desire to obtain respect. They've murdered for it, stolen for it, turned brothers against brothers for it, committed every human and depraved act to acquire this illusive respect."

Dolcetto cast a sidelong glance at his counselor. *"Managghia*, you're hellbent on expiating yourself, today. Look how beautiful and serene everything looks from this height, how small and insignificant everything becomes from up here. No wonder God shuttles us around like toys, eh? Nothing looks real." Rome's airport loomed beyond the right wing. "We're almost there—"

"—and this is where you aim your well-thrown darts! Right at the point of their vulnerability. Fooling with a man's pride, especially that of a Sicilian, can very well mean retaliation of untold horrors, no matter how long it takes. I've read Marco's papers very carefully and one thing stood out, Dolcetto. Vendetta is one thing a Sicilian could wait a lifetime to exact."

"Trouble with you, Giorgio, like all lawyers—you worry too much. Listen," he said, changing the subject. "Find out more about this—uh—what was his name?"

"Who?"

"The fisherman."

"Nicosia?"

"Yes, Nicosia. I'd like to know how he gets along with the boat. Incidentally, it was a beauty! Wouldn't have minded having it myself."

Giorgio nodded glumly. "What's the use talking with you? You never listen. Why the fuck you need an *avvocato* is what puzzles me."

Dolcetto laughed his infectious, happy laughter, and began radioing for landing instructions as he circled the field.

Paolo Nicosia was like a child who'd been given Aladdin's lamp. All his life he believed with conviction he was one of those men who just didn't count in this world. Doomed at birth, he'd been born with a yoke around his neck; he'd lived by it, and would die because of it. Because he believed God had a personal vendetta against him, religion escaped him. He refused to pray, refrained from entering a church despite admonitions by Padre Bonaventura at the Villa de Leone and the many priests who came to him pleading that as one of God's children he should pay his respects to the Deity.

"How can I be one of God's children when He hasn't seen fit to equip me with a man-sized cock and balls so I could do a man-sized job on a woman, eh?" He had shaken his fist angrily at the priest one day and yelled, "You tell God to do his part, then by God, I'll pray! I'd kiss his feet!

Until then, don't expect Paolo Nicosia to pray to this bumbling architect who couldn't construct me properly! For all I know God must have been drunk the day he created me!"

Traumatized after his first attempt with a woman, he never tried again. Word of his fiasco was spread by the whore who laughed in his face, and he was subjected to the cruelest torment and ridicule by his associates.

Marco de Leone had this very fact in mind when, shortly before Dolcetto's baptism, he financed the former captain of the *Marchessa* in a business across the island, thinking he could make a fresh start. "You've too much to offer the world to be intimidated by this freak in nature. Somewhere there's the right woman for you, you'll see."

"Listen," he confided in his benefactor, "with what God did to me, Excellency, He could only have had in mind coupling with a two-year-old . . ."

Nicosia had found no such woman to ease the aches and pains in his groin. He bought the fishing scow *Baccala,* had little intercourse with his fellow men, and became a loner. Those few men who went to sea with him suspicioned he was a bit *pazzu*—daft. Loneliness, self-abasement, and the total annihilation of his ego forced him to create a make-believe world, less threatening to him than the real world. In this fantasy world, he could create people from all walks of life. He held conversations with them, dined with them, even fished with them. How easy it became for him to conjure up a two-sided conversation tailored to fit any mood. Even at card playing.

Often his performances were so skilled that his real companions, watching and listening to him talk with these imaginary characters, would wonder whether they were the blind, unhearing ones? His antics became more appreciated than a stage play.

"Listen, I wasn't always a fisherman! I, Paolo Nicosia, once captained the *Marchessa* for *El Leone!*" he'd tell his workers in rare moments of clarity.

They laughed at him and his absurdities, and such statements earned for him the title of "Paolo u' pazzu!" Paolo the crazy man! A real crazy fool! His reputation as an eccentric spread. *Paolo u' pazzu,* the crazy, impotent, harmless fool! On the other side of the coin, his expertise as a fisherman, navigator, and prince of the sea was unmatched. Coming from a long line of fishermen who navigated the seas around Sicily, there wasn't a cove, current, or wave Paolo didn't know personally. "Listen Boreas, you keep your northern breath away from my ship!" he called to the north wind in a squall. "And you, Zephyrus," he'd command the westerner in the Gulfo de Castellamare when the wind played havoc with the boats in the harbor, "Go home and make love to Vulturnus, and leave us poor fishermen to earn our living!"

An expert at celestial navigation at ten, he also knew instinctively where fish were plentiful and caught them with nets made by his own hands. Muscular, well-built, he stood about five feet ten inches, his warm, compassionate brown eyes showing little of the internal anguish he endured. His skin, tan and well-leathered, gave expression to his pacific nature. He looked ten years younger than his fifty years. When the anguish of his plight grew unendurable, ruby red wine, kept handy in a goatskin *botta*, helped anesthetize the pain. In a drunken stupor once he'd babbled of his impotency and the news spread.

Uneasy in his company, men would find themselves casting sidelong glances at him. *Managghia!* A man who's not a man? *Povero meskino!* Poor soul! A man without *fegato* is bad enough, but to be without *culjiones! Managghia.* Ah, *Paolo u' pazzu!* You are even less than a eunuch! Eunuchs at sometime or another experience manhood before castration! You, poor man, have experienced nothing!

Despite his sorrows, self-hatred, and failures as a man which he began to magnify out of proportion, Nicosia was a gentle, temperate, and loving man who should have been blessed with a family. What a good father he'd have made. God, that wicked power of all had seen fit to deny him this. Whore of the Devil! Other men had sired bastards! Nicosia hadn't sired an egg! Oh the shame of it all! But, he wasn't totally without guile. In his fantasy world, Nicosia had outsmarted God! He'd created for himself a son. Not a real son, but a Godson he'd always wanted. *What do you say to this, eh, God,* he'd say with a perverse wickedness at times. *I put one over on you!* His Godson had become Dolcetto de Leone. Amazing, wasn't it, every time he concentrated on a Godson, only one face would materialize, only one name, Dolcetto de Leone.

Nicosia had long forgotten any ties existed between the Royal Lion and himself, or that it was he who'd given the golden lion that Dolcetto wore around his neck constantly. Those memories, like most others, had been tucked away in some lost drawer of his subconscious mind, after being struck with a heavy block and tackle aboard the *Baccala*, two years after he bought the scow. The impact of the massive equipment sent him flying across the deck; his foot, caught in tackle lines, held him suspended in midair and his

374

head struck against the hull of the boat time and again in the winds of winter, until some of his men found him many hours later, unconscious and nearly dead.

In time he was able to return to his boat and eke out a living. Although he had difficulty sifting fact from fiction, his memory of the sea never left him, and his agility with a boat never diminished.

"I don't understand! You were given a simple task to perform, now you tell me someone else ended up with the cruiser!" Don Barbarossa's voice contained his rage. "If this is the civilized way, it is finished! From now on we do things Barbarossa's way!" He bit off the end of a cigar and rammed it savagely between his teeth. Garibaldi shifted awkwardly in his seat and leaned forward to light the Don's cigar. Ignoring it, the Don lit his own. The *consigliori* shrugged and fanned out the match.

"Incompetent boobs! What should have been a simple matter turned into a fiasco! A humiliating blunder of errors. I didn't attend the auction, assured all would go as planned. Who could have anticipated de Leone's presence?"

Watching this scene, Don Salvatore—Lucky Luciano—sat in a chair opposite the *capomafia* filled with marked annoyance. Gross stupidity is what it was. Nothing else! He glanced at his companions who'd made the trip to Monreale with him from Naples, trying to conceal his disgust. Luciano, a small, frail-looking man, maintained an unmistakable air of superiority about him, considering himself far above these old country Dons.

"A year ago, I brought this to your attention, Matteo, and it took all this time to bungle the job? It couldn't have happened in the States! We'd have hijacked it, changed the numbers, repainted the fucking ship, and put on new licenses in the time it took to sneeze!"

I should have known better than to get involved with these small-town losers, he told himself. *What the hell can I do! I'm stuck with them.*

"Matteo," he said, leaning back in his chair. "Look, you can't handle the stuff—forget it." His soft voice carried a distinct message to the *capomafia*. "See, I've got another boat lined up with the Ferrones in Naples. They keep bugging me to get in on the deal. They'll supply transportation both ways." When he saw the firming of Barbarossa's jaw, he added with a burst of temper, "It's your own goddamn fault! With more than a million bucks ready to roll these dumb goombahs stall for a few lousy thousand! Ain't they got no brains? I thought you had organization? These *stupidi* don't know shit from shoe polish!" His contempt for them was obvious.

Goddamn! I'd give one testicle to be back in the States, back in the saddle at the Waldorf! Fucking Dewey! Goddamn that ambitious prosecutor! Use me as bait to nab the presidency, eh? Bastard! Whether Lucky Luciano was happy or unhappy with his lot in life no longer mattered. That he'd always considered himself victimized in a corrupt political system no longer bothered him. He could control the whole fucking syndicate no matter where he parked his ass. Thrown out of Rome, asked to move from Florence, finding no vacancies available to him in Milan and with no desire to remain in Palermo, because he detested small-town politics and Dons who had the gall to think he'd muscle in on them—what a laugh—it was Naples that became his permanent address for a time. Shit! Back in the States he ate little men like these for breakfast! Chrissakes, the money they made in a year, Lucky tipped in a month.

One thing Lucky Luciano didn't know was that behind every eviction from each city, had been the silent shadow of Don Barbarossa's power, moving him wherever it suited his fancy. No one cheated Matteo Barbarossa and lived—unless it was at his sole discretion, a fact Luciano would one day discover.

With no apology in his voice, the *capomafia* selected his words judiciously and spoke with overt respect.

"Don Salvatore, I was assured the boat was ours. Not once, but nearly every day for the past month. All this came as a surprise. You leave it to me. We'll have the boat. I myself will attend to this matter, personally. You're painfully correct when you suggested that my men didn't impress the court with the proper offer."

"There's no other boat like her in these waters. I thought I made myself clear."

"You did. It was my orders that weren't clear, eh?" He glanced once again at Cacciatore and his aides with the proper amount of menace. "The *Arcturus* will be ours. Make no mistake . . . *Capeeshi?*"

"Who the hell are these Lions you speak of? They give *you* a bad time, Matteo? Don't you know how to handle them? You want I should take care of them?"

"You just make sure the merchandise is ready at the appointed hour. I'll take care of my end." The Don burned internally at the suggestion.

Luciano stood up, nodded to his men, and shook hands with his cousin. Earlier they had come to terms, terms the *capomafia* dictated. If Lucky wanted to prosper in his old country, he learned that outside the village in which he was born he'd have to march to the tempo set by Barbarossa. Take it or leave it! Even Vito Genovese had left Italy remarkably impressed with the power of Barbarossa. *"Aloura —in two days. Ni videmo."*

For the rest of the afternoon, Don Matteo saturated himself with the report on Paolo Nicosia, containing besides the usual facts compiled in such a report, the hearsay, and conjectures about the man called *Paolo u' pazzu.* He made his decision. On the afternoon of the next day, he would meet this man Nicosia.

Long after Dolcetto de Leone left the auction site, Nicosia pondered the events of the day with an older man's skepticism. He examined the papers, time and again and crying tears of joy, sat on the dock as if he'd never be done staring at this luxurious mistress, the *Arcturus II.*

Much later, when he felt certain it hadn't been a dream, he reexamined the bill of sale, then returned to the *Baccala* and put a for sale sign on it, packed his few meager belongings, and returned to the *Arcturus* to make it his home. Oh joy of joys!

What happiness! Now, there was no mistake the boat belonged to him. Didn't he have the paper to prove it? The young excellency was right. This *Arcturus* was the brightest star to ever shine on Paolo's horizon. That night he celebrated his good fortune by getting stinking drunk. He tried to forget the auctioneer's parting remark: "Listen, Nicosia, *pescatore,* I wouldn't give a counterfeit coin for your life and what might happen to you. The *mafiosi* are still to be reckoned with. You can believe me!"

Nicosia made an obscene gesture as he engaged in his fanciful imaginings.

35

It was hot. Palermo sweltered under the scorching sun despite the spurts of ocean breeze. Adjusting his dark glasses into place, Don Matteo Barbarossa sat stiffly in the aft position of the flat-bottomed rowboat transporting his *consigliero,* Cacciatore, and himself out to the *Arcturus II.* It wasn't difficult to locate the American sea craft for even among the colorful profusion of vintage vessels surrounding her, she stood out like a sleek white snowbird in a green sea.

They saw a well-muscled man, stripped to the waist, suspended on a pulley, with a thick line coiled about his middle, hanging rakishly over the starboard side of the vessel, sanding out a few scratches. Nicosia was singing happily as he worked.

"Ahoy!" called the oarsman. "Hola, Nicosia! You have company!"

Nicosia heard the voice call to him and turning in the direction of the sound, his ready smile disintegrated. Unmistakable gray fedoras, thick brown cigars, and those sunglasses they wore chilled him; almost as if they took on an evil life of their own and compounded the evil in the men behind those dark lenses. Nicosia pulled himself up on the line, swung over the bow onto the deck. There were bound to be reprisals. The auctioneer warned him. *You can't begin to know the mess you're in, pescatore. Those* mafiosi *wanted the boat!* His words left little to be imagined. He watched the trio board the cruiser with mixed feelings.

"*Buon giorno, pescatore,*" called Don Barbarossa amiably. "*Managghia!* This is some boat! You think we could examine it without too many complications to you? With your permission, of course," he added with just the right amount of propriety.

"Do you know me?" asked the Don, removing his fedora and wiping his face free of sweat, then swiping at the hat band. He left the hat off.

"I don't know you."

"I am Don Matteo Barbarossa."

"*Piacere,* Signore Barbarossa," he said unimpressed. "I am Paolo Nicosia."

The Don smiled internally and introduced the others with cordiality.

Nicosia nodded. He did not extend his hand. He had no opinion of Garibaldi, disliked Cacciatore on sight, and hadn't made up his mind about this man who talked to him like a man ready to pluck another's feathers. He wanted something.

"I never seen the likes of such a ship," said Garibaldi appreciatively.

Nicosia nodded. The three men assessed the cruiser and found it even more appealing than had been rumored. The Don's eyes telegraphed a message that instilled an uncomfortable feeling in his companions. Cacciatore, retiring to a corner of the aft deck like a cornered rat that sees and hears everything in a world of hatred and hating, sulked visibly.

Nicosia walked inside the cabin and from a galley cupboard he removed a wine bottle and four glasses, and setting them down on a fold-down table, he poured the wine.

378

"Chienti anni," toasted the Don.

"Chienti anni a lei." Nicosia drank with the others.

Don Barbarossa, who trusted no man, encountered few men whom he liked, found Nicosia refreshing, and approved of his manners. For nearly two hours he engaged Nicosia in conversation and the seaman kept them entertained with his seafaring tales. In this time the Don evaluated Nicosia. *This is no common fisherman,* he told himself. A mark of gentility was indelibly stamped upon him. Three centuries of seamanship were in Nicosia's blood and bones, and the Don was certain he was a seaman of worth.

"Listen, fisherman, you've told me you are the finest navigator on the Mediterranean, and I believe you," began the Don. "I've heard tell among many seamen that there's no one like Paolo Nicosia. Now, I wish to see with my own eyes that Paolo Nicosia is first-class. Perhaps without too many complications you could take us for a little ride in this ship?"

Who could refuse such a request? Certainly not Nicosia, who was both flattered and delighted. Perhaps these *mafiosi* were not as bad as they were stamped, eh, he asked himself, never knowing he played host to the once dreaded Mazzarino bandit, the *capo de tutti capi.*

With the agility of a youth, Nicosia weighed anchor and moved behind the helm. Both engines purred smoothly as he nosed the *Arcturus II* past the scenic harbor, out onto the calm, sapphire-blue sea. The boat sliced through the water like a thread through butter under Nicosia's proficient guiding hand.

Nicosia himself took on a different pose behind the helm. He looked a pillar of strength on the sea, poised, self-assured, and knowledgeable. The Don was struck by his professionalism. Later when he pointed out the various landmarks, he pointed to one in particular, an impressive structure on the crest of a mountain of stone. It was a grand palace that appeared to have been carved from the mountain itself.

"That's the Vanzini Villa," shouted Paolo over the roar of the engines. "A beacon to sailors at sea for centuries, during stormy weather they light the tower . . . there in Porto Tomasso—a little to the left of the cliff . . ."

Don Barbarossa's twofold mission was half over. Satisfied that Nicosia was an expert seaman, he set about to examine the second half of his plan. At sea for approximately forty minutes, Nicosia suddenly glanced at his fuel gauge.

"With your permission, Don Barbarossa, we must return to port."

Don Barbarossa reluctantly tore his eyes from the magnificent panorama. Porto Tomasso, with its craggy inclined village built on a high peak of layered color strata of flaming crimsons, oranges, and burnt umbers against celestial skies, had commanded his attention for the better part of many long minutes. He looked questioningly at the uneasy skipper.

Embarrassed, Nicosia explained his dilemma and in so doing gave the Don the lead he had wanted.

"Gas is very expensive and I must be prudent with its use," he said, scanning the fuel gauge again. Paolo hadn't had time to consider all the costs involved in keeping up this mistress as Scarpino the baker had intimated the other day. To be disgraced now, before strangers, deepened his embarrassment.

"Don't concern yourself, I can supply you with all the fuel you need," said the Don with a glint of triumph in his eyes.

"I must be cautious with the little money I have."

"Yet you bought so expensive a boat?"

"Buy it?" Nicosia laughed. "Me buy this ship? *Annunca*— I didn't have enough money to negotiate the mooring lines!" He relaxed some. "My Godson bought this for me, as a gift."

"Your Godson?" The Don spun about and glanced questioningly toward Cacciatore and his *consigliori*. Both men moved in closer with puzzled eyes.

Che demonio? What devil's game was this? Nicosia, Godfather to the Lion? What madness is this?

"Just who is this Godson who thrusts such an expensive hardship on you, then walks away, leaving you burdened with upkeep, repairs, and what it takes to preserve it, eh?" His marked benevolence was spiked with bold innuendo and guile.

Confused by the way in which the Don twisted the facts, he tried to sift through those words. Never once did his eyes leave the instrument panel. He couldn't answer. He didn't know what to say.

"Who is this Godson, eh?" he prodded.

The skipper tried to clear the sudden confusion in his mind. He couldn't think. In desperation, he pulled open a drawer at one side of the helm, shuffled through papers, located the bill of sale and pointed to the signature affixed to the document and said, "De Leone."

"Who?" shouted the Don.

"De Leone! Dolcetto de Leone! Here, see for yourself!" The *mafiosi* were baffled. Cacciatore shrugged in an I told you so manner and twirled his forefinger in a rapid circular movement next to his temple and mouthed the words *Paolo u' pazzu!*

Don Matteo scowled and averted his head. "So! de Leone is your Godson, eh, Nicosia?"

The seaman nodded.

"Ahhhhh. You baptized him?"

Nicosia took a moment to glance at the Don. Images rushed at him. A baptism, years ago at the Villa de Leone. A jeweled, golden lion . . . a sleek boat . . . the *Marchessa?* The fleeting images departed. "No," he replied.

"No? Ah, then you confirmed him?"

Paolo frowned in thought. He shook his head.

"Then how? How is the son of the Royal Lion your Godson?"

Once again images of a jeweled lion entered his consciousness, but puzzled by both the questions and the images, Nicosia again remained silent. His concentration was fixed on bringing the boat into the harbor. He began to ease up on the throttle.

Persistent as ever, the Don repeated, "How long, Nicosia?"

Paolo dropped anchor and turned off the engines. "Since yesterday."

The Don nearly choked on his cigar. He coughed and sputtered and finally managed to clear the smoke from his lungs.

Garibaldi moved in close to the Don and muttered, "We're wasting time here. He's a senile old dolt. Perhaps I can register a complaint with the Bureau of Licenses and . . ."

The Don said, "We do it my way."

The *consiglioro* shrugged. *The Don must have something in mind.*

"We'll be finished with our business soon enough. Be patient," he told his men. He rammed his cigar back between his teeth and walked out on deck. Sitting in a deck chair in the shade, he smoked in silence and decided that the man really did live in a fantasy world. *What a pity! Such a sad fate to be handed any man. To live a life without ever tasting the joys of a woman?* He wondered how he'd fare under such an irrevocable life sentence.

"Please take another glass of wine with me, signore," said Nicosia, handing him a full tumbler.

The Don thanked him. "Tell me, did your Godson provide you with funds to keep this craft in condition? You know, for the petrol, upkeep, license . . ." The Don used his hands constantly for emphasis. He sipped the wine.

"Isn't it enough he bought the boat for me?"

"It was you who pointed out she has some big appetite, no?"

"Phew! What an appetite!" agreed Nicosia.

The Don's repetitious suggestions were solely to be sure that Nicosia got the point. He continued to magnify the liabilities in the ownership of such a seaworthy craft, and as he talked he could see the fisherman's troubled eyes travel slowly over the plush accessories, fine-grained leather work and upholstery, blended walnut interiors polished to a glossy finish, ornate brass appointments and late model equipment; all a billionaire's plaything. With dismay, Nicosia said, "How could I have been so foolish to think I could care for such a costly boat? Without money to support her the *Arcturus II* will be reduced to less than a seafaring whore."

"Certainly you wouldn't fish in this boat as you did the *Baccala*?"

"No . . . Are you crazy? Fish in the *Arcturus II?*" Suddenly Nicosia realized. "How will I earn my living?" The insecurity of old returned to plague him. He felt more impotent than ever.

"Now, what do I do? Damn that de Leone! Why didn't he mind his own business? I'd have gotten over losing the *Arcturus*. I'm used to disappointments. What would another have mattered?" he said bitterly.

"Listen, fisherman, you think we can help each other?"

Nicosia turned to him. "What are you saying?"

"My business is to travel to the nearby islands once or twice a week," he began slowly. "For this special service, I am prepared to pay well . . ."

"Yes . . . yes . . ."

The Don outlined his plans, explained that his compensation would more than care for the boat, supply it with necessary repairs, pay for insurance and other expenses. "Besides, I'll pay you a salary. Not much, but enough to keep you in good food and *vino* . . ."

Nicosia fell to his knees and kissed the Don's hand out of gratitude.

"Get up, Nicosia," said the Don flatly, after casting triumphant glances to his companions. "Between us is purely a business arrangement. You mind your business and discuss ours with no one. Show me your loyalty and I, as your *capo*, will see you have no worries about the *lira . . . Va biene?*"

To Nicosia, this left no question but that God had decided to favor him once more. Excited and filled with optimism and a youthful naiveté, the seaman blurted, "You'll never have to worry about Nicosia, Excellency! As of this day I pledge my life to you!"

382

Nicosia would have kept a pact with the devil for the privilege of keeping the *Arcturus II*. Trouble was, he didn't know he had done just that.

Cacciatore watched the goings-on with mixed feelings. He'd have preferred killing Nicosia and confiscating the boat rather than going through such time-consuming discussions. Garibaldi, on the other hand, was clever enough to see the Don's strategy. Killing off Nicosia would have brought on the wrath of Dolcetto de Leone, and they'd have been subjected to a full-scale investigation. No doubt a suspension of the narcotics traffic would have followed, just when profits were high. But there was something even more ingenious in all the Don's crafty plans, something which filled him with more satisfaction than he'd felt in years.

Whether the Lion realized it or not, in buying the *Arcturus II* for Nicosia, he had done the *mafia* a tremendous service. Who would question the activities of a boat bought with de Leone money? Let Nicosia rant and rave about being Godfather to the Lion. Who'd dare question the Godfather of the son of the Royal Lion of Italy? Don Barbarossa chuckled to himself; it hadn't taken *him* long to ascertain that no real bond existed between Nicosia and his fantasized Godson. The man was fanciful all right.

Finished with his business, the Don prepared to leave.

"You're a smart man, Nicosia. We'll be in touch with you soon. Whatever you need in the way of supplies or food, get them at this *negozio*." He handed Nicosia a card which read: Tedesco's Marine Supplies. "Charge them to my account and tell Tedesco to call me. *Va biene?*"

The Don left the *Arcturus II* followed by a dour-faced Cacciatore and a pleased *consigliori* who later congratulated his Don for such shrewd thinking. "You got the boat, a fine skipper, and a perfect veil of protection."

Thus *Paolo u' Pazzu* became involved in *mafia* business. Exactly what the business was didn't interest the simple man. As long as he could keep his costly mistress in the custom she demanded, and keep himself supplied with the precious wine that anesthetized him in moments of quiet desperation, he could ask no more from life.

Ten years of his life passed swiftly and rather uneventfully, and during those years, he minded his own business and took orders.

When Cacciatore arrived at the Don's villa three weeks before the wedding and reported that the di Lucca brothers had seen the American agents with Paolo Nicosia, he'd been correct. Only that morning Nicosia and Don Barbarossa had returned from Corsica with a cargo of refined heroin. An hour after the cargo had been removed and the Don had departed, Nicosia began to scrub down the decks as he always did after a voyage. He'd been surprised by a visit by Hank Rossi and Danny Moreno.

"Captain Nicosia?" called Danny Moreno from a motorboat bobbing up and down in the water. "May we come aboard? We wish to speak with you about an important matter." They flashed their I.D.s and international permits.

"You must have the wrong man. I know of no important matters."

"It's you we wish to speak with," said Moreno, climbing aboard. "Where can we talk?"

"No place. I know nothing. Now stop bothering me. I have work to do that can't wait."

"You don't understand, old man," said Moreno, baffled by his rudeness and lack of respect. No one ignored them like this. No one in his right mind. "You're in deep trouble. Either you talk to us or to the *Questura*. Take your choice."

The scrub brush in the seaman's hand fell to the deck. He stood erect and frowned. "I don't understand. What is it you want of me?"

"Get your log. We wish to inspect it. You do keep one, don't you?"

"That's all you want?" He breathed easier. "*Managghia!* You scare a man half to death and that's all you want. My log."

"Get it, please."

"Now you stay on deck. I don't want any trouble." He patted the gun at his hip. "I can use this if necessary," he cautioned them.

"You're in enough trouble to last you a lifetime, *paesano*."

Glancing at them sharply, Nicosia said, "What do either of you know of trouble?" He walked into the cabin and returned in moments with the ship's log.

"Are you on anyone's payroll?" asked Moreno while Rossi studied the log.

"I don't understand you." Nicosia felt strange with these men.

"How do you earn your money?"

"I have a charter boat. I hire it out to anyone who wants one and can pay."

"Who's your best customer?"

Nicosia shrugged. "Many people. What do I know?"

"With whom do you do the most business?"

"Whoever needs a boat." The seaman scratched his head, eyeing the deck.

Rossi shoved the log at his partner. His voice was stern, full of reproof. "Let's stop the child's play, old man. We know you work for Don Barbarossa. There's no use denying it. Now let's have some straight answers."

"I've done nothing wrong."

"Do you wish us to impound your boat? We'd like to avoid such action, but your lack of cooperation leaves us no alternative."

"What is *to impound*? I don't understand. You want to take Nicosia's boat? Why?" He grew agitated.

"For transporting illicit narcotics to and from Corsica, Turkey, and Lebanon."

"I know nothing," insisted Paolo. "Nothing!"

"Look, we know you're a good man," began Moreno.

"Yes, yes! I'm a good man. I never hurt anyone, not even a fly. Just leave me in peace with my boat. That's all I ask."

Rossi grew impersonal. "It's all in the log. All the evidence we need, documented by your own hand. But if you cooperate, we promise no harm shall come to you."

"*Tu si pazzu!* You're crazy, both of you!" *No harm shall come to me, hah! What do they know? They must be simpletons.* "I know nothing. My job is to take people where they want to go. I don't ask questions. What they do, what they don't do, is not my affair. Can't you understand?"

"All we want you to do is to tell us in advance when your boat is hired out."

"You're crazy! You hear? Crazy!" Nicosia's face turned purple in rage.

"All right, if you don't want to cooperate . . ."

"How can I tell you when I don't know myself?" Nicosia shook as his temper flared up. "I never know. Sometimes I get only ten minutes' notice."

"That would be sufficient."

Nicosia slapped his thigh in exasperation. "In those ten minutes, I have more important things to do than run errands for you." He glanced about the boat and grew uneasy. He knew how many eyes the *mafiosi* had around him. Faster than the agents could collect their wits, Nicosia, in a moment of genuine clarity, pulled himself together and spoke coldly, with authority, in a manner emulating the *capomafioso*.

"Unless you have a warrant to arrest me, you will please leave my boat and give me peace. I mind my own business. It would be better if you did the same."

The American agents exchanged glances. In only moments, they had witnessed a complete personality change in the captain. They looked about the boat in every direction, wondering who, if anyone, had given Nicosia this sudden burst of courage. Rossi grew disturbed.

"Very well, captain. We shall authorize the *Questura* to issue a warrant. Then you'll testify under oath."

Nicosia finally understood. They wanted him to be an informer. *Maria Santissima! Nicosia an informer? My life would be worth nothing.* He spat into the brink and glared at them stubbornly. He wouldn't talk. Never!

"Do you know what heroin is?" asked Moreno.

"No."

"Do you know what it does to people? The agony it can bring through addiction?" Moreno explained in fuller detail.

"I know nothing," insisted Nicosia, his watery eyes growing more distant.

They got no place with him. Their investigation indicated Nicosia had been a loner, an industrious worker with no vices or criminal involvements; it was only after he acquired the *Arcturus II* that he'd come under the scrutiny of the *Questura* and later the *Guardia*, while they pursued leads in narcotic trafficking along with the American agents who had initiated the investigation.

Agents in the field, reporting frequent trips to Corsica by Don Barbarossa and Mario Cacciatore, whom they knew tied in with Lucky Luciano, were well aware of the cargo they carried. What they needed was someone on their side who could tell them in advance when the trips were planned so they could set up their phase of operations to get the suppliers or the top men, even the *fattoria* that converted the opium to heroin.

It was the same everywhere the agents went. No one gave a good goddamn! The average peasant couldn't begin to comprehend the problems heroin use presented. "It's not our problem. None of our people indulge," they'd say. "Why should we care?" The answers were always the same.

Appalled by Nicosia's sense of loyalty to the evil that permeated Sicily, Rossi reached into his pocket, pulled out a stack of liras, and presented them to Nicosia, "Thank you for your time, captain," he said.

The unsuspecting fisherman took the money. He'd never refuse money. He tipped his hat and shoved the bills into his pocket, thinking they weren't such a bad lot after all. The agents knew exactly what they were doing. And they were right. Not far from the *Arcturus II* on another smaller boat, the di Lucca brothers had been watching the scene through powerful binoculars. It would be only a matter of time before the Don received their report.

A week before the Vanzini-de Leone wedding, Mario Cacciatore paid another visit to the *Arcturus II* to talk with Nicosia.

"Purely a social visit," said the frog-eyed butcher benignly. "I should have taken more time to get better acquainted with you, Nicosia. But, a man with pressing duties has little time to socialize. You understand . . ." he said with a little *too* much respect, a little *too* much concern.

This change in Cacciatore's manner was terrifying to the seaman. His past behavior was cold and aloof. He'd treated Nicosia like an insignificant bug. Why should this viper suddenly pay him a call, social or otherwise? Mechanically, the seaman brought out the wine and a cold dish of *polpetti*. *Why does he make me feel like a cornered animal?*

"Perhaps on this night we can make up for lost time, eh, Nicosia?" He glanced about the boat, surprised at its mint condition, and when he caught sight of the array of newspaper clippings of Dolcetto de Leone which the seaman kept religiously, he shook his head with disgust. The simple old man still clung to his fantasy after all these years? He was a true loony.

"You're all alone in the world, eh, Nicosia?"

"More or less. I'm alone . . ."

"You don't have any friends?"

"Do you?" asked Paolo icily.

Cacciatore checked the impulse that rose in him. Time for that later. "Who do you talk to when you feel like chatting a bit?"

"No one. I have no friends," he said mockingly.

"I'll be your friend, old man," said Cacciatore, leaning forward a bit too eagerly. "Would you like that?"

In a pig's eye! Who does he think he's fooling? He treats me like a dim-witted child . . . Relax, Paolo. This bloodthirsty viper can kill you in cold blood and not be in the least concerned with conscience. My friends told me about this murdering devil. Beneath the table, he made the sign of *cornu*, his first and little finger thrust downward like horns.

"I have no need of friends," said Nicosia. "I have nothing to say."

Cacciatore picked his teeth and sucked on the particles of food lodged between them. "Isn't there something you want to talk about—to get off your chest?"

The seaman shook his head and sipped his wine.

"You have many visitors on the boat?"

"Here? On the boat? I have no visitors."

"Ingrate!" shouted the *sicario*. "Patience isn't my virtue.

I gave you every chance to tell me in your own words. I see by your stubborn silence, the di Luccas spoke the truth."

"The di Lucca brothers? What are you saying? I don't understand."

"You deny you were seen accepting money from two American narcotics agents several days ago? Don't deny it, Nicosia. You were observed." He slapped his hand down hard on the table. "I'm not sure why Don Matteo wanted me to talk with you. If it was up to me, you'd be face down with your head blown off!"

Nicosia paled and swallowed. "You will relate to Don Matteo that Nicosia has said and done nothing. I am *no* informer. The Don *knows* I'm loyal only to him." He shook under the scrutiny of Cacciatore's accusing eyes and slowly what little courage he had left began disintegrating.

"It would have paid to have shown your loyalty before this," said Cacciatore indicating the news clipping of Dolcetto de Leone. "One can't be a slave to two masters."

"And if one chooses not to be a slave at all?" countered Nicosia in a rare moment of clarity.

Cacciatore slipped the toothpick into his vest pocket, sipped the remains of his wine, and affected a pose much like that of the Don filled with benevolence.

"Ah, Paolo . . . Paolo . . . Paolo . . . You did choose. When you took the job offered by the Don, you became his property, body and soul. He will do with you as he wishes!" He rose to his feet.

Nicosia rose to his feet as a shudder passed through his body. And when the vile frog leaned in to kiss him, he couldn't recall when such cold terror gripped his heart. "Why do you give me *la baccia de morte*? The kiss of death? You don't believe Nicosia!" It took all his courage to speak.

"Listen, what I believe is of no importance, whether you speak the truth or not. What you told the agents is of no consequence. What concerns the *capo* is that your movements have been observed. *Capeeshi?*" Cacciatore grew impatient. *"Aloura, pescatore,"* continued the frog. "I have no quarrel with you. My orders were to investigate the report. If you'd made my job easier with the truth——? Well, no matter. Your lack of cooperation means one thing. But since I've taken a liking to you, its only right I should tell you your existence threatens our organization."

Nicosia couldn't believe the man's words. What had he ever done except keep his mouth closed? He'd given those 'Mericanos nothing! No aid at all. This is the thanks he got in return?

"There's nothing I can do, old man. Accept it." He bit off

388

the end of a cigar and rolled it over his tongue and lips while striking a match on the galley stove; it flared brilliantly as he lit it. His cold, cruel eyes remained impersonal, as if Nicosia didn't exist.

The veins of Nicosia's throat and temples throbbed. To be told so calmly he was going to die angered him. *Why didn't the bastard do it and get it over with instead of dawdling?* His anger gave rise to new courage.

"Schifoso!" spat Nicosia. *"Fittuso!* You think I'm afraid of the *birbante* who hides behind dark glasses? Or you?" He spat at the man in his contempt.

Cacciatore's iceberg eyes narrowed to slits. Slowly he wiped the spittle from his face. "Poor beggar! Poor excuse of a man! You just signed your death warrant and no one shall mourn at your grave. You hear? No one!" The *mafia* butcher left the *Arcturus* in a blind rage, both at this castrated fool and at his *capo* for not giving him license to erase Nicosia from the earth.

Nicosia sprang forward at the sound of the motor launch taking Cacciatore back to shore. He bolted the cabin door, doused the lights, searched the area for all the firearms he could locate. Four guns, most of which malfunctioned or had rusted, were all he had. Wiping the sweat from his face and neck, he crept to the portholes and gazed at the waters below. Nothing stirred. Unlocking the cabin door, he went out on deck, raised the ladder and inspected every inch of the cruiser; satisfied, he returned to the cabin and relocked it.

Villainous bastard! Who is Cacciatore to frighten me? He poured himself a glass of wine and gulped it down to brace his courage. *In their way, the* mafiosi *are fiercer than God's wrath,* he told himself. He hadn't minded the threat of death as much as he minded being told no one would mourn him. How much longer would he live, eh? What did it matter if they killed him? But to be told no one would mourn him at his grave paralyzed his mind. It was true, Sicilians didn't worship life; it was death they idolized. Death sat on the throne in their secret rooms of worship. Why even bother with God? In the hearts and minds of all Sicilians, Death reigned supreme. Death is what they prepared for, why they scrimped and saved money all their lives, denying themselves the fun of living to buy cemetery plots. All so they could die in style. No one thought to *live* in style, only to die that way.

Is the mafia *so powerful they can remove Nicosia's name from the register of life?* he asked himself. *No tombstone to mark my grave or my very existence?* These thoughts shook him to the core. Nicosia began to drink himself into a stupor that lasted another two days and two nights.

In moments of alternating clarity, he couldn't understand why Cacciatore hadn't killed him immediately. Why had he been given advance warning? Was it possible Don Matteo hadn't really ordered his execution? What if that bloated frog had acted on his own initiative? He had never liked Nicosia.

These and many other thoughts pursued the seaman until he was convinced he'd lost all his senses. On the fourth day after Cacciatore's visit, when no amount of wine could dull his senses and the intolerable paranoia he experienced began to ease up, Nicosia went up to the flying bridge and started up the engines. He had to get out to sea to do some thinking. Somewhere in his mind lay the key to this problem with Don Matteo.

The cool salt air refreshed him on this October day. In the bay at Porto Tomasso he dropped anchor and watched the hungry gulls dive for food. It seemed they never came up empty-handed. He glanced high above the colored layers of rock and stared at the Vanzini Villa; it gave him a feeling of security to see it, as if nothing could change in his confusing world.

Everything had gone so well these past ten years. Was this to be the year of change, the year the pendulum would move back into the negative zones in his life? He'd kept his bargain with Don Matteo and performed his duties diligently, remaining as loyal as he had when he worked for His Excellency the Marquis de Leone.

Nicosia gave a start. The fog banks in his mind began to lift, and he suddenly felt as if his life had cleared in the mirror of his mind.

I did work for the Royal Lions! I captained the Marchessa!

Images came at him. He saw the luxury cruiser, recalled the honeymoon of Marco and Mariolina and how they had seen her villa in flames.

"I'm not crazy!" he shouted aloud. "It was all true!"

Inside the cabin, he unlocked a closet door where he stowed all the junk he brought from the *Baccala*. He searched through the boxes and cases and was about to forget the nagging thoughts that persisted, when he caught sight of a small metal chest that had been given to him by his father. *Something to keep your treasures in, my son.*

He wiped the dust from the long-forgotten chest, pried it open with a tool from his kit, and took it to the galley table where he lifted the lid with trembling hands. So many things

390

rushed into his mind that he had to force himself to remain calm. *Steady . . . steady now, take your time.* He was like a new man and not knowing how long this revelation would last, he wanted to make the most of it.

Amid a small collection of mementos and faded tintypes and artist's drawings of the *Marchessa,* he found a worn ship's log. He opened it and began reading the daily entries he had made so long ago. On a faded photograph of Marco de Leone and his bride taken in Marseille was inscribed: *To* Capitano *Paolo Nicosia with our deepest thanks and affection for three of the most memorable months in our lives.* It was signed: *Marquis and Marchessa de Leone.* There was also a letter from the Royal Lion thanking Paolo for the magnificent golden lion he'd given to the infant Dolcetto de Leone. Paolo's eyes rested on the phrase, *Your Godson, Dolcetto, will wear it the rest of his life and always remember the fine man who gave it to him.*

Paolo Nicosia paused to pour himself a glass of wine. Was it possible that Dolcetto really was his Godson? He turned his attention to the news clipping of Dolcetto tacked to the wall in the cabin and wondered. He clearly recalled Dr. Alberto Pietro holding the infant during his baptism. *Dr. Pietro is his Godfather, not me,* he thought, dusting away a few more cobwebs.

He poured some water into a basin and washed his face and neck. He felt feverish. When he had cooled off sufficiently, he returned to the table and sorted through more memorabilia. He picked up a letter that bore the seal of the Royal Lion on the envelope. He removed the letter and read its contents:

> *My dearest friend,*
> *Never will I be able to repay you for what you've done for me. To have returned with Calo on such short notice in my time of need, and to have then assisted me with my heavy burden, is more than I could have expected from my own flesh and blood. You've succeeded in rekindling my enduring faith and belief in you, Paolo. You are truly a great human being. Never shall I forget what you did for me and my friend. It has come to my attention that he is safe and has found contentment and refuge in this world of uncertainties. If ever you have need of anything, never forget I am as always your loyal friend.*
>
> > *Humbly,*
> > *Marco de Leone*

Paolo dropped the letter to the table. For several moments he sat in silence contemplating the contents. These broken bits and pieces meant little or nothing to him. There was a giant hole in his memory and he couldn't bridge the gap. No matter how hard he tried, he couldn't put all the pieces together.

Who was the *friend* the Marquis spoke of? What did it all mean? The golden lion around Dolcetto's neck flashed before his eyes, and he blinked several times and paused in reflection. He found the bill of sale and studied the frayed, yellowed document, hardly legible after ten years of handling, but there it was, somewhat dim and water-marked, but nonetheless the signature of Dolcetto de Leone.

An hour later, Paolo's mind had clouded. He replaced the items in their box with mixed feelings. The letters said there was a connection between Paolo Nicosia and the Royal Lions. But if he, Paolo Nicosia, could remember nothing, what should he believe—his mind or the information in the letters?

Paolo locked the cabin and lowered the dinghy into the water. He'd go into Porto Tomasso for supplies. He was out of many things, and if he decided not to go right back into Palermo, he didn't want to run out of certain necessities— namely wine.

In the village square, he found a huge crowd of cheering and waving people packed like fleas in the fur of a sheep dog. What appeared to be a motorcade, complete with security officers and motorcycle escorts, was winding it's way up the serpentine roads.

"What is it?" asked Paolo, shading his eyes with his hand and looking out into the distance. "What's going on?"

"Can't you see, stupid? Look at the car. It's *El Leone* and his family. The wedding is Saturday," shouted a woman filled with excitement. "A wedding! A *festa!*" she cried joyously.

Paolo Nicosia stood on a huge rock to get a better glimpse of the motorcade. He saw a white-haired man sitting in the back seat of the elegant Mercedes limousine, flanked on either side by two younger men. They were escorted by the security police, special details of *carabinieri*, and other secret service men who looked like Italian officials.

For an instant, he thought the white-haired man in the back seat of the limousine had looked at him, and for a time, Paolo felt a peculiar sensation shiver through him. The car passed. The people cheered and waved and shouted, so Paolo Nicosia cheered and waved and shouted. *"Viva El Leone! Benvenuto, El Leone! Benvenuto! Welcome!"*

The motorcade faded from sight, winding its way toward

the Vanzini Villa. Slowly the excited crowd began to disperse. Inside the *negozio*, Paolo picked up the necessary supplies and returned to his boat. He cooked himself a supper of green peppers and eggs and fresh tomato sauce, and after supper he began drinking again.

36

"El Leone! El Leone!" came the cries. Shepherds and peasants dropped their work and ran to the walls along the road and waved to the occupants of the limousines as they made their way to the Vanzini Villa at the crest of the mountains. Marco couldn't have been more pleased that here in the heart of *mafia* country, he was known and revered.

Stepping from the limousine into the glaring sunlight, Marco's tear-filled eyes continued to play tricks on him, and when he saw the dark-haired young beauty running toward them, he felt a strange fluttering over his heart.

Mariolina! The name caught in his silenced throat.

As his eyes adjusted to the light, the inevitable happened; the woman was no longer Mariolina. He watched with a fluttering of excitement as the raven-haired woman embraced his son. Dolcetto turned to his father happily, with shining eyes.

"This is Francesca, father. Francesca, this is my father."

"Piacere, Excellency," she said in her marvelous voice. She bowed, and curtsied with decorum.

Marco leaned over her, touched her shoulders, and lifted her from her curtsying position. She slowly raised her luminous dark eyes to meet his and for moments they regarded each other in silence, each overwhelmed by the other. Then, Marco drew her to him and held her close to his heart.

How lovely you are, he would have said to her if he could speak. But words were superfluous, for Francesca saw the love and acceptance in his eyes and she radiated even more joy and happiness.

"This is Antonio," smiled the bridegroom, introducing her to his cousin.

Before she could speak, Antonio gathered her into his strong arms, spun her about in a wide arc, and kissed her. "At last! We finally have a woman in the family! Welcome, Francesca!"

Unfamiliar with his continental manner, she flushed with embarrassment. "I've looked forward to meeting you, Antonio. I feel as though I've known you all my life." She slipped one arm through Marco's and held Dolcetto's hand with the other. "Come, let's go inside out of this hot sun. You must be tired from the trip."

Inside, the villa was filled with scurrying servants preparing for the wedding. Activity was everywhere in the grand ballroom, Peacock Court, smaller salons—all over. At their entrance, the hushed whispers began, *"El Leone! El Leone!"* they cried, clapping their hands. Marco bowed at either side and nodded to the pleasure-flushed faces of the peasants. He was terribly affected by their adulation and attention. Francesca steered them right through the foyer toward the small sitting room beyond the study, and closed the enormous hand-carved doors to shut out the sounds and provide them with privacy, and the opportunity to get better acquainted.

Marco could never be done roaming about the splendid villa. *If I stayed a year, I'd not see everything,* he told himself. *It looks like a temple carved from the landscape, and isn't it remarkable how the Greco-Roman, Moorish, Spanish and French influences could be combined so successfully into a giant complex.* The Lion stood on the thick stone wall overlooking the sea below and thought to himself, *how strange I didn't settle near the water, it's so peaceful.*

Two days before the wedding, Dolcetto searched for his father and found him with the Vittorio brothers checking out the central alarm system on a ceiling panel in the master bedroom. He listened as Gino explained the complicated alarm system.

"The panel consists of seven rows, each a different color when lit up. Each row represents a checkpoint that triggers an alarm the instant a trespasser violates that checkpoint. Opposite each of the seven colored lights are three smaller lights of the same color. These represent a three-minute interval before a progressive device triggers a light on the next row, meaning the trespasser nears in his approach to the villa. Anyone watching the alarms can accurately judge the distance and time between each alarm, and gauge how far the interloper has penetrated the villa.

"An audio system works simultaneously with the rows of colored lights. The seventh row, indicating the trespasser is furthest away, is violet and it's accompanied by a series of slow beeps, two per second. The orange lights in the sixth row are joined by chimes that ring once in a full second. The fifth row—light blue, five fast chimes per second. Fourth row—green—four fast beeps per second. Third row—yellow—three rings. Second row—white lights—two chimes. Finally the last row, a flashing red light, indicates the trespasser is inside the villa proper. A combination of beeps, chimes, and rings sounds the warning in a loud staccato."

Marco scribbled notes all over the plans as he listened.

"Well, Papa, how is it so far? Meet with your approval?" asked Dolcetto, smiling at his father's precautions.

Marco nodded.

"He's remarkable. I've shown His Excellency the alarm system and by tomorrow he'll know it better than either Pepino or me," said Gino, smiling at the Royal Lion. "Later we'll take you underground to show you where the signals originate."

Dolcetto put an arm around his father's shoulder and studied his notations on the blueprints. Suddenly his arm fell to his side and a mask of disturbance crossed his face. He reached over and took the plans from his father.

"Papa, where did you get these plans?" he asked quietly.

Marco shrugged. *Why does it matter?*

"Where did you get them?" insisted Dolcetto.

Marco spread his arms in an open gesture. *Why?*

"Because there was only one set of plans and I already returned them to Francesca. Now where did these come from?"

Marco wrote in his notebook, *I had them made.*

"Where?"

Marco scribbled, *In Messina. I asked your Godfather to have these made up for me.*

Dolcetto filled with dismay. After all his precautions, he hadn't counted on this. Knowing all the Lions would be gathered under one roof, he had planned everything carefully. Marco placed a slender hand on his son's arm to reassure him.

"Don't you see, Papa? There was only one set of plans. Now there are two. Who knows, perhaps there's a third or a fourth."

Marco's smile froze. *So that's what Dolcetto is driving at. How could I have overlooked such a possibility?* Marco filled with self-reproach.

"Perhaps I'm alarmed over nothing." Dolcetto hugged his father and walked out of the master bedroom visibly disturbed.

Listening intently, the Vittorio brothers took in every word. *Francesca's always been so protective of the plans,* thought Gino. *Should I inform her? No, her future husband will tell her. It's his place to tell her.*

Marco felt terrible. He brooded over the matter but convinced himself Alberto Pietro would never betray such a confidence. *We've known each other over thirty-five years. He would never cause harm to the Lions.* He continued to go over every detail of the security with Gino and Pepino.

The next afternoon a frightening blow was struck at the villa! Marco de Leone disappeared! The estate was turned upside down with security men searching everywhere for him. Dear God, what could have happened? Everyone filled with panic! Calo and Ciccio had been walking a few feet ahead of the Lion as they usually did to make sure they encountered no foul play.

Long, exhausting searches in every possible nook and cranny resulted in total failure to locate the Marquis de Leone. Everyone feared the worst—kidnapping or death. Dolcetto questioned the despondent Calo and Ciccio.

"Excellency—it is not believable! He was there one moment, the next with no warning—whooooosh! He was gone! Only a sorceress could have made him disappear! We were strolling along the trellis under the domed archways, Excellency, right here." Calo pointed out the exact path they had taken. "Right at this place, where the outer portico connects one wing of this old palace to another old section east of the main villa—over there—he disappeared!" Over and over they repeated their stories until they were exhausted and could no longer speak to Dolcetto about their ineptness.

At the point where gloom descended upon the Vanzini Villa, and heartache and concern and guilt poisoned the air, the Royal Lion of Sicily entered the study where all had gathered, covered with dust, his clothing in total disarray, exhausted and hungry. His hazel eyes lit up feverishly and he exuded the inner turbulence of a man who had stumbled upon the most earthshaking news.

"Papa! Uncle Marco! Excellency!" came the cries. "Where have you been? What happened? Are you all right?"

Marco walked to the desk and wrote on his pad, "I fell asleep under a cool arbor. Forgive me if I caused anyone undue concern. I'd like to be alone."

Alone in his suite, Marco allowed his thoughts to snake back over what had happened earlier. Under the domed archway, not more than four feet behind his bodyguards, at the far end of a deserted courtyard, he'd taken a quick right turn through a bower of ivy, when he chanced to see a long passageway. He would have turned back onto the original path when suddenly an adventurous spirit urged him on along the passageway.

He passed through old, musty, unused corridors, opening one door after another, peering through ivy-covered grilled windows, until he finally entered what once must have been a magnificent ballroom. The floors were thick with dust, spiders and rats scurried. But in the light that penetrated through open grill work, he saw that the room was full of art objects. He glanced up at the hand-painted ceiling with its delicate celestial angels. Then Marco allowed his startled, appreciative eyes to gaze in wonder at the sumptuous collection of rare furniture and works of art. He took the dust cover from one of the shapes; the material, disintegrating in his hands, revealed what appeared to be a curio cabinet of a baroque design. As he dusted it off lightly, he could see it contained objects of art and other treasures more exquisite than any he'd ever seen.

The small curved doors had swollen shut with mildew but he gently forced them open and removed a golden chalice studded with gemstones worth a king's ransom. He blew off the dust and held it up to the light. Even without his glasses, he could see the exquisite filigree work and stone setting of another era. He carefully replaced the cup and shook his head in disbelief. Removing a few more dust covers from the other bulky shapes, he saw magnificent statuary and furniture as well as a collection of oil paintings bearing signatures that dazzled his senses: Titian, Michelangelo, Botticelli, and on and on.

He didn't dare dust the oils for fear he might do permanent damage, but he looked for signatures and literally shook when he read the name Raphael. The next few hours sped by and he grew absorbed in studying the wealth of works by old masters.

A glance at his watch returned him to the present. Covering the objects as best he could, he found his way back through the endless turns and corridors, trying to memorize the way and jotting down directions in his little black book. He emerged into the late afternoon sunlight, never thinking of the uproar his disappearance had created.

"Papa, next time let someone know where you are. Half the countryside was out looking for you," Dolcetto scolded gently.

Marco left his room after he'd cleaned up and returned to the study. For a time he sat behind the desk buried in thought. He scribbled several notes and set them aside. Later when Dolcetto came into the room, Marco waved him over and handed him a note.

Dolcetto read: *Ask Francesca for deed to property.* "Why? Is something wrong?"

Marco shook his head and pointed again to the note.

"All right, Papa. All right. I'll ask her right away."

Marco nodded with satisfaction.

Moments later Francesca returned with Dolcetto and

smiled at Marco. She walked to a wall safe behind a painting, opened it, and removed a metal box. "If there's anything of importance, it will be in this box."

Marco searched the contents twice and didn't find what he wanted. He handed Dolcetto another note: *Call Giorgio Bocca in Rome. Tell him to bring all data including title searches when he arrives for the wedding tomorrow.*

"Why?" asked his son.

Marco waved him off and scribbled another note: *Later!* Dolcetto shrugged and left the room to make his call on another phone.

"Is there something special you are looking for, Excellency?" asked Francesca. "Perhaps I can help in some way?"

Marco smiled gently. He nodded and wrote on another pad, *I want to know more about the history of this villa. Who owned it before your father and before him. And call me Papa.* Va biene?

Francesca smiled warmly. "Is that all? I think I might have what you're looking for, *Papa*. My father was somewhat of a historian himself." She crossed the room and rolled a small library ladder to the far end of the bookcase. From the top shelf, she selected five thick, dusty volumes and handed them one at a time to Marco. "There's enough history in these books to occupy you for a year," she smiled.

Marco began to thumb through the books and almost immediately he was lost in another world. He was so absorbed he didn't hear his name called for dinner two hours later.

"Papa!" called Dolcetto. "Have you forgotten dinner?"

Marco raised a restraining hand and waved Dolcetto off.

"I'll have Maria Antonia bring him a tray," whispered Francesca. "I'm happy he's enjoying himself. It's the first time since he arrived that he hasn't been concerned with the alarms."

"What are those books all about?" asked Dolcetto, filled with curiosity. "I haven't seen him so absorbed in years."

"The history of this estate," she said softly. "It must be interesting; my father paid handsomely to have the titles searched and bound."

Dolcetto shrugged, put his arms around her, and kissed her. "We've got work to do, *cara mia*," he said. They returned to the salon where they'd been opening wedding gifts with Antonio. Oh, God! How many times Dolcetto would ruefully regret giving this matter so little importance. Why hadn't he had the foresight to have examined these books, he would ask himself.

For hours the Royal Lion paced the floor after reading the contents of the books. He wanted to sing, cry, rejoice, and wake the entire villa to tell them of his discovery! But Marco de Leone wanted nothing to interfere or distract from the nuptials of the bride and groom. Tomorrow would be their day, and theirs alone! He clapped his hands with the delight of a child, wondering what Alberto would say when he read the letter he intended to write him. Expectation of that very moment motivated him to sit down and begin to write a lengthy letter. *Dearest Alberto* . . . it began.

Later, Marco took the fifth volume to his bedroom, reread his letter, placed it into the book, and didn't fall asleep until dawn crept over the horizon.

The wedding had been spectacular! Five hundred guests had been served at an elaborate sit-down dinner created by creative artists imported from Rome. The villa, a profusion of magnificent flowers and decorations befitting a royal wedding, was the setting against which Father Bonaventura, now a Monsignor, performed the wedding ceremony after obtaining special dispensation from the Vatican to attend to the rites in the villa instead of a church.

From the mainland and other points distant came titled nobility, high powered politicos, ambassadors and their families, business affiliates, and friends. Wedding invitations, themselves works of art, had been individually scripted with special ink and upon presentation were scrutinized under a unique lamp to detect forgeries. No one was permitted within miles of the Vanzini Villa without one.

Security police were everywhere. A special squad, numbering nearly thirty men in all, immaculate in formal attire, who knew every *mafioso* on sight, mingled with the guests keeping sharp eyes alerted for anything unusual.

Now, it was nearly over. As Marco stood with his son, new daughter-in-law, and nephew, shaking hands with departing guests, he found himself somewhat relieved that the day had passed without incident. *Santo Dio!* No mishaps. No troubles or disturbances. It had all worked out better than anticipated. Tomorrow, he'd visit Fregossi's vineyards for the promised vines. That, and what he had in store for Alberto, occupied his senses. Finally the last guest departed. The newlyweds had kissed him and retired to their suite where they planned to stay the night, then leave for a European honeymoon the following morning. Antonio had disappeared on the arm of some enchantress.

Calo and Ciccio were the last to pay their respects to the happy couple, and informed the Royal Lion they were joining the peasants outside where the real celebration would soon commence. Marco smiled and nodded, and suddenly he was alone. Glancing about the enormous salon, force of habit made him begin to turn off many of the bright lights. Servants scurried about him, in a hurry to complete their chores so they could join the others. Already the music of Sicilian peasants echoed into the great villa. Walking into the guest bathroom off the foyer, Marco paused to dampen a towel and place the cool cloth on his burning eyes. How many cigars had he passed out? Thousands had been ordered. The smoke or something continued to irritate his eyes; he noticed they were red streaked when he glanced critically at them in the gilded oval mirror. He turned off the light, left the room, and crossed the foyer to the spiral staircase. He stopped suddenly as if he were looking for someone.

"Ah, *compare*, there you are," called Alberto Pietro, approaching Marco from the study, smiling warmly. Marco smiled back. He'd hardly seen Alberto all day. With so many guests . . .

"Come, join me for a cup of espresso . . ." Together they walked into the small anteroom where the espresso machine remained on the table. Dr. Pietro retrieved two cups and saucers, poured the black fluid into demitasse cups, and handed one to Marco. He sipped from the other and they sat down in the comfortable leather sofas, nearby. "Did you enjoy yourself?"

An ineffable grin on Marco's face turned into a pleased smile. But it wasn't thoughts of the wedding that brought this smile to his face—it was the thought of the letter Alberto would receive tomorrow morning that brought a wicked gleam of delight into his eyes. His glee, interrupted by two chimes from the golden-faced clock on the mantle, where two cupids encrusted with mother of pearl indicated it was 10:30 P.M., brought a look of perplexity to his face.

"Antonio?" asked Alberto, who knew his friend well.

Marco nodded.

"The rascal is with the young daughter of Signor Carmen Lucca of Milano. Remember the *biondella*? Well, don't count on his coming home for a long while," he smiled knowingly. "You know Antonio. But don't worry, I took the liberty of requesting one of Francesca's trusted men to keep closer to him than a shadow." He studied Marco's appreciative, but drawn and tired face. "Drink your coffee . . . you look pale. Did you drink too much?"

Nodding, Marco thought, *I'm really tired.* The wine had been too heady, much too heady. Felipe had sent a dozen cases of his special wines. *Wait until I tell him,* he thought, *that the wine wasn't like Fregossi's.* He smiled, then as quickly, his smile faded. All week he'd expected his old friend the Falcon to show up for the wedding. They had so much to talk about. But a letter came with the wine; he'd had an accident, a fall off his horse, received some spinal injury. Marco shook his head sadly, hoped Felipe would recover speedily. He turned expectantly to Alberto. *What was it he'd said?*

"I said, perhaps I should give you a tablet to keep your head from spinning. Nothing's worse than going to bed with too much *vino* mixed with champagne and what else?" Alberto chuckled. "Well, it's only once that Dolcetto marries."

Marco nodded, untied his four-in-hand, opened his collar, and breathed easier.

"Next will be Antonio's wedding, no?"

Marco's face brightened. *What a godsend! I'd be a happier man knowing the young scamp had settled down, married and started a family. It's uncanny how much like Guillermo Antonio had become. What energy! And so possessed with women!*

"Don't concern yourself, *compare.*" Alberto opened a small silver case he took from his inner breast pocket and removed a small vial of white tablets. "Two are the prescribed amount, Marco. Take two now, and no more than two later, if you should awaken. It will reduce the dizzy spells. *Capeeshi?*"

Marco nodded wearily and yawned.

"Here, take the pills now," said Alberto. "I'm going into Palermo tonight."

Marco glanced questioningly at him. He swallowed the two pills, then waited with an expectant look on his face.

"Why am I going?" he laughed. "It's about the clinic I'm going to build. You made me a wealthy man, *amico,* and with it have come responsibilities and obligations, hospital boards, charity organizations, homes for orphans—need I tell you? But have no fear. I shall return in the morning in time to go to Fregossi's with you. Then we'll motor across the island back to your villa."

Marco smiled complacently and nodded. *Talk about energy. Alberto is five years my junior and he only looks forty-five.*

"You're sure you'll be all right?"

The Royal Lion nodded. *Of course, I'm all right. With Dolcetto upstairs, a house full of servants, an arsenal of*

*men and weapons outside, what could go wrong? The entire
week passed without incident. What could happen now?*

"The alarm system is on, isn't it?" asked Alberto.

Marco nodded. He glanced at Alberto strangely. *How
does he know about it? Oh yes, he heard us talking at my
villa.*

"You're sure? Let's check on it just in case. I wouldn't
feel right, if I hadn't at least checked it out with you."

Managghia a miseria! Marco shook his head impatiently. *I'm not an idiot! I just don't have a tongue! And tonight
I'm too tired to be writing my questions.*

"I'll wait until you make sure it's in order. I wouldn't rest
all the way to Palermo with the thought nagging at me."

Managghia a miseria! No use protesting. Marco walked
resignedly into the study and checked the replica of the intricate sound and lighting system upstairs in the master bedroom. It was fine. He took a few steps away, then stopped
abruptly. A distorted afterimage registered in his mind. He
retraced his steps and peered cautiously at the panel. He
felt slightly dizzy and he didn't have his glasses with him, but
he didn't have to see. With his eyes closed, just by feeling,
he knew the main alarm hadn't tripped to go on at 10 P.M. He
pulled on the handle and it fell into place. Odd, only that
morning he had checked with Gino Vittorio. Oh, well, it
was secure now. He decided to say nothing to Alberto about
the alarm. He might insist on canceling his trip to Palermo.
But because he felt a charge of inner excitement, he scribbled him a note.

Dr. Pietro read: *Tomorrow tell me more about your Sardinian prince.*

Alberto glanced sharply at his friend; his questioning eyes
searched the tired, glazed eyes of the Lion, who managed an
impish grin.

"My Sardinian prince? I don't understand, Marco."

Marco pointed to the word *tomorrow* and smiled again.

Dolcetto's Godfather nodded and walked out into the
night. Suddenly Marco felt totally fatigued. His eyes grew
dull and clouded. Leaning heavily against the door, after Alberto left, he barely found the energy to slip the bolt lock
into place. Difficult as it was for him to move in a room that
began to spin and rock, he slowly, inch by inch, managed to
cross the Peacock Court, holding onto the wall for support.
Outside the merrymaking picked up in tempo and the music
totally discordant to his ears sounded like a cacophonic
nightmare. He climbed the spiral staircase to his room.

Outside was music and gaiety, smiles and songs, laughter
and happiness and countless toasts to the newlyweds. Peas-

ants clapped hands, stomped feet and danced frenzied taran-
tellas. It seemed everyone, but everyone, in that overfilled
party was contented and joyous—except one. Only one person
seemed isolated from the festivities. Gino Vittorio, against
his brother's instructions, had been drinking heavily. The
rejected soul floundered like a wounded tiger, unable to adjust to Francesca's marriage. Inflicting the role of a spurned
suitor upon himself, he berated and upbraided himself for
thinking he had had a chance with her. *The wine will numb
my feelings and still my emotions,* he told himself. But Gino
was wrong. He grew more tempestuous and full of self-pity.

For weeks he'd rehearsed the musicians in learning Francesca's favorite song, "Shangri-La." Moments ago he gave
them the signal to play the music. As the night air filled with
sounds of the *cansona,* the more romantic couples snuggled. Overhead the stars clustered together like shimmering
confetti of diamonds glistening brightly on thick carpets of
midnight blue hanging low in the heavens. Gino had wanted
to hurt Francesca as she had hurt him. But it was Gino's
heart that felt like a dartboard at the familiar sounds of the
music. *Demonio!*

Upstairs, a light went on in the bridal chamber. The
French doors swung open and Francesca, still in her pale
shimmering satin gown, stood at the balcony railing. Dolcetto joined her, carrying two glasses of champagne. He
handed one to her and placed his arm around her waist. Together they stood in silence watching the *contadini* in the
gaily decorated courtyard. It was at this moment that
Francesca caught sight of Gino Vittorio's eyes when he
raised his glass in a toast to her. For an instant her face
turned the color of the pink roses that grew around the
balcony. Her husband nudged her. "There's Gino, cara mia,
drinking a toast to us."

"Yes," she replied quietly, lowering her thick lashes.

They raised their glasses to him, when suddenly another couple spied them. In a few seconds a wave of delight
swept through the crowd and everyone reached for wine
glasses to toast the newlyweds.

"As long as we remain out here, dearest, they won't continue their merrymaking," whispered Francesca in her husky
voice. "We wouldn't want to be responsible for spoiling their
fun, would we?"

They waved to the crowd below and disappeared inside.
As the music resumed and the couples began to dance, Gino
threw his glass violently against a brick oven at the rear of
the tiled courtyard.

Across the courtyard, Ciccio Pontiface nudged Calo La

Bolla. "See how the young bull flares his nostrils and scrapes his foot into the dirt?"

"That's what he's doing?" Calo's glaucomic eyes couldn't see that far.

"I look at him and I see trouble," Ciccio insisted.

"No, he's a good lad. All week long I've talked with him. He and Pepino are very devoted."

"I don't deny that, but I learned it was he who urged the musicians to play the *cansona* that they now are playing for the *third* time. That's no polka or mazurka!"

Calo understood immediately. He turned around and tried to watch Gino's behavior. He did seem to stagger a bit. Calo looked at the others, studying them with measured certainty. "Tell me," he asked Ciccio. "Who else looks like they've had too much to drink?" The old antenna was up and working.

"Wait here. I'll return in a few minutes." Ciccio's calculating eyes scanned the area. He sauntered casually through the lively courtyard. The scent of fragrant orange blossoms filled the air. Next to the musicians' stand, a huge table was laden with wine and champagne, sugar-coated almonds, cake and *canolli* and *sfinghi*. In the center stood a two-tiered miniature of the enormous wedding cake which had been served earlier.

Ciccio picked up a bottle of champagne and two glasses and returned to his table, smiling and nodding to others in passing, studying their faces. He missed no one and nothing, including the guards who stood along the outer wall of the estate.

"No," he told Calo. "Gino looks like the only man with good reason to drink."

"*Aloura,* go get him. We shall have a little talk, eh?"

Ciccio moved to Gino's side, placed a friendly arm on his shoulder, and steered him back to their table. "Come, *paesano*. Drink with us."

"Ah," said Gino with a rubbery tongue and loose lips. He glanced unsteadily at Ciccio and said, "Calo?" He had trouble focusing his swimming brown eyes. "No, you're Ciccio . . . Well, which one are you?" He seemed totally confused.

"I'm Ciccio, he's Calo," explained the smaller man, pointing to the grinning Calo. They both looked like benign bears and pretended to be as jovial as Gino Vittorio.

"*Managghia,*" giggled Gino with a display of humility. "To think I'm really in the company of *El Leone's* legendary bodyguards," began Gino. He blinked heavily lidded eyes and sat down with a thud. He weaved back and forth and watched as Ciccio poured him a glass of champagne.

404

"To the bride and groom," toasted Ciccio.

"To the . . ." Gino faltered. "To the . . . to them!" Before Gino could raise his glass to his watery lips, a dull expression came over his face and his head fell forward, unceremoniously hitting the table with a dull thud. The wine glass fell from his outstretched hand and shattered on the terra cotta tiles.

Calo and Ciccio exchanged startled glances, then both broke into gales of laughter. Ciccio grasped a handful of hair and held up Gino's head.

"The bull's been castrated for the night," he said, noting the sappy expression of drunken stupor. He laid Gino's head back on the table. He removed a small black case from his pocket, opened it and took out a knife with a sharp tip. He jabbed it quickly into Gino's wrist, and when there was no reflex, he was satisfied. "It's best to make sure he's drunk, eh?"

Calo indicated his admiration for his partner. He gazed about, seeing nothing, yet sensing a disturbance. He said, "When we're safely in Lion country, I'll breathe easier."

Ciccio lit up a cigar and studied his companion of so many years. "Tell me what you feel. You may be blind as an owl in daylight, but with my eyes and your instinct, I'd match us against twenty men with all their senses working."

Calo shrugged. "When have things been so perfect? No complications? Nothing's been wrong all week. Nothing. *Che demonio!* At home it's not like this. When things go too smooth, Calo worries."

"Listen, old rooster, could it be we're growing old? The young plan things to the last detail. What's this? Everyone leaving so soon? How come?"

Pepino Vittorio walked toward them. Behind him the peasants were leaving for the night. Musicians were packing their instruments.

"You look for Gino?" asked Ciccio. "He's here. Better to take him to his bed. He's finished for the night."

"I told him to be careful, not to drink. Tonight of all nights he has to screw up! He's never tasted wine except at mass," laughed Pepino. He picked his brother up and tossed him over his shoulder. *"Buona notte,"* he began, then stopped. "How many guard the wall tonight? Will you need any extra men?"

"The same as usual. We expect no trouble tonight. If it comes it might come before flight time, tomorrow," said Calo.

Pepino touched his beaked cap and walked off with his heavy load.

"Everything all right here?" asked Calo of the guards in the garage where the Mercedes was watched around the clock. The men nodded and gave the signal.

The Lion's bodyguards made the rounds with all the guards; once assured of the security they retired to their quarters. It was a modest room with two beds and a bathroom. Ciccio padded about the spacious room intent on looking for something. He scowled, walked to his suitcase, opened it, rummaged through its contents. He paused reflectively, walked to the nightstand next to the bed, and opened the drawer in brooding silence. In the bathroom, Calo could hear him fumbling about and cursing aloud. He returned to the bedroom, a look of panic on his colorless face.

"Mah che c'e? What's wrong?" asked Calo.

"My insulin case is missing."

"It must be here. Where did you put it?"

"Where did I put it? Where I usually put it!" he snapped impatiently.

"Look again," Calo said calmly, removing his shoes.

"I already have, *porco diaoro!!"*

Calo slipped out of his tuxedo jacket, loosened his tie, and began to remove the studs from his shirt. "When did you see it last?"

"This morning at six, when I usually take it."

"You need some now?"

"I drank too much wine. Already I feel shaky. I'm sweating too much."

Calo joined in the search. He knew the signs. "You brought no other with you?" The syringe and insulin were nowhere to be found.

"Listen, Ciccio, you lie down on the bed. I'll find Dr. Pietro."

"I saw him leave over an hour ago."

"Where the hell did he go?" Calo frowned. "He was supposed to check with us! *Che demonio!"* He slipped back into his shoes, grabbed his jacket.

"I'll drive to Palermo. I'll find a pharmacy if I have to break into one. I'll call Pepino Vittorio and have him post more guards. Now you stay quiet, *me siente?* Try not to get excited!" Calo was gravely concerned.

"I'd better go with you," said Ciccio.

"No. You stay. I'll return as soon as possible." On impulse he picked up the intercom that connected him with the Royal Lion's suite. As soon as he pressed the button, he changed his mind. No sense in disturbing His Excellency. Poor man must be exhausted, without sleep the night before. He flung the jacket over one shoulder and walked into the night.

The night was filled with sounds: the pounding of the surf below the cliffs; a slight movement in the brush, caused by an animal or a waft of wind; the lights and lanterns swaying in the cool ocean breeze; noises different from those he was used to at the Villa de Leone. A soft, silvery shaft of moonlight flickered through the thick shrubbery in the courtyard, casting dark, shadowy patterns. Calo slowed down, paused, and looked about. Then he continued on.

Instinctively, Calo stopped abruptly. He listened with catlike ears, cocking his head in each direction and peering with his nearly blind eyes. The uneasiness he felt earlier mounted. He struggled through failing eyes but he couldn't see beyond the dim shadows. *Managghia! I might as well be blind for all I can see.* He moved forward with slow precise steps. Up ahead he waved a greeting to a sentry. The man didn't wave back. Calo wouldn't have seen him if he had. Nor did he see the fine wire stretched across his path. He stumbled over it and fell down. His glasses fell off and landed several feet away.

"Butanna u diaoro!" he cursed, fumbling about the dark, groping for his glasses.

As a shadow moved before him and stopped a few feet away, Calo rose to his knees. "Who's there? Who are you?"

He heard the crunching sound of broken glass as the heavy, thick heel of a man's boot came down and ground out the lenses in his glasses. His head darted swiftly in the direction of the sound.

Before Calo could get to his feet, he felt the dull thud of an impact at the base of his skull. He was stunned for an instant, then came an onslaught of excruciating pain as blow after blow struck him with the force of violent explosions. Then all was darkness. He gasped desperately for air and felt his heart pound as if it would burst in his body. Somewhere a clock struck the half hour. It was half past eleven and Calo La Bolla—that wild, crazy bull of a man—was dead.

In his room Marco prepared for the night. Although he felt very tired and dizzy, he forced himself to walk down the hall toward the bridal chamber. He heard music coming from the room and the sound of Francesca's fluttery laughter. He smiled, then turned into a small alcove off the hall and unlocked a well-camouflaged door. A light went on automatically, revealing a small arsenal. He examined the weapons, then yawned and locked the door again. Back in his suite of rooms, he removed his robe and placed the two remaining tablets Dr. Pietro had given him on the table next to his bed. The alarm system overhead caught his attention, and he checked it out once more. Overcome with a dullness, he sat down on the bed. Then Marco gave a sudden start; his head shot up and his face paled visibly. Despite the drowsiness, he was filled with an ominous premonition. His head cocked from side to side, listening. Was that a flash of light he saw on the phone? Nothing . . .

Strange . . . this icy coldness I feel. It's come upon me like a fever.

He saw Calo La Bolla as clearly as if he stood in the same room with him. Instinctively, Marco picked up the phone. About to press the intercom button, he suddenly remembered. Slowly, he replaced the phone. *What's wrong with me tonight? Can't I remember I have no voice to speak with? I must be growing old. Yes, that's it. The old Lion has seen better days. Don't imagine things. Everything's been perfect all week.*

The clock on the bureau chimed 11:30 P.M. Marco picked up the fifth volume of the Vanzini Villa history. In it was the letter he'd written to Alberto Pietro. Before he opened the cover, he passed out in a heavily drugged sleep.

37

Earlier that day on Saturday, October 15, in the early evening, after the terrible hangover had passed, Nicosia shoved the metal chest to one side of the berth. He lowered himself over the side of the boat and bathed himself. Back on board, he dressed in an outmoded pin-striped suit he had saved for his burial, then piloted the *Arcturus II* back to Palermo where he intended to visit Don Barbarossa to plead for his life. He wasn't ready to die yet. His affairs weren't in order.

He stopped at Tedesco's Marine Supply and bought a box of cigars for the Don. On the way out he chanced to see the newspaper headlines: *SON OF ROYAL LION TO WED TODAY.*

Nicosia picked up the paper and glanced at the photos of Francesca Vanzini and Dolcetto de Leone. The photo of Marco de Leone arrested him. It had been taken in earlier days when Marco was a Senator. Paolo could have related to it if his mind had functioned properly. Instead, he laid the paper aside and walked spryly out of the store. He hailed a cab to Monreale.

"I'll just tell him, straight, Paolo Nicosia is no traitor! I'll tell Don Barbarossa, Nicosia is no informer to the police! He'll believe me!" By the time Nicosia had summoned the courage to confront the *capomafia*, it was midnight. The cigar box tucked firmly under his arm and a helluva lot of belts lacing his courage, he entered the south entrance of the estate and proceeded to the servant's entrance. In the clear night air, voices drifted out to him from the open French windows, familiar and recognizable. About to turn the corner, he changed his mind and drew in closer to the windows. The remarks he heard stopped him. The voice was Don Barbarossa's.

"Tonight the family of Royal Lions will be wiped out once and for all, then, my friends, we have real cause to celebrate. Before daybreak the job must be completed, *capeeshi?*"

Peering over the hedge, through the open doors the fisherman recognized Cacciatore and the two di Lucca brothers through the smoky haze.

"They are gathered under one roof—all of them. All the Lions from this night forward will become part of the past," said the Don who appeared triumphant and in light spirits as he raised his glass in toast.

Moved by profound curiosity, Nicosia inched in closer and saw the Don pacing to and fro. In the shifting pockets of cigar smoke he recognized consigliori Garibaldi and another man, Dr. Pietro, whom Nicosia couldn't place in the haze of his mind. This stranger to Nicosia spoke out sharply.

"Let's wait until we have something to celebrate before we drink a toast," he said tersely.

The Don turned and focused his attention on Cacciatore. "This time, there can be no excuses, no slipups, no failures! You've had the plans long enough to do the job blindfolded. You took care of Nicosia, no?"

Ah, thought the fisherman with a measure of elation, *now he'll tell that malevolent scum that no harm must come to Nicosia.*

"It's arranged!" said Cacciatore. "Nicosia will be dead before morning!"

The fisherman froze. Just like that! *Nicosia will be dead before morning!* What the hell is that? He felt sick, and leaned against the building, hoping his stomach would unknot. There was no mistake. The words came from Matteo Barbarossa himself. Hadn't he heard? Hadn't he seen the man's lips move? He heard. He understood. The words came at him like stinging bullets searing his mind.

The Royal Lions wiped out. Nicosia dead before morning!

Like a cat he sprang away from the window, numb and still filled with disbelief that the Don had disregarded ten years of loyalty in one breath. He crouched cautiously in the shadows to make certain he was undetected. All the way back to Palermo his conflicting thoughts baffled him. The cold-blooded orders issued to kill the Royal Lions ate away

409

at him and the cobwebs in his mind cleared and thickened as images of Marco and Dolcetto, his Godson, waxed and waned in his mind.

It was 2:30 A.M. by the time the fisherman boarded the *Arcturus II* and started the engines, heading his craft into deeper waters, toward Porto Tomasso. Intolerable wretchedness tore at him and his only thought was, *They are going to kill my Godson.* Never mind his own fate. He wasn't about to let harm befall his Godson!

At 2:30 A.M the black Alfa Romeo, filled with the couriers of death, left Don Matteo's villa heading in the general direction of Porto Tomasso.

At 2:45 A.M., having guzzled the contents of his goatskin *botta*, Nicosia refilled the wine container, slung it over his shoulder, and dropped anchor in the drifting shadows of the sleepy Porto Tomasso harbor. The grizzled old man with bloodshot eyes piloted the dinghy along the shore and pulled it up out of the water onto the beach. He swung up to the rickety old pier and moved swiftly toward the rusty gate at the end of the wharf. A putrid odor emanated from the murky waters, brimming with sewage, but tonight the fisherman was immune to any stink.

Lights from a few fishing boats in the harbor winked deceptively at him while the asthmatic raspings of fog horns gave life to the impotent night.

They want to murder the Lions! Murder my Godson! was all the fisherman's brain telegraphed to him. *Well! We'll see about that!*

Under the topaz glow of the dim street light on the Strada Pescatore the old seaman squinted his red-veined eyes at his pocket watch. He held it at arm's length, drew it closer, then pulled back and cursed aloud. "Fucking old age! I can't see a blasted thing!" He fumbled; after a few misses, he managed to replace the watch in his vest pocket.

Another gulp from his goatskin flushed through his throat and chest. At the corner where the road makes an abrupt hairpin turn and the harbor is hidden from view, Nicosia leaned heavily against a decaying lamppost, panting breathlessly. His body felt wet and clammy. *Why am I so damned tired? I feel weak as water.*

He'd walked double this distance without such a weak feeling. A curious numbness passed over him and his mind became blank. He felt disassociated from his mission. He stared about his surroundings, struggling to recall why he'd come here. Images came at him, vague and indiscernible, then, as quickly, they vanished. His eyes, hot and swollen, burning like fire, were unable to focus. Bewildered, he clung to the lamppost. Fumbling, he reached again for the goat-skin, sipped more wine, and hoped his vision would clear.

The clock in the Norman tower struck 3:00 A.M. as the couriers of death approached the outskirts of Porto Tomasso. Fog banks rolling in over the patchwork of flickering harbor lights added an eeriness to the black night. The dense fog made it difficult to spot the Alfa Romeo as it turned off the main road, onto the narrow corkscrew road that spiraled to the village high atop the breast of the mountain. The headlights were heavily veiled, hardly detectable.

Tonight *Paolo u' Pazzu* will show God he's a real man! He affected an air of bravado. Deep in his heart it was really God he wanted to get even with. For his vendetta with God had been of long standing. The hatred he felt for the *mafiosi* was comparatively new and violent since he discovered they had no further use for him and in addition intended to wipe out the Lions. *"Che demonio!"* he shouted, then had to pause to catch his breath. "I'll show the world that Paolo Nicosia was here and left his mark upon the earth!" In a sudden rage of potency he shook his fist at the heavens.

Now the fisherman stood still as an image. He breathed with Herculean effort and in a quick movement clasped his hands over each ear to drown out the savage pounding of his heart. He had arrived at the south entrance to the piazza and as he looked about, the time-worn structures of broken walls and musty smells danced before him in a vast, sweeping, circular movement that made his head reel. His hand on the goatskin *botta,* Nicosia glanced at it for a moment and thought, *Sonofobitch! This wine has some kick to it!* He raised it to his lips, swilled more of the ruby red and felt a hot glow course through his body. That's when he enjoyed the wine most; that first glow, that inner surge of warmth that filled him with a certain *maschiezzo*—manliness. Wiping his slobbering lips with the back of his hand, he began to shiver. Waves of nausea spread through him and he clutched at his stomach trying desperately not to vomit.

The moment passed. With some semblance of equanimity he suddenly shouted aloud, *"Cornutti!"* His voice bounced off the cobbles, reverberated from building to building, then faded into nothingness. Sweating profusely, he loosened his collar and shouted another obscenity; shook his fist.

"Goddamnit, you bastards! Come and get me if you've got the balls! It's me, Paolo Nicosia! I know you're out there, you obscene sons of whores!" His laughter rang out through the *piazza.* Suddenly he found no humor in the situation. Was there no one to hear the bungling old fisherman in his hour of bravado? The empty streets were his answer.

411

But the fisherman was wrong. There were some who heard. Across the street in the dark unlit interior of the cobbler's shop, Giacomo Casabiano and his paramour of the evening had been passionately joined when sounds of the commotion outside forced Febronia de Lucca to jackknife her legs and spring away from her lover's embrace. Petrified, her dark eyes filled with terror and in a swift movement she thrust him from her hot, wet thighs. "Go, see who it is! Quickly!" she insisted in a highly agitated manner. "All I need is to have my brothers find me here with you, a cobbler's son! *Demonio!* There'd be the devil to pay!"

"Cammoria!" exploded her lover, furious at the untimely interruption. One more second and he would have exploded. Then, he could have run like hell out the back way! His trousers in an awkward heap at his ankles, he shuffled reluctantly toward the window and swiped at the grimy glass, peering out at the deserted square. Recognizing the old fisherman swaying under the dim street light, he glanced with annoyance at his watch. It was 3:15 A.M.

"Whore of the devil! It's only *Paolo u' Pazzu! Povero meskino!* As usual he's drowning his sorrows in wine!" He hurried back to Febronia, anxious to pick up where he had left off. The lust-filled girl clung tightly to her lover. "Wouldn't the crazy old fisherman give anything if he could stick his cock into a sweet hot thing like you, *bedda?*" he whispered. "Come on, little cat, show me your claws," he cooed. She was a hot one, this fireblooded peasant, and no one had pleased her like this strutting rooster. "How's this, eh? How's this? Ahhhhhhh . . ."

Unknown to the old fisherman, the American agents Rossi and Moreno had put a tail on Nicosia and for the past week he'd been under surveillance. Sticking to his man like glue, Miguel Camarata, a local undercover man with the *Questura*, was no less than twenty feet from the old seaman, and right up against the cobbler's shop wall. Having heard movements coming from inside the building, he crept close to the exterior and peered in through an open window and saw the shadowy forms of the two lovers. Thin walls and open windows amplified their voices and Agent Camarata smiled enviously. Damn! He wouldn't have minded changing places with the cobbler's son in that instant. He turned his attention back to his assignment, wondering at the crazy man's erratic behavior. This unusual break from normal behavior baffled Camarata. Why the hell is the old man here in the first place? And at this hour? Where is he headed? Or is this simply a binge! It's a helluva time for a drunken spree! Goddammit! The man was known for his crazy, crazy behavior! He belonged in a home, not turned loose on the streets. But, Camarata rationalized, he wasn't paid to think, only to follow the poor bloke.

Paolo Nicosia's mood shifted like a kaleidoscope from self-abasement, to light gentle humor, from anger to guttural sensualities. Losing his inhibitions he began to sing pornographic lyrics to an old Sicilian song:

"... *Nofrio, Nofrio with his cock so fat, could only fuck whores when he sat* ...

"... *Sucking cowlike tits and asses so round, he could shoot ten loads into their mounds* ..."

Suddenly he burst into tears, as if the song typified his loneliness and wasted life. His emotions shifted. "What's a man without *maschiezzo*? Nothing! Nothing! Nothing!" he wailed in a heart-rending sob. He sat down on the curb and cried. The fisherman dried his eyes on his coat sleeve. Through the drunken haze came a split second of clarity.

"Dolcetto!" he called. "Dolcetto! I'm coming! I'm coming to save you!" His words, loud enough for Agent Camarata to hear and perplex him, were quickly scribbled in a small notebook. Suddenly the agent paused and turned his head, cocked it slightly, straining to hear. He glanced at his man some ten feet from him and noticed the fisherman also strained to listen.

Death's couriers in the Alfa Romeo had begun to make the ascent up the spiraling road to the *piazza*. The men leaned forward in their seats trying to pierce the darkness, to make the right turnoff toward their destination.

In the *piazza*, the glow of illumination from two lampposts cast oblique shadows in the mall. By no stretch of the imagination could they be construed as anything other than what they were, mere shadows. To Nicosia, they became monstrous and threatening. His hollow eyes, anguished and tormented, glanced about the village square. He drank greedily from the goatskin, his aim all wrong, he spilled the liquid past unmanageable lips onto his chin and white shirt. He blew his nose into the cobbles, dabbed at his hot stinging eyes, inclined his head in the direction of the east entrance to the square, to the road that led to Palermo.

The fisherman drew himself up and in that instant he knew everything. He was *Capitano* Nicosia, skipper of the *Marchessa!* He was Paolo Nicosia, fisherman extraordinaire of the *Baccala!* He was Nicosia, worthy seaman of the *Arcturus II*. He was *Paolo u' pazzu*. He was an impotent zero; a nothing! He was a dead man!

Chills and fever alternately plagued him. He held the goatskin rakishly in the air, and he knew. *Something in the wine!*

413

His legs, like dead weights, refused to function. He was rooted to the ground. He was a dead man all right. A poor, dead fish!

Agent Camarata knew something was wrong with Nicosia, but he had no time to make a move. The sounds he and the old fisherman heard drew nearer and when the bright, blinding headlights of the Alfa Romeo lit up the square, he retreated quickly into the shadows.

In a frenzied moment, Nicosia saw the car snake around the corner into view. He clutched at his chest, contorted with pain, and made a series of disordered gestures of a prostrate and broken man.

The coroner was to later say that death came as a result of poisoning and not from the lethal lupara pellets. But, for now, blasts of a lupara shot from an open window of the death car caused his body to jackknife, lift into the air, and bounce back several feet. He fell to the ground like a puppet whose life strings had been severed.

The couriers of death hastened the Alfa Romeo along, turned, wheeled, and disappeared down the road leading to the waterfront, but not before Agent Camarata noted the license number and make of the sedan.

Camarata hastened to Nicosia's side. He raised the dying man's head. Blood spurted from the massive wounds and mingled freely with the lethal wine that trickled from the goatskin sprawled next to his body. He listened. The old man was trying to say something. "Dolcetto! Dolcetto! My Godson! They'll kill him tonight! They'll kill him!" Nicosia grabbed the agent's lapels, his eyes fired with bright mania, then he fell dead.

It was 3:30 A.M. Camarata clinically noted the time and jotted down the fisherman's last words, meaningless to him at the time. On his feet he ran to the cobbler's shop and knocked sharply on the door. Once again he knocked harder. "Open up! I know you're in there! I'm an officer of the law!" he ordered brusquely.

The door opened a sliver. Giacomo peered at him hesitantly.

"A *telefono!* Where can I find a telephone?"

"Across the *strada* . . . Over there," pointed the cobbler's son. He slammed the door and bolted it tight.

Having finished their lovemaking earlier, they had watched Nicosia's antics from the darkened window. They had laughed and giggled and nudged each other playfully as the fisherman sang his song of lament until the sound of a car's motor laboring up the hill had drawn their attention. Everything

414

happened so fast that they were both startled to realize they'd witnessed the fisherman's murder.

Febronia, who recognized her brothers' car first, and then their faces, went into hysterics. She panicked. Crossed herself over and over again religiously, then broke into tears. Giacomo, an aspiring young *picciotto*, who knew the score, quickly assessed the situation and slapped the girl until she quieted down.

"We've seen nothing, understand! Nothing!" Hurriedly he tucked in his shirttails and kept his feverish eyes on the girl who wept softly.

"My brothers—murderers! They killed that crazy, crazy, poor man! Sainted God! By the unholy balls of Lucifer, my brothers are murderers!"

Giacomo grabbed her, shook her roughly, and declared, "We heard nothing! We saw nothing! We weren't even here! *Capeeshi?*" Filled with bravado, in that moment of decision he'd altered the course of his destiny. Watching the agent bending over Nicosia's body, he knew that soon he'd no longer remain the son of a cobbler. He knew how to keep his mouth shut until the right time.

38

The sloe-eyed bride turned to her bridegroom of a few hours. The joy she felt overwhelmed her, as if her heart would burst with happiness. At first, Dolcetto had treated her like a fragile doll. When she responded to his erotic touch without inhibition, his startled expression turned to one of immediate joy. With both their passions fully aroused, the lovers achieved mountains of ecstasy, again and again. Dolcetto poured more champagne for her.

"I've had too much already, dearest. Already my head is spinning."

"Here," he insisted. "Not every night is a wedding celebration."

"Are you very upset I wasn't a virgin?"

Dolcetto avoided her eyes for a moment. "That's never been of earthshaking importance to me." He sipped his champagne. "After all, I wasn't a virgin either. I haven't been one for many years."

She smiled mischievously. "I'm happy for both of us you weren't."

"*Salute.* I'll drink to that."

"You're not curious as to who deflowered me?"

"No."

"I want to tell you."

"Why?"

"So that you can understand me better."

"*Cara mia,* I don't want to understand you. It would spoil the illusion. When people understand each other, they've nothing to look forward to. The mystery is gone and the relationship grows dull. It stagnates."

"Aren't you just a *little* curious?" she teased.

"You won't let me off until you tell me, is that it?"

"Perhaps."

"All right, tell me." He exaggerated his impatience.

"Later," she said.

He threw a pillow at her, feigning exasperation. They frolicked on the bed, then he grabbed her and held her tightly until, clinging to each other, they melted into love.

Francesca snuggled up to her husband and thought back to the earlier part of the night, when they were alone with each other for the first time since Rome. She had removed the crown of orange blossoms with its sheer silk illusion veiling, and tossed it on the pale ivory love seat near the marble fireplace. Across the room, Dolcetto poured two glasses of champagne and watched her remove two large hairpins from her hair, allowing it to cascade softly past her shoulders.

Aware of his eyes on her, she premeditated every move especially to increase her husband's rising excitement. Suddenly she began to giggle. Dolcetto rushed to her side, picked her up, and whirled her joyously about the room. Pulling his head closer to hers, she kissed him lingeringly. Slowly, he allowed her body, pressed firmly to his, to slip down—down—down—until her toes almost touched the floor. He picked her up in his arms, carried her to the enormous bed, and fell against her, holding her pressed tightly against him. Caught up in his mood, she laughed throatily in that wild provocative voice that drove him into rapturous delight. Dolcetto sobered. He looked deeply into her eyes, filled with another mood, one less playful, more amorous.

His strong, tender hands caressing her face, stroking it gently, sent shivers up her spine. He cupped her velvety face until she too fell into his mood and a silence filled the room. "I love you, *cara mia.* I love you with every breath I draw, with every heartbeat, so much I'm bursting this very moment," he whispered hoarsely.

"And I love you," she replied in that magical voice. Their eyes melted into each other's, then, with tenderness, such sweet tenderness, he kissed her soft, sensuous lips, lightly at first, then with the deep passion of a totally committed man. Their souls had begun to soar above the mundane.

It was just at this moment, the refrains of her favorite

416

song, "Shangri-La," filtered through the open windows. Far away at first, it suddenly pierced their mood. Delighted and amused that someone should think to play her favorite song, she glanced at her husband. His expression was one of innocence. She pushed Dolcetto from her for a moment.

"*Aspetta, amore,* wait a moment." Much to her bridegroom's consternation she arose from the bed, smoothed the folds of her gown, and pushed her long hair off her face. She walked regally to the balcony and stood for a time glancing at the peasants who tried dancing to the unfamiliar tempo. Dolcetto joined her, carrying two glasses of champagne, and kissed the back of her neck.

At that moment, Francesca caught sight of Gino Vittorio, his hand raised with a glass of wine in a mocking gesture only she could perceive.

"Look! . . . There's Gino, toasting us," said Dolcetto, pretending to be pleased. Brooding for a split-second as only a man who knew that look could have brooded, he told himself, *Stop it! You're seeing things that aren't there. Forget it before it grows into a malignancy!*

Inside the bridal chamber Francesca's mood had altered considerably as she undressed and prepared herself for Dolcetto's loving arms. She had had many misgivings about that night she let Gino make love to her. After she'd killed and castrated the men who betrayed her family, she experienced curious, overwhelming sensations inexplicable to herself, which she felt sure would leave her as she walked endlessly about the estate. But nothing eased the insatiable physical need. Nothing! Gino just happened to be there. She never dreamed he'd expect more or that he'd become so possessive afterwards. To discourage any further ideas he might have she went out of her way to avoid him.

"Damn!" exclaimed Francesca, catching a fingernail in one of the many looped buttonholes of her gown.

"Here, let me help you," laughed Dolcetto, kissing her injured fingernail. Seated on the bed, he turned her around with her back to him and began to undo the long line of buttons. Despite her constant wriggling, he completed the task, then, gave her a playful smack on her buttocks to keep her still. In moments she stood before him, naked and unashamed.

Dolcetto devoured her with his eyes. She moved across the room to turn up the wall stereo unit, and the music she loved so much flooded the room. He walked to her side, gathered her into his arms, and they began to sway rhythmically to the music as they gazed into each other's eyes.

"Why didn't you tell me you were here all the time? I'd have come for you much sooner," he told her.

They kissed in a rapturous embrace.

The black Alfa Romeo pulled to a stop before an old, run-down warehouse in a slum section along the waterfront. Mario Cacciatore beckoned his companions, Nino and Stefano di Lucca, to follow him as he stepped from the car. The stench of dead fish filled the air and the *mafiosi* screwed their noses in disdain. Cacciatore cursed silently. Tonight he had to deal with the Royal Lions using men he had never worked with before. As he turned around to hurry them along, something in the distance suddenly caught his eye. When he recognized the *Arcturus II* laying at anchor in the bay, he nudged Nino. "Quick, get the binoculars."

"Why? What's wrong?"

"*Cammoria!* Do as I say!"

Nino returned with the high-powered lenses and handed them to his boss. Cacciatore focused them on the cruiser, but he saw no movement, no sign of anyone aboard.

"I'll be back in a moment," he hissed, walking across the street to a telephone booth at the end of the pier.

"*Botta de sanguo!*" he barked into the phone. "The *Arcturus II* is in the harbor at Porto Tomasso. Have someone pick it up immediately. Yes, Nicosia is dead!" He hung up the receiver, glowering at the ineptness with which he'd handled Nicosia. *Who'd have thought the old man could survive the effects of the poison long enough to come to Porto Tomasso? Why had he been there in the square? Lucky for us I spotted the cruiser. It must be out of the harbor before we finish off the Lions.*

Cacciatore returned to where the di Lucca brothers waited for him. *Damn! They act as if we're out for a social evening.* He nodded and they fell into step behind him. He tried to force the shabby old door on which a faded sign read: *Vanzini Chemical Company.* The handle, rusted from years of neglect, wouldn't budge. He jerked his head toward Stefano and the young man stepped in and shoved with his powerful shoulders. The decayed wood gave way like crumbling matchsticks. He kicked the rest of it in and permitted Cacciatore to enter first.

As Cacciatore's beady black eyes darted about the unlit interior, he motioned the others to follow. He crushed his cigar against the word *Vanzini* on the fallen sign and tossed away the stub. Stefano kicked aside a few empty crates and proceeded with the others toward the entrance to the underground tunnels. The air was thick with cobwebs. Stefano tapped the wall with the butt of his .45 automatic until he heard a hollow sound. Slipping the gun back into his belt, he leaned heavily against the wall and motioned the others to help. Together, they pushed and shoved until the concealed door began to move. Finally it creaked on its rusty hinges and opened.

Cacciatore motioned them forward into the shadowy alcove to begin their descent through the ancient underground tunnels which led up the hill to the top of the mountain. With a powerful flashlight to light their way, they moved through an endless series of twists and turns and sharp-angled paths, walking for what seemed an eternity.

Cacciatore's thoughts turned back to Nicosia and how shocked he'd been to see him in the square. Earlier that evening while Nicosia had been en route to Barbarossa's villa, Cacciatore himself had slipped aboard ship and poured Luminal poison in his goatskin *botta*. The chemist had assured him the victim would be dead in less than an hour. Recognizing Nicosia in the piazza had so astounded him that he grabbed the lupara from the sheath in the car and fired without taking time to aim at the head to make identification difficult. What was important was Nicosia was dead!

It was this cold, detached, quick thinking that made Cacciatore the envy of every aspiring *picciotto*. Such a *picciotto* was Stefano di Lucca. When told he and his brother would accompany Cacciatore on this special assignment, he became so excited, the nervous tic that pulled at the left corner of his lip became uncontrollable. He unbuttoned his jacket and slipped the .45 into his belt next to the sheath containing a sharp knife. His tic continued to work in rapid staccato. He was so annoyed, he unintentionally shoved his brother Nino, who stumbled forward and bumped into their grim-faced leader. Cacciatore turned and glared at him. "Watch where you walk, idiot!" Cacciatore fumed inwardly. *Fucking lamebrains, these two! They were fine for wine, women, and song, but not for jobs like this. What the hell was the Don thinking of to have wished them on me tonight of all nights?*

In the beginning these icy, arrogant stares and repeated insults angered Nino. Tonight he didn't give a damn. Tonight he'd prove to Don Barbarossa how good a killer he was. Up till now he'd been a glorified errand boy. A cocksman of the first order, his physical endowments made him king with the opposite sex, but Nino wanted more than recognition for his *machiezzo*.

They arrived at a spiral staircase made of flat stones which hugged a wall of layered rock. It was unbearably hot and humid. Cacciatore stopped, groped along one wall with one hand and flashed his light in a wide arc of light with the other. His stony expression remained unchanged as he located a small knob on the wall. He turned it. A small opening appeared accompanied by a squeaking, straining sound.

Inside the villa, Marco de Leone had fallen across his bed in a deep drugged sleep. The violet light on the alarm panel lit up, accompanied by two beeps per second. He didn't stir.

Lost in each other's arms, Dolcetto and his bride continued to make passionate love. The music played over and over, but neither made an effort to change the records.

Breathing laboriously in the stifling heat, Cacciatore and his men forged on through endless tunnels that twisted intricately in the darkness. Cacciatore again stopped and scanned the map in his hand with the flashlight. Then he examined the damp stone wall on his left. Locating a rafter, he signaled his companions to help push the cumbersome beam into position. Straining under the weight, the men groaned, grunted, and pushed until a door squeaked open enough to permit them to squeeze through. On the other side, a long corridor, filled with several inches of water, wound on endlessly. Offended by the unbearable stench, the men placed handkerchiefs over their noses.

Marco de Leone stirred slightly on the bed as the light panel progressed to the orange light and one chime per second. The pallor left his face and he grew flushed. His breathing was deep and steady. It seemed that nothing short of an earthquake would awaken the Royal Lion, not even the blue light which now blinked above his head.

At the end of the underground tunnel, the *mafia* trio began to climb a flight of spiral iron steps.

The newlyweds lay back fully spent, overflowing with love for each other. Francesca moved voluptuously across the oversized bed with its shimmering silk sheets. She propped herself up against the thickly tufted headboard and pinned her thick hair high atop her head. Her eyes were fastened on her new husband in the semi-darkness. He lay still, eyes closed, breathing deeply with contentment. Feeling her eyes upon him, he opened one eye, then the other. They both smiled and Francesca began giggling.

Dolcetto got to his feet, turned on the light, changed the records on the turntable, and poured them each a glass of

420

champagne. With the exaggerated movements of a mime, he moved toward her, trying to keep his hands steady. The towel around his hips came undone and he missed his footing, spilling the amber fluid all over his bride. She squealed with delight, writhing and squirming all over the bed. He picked up the towel and began to blot the champagne from her body. *"Cara mia,"* he said. "Forgive me. I'm tipsy."

Francesca reached for his hand to stop him. "There's nothing to forgive," she said huskily, encircling his neck with one arm. With the other she groped for the light switch that once again thrust the room into darkness, as she felt him harden against her flesh.

"Carissima, carissima mia," he sighed. "I love you . . . love you . . ."

Cacciatore and his men entered a shadowy wine cellar. Stefano located a large candle and when he lit it, both brothers stared about in open-mouthed fascination. Nino removed a bottle from its niche, blew off a layer of dust and, holding the bottle up to the light, uttered a low murmur of approval.

Cacciatore snapped his fingers impatiently and prodded them. "Move, goddammit, move! You think we're touring the king's palace?"

They were all soaking wet, and they carried their jackets slung over their shoulders and shoved their fedoras back on their heads. Thinking he had Nino's attention, Cacciatore suddenly flung him the flashlight. Nino missed the catch and froze. It fell to the floor with a loud crash, rolled along the stones, and came to an abrupt halt where one stone protruded above the others. The men instinctively reached for their guns and stood flush against the walls, not daring to breathe or move.

Red-faced, Nino reached to retrieve the light and in so doing, unwittingly stepped on the protruding stone. He felt a peculiar cushioning under his foot, but he said nothing to the others as he fell into step behind his brother, wondering at that odd sensation.

Upstairs, the Royal Lion yawned and stretched, then rolled over on the bed and fell into a deeper sleep, unaware that the blue light had progressed to the green. The next light flashed yellow. Three rings per second followed. Marco de Leone slept as sound as a baby.

Downstairs where the wedding ceremony had taken place, the room filled with partial shadows as moonlight filtered through the large windows. The floral-banked fireplace and wedding decor remained untouched. Fine paintings, wall tapestries, and thick Kashmir carpets added elegance to the luxurious room. Opposite the marble fireplace stood an enormous breakfront of exquisitely carved rosewood. There was a slight creaking as the magnificent piece began to move away from the wall. It swung out in a full arc, revealing an opening behind it.

With Stefano and Nino at his heels, Cacciatore entered the salon cautiously, peering about the shadowy darkness. Once inside the salon, the di Lucca brothers could see well enough to be stunned by the opulence. Stefano nudged his brother and whistled softly in full appreciation. Never having seen such grandeur, they stared like gawking tourists. Did people really live like this?

Wiping the perspiration from his face, Cacciatore pulled out his gun and tossed his jacket on the nearby chair, making a mental note to pick it up on the way out. They swiftly crossed the room, stepped lightly through the foyer, and began to climb the spiral staircase. The thick carpeting absorbed their footsteps, silencing their deadly movements.

Upstairs in the bridal chamber, the newlyweds lay fully spent, drained of energy, in the repose of a Lion and his Lioness, curled up in each other's arms.

By now, the ominous red light flashed angrily as the full alarm of rings, chimes, and beeps made a cacophony of discordant sounds in Marco's bedroom. Beneath the active alarms, the mighty Royal Lion slept, unstirring.

39

The music emanating from the bridal chamber drowned out any sound that might have permeated the upper hallway. The trio of death crept cautiously to the right at the top of the landing and walked toward the bridal chamber until they stood abreast of the large, thick double doors. Very slowly, inch by inch, Cacciatore turned the finely scrolled brass handle until the hand-carved oak panels moved. Then, in a quick gesture, he opened both doors. The men moved in swiftly and soundlessly with animallike movements. They crept along the sides of the bridal bed, staring at the sleeping couple with deadly eyes.

Under their hostile scrutiny, the unsuspecting couple dozed, wafting in and out of a satisfied reverie. Francesca yawned and lay back on the silken pillows as Dolcetto, feeling her movement, moved in to close the gap between their bodies. The ornately gilded cupids on the clock over the mantel stared angelically at the room's occupants. The clock chimed. It was 4:30 A.M.

The men stared at the partially naked body of Francesca, who had, moments before, cast aside the silken sheets. In the moonlight, her body shimmered like pale ivory. The golden lion around her neck glittered defiantly and caught Cacciatore's attention. He stared at it with contempt and a hatred for the memories it conjured up. Stefano nudged his brother and they both saw the grimace on Cacciatore's face. They puzzled over his reaction.

Almost as if a sixth sense nagged at her, warning of impending danger, Francesca's eyes fluttered open. She blinked a few times until she was able to focus clearly. Impulsively, her hands went to her eyes and she rubbed them in disbelief. She bolted upright in the bed. Her exhausted bridegroom, intoxicated by both love and alcohol, slept soundly at her side. Francesca recognized Cacciatore and filled with terror. She tried to scream to warn Dolcetto, but no sound came forth. Her eyes shifted from one shadowy form to the next. Then Nino, moving in quicker than the eye could follow, placed a foul-smelling hand, wet with perspiration, over her mouth. His other hand held a gun to her temple. Her dark luminous eyes widened in horror. Nino's lascivious eyes lingered longingly over her body, while his brother pulled the drowsy, protesting Dolcetto off the bed.

Groggy, the Lion tried with difficulty to force his eyes open. The room became cyclonic; everything moved. His eyes couldn't focus through the film over his eyes. Slowly, like a recurring dream, the image of Nino holding his wife in a viselike grip began to take form and hold. He blinked several times. He saw Cacciatore, whom he didn't recognize at first. The unmistakable, cocksure pose of a *mafioso* sobered him instantly. His eyes narrowed and he forced his mind into action. Vague images came to him. The pose was the same! The man was the same! Older, but still the arrogant bandit he'd branded! Hatred and black fury mixed with adrenalin combined in an instant, and without realizing he was held in check by Stefano, he lunged wildly at the *mafioso*. Stefano flung Dolcetto into a chair and quickly tied him with the sash of his robe, hurled to him by Cacciatore. Helpless and stunned, he stared at his terrified wife, filled with a sinking feeling of gloom.

Cacciatore moved boldly toward Francesca and allowed his hand to caress her body. She recoiled with the instinct of a frightened animal. Dolcetto's eyes followed his every

423

move. With immeasurable hatred and rage, he strained furiously against his ties.

"Schifoso!" he spat at the *mafioso.*

Stefano clouted Dolcetto with a powerful fist. His head fell heavily to one side. A variety of constellations exploded inside his head. He shook his head in an attempt to reorganize his senses. Words of protest formed on his lips. Instantly, he was judo-chopped from behind by Stefano. His tic more pronounced now, he laughed sadistically at the limp, sagging head of the trapped Lion.

Enraged at this brutal display, Francesca squirmed free of Nino's hands. She scurried across the bed, only to be headed off by the quick-thinking Stefano, who leered defiantly at her. Her dark, horror-stricken eyes flared like a wild woman's. She glanced from him to the sick and depraved-looking Nino and her fears intensified. She retreated to the headboard of the bed, clutching savagely at the slippery sheets, trying to cover her nude body.

Why can't I scream? Coraggio, *Francesca,* coraggio. No matter how she tried no noise would emanate from her throat.

"You should have accepted the Don's generous offer, Signora de Leone." In a quick, furtive movement, Cacciatore tore the sheet from her body. "You could have avoided all this," he added with a smug half-apologetic voice.

"Filthy, impotent pig!" she lashed out in a moment of sudden courage.

In his black, brutal eyes were culminated the many years of hatred for his emasculation suffered at the hands of the Lion. His voice was deadly. "Take her, she's all yours. I'll sit and watch until her husband comes back to us."

In a flash, Nino tossed off his jacket and jumped onto the bed. His eyes were fixed greedily on the exotic beauty under him. When he entered her, Francesca screamed out in agony from the size of him. She clawed at him with her long fingernails, leaving bloody trails on his face. She bit and scratched and clawed and kicked until her strength gave out. Each thrust of his pelvis sent excruciating pains shooting through her body. She cried out in agony and fell faint under him.

Stefano watched for a time, then, as an evil glint appeared in his eyes, he stepped behind the unconscious Lion and savagely pulled back his head. He tried to revive Dolcetto and force him to watch, but no matter how many times he slapped the inert man, his victim failed to respond. Stefano looked about the room and saw the open champagne bottle and the ice bucket. He picked up the bottle, shook it, and squirted champagne in Dolcetto's face, then finally poured it over his head. The cold liquid partially revived him in time to hear his wife's agonized screams.

When Dolcetto realized what was happening, he closed his tortured eyes and tried to avert his head. He retched violently at the sick and depraved act, struggling in vain against his bindings. His head was forced back by the psychotic Stefano.

Cacciatore's face remained hard and expressionless. He tore open his shirt so that the Lion's brand was visible as he walked to Dolcetto's side.

"At last we meet again, eh, *El Leone?*" he hissed. "It's taken a long time, but I've been patient. Now, I shall be avenged for what you did to me."

This was all new to Stefano. He gazed at Cacciatore's chest, saw the Lion's brand, and stared with profound interest. Never had he heard mention of this story.

"Now you'll crawl as you made me crawl that night. Before I finish with you, you shall beg for mercy. If not for yourself, for your wife."

"I should have killed you that night."

"See, Stefano! Even now, with his life hanging in the balance, he shows no fear. We'll soon see who shall live to tell the story *this* time." He made the sign of a cuckold, and Dolcetto backed away from the grimy fingers thrust at him. Cacciatore moved deftly to one side, forcing Dolcetto to gaze upon the animalistic ravaging of his unconscious wife. For an instant, even Stefano and Cacciatore were drawn with curious interest by Nino's loud grunts and groans and animal cries as he climaxed.

Suddenly, the unexpected happened, as if Destiny herself stood in the room to help Dolcetto. In a violent burst of energy, he backed the chair into the unsuspecting Stefano. Knocked off balance, he fell against the fireplace, struck his head against a heavy, ornamented andiron and blacked out. Cacciatore stared mutely at the still form of his aide sprawled unceremoniously on the floor. He took a menacing step toward the Lion, then, in afterthought, walked to Nino's side and pulled the protesting, depraved, and sexually excited beast off Francesca's unconscious body. The incensed, disturbed look on Cacciatore's face, halted Nino's protest. Cacciatore jerked his head toward Stefano's still form with a clear order behind his silent, icy look.

Nino pulled himself up and buttoned his trousers, then he quickly sprang to Dolcetto's side. He cut the ties with his knife and stood back, poised to strike. Dolcetto's arms felt like dead weights, numb from the tight ligatures that had bound them. When he caught sight of Francesca on the bed, he filled with indescribable anger, but just then Nino's fist came at him. The blow knocked him backwards and he toppled over a chair. As he staggered to his feet, both men moved in toward him. For what seemed an eternity, Dolcetto took their savage blows.

How Dolcetto, bruised, battered, still feeling the effects of so much champagne, still had his wits about him was a miracle! Somehow he maneuvered the men along the wall housing the stereo unit, seemingly unaware of the physical pain inflicted upon him as blood squirted from his nose and badly cut lips. Nino connected with a right upper cut to the jaw and sent the Lion flying backward. His body, flung like a limp rag doll, covered one end of the stereo cabinet. The impact of his fall agitated the phonograph needle. It jumped over the ruts and grooves with a whining raucous scratching sound until it landed in another groove where it remained to drone on and on and on, in a monotony of repetition. Unnoticed by his assailants, Dolcetto's hands groped blindly for a set of switches. Locating them, he pushed hard against them, hoping as he did his movement would go unnoticed by these men.

Cacciatore reached for Dolcetto and pulled him away from the stereo with strength unusual for a man his age. He was about to strike the Lion again, when Dolcetto's body sagged heavily and slipped through his hands like a stone weight. For a moment, he stared dumbly at the swollen, semi-conscious face with its puffy, bleeding eyes. Then he turned him over to Nino, who came at Dolcetto fully enraged. Time and again, he slashed out with his razor-sharp stiletto.

If he lived forever, Dolcetto would never forget the sight of Nino di Lucca coming at him with the fixed, glittering eyes of a psychopathic killer, with gleaming white teeth frozen in a smile more chilling than the outthrust jaws of a shark. *From where do those moans and groans come,* wondered Dolcetto. *From me?* Whirlpools of hot blood erupted and gushed over his face. Swollen eyes rolled upward and back into the darkness of his mind as agonized eyelids tried mercifully to shut out the sight of his attacker. He felt himself thrash wildly about the floor unable to control the violent spasms that shot through his body. Why couldn't he stop the twitching, jackknifing of his body? He clutched savagely at his face trying in someway to hold back the flow of blood. *God, he had to do something! What?* The last he saw of consciousness were the two shadowy figures of Mario Cacciatore and Nino di Lucca who stood over him with frozen expressions, staring down at his writhing body in its struggle with death, until merciful darkness came.

Cacciatore spat contemptuously at the prostrate form at his feet, a gleam of triumph in his vengeful eyes. Strutting to Francesca's side, he grabbed a shock of her black hair in his grubby fist and yanked hard. He stared long and hard at her silent, limp form, then, thrust her violently from him. She fell over the side of the bed in a sagging mass, the golden lion at her neck falling away from her body, swaying back and forth on its chain.

Nino picked up the unconscious body of his brother, slung Stefano's limp form over one shoulder, and waited impatiently for Cacciatore.

"Now, for the mighty Royal Lion, himself, eh? According to the *capomastro* he should be sound asleep. *Amonini,* let's finish him off!"

They both crossed the room to the door and stopped frozen in their tracks. A look of astonishment on their sweaty faces transformed to looks of fear.

The mighty Royal Lion of Sicily stood poised in the doorway. His eyes smoldered darkly, filled with the revulsion of a centuries-old loathing. In his long, thin hand, he held a menacing burp gun. With a sure, steady movement, he squeezed the trigger. Marco de Leone's body shook from the vibration of the gun as its bullets spewed forth at his targets.

The impact of the bullets spun Nino around like a dervish. Stefano's body, filled with bleeding craters, fell to the floor. His own, ripped apart by the missiles, fell back and landed in a heap over his brother's. Clutched tightly in his hand was the gun he'd been too late in using.

Cacciatore managed to whirl around and find cover behind an overstuffed chair. He whipped out his gun and began firing as bullets from the burp gun followed and hit their mark. The terror of the Mazzarinos and of Sicily fell shaking to his knees. He managed to fire three wild shots before he pitched over and died, a look of surprise still on his face.

Marco still stood in the doorway. His bewildered eyes traveled slowly over the bodies sprawled on the floor; his mind refused to accept it as truth. Marco stared dumbly at the gun in his hands. He relaxed his fingers and the gun fell noisily to the floor. Marco took a step forward and fell heavily against the wood-paneled door. Blood spurted from his lips and he clutched at his stomach where two of Cacciatore's bullets had caught him.

His tormented eyes traveled from his son's body to that of his new wife, and the Royal Lion fell to his knees. He crawled along the floor, inch by inch, pulling his numbed body after him as excruciating pain shot out in hot licking flames. He reached with a helpless, outstretched arm toward his son. Tears like liquid fire sprang into his eyes, and they grew dimmer until he could barely distinguish the forms about him.

Dear God, let Dolcetto live. Take my life—but let him live. Keep Francesca alive—let her live. It's all over for the Lions. The Royal Lions are no more.

As the moment of truth approached, he knew Alberto Pietro for what he was. The tablets, the plans, even Roberto's unheeded warnings came to him, too late.

You must let Dolcetto live, God! If only to learn of Alberto's treachery!

The Lion was dead. Long live the Lion.

Antonio de Leone whistled happily as he sped along in the Giulietta Spider. Soon it would be dawn. But, what a night! *Managghia!* What a night! He wheeled the Spider up the steep incline leading to the Vanzini Villa and geared down, thinking how much he'd missed confining his amorous escapades to the Continent. Phew! These Sicilian wenches were something else! Voluptuous breasts, small waists, wide-hipped like brood mares in heat! Very discerning of Dolcetto to pick a Sicilian for his bride! If the Lion enjoyed his bridal night half as much as Antonio had enjoyed his night— Antonio laughed aloud at the speculation. A pulsing light broke in the eastern sky.

Almost immediately an inexplicable shudder passed through him, a sense of foreboding. He no longer smiled. His whistling ceased. He saw no guards, no sentries, not even an early rising peasant, who by now would have filled the roads with their gayly painted carts en route to the feudal estates. Nothing! For too long, he and Dolcetto had been indoctrinated to the unusual as it occurred in the landed estates. He knew what to look for and it wasn't there. He left the Spider some distance from the main gate, and crept cautiously toward the entrance, his eyes darting all around him.

Antonio had forgotten many things since his accident, but this instinctive reaction to trouble remained. He could smell it in the air and feel his senses recoil. The villa seemed deserted. What's more they'd locked him out! His only means of access would be to scale the treacherous sea wall. Goddamn! That was a sheer drop to eternity, he thought, trying not to focus on the shimmering waves that seemed to beckon far below him.

Having scaled the wall, he drew a deep breath of gratitude. His patron saint was smiling on him. Now he moved cautiously in the weird, predawn light, along the rear of the villa, past the kitchens and outside ovens. Advancing toward the terrace he tripped and fell over a cumbersome object. Breathlessly, he peered about, and when he saw the prone figure of Marco's bodyguard, Calo La Bolla, he didn't have to look twice to know the man was dead. Shocked, and filled with disbelief, he backed away, slowly, looking for possible traps or treacheries. To gain entrance into the villa, he broke a pane of glass on one of the French doors, reached in, and unslipped the bolt. He let himself into the house, stealthily, like a cautious tiger.

Upstairs in the death-filled bridal chamber, Dolcetto felt the stirrings of life. His body, a bloody mass of purplish welts and abrasions, moved slightly. One eye was grotesquely swollen shut. The other forced itself open into a hairline slit. Desperately he tried to move. The room swayed and moved with frightening momentum. Memory came and left him. He drew his hand finally up to his face and stared mutely at the profusion of warm sticky blood dripping over it. Somewhere in a far off distance he heard the scratching monotone of a phonograph needle. It cut into his consciousness and became the only link to the sudden, unreal world in which he found himself.

It took the strength of a god to raise his battered, bloody head and to piece together the broken fragments of a shattered nightmare. It would have been difficult for two good eyes to pierce the deceptive predawn light. Had it not been for a shaft of light striking the jeweled lion around Francesca's neck, making it glitter, he might have missed seeing her body sprawled across the bed, her raven hair spilled over her face.

God knows how he got to her, but he did, straining, crawling, clutching frantically at the bed covers to propel him, he reached out and drew her to his bosom, cradling her limp form, rocking her in a monotonous motion. His tears and his blood dropped onto Francesca's nude, motionless body.

"They'll pay for this . . . they'll pay! Oh, *cara mia,* if it takes all my life, they will never get away with this! My heart, my life, my very dearest wife, oh, how they'll pay! Your death, they will find the costliest deed of their life!"

Just before Dolcetto collapsed over the lifeless form of his wife, he caught sight of his father's leonine white mane at the edge of the bed. His heart stopped. "Papa?" he gasped hoarsely. "Papa! No—not you!" He fell into a pit of icy blackness.

Noises from Marco's bedroom struck Antonio the moment he reached the spiral staircase. Taking the steps three at a time he rushed first into Marco's room only to find it empty. He gazed about and swiftly shut off the clanging alarms. Now he moved furtively. He flung off his tuxedo jacket, crept along the upper corridor, pausing at the long console table where he reached behind a vase to pull at a cord. He asked himself where the servants were? His uncle? Anyone? He didn't delude himself into thinking any servants were around. Something or someone either frightened them off or made certain they were no place to be found. Heading for the bridal chambers, he paused when he saw the arsenal door open. He shoved a Belgian-made Browning into his belt and took down a war surplus M-1 rifle and checked them for action.

The scratching of the needle struck him first. The partially open door offered him no visiblity, so he gave it a savage kick and fell into a crouch position, his gun poised in mid-air ready for any encounter.

Only silence greeted him. It was difficult for him to see in the dark. Slowly, he stood up and groped behind him for the light switch. Light filled the room giving life to a horror that could hardly be tolerated even in darkness.

Antonio moved like a zombie to the stereo unit to turn off the droning, scratchy sounds of the rutted phonograph needle. When he saw the outflung body of his uncle, a sob escaped him. He moved swiftly, knelt at the dead man's side, gathered him into his arms, and studied the waxen face, unlined and peaceful in death. Slowly, he rocked Marco back and forth. When he could he reluctantly pulled his eyes away from the face of his uncle and glanced about the room, dazed and numb and stupefied. Suddenly every nerve in his body stopped. He swallowed hard and fixed his eyes on Dolcetto's body. Had he seen movement? Was it possible his cousin was alive? His heart raced.

Gently he lay down the body of his uncle and stared at Dolcetto, not daring to breathe or move. There! There it was again! A sight movement, like a muscle spasm. His senses came alive. He moved swiftly to his cousin's side, daring to hope, praying, *Sainted God! Let him be alive!*

"Dolcetto?" he whispered. "Dolcetto! Can you hear me?"

A finger on his cousin's hand moved a hair. He lifted Dolcetto off Francesca's nude body. Dolcetto moaned softly. Antonio felt his pulse. Leaned over to listen for a heartbeat. It was faint, hardly discernible, but merciful God, it was there! When he cleared Dolcetto's body off the bed,

Francesca fell limply to one side. Covered with Dolcetto's blood, she looked horrifyingly still and dead.

Antonio turned his sickened eyes away. *What shall I do first? What shall I do first,* he asked himself.

"Dolcetto! I must get Dolcetto out of here! I must save him. I must! Someplace, where he'll be safe. Where?" He snapped the silken comforter off the bed, wrapped the Lion in it, flung him over a shoulder like a limp carpet and made his way downstairs and out the villa with no other thought in mind but to save Dolcetto. He stuffed his cousin into Francesca's Spider convertible, pulled the top up and snapped it into place.

Feeling lost, shaken, confused, and filled with dread, he headed toward the only place and person he was sure would help them. To the villa of Dr. Alberto Pietro.

40

Lt. Santino Domingo sat at his desk in a daze. His face blanched and puckered like a creased white fig set out to dry. He read the words but didn't believe his eyes

THE HOUSE OF LIONS HAS FALLEN

What appears to be a vendetta murder occurred at the Vanzini Villa in Porto Tomasso a few miles northwest of Palermo. The Honorable Marquis Marco de Leone, former Senator; his son, the Honorable Dolcetto de Leone; and his young bride of a few hours, Francesca Vanzini de Leone, were killed in what appears to have been a fiendish and savage murder rite.

A few hours before, the historical and picturesque villa had been the setting of an elaborate wedding attended by the crème de la crème *of society from the mainland of Italy and Sicily. Six years ago, the bride's parents and younger brother were found slain under similar circumstances. That case still remains unsolved.*

The bodies were discovered by two of Signora de Leone's most trusted servants, Gino and Guiseppino Vittorio. Two of His Excellency's bodyguards were also found slain.

"Dammit to hell!" cursed Lt. Domingo, glancing at Hank Rossi who sat across the desk from him. "And I had to leave Palermo at the wrong time!" He filled with recrimination. "The last thing I told those idiots in Palermo was to make sure the family was guarded around the clock. Mike

431

Camarata assured me he'd sit on all the security guards to be certain my instructions were followed to the letter."

"Perhaps he's still sitting on them," said Hank Rossi absently. He was busy reading another newspaper account.

"That's not funny, Hank. Not funny at all."

"Sorry. I didn't mean it the way it sounded." He waved an apologetic hand in the air. "I guess that blows our case to hell." He slammed the paper down hard on his desk. "Geezus to hell!" He removed a bottle of Scotch from a drawer and poured himself a shot. He raised a glass to Lt. Domingo, who shook his head in a silent no.

Rossi walked to the wall and studied the chart indicating locations of all their undercover narcotics agents in the Middle East and Mediterranean countries. There was a strained expression on his face.

Lt. Domingo moved his swivel chair from side to side trying to piece together what might have happened after he left Palermo. On impulse he leaned over and picked up the phone.

"Get *Avvocato* Bocca on the phone," he told his secretary.

"He is already on the line calling you, lieutenant," came the astonished voice.

"Santino?" asked Giorgio Bocca.

"Speaking. Giorgio?"

"Have you heard the shocking news? I can't bring myself to believe what I read or hear on the radio."

"You aren't alone, *amico,*" said the lieutenant.

"When did you leave the wedding?"

"About four. I couldn't stay for all the festivities. And you?"

"I stayed until half past seven," replied the lawyer with a noticeable catch in his voice. "It's all so utterly inconceivable. I still can't believe it. Nothing I've read makes sense. Do you realize the kind of security they had? I was with Dolcetto and Francesca most of the afternoon; they were so happy. Even His Excellency was in splendid spirits. If something disturbed them, they gave no indication of it . . ." Giorgio's voice broke. "Just two days ago . . ."

"Have you tried reaching anyone?" asked Lt. Domingo.

"The lines are all jammed. You know what it's like getting calls through to Porto Tomasso. So far we've been unable to get anyone. Have you heard anything from Antonio?"

"No, why?"

"I haven't been able to locate him. You'd think he'd call me right away," agonized Giorgio. "Someone has to make funeral arrangements."

"Funeral arrangements?" The words made the tragedy

432

seem more real. "Yes, of course, the funeral," muttered the lieutenant *sotto voce*.

"I'm flying to Palermo in a few hours . . ."

"Why not join us, Giorgio? Our flight leaves in three hours. Enough time for you?"

"I'll be waiting at my office, Santino. It's on your way. *Va biene?*"

"*Va biene. Ciào, amico.*"

"Include us in the flight," said Hank Rossi, when Domingo hung up the receiver.

"Already did," he mumbled. Lt. Domingo lit a cigarette, took a few long puffs, then snapped on a tape recorder. He listened to the voices of Primo Garibaldi and Dolcetto de Leone. Garibaldi's voice was loud and clear.

"Look de Leone, we intend to divert better than ten million a year to de Leone Shipping."

Across the island of Sicily, several kilometers north of Messina in the modest, well-kept villa belonging to Alberto Pietro, Antonio de Leone stared red-faced and angry at the newspaper.

"That's not the way it happened! There were *six* bodies, not three. What happened to the three *mafiosi* I saw dead on the floor? Why is there no account of their deaths?" He slammed the newspaper down on the table and paced like a bull in heat.

"Be quiet, Antonio," cautioned Dr. Pietro. "Do you want to worsen your cousin's condition? He's critical now. He mustn't be disturbed by any shouting, understand?" The concerned physician crossed the hall to the bedroom at the end of the corridor. He cautiously opened the door and peered inside. Apparently satisfied, he retraced his steps to the living room.

"You don't understand. *I* discovered the bodies, not the servants," whispered Antonio. "The paper distorts the facts. From what I could tell, it was obvious Uncle Marco surprised them in Dolcetto's room and killed all three. He was a hero to the end."

"Does all that matter so much, now? Will the information bring back Marco or Francesca or Dolcetto?"

Antonio frowned. His eyes quickly darted to the physician's face. His own face took on a brooding expression and his fiery brown eyes reflected a fierceness rarely associated with him.

"Dolcetto's not dead!" he stated emphatically. His expression was hard as granite.

Ignoring his statement, Dr. Pietro asked, "Do you want

to be next? What do you think your life is worth, when it's known you're still alive?" Obviously, whoever planned this *infamita* did so in the hope you'd all be eliminated at one time. If it's discovered that you found the bodies and brought Dolcetto here to me . . ." His expression and a significant hand gesture were enough to quiet Antonio for a time. He handed him a glass of wine.

"Look, my boy, you've a duty to perform now. As sole survivor of the de Leone family, you must attend to the funerals. You must return to Palermo to claim the bodies. Take along two bodyguards from the villa."

"But Dolcetto's still alive!" he insisted. "The authorities must be told. The papers must be informed."

"*Is* he still alive?" Dr. Pietro cut him off abruptly.

The two men regarded each other silently. The sensitive, confused Antonio was no match for the crafty physician.

"Do you realize what your cousin's condition is? He was nearly dead when you brought him to me. Only time will tell if he survives. And we need that time." Dr. Pietro rolled back his calculating blue eyes. "If they knew he was still alive and here . . ." he conjectured. "*Maria Santissima! Our lives would be worthless!*"

Antonio got the point, but it didn't placate him in the least. He exploded. "How can I keep up the farce when I'm asked to identify the bodies? The papers said there were three. Who is the stranger I must identify as Dolcetto?" He wrung his hands. "No! I can't do it. Someone's bound to discover the truth."

"Who'll know, save for you and I and Dolcetto—if he pulls through?"

"I won't know what to do in Palermo. I'm not good at such things. You, better than anyone, should know that," he retorted belligerently.

"Pull yourself together, Antonio. You're a de Leone. You'll have to work things out. I must stay here with Dolcetto, if you expect him to live. He needs constant attention." Alberto glanced easily at Antonio who grew more wretched by the moment. He spoke in a gentler tone. "Don't worry, *nepoto*. I'll be here to help you. I'll outline each step you must take. The most important thing to remember is— *trust no one*. Keep your mouth shut about all you know. Take no chances. Tell no one that Dolcetto is alive. *No one!* Understand?"

"I don't know," replied Antonio, shaking his head. "I'm not sure I can remember everything."

"You will. Just don't worry about anything. No one will

question your actions or think it strange you can't communicate with so heavy a heart."

Antonio shook his head and stared at the floor.

"I'll do all in my power to see that you honor the name of de Leone. But you must be cautious. Watch yourself like a hawk. *Say nothing, do nothing* to betray your cousin's whereabouts. The world must believe him dead. You do understand, don't you? If you break under the strain, you'll be signing three death warrants: Dolcetto's, yours, and mine."

Antonio shook uncontrollably. His breathing grew labored. His lips parted and trembled. Perspiration broke out on his face. Alberto studied him closely, then left the room briefly and returned with several white tablets.

"Here, my boy, take these. Try to get some rest."

Antonio popped the pills into his mouth, chased them down with water he poured from the tumbler on the table, and shook his head stubbornly.

"I'm all right. It's Dolcetto who needs your attention."

"*Aloura*, Antonio. First, contact Giorgio Bocca in Rome. Then call your office and Dolcetto's. Your associates must be told that you're alive or else they may panic."

"The board of directors will know what to do in our absence. They've been primed for such an eventuality."

"That may well be, but they should be told you're alive, shouldn't they? It will be easier on them."

Antonio shrugged indifferently, then he reluctantly agreed.

"Now, go and rest for a while. The tablets were a relaxant. I'll call and make necessary arrangements at this end for the funeral."

"Would you? I would appreciate that."

"If you feel peculiar, let me know. I'll fix you another injection like the one I gave you yesterday. It will help dissolve all your fears."

Dr. Pietro sat down in his favorite chair, propped his feet on the stool, and was soon immersed in writing out a list of instructions for Antonio as one would for a child.

Giorgio Bocca, Lt. Domingo, Hank Rossi, and Danny Moreno, accompanied by the local agent Mike Camarata, walked briskly into the dismal, foul-smelling funeral parlor where they were quickly ushered into the equally dismal office of Tanno Baccamorto, the funeral director. The short, thin-faced man had a slender, waxed mustache that gleamed like patent leather and matched the sheen of his dyed black hair. His nervous eyes expanded and contracted when agitated. His shiny black suit, a size too large, flapped and shimmered as he walked in his bowlegged, pigeon-toed manner. It was the mortician's eyes that arrested their attention. He had the eyes of a bug.

Lt. Domingo shoved his I.D. at him. "We're here to examine the bodies of the Honorable de Leone family. You were called by the commissioner's office . . ."

"Ah, 'Tenente." His grotesque eyes scanned the card, expanding and contracting in their whites. Impressed by the emblems of the *Guardia de Finanzia*, he returned the card and turned his strange eyes questioningly upon the others.

"This is *Avvocato* Bocca, *consigliori* to the family, and these are my associates, Rossi, Moreno, and Camarata."

They nodded at each other. Satisfied, the mortician opened his files, removed the death certificates, and handed them to Lt. Domingo. His voice was thin and he spoke with measured words.

"There's very little to see, gentlemen. All were mutilated beyond our repair. We do pride ourselves in making our departed souls look as natural as they did in life. But we are limited in our talents. We need something with which to begin our artistry." He cleared his throat. His eyes fascinated the others.

Lt. Domingo shuddered. Giorgio Bocca felt indignant revulsion sweep through him. He averted his head, unable to gaze upon the bug of a man.

"Nevertheless," snapped Camarata gruffly, "we must inspect the remains."

"As you wish." He kept his hands clasped together in an effeminate manner. "Follow me."

He led the way down a musty hallway to the rear of the building. Together with the odor of formaldehyde, the smell of death prevailed, clinging to the walls and ceilings like a thick, scummy mold. Baccamorto opened another door that led to a quiet, dimly lit room, fully carpeted and draped in black and deep purple satin. The candles on the altar flickered and flared, casting bizarre shadows into the frightening, nauseous room. In the center of the room stood three crude wooden boxes.

"We keep the departed in these containers until we know what to do with them. So far the family has not contacted us."

Giorgio Bocca felt incensed and a slowly rising anger began to eat away at him. He watched the bug-faced roach of a man unsnap the hinges and lift the cover of the first box.

The visitors drew back at the hideousness that greeted them. They were sickened and appalled to see that the entire face of the corpse had been blown off, leaving a gaping hole, the flesh torn and shredded about the skull, a snow-white leonine mane of hair, matted with purple-red blood, dried and caked about the faceless head. The body could have been anyone's.

"Marco de Leone," read the mortician. "We assume it to be his body because of the age."

Giorgio Bocca stared with sick humiliation at the offensive, mutilated body lying naked in the stark wooden box. He closed his pain-filled eyes, trying to obliterate it from his mind. *Was this the end he'd been destined for? My God, how could anyone have performed such a macabre act upon the Royal Lion!*

The mortician opened the second box. He read from the name tag, "Dolcetto de Leone."

The accumulated mass of remains was no more distinguishable than the first. Giorgio forced himself to approach the second box. He peered closer at these remains than he had the first. The body was that of a younger man. It was crusted with caked blood and covered with massive wounds. The hands were unrecognizable, coated with dried blood. The man's genitals had been gouged out and left hanging like limp, dried hunks of liver. The man's eyes had been plucked out of his head. Giorgio averted his head and caught the sickened revulsion in Lt. Domingo's eyes as they all shuddered and looked away.

"Couldn't you have at least cleaned up the bodies?" Giorgio Bocca growled angrily, venting his fury at the mortician.

"Unless we're given permission by the family or responsible parties, we can't touch them. With no word from the authorities, the families must instruct us."

Incensed beyond endurance, Giorgio Bocca wanted to take the Royal Lions away at once, to some other place where they could lie in the dignity they deserved. He bit back a mounting desire to strike the supercilious mortician.

"And this is the Vanzini woman," said the embalmer with a touch of sarcasm. They all turned to stare coldly at him. "Forgive me, she was the Signora de Leone, no?" He threw back the lid of the third wooden box.

"Dio buono!" Bocca stared horrified at the remains of what could barely be judged a woman. As with the others, the face was missing. One breast had been completely severed, leaving an open crater in its stead. Blood, coagulated and thick, was matted over the body. Especially thick was the concentration near the pubic area. Portions of visible skin were a bruised purplish hue. The stench violated the nostrils. Around the woman's neck hung Francesca's golden

jeweled lion. Giorgio Bocca turned away sick, his composure reduced to nothing.

"I've seen enough. Let's get the fuck out of here!"

Lt. Domingo turned to the mortician. "Please remove the golden amulet from the body. I'll be responsible for it."

"My dearest friend, Dolcetto! How could this have happened to you?" Bocca cried, slamming his fist hard on the wooden coffin.

Rossi and Moreno, quietly outraged, moved in quickly toward Bocca. "Are you all right, counselor?" asked Rossi with grave concern.

Moreno took Giorgio's arm. "Steady now," he said softly.

"I'll be fine," replied Giorgio after a few moments. "I need fresh air."

As they moved toward the exit, Lt. Domingo remained behind. "You say you haven't been contacted by the family?" he asked. "Who gave you orders to pick up the bodies?"

The man extended his arm toward his office at the other end of the hall. When the men filed into the room, he looked through a small book on his tidy desk. "Gino Vittorio," he responded. "An employee at the Vanzini Villa. I believe he's the woman's bodyguard."

"Was," corrected Lt. Domingo.

"Yes, was. Before you arrived I received a call from Messina. I believe he said his name was Antonio de Leone."

Instantly they all trained their eyes upon him. He hesitated, then continued. "Said he'd be here tomorrow to claim the bodies, prepare for their transportation to Messina."

"Grazie," said Domingo as they prepared to leave.

"Prago," said the creepy mortician. "If I can be of further assistance, please call upon me."

Unable to control himself, Giorgio hissed at the cold, slimy man. "Do you realize just who those people are who lie degraded by your apparent lack of concern?" He stared angrily at the man.

"They are dead bodies," replied the absurd mortician with a sense of propriety.

For a wild moment, Giorgio felt like punching the man's face. His blood ran cold and his body sagged under the simple truth. Again he stormed angrily, "Get them out of here, Domingo! Get their bodies out of this filthy hole! I don't want them to remain another second. Out, get them out of here!" His voice climbed hysterically. With that, Giorgio turned and stalked out of the putrid death parlor, followed by Hank Rossi, Danny Moreno, and Mike Camarata. Lt. Domingo tarried. He placed copies of the death certificates in his briefcase without glancing at them. "I'll need these."

Baccamorto protested. "They are the property of the family."

"Tell Signore de Leone that his *avvocato* has them. They'll be available whenever he desires them."

"I'm sorry. I can't permit them out of my sight."

Domingo gave him a long, burning look. He quickly removed the certificates from his case and examined them with more care. He scanned the name: *Marco de Leone. Cause of death: Old age, heart failure.* Outraged, Lt. Domingo looked up at the red-faced mortician and gave him a scathing look. His eyes dropped to the second certificate. He read: *Dolcetto de Leone. Cause of death: Peritonitis, insulin shock.* Domingo quickly shuffled to the last. *Francesca Vanzini. Cause of death: Rupture of uterine wall, burst appendix.* Domingo's face swelled with anger.

"How dare you! How dare you falsify these death certificates?"

"Are you addressing me?"

"No! I'm addressing the imbecile who stands in your shoes!" He scribbled on a piece of paper and thrust it at the man. Domingo stuffed the certificates back into his case and snapped it shut.

"But you can't!" Baccamorto glanced at the paper in his hand. "What's this?"

"A receipt for the certificates. Can't you read either?"

"I order you to return those certificates to me instantly."

"You *order* me?" Lt. Domingo opened the door and left, slamming the stained-glass panes in the mortician's face.

Baccamorto rushed to the phone on his desk, gave the operator a number, and waited for his party to respond.

"*Consiglioro?* This is Tanno Baccamorto. Is Don Barbarossa with you?"

"No," answered Primo Garibaldi. "*Mah che c'e?*"

"They were here, all five of them. Bocca, Lt. Domingo, and three other men, all officers, I believe." Baccamorto wiped the perspiration from his face with the back of his hand. "They took the death certificates."

"You explained they were the property of the family?"

"*Si.* I did everything you told me to do."

"*Va biene.* Don't worry. There is little they can do."

"Tomorrow, a member of the family arrives. Antonio de Leone."

"Antonio de Leone!" shouted Garibaldi, aghast. "How can that be?" It was the first he'd heard that the entire family hadn't been wiped out. He'd already sent Don Matteo out of the city on an extended vacation. No one had seen fit to inform him. "You make sure it is Antonio de Leone, understand!" He slammed down the phone. *This development will have to be carefully studied,* thought the *consigliori.*

"*Si, grazie,*" said the mystified mortician. "*Botta de sanguo!*" *How can I make sure? I never laid eyes on Antonio de Leone before.*

Consiglioro Primo Garibaldi had sent Don Barbarossa on an extended vacation. News that Antonio de Leone was still alive increased his own agitation. *This is as good a time for me and my family to take a vacation,* he told himself. *We'll go to Capri! It's best we're all away while investigators prowl around Palermo and Porto Tomasso. The less we know or pretend to know in these matters, the more believable would be our shock and feigned sadness over the terrible tragedies.*

Why hadn't he received word from Cacciatore, he wondered. Even the di Lucca brothers hadn't shown up. Di Lucca? Suddenly he remembered that a young woman who claimed to be sister to the di Lucca brothers sat in his outer office demanding to see him. He pressed the intercom. "You may send the young di Lucca woman in to see me."

Febronia Angela walked slowly into Garibaldi's office, intimidated by her surroundings. She felt out of place in her modest black dress and black lace shawl. He smiled to put her at ease. "What can I do for you?" he asked.

"It's about my brothers. They haven't returned home since they went out on a job for Don Barbarossa," she began in a hesitant, unsure manner.

Garibaldi was annoyed. "What makes you so sure they work for Don Barbarossa?"

She smiled subtly. "Four nights ago, I saw them commit murder. They killed *Paolo u' Pazzu.* Actually, it was Cacciatore, but they drove the car. It's as if they killed him themselves. I know now that they all killed *El Leone* and his family. But they are still my brothers. Where are they? That's all I wish to know. They never returned home that night."

Garibaldi regarded her in a deep silence. He smiled a forced, superficial smile, hoping to disarm the girl. "Signorina, I have no idea where your brothers might be. I hardly know them. As for Don Barbarossa, he's been away on a holiday. I don't know what gives you the idea they work for Don Barbarossa. Certainly Don Matteo wouldn't use your brothers to commit a crime." His voice was sugary.

She regarded him with mixed emotions. Her naiveté in such matters showed on her face. Garibaldi took that moment to deceitfully assure her that her worries were premature. "Perhaps they are on a holiday also?"

"Without taking any clothing? They left their car near the old Vanzini *fabbrica*. No, *consigliori*. Don't make fun of me. I'm not a bright girl, but certainly I am not *stupida!*" She drew herself up indignantly.

"What is it you want from me?"

"Compensation."

"Ah," said Garibaldi. Now he understood her. *"Quanto?"*

She shrugged. "They were the sole support of our family. There are six of us at home, left to starve without their income."

Garibaldi opened a safe behind him, a floor safe that stood next to a wall console. He removed one hundred dollars, counted it out, and handed it to her.

She glanced lightly at the money, but she wouldn't touch it. Garibaldi had made his first mistake.

"Signorina?" questioned Garibaldi. He knew the answer. He sighed with marked annoyance. He reached into the safe and removed a like amount. "That's all you get until I discover what happened." That was his second mistake.

She took the money, recounted it, and wrote the amount into a small book.

"Just what the hell do you think you're doing?"

"Keeping a record. If the same amount doesn't arrive each month, on the first day, I will send this account to the authorities." Her sudden astuteness astonished him.

Primo Garibaldi's eyes narrowed with grim disgust. It was the first time he'd been involved with these people at this level. Without the Don here, he felt he had to do something to keep her quiet until he returned and handled the matter himself. He didn't like the involvement. He hated more the festering thought running wild in his mind. Could her brothers have masterminded this?

"Let's understand one thing, Signorina di Lucca. I know nothing about your brothers. I am assuming that your story is true. I have no proof of this. Until Don Matteo returns from his vacation, I am only doing what I think the Don would want me to do. If your family is destitute, you must have some money to live on."

Febronia Angela smiled. Her lover had been right. It was easy to extort money from them, if you knew how. If he hadn't been as guilty as her brothers, he wouldn't have given her any money. "I understand you perfectly. Just give the information to the *capomafioso*. But make sure the money continues to arrive the first of each month."

The bitch! The stupid, little bitch! How dare she give orders to me!

Garibaldi said nothing. He stood up, ending the conversation. The di Lucca girl collected the money and walked out of his office. He sat down heavily and regarded the entire incident. Now he *had* to contact the Don. Normally he'd have turned the matter over to Cacciatore. What could have happened to him, he wondered.

41

Two days later, when the body of Febronia Angela di Lucca was found, a totally confused group of *carabinieri* shook their heads in wonderment at so brutal a crime. It was only coincidence that Mike Camarata happened to be there asking about the cobbler's son whom he'd tried to locate, that he happened to catch sight of the name di Lucca on a D.O.A. sheet. He stared at the cold white body for some time as images rushed at him of that night in the dimly lit cobbler's shop. *It is the same girl,* he told himself. He'd stake his life on it.

Later in his office, the American agents, Moreno and Rossi, had gathered with Lt. Domingo and *Avvocato* Bocca, discussing pertinent facts of the crimes. Danny Moreno had been intrigued about the curious circumstances involved in the death of Paolo Nicosia.

"Paolo Nicosia?" Giorgio Bocca tried to stimulate his memory.

"Go ahead, Mike," suggested Lt. Domingo. "Tell them what you observed when you tailed the old seaman."

Mike Camarata told the others what had happened from the moment he picked up Nicosia's trail to Barbarossa's villa. "He didn't stay long, but left highly agitated, and returned to the *Arcturus* where he started the engines and headed for deeper waters. We lost him in a fog bank. Luckily one of our men spotted the cruiser in the Porto Tomasso harbor. Most of the yachts and other craft transporting the wedding guests had already departed, so there was little activity. But there she was, bold as ever, that *Arcturus II* . . ."

"*Arcturus II?*" muttered *Avvocato* Bocca. Why did that sound familiar?

"The *Arcturus II* is a fifty-two-foot cruiser used by Don Barbarossa to transport narcotics to and from various ports in Lebanon and Turkey, then to Corsica and back," said Domingo.

Unable to make the connection, the two names *Nicosia* and *Arcturus* rammed at him. It had been ten years and nothing gelled at the moment.

Camarata continued. "I picked up Nicosia's trail at the

dock and followed him up the rocky incline to the village square. He was certainly headed in a definite direction. Halfway up the hill he began to drink from a goatskin bottle that hung suspended about his neck. By the time he reached the square, he was noticeably drunk. In the middle of the square, he shouted obscenities into the darkness. It was very late, nearly three in the morning. I heard what he said, but I couldn't make sense of the disjointed bits and pieces of his conversation. He mentioned Dolcetto. Called him his God-son.

"At 3:30 A.M. by my watch, a black Alfa Romeo, which we later established as being the property of Stefano di Lucca, drove through the village square. It turned and came around the fountain. I'm sure the subject recognized the auto. Blasts from a *Lupara* cut him in two. The car swerved, turned around, and headed south toward the waterfront."

"That's it?" asked Lt. Domingo.

"One more thing. His body's at the coroner's office. The post-mortem indicates that Nicosia died of Luminal poisoning; the gun wounds were secondary."

"Another falsified death certificate," mumbled Lt. Domingo bitterly.

"No. The findings came from our own men, not a private physician," insisted Camarata.

"Then it appears that two separate factions wished him dead?"

Camarata shrugged. "I just don't know at this point. There are too many contradictions."

"First he was poisoned, then he was shot?" Domingo shrugged. "Poisoning isn't a *mafia* M.O." He brooded for several moments. "Let me see the map, Moreno." Domingo studied the map while the others glanced over his shoulder. "The car turned southwest and ended up at the docks, where you found the Alfa Romeo? Right?"

Camarata nodded. "Right. It was the same car that came after Nicosia and shot him. There were three men in the sedan."

"And you say this Febronia di Lucca was in the cobbler's shop?" asked Giorgio.

Mike Camarata nodded. "I'd stake my life on it."

"Then it's possible she could have been a witness, who knew the car's occupants?"

They all glanced at Giorgio. "What about the man she was with?" asked the lawyer. "Do you know who he might be?"

"I could only guess it was the cobbler or one of his sons.

I've already checked on that. One son is missing. Rather his father said the lad was on a holiday."

"A lot of Palermitans are on holiday, it seems," said Lt. Domingo dryly.

"Let's get back to Nicosia for a moment," urged Giorgio as the machinery of his mind shifted into high gear.

"Lt. Domingo has a theory," said Camarata.

"What theory?" asked Bocca, rolling a cigarette over on his lips.

"He feels there's a tie between Nicosia's death and those at the Vanzini Villa. They were all *mafia* killings, unmistakably. But here, see for yourself, the sedan went in the opposite direction from the villa. From my point of view, although I can't prove it at this point, Nicosia was headed toward the Vanzini Villa. Another moment or two and I would have known for sure." Camarata paused to light Giorgio's cigarette with his lighter. "It's all very confusing. Too confusing."

As Giorgio puffed on the cigarette, he asked to see the map. The connection in his mind even astounded him and became more obvious by the moment. "This is where Nicosia died?" He pointed to a large X on the map.

Moreno and Camarata nodded.

"The car was found—where?"

"Right here." Lt. Domingo traced a dotted line outlining the possible route the sedan had taken. His finger stopped at another point marked with a larger X. "On the waterfront."

Giorgio slapped the table with a loud bang. "The former Vanzini chemical plant!"

"Yes, that's right," replied Camarata expectantly. "The building's been condemned for nearly five years."

Giorgio wasn't listening. He pointed to another area on the map. "See, this is the Villa Vanzini, here at the top of the hill."

"Yes, yes, go on," urged Domingo.

"Did any of you know there are underground passages that lead directly up the hill to the villa from the old factory?"

The others looked genuinely astonished.

"No? But then, how could you have known? The family went to great lengths to keep it secret. In any event, gentlemen, that's how your murderer or murderers gained access to the villa." Before the agents recovered from that bit of news, he threw them another curve. "For whatever it might mean, the cruiser *Arcturus II* was purchased by Dolcetto shortly after the war. He made an outright gift of it to your man Nicosia."

"Are you sure?" asked Domingo, puzzled. He glanced quickly at Hank Rossi and Danny Moreno, who strangely enough weren't as disturbed as Lt. Domingo over the news. He removed his thick-lensed glasses and cleaned them with a handkerchief. Without the glasses, Santino Domingo was a fairly good-looking man. His eyes were considerably smaller than they appeared through the lenses. He replaced them on his nose and glanced at the lawyer. "What makes you sure of these facts?"

"I handled the papers on it, *amico*." He proceeded to tell them what had occurred the day of the auction. "That's all there was to it. Dolcetto felt sorry for the old fisherman. To this day, I never learned the particulars. All I know is, after the purchase, Dolcetto turned it over to the old man. You know Dolcetto. Whenever he could outsmart the *mafiosi*, he did." He smiled for a moment, then filled with anguish when the thought struck him he'd never see his dear friend again.

Don't worry about me, I'm invincible, Dolcetto had told him that day.

"You don't appear surprised by this information, Hank," persisted Domingo.

"We learned early in our investigation the *Arcturus II* was purchased by de Leone."

"You never mentioned it," scowled Santino Domingo darkly.

"It wasn't important. Further, we discovered the boat changed titles three or four additional times, on paper only. An obvious attempt to divert or conceal the true owner's identity." Rossi loosened his tie. It was hot in Palermo. The office had no air conditioning.

"Where's the cruiser now?" asked the lawyer.

"That's a good question," responded Camarata. "Immediately following our delivery of Nicosia's body to the local coroner in Palermo, I dispatched two of our Marine officers to where the *Arcturus II* lay at anchor in the bay. When they arrived, it was gone. Vanished into thin air. No one has reported seeing her since."

"A boat that size doesn't just disappear. It must be someplace. Find it!" exclaimed Lt. Domingo, growing increasingly agitated. "Send messages to all Marine units. Search every port, every bay and cove in and around Sicily and the surrounding islands. Search the mainland if necessary."

"We've done that, lieutenant," responded Camarata. "You know in five years of trailing the *Arcturus II* we've never known another man outside of old Nicosia to pilot the craft."

Giorgio asked to see the reports from the *carabinieri's* office. While he skimmed through them, he paused as a sudden thought struck him. He stared hard and long at his friend Domingo. "I'm not sure I can be involved here without causing a legal problem." He handed the file back to Domingo.

"You're Dolcetto's friend, aren't you?"

"Also his attorney, personal and corporate."

"I can't see that that changes anything. You also represented Francesca Vanzini. You attended the wedding as a very close personal friend. At this juncture, you're helping to reconstruct certain facts. If we get in too deep, I'll advise you."

"Good. I wouldn't want to find myself in any international entanglements."

Rossi and Moreno smiled easily. Both agents liked Giorgio Bocca, respected his professional reputation. Rossi said lightly, "Domingo knows his job."

"Va biene."

For a time, Danny Moreno read and reread Camarata's reports. "Wonder what the old man meant when he muttered he had to see his Godson?"

Camarata shrugged. "Listen. I was there. I'm damned if I know. It's rolled about in my head ever since. What does it tell you?"

They decided it was time for lunch, so they all left except for the persistent Danny Moreno. "Go ahead without me. I want to reread this report. Something about the word *Godson . . .*"

"C'mon fella," ordered Hank Rossi. "Sleep on it."

"I'm not hungry. Mind if I give it a go?"

"Suit yourself. No sense arguing with him when he gets like this," Rossi said to the others.

Antonio de Leone had never felt so bewildered, so alone, or so full of inconsolable grief as he did on that dreaded return to Palermo. No matter how he fought against returning to claim the bodies, he was duty-bound to perform the painful chore. He was grateful he had the foresight to contact Giorgio Bocca's office in Rome. They informed Antonio that Giorgio was in Palermo and that they would arrange to have Giorgio meet him at Baccamorto's funeral parlor.

Antonio's courage, what little was left by the time he was ushered into the macabre funeral parlor and asked to identify the bodies, dissipated and he collapsed. Trembling, he hung onto the *avvocato*'s arm, his face a white mask of terror. He wanted to scream, to protest, to remove the heavy burden from his shoulders. They weren't like this when I last saw them, he wanted to scream, but the words stuck in his throat.

Together, he and Bocca ordered the immediate removal of the bodies to Messina by private railroad car to be prepared for burial. The caskets, of course, would remain closed, the bodies would lie in state for three days before burial in the family crypt at the Camposanto at the villa. Antonio rushed through the business, hurried to get outside where he could breathe clean air.

Antonio explained that the two men who followed them were Calo and Ciccio's sons, trusted bodyguards from the Villa de Leone. Giorgio hardly trusted anyone at this juncture. He nodded in acknowledgment.

"You'll come to the Vanzini Villa, now, Antonio. Your presence is requested on certain matters," said Giorgio after Antonio smoked a cigarette and popped a few pills into his mouth.

"Are you crazy? You must be insane to suggest I go back to that hellhole!"

"You must," said the lawyer simply, watching the state of agitation in the other. He could understand his reluctance, but his choice of words alerted Giorgio.

"No! I won't!" Antonio had a clear mental image of the violence that greeted him on that night of horror. "Why do you insist? I tell you I'll never go near that death trap!"

"Look, *amico,* I can understand your feelings. The shock has been staggering to all of us who loved the Lions. Your grief has to be all consuming. But, life goes on, as does business. You are the sole survivor to de Leone properties and I as your counsel and *caro amico* am here to guide you at such a time. Now, you are responsible for many things."

"Fuck the responsibilities, Giorgio! I never wanted them."

"Times were when I've agreed with you. But now isn't one of them. Take courage, Antonio. Other people depend on you. It's not so bad. Soon you'll put someone in charge of the villas, someone who'll report to you directly, a trustworthy, responsible person . . ."

"Who—you?" Antonio snorted. Contempt dissolved into painful confusion.

Giorgio stopped a moment, stunned by the uncalled-for remark. He let it pass. "Later, do what you wish with the properties. Sell them, lease them, whatever." Giorgio took a grip on himself, became efficient. "The world is waiting to hear from you. The villa swarms with reporters and police."

"Fuck the world!" cried Antonio, his dark features livid. "What do they really care? Fuck them all!" His dark eyes were veiled in anger.

"You know, *amico*," said Giorgio sagely, "you're one of the world's wealthiest men . . ."

"What the hell's that supposed to mean?"

"I thought you might like to know, that is, if you didn't already know."

The last of the Lions bit his lips, said nothing, but his features jerked.

They drove along in silence, the second car following closely, noted the lawyer. He had convinced Antonio of the necessity of returning to the villa and promised it wouldn't take long. He would then accompany him back to the Villa de Leone to help with necessary arrangements.

"Where were you when the killings took place?" he asked Antonio.

"Why, I was right—" he caught himself. "I left Palermo before nightfall and returned to Messina," he said as if by rote.

"Without your clothing and in Francesca's car?"

"You know me by now, Giorgio. I go where and when I want without thinking or planning ahead sometimes. Isn't that part of the old syndrome?"

Giorgio glanced sharply at his friend. "Yes, yes, that's true," he nodded, trying to convince himself. "Did you drive directly to the villa?"

"Yes."

"That's odd. When I called the villa, the caretaker told me you weren't there. Hadn't been there since before the wedding. In fact it was I who broke the news to old Vincenzo, about Calo and Ciccio and everyone."

Antonio stammered. "I—didn't go directly to the villa. I stopped at Faro to get medication from Dr. Pietro and he suggested I spend time with him."

"Ah, then Dr. Pietro left Palermo when you did?" Giorgio shook his head. "He had plans with Marco to go to Fregossi's vineyard the following day. I wonder why he changed his plans?"

"Yes, I suppose he did. No! I don't know. You're confusing me! Listen, I only know Dr. Pietro was there when I got there." The confusion in Antonio's mind lifted. Dammit! Alberto *did* have an appointment with Marco to go to Fregossi's! He'd be sure to ask him about it. How the hell *did* Alberto return so swiftly to his summer villa? He said nothing to Giorgio except to ask, "Why are you asking me all these questions?"

"Just priming you for what you can expect at the Vanzini Villa. By the way, how did you learn of the deaths, Nino?" he asked quietly.

"Newspapers at Dr. Pietro's villa," he lied, drumming the fingers of his hand on the car window with increasing nervousness. It seemed as if an iceberg separated these old friends who'd caroused together, gone on drunken sprees together, and even attended sexual orgies together. *He acts as if I'm his most lethal enemy,* thought Giorgio. Puzzled by Antonio's inexplicable behavior, he moved onto a different tack.

"It's a terrible tragedy, Nino. Terrible! I still can't believe it happened. Not to Dolcetto! He was invincible! Invincible! He always told me that."

"*Si,* Dolcetto's invincible," said Nino with bitter irony.

"*Was,* Antonio. *Was* invincible."

"Hummmmn? Oh, yes. *Was* invincible." Antonio's attention was focused up the hill near the entrance to the Vanzini Villa. Vying for attention were crowds of reporters, photographers, and investigators. *Carabinieri* were stationed to hold back the hordes of nosy spectators who milled in and around the grounds, attracted by the morbid happenings. By the time the limousine scaled the short incline, Antonio slunk further into his seat, unreasonably frightened.

"Giorgio! I can't face them! I can't!" he shouted.

Alarmed at his friend's erratic behavior, he took command. "All right. Calm down. Drive through the rear at the servant's entrance," he told the driver. "I'll do my best to avoid them," he told Antonio. "I'll think of some excuse. But, for Christ's sake, take hold of yourself, Nino. You hear? Take hold of yourself. What are those pills you were taking? Tranquilizers? Take another!"

They got through without too much commotion, entered through the kitchen facilities and made their way to the den. Antonio spoke briefly with a few servants who offered their sympathies. He nodded, "Please, please, tell no one I'm here. I cannot give out any statements."

Taking advantage of their privacy, Giorgio, filled with conflicting emotions, purposely baited Antonio de Leone. "Would you prefer I read the wills now, or later? There were several predecease clauses in both Marco's and Dolcetto's wills . . ."

"By the sainted balls of St. Sebastian, Giorgio! Not now! In God's name, not now!" he shouted hysterically. "Do you think I give a fuck what the wills say?"

Giorgio breathed easier, even at the expense of Nino's shattered nerves. "All right, all right, calm down, *amico*. You've been through enough for one day. Goddammit! I've never seen you in such a state!" He poured him a tumbler of whiskey from a nearby decanter. Greedily Antonio gulped it down like water, while the lawyer replaced the papers in his case.

He felt the walls close in on him. "You know I'm no good at these things, Giorgio, you of all people should know how I am. I want to leave this place, I can't stand being in it knowing what happened," he cried, raising his hands to his face as if to shut out some demoniacal sight.

If the Roman lawyer was disturbed earlier, he grew more so as he studied Antonio's physical actions. He knew more than he was telling and what gravely concerned Giorgio was that for the first time in years, Antonio wouldn't confide in him. He placed a comforting arm around Antonio's shoulders, led him to a chair, where he sat down heavily, his face the color of snow.

"I know this is painful to you, but so many questions remain unanswered. The agents wish to talk with you, hoping you can shed some light on the situation. They want to reconstruct the crime and vital information lacking, they can only look to someone like you to help fill it in."

"No! Not until after the funerals. Sainted God, can't they even respect the dead?"

Giorgio shrugged. "That's fair enough. I'll tell them. By the way, what time did you leave the wedding festivities?"

"Before you did."

"Did you return here at all? Or did you go directly to Dr. Pietro's villa?"

"Why?"

"Just a few questions you'll be asked. I want you prepared for them."

"I left Palermo and drove to Faro."

"You never returned here? You saw nothing unusual? Nothing?"

"No."

Antonio had never been a good liar.

"You want to tell me anything?" asked Giorgio gently in a disarming voice that had oftentimes led an unsuspecting jury down the primrose path resulting in laurel wreaths of victory for him.

Antonio's lips moved tremblingly. He'd burst if he didn't confide in someone. But Dr. Pietro's programmed voice, pierced through his consciousness, *Be careful what you say or do or you may be signing Dolcetto's death warrant. Say nothing to anyone. Trust no one!*

In a quick transition which didn't escape the lawyer, Antonio shook his head. "I'm going back to Messina, to the Villa de Leone. You take care of things here, won't you?"

"Don't you care to know what happened here?"

"I know what happened."

The *avvocato's* brows shot up, his searching eyes probing the other's.

"They're all dead," he said simply. "That's what happened."

"I refer to the technicalities involved. Aren't you curious as to why the servants didn't hear the alarms? How the murderers gained access? Did you know they'd been drugged? Calo was murdered. Ciccio died from insulin shock even though his insulin kit was right alongside of him."

Antonio hung on every word. "Did you arrange to ship Calo and Ciccio's body back to the villa?" he asked matter of factly.

The lawyer nodded.

"Dolcetto's men, from Rome—what of them?"

"Also drugged. They're waiting to talk with you."

"No! Send them back to Rome with the limousine. I'll fly to Messina with the two bodyguards."

"You should at least talk with the Vittorio brothers. Give them instructions on what they should do here. The villa is yours now. You know it was Gino Vittorio who discovered the bodies. Don't you even want to know how?"

"No!" insisted the new, disoriented Lion. He stopped suddenly. *"He* found the bodies?" A strange impulsive daring crept into Antonio's dark, glittering eyes. "Gino found the bodies, eh? By all means, this I've got to hear!"

Antonio's sudden boldness, plus those glittering black balls his eyes had turned into for the past several moments fascinated him, but Giorgio chose to veil his thoughts under a deeply furrowed frown. He took a last puff on his cigarette, then ground it out slowly in an ashtray. Too many things he hadn't bought. Nino's going to Faro following the wedding was one. Neither, he felt sure, would Lt. Domingo buy it. While he rang the damask cord summoning Gino Vittorio, he pondered on Nino's sudden change of attitude. Perhaps in this confrontation he might learn something.

Moments later Gino Vittorio stood before Antonio and reconstructed the story he'd told the investigators following the deaths. Giorgio Bocca, studying Antonio's face during the story, sensed the worst. He'd known Antonio too long and too intimately not to realize that something was dras-

451

tically wrong. He smelled a rat and was more concerned with why, than who.

". . . I found His Excellency in bed with his head blown off," related Gino, displaying a genuine agonized sadness. "My mistress and her bridegroom were in their chambers in a similarly mutilated condition—beyond all recognition. It was ghastly! I couldn't believe my eyes." Gino crossed himself religiously. "I don't know how to express my sympathies to you, Signore de Leone, I want you to know that we here at the villa would have gladly died that *El Leone* might have lived. You have our most profound regrets . . ."

Antonio pounced on the man. "You lying sonofawhore! You blackhearted monster!" He began to swing at the dumbstruck Gino, who refrained from striking back. Giorgio jumped on Antonio and pinned his arms down.

"Antonio! Antonio! Are you crazy! Stop this! Stop it at once!" He jerked his head at Gino. "Leave us! He's out of his mind with grief! He doesn't know what he's saying!"

Gino glanced apprehensively from one to the other, and backed away rapidly, shutting the door behind him.

"He's lying!" cried Antonio. "He's lying through his teeth!"

Giorgio asked quietly, "How do you know? What makes you say he's lying. You weren't even here, remember? What the hell provoked that?"

Antonio covered his face with his hands. Sweating excessively, yet shaking with cold chills, he pulled himself together. "I don't know. I don't know what got into me. I just don't believe him, that's all. Call it Sicilian instinct, anything you want. These westerners can't be trusted. Goddammit they're all *mafia* here!" Antonio changed again, grew defiant and aggressive. "I'm leaving for Messina. You'd better fly back with me now. We can talk better at the Villa de Leone. I don't like the feelings I get here."

Giorgio grabbed his briefcase. "I'm traveling light. Let's go."

Spotting them as they left the study, Lt. Domingo broke away from his activity and walked toward them with outstretched arms and a look of profound sympathy on his face. His expression froze. Bocca, steering his client, brushed right by him through the throngs of reporters and photographers who kept their lenses clicking and bulbs popping.

"Sorry, gentlemen. My client has no comment. He's in a state of semi-shock. You can understand. Please, no more pictures!" ordered Bocca. "Signore de Leone will make an official statement *after* the funerals!"

They drove off in a swirl of dust, leaving four confused agents and a disgruntled mass of reporters staring after them.

"What the hell was that all about?" Hank Rossi said as he popped gum into his mouth.

"Damned if I know," said Lt. Domingo, shoving his pork-pie hat off his forehead. "Well, what say we get started, eh? I want to look again at the photographs taken at the scene of the crimes."

"What about the funeral? Don't we go to Messina?"

"When someone sees fit to tell us," said Domingo.

"Listen," said Danny Moreno, "you wanna really hear a ballbuster? Molinari sent a letter of resignation to de Leone Pharmaceuticals a week ago."

"He what?" Hank Rossi swallowed his gum. "How the hell can that be?" he said after the lump went down.

"Someone tipped him off! That's how the hell it could be!"

Domingo's mouth fell open. "How? But, how?" asked Domingo. "Dolcetto made no mention of this to me. A week ago, you say? He mentioned nothing at the wedding, not to me or Giorgio. We talked about the Garibaldi tape recordings—but no mention of Molinari passed our lips." Domingo regarded Rossi frankly. "Sure there's no leak among your men?"

"Goddamned if I know! But, you can bet your sweet ass we'll check every mother's son!"

The investigation proceeded rapidly, each agent attacking those portions which held the most fascination for them and which directly affected their personal involvement.

Agent Camarata was to learn after extensively interrogating the servants and many peasants who attended the wedding that although they had been drugged, the wedding guests who left the villa earlier reported no such fact. So, he concluded, an inside job! Who among the servants? Who? Wine for guests and peasants had been separated and doctored *after* it arrived at the villa. Among other things bothering Camarata were the disappearance of Mario Cacciatore and the di Lucca brothers. He'd give them a reasonable time to be out of town on business, then really tackle the mystery.

Hank Rossi brooded over Molinari's resignation. Eight long months down the drain! To make matters worse, now, Antonio and Giorgio Bocca play lawyer and client! Damn! Damn! Damn! What the hell are they trying to hide? He had so many questions to ask Antonio, about Paolo Nicosia, about Molinari, about a lot of things! Then, there's the matter of the *Arcturus II*. Where in the hell could a cruiser that size disappear unless it had been scuttled? And if so—why? They knew of the link between Nicosia and Don Barbarossa. But, what of Nicosia to the Royal Lions?

Lt. Domingo's mind wrestled with the possibilities of *too* many clues in this abominable multiple murder mystery. First, he didn't believe Marco de Leone had been killed in his bed where he'd been found. Camarata echoed his sentiments. There hadn't been enough bloodstains on the bed to support this claim in Gino Vittorio's statement. What clues they did find indicated that more than two people had been murdered or done away with in the bridal chambers. Blood found on the andirons near the fireplace didn't match the blood from either two bodies found on the bed. Large spots on the carpeting had been recently scrubbed down. Ballistics reported bullets fired from more than three separate weapons had been found embedded in chairs, headboard, and door panels.

In the underground tunnels they found cigars, half smoked, a flashlight, and a few boxes of matches from Nunzzio's Birreria.

Obviously, thought Lt. Domingo as he paced back and forth in the bridal chambers, someone had gone to great length to distort the crimes. Gino Vittorio was either lying or someone had discovered the bodies before he had and moved them before he'd come upon the scene. The manner of the crimes was *mafia*-inspired. The attempt to distort and cover up was not!

Sifting the facts over and over in his mind, he addressed himself to Mike Camarata. "Call Baccamorto. Find out if Antonio de Leone was able to make positive identification. How the hell he could would be short of a miracle," he mumbled. "Then send Gino to me. I've more questions for him."

"What's up?" asked Danny Moreno noting his concern.

"'What's up?' he asks me, 'what's up?' I'll tell you what's up. The whole setup stinks! Nothing's falling into place. You know what I want? Autopsies! That's what I said! Autopsies on all the bodies. If I have to get court orders I will! I owe Dolcetto that much! And I wanna talk with Francesca's bodyguards! Goddammit! I *really* wanna talk with them!" Lt. Domingo stood before the complicated stereo wall unit and studied it with appreciation. He noted the neatly stacked albums and the pile stacked on the turntable. It must have cost a small fortune, he thought. He turned around and asked Hank Rossi, "How does a man die from lack of insulin with a full kit next to the bed?"

"Tell me," said Rossi wryly.

"Tell Camarata to make sure the coroner from the Procurator General's office performs and signs the autopsy records, *capeeshi?*"

454

"Too late for that," said Mike Camarata walking back into the room. "The bodies were shipped to Messina an hour ago by private railroad car."

"That's so?" said Domingo with irritation. "Call our office in Messina. Tell them to prepare court orders. Have the coroner from the P.G.'s office ready when the train pulls in. I want those bodies autopsied no matter what the last of the Lions says. *If* and I repeat—*if*—Giorgio Bocca interferes use every means at our disposal. Listen, charter a plane for us. Make sure we arrive when the train arrives and keep me posted on the time."

Lt. Domingo turned his attention back to the stereo. He glanced at one of the fingerprint technicians, "You get what you need from this?" The man nodded and continued his work across the room. Domingo flipped on the switch.

"Look at this, Hank. Amazing how it works."

The room filled with the refrains of Francesca's favorite music. It was at this moment that Gino entered the room. Greeted by the familiar music, he turned excessively pale. His reaction was measured by the room's occupants, who noticed he glanced uneasily from time to time at the phonograph.

"How are you today, Gino?" asked Lt. Domingo warmly.

Gino shrugged and shoved his shirt sleeves above his elbows.

"You know everyone here, I'm sure."

He nodded to the others respectfully.

"I've a few questions to get straight in my mind," began Domingo. He offered him a cigarette and took one himself.

"You've worked for Signora de Leone for some six or eight years, no?"

Gino nodded. He leaned on one leg in a lazy pose with one hand hooked on the back pocket of his trousers.

"You and your brother have been here all those years?"

The bodyguard nodded and puffed on his cigarette.

"You're both devoted to her." He corrected himself. "*Were* devoted." Domingo watched him closely. "You found the bodies? Discovered them?"

"I already told you I did."

"Bear with me, Gino. Tell me in your own words exactly how and when you found the bodies. What were you doing in the villa? Is it customary to come in unannounced?"

Gino sighed resolutely and commenced. "It was about six in the morning when I awoke. I had drunk more wine than I should have the night before at the wedding. I don't drink, you see. It was the first time . . ."

"You don't drink?" Domingo picked up on that. "You

don't drink?" He was appalled. "Yet on that night, when you should have been sober, perhaps the soberest you've ever been in your life, you chose to get drunk."

"I don't know." Gino averted his eyes. "I don't know what possessed me. Perhaps I was depressed."

"Why? Why were you depressed?"

Gino shrugged and shook his head stubbornly. He put his cigarette out. "It's a personal matter."

"Then let's talk about something that isn't so personal. You awoke at 6 A.M. Then what did you do?"

"First, I made some coffee. My head felt like a stone weight."

"Si, aloura."

"I drank the coffee, went outside, and walked along the high stone wall that overlooks the sea. The cool air felt good. I must have stood there for ten minutes. I returned by way of the courtyard, made a complete turn around the villa, and ended up near the outdoor ovens. When I got there, I saw the body of a man lying in the bushes. I ran to his side and discovered it was Calo La Bolla, one of His Excellency's bodyguards. Instinctively, I looked about for the other guards—along the inner wall, around the fountain courtyard, at the main gate—but there was no one in sight. I ran into the small apartment occupied by *El Leone*'s bodyguards. That's where I found Ciccio Pontiface, lying on his bed. I didn't have to look twice to realize he was dead. My immediate thoughts were of Francesca and the others."

"Francesca? You mean *Signora de Leone?*" asked Domingo with a slight edge to his voice.

"Yes, yes." Gino was visibly annoyed. He grew more agitated at the music. Finally, he said, "Do you have to play that music?"

"Why? Does it disturb you to hear it?"

"With your permission, lieutenant, it's my mistress' favorite music. She played it day and night for the past many months. It brings back painful memories to hear it—now."

Domingo lowered the volume and switched the indicator to repeat. He wasn't about to turn it off now. *"Aloura,* your first thoughts were of Signora de Leone."

"I rushed into the villa and I rang the bell connected to His Excellency's room. Signore Marco didn't respond. Every day since His Excellency arrived, we rehearsed this very alarm three times a day. He had assured me he was a light sleeper and could hear a mouse three hundred yards away. But he didn't hear my ring. Naturally, I went to his room first. I knocked. There was no answer. I opened the door

456

to the bedroom and there he was—lying on his bed with his face blown off." Gino paused, overcome with grief. *"Povero uomo.* Poor man."

"Go on, Gino."

"Of course, I was shocked, but he was dead. I had to see if anyone else needed me. I ran out into the hall and knocked at the door of the bridal chamber. There was no answer. I called to my mistress, Francesca."

Domingo noted with some annoyance that Gino again called Dolcetto's wife by her first name. "Go on."

"There was no answer. I waited a reasonable length of time. Then I opened the door and found them—*both of them*—dead." He hung his head sadly. "Only a few hours before they had been so alive, so in love." Gino's voice broke at that point. After a moment he continued. "I didn't know what to do. I ran out to get my brother."

"How long did you say you worked for Signora de Leone?"

"I told you. Six, maybe eight years. Who keeps track?"

"In all this time, you maintained this place like a fortress," began Domingo. "You drilled daily with *Lupara* and knives. I understand you and your brother are experts. You've seen the Signora shoot off the heads of two traitors and then further mutilate them." Domingo paused thoughtfully. He turned away from Gino, stared at Hank Rossi and Danny Moreno. By the looks on their faces, they didn't pick up on what he'd said. Was it just possible? *No. No, Domingo. Be sensible.*

"In this atmosphere, do you really expect me to believe that you were bewildered and didn't know what to do?"

"In truth, I swear it. I found myself reacting as if I'd never seen death before." Gino began to perspire.

"Come, come. I've been told you and your brother and your small army are feared in these hills. That even Salvatore the bandit profoundly respected your courage. Now, tell me again you didn't have a better awareness of the situation! This is your profession! Permitting yourself the luxury of drinking when you never drank before in your entire life? At such a time?" Lt. Domingo scoffed at the mere suggestion. "In your words, you said you never drank before! Then why, by the horns of Lucifer, did you drink that night?"

"I told you before. I was depressed."

"Why? Why were you depressed?"

Gino's face was wringing wet.

"Where exactly did you find the Signora's body?" asked Domingo in a softer, more modulated voice.

"On the bed, next to her husband."

"Which body was on the right? the left?"

457

Gino glanced in the direction of the bed for the first time since he entered the room. "Husband on the left, wife on the right."

"You're sure?"

The officer's question disturbed Gino. He glanced with marked hesitation at the bed stains and disorder as it was that never-to-be-forgotten morning. "Yes, I'm sure," he insisted, perplexed by Domingo's line of questioning.

"How do you explain these then, Vittorio?" He handed a set of photos to the bodyguard. The photos showed the position of the bodies to be exactly opposite to that described by Gino. He shook his head wondrously. He walked to the side of the bed and turned his body around in an attempt to get the proper perspective.

"No," insisted Gino. "These aren't right. The bodies weren't like this. I swear!" He moved to the opposite side of the bed as the agents watched him and continued to study the pictures. *"Your pictures lie!"* He pointed to the right side of the bed, stared solemnly at the blood-stained, rumpled sheets that hadn't been changed since the investigation began. "This is where I found her. Francesca was lying on the bed, dead. I walked to the opposite side of the bed. This is where her husband lay. I know because I put him there."

"You moved the body?"

"He was half off the bed and half on. I just raised his feet and placed him alongside his wife. It was the decent thing to do."

"What made you call the *carabinieri?* You people don't usually call in the law in such personal matters."

"This wasn't a personal matter, lieutenant. If it had been, you could wager and win, the assassins would have been apprehended and taken care of before this." Gino lit another cigarette. "Besides, I followed instructions."

"Instructions? Whose instructions?"

Gino reached into his pocket. "I forgot to mention it the other day. His Excellency's instructions. He was a thorough man." Gino reached in his pocket and pulled out a rumpled piece of paper which he handed to Domingo.

To Whom It May Concern

In the event of my death and or the death of the de Leone family, you will proceed as follows:

1. *Contact the* carabinieri. *Make a full report to them.*
2. *Call Baccamorto's funeral parlor. Arrange for them to pick up the bodies of the deceased and prepare them for burial.*

3. *The bodies are to be transported to Messina for interment at the family* Camposanto *at the Villa de Leone.*
4. *Notify Giorgio Bocca, our attorney in Rome. He'll take over at that point.*

The instructions were signed in the flowery, decorative script of Marco de Leone. Finished with it, Domingo handed it to Hank Rossi.

He glanced at the ornate script, read the words several times. If what he'd heard about Marco de Leone was true, he couldn't believe the Royal Lion would write such a note. The person or persons who'd composed this list knew in advance what the outcome of the evening would be. Hank folded the paper and gave it back to Camarata, biting back an impulse to contest it.

"Did the Signora receive any threats prior to the wedding? Perhaps there was someone who felt malice toward her?"

"It's disrespectful to talk about the dead, lieutenant."

"Disrespectful, my ass!" he retorted. "We're trying to solve murders here, not conduct a eulogy!"

Gino shuffled uncomfortably. It was against his nature to discuss such matters so freely with the authorities, a violation of an island law of *omerta*. Had he not been under strict orders, he'd have done what most had done—seen nothing, heard nothing, told nothing. "Only by the *mafiosi* who wanted the property," he began, well practiced. "For six years they've tried to buy it. These past three months they've been like hungry, ravishing tigers wanting to devour it. One day, Don Barbarossa sent his men . . ." He told them of the meeting with Cacciatore and the other Dons. All the while Gino's eyes were everywhere, unsure of the men who interrogated him.

Listening intently, Domingo recalled the luncheon conversation at Alfredo's with Dolcetto and Bocca. He remembered the magic between Dolcetto and Francesca, then his brooding eyes fell to the grotesque photos of the brutally murdered victims spread out on the bed. A shudder escaped him.

"Our mistress made fools of those obscene swine that day. Even that malevolent frog Cacciatore seemed in awe of her."

"Cacciatore was here? In this house?" asked Camarata. "You're sure?"

"I was here with my brother Pepino. In the same room. After they left Francesca ordered us to tighten the security.

459

She wasn't herself until Signore Dolcetto arrived over a week ago. Only then did she appear content."

Domingo glanced inquiringly at Camarata. The Palermo investigator shrugged. "The jacket we found downstairs could very well fit Cacciatore. We're tracing it through the tailor shops at present."

Domingo nodded. "Very well. Keep checking. Meanwhile try to locate this Cacciatore."

Camarata gave him a meaningful look, indicating that might be more difficult than intended. "He hasn't been seen since the wedding."

Domingo turned back to Gino. "Will you be in charge until you hear from the estate?"

"No one has approached me, Signore."

"I suggest you carry on as you have in the past as if Signora de Leone were simply away on a trip."

Gino glanced sharply at the agent. Domingo missed none of this. Across the room Rossi and Moreno exchanged glances. Gino wasn't telling all he knew.

Camarata took Gino to the study to get his statement. Hank Rossi picked up some of the photos. Nonchalantly, he asked, "Why didn't you press him about the difference between his testimony and the photos?"

"Take another look."

Rossi studied the photos. He glanced from the bed to the photos. "You son of a bitch! You printed reverse negatives."

Lt. Domingo laughed for the first time in three days. "You aren't the only ones with tricks in a sack."

Moreno laughed. "Bag of tricks," he corrected.

"All right, bag of tricks," Domingo smiled. "It takes a sharp eye to catch it. Vittorio isn't telling us the entire truth, but we're lucky he's even talking to us at all. You know how it is with most Sicilians, they'd as soon spit in our eyes as tell us what they really know. Chew on that for a while. Besides, the music disturbs him too much to suit me. But this thing about his drinking—on that night of all nights—is too much to swallow." Domingo lit a cigarette and puffed thoughtfully. "We'll have to question the others before we can tie anything up here. I don't mind saying we've got as fat a chance for coming by any more real information as you have for shaking hands with Don Barbarossa. Not here in Sicily!"

"Listen, Santino, is it O.K. to read Gino's statement when Mike's finished with it?" asked Danny Moreno thoughtfully.

"Danny, our only interest in this case is from the narcotics standpoint," said Rossi sternly. "We've no business interfering with Santino's case."

"Sorry, I didn't mean to presume," began Moreno.

"Presume, my ass! Listen, three heads are better than one in my book. To me it's a privilege. Now, we gotta move! I'm letting Camarata wrap up here. I'm heading for Palermo to catch a plane to Messina. Anyone coming?"

The American agents nodded. At the bottom of the spiral stairs Domingo headed toward the study. "Wait a moment, there is another question I wish to put to Gino Vittorio."

"Did His Excellency hand you the note of instructions personally?" he asked, interrupting the interrogation.

Gino appeared baffled. "Ah—*si*, the note. It was in my room the morning of the wedding."

"You didn't ask His Excellency about it?"

"The envelope stated, 'To be opened after the wedding.'"

"After you read the instructions, didn't you think it was peculiar that they were so precise, so well planned?"

"I only thought to follow his last request."

"Where's the envelope?"

Gino fished through his pockets. "I don't know. Perhaps I threw it away. I'll look for it." He ran his fingers through his hair.

"You do that, you hear? It's important," Lt. Domingo emphasized.

Gino nodded.

The agents left the room and found themselves in the midst of a group of reporters who fired questions at them.

A voice pierced the air. "Hank Rossi! Rossi!" He turned and looked with astonishment into the eyes of Eddie Paletine, one of America's crack correspondents. There was no shrewder, more aggressive reporter than this internationally syndicated columnist. He had won many awards and citations as a crime reporter, but his obnoxious behavior made a great many enemies.

"What in hell is Uncle Sam's top treasury man doing in a remote little village far from the fleshpots of the world?"

"Nothing," said Hank Rossi flatly, showing his obvious disapproval at such a stupid remark. "I'm on a three-day holiday with my friend Lt. Domingo," he said icily. *Goddamn! Of all the fucking people to run into here, it had to be this barracuda.*

"Shit, man. Don't tell me that. We all know Lt. Domingo is with the *Guardia de Finanza*. Don't tell me the Royal Lions of Sicily are implicated in something your department is interested in?" Paletine grinned with revolting sweetness. "Then the rumors do have some bearing . . ."

"Rumors? What rumors?" Hank asked innocently.

461

"C'mon, Rossi. Don't con me. You know this is a *mafia* killing."

Rossi feigned bewilderment. He turned to Domingo. "Did you hear the man, lieutenant? He said these are *mafia* killings."

Domingo went along with the game. "Then he knows more than we do." He moved away, showing considerable interest in the wall paintings.

"You bastards! Don't pull that shit on me. This is Eddie Paletine you're talking to. Look, I can print it my way or yours. Which would you prefer?"

Rossi pulled at Paletine's lapels and shoved him ever so gently into a corner of the sun-filled garden court. He was about to reason with the reporter, but, before he could open his mouth, Danny Moreno walked into the court. He was about six feet away when he saw Paletine. Simultaneously, Paletine recognized him. It was too late for Moreno to retreat.

"Danny Moreno! Now I know something's up! How's the trick knee, quarterback?"

"Oh, it's you."

"What are you doing here, dago?"

"You know better than to ask, Paletine." Moreno was blunt.

"My, my, not one, but two of Uncle Sam's narcotic agents! Was this a front for heroin traffic? Don't tell me the Royal Lions are involved, after all? I get it, de Leone Pharmaceuticals—de Leone Shipping! What a perfect tie-in! Are they involved in the Mafia connections? With Luciano?" Paletine read more into the script then Rossi felt comfortable over.

"You know I can't answer any of those questions. But you'd better not print that mess of garbage, Eddie. Are you waiting for me?" he asked Domingo.

"*Va, va! Alleste te.* We're late already," growled Lt. Domingo.

"Go ahead. Don't mind me," said Eddie Paletine all too knowingly.

Moreno took one of Paletine's arms, Rossi took the other. Together they led him into one of the anterooms off the Peacock Court. They went to extreme measures not to manhandle the press.

"You can't push me around," shouted Paletine, full of self-importance. "You know what'll happen if you do."

"Rossi, do you detect a threat in his words?"

"Sounded like that to me."

"Ah," said Moreno, "I thought so." He pulled out a small notebook and began writing.

"What the fuck are you guys doing?" asked Paletine. He'd been drinking. His breath was offensive and Moreno fanned the air with his hands.

"You just threatened Uncle Sam's T-men."

"I what?"

"You heard Danny. He said *threatened*."

"O.K. I get it. Let's cut the games. What do you want?"

Rossi sobered instantly. "Forget you saw us. Print one word that either Danny or I am involved in this matter and so help me, Eddie the Chief will take *good* care of you. Remember the expedition you covered in the North Pole in fifty-below-zero weather? That was a tropical paradise compared to the freeze you'll get from the department."

"Now, who's threatening who?"

Seeing the stern reproof on the agents' faces, Paletine held up a hand to ward them off. "O.K. O.K.," he boomed at them in a well-composed voice. "You sitting on something heavy?"

Rossi didn't answer. He just looked bored. Moreno pursed his lips. His eyes remained empty.

"You are. I know you are." His eyes lit up with a glitter of excitement. "If I lay off, will you give me an exclusive?"

"As much as it pains us," Hank interrupted, "I'll agree to an exclusive—if you lay off. If any reporters get wind of who we are, you do your best to convince them otherwise."

"When do we meet again?"

"We'll be around." Over his shoulder, Hank's electric eyes scanned the cloistered group of reporters and photographers. "Give us a chance to leave unnoticed. Wait about five minutes."

"Sure, sure, fellas." The correspondent watched the American agents walk out of his line of vision. *I'll be goddamned if I wait for them to feed me information. If I waited for those two clams, I'd turn into a pertrified mummy.*

As soon as they were gone, Paletine reread the information in his small black book. It was information compiled on Dolcetto de Leone and his remarkable father. Underlined were the names *de Leone* and *Barbarossa*. "Don Barbarossa, you're my next stop," he said aloud.

If Eddie Paletine labored under the delusion that Rossi and Moreno trusted him, he was sadly mistaken. From the time they left him at the Vanzini Villa, one of their top agents began tailing the reporter, night and day. Paletine had agreed too easily to lay off the story. They didn't trust him. They knew that in his zealous quest for a story, he'd interfere with their investigation and possibly slow them down. If Paletine got too close, he might suddenly find that his passport was no longer in good order, or that he was guilty of some minor infraction of Italian law.

42

"Just what in hell do you think you're doing, lieutenant?" demanded the red-faced Giorgio Bocca as he rushed in the door of Volpecino's Mortuary in Messina. The bodies were being taken out the rear entrance of the mortuary as Domingo, Rossi, and Moreno stood quietly by.

"My job," answered Lt. Domingo in a curt, professional manner. He handed the lawyer a court order demanding the removal of the bodies for autopsy.

After reading it, Giorgio Bocca handed it back to the Italian agent. "You didn't have to go through all this, *amico*." he said gently. "I'd have allowed it. Why didn't you ask?"

Lt. Domingo's voice remained professional and aloof. "We want to keep it legal and aboveboard."

At this point Antonio de Leone rushed in, followed by Dr. Pietro. Breathless, hostile, and indignant, Antonio held up a restraining order signed by a stipendiary magistrate.

"Stop! I refuse to allow you to further degrade these bodies, to commit further insult to their remains. Isn't it enough they've been subjected to such humiliating perverseness?"

Lt. Domingo read the restraining order, then leveled his intent brown eyes on Giorgio Bocca, who had just told them they wouldn't need a court order.

"There's no problem, Antonio," spoke up Giorgio in a compassionate manner. "I just gave them my permission to proceed with the autopsies. If Lt. Domingo requests one, I'm sure it's important."

"You had no right! You should have consulted with me. That's what you're paid for. I'll not permit the autopsies!"

Red-faced and furious, the lawyer grabbed Antonio's arm firmly and steered him away from the others. "It's time for us to talk, *friend!*" For a time they were involved in heated discussion. Having primed Antonio to do most of the talking, Dr. Pietro remained as inconspicuous as possible.

Lt. Domingo regarded them with weary but grim curiosity. He watched Giorgio, white-faced and angry, shuffle from one foot to the other. He saw the lawyer shrug his shoulders indifferently, but Domingo knew the *avvocato* too well not to see the powerful resentment and anger building inside

464

him. Finally, Giorgio Bocca left Antonio's side. He avoided Domingo's eyes.

"I'm sorry, lieutenant, but my client strenuously objects to autopsies. He's greatly aggrieved, close to shock. He insists no further humiliation be done to the bodies." At that moment, Giorgio caught the temporary light of triumph glittering in Dr. Pietro's eyes. For an instant he stared. The other agents turned to follow his line of vision but by then Dr. Pietro had lowered his eyes and walked to Antonio's side.

"I'm just as surprised as you are . . ." Giorgio's voice trailed off as his eyes followed the physician's movements. He glanced at the restraining order, then handed it to Domingo. "It appears to be in order," he said quietly. "I suggest you abide by its instructions."

As soon as Bocca finished, Antonio de Leone and Dr. Pietro made a quick exit, leaving Giorgio Bocca behind with the others. This last humiliation was almost too much for the distinguished lawyer. His anger was tempered by the many years of closeness with Antonio and his profound respect for Marco and Dolcetto de Leone.

"Will you tell me what the fuck's going on?" screeched Lt. Domingo.

"I would if I knew," replied Bocca, as stunned and perplexed as the others.

"Beats me how they found out so soon." Hank looked at his watch. "You issued the orders less than three hours ago."

The Roman lawyer lit a small, thin cigar and puffed on it for several seconds. His eyes narrowed in thought. "Santino, what are you on to that made you insistent about the autopsies?"

"I'd tell you if I knew," mocked Lt. Domingo deliberately. At the hurt expression in Giorgio's eyes, he threw up his hands in a disorganized gesture. "I wish I could tell you, *amico*. At the moment we're on opposite sides of the fence. And you can only wear one hat at a time."

"I wouldn't bet on that," said *Avvocato* Bocca with a tinge of bitterness. The men watched the bodies being wheeled back into the mortuary with crestfallen faces.

"We can wait," said Domingo with bold determination. "We'll get a court order after the funeral, if necessary. One they can't ignore. This is one northerner with as much Sicilian in him as any!"

"You're staying for the services?" asked Giorgio.

"They are," said Domingo, pointing to Rossi and Moreno. "I'm flying back to Rome. I'll return with an order from the State Department, one they'll have to comply with."

"Tread carefully, *amico*," warned Giorgio. "The de Leone name carries powerful weight."

"Correction, my friend. The names Marco and Dolcetto de Leone carried the weight," replied Domingo truthfully.

Bocca nodded. He felt many things, wanted to say even more. His present role, as nebulous as it might seem, didn't allow him to elaborate on these feelings. Instead he said, "Call me if I can be of any help." He shook hands with the agents and drove off alone in his misery.

Later, at the villa, Giorgio Bocca threw caution to the winds. He stormily confronted Antonio in Marco's den.

"You could have told me of your intent. I happen to represent the family, Antonio. You made me lose face with my friends. Dolcetto would never have put me in such a position. For that matter, neither would you a week ago. Whatever possessed you? You realize you've succeeded in making enemies of the very men Dolcetto worked with and respected? Now, either you tell me what in hell is going on, or you can get yourself another attorney. Goddammit, Nino, I'm not jesting."

No one could have been more shocked, more dumbfounded, than Bocca when he heard Antonio remark, "Suit yourself, Giorgio."

Antonio felt like a complete traitor as he spoke the words to his best friend, but how else could he protect Dolcetto? The inner torment he endured as he weighed his loyalties were catastrophic for Antonio. His emotions were nearing a breaking point. When he saw the hurt and confusion in Giorgio's eyes, he wanted the earth to open and swallow him up. At that moment, Giorgio arose, slammed shut the file he carried, and stalked out of the study.

Antonio quickly reached for the brandy decanter, filled a large tumbler, and drained the glass. Then he threw the glass against the marble fireplace across the room, collapsed in a chair, and sobbed loudly.

The funeral services turned out to be an affair of state; visiting dignitaries from Rome and major Italian cities, foreign ambassadors, top government leaders, and a vast array of friends of the Royal Lions came to pay their last respects. The eulogies performed by the Prime Minister were glowing and left a tearful group of mourners.

The bodies were laid to rest in the Camposanto on the de Leone estates. The bodies of Calo La Bolla and Ciccio Pontiface were also interred in the Camposanto of the family.

Immediately following the funeral and after every last

466

guest left, Giorgio Bocca, as a matter of legality, read the last wills and testaments of Marco and Dolcetto de Leone and Francesca Vanzini de Leone. They were of so complex a nature that it took nearly four hours to pore through them. In essence, the documents declared Antonio de Leone the legal heir to upward of fifty million dollars. Giorgio noticed Antonio had paled considerably and trembled noticeably. He paused and forced him to drink some brandy. Gravely worried over the physical and emotional state of his friend, he despaired that Antonio's face had grown pinched and haggard; it seemed he had lost twenty pounds and aged ten years.

"Call Dr. Pietro, please," he requested the lawyer weakly.

Giorgio pulled the damask cord near the window. When a servant appeared, he instructed him to summon the physician. Waiting for the doctor to appear, Giorgio decided he didn't like the physician. His arrogance, icy aloofness, and cold detachment irked him. There was something else. The overdependency Antonio had demonstrated for the man recently troubled Giorgio. In the past, Antonio had confided to him, he felt remote tolerance toward the icy-eyed, vain man. In truth, Antonio had expressed an ambivalent, somewhat passive attitude toward the man. Now, for some mysterious reason, the two were inseparable. He'd have liked nothing more than to ask Antonio about this sudden switch. But how do you make a stone wall talk to you?

Giorgio remained at the villa for three days after the funeral in his compassionate desire to help set Antonio straight on the vast duties he'd inherited with the bulk of the estate. In those three days, he was permitted to see Antonio about an hour a day. In that hour Antonio, strained and aloof, seemed unable to concentrate on anything Giorgio spoke about.

Bocca wasn't so obtuse that he couldn't see his presence was not appreciated, so finally, on the third night, he told Antonio he intended to leave for Rome. The sudden relief in Antonio's eyes at this announcement didn't escape Giorgio Bocca.

He stalked out of the study, went upstairs, packed his belongings with all the arrogant and injured pride of a spurned prima donna. By the time he came back downstairs, briefcase and satchel in hand, he had decided against taking drastic measures that might sever the relationship, at least until he found a reasonable explanation for Antonio's strange behavior.

"When you're ready to return to Rome, you can reach me at my office," said Giorgio gently.

467

Antonio embraced Giorgio like old times. When the lawyer searched his friend's eyes for the old friendliness, some sign of their camaraderie, he saw nothing.

The lawyer departed sadly, leaving a part of himself with the sadder young man who felt terrible guilt over the deception foisted on his old friend. Shivering violently and sweating profusely, Antonio ran back into Marco's study and reached for the vial of pills Dr. Pietro had given him before he left for Faro.

Antonio wasted little time in changing his clothing to casual slacks, pullover, and suede jacket. He jumped into the red Giulietta Spider and headed the car north, making certain he wasn't followed. He told himself, *I've done the right thing! It's the only thing I could have done!*

BOOK FOUR

43

"Why so soon? Why can't he stay here longer?"

"He's been here too long. He's well enough to be moved."

"We need time. More time to think things out."

"No. No more time." Dr. Pietro's voice retained a measure of hardness. "If the *mafiosi* don't discover that Dolcetto is alive, how much longer before the intelligence officers from Rome force us to exhume the bodies? You've stayed away from your duties in Rome and Milan too long."

"Don't you understand? I can't go yet," cried Antonio. "I never wanted these responsibilities."

"Life goes on, Antonio. Life goes on. The only way they'll be satisfied the Lion is dead, that Dolcetto is dead, is when you take over duties as head of de Leone Enterprises." Dr. Pietro rose to his feet. "If they discover that Dolcetto is alive, that I had something to do with prolonging his life . . ." His blue eyes rolled upward and around. He made the sign of the cross. "And mind you, *caro mio,* I'm not a religious man!" He shoved an ashtray at his guest in time to catch a long dangling ash. He continued.

"You think I'm insensitive to your feelings? You forget Marco was like a brother to me. Dolcetto is my Godson. Your family has been *my* family. I feel pain and anguish in my heart, like you. But, it's over and done. Now, we must do what is best for Dolcetto and you, *capeeshi?*"

"I understand, but, it doesn't lessen the heaviness in my heart." Antonio tossed the cigar in the roaring fireplace, rubbed his temples, and sank in the overstuffed chair close by. He closed his eyes. His head pounded. The room felt insufferably hot. He needed rest as much as Dolcetto did. For months he'd been unable to eat. The sight of food sickened him.

"Listen, you saved Dolcetto's life. We're grateful. Whatever follows is our problem."

"What's our problem, cousin?"

Both men turned in amazement to see Dolcetto entering the room.

"You should be in bed," said Dr. Pietro sternly.

Dolcetto padded slowly into the sitting room using considerable effort to maneuver about. The left side of his face was heavily swathed in bandages. His right eye, swollen and still bruised, afforded little vision. He favored his heavily bandaged and taped upper torso with every movement. Bare arms bore unmistakable welts, bruises, and healing scabs. He was a mess. In trousers only, he walked barefooted. The loss of weight had been considerable. His voice was hostile and brittle.

"I heard you say I must leave here, that I'm endangering your life."

"What your Godfather means is that your life's in greater jeopardy as long as you remain here." Antonio tried to soothe him.

"My life?" Through the restrictive bandages Dolcetto laughed bitterly. "What good is my life? I've nothing to live for except to avenge the deaths of my father and wife. I should have killed that grotesque insect when I had the opportunity. My life! Hah! I died the night Marco and Francesca died!"

"No, you didn't! You're alive! Antonio and I saved you. Long hard weeks of watching you day and night while wavering in the jaws of death is what pulled you through. And now you give me this gross stupidity, this unthinking idiocy!"

"All right. So, you saved my life. Your job is over. My life is mine to do with as I please. I choose to avenge their deaths!" retorted the Lion.

"Is it possible I risked my life for such an inane jackass? Do you think I saved you, so, you in blind vengence would go out and repeat the process of death?" Alberto slammed his hand down hard on the table. "Bah! Better I should let you die!"

"I'm a dead man anyway! You buried me, didn't you?"

"It's our duty to avenge the deaths of our loved ones," said Antonio. "Dolcetto makes sense . . ."

"Sense? You mean idiotic nonsense. Fools! Both of you. To think I permitted such imbecilic blockheads to remain on earth at the expense of my own life!" Appalled at their reasoning, he turned to them, "Tell me, how do you intend to avenge these deaths, eh? I want to hear what ingenious plans makes you two specimens of gentility and noble birth so bold that your conceit deludes you into thinking you can attack this machine of corruption? Tell me? I want to hear."

The icy truth of his words cut deeply into both young men. His reality was too complicated to contemplate at the moment. But Dolcetto countered.

"Once you called me an animal for dealing with a man at his own level, at his own reality. The time has come to deal with this—uh, machine of corruption, you called it—at their level, by their own laws. An eye for an eye, a tooth for a tooth. Perhaps the Bible had many more truths to teach me than I allowed myself to learn."

"Bah! Don't spout theology to me! I don't comprehend its senile riddles. I'm a practical man! I was born one, I live as one, and I may even die as one!" He poured three glasses of wine. "This man Barbarossa is a man to be feared. You above all should be convinced of this, Godson."

"Feared, Godfather? By now aren't *you* convinced I have no fears? Fear is an emotional enslavement I cannot afford. It clouds the judgment, deludes the senses, and—well you know how Marco raised us!" He winced as a pain shot through him.

"Are you in much pain?" asked his Godfather solicitously.

"Pain? Oh, yes, I have considerable pain. But then, that's the price of consciousness, isn't it?" He sipped the wine set before him.

Ignoring his Godson's philosophy, he asked again, "Just how do you intend to avenge the deaths?"

"How else, Godfather? How else?"

"By killing those responsible for taking Marco's and Francesca's lives," said Antonio.

"Who? The men who killed them? Those who raped and ravaged your wife? The men who mutilated you? They are all dead, Godson. Aren't they? Antonio attested to that, even if the newspapers made no mention of them."

"The hatchetmen, the torpedos, the hired killers, none of them interest me. I want the men who signed the death order. The one man responsible for this infamy—Barbarossa!"

"Barbarossa again, eh? Don't you know since the war, Barbarossa's become too powerful to touch? Barbarossa held the Allies in the fist of one hand; made them dance like puppets. Barbarossa controls the security police, the *carabinieri,* even the bandits! Barbarossa's underground spy system is so vast that a chicken can't lay an egg in Sicily without him knowing of the event before it happens! Rumors that Barbarossa controls the government aren't hearsay. Barbarossa *is* the Christian Democratic Party—second to none! The Vatican and Belasci come after him. Barbarossa is—"

"If you *Barbarossa* me once more, Godfather—" Dolcetto shook as he held his breath, one eye of murderous green fire, blazing at its center, fixed on the older man.

"Dolcetto! . . . Alberto!" Antonio sprang to his feet, bewildered at their behavior.

Alberto averted his head. "Besides, Godson, you should

471

know by now, that there is not *one* man. But, for argument's sake, let us suppose you're right. What will you accomplish, providing you get past an arsenal of bodyguards and provided you don't get killed in the attempt?"

"So, I get killed. But you can be sure I'll take plenty down with me."

"Another man replaces the devil you kill and the *mafia* goes on ad infinitum. You still think one man alone can affect the *mafia*? Your father and your father's father discovered where that road led. By now, you Royal Lions should have realized the *mafia* is a social disease with which the people seem content. No matter what you think of the man whose name incites you to murder, he's looked upon as a hero by the nation, the world."

"Our intention is to avenge two deaths, not change the world," said Antonio.

"Three deaths—you forgot mine," added Dolcetto. "Your attitude shocks me!"

"My attitude shocks you, eh?" responded his Godfather. "Shocks you?" He arose from the table, padded across the room, tugged on a portion of a bookcase that swung out, revealing some shelves. He removed several packets, closed it, and returned to the table.

While he did this Dolcetto glanced about the all-purpose sitting room banked with floor-to-ceiling bookcases containing endless books on a variety of subjects, mainly of Sardinian, Italian, and Sicilian history, economics, principles of banking and finance. There was little ostentation in the modest villa. It was the first time Dolcetto or Antonio had ever seen this place. Cheery enough, with a bright crackling fire and a circular table laden with foods and wines, it felt safe, comfortable, and secure.

"For the past ten years, Godson, you've done all in your power to defy them. You bested them in business and finance, opposed them in union disputes, insulted them in public, damaged their pride—everything on a personal basis. You were determined to blister their egos, no?" He didn't wait for an answer. "Marco worried at length over these foolhardy episodes. Did you really think you could go on provoking them without retaliatory action? You didn't fight the *mafia* as Marco did from the Senate floor, in the Legislature, or even in defending the villa. No! You did it *your* way!"

"Each man follows his own star, the dictates of his own destiny. Only fools combat the whisperings of destiny," said Dolcetto flatly.

"Destiny didn't plan *your* future with foresight, your

472

father did! Destiny left you to die at her hands. If Antonio hadn't brought you to me, you'd be buried in the crypt next to Marco and Francesca. You still trust to the fickle whims of destiny?" smirked Alberto Pietro.

"It's a matter of interpretation. I choose to believe it was destiny who brought Antonio to me, that destiny decreed I wasn't to die, that destiny guides me to my ultimate fate even at this moment."

Alberto broke open the royal seal of the Lion, opened a packet, and spilled the contents on the table. There was a passport, bankbooks, foreign currency—American dollars in the staggering sum of $500,000 in stacks of thousand-dollar bills. Dolcetto and Antonio exchanged mystified glances.

"What's all this? Why all this currency?" The name on the passport was alien to him.

"You're a dead man, Godson. You can't show your face and live. You can't draw money from any banks you've done business with. This will get you started in a new life."

"You seem certain that I'll allow this farce." Dolcetto grew more depressed.

"Your Godfather is right, Dolcetto," said Antonio suddenly. "They knew all our plans, our activities, everything. Even now, it's possible that Barbarossa knows you're alive!"

"I hope he does!" Dolcetto flared suddenly. "I want his every waking moment to be a nightmare, never knowing where or when I'll kill him."

"I'm talking to the four winds!" exploded his Godfather. "How can I convince you of the folly of such thinking? What can one man do against an organization that's held people in bondage for six centuries? Tell me! I'm a reasonable man. I want to hear! If only your grandfather had been as foresighted as the Florio family who gave up their holdings when they saw the impossibility of fighting the *mafia* and left to go north where they became the richest and most influential in the nation. I can't tell you how many times Marco reflected on this very fact and regretted not doing the same.

"Come, Godson, let's review the facts. Your father's trusted bodyguards were found murdered. You know the facts so we'll pass them for now. Your men along with Francesca's were drugged. The wine merchant swears his innocence. Why didn't Marco hear the alarms in time? Was he also drugged? By whom? Antonio claims the alarms were ringing like the *campanili* of the church, loud and clear. Antonio also tells us, when he took your nearly lifeless form from the bedroom, that three bodies in addition to Marco and Francesca's were lying dead. He mentioned noth-

473

ing of their mutilation. Gino Vittorio on the other hand gives a different account. He also makes no mention of three other bodies. Between the time Antonio left and when Gino claims to have found the bodies, could someone else have been there? And why? Possibly to mutilate Marco and Francesca and carry off the *mafiosi,* no? I'm a layman, but it seems simple enough to me."

"One was Cacciatore, the others, the two di Lucca brothers. You say Marco must have surprised them, killed them?" Dolcetto appeared satisfied for the moment. "I rang another alarm, perhaps it was the one that finally awakened my father. I can't remember after they sliced my face open."

"Yes, that's right. It must have happened that way. I saw the gun missing from the arsenal. It was close to Marco's body," insisted Antonio.

"You're missing the point. Who put Marco's body back into his own room? And why? You said yourself, Antonio, you left him on the floor."

"That's right. And someone else is buried in place of Dolcetto. We don't know who it is." Antonio was downcast.

"Ah! Then who among your servants betrayed you? Did they all turn their backs on the mighty Lions? How did the killers gain entrance to the villa? A veritable fortress, you said, Dolcetto, as I recall. What has come of all the co-operation you've afforded the *Questura* and the *Guardia* in the past? Where are they in your deepest hour of need? Tell me, who can you really trust anymore?"

The calculating Lion studied his Godfather through one glazed, red-veined eye and felt sickened by what he heard.

"Even I could be lying to you, right now, as I sit here."

"Yes," agreed the Lion. "As I recall, it was you who used the words *veritable fortress* before I even mentioned the security at the Vanzini Villa. It was you who made up the duplicate set of plans for Marco. As you said, you could be lying to me."

"And I could be setting a trap for you at this moment. How would you know?"

"Yes, how would I know?"

"Dolcetto! What are you saying? Your Godfather saved your life!" said Antonio, aghast. "It's public knowledge the Vanzini Villa is well guarded!"

"Didn't you say the killers gained access through ancient underground tunnels?" asked Dolcetto quietly. "Hardly anyone knew of the tunnels."

"The Vanzini family, father, mother, and son, were killed six years ago. The papers stated that was the manner in which the killers entered the premises."

474

Dolcetto frowned. He really wasn't sure. Unable to concentrate, he floundered in light-headed emptiness and confusion of mind. "What about Antonio? What becomes of him?"

"Giorgio Bocca has already read yours and Marco's and Francesca's wills. As sole survivor, naturally he inherits the estate, with the specific reservations you included, regarding the acceleration clauses concerning certain monies, stipulated by you to be included as income from various other enterprises, providing, of course jurisdictional supervision of the special board of directors you specified, remains intact as a guiding force—with all those other whereases and wherefores and other nonsense you found necessary to include as requisite to this special board of directors. You'd have made some lawyer, Godson! The complexities of those instruments bewildered even me."

Dolcetto was doubly astonished. First, the astuteness in which his Godfather captured the essence of the several addendums to the wills baffled him, since in the past he'd never appeared so perceptive. Second, the expression on Antonio's face as Alberto spoke seemed that of a man who'd grown in stature. Dolcetto couldn't imagine Antonio sitting at the helm of de Leone Enterprises, and he felt sure that the Antonio he knew couldn't imagine himself in the pose.

"The world must continue to believe you're dead," continued Alberto. "In our world, death certificates alone aren't adequate proof. Antonio will be that insurance to prove conclusively that Marco and you are dead, and the moment he takes over as head of the corporations who will doubt the fact?"

"Marco wanted this for me? Not to fight back as we Lions have always done?" Dolcetto found it all too incredible.

"Only under these circumstances, Godson. That you are alive will mean more to Marco—wherever he is." He turned his attention to the dark-eyed young man. Antonio leaned forward, anxiously intent on the Godfather.

"You, as the last of the Lions, will be invulnerable. They wouldn't dare harm you now. In all probability they'll consider the vendetta is finished. Especially since you stand alone." The physician winked slyly, seemingly pleased with himself. "And where Dolcetto defied them constantly, you, Antonio, will become a subtle aid in assisting them in their various enterprises."

Dolcetto froze. He stared at his Godfather uncomprehendingly. Antonio's smile faded. In that instant, Alberto's position wasn't as secure as he thought.

But, the undaunted man continued in a syrupy voice.

"Who is to blame you, Antonio, if a sudden fire breaks out in the ship's hold and their precious white powder goes up in smoke?"

The man's incredible! Dolcetto's face turned livid with anger, but his Godfather allowed him no opening to voice his fury. "If their agents, in transporting the contraband, suddenly meet with accidents, who can they blame?" he continued. "You?" He pursed his lips in mock consternation. "I think not. What if certain information leaks to the *Questura*, resulting in the arrests of those arrogant *mafiosi*, eh?" He smiled with smug satisfaction. *"This* is the way to fight, Godson. *This way!"* He slammed his fist hard on the table for emphasis.

Dolcetto lit a cigarette and puffed on it thoughtfully. He didn't like what he heard, yet he felt powerless to speak. He looked at the papers and the money spread out on the table. Marco must have prepared a long time for this.

This isn't happening. I'll go to sleep and when I awaken, I'll find it was only a dream.

"You understand this is only possible if you are in total agreement, Godson. I'm only conveying what Marco wished me to. I speak on his behalf." Dr. Pietro studied the Lion over the rim of his glasses.

"The way you put it, I have no choice."

"Ah, but you do have a choice, Godson. You can choose to remain here and die, or go to America and live."

"Some choice," he replied bitterly.

"Nevertheless, it's a choice."

"Humph," muttered the Lion. He stood up with slow, pained movements. His head ached and his body hurt. "I want to rest a while."

"It's not as bad as it might appear on the surface. You were born in America. After all, it is your country. You wouldn't be a stranger in a foreign land. There, you can take on a new identity. If ever you need anything, you have but to contact me and I'll get word to Antonio."

"What are you saying? I'm my father's son! I'm the Royal Lion of Sicily!" As soon as he spoke the words, he knew they were utterly obsolete, totally useless. A terrible depression came over him. His heart turned cold as ice.

"Were a Lion, Godson. Most important, you'll be alive." Alberto averted his head so he wouldn't have to meet his Godson's gaze. Dolcetto's eye had the stillness of gray death in it.

"Will I? Will I ever be alive again?" He limped out of the room.

Antonio rose to follow his cousin, but was held back.

"No, let him rest. He's been through so much." Alberto began to repack all the articles into the manila packet.

Watching him, Antonio began to tap his fingers on the table in a steady drone. He grew reflective. Finally unable to hold back he blurted out, "Aren't you forgetting one important thing? Francesca! What about *her?*"

Alberto picked up a slice of cheese and salami and thrust them into his mouth, chomping noisily. He glanced sharply at Antonio.

"What about her?" asked the Godfather.

"That *wasn't* her body in the coffin! Why the farce of burying her?"

Stunned by the information, Alberto stopped chewing. He stared blankly at Antonio. "Not Francesca! How do you know?" He frowned and swallowed the food whole, washing it down with wine. "Why haven't you said something before this?"

"I thought you knew."

"No! How could I know? You said . . . well, never mind. What makes you so sure?"

"I saw the body. Two days before the wedding, while Francesca showed me some of their wedding gifts, one of the knives in the silver service slipped from its sheath, cutting her little finger and the two next to it. The girl in the coffin has no such cuts. In addition, Francesca had long black hair. The impostor's hair was a medium brown shade. Francesca's was long and thick. The corpse had short hair."

"Antonio, if this is some sort of *giuoco grossolano*—horseplay . . ." Dr. Pietro's face turned to granite. His eyes turned to blue fire. He had to think swiftly and orderly. Where could he reach Matteo? Even Garibaldi had flown the coop— off on a holiday of sorts.

"You think I'd make jokes on such a serious matter? Why? What's wrong? I was certain you knew. Why else did you insist on the restraining orders to prevent the autopsies?"

"That was for Dolcetto's sake, to prevent them from learning he was still alive. To protect him from further action by the *mafiosi*." Alberto regained his composure. "But never mind, *nepoto*. It's enough that Dolcetto believes her to be dead." He lowered his voice to above a whisper. "The tombstone in the *Camposanto* will attest to it. Meanwhile you say nothing," he warned.

"Hasn't he the right to know it isn't Francesca who is buried there?"

"You said yourself, she was dead, Antonio. How could she have survived? You heard what Dolcetto told us, what they did to her? You've been through a terrifying experience.

477

In your condition, who knows where truth leaves off and fantasy begins?"

Antonio was confused. "Do you doubt my word? I saw her with my own eyes."

"*Si*, you saw her. You were there with enough *vino* in you to see Jupiter, Mars, and the entire galaxy for that matter."

Antonio started to protest. "But . . ."

"Antonio! Whatever happened to Francesca, only God knows. Do you want your cousin dead or alive? For Dolcetto's mental welfare, it's best he believes her to be dead. If there was doubt in his mind, he'd stay here. You know that, don't you?"

Knowing in his heart Alberto spoke the truth, Antonio sighed heavily and nodded. He broke out into a cold sweat and his hands shook as he started to light a small cigar.

Alberto took the cigar from his hand. "Why don't you stop smoking those things? See how they make you shake? Here, take another tablet, it'll relax you," he said with paternal warmth.

"No, no! I've taken too many already. I don't want to grow dependent on them. I'll lie down for a while. Don't know what makes me so tired lately. So very tired. Just a short nap, Alberto. My energy is not as it was."

"Soon you'll go to Switzerland. You'll see what Dr. Simoni has to say. The headaches will abate soon enough."

"*Va biene . . . Va biene,*" Antonio leaned back in the comfortable chair near the fire and closed his heavy lids.

Alberto picked up his newspaper, sat back, and scanned it. Lurking behind those seemingly benign eyes was a diabolical brain racing swiftly over recent events. So, the woman hadn't died after all! Bungling idiots! Hadn't he told Matteo, all the Lions or none? Not only does Antonio live, but Dolcetto as well! And Francesca? He wondered who had spearheaded the di Lucca girl's extortion plot. Was it possible her brothers were alive and behind this foolhardy scheme? Well, at least she was a closed chapter.

But, this new development over Francesca disturbed him. He'd heard stories about her stalwart bravery. How could she have lived after the cruelty inflicted upon her? Dolcetto had been explicit in describing that night. Well, Matteo would have to be told. If she lived, she'd be tracked down. She couldn't be permitted to live, now. Perhaps if they contacted that special friend, the one who helped them before, he might assist them again. It was a good thought. Let Matteo handle it. His skill in such matters was stellar.

44

He had listened to all their talk; to all that interminable good sense; to the benevolence behind every word his Godfather spoke; to the logic and wisdom of Marco's strange legacy. In his narcotized state, the Lion's instinct, his perception, even his roar malfunctioned. He felt like a wind-up toy with no will or volition of his own. But the decision had been made, and on this moonless, overcast, stormy night in early December, in a torrential downpour of winter rains and assaulting winds, the Lion stepped into a motor launch that would transport him to the sleek cruiser lying at anchor a few hundred yards off shore, well camouflaged in a cove between Faro and Barcelona, northeast of Messina. Wearing a black seamans' cap, turtleneck sweater, and dark trousers, bundled in a warm windbreaker, his face still heavily bandaged, Dolcetto kept his eyes fixed on the shadowy forms of Antonio and his Godfather until the darkness swallowed them up.

They had said their goodbyes. Now as the small craft navigated over choppy waters, he turned and tried to discern running lights on the cruiser. His mind hadn't cleared enough to begin contemplating his future.

Antonio could no longer see Dolcetto. He turned to Alberto, wondering what was to become of him. Alberto had given him an injection to calm his nerves, and it succeeded to some extent, but the uncertainty of what lay ahead without his cousin filled him with exaggerated terror. The medication halted the tremors but nothing could ward off that overwhelming loneliness he felt at the moment of separation. Even Dolcetto, in his own desensitized state, felt alarm at Antonio's appearance. He made him promise to return to Switzerland for his usual check-up. In parting they embraced affectionately and he said, "If you ever need me, Antonio, somehow, some way I'll be there. Count on it."

The motor launch reached the cruiser, deposited Dolcetto, turned about and headed back for shore. The cruiser's lights blinked twice. Engines fired up, roared loudly, and settled into a steady drone as the craft sliced through the night, taking the Lion toward a new life and destiny.

On land in the pouring rain, Dr. Pietro tugged at Antonio's arm. "We'd best be leaving," he shouted to Antonio. They walked to the waiting jeep.

"I'm alone now, Alberto," said Antonio. "You and Uncle Marco were very close, shared many secrets. Promise me you'll help me. Promise!" he insisted fervently.

"You needn't worry," replied the gloating physician. "I'll be right by your side, anytime you need me." He started up the jeep and headed back toward the Villa de Leone. In his eyes was reflected the sweetness of his victory.

Dolcetto stood on the aft deck of the cruiser, peering out into the inky blackness of night, watching the rough waters and sea swells slap against the hull with increasing ferocity. Although he was drenched by the whipping rains that came at him on deck, he refused to seek refuge inside the cabin and had no interest in who the skipper might be. Standing there, one arm wrapped around a supporting post, he was filled with wretchedness.

Dolcetto must have remained on deck for some fifteen minutes before it happened. Moved by instinct, he spun about at precisely the right moment to ward off a blow flung at him by the boat's skipper. In the hand of his upflung arm, held high, was a bludgeon with which he intended to strike the Lion a lethal blow. In the melee, Dolcetto managed to disengage the gruesome implement from the skipper's hand. They both slipped, lost their footing on the watery deck, and the Lion was knocked against the cabin door as the cruiser fishtailed dangerously out of control. Stunned by the impact, he shook his head, staggered to his feet, and saw his powerful opponent coming at him with tremendous force. Quickly sidestepping, the skipper missed the Lion and was flung heavily against a beam post where he cut the side of his head on a grappling hook secured to the port side. Infuriated at the sight of blood, he came at Dolcetto with murder in his eyes. Once again Dolcetto sidestepped, and his astonished opponent lost his footing and went flying overboard into the stormy sea.

Dolcetto frantically searched the swirling, frothy waters for the man overboard. He saw nothing and heard nothing. Stunned and still dazed, in a stuporous fog, the Lion tried to clear his mind. He even tapped his head several times, anything to make it work as it once worked for him. Now, the cruiser pitched and heaved and careened dangerously in turbulent waters. Aware of this suddenly, he made his way forward, hanging on for his life until he reached the bridge and grasped the helm, bringing the ship under control.

He searched about in the darkness, groping in unfamiliar surroundings for a flashlight. Finding one, he tried to take a compass reading while his other hand groped for charts and maps. They had to be somewhere. The fan-shaped ray of light focused on a life preserver. He caught sight of the name: *Arcturus II*. He stared for several moments, trying to remember.

Arcturus—Arcturus—Arcturus. Where had he heard the name before? Something out of the past tried to push its way into his mind. The agents Rossi and Moreno made mention of a boat used by the *mafia* in the transporting of narcotics.

No use pushing—the answer will come as soon as the fuzziness clears from my brain and I calm down, he told himself. It did and he did. He clearly recalled the name *Arcturus II*. This was *their* boat!

Aloura—his Godfather was right, after all! The *mafiosi* knew where he'd been hiding all the time! The newspapers had convinced the world that the Lions were dead. Yet, somehow, the *mafia* knew differently. Who were these unseen forces who knew all, saw all, and were determined to exterminate him? Who? Sainted God, let them not harm Antonio!

Dolcetto guided the cruiser expertly through turbulent waters, his concentration commanded now by thoughts of survival. Instinctively Dolcetto thought to change the course of his original plans. Somewhere between Faro and the mainland the planned destination of Palmi was discarded. After studying the charts and maps, he headed for the Gulf of Gioia. In one of many coves, he might be able to lay at anchor, providing he could ride out the storm. He rechecked the fuel gauge, checked compass readings, and rechecked the maps. With no moon or stars for celestial navigation and no sextant handy, he had to trust to the accouterments at hand.

Finally in the distance he saw a glimmer of shorelights. The sea grew calmer. Easing the throttle, taking care not to hit the shallows, he dropped anchor and cut the motors. He turned on the running lights and went into the cabin. Dolcetto wasn't prepared for the opulence that greeted him there. Moreover, when he saw newspaper clippings and photos of himself staring down at him from one wall, his astonishment turned to profound curiosity. He moved about the cabin totally perplexed, opened cupboards, nooks and crannies in the galley, over and under bunks. He stumbled over the black metal chest Paolo Nicosia had hurriedly shoved next to his berth. It wouldn't budge. He picked it up and absently placed it on the galley table. Shivering in his damp clothing, feeling wretched, he glanced at his watch. It was 3:00 A.M. Coffee is what I need, he told himself. Or a good stiff shot of whiskey—something. He found the coffee in a well-stocked larder. He lit a kerosene burner, poured water and coffee into a pot, and set it to boil. He nibbled on a piece of cheese he found in the cooler and winced at the pain as he chewed. Disgustedly he tossed it aside. For a long time he stood over the burner watching the coffee, holding his hands near the warmth.

"Va! Va! Coffee—the least you can do is boil, eh?" He sat at the galley table, lit a cigarette, and gazed about the interior. A pain shot through him and he leaned over the table and let his head drop into his hands, elbows on the table. His eyes fell on the metal chest. He stared at it with no real interest for a time, then, bored, one hand moved over and flipped open the lid. Casually he leafed through the assortment of papers, letters, and other memorabilia.

One paper in particular caught his eye, yellowed and frayed from handling. He held open the old bill of sale for the *Arcturus II*. When he saw his signature he gave a start. He read: "Paolo Nicosia, owner."

What the hell is this? Then it all came back. The boat auction, Giorgio, the *mafiosi,* the old fisherman, all of it. What was it he told Nicosia?

"Take care of the boat, I might want to go for a ride someday."

What irony! What ridiculous irony! The old goat was a *mafioso!* I made it possible for the boat to become a tool for the *mafia* to perpetuate their immoral practices! Hypercritical of his stupidity, Dolcetto shuffled through more papers.

He froze as the familiar faces of his father and mother stared up at him from faded, aged tintypes, The marquis and his bride smiling on board the *Marchessa*. Stunned, Dolcetto stroked his forehead in a daze. What is this? A nightmare vessel? A ghost ship to stir up memories? Another photo showed Nicosia as skipper of the *Marchessa*. Why should photos of the Royal Lions be stored in an old fisherman's chest?

With trembling fingers, he opened letters bearing the seal of the Royal Lions. Dolcetto read one in particular with astonishment.

Caro amico Paolo:
It was good of you to write me. I can't tell you how proud I am and pleased that your fishing business is so successful. Your kind letter stirred up pleasant memories of the wonderful times you afforded my family while you captained the Marchessa. *Your God-son Dolcetto grows faster than these old bones can keep up with. He and Antonio are inseparable, like twins. One cannot bear to be without the other.*

Dolcetto continuously wears the golden lion you gave him. No one can take it from him. It is the one thing he will not share even with his cousin. If you could see him, Paolo, you'd be proud of the next Lion of Sicily.

> With great affection,
> Marco de Leone

Dolcetto glanced at the date. He was three years old when his father had written the letter. He glanced at the next page and found a postscript added that intrigued him.

P.S. Although we never speak of it, we shall always be grateful for what you did for Antonio's father. I resist the impulse to mention his name for fear this letter might get into the wrong hands. To this day, there's been no mention of our mutual friend. Wherever he may be, I know it was because of your exceeding bravery in his hour of need. We Lions are eternally grateful to you. Dio de benedicci.

> *MdL*

Dolcetto pondered the letter at length. Was it possible Antonio's father was alive? They'd both been led to believe Guillermo was dead. The thought heightened his senses and sharpened his wits. Now he grew excited as he read and reread the letter, committing it to memory. Thumbing through the old ship's log, he thought, *How incredible. Nicosia had actually worked for my father. That old seaman gave me the golden lion.* His fingers reached up and felt for it under his sweater.

At the end of the log, a final item caught his attention. *Took my passenger to Marseille. Final destination Andalusia, Spain. Strange,* thought Dolcetto, *that's where Felipe Santiago lives.* He shrugged. *He might have transported Felipe, the old falconieri.*

Dolcetto replaced the contents of the box. Startled by the sound of the perking coffee, he got up and poured himself a cup and went at it greedily. It nearly seared his lips. He set it aside.

What does it all mean? All these disturbing facts rushing at me? He thought of the assailant who tried to kill him on the boat. *Who'd sent him? Where was the old fisherman?* He sipped the coffee and sucked in his breath. It was still too hot.

With coffee cup in hand, Dolcetto weaved forward out of the cabin and up the ladder to the bridge. He turned on the battery lantern and studied the map in detail, took a compass reading.

Suddenly, Dolcetto glanced up and peered about the darkness, cocked his head to the right and to the left, listening like a cat in the night. He couldn't quell an uneasy feeling that something was wrong. He dug into his jacket pocket for a box of pills his Godfather had given him. Suddenly a giant ocean swell struck the boat, and the pills flew out of his hands into the sea. For a few tense moments he panicked, wondering what he'd do without the pills. *Get used to it, Lion!*

The storm was moving toward Gioia. Unpredictable swells rocked the boat unmercifully and the waters grew turbulent. He moved about unsteadily, securing everything in sight. Taking the flashlight he went down the ladder to the aft deck. He opened the engine hatch, checked the fuel tanks, and flashed the light about to make certain the fuel connections were intact. Satisfied, he closed the hatch, but as he moved forward to the cabin, a sudden afterimage struck him. Something wasn't right. He returned to the engine hatch, tugged off the cover, fanned the flashlight around again. He saw what shouldn't have been there and a closer look filled him with alarm.

Sonofabitch! Why didn't I think before this? There was no time for second thoughts—nothing! Dolcetto dove off the rail into the icy waters and swam clear of the *Arcturus* as swiftly as possible, hoping against hope he'd make it in time. Thank God for the incoming tide which swept him to shore sooner then he could have made it under his own steam. On shore, he crawled, slipped, fell, and struggled to his feet, ran along the beach until he collapsed on a sand dune. His breath came in short gasps and his heart beat wildly at the exertion and panic he felt. Icy waters had chilled him to the marrow and in his shocked state of sobriety he couldn't stop the convulsive shivering. But as the medication wore off, the Lion found his mind responding more efficiently than it had in weeks. He glanced at his watch. The luminous dial showed 3:30 A.M.

Suddenly a thunderous explosion rocked the nearby area, accompanied by a blinding white light and a series of small explosions which consigned *Arcturus II* to a watery grave. She blazed brightly as she splintered and cracked. Portions of her bridge and cabin flew into the air like fireworks when the auxiliary fuel tanks exploded and caught fire. Dolcetto was grim. He stared at the destruction. Now it all came together sharply.

It wasn't meant for him to leave Sicily alive. Insurance

484

against his chances of survival had been implemented by the bombs planted aboard ship. His Godfather had to be complimented. Hadn't he told Dolcetto they wouldn't rest until the Lions were all dead? They had covered all angles. After killing Dolcetto, the ship's pilot would have been killed by the exploding bomb before he returned to Sicily. Poor bastard! Small compensation for his efforts.

Six weeks ago, Dolcetto had prayed for death to consume him. Now, he thought only of survival and vengeance. All previous plans were quickly dispelled from mind. He knew what must be done.

He yanked the soggy bandages from his face, unaware that Stefano's stiletto and later suturing done by his Godfather had severely disfigured his once handsome features. Disfigured? *Che demonio!* He looked like an apparition from hell itself! But the Lion had no way of knowing this as he set off toward a faint light he'd seen earlier, heading toward the sleepy fishing village a few kilometers away over the slight rise of beach.

A few early-rising fishermen were tying their nets when Dolcetto staggered off the rocky incline and made his way toward them. With the tricky, predawn light to heighten their imagination, a few of the older men blinked their eyes, rubbed them, then cringed back in horror. He saw terror in their eyes, saw them shrink away from him, but didn't understand it was a reaction to him.

"Pescatori!" called the Lion. "Can you tell me where I am? My boat was shipwrecked off the coast and I swam to shore . . ." He was shivering noticeably.

Several old men, trusting neither their eyes nor their ears, threw their nets down and ran from him. One lone fisherman, who stood his ground, was immobilized by the awful sight.

"What frightened your friends?" he asked innocently, walking closer to the old man. Closer up he appeared more grotesque.

The Calabrian stared stonily at him. *Doesn't he really know who frightened off my foolish friends?* he asked himself. *Managghia!* He looks like Lucifer, has the manners of a prince, and carries himself like a king.

"You said your boat was shipwrecked? You must be frozen."

"Yes, I am."

"In there," pointed the fisherman to a nearby shack. "You'll find warm clothing, nothing special, mind you, but dry. There's hot coffee on the stove and a blanket to warm you while your clothing dries. *Va! Vatini!* Go fast!"

485

Dolcetto nodded gratefully and ran toward the shack.

The old man laid down his nets, unhooked his rubber leggings, unsnapped his all-weather jacket, and scanned the pale gray early morning skies. *If I don't get these old bones moving, there won't be a fish left in the sea for old Marinello to catch,* he told himself.

In sixty years dedicated to fishing, Giovanni Marinello, who hadn't missed a day at sea except on his wedding day and the day his wife died, never dreamed when he awakened that morning that this day would be any different from any other day in his lonely life. The white-haired, grizzled old fisherman would never have to work another day in his life if he didn't want to, because of a kindness done to a curiously disfigured man.

Inside the shack, Dolcetto changed to a pair of coveralls, many sizes too large, and a moth-eaten sweater, which he tucked down over his money belt. He spread his clothing to dry near the pot-bellied stove and sipped the murky, foul-tasting coffee.

Marinello entered the shack and approached him where he stood warming himself.

"What happened to you?" asked Marinello with a jerk of his head toward Dolcetto's face.

"You mean—my face?" He raised one hand and traced the scarred tissue lightly "Ah—*il macellaio*—a butcher mistook it for a side of beef." The Lion forced a brave laugh. "In a month it will return to normal."

"This butcher did some job on you, *caro mio,* but never in a month will it be normal," he stated with unabashed honesty. "Some butcher! *Managghia!* What do they call you?" asked the fisherman.

"Dol—" he stopped abruptly. "Gino Vittorio," he replied. *Of all names why did I think of his?* he asked himself. *"E tu?"* He greedily gulped the awful coffee.

"Giovanni Marinello," he said politely. *"Piacere,* Vittorio." *"Piacere,* Marinello."

In less than ten minutes the Lion had made a deal with Marinello to transport him to Rome. Having been assured he'd be compensated for the fuel and the possible day's catch, they were off for the north.

The fishing scow *Squid* stank of the millions of anchovies once housed in its rusty pots and antiquated water holes in the thousands upon thousands of miles the old girl had traveled from sea to port and back again, but Dolcetto paid it no heed. He had felt a certain elevation of spirits until he caught sight of his reflection in the cracked mirror in the fisherman's cabin.

Suddenly, his world fragmented. He didn't recognize the grotesque image staring back at him. He stared in fascination at the angry red scars that had altered his face immeasureably; livid scars that resembled wrinkled scarlet ribbons with tracks on either side, where stitches had been removed. The left side of his cheek pulled his eye down into a pocket and the corner of his lip pulled up into the same mass of weird scarring. By no stretch of the imagination would anyone who had known the Lion before recognize him now.

This freakish appearance would come to serve as the daily reminder that he must find and come to terms with those devils who masterminded the death of Marco and Francesca.

In those few days at sea, Dolcetto's mind functioned like a computer. He sifted facts, sorted information, and deleted rumors, aided by Antonio's reconstruction of the tragic wedding night. Pumped full of drugs and painkilling medicines, Dolcetto hadn't been capable of putting his questions into the proper perspective. Guilt-packed nightmares, recurring night after night, were driving him into a state near madness. Oddly enough, these five nights at sea without medication, the nightmares had disappeared.

When the snail-paced *Squid* arrived at Amalfi, Dolcetto decided to leave the boat. Into the trembling hands of the dazed fisherman he pressed five thousand dollars and asked to be let off on a nearby quay. In Amalfi, he bought appropriate clothing—nothing like what the Lion might ordinarily wear—conservative casual wear—and decided against wearing dark glasses for fear he might be recognized in profile.

He reasoned, with the deformity exposed for the world to see, most people would avert their eyes from such a sight and the remote thought it could possibly be Dolcetto would be quickly dispelled from mind.

45

Francesca Vanzini de Leone stared numbly at the older woman who attended her for two months following the tragic wedding night, unable to believe her parting words. "You'll have to be extremely careful not to abort the child growing in your womb," she warned. "You lost too much blood—the injuries were too many . . ."

The midwife and quasi-nurse was transported blindfolded back through intricate, labyrinthian corridors of the sequestered apartments in which Francesca sought refuge. Only when she was back in her own village of Camporeale was the blindfold removed.

"If we should need you again, Signora, I shall come for you," said the dark-eyed young man. "I needn't caution you to say nothing . . ." He paid her well.

"I know nothing, Signore. So what could I say?" She waved goodbye.

Francesca wept bitter tears after the midwife left. To be handed such a legacy—a child whose father's identity couldn't be rightly established—was something she neither needed or wanted. God, let it not be the seed of one of those *mafiosi,* she prayed. She sipped the hot tea prepared for her as the irony of her predicament ate through her. Dear God, where is Dolcetto? If he was alive, he'd find some way to find her. She could bear anything with him, but alone? She had to force herself to think he was alive, since his body wasn't found. Could he have miraculously escaped? Right now he might be someplace thinking of her, needing her as she needed him . . .

How many times she had thought back to that fated night, trying to piece things together, trying to find what went wrong. After she succumbed to the brutal raping and physical abuse inflicted upon her by that beast, she had no recollection of what transpired. She hadn't awakened until dawn. Even then, she was dazed, totally disoriented to her surroundings. For a time she had no memory, no recollection. Weakened and hemorraging heavily from the assault upon her, she evidenced a peculiar numbness in her lower extremities. Then, as memory returned, fragmented, with it came the terrors experienced earlier. Her first thought was Dolcetto. Weakly she called his name. There was no response. Exerting almost superhuman strength, she pulled herself up from the awkward position she had fallen into when Antonio pulled Dolcetto from her. She had no way of knowing that only moments before, Antonio had taken Dolcetto away, presuming all others to be dead.

In the bathroom mirror she stared without recognition at her bloodied image. Mechanically, without conscious effort, she turned on the shower, stepped under it, and washed away all traces of the assault. Laboriously she dried herself, pulled on a pair of trousers, tucking a shirt inside them, and slipped into boots, still trying to make her brain function. Images of the brutal beating inflicted on her husband rushed at her. She tried to obliterate them from mind, but the images were unrelenting. The faces of her assailants came at her like a swarm of attacking bats in a cave and she shielded her eyes with hands and arms. She had to leave that chamber of horrors!

Trembling in her weakness, she knew if she let go, she'd collapse in a heap on the floor. She grabbed at anything to support her, a chair, the wall, a chest, anything that would aid her exit to summon help. Searing pain like volcanic fire shot through her body at every movement. Then she caught sight of Marco's lifeless form and gasped in sickened dismay. She averted her head as a rush of hot stinging tears erupted and splashed down her cheeks.

Santo Dio! Not *El Leone!* Not the Royal Lion! Cold dread in her heart, she moved like a silent shadow across the room to his side. With excruciating agony she sank to her knees, studied his unlined features. Recognizing the peace of death in him, she closed his sightless eyes and crossed one hand over the other over his heart. Her tears spilled onto him as she uttered a silent prayer.

Francesca had no strength to even utter a string of curses at those dead animals responsible for this bloodbath as she focused on their bodies. Sheer will alone moved her out of that room that should have perpetuated a wealth of joyous memories and instead would forever remind her of a frenzied mazurka of death.

In the kitchen, moving like an automaton, she set a pot of coffee to brew. Her fingers pulled a cord that would summon one of her bodyguards. At the sink, she poured a cool pitcher of water over her head, hoping it would revive her and aid her thinking. It did! Suddenly she panicked. The loss of blood had dulled her perception. Grabbing a towel she wrapped her head in it, and the realization of her foolishness caused a wild beating of her heart. Before summoning anyone she should have made certain the dangers were over. At the approach of footsteps, she moved behind a door in the butter room, upbraiding herself as she waited.

Dressed in dark trousers and pullover sweater with a noticeable bulge at his waist, Gino Vittorio entered the kitchen nursing his first hangover—*con molto doloro*. The sight of coffee brewing brought a response. "Maria Antonia! . . . Where are you?" he called. "*Aye yi . . . yi . . .* What a head. *Butana u' diaoro!*" He held his aching head for several moments and called out again, "Maria Antonia!" At that moment, he caught sight of Francesca as she fell against the door. He rushed to her side, his momentary discomfort forgotten.

"Gino . . ." she whispered. "Oh, Gino," she whimpered. "Come . . . Come with me . . ." She moved slowly, holding her arms wrapped about her body.

He scowled noticeably. Too much wine. Not enough sleep. A head that felt stomped on by a herd of elephants and now, this! The bride is up at the crack of dawn! Occupied with his own petty grievances, Gino didn't take a good look at his mistress, but he dutifully followed her, wondering why she couldn't move faster. Halfway up the stairs, Francesca could go no farther. She faltered and fell back into his arms. Her pale, feverish face, drenched with perspiration, alerted him.

"Signora—what is it? What's wrong?" He swung her up into his powerful arms and carried her to the second floor landing. He glanced down at her face and shook at the closeness of her.

"In there," she whispered, pointing to the bridal chamber.

Inside, Gino blinked his eyes and stared with disbelief at the carnage. He set her down gently in a chair. Quickly he went from body to body. He stopped at the body of the Lion to cross himself. "But—how?" he asked stupefied. "How could this happen? Where is your husband? I can't believe my eyes!"

She told him as best she could what happened. "After I blacked out, I don't know what happened, or where they took my husband. Judging from what they did to him, I doubt he's alive, Gino . . ." She swallowed hard, and took another deep breath. "They came to kill us, Gino. Now we shall accommodate them."

In a quick transition, she outlined precisely what she expected her bodyguard to do. She ordered, in a dispassionate voice, that he shoot off Marco de Leone's face, return the body to his room and place it on the bed. He was to do the same to Nino di Lucca and place him on the bed in Dolcetto's place.

"Dispose of Cacciatore. I don't have to tell you what to do," she said flatly. ". . . And Gino, find the body of a dead woman, my size, do the same to her. Someone who won't be missed. *Make identification impossible.*" She swore him to secrecy. "Tell no one! Not even Pepino must know. Understand? No one's to know I'm alive." her voice rose hysterically.

"Not Pepino? Why not? Is he not your bodyguard as I am?"

"Promise me!" she screamed hoarsely.

He held her in his arms to quiet her. "*Si*, Francesca, I promise. I promise."

She outlined the rest of her plan. "I'll remain hidden until I learn who betrayed us."

Gino thought he knew every inch of the villa. Later when

490

she led him through the foul-smelling corridors and rooms that had been closed for nearly a century, he was astounded. Francesca doubled over with pain at one point, was forced to slow down. He begged her to rest. She shook her head stubbornly.

"No, not yet. Just a few more steps . . ."

By the time they arrived at their final destination, Gino recoiled from the dirt and total disarray and insisted upon sending the servants to clean it for her.

She protested and reminded him of his promise. "No one must know, Gino. You can bring whatever I'll need."

He nodded obediently but he continued to protest. "You can't stay here alone at night!" His eyes swept the dismal surroundings, looking at the spiderwebs and rats.

"I'll be safer here than any place. Just make sure no one sees you come and go." Her voice grew faint. "Gino, please find a doctor, one who can be trusted, someone who can help me. I feel a numbness in me, at the same time I'm on fire, as if Mt. Etna released her fury inside me . . ."

He rushed to her side in time to catch her as she fainted.

Through the maze of stacked furniture, crates, and covered art objects he moved swiftly toward an antique canopied bed, tore off the dust covers, and yanked off the faded coverlet. Clouds of dust exploded all around him. Cursing, he waved his hands trying to push aside the dust until it settled. He picked up Francesca and laid her across the bed. "Will you be all right until I return?"

She nodded weakly. Her face was the color of death and her lips looked cracked and swollen. She fought to keep her dull eyes open.

"Take courage, Francesca. Take courage," he urged frantically.

He returned in a half hour with sheets, blankets, and a few supplies. Swiftly, he remade the bed with clean white sheets, removed her boots, trousers, and shirt and wrapped her in a dressing gown. She fell back exhausted on the bed, unable to perceive what was happening.

Gino filled an ancient brazier with coals and lit it; he placed it near the bed. She needed warmth and he couldn't risk lighting a fire in the fireplace and chance that the smoke might be seen.

"Francesca. Can you hear me?" he whispered. "I must leave to fulfill the rest of your instructions. When the security police arrive I may not be able to return for God knows how long. I've brought you extra provisions, and water, here on the chest next to the bed. *Santo Dio,* I can't leave you like this . . ."

Her eyes fluttered open. "I know . . . I know . . . Make sure you aren't followed. Let them think I died with Dolcetto. I want those *schifosi* to tremble in their own dung when Cacciatore and those two pigs don't return to their styes. Let Barbarossa worry and wonder."

For an instant her eyes glittered madly, then they darkened and dulled.

"Here, keep these with you." He thrust two pistols under her pillow. "For protection," he muttered hastily. He leaned in toward her to wipe the perspiration from her face with marked tenderness.

She smiled wanly. "Go," she whispered. "There's much to do. You understand all I've told you?"

He nodded dutifully.

"And—Gino," her voice was barely audible. "Find out who betrayed us."

Gino's eyes dilated. "And when I do . . ."

"You'll tell me, first."

By confusing the facts and distorting the evidence, Francesca de Leone knew exactly what she was doing, knew that it would throw the investigators off the track. Why should she care about the police or investigators, when had they ever helped a Sicilian? As a Sicilian she'd learned long ago to handle her own problems if she wanted justice. One day, one day, she would reckon with Matteo Barbarossa, herself. This thought alone comforted her through her darkest hours and the ordeal that was to come. He dared harm the Royal Lions!

Word came to Gino Vittorio from Rome to shut down the villa until further notice. Each of the servants received a substantial sum of money as severance pay from Antonio de Leone. The letter stated a caretaker would be hired and in the interim, would Gino make sure no trespassers looted the estate? When he reported this to Francesca, she grew thoughtful.

"Good," she said. "Now I can move back into the villa and roam about without fearing prying eyes."

"You can't stay here alone," insisted Gino.

"Why not? It's my home."

"But not alone. It may be dangerous."

"Nonsense. I'll be fine." Concerned, she asked, "What about you and Pepino?"

"The world is changing, Francesca. Pepino is buying a farm near Camporeale."

"And what of you? What will you do?"

After a moment's silence, he said, "I'll stay here with you."

492

"I can't allow you to stay, Gino. I can't ask that of you."

"Then don't. I'll stay anyway." His voice was final.

Their eyes met for several brief moments. "You know I don't share your feelings, Gino." Her voice dropped. "I've never loved anyone the way I loved my husband."

"Yes. I know."

"You've been good to me. You've saved my life. Can you understand I care for you deeply in another way—feel for you the love of a brother?" Gino avoided her eyes. "If you remain, I can't promise anything. The wound is too new, the hurt too profound."

She kept talking, but Gino didn't hear her words. Her heart told him something else. Even Francesca sensed a strange emptiness to her words.

On December 15, the day that Dolcetto arrived in Rome, Francesca abandoned all hope that he might be alive. She knew who was buried in Dolcetto's place, but did anyone know it wasn't she buried in the Camposanto at the Villa de Leone? How many times she'd picked up the phone to call Giorgio Bocca—but after careful consideration, changed her mind. Until she knew who had betrayed them, she couldn't make a move. If she knew anything, Francesca was as certain that Cacciatore couldn't have gained access to the villa without outside help as she was that a child grew in her womb.

At Christmas, Gino came to her with the news that until it was decided what was to be done with the Vanzini Villa, Gino was officially hired as caretaker at a substantial increase in wages.

"Accept," she instructed him firmly. And he did.

"Surely they don't intend selling the villa?" she asked with marked disturbance.

"Anything is possible, Francesca. It's best you prepare yourself for such an eventuality."

She was perplexed. She couldn't draw money from the bank without some repercussion. Officially she was dead. Gino assured her that with what he earned they could live comfortably. "Then, it's only a loan," she insisted. "Until after the child is born . . ."

In February Gino arrived at the villa, red-faced, angry, swollen with rage. He stormed into the kitchen filled with the aroma of freshly baked bread. He tore off half a steaming loaf, sprinkled olive oil on it, salt and pepper, and sliced fresh cheese in between, and began to chew at it savagely.

Francesca admonished him. "You shouldn't eat when you're angry. Your stomach will tie up in knots. Talk about it, you'll feel better."

"It's Pepino! That crazy fool!" He removed his gun from

its holster and moved the leather around to get more comfortable. "He wants me to help work the farm with him. Half! He said he'd give me half—for nothing. He called me *stupido!* A slothful snail, because I chose to remain here."

Swollen with child, Francesca moved toward him, enveloped with a surge of guilt. The two brothers, always inseparable, were now squabbling?

"You must take his offer, Gino. It's a generous one. You've been my strength these past few months, but, for the present, I've nothing to offer you that can compare with ownership of a farm."

"I've not asked you for anything, Francesca," he retorted sharply, wiping the corners of his lips.

A gloom of depression settled over them.

It came to them simultaneously. For a time they searched each other's eyes, hoping they were wrong. Gino brought it into the open, and asked wonderingly, "Where do you suppose Pepino found money to buy a farm? These days it takes much money to buy land."

They regarded each other uneasily. As their suspicion grew, she averted her head, shook it, not wanting to believe what she felt. Santo Dio! *Don't let it be Pepino who betrayed us!*

Gino stared as one struck totally dumb and sank back against his chair. He dropped the hot bread and cheese as if it had turned to poison. "Where then did he get so much money in so short a time? The severance pay, like mine, wasn't enough to buy a carton of cigarettes in these times." He rose to his feet and grabbed her arms roughly. "Tell me I'm wrong!" he said bitterly. "Tell me we're both wrong!" He forced her to look into his eyes.

"It wouldn't be the first time a man's loyalty has been bought with a promise of riches," she said without emotion. "Why not Pepino? To be elevated from an employee to landlord would tempt St. Anthony," she said simply.

Gino sat down again, heavily, and lit a cigarette for her and one for himself. He reflected in silence, then slowly verbalized the events of that night of October 15.

"The night of the wedding, Pepino, who loves the grape, didn't touch a drop. Not one drop. Even as others toasted the bride and groom, Pepino drank no wine at all. He even admonished me for drinking—I thought it was only to warn me that I'd become as stupid and insensitive as I became— and didn't let up on me. Pepino had access to the wines from Fregossi's vineyards. How easy it would have been for him to tamper with them, drug them. But—why? Why, Francesca? We had no quarrel with you. You've been good to us."

494

"It seems incredible Pepino wouldn't touch wine, knowing his fondness for it, unless he knew something no one else did . . ."

Gino rose to his feet, slipped his automatic pistol into its holster, then took his shoulder holster from the nearby wall peg and slipped into it. Francesca frowned.

"What are you doing?"

"What I must," he said evenly.

"No!" she said firmly. "Sit down." Her voice was surprisingly calm. "To kill Pepino will not bring the Royal Lion nor my husband from his grave, or wherever he might be."

"What are you saying? He was responsible for several deaths. Look what's happened to you and how you must live as a result of it."

"Forget that. We're not even sure he's the one who betrayed us."

"Hah!" snorted Gino.

"I want you to bring him here to me. Let him face us, first."

"I must do right by you, Francesca. It's my duty."

"No!" she insisted. "No harm must come to Pepino. Not now. Bring him to me without telling him why. Will you do that?"

"Will you be all right until I return from Camporeale?"

She nodded. "Promise you'll say nothing to him, do nothing to him!"

"I promise," he said unconvincingly.

"How can I make you understand? He's more valuable alive than dead! I want the name of the man who gave him his orders."

"The Francesca I knew would have castrated him on sight!"

"The Francesca you *knew* is dead! Now do you understand? I want the man who hired Pepino. Disappearance of three *mafiosi*—Cacciatore and the di Luccas—must have caused Barbarossa some concern. With no official news of their deaths, he can only wonder, no? We know they're dead, you and I. What we don't know is who helped them! Only one man can give us that information. Pepino!"

"What do I tell him to get him here?"

She pondered a moment. Then her eyes lit up as she outlined a plan. Gino nodded somberly, listening carefully. "You take care while I'm gone. Don't let anyone in, understand?"

Hank Rossi's interest was narcotics. While he professed vehemently that it was his only interest, he couldn't help but have a profound interest in the murders of the Royal Lions.

The obviousness of misleading clues irritated him and stimulated his complex mind. Again and again his thinking in the matter revolved on Antonio de Leone. Where in hell was he? Why had he been so evasive? Why the mystery? He'd called de Leone Pharmaceuticals dozens of times and could not make any connections with Antonio.

The many calls made by Lt. Domingo yielded the same results. One day in early spring, Santino Domingo threw all past grievances out the window and called Giorgio Bocca.

Caught between the stresses brought about by Antonio's strange behavior and the added pressures of his own practice, Giorgio was curt and formal at first. When asked about Antonio's whereabouts, he was refreshingly candid.

"I don't know where Antonio is, Santino. We haven't seen each other since my return to Rome after the funeral. Corporate matters have been attended to by mail or special courier and all documents bear his signature. As a matter of fact, it's incredible! It's as if a ghost rides at the helm of de Leone Enterprises." Bocca had paused reflectively. "I tell you, Santino, by some strange mystic power I never gave Antonio credit for, he's developed an astuteness and made several shrewd decisions I wouldn't have believed possible."

Hank Rossi had been listening in on the conversation between Bocca and Lt. Domingo, with permission of course. For days, that final remark of the lawyer's played over and over in his mind. When nothing jelled, he stored it away for posterity and focused attention on the latest communiqué from Chief Rossinger, head of the Narcotics Bureau in Washington. "Too much fucking heroin coming into the States. Not enough busts! Crack down! Goddammit! Crack down!"

Yeah, yeah, Rossi lamented to himself. He'd need more political clout than he had to do what the chief wanted, and he told Rossinger just that. "You're going to have to incite the Senators to push someone into action! Someone's gotta begin someplace! Why not try the United Nations? A lobby! Some damn thing!"

"It's not the same, is it, little brother?" asked Pepino as they approached the Vanzini Villa. Two days had passed before Gino could pry his brother away from his farm.

"Nothing's ever the same," replied Gino, *sotto voce.*

"Why was it necessary to bring me here? Couldn't we have talked at the farm? The men are harvesting the prickly pears and I should be there." Pepino felt uncomfortable at his brother's insistence on returning to the villa.

"Ten times, already, I've explained to you. I found what

496

may or may not be a fortune in paintings. You're the expert. Not I. They were hidden in a place no one knows about. We have to work fast before the estate is sold."

"It's going to be sold?"

Gino shrugged. He eased the powerful Ferrari into the courtyard. From force of habit, Pepino jumped from the auto, unlocked the gates, waved Gino through, then relocked them. He followed Gino on through to the garages.

"Vene ca," called Gino to his brother, after he parked the car. He led his brother to the isolated apartments, carefully prepared for his arrival.

"Where in God's name are you taking me?" asked Pepino, curious but tiring of the long, dark, ominous-looking passageways.

"Just a few more minutes. Patience, have patience. You never saw this part of the villa, did you? I myself stumbled upon it quite by accident." Gino flashed a light on the stone steps that led to the upper hall. Just enough moonlight filtered in through the ivy-covered, grilled window to illuminate the corridors and high-domed ceilings. Before Pepino could express his surprise at the surroundings, Gino sighed with apparent relief.

"Well, little brother. We're here!"

He pushed heavily on the squeaky oaken door which groaned and strained on its rusty hinges. Leading his brother through the grand old salon, he lit a few candles that sputtered and flickered, filling a portion of the room with soft illumination. A few of the paintings had been dusted off and turned face out. Gino turned his flashlight on them one at a time.

"Look," he pointed to the *Primavera* as the fan of light illuminated the spectacular painting. "Is this Botticelli?"

Pepino studied the painting carefully. When he glanced at the signature, his mouth dropped open in astonishment. *Porco Dio!* Is it possible? He pushed his leather cap off his face and stepped in closer to examine the signature. Slowly he turned to stare at his brother with a mixture of incredible disbelief and indescribable delight. "Go on. What else have you uncovered?"

"This one is signed Carapacio." He illuminated the exquisite nude.

"Move the light in closer," ordered his brother, waving his hand to indicate where he wanted the light. He filled with a tremendous excitement and his throat felt parched. There it was, signed in the artist's hand, Carapacio.

"What of this one?" Gino moved on to the next painting. "It says Titian."

His brother's rising excitement couldn't be contained as they moved from one painting to the next. Gino remained calm and composed, feigning complete ignorance.

"You must have them authenticated, brother. I think . . ." He hesitated, almost afraid to say what was on his mind. "I think they are genuine." His face flushed feverishly as he tried to subdue the excitement at the prospects presented by Gino's discovery. He grew animated and flustered trying to drink in all he saw.

"Look here, at this one. What does it say? L-e-o-n-a-"

"Leonardo de Vinci!" exploded Pepino as he read the signature. "His paintings were very rare. If these are authentic, *caro fratello* . . ." He rolled his eyes and whistled softly. "Do you realize what you have here?"

Gino Vittorio didn't want to be sidetracked from the main purpose of his meeting, even though he found his brother's assessment of the paintings quite exciting.

"You have a fortune here. A fortune, Gino. Do you know that?"

"You think so?" His brother's excitement was contagious.

"How did you find this old section?" Pepino stared about at his surroundings, mystified by what he'd seen and enraptured by the far-reaching prospects of this find.

Heavy of heart, Gino watched his brother examine a few art objects.

How close they'd been as children. They'd have died for each other. Long ago they'd taken a blood oath to avenge the deaths of their parents, something not taken lightly among his people. Now, Pepino was one of those vile and scurrilous reptiles. How could he have joined forces with *mafiosi* after such men had made orphans of them? How? His heart hardened against his little brother, but his feelings of torment were masked behind his bland expression.

Moving into the old salon occupied by Francesca during her convalescence, Gino flashed his torch onto another painting. "Could this be a Goya?" Before his brother examined it, Gino moved to another. "What's this one?" He moved on to another. "And this? Or this?"

"*Aspetta, aspetta!* You're going too fast for me."

"*Scuza.*" Gino spun around and flashed his light on a dusty, cobwebbed old Venetian mirror on a floor base. Reflected in it like a misty, faded vision was Francesca de Leone, dressed in her wedding gown.

"And this one, Pepino," baited Gino. "What do you say of this? Could this possibly be a genuine Vanzini?"

Pepino saw the vague reflection of Francesca's image before his brother's words struck him. He peered closely, then blinked his eyes. Puzzled, he reached out to touch the image. His fingers felt smooth glass and when he saw the clean smudge left on it by his fingers, in an instant of realization he spun around, his startled black eyes searching furtively about him. His brother's words echoed in his mind. "A genuine Vanzini?" he asked, and found himself staring into the inscrutable dark eyes of the woman he'd known all too well.

Gino wanted to give his brother the benefit of the doubt, but the look of terror, guilt, and panic registered in his face convicted him instantly. He felt a sinking sensation.

"Francesca!" whispered Pepino hoarsely. His lips trembled, his pale face appeared haunted. His eyes darted to his brother, silently questioning, pleading. "What are you doing here?" He swallowed with difficulty. "They said you were dead, the papers, everyone. I saw your body!" He turned to Gino and stared incredulously. "I'm your brother! You'd do this to me?"

Gino looked right through him as if he didn't exist.

There was an awful silence.

"What do you want of me? Why are you doing this? Why do you both look at me as something vile?" he asked feverishly.

"You'll walk away alive, if you answer some questions for the Signora. Who was it you took orders from that night? Or whenever?"

"Are you crazy? Crazy? *Che demonio!* You must be insane to ask such a question. You know what happens to informers?"

Gino snapped the gun clip into his automatic. "The same thing that happens to traitors," he said simply.

"But, I'm your brother!"

"I have no brother. My blood wouldn't have mixed with *mafiosi.*"

"Did you hate me so much, Pepino, that you couldn't have come to me if you needed money? You had only to ask if you wanted a farm, land of your own. My husband would have given you anything in the world for taking such good care of me . . ." She paused, consciously controlling her emotions. "Now, I ask you. Who gave you orders?"

"Answer the Signora."

"What's wrong with you? You're signing my death warrant!"

"And you'll sign mine over again, if you don't," insisted Francesca evenly. "All I want is the name of the man who gave you orders. Then you'll be free to return to your farm.

If anyone learns you talked, it will have to come from your lips."

"It's easy for you to say. You don't know them like I do! They have eyes and ears every place! Right now, at this very moment, don't think they aren't aware my brother took me from my farm and brought me here. In a day or so, I'll have a caller, who'll ask, 'What business did you have at the Vanzini Villa?' They know everything! When the *mafiosi* own you, they own you body and soul!"

"*Schifoso!*" spat Gino. "Knowing this, why did you let them buy you, eh?"

"Don't you act so righteous and high and mighty, Gino. What's in this for you?" He looked toward Francesca and for the first time noticed her swollen belly and smirked.

"You wouldn't understand," he said quietly. "You had to join them against the only person who helped us leave the orphanage," Gino retorted. "There's nothing in this for me except my honor."

"Nothing, eh? Hah! You went around calf-eyed, lovesick and despondent when she announced her marriage to another man! What I did, I did for you as well, *caro fratello*."

Gino grabbed his brother's arm. "You took too much for granted! You had no right!"

"How was I to know? I saw you hurting from the pain of love that wasn't reciprocated," argued Pepino.

"Don't lay your greed on my infatuation!" he countered.

"*Basta! Basta!* Enough!" interrupted Francesca. "What's been done can't be undone. Just give us the name of the man who gave you orders and you're free to go."

"That will end it?"

"That will end it."

Pepino glanced from Francesca to his brother. Gino nodded.

Pepino capitulated. "All right. All right."

They sat in the kitchen of the villa proper, drinking coffee as Pepino began his tale. "One day before the wedding, I had unlocked the main gate to permit *Dottore* Pietro to drive through. He stopped to thank me and asked, 'You are Pepino Vittorio?'

"'*Si,*' I replied.

"'*Aloura,* this is for you.' He handed me an envelope as he stepped from the car, then he walked away.

"Like a *pezzo de Shekko,* I opened it. When I saw the contents, I quickly closed the envelope and looked about to see if someone had seen me. I hurried to our quarters, made sure I was alone. I reopened the packet and saw more money than I'd ever seen in my life. Five thousand dollars was in the packet with a note that said, 'If you'll do one thing for us, the other half of this amount will be delivered to you the day after the wedding.' It was signed, *Amici de Amici.*

"They asked me to allow one man to pass through the security. The man who delivered the wine wouldn't come from Fregossi's, instead he'd come from Don Cuccio Farfalla's vineyards."

"That's all you had to do—allow one man to pass through the security?" Francesca's voice filled with ironic bitterness.

"Signora, I've had many regrets since then. How can I say I'm sorry after what happened? I had no idea what they wanted, what they intended. They said nothing to me. I can't plead innocence. God knows what went through my head when I saw all that money in my hands."

"Dr. Pietro handed you the packet with the money?"

"Yes."

"Why would *he* deliver such a message?" Her eyes clouded in thought.

"I never stopped to think or to question. Later that night I saw him and he made no move, no sign to indicate he knew what was in the envelope. He was as impersonal as he'd been when he first arrived."

Francesca recalled the sudden dislike she'd experienced when she met Dolcetto's Godfather and didn't know why she felt as she had. Francesca had set aside her own feelings and acted polite and gracious, out of respect for Marco whom she adored and her husband whom she loved with a passion.

"And he said nothing beyond that? There was no messenger who might have given him the packet, en route to the villa?"

"I saw none. Besides, Signora, no one could get near the villa while the full security was enforced. All the letters and packages were inspected by the security men before you received them, no?"

She nodded.

"Only those with passes were admitted. He must have brought it with him from Palermo."

"This man from Farfalla's winery, would you recognize him again?"

"Yes, of course. I'll never forget him."

"You didn't think to watch him carefully?"

"Whatever else I did wrong, I *did watch* him. Very carefully. He carefully set the wine he brought alongside the supply intended for guests. He placed red stickers on the bottles and told the waiters those bottles were for the peasants and servants who would celebrate the wedding after the formal guests left.

"I followed him to Calo and Ciccio's room. He stayed only a second, then he moved among the servants helping them wherever he was needed. Much later I saw him bring the *special* wine to the guards. 'Compliments of His Excellency, *El Leone*,' he told them. He did the same with the security men.

"Later I saw Calo La Bolla leave his quarters and walk outside. Suddenly he leaped into the air and fell to the ground. Before I could move, the man from Don Farfalla's struck Calo on the head, smashed his glasses, and dragged him off into the bushes. With my knife in one hand and gun in the other I went after him. Just when I thought I had him where I wanted him, I felt a heavy blow from behind, at the base of my skull and a sharp pain in my upper arm as if a needle pricked me."

Pepino showed the back of his neck to Francesca and his brother. "Look. Here. After all these months, it's still there." A slight discoloration was noticeable on the neck area.

"That's the entire story?" she asked dubiously.

"*Si.*" He turned to Gino. "Remember how difficult it was for me to get up the next day? I don't even remember getting into bed, only the ice cold water you threw on my face awakened me." He looked accusingly at his brother. "That's when you told me about the murders. You even told me Francesca was dead! You let me believe it all this time. And here she is alive!"

"No, Pepino! I am dead. Don't you forget that for one moment. I'm dead!" Francesca grew thoughtful. "Tell me, either of you. You talked with this *Dottore* Pietro. What did he ask you? Did you mention your life before coming here?"

Pepino grew thoughtful and shook his head. Gino's eyes lit up in recollection.

"He accompanied us several times when we walked about with His Excellency, but he spoke with *El Leone* most of the time."

"And?"

"And . . . nothing." Gino's fleeting thought escaped him. "*Aspetta*—I remember now. On the day everyone went to Fregossi's . . ."

"Yes, yes, *anunca* . . . go on . . ."

"*Dottore* Pietro didn't go. He complained of indigestion to the others. But, it wasn't true. He was fine. I know because he began to talk with me soon after. I found him at the north wall overlooking the sea and I told him, 'You must be careful; the drop to the sea is well over four hundred feet.' 'Don't worry,' he tells me. 'I'm a very careful man. Which brother are you?' 'Gino, the youngest,' I replied. Then he asked a strange question. 'Who owned this property before the Vanzini family?' And I replied, 'I couldn't tell you, sir.' "

"That was all?"

"That was all. I'll say one thing, Francesca, that sonofagun knew plenty."

"How do you mean?"

"He knew enough to fill a book. He told me about the underground passages and how they were used in the days of Caesar to transport slaves."

"He *knew* about the underground passages?" she asked in astonishment.

"At first, I was concerned that he knew about the tunnels. Later something else occurred which made me set aside my fears. But first," said Gino, taking a new tack, "while it's fresh in my mind, let me tell you this. He began to tell me a myth, a story handed down by his people about a prince of Sardinia. He asked me if I ever heard the story. I hadn't and I told him so.

" 'Did you ever hear rumors of a buried treasure in this vicinity?' he asked me. When I shook my head, he continued. 'Well, Gino, rumor has it that this Sardinian prince owned a palace such as this near Palermo, and the bulk of a treasure in art he absconded with has never been found.' "

"He said that?" asked Francesca.

Pepino was the first to make the connection. "You don't suppose . . . what I mean is . . ." He cleared his throat, looking from one to the other.

Realization came to all of them after that, but for different reasons and with different reactions. "Dolcetto's Godfather is a *mafioso?*" she hissed aloud. "So that's why they've wanted the villa? Why they murdered my family? Those *sciffiosi!* Is there nothing they don't claim for their own?"

"Why don't we go back to recheck the paintings?" Pepino asked. "Perhaps there are more apartments, more treasure . . ."

"Not now." Gino was firm. "You said earlier, your movements might have been observed. It's best I take you home now." He glanced at Francesca for her approval.

She nodded. "It's best you go now."

"Before I leave, signora, I beg of you. Tell me I'm forgiven."

Appalled at his request, Francesca turned away from him, filled with revulsion. *Forgive him!* The words themselves stuck in her parched, hot throat. She wrestled with her soul and her conscience. Then suddenly the baby kicked and moved about within her swollen stomach, and curiously she found herself saying, "I forgive you. Go now."

"Let's get going! It's a long way to drive both ways at night." Gino turned to Francesca. "You'll be all right until I return?" She nodded.

Half way to Camporeale, Gino pulled the car over to the side of the road. Instantly, Pepino's eyes darted about like a cornered fox. "Why do we stop? We've a distance to go yet."

"Do you really think we found the prince's fortune?"

"Mama mia, Gino, if those oils are authentic we could become millionaires ten times over."

"Si? Siguro?" He offered his brother a cigarette.

"That's the truth. With my eyes I saw Botticellis, Tintorettos, Goyas. God knows what else is buried there in a state of dusty confusion." He grew agitated. "Believe me, brother, I am glad the Fathers made me study art."

"Then you're more sure of their authenticity than you were at the villa?" He blew smoke through his nostrils.

"Only if those signatures are authentic." He paused thoughtfully. "No, brother, even *without* the signatures, the materials they used, the manner in which they work, their technique distinguishes one artist's work from another. They look like the real thing. To make sure, we'll have them appraised. They will probably need restoration—in that light I couldn't tell."

"Aloura, there's a fortune, eh?"

"More than a fortune."

"For all of us? Enough for the rest of our lives?"

"All of us?"

"You, me, and Francesca?"

Pepino was quiet, reflective for a few moments. "Francesca?"

"Yes. What about Francesca? Certainly she shares in this with us." Pepino shrugged imperceptibly. "What about Francesca?" insisted Gino.

"C'mon, be smart, Gino. You heard what she said. She's dead, no? Who needs her? Without her we could sell those paintings and live like kings, brother. Do you hear me—kings!"

They both laughed in a secret way brothers do. Then, in a slow, deliberate movement, Gino leaned toward his brother and emptied all the bullets from his gun into his body.

Gino jumped out of the car, removed all his brother's identification, and threw the body into a ditch. From the trunk of the sports car, he grabbed a *Lupara* and shot off his brother's face.

"That's for mama and papa, traitor! *Fittusso!*" He spat venomously, returned the *Lupara* to the trunk, got into the car, and drove back to the villa.

Francesca had waited up for him with a pot of freshly brewed coffee and some *companaggio*. The look on his face told her what had happened. Gently she touched his arm. "I know how you must feel. I'm tired of vendettas and vengeance," she sighed despondently. "I'd like to live in peace."

"Have you thought about the paintings, the treasure?"

She nodded. "Perhaps in a way you wouldn't understand."

"Do you realize, if they're authentic, we could both leave this place of bad memories?"

The baby kicked again, making her very much aware of life—and Dolcetto. "You might be able to, Gino. I'm a *dead* woman, remember?"

It was the second time that night she'd made this remark. Not sure of her meaning, Gino continued. "Look, a cousin of mine can get us passports in any name. You can become whomever you wish."

"I can't be what I'm not. I'm Francesca Vanzini de Leone. Like it or not."

"And you must continue with the vendetta against the *mafiosi*, despite what you said—that you're tired of vengeance and vendetta."

She said nothing. Again the baby kicked her belly. She clutched at it and a faint smile came upon her, an enigmatic smile that Gino couldn't hope to understand.

They sat in silence for a few moments until Francesca spoke.

"This Dr. Pietro. Why should *he* know so much about the villa? It bothers me that he should be so well informed. You said earlier . . ."

This is the Francesca I know. The Francesca of old, shrewd, clear thinking, and wise in the ways of life. "Yes," he answered. "When I heard him mention the tunnels. *Aloura*, it began with the plans."

"What are you raving about, Gino? What plans?"

"The plans you gave Dolcetto, *buon armo*. The plans, remember?"

"*Si*, I remember. They were returned."

"After another set was made, perhaps a third set!"

When she expressed her shock over this, Gino told what happened in the courtyard when Dolcetto discovered the extra set of plans.

"And you didn't tell me?"

505

"I thought it was your husband's duty to tell you, Francesca."

"You were my bodyguard! You should have told me! *Botta de sanguo!* You should have reported it to me!" Her voice was accusatory. "It is my home, my plans! I should have been told!" She shivered noticeably as her temper cooled, and suddenly she felt ashamed she'd spoken so sharply to him.

"Are you cold?"

"No. Goddammit! Who the hell is this Dr. Pietro?" she asked. Her thoughts ran wild. How could the Royal Lions have been fooled by this man? Should she try to get word to Antonio? Perhaps she should contact Giorgio Bocca? How could she contact anyone without announcing to the world that she wasn't dead, that she hadn't died that night?

Later in the study, Francesca sat behind the desk in the leather swivel chair and moved it from side to side monotonously. She lay her head back and her eyes kept sweeping the room, arc after arc. Suddenly she stopped the chair. She saw the five volumes on the Vanzini Villa history on the top shelf and recalled Marco's keen interest in them.

In moments the five volumes were spread out on the desk before her. Gino entered the room with a tray of coffee. "What are you looking for?" he asked quietly.

"I'm not sure," she said. "But whatever it is, it's got to be in these books." She picked up the fifth volume, and the letter Marco wrote to Dr. Pietro fluttered from between the pages and fell to the floor. Francesca glanced at it excitedly, tore it open, and sat back in the chair to read it.

My dearest friend Alberto:

You've never been a believer in Destiny. If you'd been with me today, you'd have become a believer for all eternity. It had to be Destiny herself who guided me today, when for a short period of time, I became separated from Calo and Ciccio and stumbled into a long corridor that led me back through the pages of history into another time, another century, wondering as I did, if I had lost all my senses, lost touch with reality. I felt much like that fabled character, Alice, entering a wonderland of intoxicating pleasures and incredible beauty.

For a while I gazed at what appeared to be a collection of worthless junk. Out of mild curiosity, at first, I began to see, beneath the centuries-old dust, a collection of art and sculpture of considerable worth. For some strange reason, all that came to

506

mind was the story you once told me about your Sardinian prince. I walked about the antiquated halls, peering about, studying them as best I could under the weak light. I rubbed my eyes continuously, thinking it was all a dream that would vanish like a mirage.

Soon, I left the enchanting rooms and made my way back along the corridors and secret passageways and history pages to the present and the villa. I couldn't still my excitement. You, dear friend, know only too well how unable I am to leave a stone unturned until a problem is resolved.

It wasn't until I studied the volumes, five of them, that my own dear daughter-in-law presented me with, in the form of a History of the Vanzini Villa, that her astute father, buon armo, had the foresight to accumulate, that my suspicions were confirmed.

Tears splashed down Francesca's cheeks as she read the letter. She dabbed away at them, then continued to read:

I decided to wait until after the wedding before presenting you with this letter, so that nothing could detract from Francesca and Dolcetto's pleasure on their day of bliss.

Aloura, here my good friend, after all these years you've devoted to this fascinating hobby of yours, I present you with this letter. As soon as we finish breakfast, we shall both travel a short distance to witness the fulfillment of your dream of fifty years. It's finally materialized. I never mentioned to you how much I respected your dedication to this search. At times, I must admit, I thought you'd lost your senses, that you'd become obsessed with a madness of untold proportions, especially after I learned that you'd spent three summers of your life in the Hall of Records in Rome. How do I know this? The clerk who helped you happened to be a cousin of Amelio Molinari, the manager of one of my pharmaceutical plants. He mentioned that you used my name to allow you the special privilege of examining the National Archives. I would have been happy to write you a letter of introduction. Even in a city as large as Rome, news gets around.

I never mentioned this, Alberto, because I don't wish to sound like a nagging friend who doesn't understand true dedication. But that's all in the past. Be prepared, my friend, be prepared for the greatest

507

*victory a dedicated man can experience—the fruits
to all your labor.*

Your devoted friend and servant,
Marco

Francesca sat back in her chair, allowing the last page
to flutter from her fingers and glide to the floor, her eyes
staring off in the far distance.

Fifty years? What manner of man is this who dedicates
his life to a fleeting romantic myth for fifty years? How incredible! The plan to acquire the Vanzini Villa had been of
unique strategy, employed by a man of rare vintage; a man
so driven by ambition that he'd sell his soul to acquire the
goal he sought. And all the time this cunning snake, Alberto Pietro, always beside the Royal Lions, waiting, watching, preparing the death strike, with the venom of the *mafia*
stored inside his poisonous sac.

Watching the changes in his mistress, Gino was curiously
drawn to pick up the letter and read its contents. They were
as staggering to him as they were to Francesca.

She wondered, *How can I warn Antonio? What if I call
Giorgio Bocca?* Would any of them believe her? It just isn't
possible, she told herself, that the Lions would be taken in
by this—this—she couldn't even think of a descriptive word
that would encompass her feelings for this many-sided
chameleon. Once she had learned something from her father,
who just before his death tried to explain some of the treacheries in life, "Friends may fight you the hardest—but the one
who smiles the most will take your head." That much for
treachery!

"I'm going to make several pots of coffee, Gino. It's about
time this young woman takes a look at what it took her
father so long to compile, and what he may have been killed
for! Join me if you wish," she said with renewed spirit.

46

Later, after it was over, he would tell the others how it had
been for him. Had he only listened to the proddings of
Destiny, he might have resolved this long ago. But at the
time, Dolcetto de Leone had no illusions that Destiny plotted
against him all the time he was in Rome. Nothing had gone
as he planned. He had forced his will power to move certain
things into place instead of relying on his intuition to guide
him. How many calls had he made to Giorgio Bocca, then
hung up before the calls were completed? How many times
had he waited outside the pharmaceutical plant, waiting for

some sign of Antonio? He'd even gone to Madame Roulettina's in hopes of running into either Giorgio or Antonio. Then there were times when he looked at his image in a mirror, he'd grow so depressed he was ready to fly to Switzerland for reconstructive surgery. Each time a small warning voice advised against it.

In a few weeks it would be almost the anniversary of his wedding to Francesca. He grew agitated, unable to concentrate, turned into an insomniac, was unable to eat, and all this he could take, but those dreams and recurring nightmares of Francesca dressed in her bridal finery, calling to him, softly moaning, pleading with such heart-rending sounds had convinced him he was losing his sanity.

He told himself: *It's this isolation I've imposed upon myself. I've got to go out and live again.* My Godfather was right! Go to America! Start a new life! Sever all your ties! Forget you were ever a Lion! But, whenever he convinced himself that major changes in his life were in order, the dreams of Francesca would accelerate and he could think of no one or nothing else.

It was uncanny how it worked. In these dreams Francesca would appear transported by a carpet of wind, ethereal. ". . . D-o-l-c-e-t-t-o- . . ." The voice chanted relentlessly. "Come . . . to . . . me . . ." Over and over it was always the same. "Come to me."

When the urge to return to Porto Tomasso grew unendurably strong, the vivid visions of Francesca grew even clearer in his wakeful moments. There were times when he'd swear he could feel her presence, smell her perfume. This is what first made him think he was going mad. But, in retrospect, his mind refused to accept these visions as fantasies. His reasoning was that the answers to the many questions that plagued him were to be found at the Vanzini Villa.

After making several preparations, he made his decision. In Palermo he rented a car and drove to the villa, arriving at dusk. The place seemed deserted, the enormous gates were locked; dismayed, he asked himself why he hadn't thought to inquire before making this trip. Of course, they'd shut the place down. Who'd want to live here? Certainly not Antonio!

He was about to get back in the car, when on impulse, Dolcetto moved to the side gate, opened a small cabinet only a few knew about, and pulled the bell contained in it.

Inside, Francesca had just finished bathing her three-month-old son. She had dressed him, placed him in his crib following a feeding, when she heard the alarm ring. Startled, she felt a flush of uneasiness immobilize her. With the exception of Gino, Pepino, and herself, no one knew about this special alarm. She frowned. It couldn't be Gino, he'd gone in the opposite direction to bring in some canned goods. Sainted angels in hell! Where was Gino? Surely, he heard the bell.

Gino walked into the kitchen, opened the door to the room where Francesca stood, frozen like a statue, listening to the repeated sound of the bell.

"Who can it be?" she whispered. She shoved back a few stray strands of dark hair and wrapped her son protectively in a blanket.

"We'll never know, if I remain here." He set the canned goods on the table.

She was obviously concerned. "Think you should go?"

"Calm yourself. It may be nothing. Whoever it is, I'll get rid of them."

"Be careful, Gino."

He strapped his shoulder holster in place, slipped the gun in and out of it a few times, then reached for a *Lupara* from its niche in a small storage room. He walked slowly through the Peacock Court, swaggered across the tiled courtyard to the large gates, flipped open the peephole, and peered out at the lone man, standing with his good side toward the gate. For one instant, Gino gave a start. The shadowy figure of the man bore a marked resemblance to someone out of the past.

The sound of squeaking hinges on the small opening above his shoulders caught Dolcetto's attention. He turned full face and looked into Gino's unfriendly eyes. Upon seeing the mutilated portion of Dolcetto's face, Gino found the courage to speak out. He shoved the barrel of the *Lupara* through the opening, stopping it inches from Dolcetto's nose. The Lion didn't budge or flinch.

"*Si? Che cosa voi?* Yes, what is it you want?"

Dolcetto flung out his arms to show he wasn't armed. He held a card in his right hand and shoved it through the peephole at Gino. Reluctantly, Gino tore his eyes from the stranger and read the card: *Signore Dante di Luigiano, Director, de Leone Enterprises, Land Investments and Development. Rome, Italy.*

Instantly the door was unbolted. Gino grew very hospitable.

"Forgive this reception, Signore di Luigiano. I allow no one on the estate. I am Gino Vittorio, the caretaker."

"*Piacere*, Gino," said Dolcetto in his northern accent, with a voice that disguised his own fairly well and covered the nervousness he felt at reentering the villa.

"It's good that you exercise prudence. One can't be too careful these day. I can see we put our trust in the right man. *Va biene.* This is my first trip to Porto Tomasso. I am impressed," said the Lion as he gazed about the place with the curious eyes of a tourist. He affected a light, easy manner. "Yes, indeed, I am impressed."

Gino raised a speculative eyebrow as to whether or not this emissary from Rome was fully masculine. He'd never seen such fluttery mannerisms among the Sicilians. He shrugged, then escorted his guest into the villa.

"Come in, signore. Come right in." He held the iron gate ajar for Dolcetto to enter the Peacock Court. "What brings you to the Vanzini Villa, signore?"

"Just a routine visit to assess the property. It is possible that our firm may have a potential buyer who wishes to make a resort out of the place. I'll only stay a few days, ah . . . it *was* Gino?"

"*Si*, Gino."

"I shall try not to disturb you, Gino. I'll be no bother at all. Pretend I'm not here at all."

"Well . . ." Gino hesitated. "There are no servants, very few conveniences. They never wrote to tell us to expect you. You see we . . ."

"Us?" interrupted the Lion.

Gino's face filled with color. "My—ah—wife and—ah, son."

"Is that so?" An eyebrow shot up. "Strange, my report doesn't indicate you are married."

"Only recently, Signore."

"And you have a son? So soon?"

Gino's face turned the color of pomegranates. "It was one of *those* marriages."

"Ah! I understand. You and your family continue to feel at home. I promise I shall be no bother. No bother at all. When I've completed my work, I shall leave."

Dolcetto had no idea how devastating the effect would be on him when he entered the Peacock Court. Powerful memories surfaced and he felt a strange chill pass over him. Images of his wedding day came at him. He saw Francesca descending the stairs on Marco's arm, dressed in her wedding finery. Smiling guests. Marco standing proud and tall, shaking hands with everyone.

Dolcetto forced himself out of the reverie. There was little he could do now, except go through with his plan. Thanks to the miracle of contact lenses he took to wearing in Rome, his eyes were a rich, deep brown. He glanced up and saw an enormous oil painting of Francesca midway up the spiral steps on a wall. He filled with anguish. He stood in a careless pose, one hand thrust in a high waist pocket, the other holding a cigarette.

Watching him from the shadowy foyer, Gino stopped for the second time, startled by something that shook him into an unnerving sobriety. His dark eyes missed nothing. Sharp and observant, they scanned Dolcetto from head to toe; the posture, the manner of smoking, the careless pose, all part of the Lion's characteristics. Gino's eyes smoldered in suspicion. "Forgive me, signore. You seem so familiar to me. Have we met before? Are you sure you've never been here?" asked Gino, totally unnerved.

Dolcetto turned to him full face and silently questioned him.

"No? Perhaps not." Gino told himself, *I'd have remembered that scarred face.*

From the other end of the corridor, Francesca approached them, filled with curiosity about the length of time it had taken Gino and why he hadn't returned.

"Signore di Luigiano, may I present my wife, Signora Vittorio."

Dolcetto spun about with as pleasant a look on his face as he could manage considering the scar on his cheek. When he saw Francesca, the pleasantry faded. His heart stopped and his body went numb. He stared unashamedly in complete stupefaction at the very thin figure with warm, brown eyes and dark hair pulled back away from her face in an unbecoming bun.

Francesca smiled politely. When she saw the grotesque mass of scar tissue she stared in awe, looked into his dark brown eyes for a moment, then not wanting to cause him embarrassment by staring, she averted her eyes.

"*Piacere,* Signore. Our house is yours."

Dear God. There it was, the same sensuous, throaty voice that melted my heart so many times. For one brief moment, he felt sick. The room began to swim about him in a hazy mist. Gino's voice snapped him out of it.

"Signore di Luigiano represents the House of de Leone. He's here on business from Rome."

Francesca nodded at Gino. *Why does he stare at me so? Dio buono, what a horrible face! Poor soul.* She kept her eyes trained on Gino. *Why do I feel so uncomfortable?*

"I shall make some coffee. You must be tired from your trip. Are you hungry? Shall I fix a snack?" Before he could answer, she turned and disappeared through the shadowy corridors.

Gino paused to light two of the brass hanging lamps in

512

the foyer. They instantly cast dotted fans of light on the tiles. "Signore." Gino called out to him three times before Dolcetto heard.

"Mi perdona, Gino." Dolcetto came back to life. "Forgive me for staring. Your wife reminded me of someone I once knew." He hoped the bodyguard couldn't see him shaking. *What nightmare is this? I must be losing my mind. It was Francesca. No one could resemble her that much.* He composed himself. "She greatly resembles the portrait on the wall."

"Oh, that." Gino laughed in a voice of deception. "Yes, there's a remarkable resemblance."

"Who is she?" he asked, glancing at the portrait once more.

"That, Signore, was the Signorina Vanzini."

"Vanzini?"

"Forgive me. I mean de Leone."

"Ah," muttered Dolcetto, nodding his head as if he knew about the tragedy of a year ago. "Would you be good enough to show me to my room? I should like to freshen up a bit." If he didn't get away soon, Dolcetto felt certain that Gino would see through him.

When Dolcetto was ushered into the room Marco occupied for the wedding, his throat thickened and he fought for control. His pulse accelerated with a fury.

He convinced himself he must remain calm, that if he didn't, he'd give himself away. This he couldn't chance, not until he'd had time to think things out more carefully.

"I'll rest for a while. The trip tired me more than I realized."

"I understand. May I ask, Signore, how is Signore Antonio doing?"

For a moment, Dolcetto was at a loss. Then he managed to say, "As well as expected, considering . . ."

As soon as he was alone, Dolcetto put out his cigarette and began pacing the floor. Francesca was alive! How could he have known? Antonio told him she was dead! He'd know her anyplace. There'd been no sign, no indication in her eyes that she knew or recognized him. He caught his reflection in the mirror over the dresser. How the hell could she know me with this face? How? He felt sick. He felt as if he'd been mortally struck.

He took a small case from his pocket, removed the contact lenses, placed them into the container, placed it on the bureau, then walked into the bathroom to wash. Later he sat out on the small balcony overlooking the Tyrrhenian Sea. He must have fallen asleep, for when he awoke, he found a

513

small tray next to the bed with bread and cheese and stuffed eggplant. He drank the coffee but left the rest. He sat in the semi-darkness, forcing his mind to go back over everything Antonio told him about his wedding night.

Arrived at villa . . . Gate was locked . . . Climbed high wall . . . Found Calo dead at servants' entrance . . . Grew alarmed . . . Uncle Marco's room was empty . . . Alarms rang loudly, turned them off . . . Rang servants' bell . . . Opened gun room, took out two and a burp gun . . . Went to your room . . . Saw dead bodies . . . Panicked . . . Took Uncle Marco in my arms . . . Saw Dolcetto move . . . Ran quickly to your side, tried talking to you . . . Pulled you off Francesca's lifeless body . . . Her body fell limply to one side, blood all over her . . . She didn't move . . . Picked you up, wrapped you in blanket and drove to your Godfather's.

Antonio never did check to see if Francesca was dead or alive. She could have lost consciousness. No. No. Stop! It was Antonio who claimed her body. He would have told me. Antonio wouldn't have done this to me. Could Antonio have been fooled? He swore she wore a golden lion around her neck.

He dug into his pocket and studied the golden lion. Lt. Domingo had taken it from the dead body and sent it to Antonio, who later gave it to him. Now he kept it on a golden chain circlet with a few important keys attached to the ring. How could he not know Francesca? He'd seen her face a thousand times a day for a year. And that voice! Etched in his memory for all eternity. Yet, Gino called her his wife. He mentioned a son. Dolcetto recalled their wedding night. A sob rose to choke him.

Francesca wouldn't have remarried! Not the Francesca I loved and married. It had to be part of a bad dream. He'd imagined it to be her. Tomorrow in the light of day, he'd prove to himself that it wasn't her. *Steady, Dolcetto, steady. Dear God help me!*

On the eve of the anniversary of the de Leone-Vanzini wedding, Gino had been unduly quiet and unresponsive, filled with obvious brooding. Several times Dolcetto caught Gino staring, watching his movements with curious and suspicious eyes.

"I must go into the village for supplies," he told Dolcetto. "I'll return as soon as I can, Signore di Luigiano. Is there something I can get you?"

Dolcetto gave him the equivalent of a hundred dollars. "My stay has inconvenienced you. Please buy whatever supplies or foods that are necessary. Also I need film for my camera. Will you bring back six rolls?"

"They have no film in Porto Tomasso. I'll have to go into Palermo to the shops there. Truly, Signore, it isn't necessary to give me your money. They pay me enough."

"Nonsense, they don't pay you to entertain the likes of me." Dolcetto thought a moment. "You have to go to Palermo for the film? Then forget it. I don't want you going so far."

"Far? It's but a fifteen-minute drive. Besides, I enjoy driving the automobile. It's some machine. It handles like a woman."

"Our firm takes good care of you, no? A Ferrari no less."

"Oh, it's not mine. Not even the firm's." He lowered his eyes as they walked along the path toward the old reconverted stables. "It belonged to Dolcetto de Leone, *buon armo*. It was left here and it would be a shame not to use it, such a fine piece of machinery."

"I agree. I'll say nothing of it in my report. Never fear."

Gino smiled and relaxed. "*Grazie*, Signore. *Aloura*, I'll see you later."

Upstairs in his rooms, Dolcetto grew uneasy. *Why am I so tied up in knots?* His calendar told him it was a year ago this very night that the villa was permeated with life, love, and laughter; one year ago this night that his world was shattered.

He'd planned to go into the main salon, where the wedding had taken place, to stir up his memories of that night. In the bridal chamber, he hoped he might reconstruct portions of what happened. Tonight, with Gino away, he had the villa practically to himself.

The perverse mixture of curiosity and a desire to unite himself with what had been the happiest moments of his life urged him on. He showered, changed into a white turtleneck sweater and slacks, removed the contact lenses, and slipped into a pair of soft shoes. Then he crept soundlessly along the upper corridor toward the room that once contained the greatest love of his life and the most terrifying horror he had ever endured.

He walked in the direction of the old arsenal. His hand groped for the hidden key, and finding it, he inserted it into the lock and opened the door cautiously. He wondered if Lt. Domingo or his men had located this cache of weapons. Everything was just as it was a year ago. He turned off the light, locked the door, and replaced the key. What good had this arsenal done? What good had any of the precautions done? It had all served no purpose.

Padding softly across the corridor toward the bridal chambers, Dolcetto had to pause to wipe the sweat from his face, the corners of his feverish lips. Almost reluctantly his hand reached up to turn the door handles, and before he entered, he drew a deep breath to brace himself, then crept inside. He stopped dead still, frozen in astonishment.

Methodically his eyes started at one point and traveled slowly across the room; he felt dazed and chilled to the bone. The hairs on his neck stood on end. What madness was this? What bizarre mind had concocted this? The room had been totally restored to the way it was on their wedding night. Francesca's gown and veil lay across the silken covers of the bed. Dolcetto's formal morning coat and striped trousers were draped on a clothing caddy; a table between two chairs supported a bucket containing a bottle of unopened champagne with two hollow stemmed glasses next to it; several packs of cigarettes lay carelessly strewn about the table and nightstand; two golden lion's head lighters lay side by side, his and hers.

Dolcetto stared in utter fascination as if he examined the *mise en scène* for some bizarre stage production. Everything was perfect; his gold and emerald studs and cuff links were on the bureau; his shoes, the same he'd worn on his wedding day, lay polished and set into place. The luggage they'd intended taking on their honeymoon was exactly where they had left it, alongside the enormous wardrobe closets.

Why would someone do this? Someone wanted to keep the memory alive. It had to be Francesca's handiwork. But why? Filled with mixed emotions, he moved like a shadow as bitter and tragic memories tore at him. He moved toward the wall stereo. They had missed nothing. *Misericordia!* The recording of "Shangri-La" was still on the turntable, as it had been the night it played over and over so many times.

Dolcetto grew dizzy at the powerful images that rushed at him from every direction of the room. He heard Francesca's delicious laughter; he saw her smiling face as she romped with him on the bed; he saw a sea of smiling faces gazing up at them from the courtyard below; he saw the three shadowy figures of the *mafiosi* come at him, at Francesca.

Unconsciously, Dolcetto turned on the phonograph. He saw the slender arm of the mechanism come to life, hover slightly in midair, then swoop down to fit in the record groove. The room filled with the familiar, memory-evoking melody. For a year Dolcetto had avoided listening to the recording. He had bought the record in Rome, but he couldn't bring himself to listen to it. Now it rekindled every sensa-

516

tion he fought so hard to repress. *Sainted God!* He fell heavily into a chair, and letting his head fall like a dead weight into his hands, he sobbed uncontrollably.

Dolcetto was unaware he was being observed. Drawn to the room by a tripped alarm, which rang downstairs when Dolcetto entered the arsenal, Francesca left her room, gun in hand, and crept soundlessly up the stairs. All day she'd been filled with premonition, and reflecting with resolute sadness on the anniversary of her wedding, she attributed the feeling to the bitter memories.

Only once had Francesca entered the bridal chamber. It was after she returned to the villa proper from her hiding place. In a moment of maudlin despair, she had painstakingly restored the room as it had been that one night, then she never returned to it.

Now she stood quietly at the threshold unnoticed by Dolcetto, looking and wondering at the dark shadowy figure slouched over in the chair. She didn't move a muscle, didn't breathe. She studied him while the music replayed three times.

Dressed in a modest dressing gown, her long black hair hanging loosely around her shoulders, only a faint glow of light behind her lit up Francesca's shadowy form. She staggered a moment, stifling a gasp. She studied him in profile, scarred side away from her. Trancelike, she started to deny the impressions that came at her. *Jesus, Mary, and Joseph. God. Someone help me. I'm losing my mind. Don't do this to me, not tonight of all nights.*

Francesca leaned heavily against the door. She heard him cry aloud and saw his body shake convulsively.

"Francesca, Francesca. *Sanguo dei mio cuore!* Blood of my heart!"

Good Mary, Mother of God. It's Dolcetto. I'd know that voice anyplace. She inched toward him, tears spilling down her cheeks. She stretched her arm toward him, hesitant and unsteady, until she touched his shoulder lightly. The gun slipped from her other hand and fell with a dull thud onto the carpeted floor.

Startled, Dolcetto bolted from his chair and turned to her. His green eyes fixed on her. She searched his face with eager eyes and knew him instantly. It all came together for her, ugly scarring and all. *Of course! Why hadn't I thought of it before? They cut him up before my eyes!* She uttered a low moan and fell into his arms. They clung to each other, motionless and in silence. Then she moved back away and

517

fanned his face with her dark eyes. Dolcetto averted his head and turned the scarred grotesqueness from her eyes.

Francesca reached up and tenderly drew his face back to hers and stroked it with her cool hand. It felt a relief against the feverish pulsation of his veins, but he instinctively pulled back.

"Don't turn from me."

"My face is repulsive."

"It's the most beautiful face I've seen in a year." Her sensuous, throaty voice had the same exciting effect. Dolcetto could no longer refrain from holding her. He swept her back into his arms.

"I'm dreaming," she whispered. "I'm sure, I'll wake up and find you gone."

"I can't believe it's you."

"Yes, it's me. Touch me, I'm alive."

"We're both alive. Oh miracle of miracles."

He stroked her face tenderly, smoothed back her hair, and held onto her for fear she'd vanish as she had so many times in his dreams.

"Why didn't you let me know you were alive?"

"Who could I tell? A tombstone?"

"I'm sorry, I didn't think. If you only knew what I've been thinking this past week." He shook his head and avoided her eyes. "I recognized you immediately."

"And you didn't see fit to tell me?"

"You seemed another woman . . ."

"And you," she said suddenly, "had brown eyes. Now they're green."

"Come, I'll show you."

Downstairs in the study, they sat drinking coffee. When they could bear to, they talked about the pain of their wedding night.

"Why did you leave without me? Couldn't you have taken me with you, Dolcetto?"

"I had no control over what Antonio did. He presumed you to be dead. His only thought was to save my life. He drove me as fast as the car would take us to my Godfather's house near Faro where I was nursed back to life."

Dolcetto would have had to be blind not to notice the instant change that came over his wife. Her inner radiance, the joy of their reunion dissolved instantly and her eyes clouded. Her lips formed a tight, white line. She said nothing. *There's plenty of time to tell him. When he discovers who it was. Mother of God.* Francesca lowered her eyes for fear he would see them speak.

They both heard the noise of the powerful Ferrari engine. Dolcetto, suddenly alert, tensed noticeably.

"Don't worry, *carissimo*, it's only Gino."

"Your husband?"

She glanced sharply at him. Then said softly, "No. You're my husband. Gino saved my life and that of your son."

"My son?" he asked incredulously.

"For a time I wasn't sure. I feared he might have been the seed of that *mafioso*. But when I saw his green eyes, your eyes, and heard his lion's roar at birth, there was no mistaking him. Yes, my love, your son."

He filled with silent wonder, grasped her hands and kissed them. "How much you must have suffered."

"And you?"

"For this past year, for what we both suffered, we shall be repaid! What you endured, what I lived through, for all our misery and unhappiness, Barbarossa shall pay. I swear!"

She felt her body turn cold as ice. She trembled and her face faded to a deathlike pallor. With trembling lips, she shook her head and managed to speak out. *"Basta,* Dolcetto. *Basta!* I'm tired of vengeance, sick of vendetta, frightened of retaliation. Can't we leave well enough alone? We've found each other, *caro mio*. Isn't it enough? A miracle neither of us believed possible."

"Yes, a miracle. I see my duties more clearly now than ever. After what they put us through, what they did to Marco, I must strike at them. I swore an oath, Francesca."

"Isn't there another way? Let the law take care of them." Even as she spoke the words, she felt them to be alien to her.

"One fights fire with fire, *carissima*."

"I don't want to lose you now that I have found you. Can't we live in peace?"

Standing in the Peacock Court in the dim shadows of night, with only the minute illumination from the brass lamps, Gino Vittorio stared at them, stony-faced, immobile. He glanced from one to the other sensing something was wrong.

"Gino," she said, "I think you should know who our houseguest really is."

Instinctively, Gino's hand slipped around his gun and withdrew it from his holster. Dolcetto was favorably impressed with his quickness. "There's no need for that."

Her voice had triggered off an alarm in him at first. Now he was confused. He hadn't seen her so easy and relaxed for so long. As the couple drew nearer to him, Gino saw the

519

amazing green eyes, the unmistakable, incredible jewellike eyes he'd never forgotten.

"Don't you recognize him behind the scars?"

"Tell him. In God's name, don't taunt him." Dolcetto's natural voice returned. "You have my undying gratitude for saving my wife and our son's life. Whatever you desire shall be yours. You have but to ask."

Gino heard the words, saw the Lion, but didn't believe what his senses told him. He turned to Francesca.

"It's my husband. It's the Lion," she said in a flat, empty voice that momentarily startled Dolcetto. "Now that he's found us, he's ready to throw all our lives away." Her voice contained all the misery and pain and terror she'd known and endured over the past year.

"Francesca!"

"Forgive me if I shock you, my husband. If I'm not the dutiful wife and obedient woman I should be. My wifely duties escape me. I haven't learned what it's like to really be a wife."

For an instant, Dolcetto's eyes filled with arrogant anger. Just as quickly he realized it was love talking to him and he softened. He reached for her, stroking her face tenderly and smoothing back a tendril of hair that had fallen across her face. As he brushed away the faint trace of an angry, resentful tear, she melted into his arms and her resolve melted with her.

"Now, may I see our son?"

"We'll be only a few minutes, Gino. Make the coffee, please?"

Gino turned and walked away, feeling like a dead man.

Dolcetto felt the mad pounding of his heart as they walked into the small room off the kitchen. There in the uncertain candlelight, he looked upon his wife's face which shone like a smooth pearl as she gazed upon the squirming bundle of motion in the center of the crib.

"It's time for his feeding. See what a good boy he is? He hardly cries. It's as if he truly knows I'm but a moment away."

She changed his wet clothing, washed him, and dressed him with marked efficiency as her husband watched with glowing pride.

"Here, hold him while I ready myself," she whispered softly.

The child was a vigorous bundle of energy with his father's vivid emerald eyes. His golden-brown hair was a mass of curls. His arms moved about in the disjointed and uncoordinated rhythms of infants. His strong, well-formed hands

520

were clenched in tiny fists of pink velvet. The proud father, whose heart felt like it would burst with love and happiness, handed the child to its mother.

Francesca lifted him to her full, exposed breast and he began to suck on it with such loud hungry noises, the Lion laughed softly. Francesca blushed in embarrassment, lowered her face, and was hidden beneath her falling black hair.

Gino heard Francesca call to him. He kept on walking through the long corridor and into the kitchen. He reached for the bundle of mail he picked up in town. There were periodicals from Rome, a leaflet advertising new apartments in Palermo, a request for a donation for several orphanages. Always there was that, he thought. Last was a letter from Rome. It was from the House of de Leone addressed to him. He opened it and began to read it as the reunited couple entered the room.

"Forgive our informality here, Dolcetto. I maintain no servants as in the past. This past year has brought many innovations to Vanzini Villa." She turned to Gino. "What's wrong? You look pale."

He avoided her eyes and handed her the letter. While she read it, he got the cups and saucers. Dolcetto offered them each a cigarette. After lighting theirs, the Lion lit his own. He fanned out the match and turned to study them both carefully. He noticed that Francesca's face turned colorless, that she grew nervous and bit her lower lip to keep from trembling. When he saw them exchange knowing glances, he felt terribly left out of their intimacy and a pang of jealousy shot through him. Gino disappeared in the other room and returned with two chairs, which he placed around the small table.

"Bad news?" asked Dolcetto when the silence grew too baffling.

"Better tell him before he reads the letter," suggested Gino.

"No. It's best he read the letter first." She handed it to Dolcetto.

Glancing questioningly from one to the other, he lowered his eyes and smiled warmly when he saw it was from Antonio. He read:

Dear Gino:

This is to inform you that the Vanzini Villa has been sold to Dr. Pietro of Messina. It's his express desire that you remain as caretaker. Next month just before Christmas, he will arrive and tell you his

plans. Thank you for your splendid cooperation.
You'll find enclosed a year's salary in the event you
do not wish to remain at the villa. If I can be of
further help to you, do not hesitate to write. Please
give my regards to that splendid brother of yours.

Respectfully,
Antonio de Leone

"Well," said Dolcetto, "at least he's kept the villa in the family, so to speak. After all my Godfather's done for us, he's entitled to the land."

Dolcetto placed the letter on the table and watched the bodyguard pour the coffee with shaking hands. He reached out and held Gino's hand with his to steady it. Their eyes met and held for a moment, then Gino set the pot down and busied himself with cookies, which he proceeded to dunk quickly.

Both are acting very strangely, thought Dolcetto. He reached for his cup, brought it to his lips, and blowing on the steaming liquid, he studied the others through veiled eyes. *I suppose they'll tell me when they're good and ready.*

Francesca and Gino exchanged nervous glances. Finally, she reached out and placed her hand on Gino's arm. Dolcetto winced at the familiarity between them.

"Now," said Francesca. "I think we both have something to tell His Excellency, my husband."

47

"Listen, *consiglioro*, who gives a good goddamn about those headlines, eh? Let the U.S. clamp down on heroin traffic! Let the United Nations bring pressure to bear! Let those *pezzonavante* Senators and Congressmen complain and promote all the legislation they want! Let them promote anything they want. You think that will stop us?"

"They threaten to cut down financial aid to all countries who won't cooperate in halting the flow of narcotics to American shores."

"And your balls are all twisted over this? You take a look at the books lately? Our profits have—quid—quad—what is this word Alberto uses?"

"Quadrupled."

"Yes, that. And you think we should worry? What a brilliant stroke of genius to use legitimate pharmaceutical plants to make the stuff, eh?"

"How much longer can we use the political umbrella of de Leone Chemicals and Pharmaceuticals? I don't usually interfere, Don Matteo. But don't you think Alberto is spreading us too thin?"

"What's been shoved up your ass to irritate you, eh? If Alberto wants to spread us over the North Pole, you think I'll complain? With these profits? Are you crazy or something?"

"If the United Nations intervenes, they'll squeeze Belasci, and you know the Premier can't stand too much squeezing. Look what happened with him and the Communists. They squeezed his balls so badly, he would have made a worse fiasco than he already did with the bandits. You bailed him out of the Salvatore affair, no?"

Don Barbarossa glanced at his *consiglioro* with a strange expression in his eyes. "I didn't think anyone knew about that."

It was a subject neither the bright lawyer nor Barbarossa discussed in the past, and Garibaldi wasn't about to bring it in to the picture to get sidetracked.

"My concern is that Belasci will be pressured so badly he'll demand you cut back on the operations. I think we should be prepared."

"Demand? From me? Listen, now I know you're either crazy or you know something you are preparing to tell me. Which is it? You been drinking the new wine, my friend?"

Garibaldi grinned sheepishly. At times he forgot the power of his Don. "It's all these reports in the papers. American agents claim they run into blind alleys, follow false leads, and in short are in a state of confusion because our government refuses to cooperate with them. They complain they haven't enough manpower to police the corrupt continent of smugglers and transporters of illicit narcotics. One of those Senators is going to listen long enough to start some kind of an investigation committee. They'll use their muscle in politics and there's going to have to be some kind of cooperation. Some of their agents have disappeared, and you know what that can lead to, Matteo."

"What you're saying is *our* organization is running in top form, no?"

Garibaldi shrugged.

"Which rag you been reading? The Red rag?"

"The *London Times*. Eddie Paletine's column."

"The mouse who roars like an elephant? The one who wants to write about me?"

"That's the one. The Americans are puritanical, Matteo, they don't believe in giving in to these cravings for drugs and the baser things in life."

"Bullshit! Where did you learn that crap? Not from me! Listen, *caro mio,* I learned plenty from the *'Mericani,* during the war. You think black marketeering would have been possible without the cooperation of top brass Army officials? Not on your life! *Primo de tutti!* First of all, they had their sticky fingers in the honey pot!" He pointed to all the photos adorning the wall in his study, all top ranking officers in both British and American armies. "From four-star generals to lowly hustling corporals, they were all on the take. You know how much money went into Zurich bank accounts for them? Eh?" The Don wagged a finger at him. "Don't tell your Don nothing about these—what did you call them—puritans? They all have their peccadillos! And those up on top of the pile, those who make the laws, are the first on the take and then they hide behind their public boasts. With me it's out in the open! I make no excuses. I do what I believe is right for my country. Someone has to lead the people . . ." He stopped in the middle of his statement and stared at a point beyond where his *consiglioro* stood.

Following his line of vision, Garibaldi said, "That came from Alberto before you returned from Palermo today. I took the liberty of hanging it for you."

Don Barbarossa ignored him, his eyes were fixed compulsively on the oil portrait of Diamonte. Speechless, he devoured every inch of the painting, of her fabulous beauty, and felt the stirrings of old surge through him.

Goddammit! She was some beauty! What a beauty! What a face! And she'd been all his, once. All his! So enraptured was he with this portrait, he failed to notice that Garibaldi left the room, wondering many things: why the Don would permit a painting made by *El Leone* himself to hang in his house, and who the beauty was? Why the total fascination with the woman?

The Don was unable for the moment to wade through the stack of business on his desk. He walked over to the painting and stood only a few feet from it, drinking in all her beauty with the intensity sparked by his memory of her.

"Too bad you couldn't have lived to see all I command, Diamonte," he said softly. "Didn't I tell you one day I'd own Sicily? I told you, 'Believe in me,' but, you had to love him more. I can see it. I can see his love in the image he painted of you." A tear spilled down his cheek as he continued to stare at the painting. Suddenly he grew critical. He frowned and walked back to his desk. Behind him on the wall he opened a wall safe and removed a small box from it, shuffled through it, and lifted out the small gold and diamond spider earring.

He replaced everything else and was just about to call to his *consiglioro,* when Primo reentered the study. Noticing the tears on the Don's face, he hesitated, fearing he'd intruded on an intimate moment.

"I—uh—forgot all about this letter from this Signore Paletine. You must sign this letter, Don Matteo. I don't want this correspondent to come to Palermo using the excuse he got no reply from us."

"You don't want I should accept the proposal, eh, *consiglioro?*"

"Not now. To enter into an agreement with such a man to do a series of articles on your life would be courting disaster to our future plans. You'd be in too vulnerable a position. Right now, they only suspect your association with the Big Five. If you flaunt yourself publicly, you leave yourself wide open for too many questions. No breed of men are more capable of adding two and two and making it come up a hundred than his type of investigative reporter."

The Don shrugged. He kept playing with the diamond earring. "You may be right. Too much focus on me might prove disastrous, I agree." He signed the letter.

Garibaldi sighed in relief. Expose the Don to a barracuda like Paletine? Not that the Don couldn't handle himself, but he was approaching that period in his life where he felt the need to bask in his past accomplishments, and it was possible he'd turn to putty in the hands of a skillful manipulator like Eddie Paletine. It was too risky.

Besides a crucial meeting was soon to take place near Palermo and nothing, but nothing, was to interfere with its well-planned secrecy. In dealing with the superegos of five distinct and diverse personalities, you have to tread carefully and use all the skill and diplomacy you can muster. Publicity showered on one and not another might cause ruffled feathers among these preening peacocks. Garibaldi needed no additional problems at this time. It was bad enough these imperial pashas were complaining bitterly over Lucky Luciano's latest fiasco.

"Listen, Primo—you know about such things . . . Who in Palermo would you say is an excellent promising artist? A painter?"

Garibaldi's eyes widened politely. "You think you have the patience to sit for a portrait, Don Matteo?"

"Never mind. Never mind. Just call one and have him contact me, *capeeshi?*"

He nodded. "It displeases me to be the bearer of bad tidings. About your cousin, Don Salvatore . . ."

"Harumph! That again? For two weeks I hear Lucky this, Lucky that! I'll believe it when he tells me himself."

"You think he'll confess his *pecatto* to you? Your associates are blistering. Trouble with the New Orleans Dons. It's gonna take a lot to square it this time."

"We'll hear the report straight from the horse, *va biene?*"

The *consiglioro* shrugged and left the office. Don Matteo thought that whatever the hell that fancy Lucky Luciano did promised to be a real bust in the balls.

A letter from Alberto Pietro caught the Don's attention. So! Alberto had turned over his medical practice to another physician in Messina and by Christmas he'd be living in the Vanzini Villa. *Managghia!* He had to give the devil his due! He finally got what he set out for. What cleverness! What manipulative genius! He had been wasted in medicine, thought the Don. Alberto should have become a financier. What amazed the old barbarian was the manner in which Alberto had received the cooperation of Antonio de Leone. How, he wondered, had the last of the Lions been persuaded to fall into line with *mafia* thinking, eh?

One thing troubled Don Barbarossa. One real problem. He detested unfinished business, and to him Cacciatore's disappearance with the di Luccas was unfinished business. He continued to worry about this facet of the whole conspiracy against the Lions, even more than he did about the knowledge that Francesca Vanzini de Leone might be alive. He'd sent his spies out for nearly six months in exhaustive searches and came up with nothing. No matter how many times Alberto had admonished him for this paranoid reaction to Cacciatore's mysterious disappearance, he couldn't dismiss his feelings in the matter. Matteo Barbarossa had been a bandit for too long.

A week later, Don Matteo Barbarossa stood before the oil portrait of Diamonte completely flushed with pleasure and satisfaction. He thanked the artist profusedly, paid him handsomely, and now in his solitude, he felt more in communion with this image. For now, suspended from Diamonte's ears were replicas of the spider earrings. *"Va biene,* my little spider? Now you'll rest easier, eh?"

In Rome, the prominent barrister Giorgio Bocca hadn't adjusted to being ignored by Antonio de Leone and probably never would. His concentrated efforts in his private law practice caused it to flourish. In recent weeks and most especially on this day, however, a peculiar depression plagued him. Only this morning he lost a simple court case an amateur would have won hands down. Angry at himself, and angrier still at Antonio, who had again chosen not to return an urgent call he'd placed early that morning, he kicked at drawers and pushed chairs out of his path like a madman.

It wasn't that Giorgio really expected Antonio to return his call, any more than he had the hundreds of other calls. But there were mounds of incompleted work concerning de Leone Enterprises piled on his desk that needed Antonio's attention. Occasionally he sent important letters with instructions to him by mail. Duly signed, they were returned. He began to think he was doing business with a phantom.

In desperation, he had even stormed over to Antonio's office and demanded a confrontation. Greeted by Dino Caruso, full of half-assed excuses, he was told, "Signore Antonio is in Switzerland. I'm not sure when he'll return."

How many times had he heard these same excuses? Antonio is in Naples or Milan or he just left for Messina. *Antonio was nowhere.* He finally accepted the excuses for what they were—polite and persistent brushoffs.

Four letters of resignation awaited Giorgio's signature. As director of each of the four de Leone corporations, he felt it best to cut the cord once and for all. His reluctance had been due to his genuine love and concern for Antonio. His respect for Marco and Dolcetto kept him anxious over Antonio's welfare, despite the lack of communication.

On this day, he paid the cab driver who'd picked him up at the *Palazzo di Giustizia* and driven him to his office. He entered the building berating himself for having lost the court case. In his office he looked about angrily for the letters of resignation. *Where in hell are they? Only yesterday they were right here on my desk.*

He shuffled through the folders, putting everything into wild disarray. He caught sight of a plain manila envelope marked: *Personal Please.* He shoved it aside two or three times before he actually took a good look at it. The postmark was Palermo, Sicily. There was no return address. He slit the end of the envelope, turned it sideways, and forced a folded sheet of paper from it. A golden amulet in the shape of a lion's head fell onto the desk. Giorgio was stunned. Staring at it dumbfounded, he felt a cold, creepy chill surge through his body. He removed his glasses, wiped them with his clean handkerchief, reset them on his nose, and carefully examined the golden lion. He laid it on the desk, picked up a cigarette from a half-open pack, and lit it with a lion's head lighter, given to him by Dolcetto. He clicked it shut, then examined both the lighter and the amulet carefully. Chills were replaced by a feverish excitement. He picked up the letter and read it as if he knew in advance what it contained.

The sender of the enclosed amulet asks that you come to where you were one year ago on October 15. You must be here no later than October 18. Say nothing to anyone if you value the life of the sender.

There was no signature.

Six hours later, Giorgio Bocca settled back in the seat of an Alitalia airliner scheduled to depart for Palermo. He deliberately took the last seat on the plane at the very rear of the airliner so he could turn his back on the other passengers and catch up on some needed sleep.

He stared absently out the window. Below him baggage crews loaded the belly of the plane with luggage. He saw the workers drive their carts off the field, watched the stewardesses walking up and down the aisle, heard their friendly canned voices: *Vietato fumare . . .* Fasten your seatbelts . . . all in well-manicured Italian.

He closed his eyes and began to doze off. Someone slipped into the seat next to him. He turned further away in his seat and blinked his heavy-lidded eyes closed. He heard the powerful motors burst into activity, felt the vibration of the plane, and as it shuddered under the thrust of the engines, he drifted off to sleep.

Giorgio Bocca awoke to the aroma of fresh, strong coffee. He yawned. *Just what I need,* he thought. He pushed the button that released his seat to an upright position and turned to stare into the startled black eyes of Lt. Domingo.

"Santino!"

"Giorgio!"

They both spoke simultaneously, "What the hell are you doing here?"

"I asked first," said Domingo with a twinkle in his eye.

They both sat in awkward silence. For moments neither spoke. They each wondered how much the other knew? They were grateful for an interruption as the stewardess brought them coffee.

Is it just by chance that Giorgio Bocca is on this plane? Santino Domingo sipped his coffee and reflected on the events of the day—it had been a day full of surprises.

Lt. Domingo had been handed a plain manila envelope, like the one delivered to Giorgio Bocca's office and also marked *Personal Please.* He opened it and heard a rustling sound as the golden lion slipped to his desk. Domingo had picked it up, bounced it a few times in the palm of his hand, and studied it. Is this some sort of a joke, he wondered as he read the letter. Domingo read and reread the letter, picked up on key words: *Be here no later than October 18 . . . Say nothing to anyone . . . Value life of sender.*

He hardly heard Moreno call to him. "We'll be back, Santino. Mark my words, we'll be back." Rossi and Moreno had been recalled and were packing up to leave for the States.

Domingo kept staring at the golden lion in his hands. He wanted to tell them. Ask their opinion. *Say nothing to anyone.* The letter had been explicit.

"Domingo!" Across the room Rossi and Moreno exchanged concerned glances.

"Lieutenant," called Hank Rossi as he strode toward him.

"Huh? Oh, yeah. What?"

"What's wrong?"

"Nothing." He jumped up from his desk, filled with sudden elation, the first enthusiasm he'd shown in months. He reached for his crumpled trenchcoat and his worn porkpie hat and headed for the door.

"Don't do anything until you hear from me." He ran out the door, leaving the two astonished men behind. Before they could move, Domingo rushed back into his office.

"Whatever you do, don't *go* anyplace until you hear from me."

Rossi looked at their airplane tickets on the desk. They were to leave the following day. He looked apologetic and was about to protest.

"Promise."

"All right. We'll postpone the trip four days. If we don't hear from you by then . . ."

"You'll hear. Believe me you'll hear."

Domingo was gone.

The third letter, addressed to Antonio de Leone, contained the identical message and a golden lion. It remained unopened along with a small pile of inconsequential mail, the bulk of which Dino Caruso had already opened and dispersed through to the proper channels. The letter containing the golden lion had somehow been shuffled around and fell into a waste basket, unnoticed by anyone except Destiny, who smiled craftily to herself.

On their arrival at Palermo airport, neither Lt. Domingo nor Giorgio Bocca wished the other to know where he was going. They shook hands and said their goodbyes, promising to call each other for lunch on their return to Rome. Giorgio rented a car, doing his best to avoid Domingo. Domingo called Mike Camarta and asked to have a car at his disposal. Each thought they had outsmarted the other and soon both were on the road to Porto Tomasso.

Giorgio Bocca was the first to arrive. Gino met him at the gate and ushered him into the study.

"Mah, chè c'e, Gino? Do you know anything about this?" He showed him the golden lion.

"Please be patient, *avvocato.* All in due time." He served Giorgio a drink. They both heard the doorbell ring. Gino excused himself to answer it. He returned in moments with Lt. Domingo.

When they came face to face with one another, Giorgio pursed his lips and delicately held up his golden lion. Domingo did the same thing. They both smiled.

Gino announced coolly, "We are expecting a third party."

"If by chance you're expecting Antonio de Leone," said Giorgio with a tinge of sarcasm, "you might as well forget about him."

Gino stared at him, astonished by the perceptive guess and dismayed by his answer.

"It's as if he's disappeared from the face of the earth," Domingo volunteered. "For nearly a year, I've been unable to reach him."

"Ah," said Giorgio with bitterness, "I see you've been given special treatment, too."

Gino walked out of the study, leaving the two men to compare notes on the illusive Antonio de Leone. They were so engrossed in their conversation that they didn't hear the door open or notice Francesca as she walked in quietly.

"Gentlemen . . ." They glanced up. "How good of you to come."

The fixed smile of cordiality on the lawyer's face froze into one of stunned disbelief. His brown eyes widened enormously. His face drained of color and the wine glass slipped from between his fingers, crashing to the floor. Lt. Domingo's eyes appeared to have expanded twice their size. His mouth dropped open in complete shock.

Giorgio walked slowly to her side. "Francesca?" he asked wondrously. "Am I dreaming? Is it really you?" He touched her lightly.

She smiled gently. "I'm sorry to have shaken you like this. There was no other way." She leaned down to pick up the broken glass.

"Signora de Leone?" Domingo mumbled. His hand shook and he set down the drink. "What? How? I don't understand? I'm afraid discovering that you're alive is quite a shock." He stooped to help her pick up the glass fragments.

"I know. But your questions will be answered soon enough." She smiled at them and tried to prepare them for the next, even greater shock.

530

"I know you are both anxious to meet your host. Please forgive us for not being more gentle."

Dolcetto stepped into the study and stared somberly at Lt. Domingo and Giorgio Bocca. Neither recognized him.

"Giorgio, *amico*, thank you for coming." He turned to the Treasury agent. "Santino?"

"*Dio buono*," cried the lawyer. "It's Dolcetto! *Madre de Dio*." He crossed himself.

Lt. Domingo, the hardened law enforcer used to bizarre and startling contradictions in his line of work, froze as if in shock, both at his resurrection and at his facial scars. "*Managghia u diaoro!*"

Dolcetto and his lawyer embraced warmly and then Santino Domingo embraced the Lion. "I never knew how much I missed you," declared Giorgio Bocca, "until now." He blew his nose, wiped his eyes, and grinned sheepishly. "But tell us . . . how? What happened? Where've you been all this time? Surely not here? Why didn't you contact us, let us know you were alive? We've so much to talk about . . ."

"We'll talk, Giorgio . . . in due time," said the Lion. He turned to Domingo. "Don't let my face intimidate you. I'll get it fixed when my work is finished. At present it suits me to look like this."

"They did this to you?" asked Lt. Domingo quietly examining his face. "Savage beasts. Savage, inhuman beasts."

And then, because the Lion knew they'd ask a thousand questions and were fully entitled to an explanation, he told them what happened to him since that wedding night. Then Francesca told them her story, how she deliberately confounded the mystery because she felt certain the police would be ineffectual in bringing the right parties to justice. Lt. Domingo smiled a secret smile, recalling he had sensed her part, but displayed a grim face.

Over dinner, then coffee, the macabre story unfolded. The Lion frowned. "I heard you both mention you hadn't seen or heard from Antonio. Any ideas where he might be?"

"Would you know what he might be doing in Switzerland?" asked Domingo.

Dolcetto's eyes lit up. He nodded.

"Don't build your hopes yet. Now, in light of what you told us, I fear for Antonio. The last report we had on your cousin indicated he was seen boarding a plane to Berne over nine months ago. No one has seen him since. Correspondence comes out of his office signed by him. Rather his signature is affixed to letters."

"Francesca, where is the letter?" asked Dolcetto softly.

She took it from the pocket of her trousers and handed it

to him. Both Giorgio Bocca and Lt. Domingo felt the tremendous love flow between them.

"He probably signed all correspondence in blank as he did before. Or else it's a damned good forgery." He handed Antonio's letter to the lawyer.

Giorgio scanned the letter. "He sold the villa?"

He looked up in time to catch the smoldering eruption in the Lion's eyes, the fiery intensity in Francesca's eyes, and their unmistakable struggle for control.

"That's another reason I asked both of you to come here. Now more than ever I fear for my cousin."

Dolcetto began to tell them the incredible tale of his suspicions concerning his Godfather. He told them as best he could all the facts, holding his own emotions well in check. He explained his plans, who and what he needed to bring about an effective end to this murdering monster.

They all listened with tremendous interest. Lt. Domingo's eyes lit up thinking especially about his two friends in Rome, Rossi and Moreno, who had just about agreed to chuck the whole affair into the stinking sewers of Venice.

In Rome, two disgruntled Americans couldn't have been happier to have received a call from Lt. Santino Domingo.

"Grab the first plane you can to the Vanzini Villa!" was all he said.

And they did. They wired Chief Rossinger in usual coded jargon: "Startling developments of an urgent nature turned up . . . they felt obligated to pursue and would contact him as soon as possible . . ."

En route to Palermo via Alitalia, both men refused to guess what it was that fired Santino so enthusiastically. Chief Rossinger in Washington had been explicit in his screams across the ocean over their inability to crack down the gargantuan flow of narcotics into the U.S.A. His disgust at their apparent failure was heard loud and clear in his last communiqué to them a month ago.

"Either give us results or you and Moreno will be on latrine duty!" Thousands of kilos poured into the U.S.A. daily and the agents were powerless to stop what first was called the Luciano connection and was now called the Mafia connection.

What really made the agents glum and disgusted was Eddie Paletine's column lambasting them daily for their ineptness. In every column barbs were aimed at them directly, and each was like a dart aimed at their asses. A thousand and one innuendos made them out to be bungling buffoons who lived high off the hog and did no work! "If these are a sample of what American tax dollars are spent on—Americans had better wake up!"

"Sonofabitch! If he mentions the Mediterranean Big Five again as having outsmarted us again . . ." snarled Rossi glancing at his column in the *London Times*.

"Well, he's gotta find some way of evening the score," grinned Moreno. "After all, we did get him, shall I say, delicately removed from Italy."

Hank Rossi slammed the paper down on his lap and tugged at the gold watch he wore in his vest pocket. In forty minutes the mystery would be unraveled.

He leaned back, closed his eyes, and reflected.

Both he and Danny Moreno were second-generation Italians born and raised in Binghamton, New York. Hank Rossi's father had been a victim of a Mafia killing, and for as long as he remembered he had loathed this breed of Sicilian who preyed on his fellowman and extorted, threatened, even killed rather than work for a living. These bums controlled the immigrants through fear just as they'd been controlled in the old country.

Danny Moreno came from an upper-middle-class family who had no Mafia encounters and didn't have the burning drive Rossi had in his heart. They had attended high school together, went on to earn college football scholarships. Danny went on to make All American and would have gone on to profootball if a trick knee hadn't fouled him up. Actually it was a flip of the coin that brought him into the study of law, then later law enforcement, with the FBI at Quantico.

Hank Rossi, tall, powerfully built, a muscular man with broad shoulders, looked like an Olympic champion. Sandy brown hair, soft blue eyes and easy-going manners gave him the deceptive appearance of being a good-natured oaf of a man who seldom gave a damn about anything. Danny Moreno, darker haired with warm brown eyes, and well muscled, had the appearance of a hard-pressed fanatic when he was on to something. He was tenacious in his dealings, and never gave up until he solved his dilemma or caught his quarry.

World War II separated these good friends. Moreno worked with Army Intelligence on the horrendous traffic in black-market commodities in Italy and Sicily. He was transferred after the war to the Lucky Luciano case when Luciano deported, set up his operations abroad. Moreno and his men had built a case against the slippery Don Salvatore from the testimony of only one man, who identified Luciano as the man who paid him money to transport the heroin. In Italy, since one man's testimony depends heavily on the size of his bankroll and his influence, it was only a matter of minutes before Luciano was released.

So frustrated that their long, arduous chase led them up the creek, their anger abated only when Moreno learned Chief Rossinger had sent Hank Rossi to Italy to join them. Rossi, who spoke Italian fluently and several Sicilian dialects, had been sent under the auspices of a newly developed branch of the Treasury Department—Bureau of Narcotics—to question a one-time deported gangster, who made a deal to trade vital information for protection and a one-way ticket back to the States.

The deported gangster had talked up a storm! He named names, times, and places! Staggering to both Rossi and Moreno were the names of people in high public office. And one more, the House of de Leone, one of the most powerful families in Europe, whose pharmaceutical firm, the gangster admitted, had been selling the illegal contraband to Mafia factions in the States. This same deportee was about to name a top mafioso the man in high, high government under whose auspices and protection these improper and immoral practices were permitted when suddenly they had a dead man on their hands. In the dingy, god-forsaken hole of a cellar, the squat, fat-necked, cigar-chomping man's hopes of returning to Chicago were forever thwarted by a blast from a high-powered rifle.

By the time the two agents scaled the iron steps to the street, only the inky blackness of night greeted them.

All they came away with was one name: Dolcetto de Leone, head of the House of de Leone. They might as well have been handed a bomb, timed to go off on contact. Could they touch such a man surrounded by political and international power? No way! Not at their level of official capacity! The Embassy laughed in their faces! They were told that to even discuss the time of day with a man of Dolcetto de Leone's caliber, they'd need far more power than their department afforded. When in turn they reported this to their Chief, Rossinger exploded, and promised to work on some form of legislation that would empower them to meet such conditions.

In the interim, Hank resigned himself with the rationale that, "all they really had was the word of an ex-gangster who might have said anything just to make a deal."

Given temporary offices at the *Guardia de Finanzia* where they met Lt. Santino Domingo in 1950, all three were sent to Trieste to conduct an investigation with political overtones and implications of such a shocking nature that the

534

American State Department demanded immediate action. What Rossi and Moreno didn't know, and were later to find out, was they were replacing three former agents who had nearly cracked the case. Through a twisted set of circumstances, the former agents had nearly created an international incident with ramifications so damaging in nature, it might have severed American-Italian relations at the height of the Cold War, when America was still attempting to prevent the Red threat from invading Italy. The ORS File had suddenly disappeared, and Operation Red Star had to go through a slow and agonizing rebirth.

They had no clues, no supportive data, no modus operandi, no names, no idea of what had occurred. Nothing! That's not quite right, they had one thing—Lt. Domingo's phenomenal memory and what he'd retained from his former associates.

In their desperate hopes to prevent a Communist takeover, America had been aiding its allies by building up war-torn countries. Behind a facade of freight forwarding firms, import and export houses, and other legitimate houses, Soviet agents were diverting to the east valuable strategic materials such as cobalt, radar equipment, manganese and farm materials, by political skullduggery. These materials, later to be used in Russian tanks, driven by America's enemies, would kill American and United Nations' soldiers. Communists, benefitting from this American generosity called foreign aid, paid for these materials with gold bars and large quantities of heroin. Skillful Mafia hands then directed these drugs into channels leading into the U.S.A. This highly lucrative racket involving fraudulent and forged certificates of such excellent quality survived an Act of Congress. The staggering rewards reaped from this graft continued, and everyone from lowly government clerks to highly respected government officials was involved in the take.

No one cared! No one gave a damn, concurred Moreno and Rossi. American agencies who should have been alarmed seemed indifferent at the abundance of forged import and export licenses sold to the highest bidder. Regulations and controls went out the window and bribes flowed like homemade *vino*.

Rossi and Moreno checked things at their end, and Lt. Domingo, working with other agents from the Italian Ministry of Foreign Affairs, questioned everyone about these diversions. At the Italian as well as the American embassies the reports were called vague rumors. They could find no one to pinpoint, and were given polite brushoffs and non-committal replies. Since the European countries had promised not to sell these American goods to the Communists, their words were good enough for the officials.

"If no one gives a fuck, why the hell were we given this assignment?" cursed Hank Rossi. Opposition from all sides, silence, and obvious indifference caused a rush of letters to Washington. "Find out what laws govern the shipping of strategic materials!" he demanded. The answer: "Not a one worth mentioning!"

In Italy, counterfeiting, forgery, and the like involved penalties less than parking tickets in America. Not only were international spies suspect, but top-ranking industrialists and houses of commerce helped keep the Communists well stocked in materials needed for nuclear research, all emanating from the United States.

No matter what Rossi and Moreno and Domingo did, no matter what they uncovered, the results were a mere wrist slapping or a small fine. But, as they worked, the American agents became obsessed with the name de Leone. Dolcetto de Leone's name came up too often in their search to halt this commercial vandalism and the narcotics traffic. Working closely with Interpol who supplied them with a list of known international drug smugglers, they learned that the big wheels invariably turned up to be giants in finance and banking institutions and officials in the diplomatic service, men who were protected by political power and diplomatic immunity!

Revolting! Again the name de Leone Shipping and de Leone Pharmaceuticals crept into the picture too often for comfort.

It was in such a climate that Lt. Domingo enlisted the aid of Giorgio Bocca, who later introduced him to the Lion, Dolcetto de Leone, and promoted the later encounter with the American agents.

In the year Dolcetto had been clandestinely moving about Rome, they had given up all hope of cracking the de Leone pharmaceutical plant and were unable to get a thing on Molinari. Dejected, the agents directed their interest toward the Lebanon and Marseilles connections in an effort to impede heroin sales at those ends. Repeated efforts were made through Chief Rossinger to promote new legislation, to find some way to enable them to pierce that veil of silence permeating de Leone investments in this past year.

Hank Rossi wasn't sure when it happened, or why, or how it suddenly flashed on his consciousness, but he began to draw a parallel between the ghost who sat at the helm of narcotics traffic and the ghost who masterminded the diversion of strategic materials to the Communists; he had found a similarity of method. Someone with fantastic organizational ability sat at the helm of each endeavor, he was certain. And when that day, he listened in on the conversation between Lt. Domingo and Giorgio Bocca and the lawyer said, "It's as if a ghost sits at the helm of de Leone Enterprises," then it all fell together into a pattern.

Who was the omnipotent Machiavelli who rode all three horses with the skill and dexterity of an ancient charioteer? Who was the plenipotentiary?

Dr. Alberto Pietro, of course!

"Dr. Alberto Pietro? You've got to be kidding!" said Hank Rossi when he heard Dolcetto de Leone's story. "Who the hell is he?"

"My Godfather," said the Lion, grim-faced.

Rossi vaguely recalled the elderly, white-haired, blue-eyed man who greeted them at the Messina railroad station when Domingo requested an autopsy on the bodies that day, nearly a year ago. "You've got to be kidding! That mouse?" He laughed. "In all my recollection the name Alberto Pietro has never come up!"

"Nevertheless, you will employ all measures of surveillance on him while we attend to our other plans," said Dolcetto crisply, without any attempt to further convince Rossi.

"We'll comply with every directive," said Lt. Domingo. "You can count on it."

48

An orange sherbet sun rose to its zenith as the jeep driven by Felipe Santiago bounced and zigzagged its way over the dusty roads through the rambling Andalusian hills of Spain. Several yards ahead of him, Dolcetto de Leone rode at full gallop astride a swift black stallion, breathless and full of excitement. Both jeep and rider headed toward a modest hacienda nestled in the cradle of two hills.

At the outer gate of the villa, Dolcetto flung himself from his horse, just as he'd done as a boy when he drove Marco to distraction by pulling his right leg over the saddle and sliding off in a full swoop. He tied the horse to an old-fashioned hitching post used by traveling monks who hitched their donkeys here centuries before. The old mission had long since been converted to a modest hacienda.

Waiting for Felipe to park the jeep, he walked toward him watching the old falconer limp as he did, favoring an aggravated back condition. With arms about each other, they entered the immaculately kept courtyard banked with flowers and green shrubs.

Standing on the portico steps, looking amazingly like Marco de Leone, with flowing white hair, lean tanned features and exciting brown eyes that grew vibrant when he saw his nephew, Guillermo de Leone startled Dolcetto. Dressed in a beige monk's cloth robe, belted with rope, and wearing thonged sandals on his feet, he moved toward Dolcetto. The quiet, unlined face looked peaceful and incredibly magnetic. Still handsome at the age of sixty-five, he startled Dolcetto because he looked forty. Guillermo extended his arms and the two men embraced each other with warmth and love and tears.

"I'd know you anyplace," he told his nephew.

"With this face?" Dolcetto smiled.

"I see more than the outer flesh, *nepoto*. What I see is invisible to the naked eye," he said cryptically.

It hadn't been easy for Dolcetto to grasp what Felipe Santiago told him about his uncle, and it was more difficult to understand him in person.

"You'll find him unlike any human you've ever met," the ex-falconer told him on his arrival. "Guillermo's lived alone for a long time. He retired into himself, lives the life of an ascetic, has remained celibate for well over ten years that I know. He's a mystic, a student of the occult. You'll see for yourself. He's an amazing man. If I had the sense of a jackass, I'd have written to *El Leone* about what he foretold."

"I don't understand."

Felipe's face turned ashen. He hung his head sadly. "He begged me to write His Excellency to tell him he foresaw doom and inescapable dangers for him at the time of your wedding."

"He did that?"

"Yes. I couldn't find a way to tell Marco. You see, we never spoke of Guillermo in our letters. He was always referred to as *our friend*. To suddenly tell Marco that *our friend* had turned into a clairvoyant, a psychic, without my having spoken about it previously, would have been cause for great skepticism on Marco's part."

Dolcetto nodded. He could see how Marco might have doubted the validity of this side of Guillermo's nature.

Inside the cool room, furnished with heavy Spanish wood and leathers polished to a soft gloss, Dolcetto sat down to a meal of wine and a small *companaggio* of bread and cheese and boiled peppers.

"You've come a long way, *nepoto*," said his uncle with a peculiar light in his eyes, almost as if he knew the purpose

538

of Dolcetto's mission. "What made you think Felipe might know of my whereabouts?"

Dolcetto told them both the amazing story of Paolo Nicosia, the *Arcturus II,* and the incredible events following the murders.

"Yes, it was Nicosia who saved my life by risking his own. That was a long time ago," reflected Guillermo.

"How remarkable that Destiny steered me to the auction that day," marveled Dolcetto. "At least I was able to do something for the poor old man."

"Not so remarkable when one understands the laws of attraction. He never severed the cord. His mind must have been saturated with love for Marco. You see love is a most powerful magnet."

Dolcetto found himself floundering in this sea of mysticism. "I'm sorry, I don't follow your reasoning."

"No matter," insisted Antonio's father, smiling enigmatically. "Most men don't use their phenomenal brain power except for the obvious—reading, writing, physical action, and superficial thinking. They never learn to heighten their senses to that exciting level, where they could employ the super-conscious mind and give birth to perception and clairvoyance. It could open a new world to them, put them in tune with other dimensions in time."

Dolcetto felt a sudden depression and a sense of dismay. He hadn't traveled these many miles to be talked to in abstractions. *Dear God. To have come this far and find a senile old man.* He sighed noticeably.

Guillermo nearly laughed aloud. It was as if he'd just read Dolcetto's mind. There was no way for Dolcetto to know that he really was sitting in the presence of an amazing man. In the next few moments, he was to learn much that would astound him.

"You've come about Antonio?"

"Yes, but how did you know?" He stared at Felipe. He hadn't even told the ex-falconer.

"I've known for a long time he's in trouble. I'm vague about the nature of the trouble at the moment."

"He knows, Dolcetto. Guillermo knows," said Felipe when he saw the astonished reaction in the Lion. "Just accept it."

"You want me to go to another country with you?" Guillermo sat back in his straight-backed chair, his elbows resting on its padded arms, touching the tips of his fingers together in a meditative manner. His brown eyes were veiled in thought.

"Yes, to Switzerland."

"Muy biene."

539

Dolcetto told him of his fears about his cousin. "No one has seen him or heard from him in months. The authorities haven't been able to pierce the thick veil of silence concerning his whereabouts."

"When do we leave to meet with your people?"

Dolcetto stopped being astonished at his uncle's amazing perception. He answered each question as simply and expeditiously as possible.

"Two days hence. We can leave whenever you're ready."

"You've taken care of the visas, the identification?"

The Lion was baffled. "How do you do it?"

"It's a gift," he said simply. "One that comes only after great sacrifices are made." He turned to Felipe. "You'll see that someone takes over my duties at *Passa Tiempo*."

Felipe nodded. "No one can replace you at the hospital, Guillermo. But we'll manage, until you take care of this personal matter."

In Rome they met Lt. Domingo and Giorgio Bocca and boarded a special flight to Berne, Switzerland. Once airborne, Dolcetto made the introductions. The four men took seats at the rear of the plane where they could face each other.

"Picked these up at Madame Roulettina's. Should have returned them sooner. Would have if I knew you were alive." He handed Dolcetto a small package. "They belong to Antonio," explained Giorgio.

Dolcetto smiled at the lawyer, opened the packet, and tossed the contents on top of the briefcase resting on his knees. Several pairs of the gold cuff links Antonio constantly lost, a set of car keys, and a white handkerchief with a crested lion embroidered in a corner spilled out.

"One thing about Madame Roulettina is her unabashed honesty."

Dressed in a suit and topcoat of contemporary style, Guillermo sat back in his seat, his eyes fixed on the several items spread out before his nephew. Before Dolcetto could gather them up and return them to the envelope, his uncle reached over and picked up a pair of the golden links.

"Antonio's?"

The Lion nodded. His uncle's sudden interest startled him.

Guillermo sorted through the other items, feeling them caressingly, tracing the texture of the gold and rubbing the gems in the palms of his hands. He closed his eyes and his features jerked. His head tilted to the right, then to the left. He appeared to listen momentarily, then his eyes snapped open.

His companions watched a deep furrow of concentration crease his brow as he put down the cuff links and picked up the keys. Perspiration broke out in tiny beads on his face. Giorgio Bocca and Lt. Domingo sat forward in their seats.

Concerned over his uncle's well being, Dolcetto grasped his sleeve. "Are you all right?" he asked.

"Dolcetto," hissed Domingo, leaning forward in his seat. His voice arrested the Lion. Domingo shook his head, silently signaling him not to interfere.

Lt. Domingo knew exactly what Guillermo de Leone was doing. He'd seen this very same procedure during training as an investigator before joining the Treasury Department. Police investigators had called upon a psychic to help them solve a series of bloodcurdling crimes that occurred in northern Italy shortly after the war. He'd never forgotten the incident. He had originally scoffed at the idea, but later retracted his foolish statements when the findings of the psychic ultimately led to a series of arrests in which the psychotic culprit was finally apprehended.

Shaken by Domingo's abruptness, Dolcetto stared at both the agent and the lawyer whose rapt attention was focused on his uncle. He, too, turned and watched the saintly man with fascination.

When he finished, Guillermo sat back in his seat. Perspiration poured down his face. He blotted it with his handkerchief.

"Are you all right?" asked Dolcetto softly.

"Yes, of course."

He didn't say another word until the plane landed. Then he spoke with marked emotion. "It may take considerable time before we can help Antonio. Your cousin is very ill. Gravely ill. God willing, we'll reach him in time." Guillermo remained silent for the remainder of the trip to Dr. Roman Simoni's clinic.

Up on the flats of a high, craggy tor in the Swiss Alps just outside of Berne, was a building resembling a French chateau built during the Renaissance. It had been converted into an exclusive sanitarium where people of means sought rejuvenation, secret surgeries, and where foreboding family skeletons could be kept from the prying eyes of the world.

The four occupants of the rented auto traversed the dangerous, narrow road that led to the summit of the tor. The air grew crisp and fresh and the bright sun dazzled their senses.

Arriving at the heavily guarded gate that encircled the enormous estate, they were stopped by two burly guards wearing snow goggles.

"No one is admitted without a letter from Dr. Simoni," announced one of the guards in a distinct German accent.

"We're here to see a patient. Antonio de Leone. See to it that we're admitted at once," instructed the Lion with a tone of authority.

"You're a relative?"

"Yes." He indicated to Guillermo. "Father." Guillermo looked straight ahead, unsmiling.

"You will wait a moment," ordered one of the guards. He huddled with his companion before making the call.

Several weeks before, when Dolcetto's efforts to reach Dr. Simoni failed, he enlisted Lt. Domingo's aid, and with the help of Giorgio Bocca, several legal documents were prepared. They had to work swiftly. Through the ministry they were able to construct official documents that the Swiss officials would honor. Now they were prepared for nearly every type of resistance they might encounter.

While the preparations were being made, Lt. Domingo arranged to pick up Dino Caruso. Spirited into the Excelsior Hotel, held incommunicado and in protective custody, he remained there until Dolcetto arrived to talk to him.

Dino was uncooperative. Ingrained in the Sicilian mentality is the timeworn wisdom of keeping strictly to oneself. You saw nothing, heard less, kept your own counsel, and let the other man solve his own problem. Dino was no different. After a lengthy interrogation, Dolcetto entered the room. He nodded to Domingo, who left the room.

Dolcetto sauntered lazily to the open bay window. He looked down on the square below where people milled about in the afternoon sun. A swarm of doves, frightened by something in the square, took flight and flapped their wings in wild protest. Dolcetto opened a pack of cigarettes and offered one to Caruso, after taking one for himself. Dino refused.

The Lion could feel the other's eyes upon him. He pointedly remained quiet. He turned slightly and saw Dino's dark eyes scan him up and down with marked curiosity. Slowly, with measured movements, Dolcetto lit his cigarette. He heard Dino gasp. Now he faced his former secretary head on, the scars visible and frightening to behold. Dino Caruso stared at the scarring, then looked into the camouflaged brown eyes and appeared to relax.

"Where's Antonio de Leone?" he asked in his own voice.

The startled man reexamined Dolcetto's face. His own face became a mask of uncertainty. "Who are you?"

"Don't you know me?"

"No, I don't. I demand to know why I've been brought here?"

Dolcetto leaned over and spread his eyelids open, allowing the contacts to fall into his hand. He blinked several times to clear them, then turned his vibrant, green eyes on his former secretary.

"Now will you tell me where Antonio has disappeared to?"

It took several moments before Caruso understood the man standing before him was really Dolcetto de Leone. The voice, the profile, the inimitable manner, the incredible eyes, he totalled all this and then the realization seized him. Even with the hideous scars, he knew Dolcetto. The shock was too great and he fainted.

He came to with the help of Lt. Domingo who poured cold water on him, rubbed his hands, and slapped his face.

"*Misericordia*. May God have mercy on our souls. It's you, Dolcetto. You're alive." He began to cry. "I can't believe it. Why didn't you let me know? You have no idea what we've been through."

"*Aspetta, aspetta, amico*. Take hold of yourself. I realize the shock is immense. Calm yourself, eh? Later, I'll answer your questions. Right now there's no time. We must find Antonio."

Dino tried to hide his feelings. "Signore, it's been a very long time since anyone has seen him. We were told he'd never recovered from the shock of your death. And that of your father and wife." He paused suspiciously. "Are they also alive, signore?"

"You'll know soon enough. Tell me what you know of Antonio. I can't impress upon you how urgent it is that you tell me all you know."

Suddenly, Dino remembered his Sicilian heritage. "I don't have to tell the *polizia*? Only to you?" He wrung his hands. "My family, will they be safe?"

"They'll be in protective custody before the day is over. Don't worry." The Lion was adamant. "*Aloura*, tell me what you know about Antonio."

"It was eight months ago. The last I heard he was in Simoni's clinic in Berne."

The clinic, Dolcetto thought, *all that time. I pray God, he's all right.* "Now, tell me who runs the store? Who sits at the helm in Antonio's absence?"

"Signore Molinari sits at your desk." He spat. "He takes orders from someone else. Someone I've never seen. I only have a telephone number. Two in fact—one in Messina and the other in Palermo." He wrote them on a piece of paper. "I have them memorized. You see, only I can be trusted with them." He winked and smiled a secret, wicked grin.

"Good." Dolcetto glanced at the numbers and turned pale. "The number in Messina, how often does Molinari call it?" It was his Godfather's number.

"Often. He doesn't make a move until he clears it with the person at the other end of the line. He calls him the head teacher, *capomastro.*"

"And the number in Palermo, who does he call there?"

Dino shuffled awkwardly and stared about the room. His eyes were fixed on Domingo. "The walls have ears, signore."

"You don't have to concern yourself with Lt. Domingo."

Dino paled considerably. "I only learned it a month ago. He calls the man Don Matteo." Dino continued to stare at Dolcetto who had replaced his contact lenses. "Amazing, signore, simply amazing. I'd never know you."

"You're sure he'll be all right here?" Dolcetto asked Lt. Domingo.

"One of my best men will be on the job. Danny promised to look in on him."

"*Va biene.* In less than four days we'll meet again."

Now Dolcetto grew impatient with the delay. "Where the hell are those guards? What's holding us up?" muttered the Lion as he waited at the gate of Simoni's clinic with Guillermo and Lt. Domingo.

The first guard returned with his companion who tied two snarling, vicious dobermans to a nearby post. Then he released an electronic device that opened the iron gates. Dolcetto gunned the motors and drove the high-powered sedan up to the administration building. He parked the car and they walked into the imposing structure.

"Signore de Leone?" A tall, blonde woman wearing a white nurse's uniform over a sensuous body called to them. She flashed cool azure eyes with pinpoints of cold steel at their centers.

Dolcetto spun around at the sound of her voice, surprised by the incongruity of her appearance in a place like this. For a moment, she stared at his scarred face, then averted her eyes. *Another face job. Frightful scarred tissue. Horrid lacerations. Shouldn't have waited so long before coming here.*

"I'm Hulda Schmidt," she announced in a German-Swiss accent. "Please follow me." She led them to a small, antiseptically white anteroom and indicated the stiff chairs. "Be seated." She took a seat behind a sterile-looking white desk beneath a picture of a snow scene framed in white on the wall.

"Is this your first admission?"

Dolcetto stared blankly at her. Then he understood. Before he could set her straight, she rambled on. "Who referred you to us?" There was no stopping her. "I have pamphlets here that explain the entire process. You needn't worry. Too bad you didn't contact us sooner. It would have been easier for you."

"But . . ." He tried again to interrupt.

"Do you want me to fill the form out for you? I can understand your reluctance."

"Please." He grew more forceful. "You don't understand." Dolcetto threw his hands up into the air. She was like a machine.

"Signorina," boomed Guillermo. "Do me a favor and shut up!"

Her face flushed a livid purple, giving her a bizarre appearance.

"Young woman, we've flown a great distance on a matter of grave importance to see my son, Antonio de Leone. If you please, see to it that we see him immediately." He spoke slowly, enunciating each word.

She lowered her eyes and sorted through a file at her fingertips. She glanced at the card, then with a look of confidence she glared at Guillermo. "Who are you?"

"You are obviously as deaf as you are impertinent. I am the patient's father."

"You are, are you?" She pressed a buzzer at her desk. Instantly two attendants entered. They looked like carbon copies of the two guards seen earlier at the gate. "Tell me, sir, why does my card indicate the patient has *no father? Father—deceased,* it says here."

"Lt. Domingo, show the young woman our credentials."

"By all means, Excellency."

The nurse was impressed by the title, but immovable until Domingo showed her the court order. Her eyes scanned the contents. She demanded to see Guillermo's proof of identity and relationship to the patient. They were all there, all the necessary papers were in order. Still, she was reluctant.

"Dr. Simoni is not here and I can't act on this court order." Her German accent seemed more precise.

"I'm afraid you must," insisted Giorgio with a syrupy voice.

"No, I won't. This order specifically calls for an officer or a director to be served in Dr. Simoni's absence. I'm neither." The girl knew her law.

Domingo frowned. "I can easily call the local police. You'll be held in contempt."

"Never mind, lieutenant," said Dolcetto in an easy and disarming manner. "If the young woman wishes to be responsible for shutting down the clinic, let her deny us the privilege of seeing her patient." He turned to her easily and lit a cigarette with the lion's head lighter. "Before you decide, I suggest you check your files to see how much is involved. Check the contributions made to your institution by the House of de Leone from Rome," said the Lion gently.

Not to be bested, yet concerned with that extremely over-polite manner, she got up went into the adjoining room, leaving the two guards to watch them. Through the partially opened door, Dolcetto saw the girl glance through several file drawers. She returned apologetic and blustery.

"I'm sorry, signore. I certainly don't want to do anything to offend you or Dr. Pietro. He's one of our more staunch supporters." *Damn! Where in hell is Dr. Simoni. The House of de Leone is our largest sole contributor. Now what do I do?* The patient's name was Antonio de Leone. And written across the card in Dr. Simoni's own handwriting was ABSOLUTELY NO VISITORS. Nurse Schmidt faced a true dilemma. On one hand, she had a court order; on the other, the wealthiest contributor whom she dared not offend; and right in the middle, strict orders from Dr. Simoni, director of the clinic, and the patient's own physician, Dr. Pietro. *Damn! Damn! Damn!* She glanced down and read over Antonio's record:

A confirmed heroin addict. Paranoia, manic depressive, suffers from delusions. Needs constant restraint. Patient is dangerous to self and others. Keep in strict isolation, by orders of personal attending physician, Dr. Alberto Pietro of Messina, Sicily. Prognosis: Extremely doubtful he shall recover, continuous remission of psychosis.

Dolcetto saw the look in her eyes before she spoke. "I'd like to help you, Signore." She spoke directly to Dolcetto, avoiding Guillermo. "In all good conscience, I can't see how it's possible in view of the patient's record." She shrugged helplessly.

"May I see his record?"

"Well, it's not permitted." She hesitated. "I can't see the harm of it."

As he scanned the card, his face paled, then as anger set in, he cursed in Sicilian and handed the card to Giorgio.

"I don't believe it," Dolcetto seethed.

"I insist on seeing the patient immediately," ordered Giorgio Bocca, whose anger matched Dolcetto's. He handed her the card. "You have the court order. Now if you don't

546

want more trouble, you'd better take us to the patient immediately."

"Take these men to building four," Nurse Schmidt instructed the guards. She had never seen four more angry men.

They walked in silence through the main building out onto the grounds and headed toward a complex sixty yards away. A few recuperating patients were seated by a heated pool, enclosed by glass panels. Some turned away from the visitors, others waved to them. They continued along the narrow path between two buildings.

Against this background of barred windows, empty, staring eyes, faces with no expression, some with uncontrolled muscle spasms, salivating tongues, and uncoordinated movements, Dolcetto sickened, fearing the worst for Antonio. He stole a sidelong glance at his uncle Guillermo who appeared unmoved by the environment.

49

They saw him through the small opening in the center of a thick, wooden, locked door. He was filthy and unkempt, bearing little or no resemblance to the Antonio they knew before. His black hair was long and matted. A messy, black beard covered his face. He sat on a cot, too small for his large frame, wearing a soiled, abbreviated hospital gown.

Antonio's dark, haunted eyes darted quickly toward the sound of the opening window and stared suspiciously. Recoiling violently, they saw he was chained to the bed like a mad dog. He snarled like a vicious animal and his eye's glittered madly. He was terribly emaciated and his skin clung to his bones like stretched hide around a bamboo pole.

Dolcetto closed his eyes and leaned heavily against the door. "Antonio," he muttered. "My poor Antonio, what have they done to you?" His knuckles whitened as he clenched and unclenched his fists. *"Dio malodetto!"* he cried hoarsely over and over again. "Goddamn them! Goddamn them!"

Guillermo's dark penetrating eyes fastened themselves upon his son. He saw the animallike movements, heard the grunts and groans, saw him tear at the steel chains on his bloody, scabby wrists. He, too, shut his eyes for a moment, unable to believe his eyes.

Bocca was physically sick. He reached out to hold onto Lt. Domingo's arm, to steady himself. The Italian agent felt the intense shock no less than the others.

"Open the door," ordered Guillermo.

"I don't think it's advisable to go in there," cautioned the attendant. "It's not safe."

"Open the door," ordered Guillermo.

The key turned in the lock and the door swung outward. A foul stench rushed at them.

"Che demonio," exclaimed Dolcetto, quickly reaching for a handkerchief to hold over his nose. The others, with the exception of Antonio's father, did the same. As the Lion watched his uncle walk calmly into the room, he turned to the attendant with fierce indignation. "Get the records. Instantly." His green jade eyes were slashed with fire.

"But I . . ."

A shaking Lt. Domingo stepped to within inches of the attendant, shoving the court order at him. "While you're at it, call the administration office. Tell them to locate this Dr. Simoni. *Subito,* you hear?" The lieutenant's voice was starched with white rage.

Inside the small cubicle, Antonio cowered away from the threatening figure of the man that walked slowly toward him. He studied Guillermo through suspicious and demented eyes that dilated like those of a frightened, angry, and mistreated animal. He withdrew, retreating further up on the cot.

"Antonio," said his father gently. "Antonio."

Antonio blinked his wild, frightened eyes several times as he regarded this new potential enemy. He turned his head from side to side like an animal. He snarled and made loud gutteral noises as Guillermo approached.

"Don't be frightened, my boy. No one will hurt you any more." He inched his way cautiously, lest he alarm him or startle him into further withdrawal. Guillermo's voice, soft as velvet and filled with love, was reassuring. "Dolcetto is waiting for you. You remember your cousin, Dolcetto, don't you? Antonio, try to remember." His voice reached out to his son like a warm blanket, engulfed him, subdued him. *Sainted God of the Universe, what have they done to him? What?* His hand was inches away from Antonio's unrecognizable face. "Look into my eyes, Antonio. Try to focus on my eyes. No one will harm you. Trust me." With both eyes fixed firmly on his son, Guillermo beckoned to Dolcetto. He kept his voice on an even keel, careful not to change in pitch or volume, a steady monotone of soothing sound. He called to his nephew.

"Come, Dolcetto. Walk quietly toward us. Give me the golden lion about your neck," he whispered.

Once the amulet was removed, he handed it to his uncle. With the golden jewel in one hand and his other close to Antonio's distrusting face, he began to twirl the lion in a circle before Antonio's bewildered eyes.

"Look, the golden lion. Keep your eyes fixed on the golden

lion, Antonio. Fix your tired eyes upon it. See how it glitters? How it spins? Soon your eyes will feel heavy. They'll want to close. That's it, close your eyes. Just relax." He placed his cool hand against Antonio's feverishly hot forehead. "Lie back, Antonio . . ."

Against his will, Antonio's eyes fluttered closed, then opened as they darted furtively about the room. He tried to move his lips. Only guttural sounds came forth.

"Try to close your eyes. Soon you'll feel drowsy, then sleep will come. Sweet, peaceful sleep. Your memory will clear, and you'll remember everything I ask."

Antonio found himself slowly slipping into a state of relaxation. Everything seemed to fall away into a world of shifting confusion. His heavy lids finally closed.

Guillermo continued the monotoned suggestions. "You'll go into a deeper sleep now, Antonio. Dream about the Royal Lions, picture them in your mind. Dream of your home and your cousin, Dolcetto. Your Uncle Marco. Ride Empress again as Dolcetto rode Imperator over the rolling hills of the *latifondo*. Dream of Sicilian sunsets. Smell the flowers, sweet as the morning dew from the Madelaina Gardens. Think of your school days with Dolcetto. Think peaceful, restful thoughts."

Guillermo's eyes were like braziers full of fiery coals. Behind him, Dolcetto, Lt. Domingo, and Giorgio Bocca stood immobile. Their haunted eyes were fastened grimly on Antonio's scrawny shell of a body as he twitched spasmodically on the cot.

"Sleep, Antonio, sleep . . . Let peace flood through your body . . . Give rest to your soul . . . When you awaken, this nightmare shall have passed."

Soon Antonio relaxed, his muscles stopped flexing and he grew limp. Guillermo sagged forward in his chair, drained of energy. He returned the golden lion to his nephew.

"What is it, uncle?"

"I'm not sure. He's heavily drugged . . . enormous amounts." He frowned. "The nurse said heroin. I think not. Heroin doesn't cause a reaction like the one we just witnessed. He's been given some type of hallucinogen. Did you notice the dilated pupils?" he whispered. "The animallike characteristics?" Guillermo reached in toward Antonio's face, tracing lightly with his fingertip the area around his temple. "Notice the swelling, the pulling to one side of his features? Whatever they've given him, it is toxic to some degree."

Dolcetto studied his cousin as objectively as he could while Guillermo spoke. He felt sickened by what he saw. The stench was unendurable and he felt nauseous. He felt a strong hand on his arm, like a steel band, steadying him. He looked into his uncle's compelling dark eyes.

"Steady . . . steady, now." He removed his hand when he felt his nephew take a firmer grip on himself. "Don't worry, I'll reach him. By God, I'll reach him. You and Giorgio make arrangements to get him out of this filth, *subito*." He turned his attention back to his son.

Dolcetto nodded to the lawyer and to Domingo. They both backed away. Dolcetto couldn't leave. He was compelled and fascinated by the mysterious force his uncle demonstrated.

"You're in a deeper sleep now, Antonio. Relax . . . Go deeper and deeper. Let go completely . . ." He paused. "I want you to think, Antonio, and try to answer me. Do you remember Dolcetto? You know who Dolcetto is, don't you?"

Antonio squirmed on the cot. His face screwed up in a painful attempt to mouth the word. His lips trembled, "D-o-l—cett—o," he muttered almost incoherently.

Guillermo shook his head sadly. "It won't do," he told Dolcetto. "He's not deep enough. He needs expert medical attention. If only I knew what they've given him." He grabbed Dolcetto's arm. "We must get him out of here."

He turned back to his son. "Antonio, soon you'll awaken. When I tell you to open your eyes, you'll do so and feel better than you've ever felt in your life. You'll feel as if you've never been ill before. When I count to three, you'll open your eyes. One . . . two . . . three. Open your eyes! Now, Antonio!"

Slowly Antonio's eyes fluttered over inert eyeballs. They felt like lead. He tried to respond to the suggestion, using tremendous exertion. His face filled with a deathly pallor and he lay motionless. Only his eyes were alert.

"Talk with him, Dolcetto. Tell him who you are. Speak softly, as you usually did to him. Keep your voice on an even keel. Try to show no emotion," urged Guillermo.

"Antonio? It's me, Dolcetto. You remember me, don't you, Nino? I didn't go to America. I'm here by your side. Remember Giorgio Bocca? He's here with us. We've come to take you home with us."

There was movement in Antonio's eyes, a faint flicker of recognition. Again only his eyes moved, his body remained inert.

What are they doing to me now? These lousy bastards will tell any lies to get me to believe them. Who is this gargoyle talking to me? This ugly devil who claims to be my cousin? My cousin? I have no cousin. I have no one. I'm all alone.

Antonio curled up quickly into a fetal position, withdrew and shrank away from them, recoiling in terror. He howled like a raving banshee and spat at Dolcetto. A low, snarling sound emanated from his throat. Soon the room echoed with wild, inhuman shrieks. He strained at his shackles and grew uncontrollable.

Dolcetto jumped back away from him. His eyes stared in utter horror at what Antonio endured. He wiped the spittle from his face, and hot stinging tears brimmed his eyes. "How could he know me?" he asked Guillermo. "He wouldn't recognize this face if he were well," he cried in despair.

"Talk more! Tell him what happened!" commanded Guillermo. "Tell him what they did to your face, that it was he who saved you. He'll know your voice! Talk, for God's sake."

Dolcetto wasn't that detached that he could make the transition his uncle urged. Guillermo's concern grew as he watched Antonio writhe and spit as one possessed. He shook his head. "Somehow they've induced a psychosis. We must get him out of here into the hands of specialists. He's to be given no more medication. Did you obtain his medical records?" Before any of them could answer, he issued another stern command. "Domingo, see if you can charter a private plane to Rome, *subito!*"

"The records will be here momentarily. I already sent for them. I don't see how we can get him out of here in this condition."

"If we don't, you'll have no cousin. My son will be lost forever."

The attendant returned, flanked by the two burly guards.

"Where are the patient's records?" asked Dolcetto. "Didn't I ask you to bring them to me?"

"Sorry, sir. We can't do anything unless we have clearance from Dr. Simoni."

"You can't, eh?" snarled Domingo, who paused en route to the phone. "We'll see about that."

"I suggest you prepare the patient for immediate discharge. We're taking him out of here with us," snapped the Lion.

"Sorry, signore. That's impossible. No one leaves the clinic without a release and then only upon orders from the patient's physician. This patient cannot be moved." His caustic, unfeeling voice and his clipped German accent cut into Dolcetto.

"We'll take full responsibility," he said in a lethal, controlled voice.

551

"No one leaves unless they've conformed with our rules and regulations."

"They don't, eh?" stormed the Lion. "Well, we'll just see about that!"

Bastards! They were killing Antonio in some monstrous, terrifying manner. *Was it possible that Antonio hadn't needed brain surgery at all after his fall?* His Godfather had suggested this den of horrors in the first place. *Could he have planned the annihilation of all the Lions that long ago? Some six years ago?* Dolcetto shuddered involuntarily and trained his eyes on his cousin.

Only God knew what Antonio saw at the moment. In a mixture of shapes, sizes, and forms, the dimensions of his reality mingled with the unreal, producing stark terror in his stricken eyes and soul. He continued to cower away from Guillermo.

Finished with his call, Lt. Domingo reentered the room and gestured to Dolcetto with a short jerk of his head. "Dolcetto, *vene ca.*" Out in the hall, he spoke in low tones. "It will take two hours before they can arrive at the airport. Meanwhile, we'll have to take it from here on our own." He switched to a thick Sicilian accent when Giorgio approached them. "Can you both handle these three *citrolli* with me? Giorgio?"

Dolcetto glanced calmly over his shoulder at the three guards. "I'm with you, whenever you say." Giorgio nodded in agreement.

"The plane will be ready for take off in two hours. *Aloura,* I requested a stretcher with proper restraints. Another court order is waiting at the plane in case of further trouble from the authorities. Make sure they don't inject him with any more drugs. Our only hope is that whatever is in his system now will wear off. If we only knew what they gave him, a blocking agent could be administered. But since we don't know . . ." Domingo wiped his brow. The nausea from the intolerable smells created havoc with his sensitive system. "We'll be met at the airport in Rome by an ambulance and official escort to speed us to St. Angelo's Hospital, where the chief of neurosurgery and head of the psychiatric clinic will await us. If anyone can help, he can."

"*Va biene,* Santino." Dolcetto took a firm grip on the agent's arm. "I'm deeply indebted to you for all you've done." His voice filled with emotion. "You also Giorgio."

"It's not over yet, *amico,*" replied Domingo.

The sound of angry voices came from inside Antonio's room. The men searched each other's eyes, made a dash into the room, and quickly sized up the situation.

"Take your hands off me," shouted Guillermo. The cords in his neck bulged like purple ropes. "No one administers any more drugs to this patient," he shouted hoarsely in a voice unlike his own.

The two attendants wrestled with him, while the third, syringe in hand, was ready to inject Antonio with it.

"Stop," shouted Lt. Domingo. "Our court order stipulates that the patient is our responsibility. We've tried to be lenient with you and do things properly. Now, if we have to, we'll enforce that order ourselves." Domingo tossed his automatic at Dolcetto. "Make sure you aim straight when you use this. Kill if necessary." He winked slyly at the Lion, without their seeing him. He pulled out a .38 caliber service pistol and aimed it at the attendants. Instantly, they released Guillermo. Giorgio moved in quickly and disarmed them.

"He's your responsibility, eh? You'd better know what you're doing. His withdrawals will begin soon, and when he grows more violent, don't look to me for help!"

"What's in it?" asked Guillermo, his eyes on the syringe.

"You know we can't tell you."

"What's in the needle?" asked Dolcetto quietly, the gun placed at the man's temple.

"You can't frighten me," grinned the attendant with revolting assurance.

"I can't, eh?" smiled Dolcetto back. He connected a swift kick to the man's groin. First came the loud groan, then the tray went flying from his hands, its contents scattering in all directions. He doubled over in pain. Dolcetto's upflung arms came crashing down on the man's neck with a heavy blow. One more knee kick staggered the attendant, who blinked his eyes and struggled to prevent the inevitable fall.

"Now perhaps we understand each other."

Behind him, Giorgio jumped in to retrieve the gun that fell from Dolcetto's hand and trained it on the men.

"Move a muscle and you're dead, both of you," said the lawyer in a new voice that surprised the Lion. "Now walk to the other side and get into the closet."

Reluctantly, they obeyed. Domingo moved in behind them and gave them a little assistance. He shoved them hard, forcing them into the small cubicle. "You too," he instructed the third man who still hadn't recovered from Dolcetto's crushing blows. He walked painfully, doubled over, clutching his groin. Domingo locked the door behind him.

"Don't forget for a moment, we're on the other side of this door," he warned them. "Good work, Bocca." He smiled at the lawyer.

Dolcetto had picked up the broken syringe from the floor. He touched his fingertip to some of the remaining drops and tasted the fluid. "No taste," he said aloud. He handed the remains to Domingo. "What do you make of it?"

Domingo smelled the syringe, tasted a tiny drop of it. "Tasteless and odorless," he agreed. "Difficult to tell." He wrapped it with great care in his handkerchief and placed it in his breast pocket. "I'll have it analyzed when we get to Rome."

"If we get there," Dolcetto said wryly.

"We'll get there. We'll get there," Santino muttered.

Guillermo de Leone and Giorgio Bocca sat vigil with Antonio. The lawyer watched Antonio's father sniff and taste the contents of the drug vial he held in his hands. He noticed the elderly man's reaction vary as he weighed various factors in his mind.

Guillermo spoke hesitantly. "If it's what I think—a substance discovered by a chemist here in Switzerland a few years ago—we'll have to find an antidote or blocking agent. It's called lysergic acid diethylamide, commonly known as LSD 25. I've read several papers on this comparatively new experimental drug."

"Botta de sanguo!" shouted Giorgio Bocca. "Look at Antonio!" The men turned quickly in his direction!

From where he sat, crouched into a small corner of the small cot, Antonio stared at the intrusion of strangers in his room. His agitation accelerated rapidly. His temperature shot up by degrees. Tremors shook his body, his pulse raced, and the bed under him shook violently.

Why are they glaring at me, these strange creatures, asked a portion of the less dormant part of his mind. Images, frightening and distorted, came at him. The form of an animal, shadowy and vague, came toward him. Only when it was nearly upon him, did his mind discern it as a lion. Its enormous head with a shaggy mane, raised with pride and a certain fierce dignity, leveled its red-green incandescent eyes upon him; its paws were flexed; wet fangs and white claws reached out at him. Antonio continued to recoil. *Can't anyone see it? It's coming to get me!* Antonio saw the animal's dilated pupils, heard the hissing of its breath, and saw the gleaming white fangs as it opened its jaws wider and wider. It came closer and closer.

He gasped for breath. For what seemed an eternity, perhaps longer to Antonio, he hovered precariously beyond the realm of sanity and reality. He was only dimly aware of the others. He heard their frail, thin voices like incantations out of the dim, dark past.

His face ran wet with sweat. Spewing forth black bile and spittle, he flung out his arms, only to be restricted by the steel shackles that cut into his wrists over and again, reopening the sores, causing them to bleed and splatter him with blood. He was possessed with a violent surge of energy. Then he lay back, fully spent, and silence filled the room as blackness fell over his eyes.

When Antonio lost consciousness, Guillermo wet a towel in the basin across the room and wiped Antonio's face and neck and hands. He moistened the cracked lips, parched like the rest of his poor dehydrated body.

Then, in a quick transition, Guillermo grew rigid. He appeared to be listening. After a few moments, he spoke barely above a whisper. "Antonio will be dead in less than forty-eight hours unless we can get help."

Dolcetto unlocked the closet door and shouted to the captives, "Quickly, the keys to his chains. Where are they?" No one replied. Dolcetto reached in and grabbed a guard. "You think I'm kidding, you fuckin' sonofabitch?" He pressed the gun to his temple. "Give me the keys or I'll kill all of you!" His voice was too quiet, too intimidating.

"Out in the hall, top drawer on the left, key number seven."

Dolcetto released the man, shoved him back into the closet, slammed the door, and locked it. Behind him, Lt. Domingo had already left to retrieve the key. He took off his trenchcoat, and when he returned with the keys and tossed them to Dolcetto, he helped as the chains were removed, one by one.

They worked swiftly, wrapping Antonio in Domingo's coat, which they put on backward like a restraining jacket. With the belt, they tied his arms to his body to avoid the possibility he might do himself injury. Then they wrapped him in a blanket. Guillermo tore a sheet into strips to bind Antonio's legs from the knees down.

Dolcetto heaved his cousin's body over one shoulder, and with Giorgio and Lt. Domingo running interference, the men walked from building four, avoiding all main exits and entrances, and luckily soon arrived at their car. They lay Antonio on the floor of the back seat; Guillermo sat in back, the others in the front. Seated in the middle, Lt. Domingo had his gun ready for any action. Once again luck smiled at them. The guards, involved in a heated conversation over something personal, allowed them to pass without incident.

555

In Rome, Agents Hank Rossi and Danny Moreno met with Lt. Domingo and mobilized for what they hoped would be a deathblow to the *mafia*. They had managed to slip agents into de Leone Pharmaceuticals as employees, where they maintained an around-the-clock surveillance. Molinari and other well-known *mafia* Dons were also put under surveillance.

In Messina and Faro and at the Villa de Leone, where Alberto Pietro spent proportionate periods of time, listening devices had been installed and his comings and goings and his telephone conversations were closely monitored.

A group of specialists had been put in charge of Antonio's case. They conferred with Guillermo de Leone and listened with fascination to his theory. It was learned, just as Guillermo had suspected, that through gradual overdoses of LSD, a psychotic state had been induced that could easily drive Antonio insane, kill him, or both. The indiscriminate use of this experimental drug could also cause severe brain damage.

Fortunately, Dr. Ferraro, chief of neurosurgery and in charge of Antonio's medical team, had been doing case studies in controlled experimental psychiatry and was familiar with the counteracting drugs and blocking agents necessary to arrest the effect of LSD 25. Dr. Ferraro began with sodium Amytal and pervitin. However, the effects weren't completely eradicated at first. Chlorpromazine seemed the more potent and effective antidotal agent when administered intravenously at the height of a recurring psychotic reaction. Dr. Ferraro stayed with this prodecure until Antonio no longer seemed as anxious and agitated as he'd been initially. He had to be fed intravenously. In two weeks he began to resemble the Antonio of old. Although he was still emaciated, he looked much improved without his beard and with his hair cut shorter.

Return to reality was done gradually to prevent further shock to Antonio's nervous system. To date, he had no idea Guillermo was his father nor had he recognized Dolcetto.

One afternoon Dolcetto and Giorgio Bocca sat across from Antonio in the hospital room, discussing the progress being made by the agents. Antonio sat up in bed with an affable grin on his face and asked, "What are you doing here, Giorgio?"

Startled by the sudden recognition on Antonio's part, they filled with joy and relief.

"You know me?" asked Giorgio with an incredulous look on his face.

"What kind of question is that? Of course, I know you.

Why shouldn't I? What I want to know is what in hell you're doing here in Switzerland?"

"You know me," cried the lawyer. "He knows me! You heard him. He knows me! Goddammit, *amico,* he knows me!" grinned Giorgio.

"And you *don't* know me?" asked Dolcetto, moving in closer to him.

The young man shook his head. Dolcetto held a handkerchief over his scars and looked at his cousin. His vivid green eyes shone bright. The smile on Antonio's face froze. His lips trembled and he clutched the sheets. He blinked his eyes time and again, glancing at the lawyer for some word, some assurance. Giorgio moved in closer to him and held his hand in a comforting gesture. "Yes, Antonio. It's really Dolcetto."

"He . . . uh . . . told me you died in an accident at sea," said Antonio, trembling.

"*He* said many things," replied Dolcetto.

"It's you? It's really you?" He held out his hands to his cousin.

"Yes, it's really me, Nino."

For several moments they just stared at each other. Antonio raised his frail, bony arm and touched Dolcetto's face with his hand. "That's what those beasts did to you?" he gasped.

Dolcetto changed the subject. "Do you remember much of what happened to you?" Antonio shook his head.

Dr. Ferraro had warned the Lion it might be a while before Antonio could recollect what happened to him before they found him. "Just don't press him. One day he'll remember."

The door opened and Guillermo walked in, led by one of the security guards who flanked the entire wing of the hospital. Under orders from Lt. Domingo, no one was informed of the true identity of the patient and the distinguished visitors who came to see him daily. Not even the attending physicians were told.

When Antonio first laid eyes on his father, he cried out in a muffled sound, "Uncle Marco! You're alive, too?"

"No, it's not Uncle Marco." Dolcetto wanted to assure him that two ghosts hadn't suddenly come to life. The Lion turned to his uncle and said softly, "He knows us. Recognized Giorgio. I explained who I was. He knows."

Dolcetto felt dismayed that Guillermo didn't appear to share their joy and enthusiasm. Exercising noticeable control, he turned from his nephew and focused on his son.

"I'm a relative of the family, Antonio," he said soothingly. "You're looking fine today." He studied the chart at the foot of the bed. They talked a few moments and during that time, Antonio stared at Guillermo.

"You've been through a terrifying experience. Can you tell us, as best you can remember, what happened after you and Dolcetto's Godfather took him to the boat?"

Antonio closed his eyes. Dolcetto and Giorgio moved in closer to hear his words. The lawyer snapped on a small tape recorder.

"I became increasingly ill after we left Alberto's home. We both went to the Villa de Leone, where I packed a bag. He insisted on accompanying me to Rome. Wouldn't let me out of his sight, because I grew weaker each day. In Rome, I was able to meet once with the various boards, asking them to continue running things as they had. At one of the meetings of the board of directors, I assigned my power of attorney over to Dr. Pietro to act on my behalf." He looked at Giorgio. "I'm sorry, *amico*, but you must know why I couldn't confide in anyone. I was trying to protect Dolcetto. His Godfather insisted we could trust no one. But now that you're back, Dolcetto, you can run things again. I'm well enough now to return to Rome, aren't I? Dr. Simoni told me I'd only be here a month."

The three men exchanged curious glances. "You're not in Switzerland, Antonio. You're in Rome."

"Rome?" He stared at them. "How . . . when did I get back here?"

"Do you have any idea what day this is? What month? Year?" He looked from one to the other. "You were in Switzerland for nearly nine months."

Everything seemed more incredible than ever to Antonio. Dr. Ferraro came in to check him over. After he administered a sedative to his patient, Dolcetto drew the physician away from Antonio's bed and spoke in hushed tones. "Is it all right if we continue to talk with him? To attempt to bring certain things to his mind, to jog it a bit?"

Dr. Ferraro nodded. "Make sure he doesn't become agitated. He's doing splendidly. Better than we expected."

"Thank you, doctor. In due time you'll see how much we appreciate the effort expended on our behalf," said Dolcetto.

The physician left and the Lion returned to Antonio's bedside.

Dolcetto nodded at the others, and then he began to tell Antonio what had happened to him and the others at his Godfather's hands. How Alberto Pietro had even plotted Antonio's death.

He understood Dolcetto's words, but his span of interest began to splinter from the sedative administered earlier. Antonio stared in fascination at Guillermo, silently questioning the presence of the man, a stranger to him, who looked remarkably like Marco. Noting this, Dolcetto identified Guillermo.

"Antonio," he said quietly. "This man is Guillermo de Leone, your father, presumed dead all these years . . ."

Antonio's heavy lidded eyes snapped open in his attempt to fight off the sleepiness. "My—father? . . . My father?"

Dolcetto and Giorgio left the room to allow father and son to bridge the gap of time and separation.

50

At 4:45 A.M. the next morning Antonio de Leone was dead.

Weary and exhausted from the strain of the past few weeks, yet having anticipated his son's death, Guillermo had remained by his side at the hospital all night. When Dolcetto entered the room, only partially dressed, having been summoned so quickly, Guillermo bowed his head and sobbed convulsively. A priest stood over the body of Antonio, administering the last rites. The shock, the utter incredibility of the senseless tragedy left Dolcetto inconsolable.

Dazed, he listened as Dr. Ferraro sorrowfully explained, "The properties of the drug administered to Antonio and their total effects are not still fully known. We were hampered by having to conduct our work blindly, without knowledge of qualities of drugs administered over an unknown period of time. We didn't foresee . . ."

"Those are words, doctor. Words! Can't you simply explain?"

"During the night he had another attack; an unexpected, reinduced psychosis manifested itself—an inherent danger when one works with experimental drugs. Whatever delusions his mind manufactured, whatever torments pursued him in this induced state, Antonio's heart was unable to withstand the shock done to his nervous system . . ."

"He was doing well," said Dolcetto sharply. "You told me yourself! Why didn't your staff watch him more carefully?"

"None of us have the power of God, our powers are limited," said Dr. Ferraro.

"Dolcetto, they did the best they could," said Guillermo. "The best within their knowledge. We couldn't have asked for more. At least we had him for a time."

Dolcetto confronted Guillermo and said accusingly, "You knew, didn't you? You knew he wouldn't live through this!

559

Why didn't you tell me? Why did you allow me to go on hoping?" Dolcetto wept bitterly.

"Yesterday," said the doctor. "He *was* doing exceptionally well. My colleagues and I were favorably impressed. All tests were normal. We all held high hopes. Where LSD 25 has been induced to precipitate psychosis—"

Dolcetto cut him off. "Surely you could have done something more! A counteracting drug, something!"

Dr. Ferraro shook his head. "Metabolic changes in his system . . . sudden rush of adrenalin . . . changes in his vital organs . . . all too fast. By the time they reached me it was too late." He rubbed his tired eyes as the nurse covered Antonio.

"Don't do that!" shouted Dolcetto angrily to the woman.

The nurse, frightened by his tone of voice, jumped back, clutched the crumpled sheet in her hands, and stared dumbstruck at the disfigured man.

"I want to stay here with him for a while. Don't anyone touch him!" He waved everyone except his uncle out of the room. Disconsolate with grief Dolcetto became mechanical. Earlier when the Chief of Neurosurgery explained the situation he nodded as if he understood. But he didn't. Nothing made sense to him. He sat in the chair next to the still form of his cousin on the bed and wept unashamedly. It was a horribly insane feeling this: Everything going downhill like a runaway train heading for total destruction. No one able to stop it. Not even the Lion. Dolcetto picked up one of Antonio's cold hands, already stiffening, between his warm hands.

"I swear, Antonio. I swear on my soul to avenge your death! Alberto Pietro has only a few numbered days in which to boast of his triumph!"

Later that afternoon when it became Dolcetto's duty to tell Giorgio Bocca and Lt. Domingo that Antonio was dead, he buried his face in his hands and felt mortally sick. Hank Rossi and Danny Moreno had arrived to pay their respects after a call from Lt. Domingo. Having heard the Lion and now watching him they exchanged gravely concerned glances, both for Dolcetto himself, whom they had grown to respect, and for the status of their involvement.

"What do you intend doing now?" asked Hank Rossi.

Dolcetto shook his head and composed himself. "Not sure at this point." Inwardly he had longed to confront his Godfather with Antonio, Francesca, and himself just to see the expression on the man's face when he saw the Lions were no longer an endangered species. How rewarding that would have been! God!

"Look, my dear friend, don't you think it's time you ceased this senseless endeavor?" suggested Giorgio Bocca. "Let the law take over now. They have enough on Molinari and the other *mafiosi* to shut down all the pharmaceuticals and announce to the world the fraud perpetrated upon the House of de Leone. Let Santino and the Americans take over. They'll put the *capomafia* and his kind where they belong, without exposing you and your family to any more dangers. Think of them, *amico*, of Francesca and your son."

"Giorgio's right," insisted Lt. Domingo. "The commissioner's screaming for action ever since we turned in our preliminary report. We want them even more than you do."

"Are you all crazy? Insane?" the Lion said desperately, staring, as if they'd all taken leave of their senses. "After this? After Antonio's brutalizing and his death? Hah!" He had a diabolical gleam in his eyes. "Perhaps if Antonio had lived, I might have been more forgiving, more easily persuaded. But now, I have a special duty to perform. A very special duty."

"Haven't you been through enough? We'll get them! So it may take a week or so longer, but we'll put them all away for life," said Rossi.

Danny Moreno echoed his partner's words. "We'll get them all. We've taken special steps to take care of Dr. Simoni and his clever staff . . ."

"I hear names, gentlemen, but, none are the correct ones," said the Lion.

Rossi took the position of devil's advocate for a moment. "About this Alberto Pietro, we've got nothing tangible to go on, Dolcetto. We can't make any move in his direction."

Dolcetto froze. "Tell me that again. I'm not sure I heard you correctly."

"You heard right," said Santino ruefully. "All we've got on Alberto Pietro wouldn't stick to a postage stamp."

"You disbelieve all I told you? You think I made up the story? What the fuck's wrong with you? Santino? Giorgio? Surely, you don't disbelieve my story? The man's a raving maniac! A cold-blooded, heartless killer!"

"All right, Dolcetto! All right! Now you listen," said Hank Rossi sternly. "Ever since we heard your story, and even now, there's no doubt that you speak the truth. We've never doubted you. But, you must understand we deal in facts! Facts that will stand up in a court of law! Facts upon which we can bring an indictment! All we've got to work on are fantasies and conjectures and your suspicions! No, no!

561

Don't argue yet, just listen to the facts we do have on this man, Alberto Pietro!" insisted Rossi.

"Alberto Pietro, male, in his sixties. Flourishing medical practice in Messina over thirty years. President of Medical Board, Sisters of Charity Hospital, patron of many charities, financially well heeled . . . Over the years has served as faithful friend to House of de Leone. In early days of practice, his skill saved the life of Marco de Leone and his brother Guillermo de Leone, not once, but twice at least. He helped establish a medical dispensary on the Lion's estate. After a brutal assault by bandits on the Royal Lion, this doctor remained diligently at the side of Marco de Leone and nursed him through the trauma of a violent atrocity when his tongue was cut out . . . For many years Alberto Pietro had been the personal friend and confidant of the Royal Lion. He is Godfather to Dolcetto de Leone. Approximately a year ago he saved his Godson's life running considerable risk to himself, and having nursed him back to health, later arranged for his escape. Pietro saved the life of Antonio de Leone by recommending brain surgery which in all probability saved him . . . You know, we couldn't find that Alberto had ever frequented a bordello? No love in his life! No hint of a scandal, nothing! What kind of a man is this? The only derogatory remark we could uncover was that he doesn't attend church services regularly!"

"Stop! That's enough! I'm beginning to vomit with all this sugar-coated veneer you spread upon him," snarled the Lion.

"I'm only telling you the facts, Dolcetto. We haven't been able to make a tie-in to the *mafia* with Don Barbarossa, Garibaldi, no one. He's either too smart, or . . ."

"Or he's not guilty. Is that what you're thinking?"

"Be reasonable, Dolcetto. We want him as much as you do. But, goddammit! We've nothing to go on. Even that coding you gave us could very well be that V-Sp stands for Spain! Not Sardinia—Pietro!"

Dolcetto was tied in knots. For hours they argued back and forth. No matter how many arguments he gave, including Marco's letter written to Alberto, Rossi was adamant. "Unless we have something concrete, we can't touch the man. His lawyer, any lawyer, would laugh us out of court! Even an Italian court!"

"And you want me to step out of the case? Let you take over? Take over what? With the evidence you've got you can't even get Barbarossa! The only way you people can make an arrest is to catch a culprit with drugs in their possession or a trainload of strategic supplies! It's no wonder you never catch the big fish when you only bait anchovies!" he said disgustedly.

Moreno and Rossi exchanged embarrassed flushes. Giorgio stood by only as a listener, but, goddammit! Dolcetto was right. All they ever jailed was the small fry, the little offenders.

"It takes a Sicilian to figure this out," began Dolcetto. "By the burning balls of Lucifer, I'll deliver Barbarossa, Pietro, and the rest, including the Mediterranean Big Five!" The hot and heavy words were interrupted by the ringing of a phone. Dolcetto grabbed it. *"Pronto! Pronto!"* he said. He turned to Rossi. "It's for you."

The Lion walked to the window and took time to light a cigarette. His hands trembled. So there was no way to catch Alberto, eh? He was too smart! Very well. He'd think on the matter and when he was finished, when he was finished thinking and had readied his plans, he'd let them know.

Muffled sounds behind him grew louder and when he heard his name called the Lion turned. Hank Rossi's face was flushed with excitement. "Dolcetto, I think we have something. One of our agents intercepted a call to the Villa de Leone. Not by phone, one thing we didn't consider—by shortwave apparatus!

"There's to be a meeting of the Mediterranean Big Five on December 26 at the Vanzini Villa," he said.

"Who made the call? Could they tell? Who answered?"

Hank Rossi was so excited, he found it difficult to swallow. His hand, still on the telephone, appeared to be stuck to it. All eyes were on him as he said, "Plato Aristopheles called Alberto Pietro and judging from the report, it appears they know each other very well."

The Lion's green eyes fired with a look of triumph. "I'll contact you all as soon as I return from the Villa de Leone where I intend to bury my cousin."

"Are you crazy? To go there at such a time. What if you encounter this Godfather of yours? Or any of his people?" said Giorgio Bocca, gravely concerned.

"You forget, I'm a Sicilian. I know how to handle myself."

For a long time after they left, Dolcetto lay on the sofa, chain smoking, and staring at the high ceiling with its dated decor and fancy ogee moldings. For weeks now he'd had less than three hours' sleep a night. Hardly anyone stirred in the hotel, and far below him it seemed the Eternal City had turned to stone. His mind roiled with thoughts. *Marco is dead. Antonio is dead. Legally he and Francesca were dead. Even Guillermo was dead. All the Lions were dead.* Was this to be the fate of the Royal Lions? The end for a family who wanted only the best for their people? No! This was not the end! Not yet! Not as long as there was breath left in him.

This final atrocity heaped upon the Lions couldn't be ignored. The cold-blooded, premeditated murder of Antonio, planned with such cunning by a ferret of a man to sate his selfish desires, had to be avenged. What manner of a man was this who could willfully annihilate the only people who befriended him? Taken him to their bosom, treated him as their own blood? This ruthless madman who demonstrated genius in murder, crime, and business had to be involved with Don Barbarossa's factions! Odd these American agents couldn't see the genius of the man behind Don Barbarossa. Rossi's and Moreno's concepts of the Mafia were the cheap imitators in America, the Cosa Nostra, the Black Hand imposters who had emigrated to their shores. *What fools! What fools!* thought Dolcetto. They just didn't know.

Following its resurgence after World War II the Mafia had become the government. Under the guise of big business and a penumbra of respectability, mergers formed with other Mediterranean syndicates had caused the Mafia to prosper like Midas. Dolcetto's personal files on Mafia activities had produced a wealth of information that he one day intended to turn over to the government archives for posterity.

Prior to his marriage to Francesca, a personal contact of his working in the Banco Nacionale in Zurich, Switzerland, had sent him a card containing the following:

V-C ... V-G ... V-L ... V-S ... V-S p

At the time it meant nothing to Dolcetto and when he turned a copy of it over to Lt. Domingo, the persevering agent pondered it zealously but was unable to come up with anything. During Dolcetto's unproductive year in Rome, he managed with the aid of the newspaper morgue to pierce the code, all expect the V-Sp which he first referred to Spain. Rumors of a so-called Mediterranean Big Five, a business cartel with diversified financial interests in the fields of oil, narcotics, finance, war supplies, and munitions were whispered about and hinted at in newspaper columns. Also rumored was the fact that the Big Five were protected by the highest offices in each nation they represented. The extent of this protection was unknown.

Dolcetto's decoding had produced the following results: The letter V before other letters he interpreted as the Roman numeral V meaning five. The rest was easy. V-C stood for

Five—Corsica. V-G represented Five—Greece. V-L was Five—Lebanon. V-S was Five—Sicily. V-Sp stood for Five —Sardinia-Pietro. After that it wasn't difficult to discover the identities of the Mediterranean crime cartel.

And the agents had asked him to give this all up to them? They didn't know it then, but without Dolcetto, they wouldn't stand a ghost of a chance in effecting a sweeping victory. Dolcetto never felt the spurs of fear and didn't now.

But he had to think. He had to take time to think it all out.

Immediately following Antonio's burial in the Campo-santo at the Villa de Leone, in a quiet ceremony performed at dusk where they wouldn't be too obvious and bring at-tention, Dolcetto saddled up and rode out to Terra d'Oro, where in the manner of his father, he meditated over his future plans. Guillermo wandered about the estate, noting the changes in the place since he'd been there last.

Dolcetto's first thoughts were of Francesca and their son whose future must be determined. Francesca, no longer possessed with the need for vendetta nor the desire for it, fought her husband at every turn in her desire to convince him to set aside his plans.

In a year what had the law done to bring the culprits to justice? Dolcetto argued. To simply place Barbarossa and his Godfather behind bars until some clever political lawyer freed them wasn't enough to satisfy the Lion. Not now! Now, he wanted a Sicilian's justice! The only kind barbarians understood!

I'm a Sicilian no matter how hard my mother fought against it. Being born on foreign soil doesn't alter centuries of inherited traits. If I permit these deaths to go unavenged, I'll be no better than countless other Sicilians who've buried their heads in the sands of time, pretending there is no mafia. Someone has to oppose all they stand for and fight them at their level with their own weapons.

Dolcetto's fiery green eyes reflected the glare of the late afternoon sun as it blended into a sea of vibrant colors. His concentration centered on his Godfather, Alberto Pietro. *I must find the key to his thinking. I must.* He recalled the time his father reprimanded him as a child for saying that he didn't like his Godfather, that he was a cold, calculating fish that never gave any warmth or emotional response.

"He's a man of medicine, my son. Remember that in judg-ing your Godfather. Men such as he have seen too much of life and considerably more of death than the average man. Controlling their emotions is their chief stock in trade."

"But I feel no love from him, father."

"It's there, my son. It's there. Some men are not articulate in expressing their feelings, however deeply they feel. Alberto is an intense man, possessed by a dream that has eluded him all his life. Unfortunately, in pursuing this dream, he's overlooked the fact that he's also a human being. It's not up to us to judge the vision another man is led by. He's a lonely man. I can't forget that it was he who saved our lives, your uncle's and mine. In his own way, he contributed to the success of the *latifondo,* helped my own dream become a reality."

But even Roberto hadn't taken to Alberto, recalled Dolcetto. He had tolerated him only to appease Marco. He usually made himself scarce when Alberto called.

"You don't like Alberto, do you, Roberto?" Marco asked one day.

Roberto had taken his time in answering. "I get the distinct impression that if you weren't the Royal Lion of Sicily, he'd not give you a second look. Besides, he drains you like a blood-sucking leech!"

"Roberto!" Marco's eyes had flared angrily. "I'll not have you talk about my friend any more than I'd tolerate his saying things against you!"

The gentle Roberto had shrugged his shoulders and said simply, "You asked, Marco. You asked." Then he explained further. "I don't mean to question his integrity or to say he takes materially from you. It's just that he drains you mentally. Think. Think of the endless questions he asks. Always about investments, Mafia legislation, the laws and their amendments, and how you blocked certain Mafia legislation, who were your compatriots and who opposed you!" Roberto had smiled enigmatically, recalled Dolcetto, when he continued.

"You offer Alberto a profound statement. Next time you see him and enter into dialogue, he reuses *your* words, *your* thoughts verbatim as if he alone had given birth to them. You asked why I don't like him, I'll tell you! He's a blotter! Yes, a blotter who soaks up all *your* strength, *your* knowledge, and *your* memory, then, no doubt presses it on to someone else as *his* knowledge, *his* memories . . ."

Dolcetto came to several conclusions at the end of his meditation. That he would exact the deaths of his Godfather and Matteo Barbarossa was a foregone conclusion. He had other considerations.

I may never be able to liquidate the mafia as it exists. Only time and man's evolution can achieve that miracle. But, by God, I shall rid the world of two of their most dangerous tentacles.

566

When Guillermo saw the look of decision on his nephew's face upon his return to the villa, he despaired for him. "I can't dissuade you, can I?"

"No, uncle."

"Well then, even though it's against every principle I've come to believe in, I shall aid you in this."

"No." Dolcetto smiled enigmatically. "It's my battle. I shall attend to it."

The two men walked into the villa toward Marco's den.

"If, indeed, I am the last of the Lions, the Lion of all Lions, it's up to me to sever the cord, once and for all time. I shall not allow the Royal Order to be perpetuated. It ends with me. I refuse to pass on such a heritage to my son, to allow this monumental burden of vendetta to motivate his life. With these, my last deeds of vendetta, it will be finished."

"What are your plans?"

"The less you know, the less you'll be troubled."

"You know that isn't possible. My curse is that I know too much. Already I see the seeds in your mind of the devilish plot you embroider."

Dolcetto removed his leather jacket and tossed it on a nearby chair. He glanced about the room and studied the familiar portrait of his mother. "Our family's never truly known more than a few minutes peace," began Dolcetto. "It's time for us to live as human beings should." His eyes rested on the lovely face of the woman he'd never known. "I wonder what our lives might have been if we'd all left this land years ago," he said wistfully. "But that's all behind us, eh, uncle?" He poured two glasses of wine from the decanter on the desk. "Here, let's drink to the future." They touched glasses. "Now is the time of the Lion. Now is the time to let these *mafiosi* know their laws are not eternal, that they, too, are mortal along with the Royal Lions."

Guillermo put down his drink. "If you want the lives of Don Barbarossa and Alberto Pietro, why not let the law do the job for you? Why is it so important to have their blood on your hands? Why do you wish to place yourself on their level?"

Dolcetto spun around angrily. The scarring on his face turned livid, his eyes sparked like flint, a white line of hardness appeared about his set lips. "Someone else said those words to me," he said through clenched teeth. "I maintain that only on their level can those *schifosi* be reached. That's exactly what I intend doing."

Seated in a soft leather chair facing the desk, Guillermo watched Dolcetto walk behind the desk and sit down in

Marco's old chair. For the first time Dolcetto gazed at the desk and noticed the appointments weren't the same, not Marco's nor Antonio's. The portrait of Diamonte no longer hung in its usual niche, now that he thought of it, and the initials on the leather-trimmed desk set were A.P.

"Whoring son of Lucifer!" he cursed aloud and banged his fist on the desk. "Already the villa is his! Soon the Vanzini Villa will be occupied by him and all that ever belonged to the de Leone family will belong to that bloodsucking son of a whoring vulture!" Dolcetto picked up the sharp letter opener, slashed at the desk blotter, made a few frustrated stabs at the offending initials, then stuck the knife into the desk where it quivered before coming to a full halt.

"He'll never own all this! Never! I'll use their distorted code of ethics to beat them, their own weapons to remain invincible and their own sense of immorality, the same devices of trickery, deceit and cunning—something they understand!"

"All this for vengence?" said Guillermo sadly.

"All this—but, don't worry, uncle. Everything will turn out just fine," he grinned a wicked, devilish grin, that made his scarred face too grotesque to contemplate. "I shall allow them to annihilate each other. But, just before the end comes they will know it was I, Dolcetto de Leone, the Royal Lion of Sicily, who avenged the deaths of my father and Antonio. When they draw their last breath they will see and recognize their own evil, their own blackhearted sickness heaped upon themselves."

51

December 22nd. Heavy flurries of snow fell on Berne, Switzerland, on this cold, blustery day. A spanking new white Rolls-Royce pulled up before the enormous gates at the entry to the Simoni clinic. Before the chauffeur came to a full stop, two warmly-padded guards nodded and swung open the spiked iron gates. The Rolls moved forward with ease and drove along the winding road, finally stopping at the main entrance to the administration building. Dressed in a spiffy mink-lined chesterfield and homburg hat, Dr. Roman Simoni, gray haired with dark glasses, stepped from the Rolls and entered the building. The doctor had no way of knowing that a second car shot out of a secluded niche in the road and drove through the gates immediately behind him. He didn't see four agents jump from the moving vehicle and take the two guards by surprise. A third car full of Swiss police moved in behind, followed by a fourth and last auto containing Italian officials. The second car drove on through and pulled alongside the white Rolls. Within the space of minutes, Dr. Simoni, Nurse Schmidt, four male attendants, and a galaxy of other employees were arrested, served with international warrants, and jailed on a variety of complaints ranging from kidnapping, illegal use of experimental drugs, conspiracy to commit murder, and so on. Special agents immediately manned the phones, while an emergency crew was detailed to handle the inmates.

In Rome, the weather was balmier and the spirit of Christmas was in the air. By 4:30, when employees were leaving to spend the holidays at home, Amelio Molinari was whisked away along with ten top executives at de Leone pharmaceutical and chemical plants and held incommunicado on charges of the illegal manufacture of heroin, its illegal transportation, and ten counts of conspiracy and intent to commit murder. Special agents immediately manned the phones with specific instructions well ingrained in their minds.

Their watches synchronized at 5:00 P.M., special agents moved into Milan, Rome, and Naples, removed all top executives of de Leone Shipping, and at de Leone Enterprises, under the able guidance of Dino Caruso, telephone lines were manned by agents with intercepting devices tied in directly to the homes of all those men involved. Ten top government officials, including some prominent cabinet ministers, were under minute scrutiny in these next few days.

In Naples, Don Salvatore (Lucky Luciano) was picked up and held in custody on a variety of charges. He was to later say, "It sure screwed things up between me and Igea. A helluva thing to be denied a Christmas!" Later he was to be absolved of any part in the conspiracy, and due to insufficient evidence, charges against him, in this instance, were dropped.

Very special agents had already been dispatched to keep a strict surveillance of the Corsican, Jean Louis Canticcio, the Greek tycoon, Plato Aristopheles, and the Lebanese Sheik Ahmed Abou, who were scattered all over the Mediterranean.

Christmas holidays were to prove highly conducive for the Day of the Lion. Communications were jammed, phone lines overloaded, and transportation was at a standstill.

Lt. Domingo, Hank Rossi, and Danny Moreno had chartered a special government plane to fly to Palermo where they were met quietly by Gino Vittorio who drove them to the Vanzini Villa for their final preparations for L Day.

Dolcetto de Leone stood at the entrance gate to Don Matteo Barbarossa's villa in Monreale, dressed in conservative navy blue, wearing brown contact lenses, the touch of gray at his temples expertly added by Danny Moreno's make-up techniques, and carrying a briefcase in his hands. He waited patiently for a servant to admit him to see *capomafia* Barbarossa. His business card, the same that he'd presented to Gino Vittorio, read Dante di Luigiano. He gazed about the courtyard, colorfully lit for the Christmas season. In the distance he heard familiar strains of the famous Sicilian bagpipes.

Two burly guards appeared from nowhere and searched him for concealed weapons. Dolcetto smiled when he noticed one of the thugs studied his scarred face with more respect than alarm.

Then, suddenly, there he was, face to face with the man who once sent shivers down his spine. He remembered thinking, *why he's nothing but an old man.* Yet behind those tinted glasses, the greed and craftiness still showed in his quenchless black eyes. Don Barbarossa's voice filled with hostility and suspicion.

"What do you want, eh, di Luigiano? No one told me to expect you. I don't like surprises. Why are you here?" He stared pointedly at the grotesque scarring, then avoided looking at the Lion's face for the remainder of the visit.

"Signore Molinari felt it inappropriate to write or call you concerning this grave matter which must be presented to you." He caught sight of the portrait of Diamonte and tried to mask his surprise.

"You like it. She was my woman, once . . ."

"My, my, what a beauty! Simply ravishing! Did you commission the painting? Who was the artist that painted with such soul?" He moved in closer to the oil, puzzled. "Spiders? Are those spiders on her ears? Dear, dear, how strange."

The Don refrained from answering on two counts. One, he mistook the question for disdain, two, the Lion's effeminate mannerisms startled him. The door opened and *Consiglioro* Garibaldi entered. "This is Primo Garibaldi," said the Don, handing the card to his counselor.

Dolcetto froze. He hadn't counted on this. He nodded and made certain the scarred side of his face remained toward Garibaldi as often as possible.

"*Aloura,* what is it? This grave problem that prevented Molinari from calling me himself, eh?"

Dolcetto indicated a marked hesitancy to speak in the presence of the lawyer.

"It's all right. Talk! We have no secrets from each other."

Dolcetto shrugged. "You know the stuff delivered by Luciano to New Orleans, Chicago, and Kansas City, was adulterated radically and must be made good?"

"That greedy whoremaster is going to ruin everything!" snapped the Don. To Garibaldi he said, "You've taken care of everything?"

"Yes, but Amelio alreadys knows this. We've discussed the seriousness of the situation and the possible prognosis." Garibaldi's annoyance was evident.

"Prog— what? What's that word? What the hell does that mean?"

"The remedy," replied Garibaldi, staring icily at their guest. "Surely Molinari didn't send you here for this old business." He grew suspicious.

"No, of course not," replied Dolcetto in his northern accent. "He wanted only to assure you preparations are underway to replace the adulterated shipments with the pure stuff. And that it won't be sent through Luciano's usual channels as indicated to you previously, but through one of the Greek freighters that will dock in New York. From there it goes to New Orleans, forwarded by the Shortino Brothers . . ." He made it a point to read the information from a small black book. "You are to take care of Don Salvatore from this end. He says, 'No one will touch Lucky or go near him.' They fear reprisal."

"Why do you read from a book, eh? You got no head to remember?" asked the Don, watching his movements and comportment with curious fascination.

"I'm sorry, Excellency, I wanted to make sure I got the names correct. They are all strange to me. This is new, you see. I'm not acquainted with this business."

The Don was outraged. "Why do you call me Excellency?"

Dolcetto appeared nonplussed. "I mean no disrespect. I only supposed that a man with your stature deserved the title of respectability."

"Just don't be clever with me. I hate clever people. Now tell me, was this the heavy news that took a special courier to fly from Rome to tell me?" His annoyance served to increase a rising paranoia. "Why haven't I heard of you before? Amelio never mentioned you before. And talk straight!"

"He'd have no cause to mention me, I suppose. We don't work in affiliated fields. That is until recently. Bear with me, Excell—I mean Don Barbarossa." Sensing Garibaldi's distrust of him, as he removed papers from his briefcase, he played on it, accentuating the effeminate gestures.

"You're sure I can speak freely?"

"Talk!"

"Very well." He coughed and made a move toward the water carafe. "With your permission."

The Don nodded and with a short brushing movement of his hand gave his permission. When he finished sipping the water, Dolcetto cleared his throat.

"Signore Molinari wishes you to know that through certain channels of information available to him, word reached him that a certain *special* partner of yours intends to deceive you on a vital business deal. For years, he's plotted and planned. Since this man is . . . not one of us . . . Signore Molinari felt you should be informed of this vile treachery underfoot."

"Not one of *us?*" exploded the Don, annoyed by the other's effrontery.

"With your permission," said the Lion humbly. "What I mean is this man is not a true Sicilian."

"And you, I suppose, are a Sicilian, eh?" *This powder puff is too much,* thought the Don. "Listen, between you and me there's no agreement. Tell me what you came to say. My patience wears thin."

Dolcetto raised himself up indignantly. "I, sire, was born in Bronte. My family was killed by bandits; my relatives were forced to send me to Florence to be raised. At heart and by birth I am Sicilian. A true Sicilian! Signore Molinari knows this. I've done him many favors. Over the years he's come to know I am reliable and can be trusted." He spoke with patriotic fervor.

"All right! All right, I believe you!" The Don was exasperated. "Now tell me who this traitorous devil is. No one deceives Don Barbarossa and lives!" He spoke with double meaning not lost on Dolcetto. Both the Don and his *consiglioro* now fastened their eyes on the Lion, unable to take their eyes off the inescapable mannerisms of a man with no *maschiezzo.*

Lowering his eyes to the papers in his hand, Dolcetto read the name: "Alberto Pietro, physician from Messina, friend and confidant to the family of Royal Lions . . ."

The Don's glum face began to pucker to suppress the laughter forming inside his belly. He glanced at Garibaldi. Both exchanged tight smiles over what they both considered utter absurdity. The sight of Dolcetto's serious face staring at the two of them seemed to infuriate the Don.

"*Va! Va!* You tell Signore Molinari to take care of his junk and I'll mind my own store!" The Don had to wipe away the tears of mirth he tried to keep back.

"The Vanzini Villa," continued Dolcetto in his overly polite, disguised accent, "has been identified as the former

572

grand palace of the Prince of Sardinia, where once the prince buried a treasure in art and jewels . . ."

"Now, look, di Luigiano, the Don is a very busy man and can't be wasting his time on . . ." Garibaldi's ears perked up. "A treasure in art and jewels?"

". . . and relics valued at today's market in the area of a billion or more."

It was difficult for them to contain their astonishment. Garibaldi grabbed the document from the Lion's hand and studied it intently. He handed it back to Dolcetto and his eyes caught the Don's with just a flicker of amazement.

"Don't fuck around with me, di Luigiano," shouted the Don. "I'm no fool." His voice was loaded with all the menace collected in a lifetime.

"I assure you, I have no such intention. I know your reputation, Don Barbarossa. And a fool, you are not."

"Talk!"

"Alberto Pietro has been a close confidant and friend of the Marquis de Leone," he continued.

"Yes, yes, yes! We know all that."

"About this alleged treasure," interrupted Garibaldi. "A billion you say? Has this sum been substantiated?"

"Most assuredly. I have photocopies of the inventory listed in the historical records from the 1800s when they were discovered missing. This is a copy of the list presently located in the National Archives in Rome."

"Molinari is sure of this information?" asked the Don when he saw Garibaldi's somber and profound interest. "He's certain that Alberto Pietro has these treasures?"

"Until the list can be checked against the genuine articles, this list is as accurate as if the former King of Sardinia wrote it himself. Of course, they will have to be found first. But our records prove they are somewhere in the Vanzini Villa. You see, Excellency, a first cousin of Amelio Molinari works for the Court of Records. He met Dr. Pietro one day while lunching with his cousin, and the two men knew each other instantly. Later Molinari's cousin told him how they came to meet. For three years, this Dr. Pietro spent entire summers in the archives doing title searches on the properties in and about Palermo and Monreale. He'd been granted special permission to enter the archives under the authority of His Excellency, the Marquis de Leone.

"Out of curiosity and upon seeing so dedicated a man, Molinari's cousin scanned the documents, thinking he was a scholar who would one day write a book. Most of the documents referred to the historical data compiled by monks during the period of the Kingdom of Two Sicilies and the lost fortune which the prince reputedly stole from his father. When he later saw documentation of the lost fortune, he made copies of the records contained in the archives and submitted them to Molinari as proof that he wasn't embroidering fanciful tales." Dolcetto cleared his throat and sipped more water.

"For this information Molinari paid his cousin a bonus, but said nothing to anyone. He wanted me to assure you, Don Barbarossa, that he wouldn't present you with such information unless his facts were supported by evidence. And it wasn't until recently—some two months ago—that Dr. Pietro, whom you know has Antonio de Leone's power of attorney, transferred title of the Vanzini Villa to himself. Oh, he paid some token amount for it, some small pittance," said Dolcetto, affecting great disdain.

"You knew this, Don Matteo?" asked Garibaldi softly. "That he held power of attorney and with it he implemented transfer of the Vanzini Villa?"

"Yes, of course I knew it," said the Don, scowling over the fact that his *consigliori* should question him in the presence of a stranger. "Perhaps not in the manner you indicate. You knew that, Primo. He's wanted the property for some twelve years."

Twelve years ago, thought Dolcetto. *That's when it all began?* He filled with dismay that in all that time neither he nor his father had the faintest suspicion of Alberto's double life.

The Don filled with brooding. He'd tried for a long time to find a weakness in Alberto, but he'd found none. Now it was evident the villa was his one weakness all the time, the one thing that possessed him. This is what Alberto had wanted from the first day they met at Nunzzio's. He recalled that Alberto had ordered the death of the family when their efforts to induce old man Vanzini to sell failed. The Don complied because by then, Alberto had become important to the brotherhood.

This is why Alberto had always refused a substitute. Count Carozza's *palazzo* was more beautiful and a more valuable property, but Alberto had rejected all attempts by the Don to appease him. To have waited so patiently for twelve years to acquire the property, and then to acquire it through such guile, impressed Don Matteo. It was this unique facet in Alberto's personality that unnerved the *capomafia.*

"A billion dollars you say, di Luigiano?" he asked with calculating eyes.

"Perhaps more in today's market. Who knows?"

The Don studied Dolcetto; regarded him as though he

could never be done staring at him with curiosity and wonder.

"You have other data to substantiate this . . . uh . . . hearsay?" asked Garibaldi.

"I beg to differ with you, signore. It isn't hearsay." Dolcetto held his hands together in an insufferably effeminate manner. "I worked for de Leone Land Development for many years and had access to the confidential files of *El Leone* himself. I was the only man entrusted to this division, but, after his death, the department was more or less abandoned, because the heir, Antonio de Leone, hasn't been around to really check into its worth.

"In this division, many of the records kept by His Excellency himself were compiled. And I myself recall turning over records on the Prince of Sardinia. The involvement escapes me, but somehow the de Leone family was involved through a planned marriage alliance of the two families. Then the marriage was called off by order of Louis Napoleon, so she could marry one of the Napoleons. The de Leone family were personally affronted and sought to discredit the royal family of Sardinia."

When Dolcetto filled them in on the remaining story, the connection struck him at the same time it struck the Don, and both grasped the significance. Dr. Pietro must have known this, so he nurtured the friendship between himself and the Royal Lion of Sicily.

Don Barbarossa thought, *Alberto's entire life had been premeditated and calculated to pursue this dream of his.* Then when he remembered his own life, how he had planned to become what he eventually became, he felt more tolerant toward Alberto Pietro. He watched as his *consiglioro* picked up the documents and read and reread them. He noticed the rising excitement in the lawyer and how he struggled to maintain a cool, complacent manner. The Don himself felt an increasing disturbance, and it showed clearly in the way he crammed a cigar between his teeth, struck a match, and puffed furiously on it until it glowed like a Roman candle.

So, Alberto has kept this a secret from me all these years. The money-hungry Don, who had more money than he could count in a lifetime, grew envious and filled with greed just as Dolcetto predicted he would.

"You asked for more substantial information," began Dolcetto. "Well, one of our men, who works for the *carabinieri* on special assignments, presented to us—on the quiet, you understand—this book found among the effects of . . . uh . . ." He glanced at his little book again, knowing how this angered the Don ". . . uh . . . Mario Cacciatore, shortly after the assassinations of the Royal Lions . . ."

"Assassinations?" asked Garibaldi indignantly.

"Mario Cacciatore!" The cigar fell from the Don's lips and landed on the desk. Ashes spilled down his shirt and vest, and he was unable to contain his astonishment.

Dolcetto glanced blandly from one to the other.

"Why do you call their deaths, 'assassinations?' " asked the *consiglioro* coldly.

"Deaths, assassinations, murders—they're all the same, no?" He watched the Don, who was brushing ashes from his shirt front, retrieve and relight the cigar.

Dark clouds suddenly hovered over Don Barbarossa. "What was found among Cacciatore's things?" Suddenly wary, he became gracious and poured three glasses of Valpolicella and handed one to his guest, another to his *consiglioro*, and the last he took for himself.

Dolcetto reached into his briefcase. "This book, Excellency. Molinari claims that Alberto Pietro has the other four volumes in his possession." He handed them one of the books from Francesca's library, embossed in gold letters with the words: *Property of A. L. Vanzini.*

"Here's a note in the book written by the Marquis de Leone to Alberto Pietro dated the evening of the wedding, a year ago. Do you wish me to read it to you?"

"Yes." The Don chewed his cigar savagely. "Yes, yes, read it!"

When Dolcetto finished reading the letter, he sipped his wine and made loud, smacking noises of appreciation. He glanced at Don Barbarossa and saw for an instant, the thick, twitching lips, the glistening black eyes, and the same self-contained look of evil he saw in the Mazzarino bandit just before he raised his outstretched hand to decapitate Roberto Argento. He shuddered.

So Cacciatore lived to return to his casita? *Why didn't he contact me? What really happened?* The Don filled with brooding. "Molinari and you have done well in your research, di Luigiano."

"It was these papers your man Cacciatore took home with him and were later discovered that convinced Molinari, Don Barbarossa."

"Ah. Why is it, di Luigiano, that Molinari's man, not mine, would have been given these important papers?" he asked testily, not trusting Dolcetto at all.

Dolcetto bounced back. "I'm sure you would have, had you been here. Even the *consiglioro* was away. Your contacts forwarded them to Molinari. Weren't those your instruc-

576

tions, Excellency? You were wise not to have directed these to Alberto Pietro, or we may not have stumbled upon such a plot."

This son of a bitch has an answer for everything, thought the Don. And before he could pick up on Dolcetto's last remark, the Lion placated further.

"By the expression on your face, Don Barbarossa, I can see this comes as no surprise to you. You must have known all along what Pietro was up to." He wagged a finger at him playfully. "I told Molinari no one could put anything over on you—that you'd know everything before I even opened my mouth."

The Don glanced at his *consiglioro* with a modicum of surprise, then glanced at Dolcetto with sudden amiability.

The *capomafia* shrugged indifferently. "It's nothing new to me. Pietro confided in me years ago."

Both the Lion and Primo Garibaldi knew the crafty, guileful man was salving a humiliated ego.

The lawyer buried his head in the inventory sheets and bit his lower lip to keep silent. Dolcetto smiled to himself, amused by the feigned deception. The first phase of his work was nearly over. The wheels had been set in motion.

"Signore Molinari instructed me to tell you he's taken a few days holiday to be with his family," said Dolcetto, repacking his briefcase.

"Will you leave these documents with me, di Luigiano?" asked the lawyer. "I'd like to browse through them and make some inquiries of my own."

"You may keep them all. I have copies in my files. Are you an art lover?"

"Yes, some of these pieces interest me tremendously. Your list is quite formidable."

"It's not my list, signore. It belongs to history." He clasped his hands together in that infuriating manner calculated to madden most men.

"Yes, yes, of course," glowered Garibaldi, tossing the Don a long-suffering look behind Dolcetto's back.

The Don rang a buzzer and his two bodyguards suddenly reappeared.

"Thank you, di Luigiano, for the information. Give my personal wishes to Amelio for *Felice Natale*."

"I won't be going back to Rome until after the Christmas holidays. In case either of you needs me, I'll be staying at the hotel noted on my card." He nodded curtly and left the Don's office.

"Whore of the devil!" cursed the Don. "Where does Molinari get these powder puffs?"

"Rome is full of them," replied his *consiglioro*.

The *capomafia* got to his feet and padded across the room to the bay window that overlooked the courtyard. He watched Dolcetto walk across the tiled enclosure. Something about his manner arrested him, the way he strode to his car, the way he held his head, different than the man in his office moments before.

He called to his lawyer, but by the time Garibaldi crossed to the window, it was too late. Dolcetto had already stepped into his rented Alfa Romeo.

"What's wrong? What is it?"

"It's too late. He's gone. But do me a favor, will you? Get Molinari on the phone. I got plenty to say to him, hear?"

The Don sank back in his chair heavily. He was filled with brooding and bitter resentment. *Why,* he asked himself, *didn't Alberto confide this to me? In twelve years, not one word! What do I care for art treasures,* he told himself. *Yet a billion dollars is a lot of money and according to this powder puff, maybe more, eh?* But, there was more than just money involved in all this treachery and deceit, much more. If Alberto had kept this secret from him—how many other deals had he kept to himself, that he hadn't shared with the Don? Lies, treachery, deceit, and murder are only the beginning—there is no end!

Who knew all this better than Don Matteo Barbarossa?

There was more. Things the Don had been annoyed over in the past, but had refrained from discussing with Pietro because of their successes. The fact that Alberto alone was the connecting link with his international partners in the combine known as the Mediterranean Big Five had stuck in his craw for a long time. All deals made with Aristopheles, Canticcio, and Sheik Abou had to be done through Alberto. His inability to communicate with the other moguls disturbed him and deflated his ego terribly. He, Barbarossa, the man behind the man who ran the government—had to subordinate himself to these *pezzinovante* from other countries! Hah! But he took it before. Now, he filled with a keen distrust. On top of all this was the matter of Cacciatore and the letter! All this stirred and infected him more than if he endured boils on his testicles!

"Goddammit! What's the matter?" he directed his fury at the *consiglioro*. "Can't you get Molinari?" He rose to his feet and paced the floor in his study.

"The lines are all busy—you know, with the holidays . . ."

"Porca miseria!" The Don tossed his cigar on the carpeted floor and stomped on it angrily.

"How long have you known about Alberto?" asked Primo Garibaldi testily.

"You think I wanted this powder puff di Luigiano to return to Rome and broadcast that I, Don Barbarossa, knew nothing of this matter? Are you crazy? You think we can afford to lose such respect?"

Garibaldi nodded perfunctorily. He'd guessed as much. Gathering his papers, he prepared to leave. "Is there something special you want me to do in this matter?"

"Not yet. I must think about this and the other matter, Primo. You know what I mean?"

"Yes, I know. I'll be at my villa, if you need me." He took his leave.

52

Dr. Alberto Pietro rose at his usual hour of 5:30 A.M., drank the orange juice and hot coffee placed at his bed for the last time in his old villa at Faro, bathed, dressed, and with bags fully packed, he closed the door on the old place and his old life.

By 9 A.M., seated in the back seat of his newly acquired Mercedes limousine, he had already passed the Greco-Roman ruins in Tindari. Here holiday visitors were already toiling up the steep hill leading to the sanctuary that reputedly contained a miracle-working, Byzantine black madonna to whom the natives and tourists made supplication.

They drove through Cefalu, past the sweeping Bay of Imerese, and approached the dusty little city of Bagheria, once the summer residence of wealthy Palermitans in the 17th and 18th centuries. They passed the famous villa containing a garden of grotesque, half-animal, half-human statues, standing in a sad state of neglect, overrun with weeds. One day, Alberto promised himself, he would come and spend a full day in this enchanted land. Before noon, he could see the famed *Conca d'Oro* in the distance, and when they drove through the quaint streets of Palermo, the rare sounds of the *Cara Middare*—ancient Sicilian bagpipes—could be heard playing Christmas music. Everywhere the Golden City of Palermo displayed nativity scenes and holiday magic was in the air. Dr. Pietro decided to stop at Nunzzio's for a slight repast.

After lunch, which took two hours, Alberto was back in his car, ready to hasten the last lap of his trip. This would be the best Christmas he'd ever spent. When he drove past Monte Pellegrino, he glanced at his platinum and diamond wristwatch and realized that in less than ten minutes the dream of his lifetime would be realized. He sat back and reflected on the last of his duties from which he had finally separated himself.

A few days before, he had resigned as director of de Leone Pharmaceuticals, thereby forfeiting his power of attorney on Antonio's behalf. Let the board of directors decide to do what they would with what was left of de Leone Enterprises. He had his own interests to devote full time to now.

Three weeks before, in a conversation with Dr. Simoni before he left for a Chicago convention, the physician had assured Dr. Pietro that it would be only a question of time before Antonio succumbed. "It's a miracle he's lasted this long," Dr. Simoni told him. Alberto smiled. Antonio had always been as strong as a bull. He'd actually been very fond of the lad.

The most difficult chore had been convincing Don Matteo that he was no longer interested in participating in *mafia* activities. Because he'd made Matteo one of the wealthiest men in Europe, he was able to exit gracefully without arousing suspicion. After the Lucky Luciano matter, Don Matteo laughingly decided that Alberto had earned his retirement. There was no question they were on the spot with the American Dons in New Orleans due to Don Salvatore's last fiasco, and if they didn't make good, there was no question that their American counterparts would take some fast action. With the aid of Alberto's ex-classmate, Plato Aristopheles, who would send the shipment on his oil freighters, the problem had been eliminated.

Only one last obligation remained. He had offered his new home as a final *mafia* meeting place in a gesture symbolic of parting with the old, commencing with the new. What could be more perfect than the Vanzini Villa, miles from any *mafia* stronghold, with a convenient harbor at their disposal—all the others would come by boat. Three of his partners had complained that their movements had been observed of late and they needed a place no one would suspect. They must be getting paranoid in their older years.

He'd already sent a long list of instructions to Gino Vittorio, asking him to hire a staff of select, competent servants, Palermo caterers, and all the people necessary to make the event a memorable one. He'd show Don Matteo how to really live. What's the point of having wealth if you don't enjoy the pleasures that go with it?

His blue eyes glittered excitedly. *I'll show them all. After I locate the treasure, I'll move to the continent and live in real style, in the manner of an Oriental potentate.* He laughed ironically. *Rather in the manner of a Sardinian king!* He found this last amusing.

"You forget, I am also a de Leone," insisted Guillermo.

Dolcetto placed his arm about his uncle's shoulders as they walked along the wall overlooking the sea at the Vanzini Villa. "But you've been away too long to take up the cause again. Besides, if anything should happen to me, you would have to care for Francesca and my son. No matter what the outcome of these next few days, you must give me your solemn oath that those *mafiosi* will never lay their hands on de Leone money. Burn it if you will, but they must never make use of it as they did this past year!"

They walked in silence, then turned and headed back to the villa.

Dolcetto's right, thought Guillermo. *I've been away too long and lived too different a life. My thoughts and ideas are so different from what they once were.* He stole a sidelong glance at his nephew and sighed, for he saw in the Lion his brother Marco all over again. It was futile to argue with a fiercely dedicated man.

Francesca waited for them at the entrance with her young son in her arms. Dolcetto took the dark-haired infant in his arms and kissed him and held him close. Then he handed the child to his uncle. "Take my son to the car. I wish to speak to my wife."

"Why can't I stay here with you?" said Francesca after Guillermo walked away with the child.

The Lion took his wife into his arms and drew her close to him. His luminous emerald eyes filled with softness. He kissed her, tenderly at first, then with so much passion she melted in his arms. *"Carissima,* if anything should happen to you or our son, I couldn't bear it. Please do not contest my wishes." He spoke with so much love, Francesca surrendered. She wound her arms about his neck and lay her head against his heart, feeling his warmth and listening to his life pound furiously in her ear.

"If anything should happen to you, *caro mio,* there'll be no hope for me or our son. I couldn't relive a year like the last one. Is it so much to ask that we be together during these next few days?"

He raised her face to his. "You aren't to worry, my love. I promise we'll spend the New Year together and make plans . . . away from all this. With this final gesture, it all ends."

Francesca had been overcome with grief when Dolcetto returned to tell her of Antonio's fate. She begged him to end it all, to turn away from everything so they could live lives of their own choosing. But he told her his decision. Still Francesca was about to protest.

"Shhh," he told her gently. "We've both endured enough sorrow to last us all our lives. For us, it will end. I promise. The curse of the Royal Lions will soon be over. Now, be sweet. Do as your poor husband instructs—without argument. *Va biene?*"

They kissed again and held each other tightly. "Now," he said firmly, "we'll discuss this no further. You'll wait at the farmhouse until either Gino or I arrive." He walked her to the waiting car, then pulled her close again. "I love you, *cara mia.* I love you."

His tenderness tore her heart in two. All she could manage in that wonderful, husky voice of hers was, "Dolcetto, Dolcetto."

He put her in the car and closed the door. "I'll see you later tonight, *Zu* Guillermo." Guillermo nodded and started the now decrepit Fiat. Dolcetto waved his family off until the car disappeared down the hill.

Dolcetto went into the villa and joined Gino Vittorio and the other workers who were busy complying with the numerous instructions sent by Alberto Pietro. In addition to the Godfather's instructions, Dolcetto had several of his own.

"Goddammit! If anyone told me I had to do this—" exploded Hank Rossi as he put on the 18th-century costume of a royal court page. He felt ridiculous in the gold satin knickers, white silk hose, and black shoes with gold buckles, topped with a white lace shirt and a golden brocade cutaway coat.

"Look at it this way," suggested Danny Moreno as he donned a similar costume. "It beats the hell out of the way we dressed in Istanbul. Remember the filth in the sheik's tent?"

"Ugh." Hank Rossi grimaced as he recalled the episode. "You just hadda bring that up."

"Just so you don't go around thinking you're an underprivileged American," he said with exaggerated innuendo. He placed the white powdered wig on his head, then stood in a ridiculous pose for Hank's approval. "Well, whadda ya think? Do you think Sheik Abou will know us?"

"You just better pray he doesn't. It's been six years."

They both turned toward the door when Lt. Domingo came in wearing an equally comical costume.

"*Mah!* This Dr. Pietro has got to be some *melanzano!*" They all laughed.

Dolcetto entered the room and smiled at the comic threesome. "I'm sorry, my friends, but these are his express orders. Must be the realization of some morbid fantasy he's dreamed up with the rest of his madness." His smile evap-

582

orated at the thought of his Godfather. "How far away are your men?"

"A signal or a phone call away. And we're not far away either, Dolcetto," replied Domingo. "Don't take any unnecessary chances."

"You'll have to get him to admit to the crimes, definite proof of his involvement," stated Dolcetto. "You *know* that?"

"One thing's certain, this Godfather of yours is no dummy. The way he covered his tracks—" said Hank Rossi. "I'm still impressed by his brilliant machinations."

"Tell me," said Dolcetto, recalling thirty years of deceit.

Dolcetto glanced at his watch. "I'll have to get ready myself. I've an appointment with Don Barbarossa. He called my hotel and requested a second meeting with me."

"Think it's wise to go alone?" asked Danny Moreno, finding it difficult to sit in his satin breeches.

"He has no idea who I am, thanks to your tying up the phone lines."

"Well, you take care. Stay on your guard. And Christ, take a gun."

"It wouldn't help. His bodyguards would pick me clean before I got within five yeards. Besides, a weapon would make him suspicious. Good luck!" Dolcetto left the men to their preparations.

"Why does he have to take such chances? I don't like him getting that close to Barbarossa," complained Rossi.

"Don't sweat it. Three men will be on him the moment he leaves here. They'll be less than a minute away," said Domingo.

"It takes less than a minute for a knife to find its mark," said Rossi.

"Less time for a bullet," added Moreno.

"C'mon, let's recheck our plans," said Santino glumly. "And what the hell was all this about Sheik Abou? You guys meet him on an assignment?"

Alberto Pietro arrived at the Vanzini Villa and stood at the outer gate waiting patiently for someone to answer the bell. Gino Vittorio, obviously uncomfortable in the dark suit, white dress shirt, and black tie he'd been instructed to wear, crossed through the Peacock Court and opened the gates. He was accompanied by Danny Moreno, dressed in his satin costume and white powdered wig. Standing at attention behind them was a group of seven servants, including Lt. Domingo and Hank Rossi, all looking like products of a bygone era.

"Buon giorno, dottore," welcomed Gino, bowing obsequiously. *"Piacere dei videre."*

"Piacere dei videre. It's a pleasure seeing you again, Gino." Dr. Pietro glanced quickly at Danny Moreno and flushed with pleasure as he studied the details of his golden uniform. "My bags are in the car. Will you tell the chauffeur where to put the car? Also tell him where his sleeping quarters will be. Did my trunks arrive?" he asked in the manner of royalty.

"Si. They are already upstairs in the suite you designated."

He removed his gray felt fedora and his black, beaver-trimmed chesterfield coat, handed them to Gino, and walked ahead much in the style of Marco de Leone, who he appeared to be emulating. In the Peacock Court, he came upon the servants standing at attention. He smiled faintly and his celestial blue eyes seemed to lose their perpetual coldness.

"I see you followed my instructions. Very good, my boy. Very well done." His critical eyes scanned the gathered men, from their gleaming, patent leather shoes to their wavy white wigs. "Yes, indeed, very well done, Gino."

Gino clapped his hands and the staff came to immediate attention. "This is your new *padrone—Dottore* Pietro," he announced to the staff. He turned to the white-haired physician. "Do you wish to meet them now?"

Dr. Pietro studied the men carefully as he strutted by, examining them in minute detail. He straightened the glasses on Domingo's perspiring nose, ruffled the jabot on Hank Rossi's shirt as both agents froze like statues. He went on to examine the white gloves of another. Gino's eyes telegraphed relief to the agents.

"Tomorrow, after breakfast. I'm a bit tired now. I'll go into the study for a glass of wine. You did remember to get my special wine from Fregossi's, no?"

"I followed your instructions perfectly." Gino handed the coat to Lt. Domingo and shooed him away with a facile wrist movement.

Hank Rossi appraised Dr. Pietro coolly. He had to admit, this man was far from the mousey-looking, introverted, bookkeeper type he remembered from the funeral. This was a man that was sure of himself, a man with a tremendous ego who appeared far more worldly than he did a year ago. All the agents wondered why all the 17th-century drama was necessary. Their thoughts were interrupted by an audible gasp.

Alberto Pietro had come to an abrupt halt when he saw the enormous photographic blowups of Francesca and Dolcetto on their wedding day that were mounted on the vast wall behind the graceful spiral staircase.

"*Chè commedia c'è?* What manner of joke is this?" he shouted.

"*Perdonna mi?*" Gino turned a bland face to him.

"Whose idea was this?" He pointed to the photos with wide, sweeping gestures.

Gino stared confusedly from the blowups to the man next to him. "I don't understand. I followed your instructions the day they were delivered to me."

"*My* instructions?" he exploded, losing his calm. "I sent no such instructions. Take them down! Immediately! Do you hear?"

"*Si, dottore,* right away." He clapped his hands. Lt. Domingo and Hank Rossi reappeared. "Remove these pictures from the wall immediately," ordered Gino. "They offend the *padrone.*"

"I didn't say that!" snapped the irate physician. "I merely want them removed."

Gino conversed with the agents for a moment. He approached Dr. Pietro, apology written on his face. "The men tell me the photos were installed with rivets and cannot be removed without causing much damage to the walls. If you can wait until after *Natale,* we'll have the same men you sent to install them remove them properly."

"Will you stop saying that I sent the men or these pictures." He fought for control. After a moment he said, "Very well then, after *Natale.* And Gino . . ."

"*Si?*"

"Bring me the list of instructions and my letter ordering this garish display."

Gino Vittorio nodded. If Dr. Pietro had chanced to see the smug smile of inner satisfaction on Gino's face, it might have given him some indication of what was to follow.

When the physician walked into the study, his face swelled with rage. Under his bushy white brows, his blue eyes stormed like a turbulent sea as he glanced about the room. It took several moments to regain his control.

The entire room had been done over into a complete replica of Marco's den at the Villa de Leone, down to every last detail including the portrait of Mariolina de Leone. Over the desk hung the official portrait of the Royal Lion, seated on his snow-white Arabian, wearing the colorful regalia of the Royal Order of the Lion. Several moments passed before Alberto could tear his eyes away from the compelling eyes in the portrait. Dr. Pietro, who hardly ever perspired, mopped his brow.

"What manner of deviltry is this?" he asked Gino.

"Is there something wrong? Perhaps you need refreshment." He walked to the sideboard and poured wine into a delicate crystal goblet. "Here, this will refresh you."

The icy blue eyes studied Gino in silence. He'd seen apparent confusion in Gino's face and decided not to make an issue of this mad design to intimidate him. *I'll get to the bottom of this later.*

He took the drink. *"Grazie.* Now bring me the list of instructions I sent you. I want to make sure everything has been carried out properly."

"I wish to do everything to please you. Here, it's on your desk."

The meticulous physician raised his jacket so as not to wrinkle it and sat down behind the desk.

"This is the letter that came with the large pictures that went on the wall in the foyer."

Alberto shook noticeably as he read the letter. Obviously it was a forgery, one of the best he'd ever seen, next to his own.

"I suppose all of this . . ." He waved his hand about the room. ". . . came with my instructions telling you how I wanted it placed?" He nodded with pursed lips anticipating the answer.

"Si, and with pictures, too." Gino handed him a stack of diagrams showing where the items were to be placed.

Dr. Pietro didn't have to examine them. *Someone's distasteful idea of a joke, no doubt. But whose? Who had guessed? Who knew anything?* He paled considerably as he continued to sip his wine, feeling its warmth as it coursed through his body. He pointedly avoided Gino's eyes when the nagging thought struck him. *One person might have guessed . . . Yes, there was one person.* He avoided Gino's eyes.

"How's your brother?" he asked in a cool, amiable way.

"Pepino? Ah, *dottore."* He feigned a temporary sadness and a long face to match. "My brother is no longer alive."

Startled by the answer, his searching blue eyes darted to Gino's face. Slowly, he scanned the man's reactions. "What happened? An accident? Illness?"

"No, he had no accident."

"What then?"

"I killed him."

"You what?" He stared in shock, as Gino calmly poured more wine into the crystal goblet.

"I killed him," he repeated.

They regarded each other in an intense silence.

"You *killed* your own brother?" He was appalled, yet fascinated by Gino's cold, impersonal attitude. "Why? In God's name, why?"

"He was a traitor." Gino replaced the wine decanter. "It was he who betrayed my mistress, allowed the *mafiosi* to enter the villa the night they were all slaughtered, including your beloved friend, His Excellency the Marquis."

"Traitor? That's a strong word to apply to one's own brother." Dolcetto's Godfather averted his eyes, fastening them on his wine goblet. He felt the smoothness of the crystal stem as he twirled the glass in his fingers. *How much did Gino really know? Had Pepino told him anything?*

"How did you discover the treachery? What makes you so sure the *mafiosi* were involved?" His eyes still avoided Gino's.

"He told me."

No matter how hard he tried to conceal his nervousness, Dr. Pietro's features jerked. Then, in a voice that masked his real feelings, he asked, "What else did he tell you? Did he name the person who hired him? One of the local Dons, no doubt."

"Ah, *dottore*." Gino tapped his forehead. "What a fool I was. A hot-headed, stupid, blundering oaf. I gave him no opportunity to tell me. I went off like a crazed rooster. Shot him before he had an opportunity to tell me who it was. Like a hot-headed Sicilian, I lost control. At the time, it was enough I discovered him to be a traitor. To think a Vittorio worked in league with the *mafiosi*." Gino clucked his tongue in disapproval.

"You did right, my boy," exclaimed the older man, noticeably relieved. "I might have done the same thing in your place. What a loss to all of us, that wonderful family of Lions." He hung his head in a sorrowful manner, shaking it from side to side. "I shall feel the loss of my friends forever." He gulped down the remainder of his wine. He raised his hands in the air in a heavy, despairing manner, then let them drop. "A sad, sad thing to have happened."

What a convincing performance, thought Gino, biting back the impulse to smash his fist in the face of the lying pig.

"Will you need me further? I must see to dinner. Shall we say in an hour, *dottore*?"

"*Va biene. Aloura.* Gino, you may call me Excellency from now on. I have just acquired an entire dukedom, complete with title and all. I wait only for the official papers to arrive from Rome."

"Yes, Excellency. Congratulations." Gino bowed out the door.

Alberto Pietro could do nothing except stare about the room, reconsider the forgeries, and mull over the giant blowups of his Godson and his wife. Who could have been responsible for such a bizarre act? Since Pepino was dead, it couldn't have been him. Then who? His mind could only conceive of one person—Antonio de Leone. He lost no time in placing a call to Switzerland. That the call was put through immediately didn't strike him as unusual at the time.

When the clinic answered, Alberto asked for Dr. Simoni and was told he had left for the holidays. He then told the party at the other end of the line he was Antonio de Leone's physician. Would the man be kind enough to inform him of the patient's condition?

"Your code, *Herr Doktor?*"

"Virgo 828."

While Alberto waited, he opened his shirt and loosened his tie.

"Condition no better. Patient deteriorating rapidly. Dr. Simoni has someone in attendance full time. Patient under restraints. Can you be reached in case we must notify you of his condition?" came the thickly accented reply.

Alberto gave the attendant his phone number. "Let me know the moment anything happens."

"*Jawohl, Herr Doktor. Danke,*" said the Swiss Intelligence agent.

Well, that takes care of that! he thought. He marveled at Antonio's stamina. Simoni had assured him he'd be dead long before this.

Alberto blinked his eyes and turned his head as if listening to something. A peculiar feeling shot through him. He felt his pulse. It raced wildly and his respiration grew labored. *What was I doing before I placed the call? Yes, I remember now. All this nonsense—someone responsible. Perhaps I should call Don Matteo. He might offer me a possible explanation.* He dialed the operator.

"*Pronto Centralino. Voglio questo numero 661-3110.*"

"*Avete sbagliato numero, signore.* You have given me a wrong number, sir."

"Impossible! I've called the same number for years."

"*Mi dispiace—mah,* you have the wrong number."

"*Figghia di butanna!*" He slammed the phone into its cradle. He reached for his jacket and fished through a pocket for a small black book. He traced with his finger, the name and number next to it. It was blurred and he couldn't see well. He put on his bifocals, reread the numbers. They were more blurred than ever. He slammed the book on the desk.

Porca vecchia. Malodetta! *Goddamned old age! No mat-*

588

ter how young I force my mind to think, the aging process is as predictable as a whore. He replaced the telephone with precise movements, wiped away an imaginary speck of dust, then glanced at his watch. His eyes snapped open, then narrowed as he tried to read the dial. *What in the hell's wrong with me tonight? I must be very tired. More than I imagined.* He poured himself another glass of wine, drained the glass, smacked his lips, and left the study.

Climbing the spiral staircase he pointedly averted his head from the photographs covering one wall. Midway up the steps he paused, touched his head, and felt a giddiness overcome him. He caught sight of an exquisite vase of Belle of Portugal roses at the top of the stairs, and suddenly the colors came alive like magnificent, luminous jewels. Drawn by the variation of vibrant colors, he continued unsteadily to the landing. Their sweet scent was overpowering, sharper than any he'd smelled before. He shook his head trying to clear his mind of the unusual sensations that surged through him. He turned and gazed below him and became aware of a slow dance of golden lights fanning out from the Peacock Court. Turning his attention back to the shell-pink roses he felt as though he were watching the unfolding of creation. Each flower seemed to breathe of its own, pulsate with its own life as it sprang from a bud into a full bloom in the space of seconds.

Alberto Pietro shook his head as if he was attempting to put his brains in order, and gripped the railing tightly. He pulled himself up beyond the landing and turned toward the suite of rooms once occupied by Marco de Leone.

What's wrong? . . . feel pulse . . . racing . . . hot and cold chills . . . Legs like water . . . Glittering lights like diamonds blinding me . . . blinding lights . . . painful!

He staggered, held on to the wall, and crept toward the bedroom. Inside he lay prone on the bed, forced his eyes closed. Things felt worse. *Think,* he told himself. *Force yourself to think. Concentrate. Brain feels deprived of nourishment. Low blood sugar. Hallucinating! I'm hallucinating! That's it!* What he endured with his eyes closed was more frightening than what he saw with them open.

Get up! Force yourself to sit up! With great effort, he managed to sit up, swing his spindly legs over the side of the bed, and let his head fall heavy into the palms of his hands. His eyelids popped open and he caught sight of his feet. Before his eyes they began to multiply; two—four—six—until he could see hundreds of feet stretching to infinity. He blinked in confusion, and when they became two feet again, he forced his eyes to look away. They fell on a por-

589

trait of Marco with Dolcetto and Antonio as young men at his side. The photo took life and grew animated, and he saw all three de Leones as he had the day the photograph was taken in the Madelaina Gardens years ago. He heard Dolcetto's voice calling, *"Buon giorno, Godfather . . . Godfather . . . Godfather."* The words echoed through the caverns of his mind.

I'm going mad! Porca miseria! I'm going mad! He laughed loud and raucously, but the laughter abruptly subsided as a clear thought pierced through the broken fragments of his mind. *There has to be an explanation. But what?*

Godfather . . . Godfather. There was that same hollow voice.

His respiration grew increasingly difficult. His eyes refused to focus. He staggered about the room, stumbling over chairs and luggage and other furniture.

Somewhere within the strong disciplined mind of Alberto Pietro was a powerful ego trying to assert itself over the maddening confusion and gross distortions reported to his brain by his miscalculating senses. His eyesight malfunctioned and he clutched and grasped at a sensuous, writhing bedpost that suddenly came alive and bared wet fangs at him like a slithering, slimy snake.

"Ahhhhhh!" he screamed hoarsely, releasing his grip on the apparition. His perspective altered with each blink of his eyelids. Other animal forms rushed at him, then diminished in pulsating motion. Suddenly, he saw the alarm signals over the bed. He tried to wade through the schizophrenic distortions to climb over the bed to reach them. The closer he got, the further away they became. He flailed his arms wildly until he accidentally set off the alarm buttons. The sudden, clamorous noises made by the alarm intensified to several degrees more than a human ear could endure. The ear-splitting sound caused his body to bounce back across the room and the assaulting vibrations tore at him with excruciating agony. He clutched at his ears to drown out the sounds. He spun around, reaching the end of his endurance for the inhuman punishment. The door opened and Dolcetto de Leone entered the room, staring impassively at the shambles. He turned off the alarm.

"Who is it?" cried the stricken man, cowering like a frightened animal. He could see the faint outline of a motionless form a few feet away.

"Don't you recognize me, Godfather?"

Alberto blinked his eyes and growled viciously like an animal on all fours and retreated further into the corner of the room.

"It's your Godson. Don't tell me you've forgotten your Godson?" He showed the scarred side of his face to the man in the corner.

What Alberto barely distinguished through his drugged eyes formed a picture of a gargantuan gargoyle, grotesque and without shape or form. He curled up into a fetal position, inching away from him.

"No. You're dead. My Godson is dead," he said brokenly.

"Believe me, Godfather, you aren't dreaming. You recall Antonio, don't you, Godfather? You know what LSD 25 is, don't you? Sure you do? How does it feel to sample what you prescribed for another? In a short while you'll receive what you meted to your dearest friend. You do remember Marco de Leone, don't you, Godfather?"

The door opened and Guillermo walked into the room in the wake of the hall light. His body took on a mysterious glow and he looked remarkably like Marco de Leone. Behind him stood Antonio.

On the floor, prostrated by the distortion to his senses, Alberto tried with superhuman effort to force his consciousness to do his bidding. He felt as if his brain bubbled over like molten lava, as if a volcano had erupted at the center of his brain.

"Why, Alberto? Why did you betray me?" came Marco's voice.

Alberto retreated further into the confusing chaos of his drugged mind. *Am I engrossed in half-forgotten nightmares? God! End this. Don't take my sanity, not after fifty years of dedication and waiting.* He paused, listening, moving his head from side to side. Now, motionless, his eyes grew alert and he saw Marco de Leone, and he saw his Godson, and Antonio coming at him. In a burst of clarity, he cried aloud, "No! It's not you! This is a dream! A nightmare!"

"What's wrong, Godfather?" asked Dolcetto coldly. "Does it disturb you to learn you didn't destroy the House of de Leone? We're alive, Godfather. Can't you see us? Look again."

Guillermo held up the golden lion amulet before his eyes. Instinctively, Alberto drew back in alarm. The veins in his neck and face were nearly bursting. His eyes were glued to the golden lion as it swayed back and forth; it had a hypnotic effect.

"You've lost the battle, Godfather. The Royal Lions *are* invincible!"

Splintered reality grabbed hold of Alberto, and for some mysterious reason, the jeweled symbol seemed to have more of an adverse effect on him than the sound of Dolcetto's voice. His eyes fixed on the swaying lion as it moved back and forth. He cowered further and his eyes grew glassy and fixed. His breathing grew labored.

"Perhaps he's had enough," suggested Guillermo with soft compassion.

"No! Not yet!" replied the compassionless Lion whose radiant green eyes were slashed with steel points.

Guillermo grew concerned. Alberto had begun to hyperventilate.

"This is your Godson."

"Godson?" rasped Alberto; then he lost consciousness.

"Quick! The atropine," ordered Guillermo as he felt for Alberto's pulse.

Dolcetto handed his uncle the counteracting drug. "He can't die yet. Dammit, I'm not through with him."

Guillermo said nothing, but he didn't like what he saw reflected in his nephew's eyes. He administered the drug in silence. Together they placed the Godfather on the bed.

"He'll be out of it in an hour," said Guillermo.

"Very good." He turned to Gino. "You know what to do. It must appear as if nothing unusual happened. He'll think it was a bad dream." His words shot out like bullets fired in rapid succession.

Gino was struck by the remarkable coldness in Dolcetto. "Relax," he said, placing his hand on the Lion's arm. He understood the weight of stone he carried in his gut.

Dolcetto returned to reality in that split second. "You're right, Gino." He left his uncle and Gino in the room and returned to his quarters.

"Nothing will stop him now," lamented Guillermo.

"*Eh, E il suo destinu*," lamented Gino. "It's his Destiny."

Slowly Alberto awoke from his drugged stupor. For a time, only his eyes moved. They darted hesitantly about the room, and when he saw the immaculate, well-organized room, he drew his hands to his eyes, rubbed them, and blinked several times. He got to his feet, utterly bewildered by what greeted him. His eyes traveled to where the photograph of Marco and the boys hung earlier. In its place was the picture of a fox hunt. His eyebrows knitted together in puzzled furrows. *Have I been dreaming again? Another nightmare? Perhaps the memories of a year ago haven't been uprooted from my subconscious after all.*

When at last Alberto Pietro finished dressing to his satisfaction, he studied his reflection in the mirror and thought, *Won't they be surprised?* He descended the stairs and recalled the amazing effect the flowers had had earlier. Now, as he gazed upon them, they were no different from any other.

I stand fearless and free. I am without fear. No harm can befall me. Why do I think of those old Nietzsche-inspired mantras? Did I really see Marco? Dolcetto? Did I hear their voices?

Halfway down the steps, Alberto paused. *Dolcetto's voice was as clear to me as the crystal chandelier I'm gazing at.* He studied the enormous fixture, fifteen tiers of Austrian cut glass, drops, and prisms, gleaming and shimmering like diamonds overhead.

I stand fearless and free. I am God. I am God. I'm all powerful.

Alberto turned around, retraced his steps back to his room, and among his things he found a small revolver. He slipped it into the pocket of his jacket and paused once again to study his reflection in the mirror. Filled with a satisfied glow, he patted the small, pearl-handled gun and walked downstairs with the air of royalty.

In the study, he went immediately to the sideboard, removed the glass stopper from the delicate crystal decanter, and sniffed its contents. He moistened his fingertip with the liquid, licked it with his tongue, then he rang for Gino Vittorio.

The word *Excellency* froze on Gino's lips. He was so startled by what greeted him, words failed him. His simple peasant upbringing hadn't prepared him for such complex behavior. He fought with all his strength to keep a straight face.

Standing in the dimly lit study, the new Duke of Cavelli, Alberto Pietro, was dressed in the full regalia of foppish court royalty straight out of the era of Louis XIV. He wore gold satin knee breeches, a lace and satin ruffled shirt studded with diamonds, a high-collared, gold satin waistcoat with tails, and white silk stockings. Black satin pumps with gold buckles at the instep graced his small feet. The ensemble itself hadn't been the cause of Gino's suppressed mirth. It was the pasty, white makeup on his face and the heavy black eyelashes and pencilled brows that made him appear grotesque and ludicrous. *This isn't Carnivale,* thought Gino as he stared in fascination at the blood-red, kewpie-doll lips with their exaggerated points.

"Well?"

Alberto waits to be complimented on his appearance like a whore, thought Gino.

"Do you like it?"

"Excellency . . ." began Gino, searching for the proper

words. "I'm speechless!" He was spellbound by the glittering, black beauty spots at the corner of Alberto's lip and over his left eye.

"Does it meet with your approval? My ribbons—the diplomatic ribbons—are they on properly?"

Gino was taken aback. Mah! Stu citrollo! *How the fuck do I know? Why ask me?* wondered the bodyguard who began to have misgivings about his role.

"*Si*, Excellency. I believe they are."

"You see, Gino . . ." said Dr. Pietro, pointing to the medallion dangling from the purple and white ribbon draped across his chest. ". . . this is the insignia of the Duke of Cavelli. I paid ten thousand dollars for this crest." Gino gazed at the fleet-footed animal with two sabers crossed diagonally beneath it.

Gino felt uneasy and terribly uncomfortable. *What have I let myself in for? If he doesn't stop looking at me with those pursed lips, I'll give him a good* bastinada.

Upstairs, in a special area of the villa, the three agents stared through peepholes and held their breath, hoping Gino wouldn't do anything rash.

"Who would have guessed he'd pull something like this?" asked Hank Rossi, staring in fascination.

"Just pray Gino will hold his own. You don't know these hot-headed Sicilians," cautioned Lt. Domingo.

Downstairs in the study, the Duke of Cavelli persisted. "Then it meets with your approval?" The Duke strutted about and moved like a mannequin.

"Dinner is ready, Excellency, when you are."

The Duke of Cavelli studied him with eyes that turned the color of frosted skies. He poured a glass of wine from the tumbler. *I am God. I am the power within me.*

"Drink this!" he ordered, shoving the wine glass at Gino.

"*Grazie*, no, Excellency. I don't drink. Since the night of the wedding . . ."

"Drink it," ordered the Duke, much in the manner of Don Barbarossa.

Gino was about to protest again, when he suddenly caught sight of the gun Alberto removed from his inside pocket. He laid the pistol on the desk and repeated, "Drink!"

Gino shrugged. "If I get drunk, you'll forgive me. To your good health, Excellency. Long life to you in your retirement." He drained the contents of the glass, and having played the part superbly, he set the glass down.

"Now you sit here until I make a phone call," he ordered. Alberto removed the phone from its niche, dialed the operator, and gave her the number he knew by heart. The line was still busy. Alberto cursed, slammed the phone, and turned his attention on Gino who by now had begun to feel the effect of his body's intolerance to the grape. One drink to Gino was like six to most men.

"How do you feel?" asked the Duke of Cavelli.

"Hot."

"Nothing else?"

"No."

"What about your eyes? Can you see?"

"I see fine. Why?"

"We'll see in ten minutes." The Duke glanced at his watch.

Gino yawned. A sappy expression crossed his face and he slumped in his chair. Alberto crossed to his side, placed a cool hand on his forehead, and looked soulfully into Gino's eyes.

"I told you I don't drink. If this job requires that I must drink, Excellency, I must serve notice upon you."

Alberto thrust a sheet of paper under Gino's nose. "Read!" he ordered.

Gino yawned and complied with the request. ". . . The prescribed dosage . . ."

"You still feel the same?"

"Sleepy and relaxed—that's all."

"*Aloura*, you can go," said the Duke, deflated. He was sure the wine had been drugged. "Before you go, will you bring me the floor plans of the villa? I may want to do some renovating."

Gino nodded, yawned, then rolled the small ladder along the track to the bookshelves. He climbed it, removed a roll of blueprints, and the four volumes of the estate's history.

"You may find these interesting, Excellency."

"Yes, thank you. I'll glance through them. Be a good man and bring me a tray for dinner."

Strange, thought Alberto. *For years I've dreamed of the moment when, as a titled landowner, I could dine in baronial elegance. Now I thrust the dream aside as if I couldn't care less.* Alberto began casually thumbing through the books and paused to remove a lace-edged handkerchief from inside his wide-cuffed jacket. He mopped his brow delicately, replaced the lace, and from a jeweled snuff box, he drew a pinch to each nostril and inhaled as Gino watched him from the doorway totally fascinated.

"Yes? Is something wrong?" He felt Gino's eyes bearing into him.

"No, Excellency. Nothing at all."

Alberto turned back to the books with mounting curiosity, in full absorption.

595

53

It was nearly 11 P.M. when Alberto set aside the four volumes of the villa's history. Like Marco, he'd found them intriguing, but incomplete. Surely there had to be another volume around. He peered closely through the bookcases, then made a note to ask Gino about it in the morning.

Alberto Pietro sat back in the chair behind the desk and found it hard to believe the villa was his at long last. He had to pinch himself to make sure it was real and not a dream. His eye caught sight of the rolled-up blueprints. Spreading them out on the desk, he spotlighted them with a goose-necked desk lamp and studied them as if for the first time. Long ago, he discovered, if his approach was fresh each time, he'd discover something he'd missed previously.

The Duke of Cavelli poured himself the last remnants of coffee into his cup and sipped it in deep thought. He asked himself, *if I were the Sardinian prince, where would I hide the treasure?* How many times had he asked himself this question in the past? Considering the variables, he would come up with a new perspective each time.

But now he was here. Actually here. It was no longer a mission on paper. It was time to think as the prince might have thought when he decided to hide the treasure.

"If I were prince . . ." he began. "If I were prince . . ." Nothing jelled. His improvisation didn't work. How could he think like another man? He was Alberto Pietro and had to think like Alberto Pietro. He got up and paced the floor. *What would I, Alberto Pietro do, if I wanted to hide such a treasure?* He walked back to the desk, studied the map and began to plot. He underlined certain sections, followed a different line of reasoning and placed a large red dot where his calculations had taken him.

It was nearly midnight when Alberto glanced up and caught his reflection in the smoky-colored glass mirror off to one side of the bookcase. He reached up and removed his wig, placing it carefully on a small table nearby. He removed the two beauty marks he'd applied earlier. He decided that since he was by nature a nocturnal person, it wouldn't matter if he went in search of the treasure now. The servants were asleep. What better time to browse, he reasoned.

The more he considered it, the more excited he became. Off the kitchen, in a tool shed he found flashlights and battery-powered lanterns. He felt for the gun he'd replaced in his pocket. Good. It was there. Taking a lantern and a flashlight, he stepped out into the cool, crisp night air and inhaled deeply. Flushed with excitement, he wound his way to the back courtyards.

The pale moon lit his way along the path that led to the rear of a secluded, unused wing of the *palazzo*. He paused to get his bearings and check the map. *At this point there should be an opening . . . an entrance . . . something.* Night shadows played tricks on his eyes. He flashed his lantern along a white stone wall, covered with wild shrubs and unkempt vines.

He ventured cautiously near a camouflaged alcove where he stumbled upon the set of stone steps leading to the second floor and upper hallways. Slowly, with marked hesitation, he began the long, arduous trek along endless corridors and walkways, in and out of musty, foul-smelling salons and abandoned apartments. In each of the high-ceilinged rooms, he flashed his lights along the walls and peered about with mounting curiosity, filled with quenchless excitement.

At 2 A.M. Alberto Pietro decided to call it a night. He was tired. It had been a long day. He tried to retrace his steps, but in leaving the large salon in which he found himself, he turned in the wrong direction. Soon he was wandering a labyrinth of lengthy corridors and twisted halls; several sharp turns led him to the abandoned apartment that Francesca had occupied during her months of exile.

The Duke of Cavelli was lost. And he knew it! Already upset at missing the turn that would have taken him back to the main villa, Alberto's desire to locate the right path was heightened by the deceptive shadows and bone-chilling dampness that permeated the old seaside *palazzo*.

By now it was nearly 3 A.M. and he was exhausted. He had no way of knowing that the treasure room lay only a few yards away. Almost as close was the apartment that housed Lt. Domingo, Hank Rossi, and Danny Moreno. Keeping well hidden and out of sight, Gino and the Lion had been soundlessly tailing the Duke of Cavelli as he moved through the night. The Lion and his companion skirted the grand ballroom and entered the well-secured room where the agents were glued to their listening devices.

Alberto Pietro approached.

Gino carefully removed a wooden panel, enabling the others to get an excellent view of the enormous salon. He cautioned them to make no sounds, not a whisper. For reasons peculiar to the area, the acoustics were such in this section of the villa a slight whisper could be heard perfectly for hundreds of yards.

Tired, cold, anxious to return to the warmth and comfort of his suite, Alberto leaned heavily against a wooden door and glanced at his map in the illumination of the flashlight. Then he stood up on his toes and tried to see out the grillworked windows. He shook his head, folded the map, and turned about. Accidentally catching the gold buckle on his shoe in a tangle of vines, he stumbled and lost his footing, falling heavily against the door. It pushed open on its squeaky hinges and Alberto fell headlong into the room dropping the lantern and flashlight.

"Managghia!" he shouted aloud in frustration. Reaching across the tiles to retrieve his flashlight and lantern, Alberto caught sight of a painting on one wall. He grabbed the flashlight and fanned it along the wall in the direction of the painting.

A trembling sigh escaped his lips. His heart quickened and raced wildly. Holding the lantern high above his head he gazed first at one, then another, and another.

There it was! As in a vision! All around him was the end of a half century's dream! Oh, what a glorious feeling! The sun in all its glory could never shine as did those dark shadows of time-worn, dust laden treasure rooms.

Slowly, like a sleepwalker, he moved about the priceless paintings. He examined the exquisite sculpture covered with centuries' old dust, caressed the fragile glass cases containing precious gemstones and jeweled art objects. He opened heavy metal and wooden chests containing thick golden coins. Everything he saw held him transfixed in silent awe.

Nearly every item on the inventory list had been committed to memory; the Goyas, Rembrandts, Botticellis, Reubens, Carpaccio—all came to life before his very eyes. His mouth was parched. The torch shook in his trembling hands. He walked among the art works feeling as immortal as his newly found treasures, losing all sense of time.

Dawn broke as he entered the main villa. In his room he removed his soiled costume, washed the dirt and soot from his body and face, donned a silk nightshirt, took a sleeping tablet, and studied his reflection in the long mirror on the floor stand near the bed. He bowed his head to his image.

Felice Natale, Alberto. Merry Christmas, he told himself.

Hank Rossi set aside his earphones. Lt. Domingo opened the thermos of hot coffee and poured some for the others.

"He's a cool *citrollo* this Alberto Pietro or Duke of Cavelli or whatever in hell he calls himself," admitted Danny Moreno. He reached for a cup of coffee and sat back in a lounge chair.

"He suspects everything and says nothing." Lt. Domingo set his cup down.

"I can see why we had trouble tracking such a man down," observed Hank Rossi. "He's got more sides to him than a tetrahedron."

"It's a good thing you switched the wine in the study, Gino, or you'd have tasted the excitement of a new world, my friend," grinned Moreno. Gino grunted.

"Tell me, Dolcetto, what's this bit about the Duke of Cavelli and the nonsense with the drag costume?" asked Rossi.

"Damned if I know. I'm as bewildered as you are."

"I've heard of eccentrics, but this one takes the cake." Domingo removed his jacket and slipped into a thick wool sweater. He blew on his hands and rubbed them gingerly to stave off the chill. The waves on the shore below sounded as if they were two feet away. "It's almost as if he dreamed about the Sardinian prince for so long, he transported himself back to that era."

"You don't suppose he's grown senile or that his mind's snapped?" Moreno knew what that might mean.

"If so," speculated Domingo, "he would be bait for a psychiatrist, and that would mean he might escape prosecution later."

"He's not that complex," insisted Dolcetto as he sipped his coffee. "*Aloura,* my friends, let's go. Our work is about to begin. When this Duke of Cavelli awakens and goes to re-check his find, I want him to really taste the feeling of utter defeat! I want him to experience the gut-shaking feeling of hopelessness, terror, and despair. *Capeeshi?*"

A diabolical grin appeared on Gino Vittorio's face. He never dreamed that a vendetta like this one planned by this Royal Lion could be more satisfying than out-and-out murder. To drink such sweet and satisfying wines of vengeance was like sipping the nectar of gods.

The Duke of Cavelli took his breakfast of hot coffee on the balcony of his room overlooking the Tyrrhenian Sea. He smiled when he saw Gino and went over plans for the day with him.

The caterers would be there that evening to prepare for the arrival of the distinguished guests the next day. The rest of the staff would handle everything else, Gino assured him.

Before Gino left, Alberto asked him, "Where is the fifth volume of the set of books you gave me last night?"

"Ah, that one. The *carabinieri*'s special investigative squad took that one right after the *brutal* murders, Excellency."

"Why? Why would they take just that book?"

"Let me see, now," pondered Gino. "Ah, I remember. A

599

letter His Excellency, the Marquis, had written the night he was *slaughtered, buon armo.* Now that I think, it was addressed to you. Yes, it was. He'd written you a letter. It was I who found it right next to the bed in which he was *butchered.*"

"Gino! You will stop referring to that terrible night. It's not necessary that you characterize the deaths with such brutal candor. You may not know it, but His Excellency was my dearest, most trusted friend. We were like brothers. Dolcetto was my Godson."

"Your Godson, Excellency?" Gino affected mild surprise, then shook his head regretfully.

"You mentioned a letter. Did you read it by any chance?" He sipped his *latte e cafe* and daintily patted the excess moisture from his lips. "As I understand it, Gino, it was you who found the bodies."

"At such times, I'm not the brightest man. So occupied was I in following the Marquis' instructions, I paid it little heed. Besides I try not to involve myself in affairs of no concern to me. *Shhoooohhh!* It might have given you solace to read the last words he wrote to you. To think his last words were to you. How close you must have been."

"We were close, but not as close as you're suggesting," he snapped hotly.

Gino sobered and pretended to be shocked.

"I heard you followed the Marquis' orders to the letter, that's why I insisted you should be placed in charge of the villa. Loyalty has its just rewards, my boy."

The Duke of Cavelli studied Gino through veiled eyes as he finished his breakfast. As good a judge of character as he'd always been, he was baffled by Gino. He didn't know where he stood with the former bodyguard. These western Sicilians were really a breed unto themselves. Something about Gino offended him and he wasn't sure what it was. He knew Gino had studied for the priesthood like himself; he should have known the score. Certainly the Hòly Fathers hadn't reserved their homosexual practices for Alberto alone? *Well, enough time for that later, after the meeting tomorrow,* he thought. *Perhaps I'm being unfair? It's too soon to tell. I haven't given him time to test his loyalty.*

"Now, about the letter . . ."

"Perhaps," suggested Gino, "the *carabinieri* might return it to you? What use is it to them now? It is your property, no?"

"Good thinking, Gino. Good thinking."

He turned to leave.

"One moment, Gino. On the dresser in my bed chamber

there's something for you." He followed the young man into the bedroom.

Gino gave him a look of simple interest and from the dresser he picked up a check for one thousand dollars. Before Gino could open his mouth to tell him what he could do with it, the Duke of Cavelli spoke. "Give what you wish of it to the staff, the rest is for you. *Felice Natale.*"

"But . . ." protested Gino.

"Now go. I have much to do today." The Duke suppressed a devilish grin. *Now we'll see how much longer he resists me. Money always talks.*

"*Si.* And Merry Christmas to you, Excellency."

An hour later, dressed in simple, country squire corduroys and a peaked cap, Alberto strolled nonchalantly along the whitewashed stone wall overlooking the silvery Tyrrhenian Sea. He left word that he might not return for several hours, and after making certain no one followed or saw him, he retraced his steps back into the treasure room.

The dismal gray light of day heightened his excitement. He found a flat table upon which to place the special items he had secreted in the pockets of his trousers and jacket. He brought several soft brushes, rolls of gummed stickers, a tablet of foolscap, and several colored pens and pencils. He placed a large magnifying glass next to the other items as well as several soft, white linen towels and a small can of paint thinner.

He selected the *Primavera* by Botticelli, which he recognized through all the dust and neglect, marveling that it was still in such magnificent condition after God knows how many years of exposure to the dampness of the sea. He delicately brushed the dust from the magnificent painting of the three virgins. Using careful and precise movements, he brushed the thick, congested dust from it and stood back, admiring a detail he hadn't seen.

Suddenly Alberto's heart stopped. He searched in his breast pocket for his bifocals and fumbled to set them into place over the bridge of his nose as he moved in closer to examine the signature. He felt the blood drain from his body.

What madness is this? He grabbed the magnifying glass, squatted on his knees, and reexamined the signature. It read: Bottacini. *Impossible! It can't be!* He reexamined the painting. *Am I hallucinating again?* There was no mistake. It was a Bottacini. He moved like a dying shadow among the paintings. All the works that he had identified only a few hours earlier that morning were now alien to him. The paintings he identified as Titians were signed by someone named Titano. All the names of the old masters had suddenly turned into names which just sounded similar.

He felt his forehead, took his pulse, but nothing he did could remove the terrible sinking sensation that brought him down. He stumbled from painting to painting about the grand ballroom in a daze. He paused to open a delicately carved chest and ran his fingers aimlessly through the gilded coins. A child could have told him they were fake. He moved about, turning in wide arcs with the frenzied look of a madman, trying to accept the delusion.

Had he been so anxious to find the treasure that he had imagined it? Conjured it up in his inventive mind? Or had it been like those nightmares that wouldn't leave him of late? He leaned heavily against a glass case. Trembling under the impact, the fragile case toppled over and crashed loudly to the floor. Paying it no heed, Alberto sank wearily into a chair, unmindful of the dust and soot, filled with despair.

Fifty years of dedication in which I stooped to commit murder and involved myself in criminal activities and for what? Cheap imitations. Worthless junk.

The inventory list matched this list, but the names weren't right. None of them. He wiped the cold sweat from his face with his sleeve, an act he generally abhorred. He didn't care anymore.

By the time he pulled himself together, it was nightfall. He stumbled slowly back along the path to the villa, like a blind man, seeing nothing, feeling nothing except a tormented emptiness and a sinking feeling of having been cheated. The problem was now how to go on living.

Inside the villa, the Palermo caterers were busy at work when the Duke of Cavelli entered and walked past them, unseeing. He climbed the stairs like an old man. At the landing, for some inexplicable reason, he turned to the right and walked to the bridal chamber. He threw open the doors and stood frozen, like a bloodless zombie, when he saw what Dolcetto had seen on his return—everything as it was on the wedding night. He scanned the room, taking in the bridal finery, champagne, glasses and formal attire. He closed the doors and returned to his suite, shutting the door behind him. He placed a call to Berne, Switzerland. For the second time, it didn't occur to him that he was able to get right through without delays. He gave his name and code and demanded to know Antonio de Leone's condition. They told him. Antonio de Leone had died an hour ago.

He asked them if they were certain. There could be no mistake?

"Death is something ve make no jokes about, *Herr Doktor.*"

Alberto replaced the phone. In the back of his mind was the crazy notion that perhaps somehow Antonio had left the clinic and come here to cause all this devilment. Alberto didn't believe in the evil eye. There was an explanation to all this nonsense. He pushed on a lever near the alarm and rang for Gino.

Dr. Pietro was waiting for him when he arrived some eight minutes later.

"Come with me," he said gruffly. He stormed down the corridor with Gino at his heels. At the doors to the bridal chamber, he faced Gino, and keeping his eyes on him, flung open the doors. "By God, you'll tell me now or else. What is the meaning of all this?" he shouted, studying Gino's face for a reaction. He saw Gino enter the room, look about, then turn and ask, "What's the meaning of what?"

Gino's reaction shook him to the core. Reluctantly he glanced about the room. His face blanched and he stared in dumb stupefaction. The room contained no evidence of what he'd seen only moments before. It was like any ordinary bedroom, no wedding finery, no champagne, nothing.

"But . . . I . . . only moments ago." Alberto stopped abruptly. "Sorry. I made a mistake." He strode back through the hall to his room and slammed the door loudly.

Gino suppressed a triumphant grin.

Alberto paced the floor like an angry bull. He tried time and again to get Don Barbarossa on the phone. Each time the answer was the same, *"Linea e' occupata.* The line is busy." He cursed and raged. *I've called Switzerland twice and gotten the call right through. But I can't get through to Palermo, less than fifteen miles away.*

He glanced at his watch. It was time for dinner. He hadn't the same enthusiasm he felt the night before. He felt like hiding in a corner to lick his wounds, but too many years of discipline had formed Alberto's character. He glanced at his wardrobe to determine what he would wear when he sat down to his Christmas dinner, alone.

There was an outfit for every day in the week: dress suits with ruffled silk shirts fit for royalty; diamond studs and links; powdered wigs in soft pastels to match the brocade suits and satin pumps. He opened his case of cosmetics created especially for Alberto in Rome by Plato Aristopheles's friend, Enrico.

His eyes caught sight of the four volumes of the villa's history. *Why would Marco's letter have been placed in the fifth volume? Why not the first or the second or third? Why*

in any of them? Why not a Bible or a diary? Or even on th
night stand? Unless he was trying to tell me something. Yes
he had to be writing something of worth for the authoritie
to have taken both the book and the letter. He thought bac
to the day he'd given Pepino the five thousand dollars. I
was the day of Marco's sudden disappearance. Marco didn'
come to dinner that night. Later Francesca disappeared onl
to return to say that Marco had everything he needed
Could Marco have discovered the treasure room? What di
he have to say about it? Oh, if only it wasn't Christmas
thought Alberto, *I'd drive to Palermo and retrieve my lette*
from the carabinieri. *Well, it will be the first thing I do or*
the morning of the 28th, he promised himself. He felt bet
ter, and his spirits elevated somewhat.

Dressed in his 18th-century attire of lavender, the Duk
of Cavelli sat alone in a small dining room off the mai
salon. The table was set with bone china, ornate silverware
and Venetian crystalware. He ate sparingly.

The servants had all been instructed not to laugh or mak
remarks about the Duke's clothing, but despite this warning
the unsophisticated peasants couldn't help staring at the
ludicrous man. They were bewildered by his garish dress and
grotesque appearance.

Disguised in his satin livery, Hank Rossi served the *chop-*
pino with a flourish, and at the fateful moment, Alberto
caught sight of a signet ring on Rossi's finger. Faster than the
eye could see, Alberto reached up and grasped Hank's wrist.
He raised his eyes to peer into Hank's face. "What an interesting ring. What is your name?"

Lt. Domingo stood across the room as still as death. He
stared at the two of them, unable to speak. Gino, on entering the salon, sized up the situation immediately.

"Giacomo!" he reprimanded instantly, clapping his hands.
"Are you disturbing His Excellency? Go to the kitchen immediately!"

Rossi loosened the Duke's grip on his wrist, bowed dutifully, and disappeared from the hall. Dr. Pietro scowled angrily at Gino. "He was doing no harm. I wanted to know
where he got that ring. It's a university ring. Is he an educated man?"

"A university ring? On that simple-minded man? I doubt
it. And if it was, Excellency, you can rest assured it was acquired through shady circumstances," said Gino, giving Lt.
Domingo the eye.

Alberto glanced up from his soup. "You *did* take time to
check all their references, didn't you, Gino? I want no

thieves working for me. Perhaps after the holidays, I shall interview them all personally. No, why not tonight? I have nothing better to do."

"You misunderstand my meaning," began Gino, casting a helpless glance at the lieutenant.

"What he means, Excellency," said Domingo in a thick Sicilian accent, "is that Giacomo won the ring from me in a card game. I myself found the ring when I worked as a bell captain at a hotel in Capri, before coming to Palermo."

"Ah," replied Alberto Pietro, not caring. He was engrossed in the chunks of crabmeat floating about in the dish.

At half past eight he returned to his study. Shortly after Gino served him *Strega* and coffee, he locked the door. He removed his brocade jacket and hung it over the large portrait of Marco. Sipping his coffee, he settled down and began poring over the papers he pulled from a briefcase, concerning the pending meeting. He began to outline his thoughts, but he couldn't concentrate. All he could think of was the enormous disappointment he'd experienced earlier that day. *Why had Vanzini gone to the trouble of compiling five volumes? Such a project entailed a huge expenditure of money, time, and effort. What was the motivation? Had he guessed about the treasure? Had he stumbled on it and then tried to trace its origin. Marco must have stumbled on the same thing. Why else would he be so preoccupied with deeds and titles? Why, on the eve of the wedding, had he kept himself isolated from the family he doted upon? If only I had the last volume and the letter.*

He reflected on all the research he'd done and suddenly an idea struck him. *If he were cunning enough to have made off with the treasure, cover his tracks, and disappear, why wouldn't the prince have been inventive enough to camouflage his treasures. He couldn't risk having anyone rob him of those priceless treasures as he himself had done from his own father. Therefore, being a resourceful young man, why wouldn't he have had duplicates made to throw anyone off the track?*

Pleased with his line of thinking, Alberto took hope. He glanced narcissistically at his reflection in the smoky mirror opposite him and patted his wig into place. He walked to the sideboard and poured himself a glass of Fregossi's rosé wine, sipped half of it, and walked to the table upon which the maps of the villa had been placed. He shook his head in disbelief. *And I almost gave up.*

He noted the number of apartments, hidden alcoves, and grand salons that he hadn't even seen, enough to occupy him for months. He slammed his fist on the table defiantly. "As long as there's breath in me, I shall not give up until I find the treasure. I know it's here." His hand slid easily across the blueprints. "Here. In some of these rooms."

In Monreale, at the Barbarossa villa, the Don hadn't been able to eat the usual Christmas Eve supper. The insidious thoughts put into his head by Dolcetto de Leone preoccupied him. What was worse, he'd tried to get Alberto on the phone all day. His line had been busy. His calls to Rome had been fruitless. The old Mazzarino didn't like what he felt.

He picked up the phone and called his *consiglioro*. "Be at my villa in an hour!" he said in a voice loaded with menace.

"Can't it wait, Don Matteo?" asked Garibaldi. "It's Christmas."

"No!" said the Don with a finality the lawyer recognized. "And do me a favor, eh? Stop at the Albergo-Sole hotel and pick up di Luigiano. I want him with us. He knows more about it than we do."

"Yes, Don Matteo. Whatever you say."

"I thought you were going to resign, Primo," demanded his petite, blonde wife as she kissed him. Her somber brown eyes darkened.

"Let's not start that again, Katerina, please."

"All right. But if you don't do something by New Year's, I swear . . ."

"Katerina! No more ultimatums! Do what you want, hear? Enough is enough!"

Whenever he lost his temper and stood up to her, she turned docile. "*Si*, Primo," she purred meekly. "*Ciào.*"

"What am I doing?" he shouted. "I'd better call the hotel first." He walked back into his office and placed the call. The undercover agents patched into Dolcetto's private line at the villa. One of the operatives answered.

"Albergo-Sole, Merry Christmas."

"Signore Dante di Luigiano, *con permisso.*"

"*Pronto . . . Pronto,*" came Dolcetto's voice.

"Di Luigiano? Garibaldi here. Don Barbarossa wishes to see you. May I pick you up at your hotel? It's on my way."

"I'll be ready in an hour, Garibaldi. I'm finishing with a client."

"On Christmas Eve?"

"I'm so seldom here. If people want to sell their property, they see me at my convenience."

"Very well then, in an hour."

Alberto Pietro poured the last of the wine. Behind him, the jacket had fallen from Marco's portrait. Alberto blinked his eyes several times but his vision continued to blur. He rose to his feet and stared about the room. As his sense of smell became acute, he grew nauseous from the odor of crab clinging to his fingers. The room began to swirl. Arrested by the compelling eyes in Marco's portrait, he couldn't move.

"Why did you order me killed?" It was Marco's voice. But how? The Lion hadn't spoken for years. "You've forgotten me so soon, Alberto?" came the same voice.

Alberto trembled and shook like a sapling in a strong wind. "Marco? It can't be you . . . You're dead . . . Aren't you? Tell me you're dead!"

"Only my body is dead, *compare*. My soul, like yours, is eternal. Soon you'll join me and we'll have our day of reckoning."

"No," shouted Alberto hoarsely as he stumbled in the direction of the portrait. "No! Once and for all I shall expunge you from my life. All of you! You hear? Every last one of you Royal Lions!" He fell over a chair, knocked over a table, grasped at anything to aid him in rising to his feet. Sweat rolled off his face and he gasped desperately for air.

"Why, Alberto? Why?" asked the agonized voice of Marco de Leone.

In his efforts to reach the portrait, Alberto blazed a path of destruction. Finally, he reached it, tore it off the wall, and brought it down smashing it against anything and everything. Again and again the frame splintered, the canvas ripped and tore. The sounds tore at his eardrums. Finally he held his hands over his ears and lost consciousness.

The door opened; Dolcetto and Gino entered. While the Lion injected the atropine, Gino reassembled the room. He replaced the original portrait of Marco with a duplicate, rehung the lavender brocade jacket over it as it had been earlier. Gino rinsed out the decanter of drugged wine, left the coffee and *Strega* as it was, and moved to one side as Danny Moreno entered with Alberto's makeup case.

"It's a damned good thing I once learned how to do this in drama class," muttered Danny as they placed Alberto's inert form on the leather sofa and he began repairing the makeup. "Ugh!" he shuddered. "It's like working on a corpse. Just the job for what's his name? Oh, yeah, Baccamorto."

"Do you have a family, di Luigiano?" asked Primo Garibaldi after he picked Dolcetto up on the Via Roma where he waited just outside the hotel entrance. He turned at the *piazza* and headed for Monreale.

"No."

"Mine were unhappy at the interruption of our holidays. I tried to convince Don Barbarossa to wait until a more reasonable time, but when he gets a bug in his head, he's immovable. An unwritten law of his that defies logic or reason or both . . . sort of intuition."

"Really?" Dolcetto was careful to remain polite.

"You worked for the firm of de Leone very long?"

"The House of de Leone? Longer than I care to admit." Garibaldi eased the car along the busy streets and turned on the Corso Vittorio Emanuele.

"Did you know Signore de Leone personally?"

"But of course. I worked directly for His Excellency."

"No, I mean the son, Dolcetto."

The Lion stiffened. "Only indirectly, why?"

"I met him once. Never forgot him," said Garibaldi who'd never forgotten the episode in Dolcetto's office.

"Ah . . . you were friends?"

"We might have been, under different circumstances." Dolcetto fought the impulse to turn and really look at Garibaldi. "You think that strange, di Luigiano?"

"To consider a man strange for saying what he feels would only be denying my own right to my feelings." As soon as the words were out, he realized he shouldn't have spoken at the attorney's level. Garibaldi was too slick, too educated not to catch a statement that a subordinate wouldn't normally make. He said nothing for a time, then Garibaldi geared down as they neared the villa.

"My family was wiped out in the war, *consigliori*," said Dolcetto, thinking fast. "My father, a Fascist and blindly loyal to Il Duce, pledged our lands and our wealth to the cause. My brothers were killed, our home bombed and destroyed, everything was lost. I don't have to tell you what it meant. After the war, I, too, studied law and wanted to be a lawyer, but could I? No! I had to live down the stigma of Fascism!"

"You told Don Barbarossa you were a Sicilian. From Bronte." He stared with cold suspicion. "That your family was wiped out by bandits."

"I told a half-truth. We were from Bronte. But can you imagine my telling Don Barbarossa my family were Fascisti?" Dolcetto dramatized the remark.

"No," said Garibaldi, suppressing a half-smile, "I couldn't."

"Especially after what Mussolini did to the *mafia*? Please *consiglioro*, you will keep my secret? If anyone finds out all

608

my hard efforts will have been for naught. Ah, the sins of our fathers."

Garibaldi was about to tell the seemingly frightened little man at his side that secrets are seldom kept from Don Barbarossa, but Dolcetto's last statement struck home. *The sins of our fathers are visited upon the children.* If it hadn't been for Primo's father's fierce loyalty to the Mafia, he might have become the man he had dreamed of becoming. He sighed. "Your secret's not so earth-shattering that I can't forget I heard it."

"*Grazie, consiglioro. Grazie, tanto.* I won't forget your kindness."

"*Prago.* Don't mention it. It's forgotten."

They got out of the car and entered the Don's villa.

At a quarter to midnight on Christmas Eve, the Duke of Cavelli finally opened his eyes, awakened by the loud knocking at the study door.

"Excellency! Excellency! Open the door!" shouted Gino Vittorio.

Alberto's eyes blinked several times and he tried to orient himself. His eyes moved slowly about the orderly study in awed fascination. He shook his head trying to collect his thoughts. *Not again! Goddammit! It was no nightmare this time!* Standing on weak, rubbery legs, he moved across the room.

"Excellency! Excellency! Open the door!" He vaguely heard the pounding.

He reached the portrait and lifted off his jacket. When he saw the portrait hanging intact he shook his head in that peculiar manner of trying to adjust his brains. "Goddammit! I don't believe it! It can't be!" he shouted hoarsely.

"*Dottore! Dottore* Pietro! Open this door!" The knocking grew louder.

In a sudden wild and savage manner, Alberto Pietro reached up, took the portrait off the wall and tossed it hard against the furniture, the desk, the chairs. Shaking with anger, blood vessels pounding, he shouted. "Die! Die, damn you, die!" he shouted maniacally. "You're not eternal!" The portrait crushed, the frame fell away in splinters, and the canvas shredded. "Die," he ranted. "Goddamn you, die!" He had reduced the oil to rubble. "Now," he said breathlessly, "you won't haunt me any longer!"

Trembling with fury, shaking like a bewildered maniac, he moved slowly toward the door and unlocked it. Gino practically fell into the room and stopped short at the expression on the older man's face. He stared at the crushed portrait and feigned utter astonishment. "What happened? What is it, Excellency?" He moved toward the fragments and picked up portions of it in his hands, making a futile attempt at reconstructing the pieces. He gazed at Alberto with horror. "Excellency! He was your best friend! You are his son's Godfather!" he admonished the Duke of Cavelli.

"Take it away! Take it away, I said! Damn you! Destroy it! Burn it! Anything! Then, you will remove from my sight anything and everything reminiscent of the Royal Lions and do the same with everything! Do I make myself clear?"

"But—Excellency!"

"Goddammit! You heard me!" he screamed, losing control. "Everything!"

"But—" Gino's protests were lost.

"I am the *padrone,* now. You'll do as I say!"

"*Si,* Excellency. I was only presenting myself to inform you there are guests waiting for you in the main salon."

"Guests?" he boomed. "I'm expecting no guests. Send them away!"

"I don't think I could do that, Excellency." Gino shook his head, half tempted to follow orders, yet reluctant, concerned with the consequences of such an act. "That is, not and live to tell about it."

"I told you I give the orders here! If I tell you to send them away, you'll do just that!" In his rage he hadn't heard Gino's last words.

Gino shrugged his shoulders. He reached for his automatic, examined the clip, and shoved it back into place. "As you say, Excellency, you're the boss. This will be my pleasure."

Alberto reluctantly interfered. "*Aspetta.* Wait a minute. Just who are these guests?" he asked suspiciously.

"*Mafiosi!*" Gino spat the words.

"*Mafiosi?* Who in particular? And stop this idiotic nonsense with the gun!"

"Don Barbarossa, Consiglioro Garibaldi, and an ugly-faced brute named di Luigiano."

"Don Matteo?" For an instant Alberto appeared relieved. Then he considered the situation. Strange, the Don never went anyplace unannounced. For him to drive to Porto Tomasso, it had to be something very special. On Christmas Eve to have brought Primo Garibaldi? They were all to see each other in two days. Why now? He addressed himself to Gino Vittorio.

"Listen, these are friends of mine. I know nothing about *mafiosi!* In my home you will treat them with the cordiality as befits any servants of the Duke of Cavelli. Understand? If you can't comply with my instructions, go to bed and send another servant to attend us! I will be in the salon shortly."

610

"*Si*, Excellency." Gino affected a sudden humility and left the room.

54

Don Matteo Barbarossa sat at one end of the main salon regarding the opulence that greeted him with undisguised envy. He was impressed all right, but knowing the motivation behind the ostentatious display of grandeur infuriated him. The scene served only to remind him of how infinitely more superior Alberto Pietro considered himself to the *capomafia*. He chewed his cigar in silence, unable to say what he thought in the presence of the creampuff, de Luigiano. But, earlier, when Gino Vittorio greeted them in cool hostility and escorted them through the Peacock Court and he saw the lavish photographic blowups of the Lion and his bride, he couldn't contain his anger.

"Did you see those photographs behind the stairs?" He had muttered to Primo.

"It wasn't easy to ignore them."

"Why does that fanatic have them in plain sight?"

"He was the Lion's Godfather, no?"

"It's in bad taste. He should know better," glowered the Don.

If he was incensed at that point, he wasn't prepared for the pussyfooting liveried servants in 17th-century attire. His astonishment was qickly communicated to his *consiglioro*, who appeared as baffled as the Don. But this wasn't to be believed! Had Alberto turned into some strange maniac, he wondered.

A prolonged evaluation of his and Alberto's relationship after di Luigiano's visit to his villa had initiated the move on his part to confront the physician. He owed him that much at least. But, there was no doubt in his mind that Alberto had been up to something. It was at such times when Matteo felt inadequate that he cursed himself for not having become more literate. Even though he was *capomafia* and displayed astonishing administrative ability and a brand of Machiavellian politics to put Machiavelli himself to shame, he always felt inadequate when it came to putting his thoughts into the proper words. The Don's attention was caught up in the flurry of activity behind him, by the servants in powdered wigs and satin knee breeches. Only good manners and a preoccupation with all this outrageous business prevented him from laughing aloud.

"This is not to be believed," muttered Garibaldi, catching the Don's eye.

Don Matteo scowled darkly and caught sight of the Lion.

Bright lights glaring on the facial scars caused him to shudder. Looks like one of Cacciatore's jobs, he told himself. Someone had given it to him good. His thoughts were interrupted by the sound of a voice:

"His Excellency, the Duke of Cavelli!" said Gino in the voice of a court page.

One at a time they turned to the domed archway spotlighted by three powerful lights. The cigar fell from the thick lips of Don Barbarossa, ashes spilling on him, and he jumped to his feet to shake the lit cinders from his clothing. Primo Garibaldi raised his head, but removed the gold holder from his lips before it fell. He rushed to the Don's side and helped him brush off the glowing cinders. Dolcetto turned away from an art object and stared in open-mouthed astonishment at his Godfather's appearance. The eyes of all three men were fixed on the Duke of Cavelli.

"Merry Christmas, Matteo. Merry Christmas, Primo. Merry Christmas . . ." He stared at Dolcetto blankly.

Before he could ask who the stranger was, the Don who tried to regain his composure spoke up. *"Buono Natale,* Alberto."

Primo Garibaldi nodded. The words formed and froze on his lips. Then, he brightened. "Perhaps you were going to a costume ball?"

"No, no, no, no! Of course not. I'm wearing my official costume. You remember, Matteo? The Duke of Cavelli?" He pirouetted and glided about the room, moving his arms and legs like a prima ballerina.

Nothing could have jolted the Don more than the kewpie-doll lips, shiny beauty marks, and pale lavender wig. Even if Cacciatore had walked in the room, he could not have been as shocked. He stared in astonishment. "The Duke of —what?"

"The Dukedom! The Dukedom! You remember Cavelli? The Duke of Cavelli?"

The Duke of Cavelli your ass, thought the Don, biting his lips. He caught sight of Dolcetto's obvious approval of the bizarre costume. *Butana u' diaora!* What do we have here? A powder puff and *stu cazzu* dressed like a French *finocchio!*

Primo came to the point. "Alberto, may I present Signore Dante di Luigiano. He's a friend of Don Matteo's."

"It's a pleasure. Happy Christmas to you, signore." Alberto continued to float around the room, nodding.

"Grazie, Altra Tanto," replied the Lion in his northern affectation. His Godfather stopped in motion and appraised him critically as he moved in close to him. Alberto raised his fingers alongside Dolcetto's face, touched the scar tissue.

"Interesting, signore. The war? Today there's no need for

such a face. Miraculous skills in plastic surgery are performed every day."

"The war," replied the Lion.

Alberto clapped his hands. Instantly three liveried servants appeared to serve a magnum of champagne in sparkling hollow stemware, on silver trays.

He nodded graciously to Lt. Domingo; the special agent poured the pale amber bubbly liquid and served the guests.

"*Salute*," toasted Alberto. "May the New Year bring us all blessings, a long life and our heart's desire, eh, Matteo?"

They raised their glasses to their lips and were startled by a loud crashing noise. Deliberately Dolcetto's glass fell from his fingers and splintered on the marble flooring. He reached for a napkin to brush off his suit, but instantly Alberto came to his rescue. He pulled a lace-edged handkerchief from his satin cuff, brushed at Dolcetto's suit in so suggestive a manner that it brought color to the Lion's face. Alberto's eyes held a steady bead on Dolcetto's brown contact-covered eyes, and caused the Lion to squirm and pull away. He glanced at Don Matteo with secret appeal in his eyes.

The Don glanced quickly at Garibaldi, urging him on with the business.

"Signore di Luigiano has worked for many years with the House de Leone," began the *consiglioro*, filling him in on the man's background and leading him right up to his business in Palermo. "Only recently, he's brought to light several facts."

Alberto paused, holding his glass in midair to admire its form and contents. Deliberately he turned his back on his guests, finished his drink, and said, subtly, "Does the gentleman also work for you, Matteo?"

"Doesn't everyone?"

Alberto shrugged imperceptibly, walked about in a foppish manner, and scanned the contents of an exquisitely carved breakfront. "You were saying, Primo. Important facts?"

"*Consiglioro—va subito*," urged the Don. "Get on with it."

"What the Don wishes to know, Alberto, is if you have anything to tell him. Something perhaps you may have overlooked."

"I'm not sure I understand."

"Don't play games with me, Alberto. We've known each other too long to begin this cleverness all over again," said Don Matteo, lighting a fresh cigar.

Alberto's eyebrows shot up delicately.

"News of the treasure you've uncovered has reached him," said Primo. "Out of respect to you, he feels you're entitled to speak your side before he passes judgment."

Alberto removed his wig in a stagy manner. "Mind if I take it off? It's a bit warm."

"If you took the whole get-up off, it wouldn't be soon enough for me," said the Don, completely rankled by this new side of Alberto.

Alberto allowed the remark to pass. After all, what does an uncouth barbarian know of life?

"Before you, uh, pass judgment, make sure this is the way you want it to be. I can see after all these years you're still the *capo* and I'm to be the subordinate, just like all the others. My past victories for you and the brotherhood mean nothing." He approached the Don with the petulance of a spoiled monarch. He shook his head and made soft clucking noises with his tongue. "I'm surprised at you. You mean to tell me you believe all that nonsense about a treasure?" He forced a smile that bloomed into laughter.

The smile wasn't returned. "What nonsense?" Barbarossa rolled the cigar between his fingers. Finocchios *can't be trusted*, he told himself.

"The nonsense of a treasure. You mentioned a treasure. What treasure?"

"Di Luigiano!" called the Don gruffly. "Refresh his memory."

"Yes, di Luigiano, by all means refresh my memory." He grew cautious. Three against one were odds he didn't relish. One to one, he could always handle the Don, but when others were present he found it more difficult, but not impossible.

Dolcetto opened his briefcase and produced the fifth copy of the villa's history and turned to Alberto. It was difficult to observe any facial changes under the thick makeup. But he did sit heavily in a nearby chair, and his features sagged, makeup or not.

"Perhaps, *dottore*, it might be more expedient if you know that Don Matteo has known of this special hobby in which you've been engaged for so many years. You might also be interested to know that the Marquis de Leone wrote his last letter to you before he was brutally murdered!"

"Signore!" Garibaldi's tone reprimanded strongly. "We do not use such a word as murder when talking amongst ourselves!"

"I meant no offense, *consiglioro*. Perhaps you had better handle it from here on in. My part is finished. You have the information." Dolcetto began to pack up his case.

"No. You stay!" growled the Don. Then he composed himself. "You stay."

All eyes were on Alberto Pietro as he read Marco's last letter. He couldn't control his nervousness. He felt as if Marco's critical eyes were upon him. *So, Marco, the old scoundrel, found the treasure, after all.* It confirmed his earlier thoughts. Marco would have stated in the letter if he'd located only cheap imitations. Then somewhere the real treasure *did* exist. The letter brought a smile to his kewpie-doll lips. He knew now what to do with this barbarian.

"So. You found me out, eh, Matteo? Very well, I should have known I couldn't keep a secret from you. I know, I know. I should have told you long before this. But, I couldn't run the risk of having you call me a fool. And that's probably what I am—a fool. Everyone has a hobby. Mine happened to be tracking down an impossible dream. The legend of the Sardinian prince's lost treasure," he chuckled. "So, I was a fool! Will you hang me for that?"

No one else smiled.

The Don wasn't fooled. He'd judged Alberto before he entered the villa. He felt it in his bones, and seen it on Alberto's face. Even Primo Garibaldi avoided his eyes.

"Is this why you're so unfriendly to me, Matteo? Because you've found me to be a fool? It could happen to anyone. So I've wasted fifty years chasing a rainbow and found no pot of gold. That's no reason to be so unfriendly."

The Don sat motionless and deadly. "What's the treasure worth, di Luigiano?"

"In excess of a billion dollars."

"Treasure? What treasure?" laughed Alberto. "You think there's a treasure here?" He saw no one believed him. *They think they have me trapped? Well, I'll fix them.* "May I see the list, di Luigiano?"

Dolcetto handed his Godfather the list, marveling at the cunning of the man. How could the Lions have been fooled by such a man?

Alberto regarded the list with disdain and tossed it carelessly aside as if it were worthless paper. "So it's come to this, Matteo? You no longer trust me? I've entertained other visions of how we'd end our successful partnership, but never this. Have I not made you a wealthy man? Kept all the promises I made to you that day at Nunzzio's?" Alberto sighed and wondered how to reason with a man who'd remained illiterate all his life.

"You understand, Matteo, this means we can never be as we were before, either in friendship or business." He tested the *mafia* Don.

The Don glanced at Garibaldi. *What's he getting at? He acts like I'm to blame.* He glanced at di Luigiano and for a few moments there was doubt in his eyes. *This powder puff had better know what he's talking about.* But the Don lowered his eyes. Remembering how cunning and deceitful Alberto could be, he refused to be taken in. He said nothing.

"*Aloura*, said Alberto Pietro. "This farce has continued long enough. I invite you all to come with me and see the treasure you all drool over."

"That's why we're here," responded Garibaldi. "Let's go."

"Very well. I will show you all these priceless treasures."

Twenty minutes later, armed with flashlights and lanterns, the four men entered the abandoned wing of the palace, followed closely by two of the Don's armed bodyguards. Inside the grand ballroom, Alberto lit candles and with the lights trained on the paintings, he pointed them out. He walked with an outer display of confidence and a trembling sigh of disappointment toward *The Primavera*.

"Here, gentlemen. Take a good look. It looks like Botticelli's *Primavera*, no? You especially, Garibaldi, take a good look at the signature."

Primo donned a second pair of glasses and peered closely at the oil. "*Magnifico, magnifico,*" he repeated over and again.

Dolcetto stood alongside him. "Here, see the fine detail. Notice how the master used values in shading. Incomparable. Incomparable."

They moved from painting to painting, art object to statuary, almost as if Alberto didn't exist, totally enraptured by what they saw. Baffled and disarmed by their behavior, Alberto's astonishment grew as their expressions grew more and more ecstatic. Unable to contain himself, he quickly picked up a magnifying glass and scrutinized the signature on the painting of the three nymphs. His stomach constricted when he read *Botticelli*. There was no mistake. "B-o-t-t-i-c-e-l-l-i-" He spelled it out. It was difficult for him to breathe. He moved forward and studied the next oil. The signature read Titian! The Rembrandts, the Goyas, all were exactly what they were and should have been—products of the masters themselves.

He didn't have to fondle the jeweled crown to know it would be the real thing.

Another nightmare? Another bad dream? What was happening? Alberto fell heavily into a dust-laden chair like a broken man, growing disoriented and hardly noticing the others.

Don Barbarossa meandered through the dusty collection, wondering why his *consiglioro* and the power puff were so emotional over it. All he cared about was the monetary worth of all this junk. He stopped before a large chest laden with the Sardinian crown jewels. Garibaldi moved swiftly to his side, removed from the chest a diamond and emerald tiara, and handed it to the Don.

616

"What you hold in your hand, Don Matteo, is probably worth a million—perhaps more," he boasted with appraising eyes.

"Fancy that," muttered the Don. "That much, eh?"

If Alberto could have seen the expression in Garibaldi's eyes, he'd have known they were real gems. His glazed eyes melted into a fixed stare, and slowly he began to swing back and forth in a rocking motion. Catching sight of him, Dolcetto, alert to the unnatural change in him, moved quickly to his side.

"Dottore? Are you all right?"

In that quick, unguarded moment, the golden lion from around Dolcetto's neck slipped out from under his shirt and glittered in the flickering candlelight. He quickly shoved the amulet back through the shirt opening, but not before the physician caught sight of it.

"No!" he screamed and recoiled. "No! Not again!"

Instantly the others were at his side. "What's wrong with him?"

"I'm sure I don't know," said Dolcetto through tight lips.

Alberto was like a dead man gasping for life. He tried to talk, to tell the others, but their world was slipping from his grasp. *I can't hold on any longer. Can't you hear me? Help me! Help a dead man! Why don't they hear me? I'm shouting!* His face was a frozen mask of horror and he wondered why they all leered at him, why they didn't help him.

"E pazzu!" said the Don dispassionately. *"Amonini,* Primo, I've seen enough. Let's go. He's a crazy man! Crazy!"

They put Alberto to bed in his room. He was in a near state of catatonia, his body and facial features frozen into a diabolical pose.

"Call *Dottore* Borghese," the Don instructed one of his men. "We have a meeting that can't be cancelled," he told Primo. "It must go on with or without Alberto."

"Perhaps we ought to change the rendezvous," suggested Garibaldi.

"How?" asked the Don. "They come from other countries. Only Alberto contacts them, remember? In the past I told you I didn't like the arrangement, but you told me to leave things as they were."

Suddenly he stopped talking. He saw Dolcetto standing close by and he grew annoyed. *"Aloura.* What do you want? *Va. Vatini.* You can go. Your work is finished, like you said." His lips tightened in a thin, hard line.

"Di Luigiano came with us, Don Matteo."

The Don scowled. Although the powder puff had done them a service, he wasn't pleased. It might have been better if he hadn't learned about Alberto this late in the game. *I'm getting old. I find no joy in this victory,* he thought. He studied Dolcetto. There was something about the powder puff he didn't like—and didn't trust. He had no respect for informers even if they worked for him.

"Call Martino. Tell him to take di Luigiano to his hotel." He raised his shaggy white brows imperceptibly, signaling his lawyer.

The *consiglioro* gave no evidence that the Don had just ordered Dolcetto's death. He left the room to call the bodyguard while Dolcetto quietly packed his briefcase.

Upstairs in their sequestered quarters, listening through earphones, the agents tensed. Rossi nodded to Lt. Domingo and the owl-eyed *Guardia* agent left the room silently.

Barbarossa's man Martino drove along the dark highway in grim silence. Just before they reached Monte Pellegrino, the butcher made his play. Dolcetto was ready for him. As the *mafia* killer reached for his gun, Dolcetto gave him a stiff, hard jab with his elbow and moved in with his right hand to wrestle for the gun. The car swerved, careened off the road and struck a roadside shrine close to the Sanctuary of Santa Rosalia. The gun went off. Martino lost control and the auto crashed against the massive rock and overturned.

The Lion managed to free himself from the wreckage just as Danny Moreno and Mike Camarata reached him.

"Are you all right?"

"Never been happier to see anyone in my life."

"You goddamned fool," shouted Moreno. "End it now. We have enough on them to put them all away."

"No!" The Lion was firm. "We wait until after the meeting. You'll have what you want and I'll have fulfilled my promise."

"Not at the expense of your life, Dolcetto."

"Don't worry, *amico,*" said Dolcetto warmly. "Haven't you heard lions are invincible?"

Moreno instructed Camarata to dispose of the car and take care of Martino's body.

Back in the apartment at the villa, Lt. Domingo noticed it first. "Dolcetto, why aren't you wearing your contact lenses?"

The Lion blinked, spread his eyelids apart, but nothing popped out. "I must have lost them in the accident. No time for another pair. I'll manage as I am."

"You listen to me," insisted Rossi. "Your eyes are a dead giveaway. I'll have no part in this if you continue on." Rossi was incensed.

"Are the men ready for tomorrow?" Dolcetto asked gently.

Rossi threw his hand into the air disgustedly. "I'll never understand you Sicilians! Can't you ever let the law take over? Must you always exact your pound of flesh? Your ounce of blood?"

"That's what you think I want? A pound of flesh and an ounce of blood? With all due respect I never did agree with Shakespeare." He smiled tolerantly.

"Can you believe that all I wish to do is infect my God-father with something he's never had—conscience? My desire is that he'll never be able to thrust from his mind the evil done to Marco, Antonio, to Francesca, and to me, his Godson. He played with Antonio's mind, put him through mental tortures unlike anything the human mind can conceive. If they had died on a battlefield in hand-to-hand combat as mortal enemies, as a result of conflict between two opposing forces, I'd have no quarrel. This man deliberately premeditated the extinction of my family, step by step, over the years, under the guise of friendship and trust. The same way he pursued the treasure of the prince, he pursued the annihilation of the Royal Lions."

"He would have done the same thing to anyone who stood in his way," said Rossi.

"And that justifies what he's done?"

"I didn't say that!"

"He didn't do it to anyone. He did it to us! To Marco—to Antonio—to me! To Francesca's family. Two families wiped out so that one man could pursue his dream to the end? What's so special about Alberto Pietro that permits him this luxury? Not only does he violate man's laws, but God's also. Am I not his son under God? His Godson? We held him in our confidence, treated him as our blood, as one of us! Cite me one law that justifies his actions! Cite one law that will punish him and torture him as he tortured the Lions and perhaps I might listen to you.

"In all your undercover work, you have no proof he gave orders to swat a fly! You told me yourself, you have no admissible evidence. So, what's he done wrong under the law? In Antonio's case, as his physician, a court might say he acted in the patient's best interest. How can you prove he ordered the murders of Marco, Francesca, or me? The men who followed orders are all dead! Exact the truth from the *capomafia*? Hah! Study the Don's life and you'll know the folly of such a thought. Any good lawyer would throw the case out of court. Remember, Hank? Those were your words. We can't prove he's a part of this rotten entanglement of criminals until tomorrow. You know it! I know it! There's only one way to get your *mafia* connection, my man, *my* way!"

619

The room vibrated in a thundering silence. No one spoke. Dolcetto left the apartment and went into the cool night air to be by himself.

After Dr. Borghese left, Alberto Pietro lay back on the pillows of his bed staring into space. His face had been washed clean, none of the white makeup remained. He looked like any old man with tousled white hair. The doctor had administered a sedative and left instructions for rest. But his mind was relentless. He wondered, was it possible that Matteo had been behind this all the time? In all the time he'd known Marco there hadn't been once when the name di Luigiano entered into any conversation. Wasn't it convenient he had in his possession the letter Marco had written and the fifth volume of the set of books? Only the Don's men would have had access to such vital information. Had he known from the beginning? Had he planned this all along? His thoughts were interrupted when the door to his room opened.

In the partial shadows of the dim room, he saw a nurse enter carrying a small tray with water and medication.

"Who are you?"

"The nurse. Dr. Borghese ordered me to stay the night."

"That bumbling fool. What does he know? There's no need for you to remain. I feel much better. Besides, I myself am a *dottore*."

"Yes, I know," she replied in a husky voice.

"How do you know? Who told you I'm a doctor? I don't know you."

"Time for your medication, *dottore*."

"Not now, I said, I feel better."

"Yes, I know. This is just a relaxant." She handed him two white tablets and gave him a tumbler filled with water.

He swallowed the medication, yawned, and lay back on the pillows.

"Do I know you?"

"Yes."

"Perhaps if I had my glasses."

"I'll get them for you." She picked the bifocals off the dresser top and handed them to him.

He didn't recognize her at first. Francesca had grown much thinner.

"When I heard you were here, I had to return to see what manner of man would murder his best friend and family."

"Who are you?" he demanded imperiously. His vision cleared and he saw her seated alongside him on the bed.

"You don't recognize the wife of your Godson?" she pulled two long hairpins from her hair and her thick tresses fell down around her shoulders.

620

"Ah . . ." he muttered with full composure. "I wondered where you were. I knew you hadn't died that night. Antonio told me."

"He knew I was alive? But how?"

"Oh, he thought you were dead when he found your husband. It was when he identified the bodies, he discovered it wasn't you." Francesca eyed him with disdain. He averted his head. "I'm tired. I don't wish to talk further."

"Not even to say the final sacraments?"

His head jerked back. "Final sacraments? What do you mean?"

"You don't believe the tablets I gave you really contained a mild sedative, now do you, Godfather dear? You aren't *that* naive."

"I demand you tell me what you gave me." He recoiled and pushed back against the headboard of the bed.

"Demand?" she asked contemptuously. "Since you'll be joining those same souls whom you ordered killed, you might want to confess. Do you want your soul to remain in purgatory for all eternity? Confess before God it was you who ordered the death of my family."

He saw her glance at her watch and saw her concerned look, but still he wasn't sure. She could be bluffing.

"There's not much time. Soon you'll begin to feel a tingling sensation in your lower limbs. Then you'll break out in hot and cold chills." Her voice was soft and well modulated.

"Stop. Stop, I tell you. Get my bag. I need an antidote. I'll tell you anything—everything." Already his legs tingled and felt numb. He could feel his muscles cramp as the hot and cold chills began.

"No antidote. Not unless you confess to your crimes." She fixed her eyes on her watch.

He panicked. "Yes. Yes, but hurry. I ordered your family killed. Your father refused to sell the villa. My offer was ten times its worth, but his greed was greater."

"Than yours?"

Not more than forty yards away, Hank Rossi and Santino Domingo listened intently at the conversation that was being recorded. Lt. Domingo glanced anxiously at his partner. Rossi nodded and signaled with his eyes. Domingo took off the earphones and left the room.

"You'd have been killed, too, if you hadn't been away at the time."

Her heart hardened. "What of the Marquis? Of Dolcetto? Did you plot their deaths as well?"

621

"Yes. Yes. Get the antidote. Hurry." His eyes bulged i[n] fright.

"And Antonio's death also? His fiendish death was you[r] idea?"

"Antonio? How do you know? He only died yesterday."

"No, *dottore,* he died weeks ago. He's buried already a[t] the Villa de Leone."

"But, that's impossible!" His legs were cramping acutel[y] and here she was calmly studying her watch. Didn't she kno[w] the danger in prolonging the effects of poison? Soon they'[d] need a stomach pump and where would they find one?

"Yes, yes! I wanted the villa. I joined forces with Do[n] Barbarossa to get this villa. It was almost mine until Dolcett[i] announced his marriage to you! Then, I knew it would b[e] lost forever to me unless I acted. It wasn't difficult to con[-]vince them to act against the Lions. They'd have done anyway, only I prevented them. Does that sound strange? [I] made my promise to Marco and before God that as long a[s] I lived no harm would befall him. Until the announcement o[f] your marriage—when I realized I'd never own this villa a[s] long as the Lions lived—I kept my word."

"And now the villa still eludes you. The *mafiosi* will tak[e] it from you. All those years of sacrifice, plotting, and plan[-]ning were for naught. It will belong to Barbarossa!"

"No! Never! They can't have it! It's mine!" He struck a[t] his limbs, trying to prevent their cramping and curling an[d] twisting. He trembled violently.

"How will you prevent it? You're dying."

"Get the antidote! Surely you have one. There, over ther[e] in my bag . . ."

"First, you'll sign these papers."

"No! I'll sign nothing."

"Then die!" she said coldly. "You see, your legs grow worse. The poison affects your muscles first, then it spread[s] and when it gets to your heart—*pouff!* But why do I tel[l] you? You know how these things work."

Never had he experienced such cold terror. His body wa[s] drenched in sweat. He could feel the toxic substance tak[e] its effect. What had she given him? Cyanide? Strychnine[?] Dear God, let it not be strychnine. He gazed at her hands.

"It's a complete confession. The killing of the Vanzin[i] family, the de Leones, naming the men who committed th[e] crimes, under whose orders, and your total collaboratio[n] with Matteo Barbarossa on up, including the Premier."

"My legs!" he screamed hoarsely. "I can't straighte[n] them! My legs!" He struck at them, pushed his hands agains[t] them in an effort to prevent the muscle spasms that con[-]torted and twisted them. "In God's name, help me!"

"Sign first."

He grabbed the pen from her, scribbled his name across the paper, and cried in panic. By now, his legs had jack-knifed into a knee-chest position, his toes curled, and his ankles twisted inward. He was powerless to move them.

Francesca painstakingly blew the ink dry on his signature and fanned the confession back and forth.

"Hurry, damn you!" His throat cracked from dehydration. "The antidote! Hurry or I'll die!" His body continued to contort. His eyes, frantic and flickering like those of a furtive coward, stared beyond her at a point in the open doorway.

"Francesca!"

She turned to gaze into the angry and gravely concerned eyes of her husband.

"Dolcetto," she cried and ran happily to his side.

From the bed, Alberto lay precariously poised between dilemmas; one, his own safety, the other, facing him, his Godson. Alberto gasped, tried to suck in air while his face registered disbelief and horror. "Don't you know I'm dying? Don't you care? Where is your humanity?" he cried aloud. "Dolcetto!" Alberto's eyes then rolled upward and he fainted heavily against the bed.

Dolcetto moved swiftly to Alberto's side, picked up his limp wrist, and took his pulse. "Will he be all right?"

She nodded. From a small bag she removed an orange, and calmly sliced it.

"Are you crazy?" he asked, watching her movements. "Why are you here taking all these chances? How did you get in without my knowing it?"

"You forget, *caro mio*. I lived here. I came to get this." She set aside the orange for a moment, and removed the signed confession from her pocket, and waved it under his nose with a smile of triumph. "Now, you can end this vendetta. Let the law take over. Let Santino and the Americans handle everything else. Please, Dolcetto, for my sake and our son's . . ."

The Lion embraced his wife tenderly, then held her tightly. He glanced at his Godfather.

"He'll be all right. I gave him a drug that rapidly depletes the potassium from his system. It causes severe cramping in the muscular system. Guillermo instructed me carefully." She glanced impishly at her husband. "Tell Gino to make sure he sucks on those oranges. It will straighten him out in a hurry."

"You crazy, *crazy*, adorable woman," He leaned in to kiss her.

"Have you heard from Giorgio?" she asked him.

"Not yet, but we will. He's in Mexico making certain arrangements."

She smiled as they left Alberto's bedroom.

55

Dolcetto de Leone had spent two weeks in conference with Giorgio Bocca on his return from Switzerland, before Antonio's death. Together they had put certain plans in motion; now all was in readiness, with all precautions taken. There would be many complications, due to the extensive holdings. Dolcetto had actually been astonished at how profitable things had been in his absence. One of the most important aspects of his close association with Giorgio was to learn of the vast real estate holdings Marco had invested in years before. One area in particular interested Dolcetto. It was remote and inaccessible, and would be ideal for his plans. He had dispatched Giorgio to the area, and last night, Giorgio had returned to advise him everything was in readiness.

Francesca had remained secreted with him at the Vanzini Villa last night and this crisp, sunny morning of December 26 they both walked along the parapet of the high stone wall overlooking the sea. Dolcetto scanned Porto Tomasso harbor and saw three elegant yachts pull into the cove.

"They're here, *cara mia,* right on schedule. All three of them." He handed her the binoculars and pulled a walkie talkie from his jacket pocket.

"The *Gregoria, Princess Yasmine,* and the *Phaedra* have arrived, Hank. Put the coffee on," he said into the walkie-talkie.

"Roger," came his filtered voice.

Francesca trained the binoculars on a sleek motor launch moving through the sapphire waters. It stopped at the Corsican yacht *Gregoria* to pick up three passengers. It moved on, slicing through the waters, to the *Princess Yasmine,* where it picked up three more passengers. At the Greek ship, *Phaedra,* only two passengers climbed aboard the launch. It wheeled in an arc, put about and headed to shore.

"You sure all is prepared, Primo?" asked the Don. "Dr. Borghese will keep him sedated until the business is over. Business is business. We can't afford to let it go down the drain, Alberto or no Alberto. You know we can't count on Don Salvatore any more. That Lucky—I should have taken care of him the last time . . . But, that's another story," sighed the *capomafia.* He wiped his brow and took in a deep breath. "This much junk is too much for Molinari. Pero—

ou still haven't reached him? What the hell is wrong with im? He should have been here last night according to plans. Vell, never mind. What was I saying? . . . Ah, *si*. It's too nuch for the de Leone Pharmaceuticals to handle so we need hese big three *pezzinovante*—the Greek for the intercept, he Corsican to refine the opium, and the Sheik for his Mid-le Eastern and French connections—until I can reach Genovese. I want no part of Luciano, *capeeshi?*" The Don racked two egg yolks in a tumbler of red wine and gulped : down appreciatively, grunting with satisfaction. "Ahhhhh!" Ie smacked his lips. "The best tonic in the world, Primo. Vhat was I saying? . . . Do I seem talkative this day? It's all his business with Alberto. All night I've been thinking, Why do I knock myself out?' You know how old I am? No, o, don't be kind or clever with me, I am almost seventy-even. In May I will be seventy-seven."

"That's not old, Don Matteo. You're in your prime." Gari-aldi felt strangely moved.

"I said, 'Don't be kind or clever, eh?' Times I think back o those days, those twenty years during Fascism and my ebirth. *Si*, I was reborn, but it came too late. I could no onger be what I was, only what I would be. In the past welve years, I've seen Sicily become the Sicily of my dreams. 3ut, the world grows too fast and beyond my control. What 3arbarossa can't control becomes too complicated for this ull mind. Now I find myself at the mercy of three strangers. t's true I helped make these men rich and powerful, but I get no pleasure in things I myself can't control. It's not he same. Now it's time I move over. *Anunca*—you know vhat disturbs me, Primo? There is no one! No one to take ny place. A hundred men greedily eye the position of *apomafia*, but not one of them possesses *maschiezzo*—man nough." The Don's eyes took on a far-off expression.

"It would take ten or more men to fill your shoes." Garibaldi spoke the truth, but having never seen this side of is Don he felt a terrible depression.

"Once there was such a man, Primo. Once I, as *capo-nafia*, found out too late that, like me, he also was Sicily. Too late I found out. No, no, don't stop me. His ghost still aunts Belasci in the Premiership, and I tell you now that :o matter how much power I give to him, he will not win he next term. The Communists are gaining too much con-rol and, my *consiglioro*, I, Don Barbarossa, am too tired to :ontest such a force. I suppose, I am just too tired now to ven think. All this business with Alberto has been too com-licated for a man such as me, much too complicated. And his betrayal has wounded me."

Said the spider to the fly, thought Garibaldi. Here sat the

most complex man he'd ever met, and he talked of com
plications and betrayals?

"Once my little spider told me unless you learn word
well, you'll find yourself unable to control the men aroun
you. I've learned words. Perhaps not as well as my littl
spider would have wished . . . but, I know she was right, fo
in this world a man who knows words knows everything."

The *consiglioro* listened attentively and his alarm grew
Of late his Don kept referring to this mystical aberration o
a "little spider" more and more. Perhaps the time of senilit
was drawing close. Pray they finished this last job. He wa
grateful the door chimes sounded and their guests had ar
rived. He was even more gratified when he saw the Don'
shoulders pull back. He adjusted his tinted glasses into place
got up and slipped into the jacket he treated more like a
enemy than an article of clothing. Garibaldi excused himsel
and left the study to greet the three foreigners.

They greeted each other with warm handshakes and Pri
mo spoke to them for several moments in hushed tones
Their pleasant expressions dissolved and were replaced b
solemn looks of obvious disappointment. The trio dispatche
their bodyguards to another section of the villa and followe
Garibaldi up the stairs to Alberto's bedroom.

"Alberto, my friend, don't you know me?" asked Plat
Aristopheles. Suave, debonair, and a literal clothes horse
the Greek tycoon bore the stamp of elegance right down t
the fragrant scent of Kolisch Juchten that emanated from
him. He shook his head sadly and stared with intent dar
eyes on the moist, pale face of his friend lying in a deathlik
stillness.

Ahmed Abou, a swarthy, bantamweight Lebanese Sheil
wearing his native robes with a cuffiah about his head, aske
in a clipped British accent, "I say, what has happened t
Alberto? Did he show signs of collapse? You say it wa
mental, Garibaldi? How distressing . . ."

"He needs a long rest, gentlemen, that's all," said th
lawyer in hushed tones. "He's worked so hard over thi
final project that if it weren't for the respect Don Bar
barossa feels for Alberto, he might be inclined to abando
the entire project. Only for him, as a sort of memorial, wil
he consider bringing the project to a successful conclusion.
Primo affected to be stricken. "Please, let's not discuss suc
mundane things in his presence, not while he . . ." H
paused effectively, shook his head, and blew his nose. Th
men lowered their saddened eyes and followed him down
stairs into the small salon.

"Only a few days ago, we spoke," said Jean Louis Canticci
in his French-accented Italian. *"Mon ami*—he was in suc

high spirits. Promised to disclose some joyous happening to us." The dark-skinned, sparkling-eyed Corsican dressed as elegantly as the Greek and was equally well jeweled in platinum and diamonds.

"This way, gentlemen. Don Barbarossa is waiting in the salon. He spent the night in vigil at Alberto's bedside, seeing to his every need. He feels dreadful, you see—but, knowing how meticulously Alberto planned these festivities, he feels we should continue in the spirit of joy and camaraderie." Primo extended his hands at the lavish display in the salon where servants scurried about to the tempo imposed upon them by the major domo Gino Vittorio.

A buffet, fabulously laden with gourmet foods and choice wines, surrounded a carved frozen statue of ice in the shape of a lion's head with open jaws. Fresh crab, oysters on the half shell, baby squid, and an array of hot entrées, including deboned, stuffed capon, breasts of dove, and numerous other rare foods graced the sumptuous table.

"How unique!" raved the Corsican.

"What a genius to have been so thoughtful," exclaimed the Greek.

"How utterly fantastic," nodded the Sheik.

They were pleased and delighted, and expressed their appreciation as servants served them hot canapés and drinks of their choice.

The atmosphere of the meeting wasn't congenial. The strain was primarily due to the fact that although the Mediterranean Big Five had been a highly successful cartel, these men of varied and distinct backgrounds had never met personally.

It was a painful and crucial moment for Don Barbarossa. Here in Sicily, Barbarossa was undisputed overlord of the Mafia. The Mafia being all powerful, therefore Barbarossa was all powerful. But, in this consortium, Alberto had been the central pivot, something Matteo fought against because it stripped him of his omnipotence. It was this very fact that motivated him to make a deal with the Chinese on his own, when Alberto mentioned his retirement plans. Then came the many complications—the Luciano disgrace and the Sardinian prince's treasure. It all happened too fast for him to make the proper connections.

Only Garibaldi knew why Alberto insisted on keeping these men apart, and now as they entered the salon and he made the introductions, the difference in these men was so decided that he held his breath and hoped for the best. These three foreigners, all well educated, the sheik, a Rhodes scholar and genteel in manners, looked upon the Don with disdain, considered him uncouth, without polish. His back-

ground as a savage and barbarous bandit heightened thei
desire to keep their distance.

Don Matteo hadn't finished brooding over the lion's hea
centerpiece when the guests entered and after the introduc
tions, he impulsively said, "Why Alberto thought up thes
fancy get-ups on the servants is laughable. It isn't *Carnivale!*

"I think it highly imaginative of Alberto," said Plat
Aristopheles." He should be complimented for bringing ele
gance to so drab an atmosphere."

Sheik Abou nodded in agreement. "I, too, am used t
pomp and pageantry with serving girls and dancing boys an
a life of conspicuous consumption. It's only one of my mino
peccadillos, don't you see?"

"What would life be without such ingenious surprises t
help you through the dismal routine of living?" added th
pretentious Jean Louis Canticcio.

The Don cast a look of mild surprise upon his *consiglior*
and sensing he may have offended the guests, he blundere
on, "You like?"

"I do, indeed," replied the princely Greek.

"Va biene," smiled the Don deceitfully. "Then I like, too.
Lurking behind the facade of smiles was the diabolical min
of a man who had lived and who knew men. Casting specula
tive eyes about him, he studied these three powerful figure
heads and it came to him suddenly—they were all powde
puffs! That was it! He was surrounded by limp-wristed pow
der puffs! Including Alberto Pietro! Sonofabitch! It stood t
reason that birds of a feather—

Disgust was apparent in his eyes, but he caught the warn
ing look in his *consiglioro*'s eyes and knew the truth. N
wonder Alberto had kept them apart.

Now, it was Garibaldi's turn to grow uneasy. They had
lot at stake, too much! Sophisticated enough to know th
vibrations were all wrong, and seeing an icy wall spring up
he knew he had to melt the wall instantly or everythin
would disintegrate to ashes. Moving toward the Don with
goblet of wine, he smiled graciously and spoke in a thic
Sicilian accent, reminding the Don how important it wa
the meeting be handled diplomatically.

"You're telling me something I don't know?" he spok
with vitriol but kept his smile intact. "Fucking *finocchios!*
And when he caught Sheik Abou's dark probing eyes o
him, he smiled more pleasantly, held up his glass. *"A votr
santé,"* he said aloud, then muttered, *Cazzi a te!*

Don Barbarossa was on his best behavior. He tried to b
amiable. He drank when they drank. When they ate he ate
When they talked he listened politely. They boasted of thei
countries, their conquests, and their possessions. Through i

ll, the Don took a back seat. His purpose in remaining silent
was threefold: He needed all three men.

During dinner, not caring that his uncouth manners, no
matter how polished they'd become over the years, weren't
up to par with those of the refined, effeminate, elegant
dandies in whose midst he presently found himself, the Don
ate with his usual gusto, devoured his food ravenously, stuffed
into his mouth as if each bite was his last, then washed it
down with wine.

Drop by drop, inch by inch, the Don tasted and felt the
bitterness of their silent ridicule in their every gesture.
Watching them behind his dark-tinted glasses, he feigned not
to be affected by their dramatic postures and elegant manners. *Che demonio!* Nothing could be more terrifying for an
animal used to instinctive behavior to be suddenly given a
human brain and reasoning. Behavior and reactions became confused and chaotic. He was a peasant, yes! But not
an ignorant peasant. He understood many things, perhaps
more than most men. If this is what they called being civilized, the Don decided to show them exactly what he thought
of them. He belched aloud, then forced his tongue against
his teeth and made loud clicking sounds as he sucked the
food particles from between them. The noise drew their attention and the guests stared with disdain until the Don
caught their annoyance. He deliberately smiled that revolting syrupy smile reserved for such men. With full peasant eccen-
tricity he wanted to fart in their pretentious noses just to show
them that at least he was a man! The strained look on Garibaldi's face prevented him from further complicating things.

He continued to smile that false affected smile that was
as out of place on his face as skates were on a cripple.
Having finished eating long before the others, he sat back
and puffed on a cigar, rehearsing in his mind the lines and
motions for the next scene in this artful drama.

In the study over espresso and *Strega,* the moguls talked
business for nearly three hours. Reluctantly, but quite assuredly, they agreed to continue with this final project Alberto had put together. When they saw the real tears Don
Matteo shed over the condition of his long-time friend
Alberto Pietro, they considered that with all his barbarism,
the man was human, and his grief for their friend was worth
the effort expended. In addition, the profits were exciting.

Overhead the agents, glued to peepholes with earphones
over their heads, listened with avid interest. Dolcetto and
Francesca stood watching them and listening to the filtered
conversation. Hank Rossi glanced up at Dolcetto.

"No wonder we couldn't find any love life on Alberto
Pietro." He shook his head. "Did you prepare him?"

Dolcetto nodded. "He should be ready about"—he glance
at his watch—"Now."

Alberto Pietro, dressed in a pale yellow brocade costum
complete with wig and makeup, pushed open the study door
"A belated and happy holiday to you, my dearest friends,
he said in the manner of an announcement, "from his Ex
cellency, the Duke of Cavelli," he said, bowing.
Instantly the three moguls jumped to their feet, astonishe
and immediately solicitous, "Alberto! You look simply mai
velous! How divine of you to think of such a treat for u
What happened? You look simply marvelous! A few hou
ago you looked like death itself—but, my dear, what a re
markable recovery! Wait until I tell Enrico. Did he do th
wigs for your outfits?"
If Jesus Christ himself had walked through the door, th
Don couldn't have been more shocked and stunned by wha
he saw. His fascination was so fixed by the stage play un
folding before him that he didn't give a thought to how
Alberto had awakened from a drugged stupor. But Gar
baldi was thinking precisely that. Dr. Borghese assured hi
he'd sleep through the day and a portion of the night. Hov
could either of them have known there were busy eyes, ear
and hands at work overhead. How could they have know
Alberto had been injected with amphetamines to rouse him

Upstairs, watching them, Hank Rossi hissed. "Faggot
Screaming faggots. To think we've been jerked around by
bunch of swivel-hipped queens. The Don's the only real ma
in the bunch."

"And now, my friends, since you're all gathered here wit
me, I wish to tell you of my plans to retire. Last month,
told the Don, and I wanted to tell you all together, I will n
longer be involved in further business."
The Greek was puzzled. He turned to his companion
With frozen expressions they all turned to Barbarossa. "Yc
know this? Yet you allowed us to think something entire
different. In all the time we've been here, you've allowed
to think, Alberto was . . . was . . . planning to meet h
maker," said Plato accusingly.
"We haven't had time to discuss it," interrupted Garibal
"There's still several hours of business to discuss."
"I'm afraid not," stated the Greek flatly. "Our business
hereby dissolved."
"You can't do that!" shouted Garibaldi, much to the Don
astonishment.
"What my consiglioro means," said the Don with dead

630

alm, "is that it wouldn't be financially smart to walk away
·om unfinished business, not when enormous profits can be
·ade." The Don wiped his brow.

"When I speak, I speak for Jean Louis, Sheik Abou, and
·yself. No Alberto, not us." The Greek made himself perfect-
· clear.

"But, why? Alberto wishes to retire. We don't need him in
·is deal."

"Why?" asked Plato. "I'll tell you. Twelve years ago
·lberto called me. He asked my opinion about several
·eals he planned to embark upon. Up till then, my life had
·een a series of financial disasters. He asked me to enter into
· business relationship with him, which I did. I've made
·othing but money, without incident, error, or interference
·rom the law. Except for that business with that greedy
·uciano, we've done well. I saved Luciano's scummy neck
·nly because Alberto asked me to. I'm a superstitious man.
· believe in good luck amulets. Alberto has been this for all
·f us." He glanced at the Corsican. "Jean Louis?" The
·orsican nodded.

"Ahmed?" The Lebanese nodded.

Alberto Pietro flushed with pleasure. "Thank you, my
·riends. Your confidence fills me with joy." He bit his lips
·o suppress a smile as he peered at the red-faced and sullen
·afiosi. "As I understand it, you won't proceed without my
·articipation in this final deal of Don Matteo's?"

"Correct," replied the Greek.

Garibaldi spoke up at a signal from the Don. "We've al-
·eady paid a million up front to the Chinese. The largest
·upply of raw opium we've ever handled. Our couriers made
·he payoff four days ago. The goods are to arrive aboard the
·esdemona, a private yacht, scheduled for a stop in Trieste
·efore arriving in Porto Tomasso harbor. We want an-
·ther ship, preferably a Greek oil freighter, to intercept
·he Desdemona somewhere between Malta and the Island of
·antelleria, just in case the Desdemona is set up."

"Got that?" asked Hank Rossi. "Desdemona from Trieste?"
·oreno nodded, held up a thumb and forefinger in an "O"
·nd left the room.

Alberto's mind functioned clearly. It was plain to see that
·atteo Barbarossa needed his friends desperately. He needed
·lato's ship for the intercept, Jean Louis' plants to convert
·he opium, and Sheik Abou's Middle Eastern connection to
·ie in with the French connection in Marseilles. Molinari
·vouldn't handle such a load, and now it was even more
·bvious the Don planned no more business with Luciano.
·Alberto glanced at his watch. Speaking of Molinari, where
·vas he? He should have been here long before this. Some-

thing tugged at his mind. Something about Dolcetto and Francesca and some papers he had signed. But, like everything else, he thought, it must have been another of those recurring nightmares. He'd dreamed she'd poisoned him. He shuddered noticeably. Imagine that. What next? he wondered. New life surged through his limbs.

"There's one possibility," he said glancing directly into Don Matteo's eyes.

Their eyes met in silent confrontation. They regarded each other as mortal enemies. The barbarian and the civilized dandy. All that had passed before was forgotten. The Don only knew he must make a move, even if it was only to wheel about in a circle. He filled with wild exultation because he knew there was always tomorrow. What stuck in his craw was that he'd spent a lifetime engaged in the art of *maschiezzo* and now his balls were to be squeezed by an emasculated *finocchio*. But then how hard could this *finocchio* squeeze? he wondered. How hard?

Garibaldi felt a sinking sensation. He'd dreamed of the treasure all night. Studying the Don, he knew what the answer would be.

Watching this interplay, the Greek asked, "What possibility?"

"Just a small matter between Matteo and myself," said Alberto, hastily scribbling an agreement on paper. "Alberto Pietro has full title and ownership of that property known as Vanzini Villa and anything contained therein shall be deemed his property without contest." He shoved the paper at the Don. "Sign it."

"The Don signs nothing. You have my word. The word of Barbarossa is as good as gold."

"The gold market can crumble. Sign it. I'll feel more secure."

Under hooded eyes and behind his dark glasses, the Don's eyes smoldered. He signed the document and told himself there's always tomorrow, and other ways to take care of this *finocchio*.

"Now," said Alberto amiably. "Let me hear the details."

During the next two hours, Alberto and his guests discussed details of their plan. Every word was duly recorded and efficiently taped by the agents upstairs, who were still dressed in their 18th-century costumes. As the meeting drew to a close, the agents, accompanied by Dolcetto, Francesca and Gino, went downstairs.

The guests' bodyguards were overwhelmed while eating their dinner, handcuffed, and silently ushered out of the villa. Domingo picked up a briefcase initialed P.A., the

Greek's. Hank Rossi held the portfolio belonging to Sheik Abou and Moreno grasped the Corsican's.

The door to the study opened and they all filed in, led by Lt. Domingo.

"We're busy," snapped Alberto Pietro coldly. "No one rang."

"Excuse me," said Domingo, glancing at the Greek. "Is this your briefcase?"

The Greek looked up pleasantly. "Why yes. My man was tending it. Where is he?"

Domingo laid the case on the desk, opened it, and counted out several kilos of heroin. The room's occupants were struck dumb as Hank Rossi entered, followed by Moreno and behind them six of Mike Camarata's agents with guns drawn. The agents identified themselves and Hank Rossi began the ritual of reading the charges:

"*Alberto Pietro, Matteo Barbarossa, Primo Garibaldi, Ahmed Abou—Sheik . . . Jean Louis Canticcio . . .*"

Dolcetto de Leone and his wife entered slowly and walked to the center of the room.

"*. . . I arrest you on the following charges . . .*"

"Di Luigiano," bellowed the Don. "I might have known it was you."

"No. Not Dante de Luigiano!" He drew himself up with majesty and he gazed from the Don to the lawyer.

"Dolcetto de Leone," shouted Garibaldi hoarsely, staring at his green eyes.

"*. . . Illegal transportation of contraband . . .*"

Don Matteo turned to the Greek. "And Alberto's your good luck amulet? Bah! Better he should be *capo de cazzi!*"

"*. . . Conspiracy to commit murder, conspiracy to defraud . . .*"

Dolcetto turned away from the sight of his Godfather, the pitiful Duke of Cavelli.

"*. . . The Italian Government . . . The American Government . . .*"

"Surely you can understand a man's dedication, Godson?" babbled Dr. Pietro. His berry-red lips pouted and his black beauty marks glistened in the light.

Francesca tugged at her husband's coat sleeve. "*Amonini, caro mio,*" she whispered.

"*. . . Conspiracy to use illegal drugs for experimental purposes on humans . . . Conspiracy to . . .*"

The last of the Royal Lions, the Lion of all Lions, took one final look at his Godfather, unable to believe the destruction he had wrought. Then, with his wife, he left the agents to complete their work.

EPILOGUE

Destiny listened smugly to the long list of crimes committed by the unbelieving Alberto Pietro, and smiling with the premeditated evil of a spurned mistress, she determined not to permit him one night of peace. During the trial, Alberto had jumped to his feet shouting, "I am God! I am all powerful!" Raving like a madman, he was remanded to a prison for the criminally insane. He survived four years, his mind utterly destroyed, never knowing one moment's peace until his death.

Don Matteo Barbarossa died a month after his incarceration. Destiny felt a twinge of compassion for this former giant and allowed him to die from a cardiac arrest.

The Greek, Corsican, and Lebanese each spent six months in jail until their lawyers cracked the confession signed by Alberto Pietro as one signed by a raving maniac. They've retired from the public eye but are still involved in international politics.

Garibaldi spent a short term in prison on ten counts of international conspiracy and was then released on bail. For years the courts stalled and continued the case until the statute of limitation expired. He lives today in the north of Italy under a name known only to the *Guardia de Finanzia.*

The Italian Ministry of Culture was baffled one day when three enormous vans appeared containing the art treasures of the Sardinian prince. The curator stood flabbergasted in the middle of it all, quivering with excitement at the mysterious return of such a priceless cache.

Guillermo de Leone returned to Spain and continued with his work in the hospital until his death five years later.

And the Lions? The Lions are no more.

But somewhere in Baja, California, in a tropical village overlooking the Gulf of California, Signore and Signora Dante di Luigiano, along with their eldest son Antonio—whose translucent green eyes sometimes resemble the eyes of a powerful lion—their daughter, Mariolina, and their second son, Marco, live a happy, contented life. And once a year, as they have for the past ten years, the children's Godfathers—Hank Rossi, Santino Domingo, and Danny Moreno—visit the di Luigiano family. Living nearby in Mexico City, Giorgio Bocca, successful in a new law practice spends all his available time with the di Luigiano family.